In Plainest Sight

ALSO BY M. L. WINITSKY

*A Fly on the Wall: The Discovered Journals of Heinz
Linge, Valet to Adolf Hitler – Volume I*

Translated from the German by
M. L. WINITSKY

a novel

In Plainest Sight

The Discovered Journals of Heinz Linge,
Valet to Adolf Hitler

Volume II of A Fly on the Wall

Waldaur Price Simons
Stuttgart - London - New York

Waldaur Price Simons
Stuttgart·London·New York

First Edition, 2025

Editing and book design by Artful Editor, LLC

ISBN: 979-8-9922234-0-8 (paperback)
ISBN: 979-8-9922234-1-5 (e-book)

Published in the United States of America

For the unique Patrice, who spared me the chaos of real "what-ifs" in my life, so I could devote my time to fictional "what-ifs" in my writing

VOLUME TWO

1 September 1939 to 6 December 1941

1939

1 *September 1939*

THE ATTEMPT ON my life in the alley last night, so instinctive and surreal at the time, played out again in a fitful dream-sleep, but this time, it was no longer fantastical. Again, I saw myself turn and witness the dagger in the assassin Schlegl's hand swing upward, just in time for me to sidestep and pivot so the blade slid past me. I spun back as he charged like the mindless bear he was, but slipping to the side, I pushed Schlegl's elbow down and away. Grabbing his head, I threw him onto the sodden ground, causing the dagger to fly out of his reach. Before I could seize the advantage, he was on his feet, head hunched into his massive shoulders, throwing his bulk into my chest, ramming me against a wall, then moving back slightly and pulling out his pistol.

Even in my dream, I could feel the adrenaline replacing breath as I grabbed his wrist, drove his arm over his shoulder, and pulled him backwards and down. I had the gun even before he landed, and bending over, I smashed him on the forehead with it. Still on the ground, the now-bloody Schlegl gripped my ankle with his feet, twisted it, and sent me reeling back to the wall, giving him time to pull himself up, rush towards me, and throw out a stiff right. I shoved myself to the left to avoid it then reached out, pulled his head forward, and smashed his nose with my knee. Thrusting my other hand into his crotch, I put my shoulder into him, lifted him off the ground, and slammed him onto the cement. With one last grunt, he went limp, his mouth and eyes gaping. Finally, I saw myself lift my booted leg and bring it down like a piston, crushing his head as if it were a ripe melon.

The deed completed, I watched myself—clearly oblivious to my sodden, bloody, and bruised appearance—make it to the street, hail a taxi, and command the alarmed driver to take me to the Adlon. There, I booked a room, had my uniform sponged and pressed, performed some emergency cosmetic repair on my face and hands, raced back to my quarters, and hoped that my position and rank would stifle, in the womb, the inevitable alarm over my ravaged appearance.

I even felt what I'd felt then, that once I'd been delivered to the Chancellery, it would take no prodigious feat of imagination to grasp the perils of using the main entrance, with its myriad checkpoints, stunned stares, robotic demands for my "papers," and all-too-human appeals for an explanation of my ragged state. So, with a shudder I still experienced, and so violent that it drove all my wounds to erupt in agony, I moved stealthily to the relatively little-known, eremitic side entrance to the main garage. There, I expected far fewer gapes and only one interrogation.

Finally, my brain took pity on me, and a void replaced the savage images.

❦

Out of the deathlike nothingness, I felt a hand rocking my shoulder with great tenderness and heard a voice no less tender.

"Hate to do this, my lad, but it's time to face the new world, even with your face."

I must have dozed off without realising it. I shook my head to clear it, but the act only caused an eruption of pain and dizziness.

"Hey, are you sure you're okay to go up?" Kempka asked tentatively as he held me steady. "The Führer can live without you for one day."

"I'm sure he can," I admitted with a painful grin, "but I'll be fine so long as I don't have to carry him anywhere."

Kempka chuckled. "Like that Jew-lover cripple, Roosevelt? I wouldn't worry about it. Also, after seeing you, I told anybody who matters that you were in a car accident and—you know— how sensitive you are, so's not to shove it up your ass."

I eased my way out of my cot to something resembling a standing position. "My ass thanks you," I said, truly grateful.

&

At 0440, while I was still in my quarters readying myself as best I could, I listened as the radio announcer, in typical stentorian fashion, declared that the Luftwaffe had descended upon the Polish town of Wieluń, destroying seventy-five percent of the city and killing close to twelve hundred people, most of them civilians. Five minutes later came the news that the old dreadnought *Schleswig-Holstein* had opened fire on the Polish military transit depot at Westerplatte in the Free City of Danzig. At 0800, our troops—still without a formal declaration of war—attacked near the Polish village of Mokra.

Kempka was right; the second shoe had dropped.

The Führer didn't buzz for me any earlier than usual. On my way, despite Kempka's errand of mercy, I chose to circulate around strategic areas of the Chancellery to minimize the coarse comments about my battered appearance. Mouth still aching, I merely shrugged at the jeers (ranging from the martial: "I sure hope you gave better than you got," to the erotic: "That slut must be some wildcat; you got her number?"), allowing their narrow, vulgar imaginations to roam free and unfettered. I hated to think how I would have fared with such a surfeit of *schadenfreude* had Kempka not smoothed the way.

When I finally arrived at the Führer's quarters, Herr Chinless (after delivering an expression that seemed to say, "Welcome, my brother") nodded me to the adjoining conference room. Brückner was already there, as were Goebbels, Göring, Himmler, von Ribbentrop, Bormann, and top military commanders. In subdued tones, they all chatted among themselves in clusters while, at his desk, the Führer, in bathrobe and backless leather flappers, scribbled some last-minute notes for his "War Message" to the Reichstag later in the day. I glanced at Brückner, but he was—or seemed to be—concentrating on what the Führer was writing. Considering the circumstances, and since no one seemed to notice me, I laid aside my personal anxieties about my appearance for the moment.

"Those stupid Polacks still decline to light the fuse," von Ribbentrop complained a bit louder than the rest, causing all but the Führer to turn their heads, but only Göring replied.

"This is a surprise to you, Ribbentrop?" he said with no small amount of sarcasm. "You somehow feel that Poles should be rendered so despondent by the Führer's public pronouncements that they would gladly commit suicide?"

Göring was being generous. No offence to von Ribbentrop, but the sheer absurdity of his statement shocked even me, who knew—and cared for—virtually nothing of world affairs or political tactics. A moron's analysis of the relative strengths of both armies would make such a statement by the "diplomat" comically ludicrous. I could certainly see why the Führer hadn't glanced up at the fool.

"Herr von Ribbentrop," Himmler said, blank of face but caustic in tone, "I will smooth out your furrowed brow. The... fuse you mentioned has, in fact, been lit. As we speak, the Reich is under a most vicious attack by those suicidal Poles the Reichsmarschall just spoke of."

Göring's medals clanged an accompaniment to his chortling, and the rest merely smiled.

"Yes," Himmler continued, glancing at his watch and drawing it out, "Just… about… *now—*"

Just then, Dara entered to nobody's notice save for me and the Führer, who glanced up from his desk, motioned me over, winced when I came close, then told me to lay out his field grey jacket in preference to his usual brown Party tunic. He then nodded her into his bedroom, followed her in, and shut the door behind them.

Goebbels turned to von Ribbentrop. "If you wish, you can come back with me to the ministry and I'll provide further details."

There was a slight flicker of von Ribbentrop's eyelids, but Goebbels, ever the narcissistic mediator, beat him to the punch. "Joachim, the Führer, and I felt that your ignorance—as well as his own—was essential to Himmler's plan."

"B-but this is…" he sputtered.

"Yes, highly irregular," Goebbels agreed. "But regularity is for bowels, not for affairs of state. The Führer feels that it's far easier to deny something you never knew than something about which you were sworn to secrecy."

Message delivered, we all left to go our separate ways.

⁊

I was desperate to push Schlegl and the eventual discovery of his body to the furthest recesses of my brain, but still, I could not help likening myself to Poland—even more pathetic since the attack on that hapless nation at least had a discernible cause and a known foe.

"So, Göring's 'logic' aside," I ventured to Brückner as we drove to the Reichstag to hear the Führer's nationally broadcast oration, "the Führer actually did get his way with the Poles." I'd already decided to broach the Christiane matter at a less distracting time.

Brückner turned slightly to glance at the damage to my face and hands. "This is Himmler's show." He tilted his head towards his raised shoulder. "Personally produced and directed. And it'll be a rousing success, I can assure you."

"Since the Führer owns the studio?" I said, in keeping with the analogy.

Brückner laughed as he slid shut the partition between the passenger compartment and the chauffeur's. "Just so. An absentee owner, I must admit, but the benefits will accrue just the same. Who was the sage who proclaimed that ignorance renders the protagonist innocent?"

I'd never heard that one, but I had my suspicions. "Could it be a biblical passage from the Book of Brückner?"

"You guessed it. I slipped it between Exodus and Leviticus while nobody was looking."

⸙

I wouldn't recount verbatim what the Führer said, for the German as well as all the major world newspapers would carry it. Far more noteworthy was the fact that, even while the Führer was dictating his speech to Dara, declaring war, German troops had already crossed the border into Poland. Göring opened the session and introduced the Führer to the deliriously adoring crowds, a leader who spoke of himself as a man of peace, blamed Poland for attacking the Fatherland, and declared—with theatrical reluctance—that he was being forced to fight a war for the survival of the German people. The rapturous response was not unexpected.

As always, after an important speech, the Führer returned to

the Chancellery elated, exhausted, and bathed in sweat. I drew
him a hot bath, drizzled in the dessert-scented bubble bath oil,
and gave him an Ultraseptyl sedative that had been prescribed
by Morell. Before I left the bathroom, what he said to me amply
supported the Book of Brückner: "Himmler has provided me
with a propagandistic *casus belli*; its credibility doesn't matter.
The victor will not be asked whether he told the truth."

Did the Führer really expect me to have understood casus belli?
And what was the "truth" that didn't really matter? I had no idea
and had no intention of asking.

As I stood outside the bathroom door, waiting for the inevitable observation, within minutes I was summoned to the tub.

"I see you wear the decorations of battle." He shook his head
from side to side in fatherly commiseration. "Kempka informed
me of your romantic mishap. Women have that power, you
know. The men of the Nordic countries have been softened to
this point, that their most beautiful women buckle their baggage
when they have an opportunity to get their hooks into a man in
our part of the world. That's what happened to Göring with his
Karin. There's no rebelling against this. It's a fact that women
love real men. Their instinct tells them. All well and good, I
say, but difficulties invariably arise when more than one man
is involved. In prehistoric times, women looked for the protection of heroes. When two men fight for the possession of a
woman, she waits to let her heart speak until she knows which
of the two will be victorious. Tarts adore poachers. So, wear your
scars proudly, but in the future, leave the poaching to those not
pledged to serve me."

I thanked him profusely through swollen lips and began
to turn round when he said, "Quite a day, Linge, eh? Did you
see Ribbentrop's face after Himmler broke the news to him?
He looked worse than you. In any event, our Uncle Heinrich

provided me with a superb-if-dubious casus belli. And there, my son, lies a lesson in statecraft."

∞

After the Führer's triumphant war speech, all in the Chancellery, high and low, engaged in a hysterical revelry of anti-Polish sentiment. As for me, what did I personally know or care about Poland and the Poles? Absolutely nothing, save for the few I'd worked beside in the brickyard. To me, they were no more or less than ignorant, drunken louts, infinitely more anti-Semitic than their German counterparts, and prodigious carousers. Even sober, they spoke of their homeland as if it were a cesspool, and Jews, its vermin.

Oddly, my best recollection of Poles came from the jokes they told about themselves with self-deprecating impunity, and that told me as much about them as I ever wished to know. But now, everywhere I turned, the atmosphere was rife with vile ethnic wisecracks and innumerable toasts to an inevitably swift crushing of those "imbecile Polacks":

"We could solve the Polack problem easily: just declare them all wanted criminals, and they'll turn themselves in for the reward."

"Q: Why did the Polack cross the road? A: He couldn't get his dick out of the chicken."

"Q: How do you sink a Polack battleship? A: Put it in water."

"Q: Why wasn't Christ born in Poland? A: Because they couldn't find three wise men and a virgin."

"Q: Why does the new Polish navy have glass-bottom boats? A: To see the old Polish navy."

"Q: What do you do if a Polack throws a hand grenade at you? A: Take out the pin and throw it back."

And on and on, the crude mockery slithered and splattered

throughout the Chancellery, rendering an entire people ridiculous, harmful, and subhuman. Like the Jews. A nation that nobody cared about, for it had no political, economic, or strategic meaning, was suddenly, in declamatory front-page news throughout the world.

And to my shame, the jokes were clever.

⁓

That evening, while the Führer spoke with Goebbels and Göring, the only thing that registered in my consciousness was him saying, "We will now wait to see whether Britain and France will come to Poland's aid. But you can trust your Führer: they'll chicken out again, mark my words."

Only the tiniest portion of my brain took in this business because the rest was preoccupied. Goethe wrote, "Things which matter most must never be at the mercy of things which matter least." For me, what mattered most was Christiane: *Why had she stood me up? Why had she lied about her job? And where was she now?* That should have been enough, but I needed to know more: *Was there any possible connexion between her and my being followed by the leather greatcoats and fedoras—and how did the would-be assassin, Schlegl, know exactly where I'd be?* But I dared not give expression or action to my own temperature until the fever of war had subsided. To have even broached the subject then would most certainly have cast irreparable doubt on my zeal—and me.

2 *September 1939*

I DRESSED MECHANICALLY, deep in confusion and disappointment, even deeper in misery. Just when I'd managed to force Emerald and Katrin into the very hindmost of my consciousness as hallucinatory phantoms of a distorted imagination, there was still Christiane. But with Christiane, there was something more, something eating away at my brain. Of course, something was amiss with all of them, but with Christiane, it was different— because Brückner's involvement made it different.

As I attempted to make some sense of my perplexity, something from *Through the Looking-Glass* edged into my consciousness: "'Well, in our country,' said Alice, still panting a little, 'you'd generally get somewhere else—if you ran very fast for a long time, as we've been doing.' 'A slow sort of country!' said the Queen. 'Now, here, you see, it takes all the running you can do, to keep in the same place.'" Yes, I agreed, all that running and still in the same place.

I strived mightily all morning to formulate what I would say to Brückner and when, but concentration was impossible, for I was bombarded by a cacophony of Poland-Poland-*Poland!* All in the Chancellery appeared to be waiting for France's and Britain's reactions. All, that was, save for the Führer and Goebbels, who were convinced they would do nothing, as always.

When the newly informed von Ribbentrop brought him notes from the British and French ambassadors demanding an immediate cessation of hostilities and the withdrawal of German troops, the Führer howled derisively. "Tell me about the French, Joseph!" he commanded, tongue figuratively pushing out his cheek.

"Of course, my Führer," he responded with no less glee and regaled him with scornful Polack-like jests:

"Q: How many gears does a French tank have? A: Four reverse and one forward—in case the enemy attacks from the rear."

"Q: How can you identify a French infantryman? A: Sunburned armpits."

"Q: What do you call a hundred thousand Frenchmen with their hands up? A: The Army."

"Q: What's the difference between a Frenchman and a bucket of shit? A: The bucket."

At each one, the Führer laughed harder and harder, like an out-of-control automobile, but when he finally eased to a halt, he told Goebbels to forget about lampooning the British. "I have one for them," he said. "They have umbrellas stuck so far up their arses that fighting will be the last thing on their minds; they'll all be too busy searching for pliers."

This sent Goebbels into rapturous guffaws. "You should have been a comedian, my Führer," he told him.

"But I am, Joseph," he replied opaquely.

Goebbels nodded vigorously while buffing his hands.

"And soon, the world will be laughing."

Standing mute in a corner, I possessed no mental energy for all the simpleminded insult jokes. I'd heard them before, and they didn't impress me more than any other brainless and vicious ethnic attacks, whether it be against Poles, French, British, Americans, Jews, or even Germans. My brain was still fixed on Christiane—that was, until Goebbels left.

"You failed to find the humour in those jokes, Linge?"

"I apologise, my Führer, but my head was aching too severely to appreciate them." A lie but a plausible one.

"Quite understandable," he commiserated, after theatrically scanning my still-damaged face and hands, "since hooligans have little respect for rank. If you're not more careful, we may need to find *you* a double. In the meantime, we must both be sound and prepared for the trials and triumphs to come, until my ascendancy, when—" He suddenly broke off. "Now go into my bathroom," he ordered with a languid wave. "Locate a bottle containing some little blue tablets with two thin white stripes girding them. Take two, and you'll be tip-top in minutes. Another Morell miracle."

His tone was jovial, but something in his use of the word "trials" puzzled me. According to Göring, a barely trained army on foot and horseback, wielding swords and pitchforks pitted against the perfectly trained, fully mechanised, and battle-tested Wehrmacht was a massive comedy that those few Poles left standing would hardly find amusing. *And what had the Führer meant by his "ascendancy"?*

I did as he recommended and re-entered to find that Göring, Himmler, Heydrich, Müller, and the Führer's top military advisers had arrived for another briefing, whereupon I was summarily dismissed. But I could swear that Heydrich sneaked a wink at me as I passed him.

After a brief reconnaissance, I located Brückner and coaxed him into an outside stroll and chat.

"You were fortunate the Führer dismissed you when he did," Brückner said. "The Poles will not be so fortunate. Those… gentlemen you left behind will soon orchestrate an orgy of indescribable brutality upon them. I'd like to think that it was only to terrify other nations into submission or neutrality. Unfortunately, terror is the most benevolent of their motives.

Yes, it's only the barest of beginnings. Of course, the Führer will once again insulate himself from the details with which the 'Two Hs' would love to regale him."

I caught the "only," "most benevolent," and "I'm afraid," but chose to ignore anything politically controversial, despite the horrific meaning I ascribed to those phrases. I also ignored the "once again insulate himself" but determined to revisit it one day. For now, I merely nodded.

"So, Heinz, did Cupid score a bullseye?"

This, I had no intention of ignoring, but I judged that I must tread lightly, perhaps even begin with levity. *Was "bullseye" meant as humour or an admission?* "Slightly off-centre, I have to admit. On our first evening, she expressed nothing short of astonishment that I'd been circumcised. She even asked me if I was a Jew. A joke, I assumed, so I answered that, as menial as my position might be, it would be difficult to imagine the Führer selecting a Jew as his principal valet. She laughed and said *touché*, whatever that means."

"It means…" he began, then gave up on my ignorance, as I hoped he would. "Well, anyway, my friend, if she was that interested in your foreskin, you must have had a reasonably successful first meeting. So then, what is this… 'off-centre' business?"

For a while, we strolled in silence while I considered the most dispassionate way of presenting the matter and decided on the truth minus a few suspicions and speculations. "It must be some want of charm on my part, Wilhelm," I finally said, "but when she didn't show up for our luncheon date, I tried telephoning her at her flat. I let it ring beyond toleration but with no success. Failing that, I tried calling her at the RSHA,[1] where

---

[1] The RSHA stood for the office formalizing the relationship between the SS intelligence service (SD) and the Security Police, which consisted of the Kripo (Criminal Police) and the Gestapo.

she said she worked, but they told me no woman by that name worked on their staff. And since she hasn't contacted me, I don't know what to think."

There was no immediate response, so I continued. "In the beginning, you were firmly opposed to telling me anything about her, and of course, I respected your decision. However, after four dates, and one stand-up, I still know nothing, so is this not a reasonable time to relent?"

Brückner stopped abruptly, turned to the side, and gazed at the gardens, then tipped his head and shoulder for me to join him. As usual, I stepped to the side where I could check his unpatched eye for subtleties.

"Heinz," he replied, "telling you nothing fulfilled a promise I made to *her*. Now, if you're still in the dark, it must have been important to her that you remain so, perhaps until she felt comfortable to confide—I grant you, not a minor eccentricity. On the other hand, her lack of contact and your current inability to locate her are quite another matter. I'll do everything I can to get to the bottom of it. That's my promise to *you*."

I nodded with painful enthusiasm to mask my frustration. "I'm most grateful, Wilhelm, but don't you think that by this time you could give me something to satisfy my curiosity? Without breaking your promise, naturally."

At that moment, a part of me wanted to pummel him, but truly, I had to admire his sense of honour, for I was certain he would do the same for me—and in the Chancellery, such a sense was virtually non-existent. "But," I said, "might it not be better to let it go and seek someone, uh, less eccentric?"

He turned and smiled. "For you, my friend, eccentricity is normal. Take my word. However, there may be more than eccentricity at play here. I'll get to the bottom of this, and you'll be together again or know the reason why you won't be."

How could he make such an assertion and assurance? I forced myself not to ask, since from both my experience and my reading of Machiavelli, no question was far better than no answer. But at least one avenue I'd pondered was open to me. "Is it possible," I asked, "just possible, that she considered my station as a servant too lowly?"

Brückner stopped again, reached out, and turned me to him. "Heinz, you must get this status nonsense out of your head. You must have discovered by now that your duties have nothing whatsoever to do with your position. You're not a servant; you never have been."

Before I could digest his words, we were interrupted by the relatively benign pedant Schaub, Brückner's immediate junior, who marched up to us and saluted.[2] He was always perfectly SS fastidious: never a pomaded hair out of place, never a thread drooping from a button. Starched and pressed, I imagined, even in private.

"Yes, Julius?" Brückner asked.

He turned his head to stare at me, then back to Brückner.

"Julius," Brückner said, "you know you can speak freely in front of Linge."

Schaub smiled thinly. "Of course, Wilhelm," he conceded. "As you've often said." He turned to me and executed a microscopic nod, then back to Brückner. "I came to tell you that the Führer will be travelling tomorrow and all must be made ready to act on the news he's certain to receive about our advance into Poland. All very hush-hush, you understand."

---

[2] Julius Schaub was one of Hitler's many adjutants but a valued member of Hitler's circle due to having been imprisoned alongside Hitler in 1924 for involvement in the coup d'état attempt of November 1923 in Munich. Both of Schaub's feet had been injured during the war, leaving him fairly debilitated.

"I'm relatively certain that Poland already knows," Brückner joked to a stone-faced Schaub, a man of no discernible humour.

Schaub's eyebrows lifted slightly. "I believe it's the reaction from the British and the French that motivates the Führer, not the Poles."

"I understand," Brückner said. "You may inform the Führer that all shall be as he wishes and that he need have no concerns on that score."

I barely listened to the banter, far more concerned with Brückner's enigmatic comment about my status. And there was still the matter of Christiane. The French Royalist writer Antoine de Rivarol wrote, "It is the dim haze of mystery that adds enchantment to pursuit." Unfortunately, at the moment, I felt considerably less than enchanted.

I WITNESSED AN historic day for the Führer, the Reich, and Europe. This I have been told, and not having read *Mein Kampf* for its wit, I have no reason to contest it. The British and French representatives notified the Führer that a state of war now existed between them and Germany.

I was summoned to the conservatory especially early to announce Ribbentrop, Hess, Goebbels, Himmler, Brückner, Bormann, and the recently promoted General Rommel. Once settled, the Führer flew into one of his famously theatrical, spittle-spewing rages I knew so well.

"The fucking Poles are miserable, good-for-nothing, loud-mouthed scum!" he bellowed. "Those damn British understand this as well as we do!" A fraction of a second later, as I predicted, he shifted down to a conversational tone. "These… gentlemen understand from their own history that might is right, especially when it comes to inferior races. In this, they were our first schoolmasters. It's disgraceful for these fucking hypocrites to suddenly present Czechoslovakia and Poland as sovereign states, when their rabble is not a jot better than the Sudanese or the Indians—*and*"—volume up again—"only because, on this occasion, it's about German interests and not British ones!" Then down. "My entire policy towards Britain has been based on recognising the natural realities as they exist on both sides, and now they want to put me in the pillory." And then a final volley: *"This is an unspeakable vilification, and mark my words, they'll pay dearly for it. I can promise you!"* Then he turned quickly to Brückner and me. "I have Schaub preparing for our departure. Please coordinate activities with him."

I knew what that meant: we were to leave for the front.

Finally installed on the America, the specially fitted-out train that was now the Führer's mobile "Field HQ," with Rommel as commandant in charge of the Führer's security, we left Berlin for Polzin, the first stop on his "Sherman's March"[3] through Poland (with the enthusiastic assistance of our new so-called Soviet ally).

---

[3] Sherman's March to the Sea was a military campaign of the American Civil War. Conducted through Georgia, General Sherman's forces followed a "scorched-earth" policy, destroying military targets as well as industry, infrastructure, and civilian property, thereby disrupting the Confederacy's economy and transportation networks. The operation broke the back of the Confederacy and helped lead to its eventual surrender. Sherman's bold move to operate deep within enemy territory without supply lines is considered one of the major achievements of the war and an early example of modern total war.

DESPITE THE DIRE warnings of his generals, the Führer persists in behaving as if he were, again, a young and immortal corporal regarding manoeuvres in the field. He visits the front almost daily, heedlessly passing through woodland and other insecure areas where Polish snipers lie in wait. Not being even remotely martial, either by inclination or happenstance, I was grateful to be left behind, but today, that was not to be.

Normally, in any procession, I would ride with Krause and one secretary, at least two vehicles behind the Führer, but this time, he asked me to occupy the tiny jump seat facing him. Save for Kempka at the wheel, we were alone.

"Bracing, isn't it, Linge?" the Führer remarked in high spirits as we drove through a wood on the Vistula. "Nothing gets the blood racing like the threat of imminent death. I'd almost forgotten, you know? All whine about the stench of battle, the terror, the chaos, but all I remember is the exhilaration, the simplicity, the clarity."

"I was never in battle, my Führer," I said.

"I know that." He smiled indulgently. "I was merely trying to give you a sense of why a battlefield holds such, how should I say...?"

He never completed his sentence, for suddenly, we came across the bodies of a German medical team, massacred only minutes before. The Führer told the driver to stop so he could survey the scene. A part of me yearned to turn away from the horror, but another part forced me to gape at a tableaux that could only have been rendered by Hieronymus Bosch: a grotesque, twisted black-grey-and-red landscape of unspeakable stench, shimmering gore, severed heads and limbs, oozing entrails and brains. What once were human beings now glowed and crackled like firewood. *Could this be what the Führer meant by exhilaration, simplicity, and clarity?* I finally turned away from the hideousness around me to catch the Führer's icy expression.

He waved his arm like a tour guide. "Pity all this will be rendered meaningless," he muttered enigmatically, then ordered Kempka to proceed.

Since I couldn't imagine his indifference, I had to marvel at the Führer's control. This seemed to be confirmed once we arrived at the front lines, where, with the sounds of shelling puncturing the air, he chatted with the common infantrymen, telling them of his own experiences at the front. I could see the visceral joy on his face when they gazed at him with almost delirious pride. In a show of solidarity, the Führer ate with the men at the field kitchens and recommended that in future, even the lofty, self-important Gauleiters[4] should follow his example, a recommendation his generals appeared reluctant to entertain.

For example, back at the Führerwagen, one of those generals, apparently disapproving of the Führer's confidence in being physically on the front lines, remarked that the campaign was a "risky adventure."

Fixing him with a stern stare, the Führer retorted, "I congratulate you, General. You have just expressed better than I ever could the craven and timorous sentiments of your kind that cost

---

[4] Political officials governing a district under Nazi rule.

us the last war and all that came with it. Never let me hear that yellow bilge again, or I'll reduce you to cleaning latrines!"

That evening, when I was alone with him, he said to me, "Linge, Linge, I ask you. How could I have possibly achieved victory with such characters?"

His use of the modal tense confounded me. "You mean the general, my Führer?"

"Of course the general—and he's far from alone."

"I…"

"Speak up, Linge; no ceremony."

"Well, my Führer," I said with well-practiced flattery, "I've observed that in your presence, even the most accomplished of your generals become… ah… what's the word…? Anyway, I… I think that you can too easily overwhelm even generals." I ached to say they became diffident but dared not risk abandoning my persona for the sake of erudition.

The Führer nodded. "'Even generals,' eh? They beguile you too. So, do you think I was too harsh?"

"Who can possibly argue with your judgement, my Führer?" I answered with tactful ambiguity.

The Führer smiled. "Too many by far," he joked, "but no matter. Tomorrow, I'll pin a medal on the fool, and he'll be in seventh heaven. Now where is Krause with that Fachingen?"[5]

It was clear from his tone that the Führer wanted more than his usual mineral water. For some time, I'd sensed that he was growing increasingly vexed with Krause. From the beginning, the uniformed rodent appeared to be as arrogant as he was duplicitous, indulged by the Führer only through the latter's

____

[5] Full name: Staatlich Fachingen. A German medicinal and mineral water, discovered in 1740. Due to a relatively high level of hydrogen carbonate, it can neutralise excessive acid in the stomach.

extravagant loyalty to old comrades. Many times, I overheard Krause recount with a laugh several liberties that he had taken with the Führer, and I personally witnessed Krause behave as if the Führer worked for him instead of the other way round. Even before my first month at the Chancellery had passed, Krause had boasted that one morning, he'd planted himself before the Führer, and in a tone of voice that brooked no contradiction, stated, "My Führer, today you must wear the black shoes; I have forgotten the brown ones." However, with the momentous burdens of war on the Führer's shoulders, comradely indulgence quickly turned to bare toleration, and I knew the time fast approached for toleration to surrender to ruthlessness.

I located the incautious bastard on the narrow ledge between the two end cars, clearly besotted and croaking some bawdy beer hall tune to himself. For anyone else, I'd have secured the Fachingen, handed Krause the bottle, and sent him wobbling back to the Führer, no wiser but perhaps a little safer. But it wasn't anyone else, so I agonised over it. For a moment, I even considered leaving him to his own drunken devices and reporting my failure, hoping that would lay the last straw on the Führer's back. *He'd do it to me,* I told myself with no little self-righteousness. *But should I stoop to the level of a Krause?* That was the only issue I faced. Debate aside, at the very least, the Führer needed his drink, so to delay a decision, I headed for the kitchen, but on my hurriedly distracted way, I literally bumped into Kempka.

"Man," he said, sweeping some imaginary dust from his tunic, "if I drove the way you walk, you'd be tending the Führer in a fucking hospital instead of a train." He laughed to assure me he was only kidding. "What's the rush?"

I told him about Krause, the water, the Führer's attitude, and how I felt towards them.

He pursed his lips in what passed for thought with him. "Look, my lad," he said, "I still owe you one for Schreck, so take the Fachingen back to the Führer and leave that little fucker to me."

"You don't owe me anything, since I didn't do anything," I protested.

"Well, you planted the seed, kiddo; I'm only the logger. Now get your ass back with the water, okay?"

His toothy smile vanished, replaced by something narrow, cold, and malevolent, so I shrugged, nodded, turned on my heels, and made for the Führer's quarters, muttering to myself that it wasn't my job to save Krause's bacon.

⌇

When Krause finally stumbled in with an anonymous flask, the Führer was sitting at his massive table—now a multi-layered mishmash of military maps, telegrams, coded messages, coloured pencils, compasses, and protractors—his hands clasped with white-knuckled severity. The Führer's expression must have sobered him sufficiently, for he clicked his heels and saluted, walked over, and offered him the flask.

"And what might this be, Herr Krause?" the Führer asked, hands still clasped.

I'd only heard the Führer say "Herr Krause" once, a few years before, after he'd overheard the valet say, "Fuck Goebbels," without knowing he'd been caught out.

Krause brought the flask to his chest. "It… it's the Fachingen you wanted, my Führer," he blurted.

"Is it?" the Führer asked him. "Is it so? Then, may I ask, where is the bottle you always pour it from?"

"It's… in… the kitchen, my Führer," he stammered. "It seemed unnecessary—"

"Tell me the truth, Krause. *The truth!*" He shouted spittle at him.

Krause jerked a step back from the onslaught and stared fixedly at the floor. "My Führer," he said, almost in a mumbled whisper, "I swear to you, Kempka told me it was Fachingen, and I—"

"You wish now to bring Kempka into your feeble, drunken duplicity? You really shouldn't go on, Krause," the Führer said in a voice as cold as Kempka's had been. "You dig your hole deeper with each lie. For years, you've been hanging from a narrow ledge, grasping onto me with your fingernails, and I've held steady and prevented you from plummeting. Those days are over, hear me? Bormann wanted you sent to… well, anyway, for your years with me, I'm content to merely rid myself of you. Be gone by morning. Brückner will see to your next posting."

As I stood in the bathroom doorway, I could see that even in Krause's impaired condition, he'd been with the Führer long enough to know the complete futility of pursuing the matter. So after his bloodshot eyes swivelled to me with a murderous stare, which received no response, he saluted the Führer, turned, and left.

"Long overdue," the Führer said to me as I organised his table. "Have Brückner take care of Krause, will you? And have him set about getting a replacement from Himmler. I don't require a giant like you, so he won't have to part with even one of his precious Vikings. Oh yes," he added with a mock grin, "and tell him to get someone young. The old fighters are either perverts or drunkards—or both—and even if they're not, they're far too set in their ways."

❦

As I readied the Führer for bed, I couldn't help discounting any feeling of triumph in Krause's downfall. Yes, I detested the man, and truly, his faults were legion. But also, no less truly, I loathed many round the Führer equally. At least with Krause, his faults were both obvious and known to the Führer. *Who else from Himmler's fellowship of fanatics would be so vulnerable?* The Dutch Christian humanist Erasmus advised that it was better for a man to keep the sharp-tongued woman he married, rather than risk finding another who might be even worse. I dreaded the Führer's new "bride."

WE'RE STILL ENCAMPED on the "Führerwagen." After three weeks of German might and Soviet brutality, the Polish jokes have continued but lost their context since Poland is no more, at least no more than the battered ruins of Warsaw, charred and razed towns and villages, devastated fields, and prison camps.

As Brückner predicted, the masses had been abandoned to homelessness, starvation, disease, and worse—Himmler—while their leaders fled to the safety of London. And as the Führer predicted, Britain and France stood by while Poland was eradicated. The English did no more than drop anti-Nazi propaganda leaflets—thirteen tonnes of them—over Germany, prompting the Führer to joke that if Britain had wanted to punish the Reich's sanitation workers, they had succeeded admirably.

The Führer designated Brückner as liaison between all the military and civilian (to the extent there was a difference) forces operating in the newly augmented Reich and so, understandably, had little time to fulfil his pledge to me. And yet, in what scant time remained, he was able to discover that Christiane did, in fact, work for the RSHA, and yet, could arrive at no explanation for why her employment had been denied when I'd inquired or why communication between us had been discontinued, as if we'd failed to pay our telephone charges.

The top Reich officials still chuckled over Nepal, South Africa, and Canada declaring war on Germany. The Führer even quipped to General Halder, chief of the Army high command, that perhaps he should surrender to Nepal before South Africa and Canada could rally their forces. Even the stolid Halder appeared to enjoy that one.

❦

As I'd completed my morning's duties, I strolled to the commissary car, at the moment inhabited solely by the Führer's SS guards, who appeared unusually subdued. I sat alone with a cup of coffee, savouring the quiet after weeks of relentless, ear-crushing bombardment and arms fire. As I considered what Brückner had told me about Christiane, self-conscious thoughts dogged me, and curiosity almost overtook desire. *Was it me?* That is to say, *what was there about me that would cause her to vanish?* But another thought came directly on its heels: *Why would the RSHA deny her situation, then be receptive to Brückner's inquiries?* Sitting there, I determined to pursue the matter with much thoroughness when we returned to Berlin—whenever that might be, and regardless of the visibility it might necessitate—when suddenly, all the guards shot to attention and saluted, and I felt a light tap on my shoulder. When I turned my head and glanced up, it was Heydrich grinning at me like a solitary hyena coming upon a safe meal.

"No ceremony, Linge," he told me, and with a slight downward motion of his prehensile index finger, he signalled for the rest to return to what they were doing, which they did instantly. "So preoccupied with your thoughts," he remarked as he moved to the seat across from me and eased himself down, draping one long, narrow, glisteningly booted leg over the other in a languidly fluid motion. "A pity to disturb them."

Pity, indeed! So, why didn't you wait to tap my shoulder when I appeared less "preoccupied"? Typical Heydrich: gentility cloaking malice.

"Nothing even remotely important, General, I can assure you," I answered. "What can I do for you?"

His slit of a mouth widened into what passed as his smile. "Quite the contrary, my friend. It's I who would do for you. Have you ever visited Warsaw?"

"Never, Herr General," I replied. "I did no travelling before joining the Führer's service, and afterwards, I have gone only where he's gone."

"Pity," he said. "'If a work of art is rich and vital and complete, those who have artistic instincts will see its beauty, and those to whom ethics appeal more strongly than aesthetics will see its moral lesson. It will fill the cowardly with terror, and the unclean will see in it their own shame.'"

I knew he was quoting Oscar Wilde without attribution. I didn't understand the quote when I first heard it, and I still didn't understand it, so I responded genuinely with only a blank stare.

The slit spread again. "That aphorism a bit recondite for you?" he commented drily. "Of no importance. Since you missed the pre-Wehrmacht Warsaw, I thought I'd do you a service by giving you a personally guided tour of post-Wehrmacht Warsaw—and perhaps more. Are you game?"

Again, the image of a hyena and its prey flitted across my consciousness, and I almost laughed. Every cell in my brain knew that when a creature like Heydrich did one a "service," it was for Heydrich and Heydrich alone. I'd visited his cellar, and now, if he wished to show me "post-Wehrmacht Warsaw—and perhaps more," I wanted no part of it. The only issue was how to efficaciously refuse.

"Has the Führer been—"

"Linge, Linge," he interrupted, "must we bother the Führer with every minuscule matter? In his position, he must concentrate all his formidable vision, energy, and talents on the next phase, so a tour by his valet of his most recent conquest is far too trivial to even mention, am I right? Shall we say eleven hundred hours tomorrow?"

Clearly, he didn't wish me to discuss his generous offer of a tour with the Führer. Among all his other dark gifts, the monster was superbly adept at blocking exits.

HAVING NO MASOCHISTIC desire to discomfit Heydrich, I mentioned nothing to the Führer, and at precisely 1100, the former came for me. Escorted by squadrons of both military and police, we drove through what must have been a model of the picturesque, now turned into primitive rubble. This, of course, I expected, but what truly horrified me was the pitiless and bloodthirsty treatment of the civilian population. I'd over-heard the Führer being informed in the most general terms by his military advisers that the Polish September Campaign was an instance of "total war," but I had possessed no experiential vision of its meaning until now.

The city resembled a relief map of moonscape etchings or grainy photographs of Stonehenge, in England, that I'd seen in library books. Only here was not a series of static craters, obe-lisks, and sand dunes but a bombed-out hell, the air alive with the fetid stench of ashes and corpses. Ornate structures that once contained office buildings, hotels, department stores, restau-rants, and apartments had been reduced to giant, jagged, charred tombstones, some parts still glowing. Once-wide, bustling bou-levards were treacherous, skeletal mazes of debris, piles of burnt bodies, and broken glass.

Brückner had informed me with no joy that from the start, the Luftwaffe were ordered to specifically target civilians and columns of refugees along the roads to "wreak havoc, disrupt communications, and destroy Polish morale."[6]

According to Heydrich—and confirmed in countless meetings the Führer had with his advisers—Party propaganda, masterminded by Goebbels and his ministry, had been working relentlessly to convince the German people that the Jews and Slavs were subhuman, which was one of the major factors behind the relentless and extravagant exuberance in their brutality. What remained of Warsaw was now crowded with Germans being quartered in all the larger houses still reasonably intact. However, by Himmler's fiat, while it was the Germans who were trying to clean up the city, for this work, they used only Jews, who had to sweep the streets, clean the public latrines (some with toothbrushes, some even with their tongues), lug away the debris, and fill the street trenches, all to the brutal cacophony of whips cracking, shots firing, dogs snarling, orders being shouted, women, children, and old men being beaten, kicked, flogged, spat upon (the laggards and infirm shot or beaten to death on the spot). I was sickened by the sight—sickened but silent.

I succeeded in not vomiting my breakfast, but after a few grinding minutes of this particularly grotesque tableaux that would repel even Dante, I dared notify Heydrich that I had a terrible migraine (not an untruth) and would appreciate being

---

[6] Apart from the victims of battles, the German forces—both the SS and the regular Wehrmacht—killed tens of thousands of Polish non-combatants. During what they called Operation Tannenberg alone, nearly twenty thousand Poles were shot by the *Einsatzgruppen* (deployment groups) at seven hundred sixty mass-execution sites. These units of the Nazi security forces were composed of members from the SS, the *Sicherheitspolizei* (Sipo, or "Security Police"), and the *Ordnungspolizei* (Orpo, or "Order Police"), acting as mobile killing units in occupied territories. Moreover, the constant, intentional bombardment of civilian facilities, along with a lack of food and medical supplies, resulted in even greater casualties among the city's population.

returned to the train. Though he didn't look at me, I could tell that he was sorely disappointed to be denied the pleasure of giving me a tour of the cellars of what he called the "newly appointed" police headquarters. Fortunately, a perverse refinement triumphed over brutish hedonism.

"A pity you're not well enough to continue," he remarked without expression as we drove back to the railway station. "These moronic Poles will continue to defy us, devastated and defeated though they may be. But to make a virtue of necessity, that suicidal stubbornness will provide the sport at which the Aryan race is so adept."

Heydrich the virtuous! I fought mightily against imagining what such "sport" would entail, but I couldn't ward off the dread it inspired, which only made the migraine fiercer. To counteract its worst effects, I attempted to replace them with thoughts of Christiane, but all that came to my aching consciousness was Jung's warning that "a particularly beautiful woman is a source of terror." Jung was right, of course, but just one of many sources, and so it helped me not at all, especially when I glanced over at the blissfully glacial Heydrich, luxuriating in his element.

The general saw me safely through mountain ranges of rubble and corpses, the myriad blockades, checkpoints, armoured columns, and sporadic gunfire, all the way back to the mobile FHQ, without incident. Though he received reports of resistance, they merely narrowed his eyelids, and the crescent moon of his lips rose even higher: the Devil as the Cheshire cat.

Before I stepped from his armoured touring car and still without turning his head towards me, he remarked, "I understand that you're seeing one of our female operatives socially but that recently, she's proven somewhat elusive. I'll let you in on a small secret: not all who work for us do so... officially, you might say. Therefore, even though I am, as you can see, preoccupied with convincing Poles that there is no longer a Poland, I'll relieve Brückner of his well-intentioned burden and set about arranging contact at the earliest opportunity."

I wasn't particularly encouraged by such largesse. "Herr General, I—"

"It's nothing, Linge," he interrupted, still staring straight ahead. "Unlike the Reichsführer, the vast majority of Party leaders, and my compatriots at the RSHA, I have a relatively open mind about certain doctrinal matters of no great weight. And far be it for me to impede the amours of one who so directly serves the Führer—no matter how… awkwardly his needs are pursued. Now, see to your migraine," he concluded as his driver quickly exited the car, came around, and opened my door.

After I exited, the driver returned to his seat and motored away.

As I boarded the train, I was reminded of the tale I'd read long ago of the scorpion and the frog, in which a scorpion asks a frog to carry it across a river. The frog hesitates, afraid of being stung, but the scorpion argues that if it did so, they would both drown. Considering this, the frog agrees, but midway across the river, the scorpion does indeed sting the frog, dooming them both. While drowning, when the frog asks the scorpion why, the scorpion replies that he couldn't help it; it was in his nature. As I recalled, the fable was to illustrate that people and creatures cannot change fundamental aspects of their character. So, while a part of me welcomed the scorpion's offer, this frog was little comforted by it.

In what I call my own Polish adventure, albeit—and happily—limited, I experienced only one interesting "domestic" incident, and it was today. When Brückner, the Führer, and I were driving to Gotenhafen, one of the cities the Poles had defended, the Führer, for whom everything was moving too slowly, ordered our driver to go down a narrow and fairly steep road to the harbour. This created a logistical problem, in that the car carrying the SS bodyguard had to stick to our tail. Rommel, clearly knowing this, positioned himself on the street and roared like a drill sergeant, "Only the Führer and the bodyguard's vehicles are to go down! All others wait here!"

As we started up and I looked behind me, I spotted a third car in motion. This vehicle contained Bormann, who gesticulated wildly at Rommel. I knew both as resourceful, stubborn, and ambitious—the former obsessed with power, the latter obsessed with victory. In my humble view, they ought never to have squared up to each other like this, but there they were, both at it, right in view of the Führer. Bormann got his version in first. Rommel had blocked his path.

"Remain where you are," Bormann barked brusquely—and disrespectfully. "I order it as the FHQ Commandant. This is no kindergarten outing; kindly do as I have ordered!"

To Bormann's chagrin, the Führer intervened with, "No, Bormann, a kindergarten outing it certainly is not. Kindly allow Rommel to do his job."

In the late evening, when I could sneak some time with Brückner, I asked him about the incident. He replied, "This is war now, and Rommel is a pure warrior. Later, it will become a bureaucracy, and Bormann is a pure bureaucrat. Bureaucrats like Bormann never forgive and never forget. If I were Rommel, I would prefer all the enemy's forces before me to having Bormann behind me."

Accustomed as I was to Bormann's arrogance, peculiarities, and love of intrigue, the ugly thought assailed me that Brückner was right again: Bormann would indeed remember and would exact his revenge. I also told Brückner of my encounter with Heydrich.

"Intriguing," he said with a bitter laugh. "To actually divert that character from the comfort of his torture chamber, I must have set off some rather noteworthy alarms in Himmlerburg."

Then I told him of my belief that I'd been followed from the restaurant, careful to omit my encounter with Schlegl. "Am I being paranoid?" I asked.

"Heinz," he remarked through a smile, "I've been a German far longer than you have, and if there's one thing I've learned, it's that Germans are born followers—in every way. It's like that old Czech cartoon, where a faceless person is following a faceless person who's also following a faceless person, who is, in turn, being facelessly followed by another faceless follower, and so on back, until the image recedes into infinity. Unfortunately, we all swim in an ocean of faceless greatcoats and fedoras. But at this point, Heinz, I wouldn't fret, because I've also learned this: if you're caught at something, it's because they want you to be caught at something; if not, they don't. So, you'll take from Heydrich what you must," he concluded, "since he's not a man who offers."

FINALLY RETURNING TO Berlin has stirred in me conflicting feelings, especially so, being greeted by a message from Christiane asking that we meet the following evening at 0830 for dinner at Café Preising, an intimate eatery tucked into a secluded side street. When I called to confirm, using the number she'd provided (different from the one I'd called after she'd stood me up), my attempt to appear casual failed utterly, but she appeared to take it all in good humour.

"I'm flattered," she said warmly. "Absence truly does make the heart grow fonder. I can hear yours, even over the phone."

Bereft of a witty response, I attempted to shift conversational gears, but my lack of social coordination caused me to stall—something else she could probably hear.

"You don't have to say it; I missed you too, Heinz. Terribly. We'll catch up. I promise," she whispered seductively, then rang off.

I didn't have a chance to inquire why she hadn't asked me to collect her at her flat.

❧

On my way to the Führer, I bumped into Morell.

"How does he fare this morning, Doctor?" I asked.

"As a medical man," Morell said, "I'm reasonably safe in saying that you won't be running for a gas mask this morning, though I make no such assurances about this afternoon and evening, since the Führer wishes me to attend an ailing Bormann, and that means a long and numbing trip to the Berghof." He glanced slowly round him like a conspirator, lifted himself onto his toes, and cupped one hand round his mouth as he whispered, "I tell you in strictest confidence, Linge, that I'd rather quit the profession than deal with Bormann. Good God, the man is insufferable. But you know how it is: when the Führer says go, we go, eh?"

There was nothing more to be said, so we saluted in the Führer's name, and he scurried off.

The Führer's mood belied his bowels. As I readied his toiletries and tidied his study, he uttered not a word, merely staring down morosely at his splayed hands on his desk. I could discern that his silence was a sign of sullenness, not contemplation, a form of unexpected mental numbness I'd lived with all my life, so I recognised it instantly and kept silent as well.

Having put away the Führer's toiletries and shut off the bathroom light, I heard the Führer say behind me, "If, after all this time, he still hasn't retrieved it, was it all, then, just a malicious hoax at my expense?" I thought he was speaking to me. I had no idea what the "it" was, and when I searched the desk-lamp-lit room, I saw the Führer still hunched over his desk, addressing his remarks to his vice-chancellor, the cadaverous mystic, Hess,[7]

---

[7] Rudolf Hess was a German politician and a leading member of the Nazi Party. In 1919, Hess enrolled at the University of Munich, where he studied geopolitics under Karl Haushofer, an adherent of the occult. Hess joined the NSDAP on 1 July 1920 and was at Hitler's side on 8 November 1923 during the Beer Hall Putsch. While serving time in jail for this attempted coup, he assisted Hitler with *Mein Kampf*, which became a foundation of the NSDAP's political platform. Hess was appointed deputy Fuhrer in 1933.

who sat cross-legged in an armchair in a dark corner. I decided to remain in the bathroom.

"I appreciate your impatience, my Führer," Hess replied, "but I have every reason to believe that the information I just received concerning Rahn is both accurate and encouraging. We now know the location. All we need to do is retrieve it. But for obvious reasons, it's well- guarded, so it could take time but, I add, will be worth every minute."

Even sitting in shadow, I could sense Hess's sunken eyes glowing with ethereal knowledge. *In fact,* I thought, *he appeared to carry a shadow with him as a constant companion.*

The Führer raised his fist and crashed it down on the desktop. "That's easy for you to say, but time is exactly what I don't have! Those limp noodles Britain and France will finally awaken from their wishful dreaming and be obliged to act on their declarations, then, my friend, we'll be in it up to our necks. Just how much can we rely on this Rahn fellow?"

"He is an adept, has been well prepared, and Katrin still speaks highly of him."

At the mention of Katrin, my brain froze. So, she was a significant part of some plan on the highest levels. All I knew was that her words to me were no more genuine than her ambiguously amorous overtures.

(Translator's Note: The alluring and mysterious Katrin plays a prominent role in Volume One. There are too many references to recount here.)

"All well and good, Rudolf," the Führer replied, his voice beginning to ascend. "But must I remind you that it was based on your word and Heinrich's that I felt comfortable undertaking this potentially disastrous adventure? And if that's to change, I require results! RESULTS! And quickly!"

"Of course, my Führer," he replied, contritely I thought. "It takes ti—"

"There IS no time!" he shouted, cutting Hess off. "And even if your Rahn succeeds, what of the second item, without which, the one he brings me is useless, eh? *EH?*" he screamed.

"That matter is being handled, even as we speak."

I could see the Führer's face darken, and I involuntarily took a small step back.

"Handled, you say? HANDLED? If I handled things the way you all do, I'd still be an unemployed ex-corporal!" He slammed his fist on the desktop again, this time sending all the materials I'd carefully arranged careening to the floor and causing Hess to uncross his legs.

I could tell that this was no choreographed display of theatrics. I understood nothing of their "conversation," save for the mention of Katrin, but with no context, I was bereft of its meaning.

There followed a deadly silence, during which, I assumed, the Führer was giving himself time to ratchet down.

Then he spoke. "All right then, Rudolf, we wait. In the absence of Rahn, arrange a meeting through Himmler, in which I can be thoroughly briefed by Weisthor—and this woman of his. I will know where I stand, hear me?"

Hess shot up from his armchair. "It will be as you wish, my Führer," he declared with no little enthusiasm and resolve, and with that, he saluted and strode out without even a glance at me, though I again stood in the very centre of the backlit bathroom doorway.

After a few moments, when I dared venture from my cover, the Führer turned to me.

"Linge," he said, sounding somewhat raspy, "I regret that you were obliged to witness such a vulgar display."

I was startled by his awareness of me and even more by his concern. "My Führer," I replied with much awkwardness, "I was only worried about you. It seemed—"

"That I'm human after all, eh?" he interrupted, completing my sentence for me, hardly the first time.

I didn't know how to respond, since it wasn't the sentence I'd had in mind, so I waited.

"Well," he finally said with a shrug. "I don't mind *you* knowing; I just hope to God no one else does."

THIS MORNING, THE Führer, who, in his typically mysterious fashion, had learned of my intended date with Christiane, kindly told me to pursue it and not bother to accompany him to the anniversary of the Beer Hall Putsch at the Bürgerbräukeller in Munich.

"But, my Führer," I entreated disingenuously, "with Krause gone and no replacement selected—"

"Good of you to worry about me so," he said with a twinkle, "but quite unnecessary. Brückner had already arranged for one of Göring's army of attendants to accompany me. For a young strapping fellow like you," he kidded with a vigorous slap on my shoulder, "I think it far better to dine with an attractive young lady than listen to the reminiscences of homely old men."

Now, such an affair would normally (if normally is the proper word) produce internal convulsions of anticipated elation. But that was not even close to the reaction I experienced. I had no words to describe it, but a voice (from whom or from where, I had no idea) shouted in my mind's ear a warning. *Stand her up!* it said but provided no explanation. *Was it her unexplained disappearance? All the searching and waiting? The follower? Schlegl? Heydrich's "largesse"? All of these? Or was it something even more sinister that I was incapable of defining but was there just the same?*

Years before, I'd overheard Baur employ some aeronautical term he called the "point of no return." When I asked him about it, he told me that it was the point on a flight at which, due to fuel consumption, a plane is no longer capable of returning to the airfield from which it took off, so come what may, there was no alternative to going forward. *Was this the voice sounding the alarm? Would I approach that point tonight—or had I already passed it?*

❧

She arrived at the exact time she'd specified, sparing me any further disquiet through fashionable lateness. She was even more stunning than when I saw her last, and for a moment, it took my breath away. As I rose, she handed her coat and gloves to the maître d' without looking at him (a situation I'd experienced often) and waited for me to pull out her chair, her lips curled up mischievously.

"Have you waited long?" she asked.

I pushed in her chair and took my seat across from her. "No, not really. Actually, not at all," I replied with embarrassing awkwardness. "We… might have even butted heads at the door."

She glanced up at me with a theatrically dubious expression. "Ah, so this time you intend not to flatter me?"

I blew some air from my nostrils and smiled. "So, this is your game?" I chided lightly. "If I come early, I'm too eager. If I come on time, I insult you. I don't even want to consider the consequences of coming late."

She laughed. "Oh, but I love games, don't you?" she inquired playfully.

"Of course," I said, "but not when the rules are written by my opponent." In actuality, I hated games of any sort.

She reached across and touched my cheek with her fingertips for a second, then took her hand away. "I didn't lie on the phone, Heinz. No game. I *have* missed you terribly despite what you must have thought." She changed the subject. "I can't tell you how wonderful I felt when General Heydrich gave me leave to see you again."

The ambiguity of her statement aside, I hoped she didn't wish me to ask her why she hadn't been permitted to see me in the first place, since I had no intention of engaging in so potentially perilous a subject as Heydrich's agenda or her relationship to it. And yet I ached to know, despite my intense apprehension.

"No more pleased than I" was all I said with no less ambiguity.

"Shall we order?"

"Of course," I said, "on condition that you do the honours. I know of this place, but I've never been here. As I look round, I see many satisfied faces, so with you at the helm, I doubt we'll fare worse."

She agreed willingly, and with a wave of my hand to the waiter, our dinner began.

I yearned to ask her what she'd been doing since we last met but decided to let her raise the subject if she was so inclined. She wasn't, so I told her instead of my travels with the Führer to Poland.

"Yes," she said, once I'd finished. "A pity, I suppose. All round headquarters, officials high and low are scurrying to act out the Reichsführer's declaration that Warsaw must completely disappear from the surface of the earth and serve only as a transport station for the Wehrmacht. No stone can remain standing, he ordered, so every building must be razed to its foundation."

I couldn't help observing that she'd mentioned nothing about the inhabitants, the Polish Jews at the very least. *Could a fanatical racist like Himmler possibly have omitted to mention them?* But whether he had or hadn't, I certainly wasn't going to bring it up.

"Well, from what I witnessed, he certainly kept his word" was all I said before our drinks arrived.

Only once did I approach the personal, when I asked after her mother, and she told me with no discernible expression that finally, the cranky crone had become "rancid porridge for the Devil's breakfast." I quickly decided to keep any further subjects light and detached.

"So, what do you do for recreation?" It wasn't an idle question. To be frank, despite the superior quality of the food and drink and the *gemütlich* atmosphere, I was straining at the social leash to get out of there and repair to her prearranged room at the Kaiserhof.[8]

"Well," she began, her elegant index finger pushing gently on her lower lip, "my job requires so much of my time that I've even stopped thinking of leisure and recreation. That's why I treasure this moment. But truthfully, with things as they are and will be, I can't imagine that the demands on your time are any less."

I shrugged at that. "Not really. The Führer has an enormously redundant staff of menials, so I'm able to switch and swap fugitive moments of relaxation. Like tonight." I wisely omitted Madame Kitty's brothel, but for a few moments, I stared down at my drink. I noticed, for what it was worth, that she didn't contradict my use of the term "menial."

"What's troubling you, Heinz?" she asked.

I glanced up self-consciously, face feverish, pausing as long as possible, but I could contain it no longer. "I'll admit I'm

---

[8] Berlin's first "grand hotel," the Kaiserhof, was situated in Wilhelmplatz, located next to the Reich Chancellery. The Kaiserhof offered more than two hundred sixty rooms, all fitted out in a modern and luxurious manner. It was the first hotel in Berlin where every room had an electricity supply, its own bathroom, and its own telephone. The hotel also featured steam heating and pneumatic lifts. Its convenient location, luxurious amenities, and managerial discretion made it the chief installation depot for the top Nazis' mistresses and an ideal spot for other clandestine assignations.

thoroughly resentful of our situation. We want to be together, yes? And yet, you can disappear without a trace, and I, then, must go it alone, making awkward inquiries until I receive an unbidden favour from General Heydrich of all people. Our relationship—if there's to be one, and I hope there is—must be direct, honest, and continual, and no less important, within our control and not at the mercy or whim of others." Even at the time, I understood the dangerous gamble in my words. *What possible control could she or I have over her situation (whatever that was)?* It was emotional, needy, hazardous, reckless, and stupid, but there it was.

Christiane's stunned appearance was not surprising, and for a time, she said nothing, her chameleonlike hazel eyes (tonight bearing a greyish hue to match her elegant grey dress) stared at me with an expression I couldn't interpret. After a few pregnant moments, she started to reply but was interrupted by a grim-faced Schaub,[9] who rushed to our table, leaned over, and began to whisper something in my ear but was drowned out by an announcement from the restaurant's owner, informing the patrons that there had been one more "traitorous attempt upon the Führer's life."

Pandemonium followed instantly upon speechless incredulity. Christiane glanced up at Schaub, then back at me, grabbed her purse, removed a small notebook and pencil, tore out a page, scribbled a phone number on it, and handed it to me. "Please call me the moment you're able," she said, her exquisite face wearing a curious expression I couldn't decipher. "It appears we have much unfinished business." After glancing at the paper, though I had no further need of it, I took it for appearances. Then she

---

[9] Julius Schaub was Hitler's longest-serving adjutant, primarily responsible for security duties.

and I rose and accompanied Schaub out the door with the rest of the hysterical crush of alarmed patrons.

❧

Though no details had yet reached the Chancellery, frenzy had enveloped all within. Since there was nothing for me to do but engage meaninglessly with ignorant people hysterically sharing their ignorance, I retreated to my quarters and completed this entry. I'm ashamed to say that the last thoughts I had before photographing you were: *Would I still have a job come morning, and why did it have to happen when I'd just reconnected with Christiane?*

9 *November 1939*

NOT SURPRISINGLY, THE entire morning was enveloped by the assassination attempt. It turned out that the Führer had left the celebration unexpectedly early and avoided the fate that the assassin had planned for him. Truly, the man was as invincible as he always claimed to be. According to Fiehler,[10] who briefed the Führer's adjutants (including Brückner, who later told me), he had been addressing the Old Guard party members, those disciples and soldiers who had been loyal to Hitler and his fascist party since the earliest days of its inception. A masterpiece of bad timing, just twelve minutes after the Führer had left the hall, along with important Party leaders who had accompanied him, a bomb exploded, which had been secreted in a pillar behind the speaker's platform. Seven people were killed, and sixty-three were wounded.

When the Führer heard the news on his train, he went pale, gasped for air, and demanded, "Where is Himmler?"

Bormann replied that Himmler had stayed behind in Munich and was personally leading the investigation. The Führer became even more excited and commanded that Himmler remain in Munich for as long as it took to see that all those criminals involved in the business "bitterly regret their folly," adding that the Reichsführer "should proceed ruthlessly and exterminate the

---

[10] Karl Fiehler was a German politician of the Nazi Party and served as the mayor of Munich from 1933 to 1945.

whole pack of them—root and branch!" As if Himmler needed such encouragement.

As I listened, I felt a sharp pang of shame since, at the moment, I cared little about our seemingly invincible Führer. My brain was roiling with what might have happened at dinner—and afterwards—with Christiane had this ridiculous would-be assassin not interfered.

∾

News of the Führer's narrow and amazing escape spread like a gasoline fire throughout the Reich, and when approached on the subject (which he was incessantly and with congratulations), all he would say was that he was under the "special protective hand of providence." I found the entire business outlandish. I asked Brückner how this character could do all he needed to do right under the noses of the handpicked, highest trained, most thorough, and rabidly meticulous security service in the world. It made no sense to me, now as then. The life of the Führer (not to mention the destiny of the Reich) should not depend upon a minor change in schedule.

Brückner merely shrugged and said, "The road to frustration, my friend, is paved with shoulds."

Upon waking, I resolved to call Christiane (hoping, of course, that the number she gave me was still reliable), but it had to wait, for the Führerbuzzer summoned me to his conference room, in which a meeting was already in progress. The Führer, in pyjamas and robe, stood white-faced while Himmler briefed him on the latest developments. Also present were Göring, Goebbels, and Heydrich.

"We questioned the waiters… rigorously," Heydrich asserted through a smirk that spoke volumes on the meaning of rigour. "And I'm reasonably confident that they didn't know the man they saw several times. We sent their description to every—"

"Must we plod through all this procedure?" the Führer broke in. "I'm well aware of your talents—after the fact," he said with no little snideness.

Heydrich shifted seamlessly to a succinct summary. "Ultimately, my Führer, our search led us to the arrest of a certain Elser, who was attempting to enter Switzerland. It—"

"After our exacting interrogation," Himmler interrupted, "this Elser confessed fully. It appears that he acted alone and had, as his motive, a change in the political order of the Reich."

The Führer halted his circuit abruptly and, red-faced, turned to Himmler. "Heinrich!" he shouted. "Do you take me for a nincompoop? There's no possible way this character could have done this without assistance. You police the Reich; you are there to protect me. Is this… whoever he is… this Elser, such a master magician that he can assassinate me at will, without even a hint to my security services? *Unacceptable!*" he screamed. "I want everyone even remotely connected with this! I want mass arrests, you hear? I want our forests shorn of trees for the gibbets! Am I to be constantly at risk from every imbecile who has a better idea for the Reich? I must deal with the world without being hindered by the brilliant hindsight of those who are sworn to defend me and my regime from crackpots! Am I clear?"

What triggered it, I don't know, but I was standing inconspicuously at ease in a corner, when I was suddenly engulfed in a frantic collage of hideous images of my liquor-loaded brute of a father raping and ravaging my mother on the floor of our dilapidated attic hovel while she screamed and writhed uselessly under a downpour of the vile drunkard's vomit. The horror only ended when the Führer shook me violently, and I saw that we were now alone in his darkened study.

"So you've returned to us," the Führer murmured, his brow knitted with concern. "When you stood there screaming, *'I'll tear your throat out, you stinking piece of shit!'* then vomited and collapsed, you had us all shocked and deeply concerned. You even shook up Himmler—not a minor feat. I was about to summon Morell, but now it seems that all you need is a good laundress with a strong stomach."

My brain was a throbbing lump of lava. I stared down silently with indescribably intense embarrassment at the putrid, viscous acid-yellow filth coating the front of my uniform, but to my utter amazement, the Führer appeared unfazed.

"I'm no physician," he said almost jocularly, "but I suspect that you had an acute attack of Führer anxiety." Before I could respond, he continued. "I know you too well, Linge. You worry about me even more than my bodyguards. Now, that's both encouraging but needless," he assured me. "Even the luckiest cats have fewer lives. And as for tearing out throats, Uncle Heinrich hardly needs to recruit *you*."

It might have been the aftereffects of my episode, but suddenly, the Führer's face seemed to lose all colour and take on the aspect of a mask with nothing behind it. Hollow. Frightening. Then, just as quickly, his real face returned with a troubled expression.

"I have an odd feeling about things, Linge, so I'll be having a working lunch." He moved me to his desk and handed me a sheet of paper coated with a veneer of undisciplined scrawl. "Have all my maps of the West available, and make certain the people on this list know to attend. No excuses will be accepted. Now go and clean yourself up," he commanded lightly.

I exited in high embarrassment at my lack of control but, at the same time, grateful the Führer assumed it was that hapless Elser whose throat I'd threatened.

After showering, gargling, and changing uniforms, I sought out that malign fount of gossip, Schroeder, told her of my conversation with the Führer (omitting my spell), and asked her what "odd feeling" the Führer might have been referring to. For some time now, she'd managed to successfully negotiate the Führer's "request" that she kiss and make up with me. I would have preferred to munch on broken glass than ask her for anything, but curiosity vanquished self-respect.

"Can it be that the Führer would leave his prized possession in the dark?" she asked with narrow-lidded, barely controlled snideness.

"A minor lapse, Fräulein Schroeder, I'm sure. You of all people know how preoccupied he is." I wanted to spit in her face but reserved my mouth for a weak grin.

She told me with a sneer, highlighting a theatrically pained reluctance, that while he was dictating to her last night, he'd made an offhanded joke that so far, he'd gotten more of a reaction from Unity Mitford than from Britain and France. "Satisfied, Herr Linge?"

"Satisfied," I responded, still smiling, "and most grateful."

She merely nodded, said, "If there is nothing else," and went on her merry way before waiting for a response I had no intention of making.

I BREAKFASTED WITH Brückner, who, this morning, occasionally tilted his head back to receive some cloudy liquid in his eye from a small applicator. When I asked about it, he told me that he was concerned about his vision in his remaining eye, so reluctantly, he had Morell concoct one of his "magic elixirs."

I joked that if worse came to worst, he could always wear two patches and added, "Just think how alluring you'd be then."

He responded drily that he was alluring enough and preferred not to be led round the Chancellery by a dog.

More important, he was wholly sceptical about Elser and his failed assassination attempt. When I told him of the Führer's apparent need for complicated conspiracy over individual zealotry, he said that it had struck him from the beginning as "highly irregular" that obsessively meticulous creatures like Himmler and Heydrich, not to mention born snoops like "Gestapo Müller" and Admiral Canaris, could be undone by a nothing like Elser and that only fate had prevented a tragedy of incomparable proportions for the Reich.

"What are you suggesting?" I asked, bewildered. "Do you believe there was a conspiracy?"

Brückner chuckled. "Of course I do, lad, but not the sort the Führer was considering."

"And just what might that be?" I asked.

"Let's leave it at that for the present, yes?"

"I imagine it'll have to be so, if you won't tell me."

After another bout with the eyedropper, he said, "Think of it this way: sometimes, information is the enemy, but we can often keep it at bay with a shield of ignorance."

Once I'd taken leave of my reticent and oblique comrade, I telephoned Christiane, who actually answered, and we made arrangements to meet at her new apartment the following evening, where she would "prepare a sumptuous supper for us." After ringing off in a state of high elation, I was immediately brought low by the voice in my head again warning me that her reappearance was Heydrich's "gift."

14 *November 1939*

ALL NUMBING ROUTINE today, so I was obliged to dwell on my impending supper, despite Kempka assailing me with questions about Christiane. As with the Elser matter, how he knew about her was how he knew about everything, but I was able (through my cultivated reputation as ingénue) to raise Brückner's "shield of ignorance," much to Kempka's consternation and incredulity. This latter condition was not surprising to me, since I knew that he dealt only with women who, at their best, were surface clear through, so he considered transparency (among brainlessness and far more lurid attributes) to be the essence of femininity.

"You think you can pull the wool over your Uncle Erich's eyes?" he asked. "You want a thinker. Don't waste time denying it." Then he shook his head as if I were an idiot, ripe for sterilisation. "*A thinking woman?* My God, Heinz, that's like wanting a rock that does tricks. And even if you got one, it'd still be a rock."

"But, Erich—"

"Take a page from the Führer's book, eh? He could have anybody, am I right? So, who does he choose? The *hausfrau* Braun: cute but dim. The Führer's no fool. You see him chasing after that crazy Mitford?"

For temporary entertainment, I decided to indulge the dolt. "You mean you don't believe a woman can think, or just that you haven't met one?"

"My son," he replied with a smirk, "I don't give a shit if they're scientists. Give me some gorgeous whore from my black book anytime. I pay them to suck my cock, not do math problems. And soon, very soon, my lad, we'll be mobbed by dazzling Agnieszkas, from highborn to trash, and all begging for a good German fuck."

"All right, but just imagine what might happen," I teased, "if instead, you paid them to think."

Kempka scrunched up his face in disgust, then laughed raucously. "Pay Polacks to think? Heinz, you're pulling my leg so hard, I'll soon be as tall as you."

As usual, I arrived early, so I took a walk round the old Jewish Quarter where her apartment was located. As an urchin without a home and constantly on the run from gangs and police, I'd known the exteriors well, especially the alleyways, nooks, and crannies. Little had changed, except for the owners and the conspicuous absence of the once-ubiquitous, tiny metal parchment-scroll holders on the sides of the doors. For me, those little containers represented an occasional grandmotherly hug and a hot meal; what they meant for the inhabitants, I had no idea. And suddenly, as if by magic, it had all been transformed into a "perfectly intact, Aryan-occupied archaeological site, initially a mystery, then a stain, and ultimately erased from memory"— which was what I once overheard Heydrich tell Brückner with no little satisfaction.

One buzz, and the door swung open, as if she'd been listening for my footfalls. My face must have sent her a message, for her first words to me after shutting and locking the door were, "Please, Heinz," she remarked in a playfully mocking tone, "don't begin by telling me how beautiful I am. Since I had nothing to do with it, you might as well compliment me on my vision." Then she winked, to underscore the impishness of her request.

"You win," I promised in the same spirit, "but would it be all right to compliment you on your accomplishments, that is, once I know of them?"

An unaccountably grave expression darted across her face and disappeared just as quickly. "If I could boast of any, you would be most welcome to. Unfortunately, I have none, at least none worth recounting, much less boasting of." She waved me further into the flat. "But please make yourself comfortable. Let me get you an aperitif. A Lillet Vive, yes? Let me take your coat."

Intangible though it was to me, somehow, she'd become different. *Was it a slight formality? A whiff of wariness? A hesitation I'd never seen in her before?* Regardless, I let it go for the time being since I assumed that time would fill in the blank if one needed to be filled.

She helped me shrug out of my greatcoat, and I sat on the plush velvet sofa. I had no idea what Lillet Vive was, but I was reasonably confident that it could be no worse than the hazardous concoctions introduced to me by Emerald, Katrin, and Bella.

"Yes, that would be fine," I said with studied casualness, as if I drank the stuff as a matter of routine.

She withdrew with my coat and returned with two large glasses in which, besides the liquid, resided what looked to be a slice of cucumber and some small green leaves. She sat down next to me, far enough for discretion but close enough to convey that discretion would be temporary.

She raised her glass to chin height and smiled. "Would you care to propose a toast?"

In my periphery, I could see that in this apartment, the

walls were entirely bereft of the Führer. "Well," I said, "since the Führer managed to barely escape another assassination attempt, perhaps we should drink to his continued good health."

She gazed down at her drink, long enough for me to wonder whether she shared my sentiment. "Yes," she finally replied, "we do need to keep us employed, don't we?"

We both laughed at that and took small sips. It was quite enjoyable but also quite powerful, so I resolved to nurse it as long as convention permitted.

"My condolences over the death of your… mother."

Her eyes performed a slight flutter. "My mother? Oh yes. Thank you. As you could tell, she was old and feeble and took precious little joy from life. She's far better off now—as am I."

"Is that why you moved?"

"Among other things," she replied without any real clarity. "I say, shall we bring our drinks to the table? The chicken should be just right."

⁊

The food was truly wonderful. I'd managed another Lillet Vive before prudence dictated a moratorium.

"If I may say so, Heinz," she told me as we finished the scraps, "you're quite unlike any ex-bricklayer I'd ever imagined."

"And what had you imagined? An ape?" I already believed I knew, but I loved the way she described things.

"Nothing quite so sophisticated as an ape. Please don't repeat this to anyone, but I would have pictured an especially vulgar Martin Bormann, if that can be imagined."

She *had* imagined an ape. I had to laugh at the imagery of an "especially vulgar" Bormann, as I would at an especially spiny anteater. "You have an artist's gift for capturing the essence," I told her. "My only problem is that it's difficult for me to imagine Bormann any more vulgar than he already is."

More light laughter as she cleared away the dishes. It was when she stretched out her arm to take my plate that I glimpsed the burn marks.

When she returned, she had us move back to the sofa, where she stared at me for a long moment—at least, it felt long to me, and definitely long enough for significance.

"What is it?" I asked.

A shadow of uneasiness flashed across her face and just as quickly fled. "I think you know, Heinz, my feelings for you. You must have sensed them." She'd said it almost pugnaciously, as if we'd been debating the matter, then, "I hope I haven't embarrassed you."

Embarrassed? I could hardly believe my good fortune. "With remarks like that, you can embarrass me at will."

Instead of the chuckle I expected, her full lips compressed into a grim red line. "Rather than that, might we go for a short stroll?"

I squinted with incredulity. "Normally, I'd love to," I lied, "but it's freezing out there, and we're—"

She rushed her index finger to her lips to silence me, then rose, went to her sideboard, wrote something quickly on a paper napkin, came back, and handed it to me. I squinted at the scribble: *What I have to say cannot be said here. The back way. Please.*

Flummoxed, I stood and took her gently by her arms and, realising that they were trembling, used them to draw her to me, but she broke away and moved swiftly to the bedroom, where she retrieved my coat and one for herself.

Her mouth said, "Please," without making a sound.

❧

All bundled up, we walked the streets in the frigid darkness, round a neighbourhood now more history than actuality—a condition intensified by the absence of anyone on the street. Nary a sound could be heard, save the occasional EEE-ah-EEE-ah-EEE-ah-EEE-ah of a Gestapo police wagon careening through the streets. If not already herded to capacity, it soon would be. Up to that moment, it was just another Berlin street noise, easily ignored, like cacophony in a beer hall, but this time, the whooshing shrillness of it registered in me as an event, not merely an environment, and I didn't know why. As we walked, frost pouring from our noses and mouths like clouds of steam from adjoining smokestacks, I asked her why we had to leave the comfort—and promise—of her apartment.

"Perhaps I shouldn't have suggested this," she said. "I was selfish. Thoughtless. I should have urged you in my note to run for your life and never look back."

"You're so very dangerous?"

"More than you should ever know," she replied.

I walked for a time without responding. "To be frank," I finally blurted, "you've never given me anything I *could* know. I don't know who or what you are. All I *do* know is that I, too, have strong feelings, even though—or perhaps, even because—you're a woman with many secrets."

"As it should be, Heinz. Beauty fades, and intelligence becomes tiresome. Secrets, then, are the only strength we women have that gets more potent with age."

Her words reminded me of a line from Rilke: "I want to be with those who know secret things or else alone." But I had nothing of my own as a fitting verbal response, so I attempted to physically change the subject. I stopped her, drew her to me, and began to join our lips, when she quickly braced her hands against my chest and pushed back, causing me no small amount of perplexity and embarrassment.

"I believe that you're in great danger of me loving you," she said tonelessly, "and that's the complicated truth of it." She looked down as if she'd lost something, then raised her head. "So, our feelings aside, there must never be any consummation."

My perplexity magnified exponentially. "But there already has been; don't you remember?"

"Almost," she said, "but not completely, don't you remember? I made certain of that."

I remembered, of course, in detail. The comical clumsiness especially. I reached over and took her hand, but she slid it back with gentle firmness.

"Listen to me, dear one," she said, "I had to prevent a disaster. But not to me, since I've long since stopped caring. It was to you. This is what they want, what they arranged. But I can't go through with it. You must keep walking when I turn back and never attempt to contact me again, whether by yourself or through any intermediaries. You understand me?"

They want. What they arranged. Who were "they"? Despite the bitter cold, I felt as if all the blood in my body had rushed to my face, causing it to burn. "Please" I urged, "if you care for me as you say, then at least give me something—anything—to justify what you're asking."

She turned to the front and began walking again, and I did the same.

"All right," she finally conceded. "I'll give you this, and it will have to do: It's all planned; they've planned it. They want you for themselves and are using me to ensure it. But what they failed to consider is that my feelings for you would grow. I've given them everyone else, but I won't give them you."

I'd been wrong again. She was no different from my other

two phantoms, not the least being the uncanny ability to take something elementary, render it enigmatic, and transform the enigma into something even more abstruse when asked to explain it.

"Please," she said, almost a cry, "don't make this more difficult for me than it already is. I know I can't expect your trust and don't deserve your generosity, but I'm begging you for both just the same. Go. Go now, and find someone who hasn't sold off her humanity."

Self-preservation would normally have controlled my actions, but a sensation I couldn't explain overtook my confusion and apprehension. "No, Christiane," I told her in a tone as firm as I could make it. "If I'm to go out of your life, it will have to be with full knowledge. If I'm running a high risk, that's my choice to make." I crossed my arms pugnaciously to underscore my resolve, hoping that if she were motivated by altruism, even affection, then what I'd just said would relieve her of any guilty feelings.

She shrugged and moved back to where I stood. "I can tell you no more than I already have."

We continued walking in silence. I no longer felt the bone-cracking chill and merely waited.

As we turned the same empty, bleak corner for the fifth time, she said, "Yes, all right. But please don't glance over when I speak. Will you do that for me?"

"Of course," I said, having not the faintest idea why.

"All right, I'll tell you a particularly German fairy tale. I'll tell you of a young woman named Dvora Hirsch, born in Berlin, an only child, beautiful, gifted, Jewish (from a family even more Jewish, as if gradations mattered). However, this Jewess was unlike her sisters in Abraham, for she looked more Aryan than Himmler's wettest dream. However, in a time when to be a Jew ranked somewhere below sewer rat and to be treated even worse, most were rounded up and transported to concentration camps. The "lucky few" were merely flies on flypaper, trapped in Germany, for they could not get visas to any other country. Having no alternative, they, like many others, eventually went underground, using a forged "Proof of Aryan lineage" to manoeuvre in public. Unfortunately, while such a device might work indefinitely for some essential few, it could be only temporary for those who fit Goebbels's and Streicher's pernicious depictions, including Dvora's own parents.

"When she and her family were eventually found out and arrested, the Gestapo offered Dvora a devil's bargain: if she helped catch other Jews who had gone underground, her family would be spared, kept safe, and even provided with normally forbidden luxuries. Not being a masochistic or suicidal fool, she took the offer and, in so doing, helped the Gestapo catch hundreds of Jews by gaining their confidence and offering to help them escape Germany—before turning them in, of course. However, as she should have expected, the Gestapo reneged on their agreement and sent her family to a concentration camp—but not their prize possession, whose name they changed to make her more acceptable to their bosses. She was spared—and even recompensed—so she continued to work for them as a 'catcher.'

"Now," she went on, "imagine being forced to live someone else's life. Imagine losing your sense of identity. Imagine being forced into a society that has turned its hatred for your former self into your own hatred, and has made you complicit in the deportation, torture, and death of your own people. Imagine living every day in fear that the life you are trying to lead will be found no longer necessary and might lead to your own horrible demise. Imagine doing whatever you must to save yourself, at the cost of your soul and the certain fate of those you've betrayed.

And further, imagine her falling in love with an Aryan who associates intimately with the same people determined to eventually exterminate her. And now, all the horrors they had her perform seem insufficient, for her handlers have commanded her to betray her lover by trapping him in a charge of miscegenation.[11] Now, my dear Heinz Linge, principal valet to the Führer Adolf Hitler, what do you think of my fairy tale?"

Her story, in tandem with my experience with Adelsheimer and my own clandestine persona, drove me to renege on my bargain. I gently took her arm, causing her to halt abruptly, and turned her towards me. "Please forgive me, but I can only say this while looking at you."

As she looked back at me, tears welled in those mutable hazel eyes. "Yes, Heinz?" Her voice had lost its edge and now seemed resigned.

I had no doubts about what she was confessing, but the way she told it created a shadowy ambiguity that followed my reply like a spectre. "If your 'fairy tale' were no more than that—a concocted yarn for a Hitler Youth campfire—I would caution this... Dvora to forsake her Aryan lover, but that would be dangerous for her. Instead, I would urge her to let him see if there is anything he could do to spirit her and her parents out of Germany, where she could deal with her mutilated conscience from a position of safety. I assume," I said guardedly, "that her lover is also

---

[11] An anti-miscegenation law was enacted by the National Socialist government in September 1935 as part of the Nuremberg Laws. The "Law for the Protection of German Blood and German Honour," enacted on 15 September 1935, forbade sexual relations and marriages between Germans and Jews. On 26 November 1935, the law was extended to include "Gypsies, Negroes or their bastard offspring." Such extramarital intercourse was marked as *Rassenschande* ("race defilement") and could be punished by imprisonment—later usually followed by deportation to a concentration camp, which often resulted in the inmate's death.

her friend and would do this for her despite the enormity of the risk. A reckless fool, perhaps, but a blindly romantic one for all that." By the time I had finished, I'd convinced myself that I'd flung myself into a whirlpool, heart first.

Her eyes confirmed my worst fears. So, while barely remaining within the flimsy boundaries of her tale, I asked her if this Dvora ever learned why her handlers wanted to betray her lover.

"You're asking me if there's more to my tale than I've told you?"

"Yes."

After a few moments of knowing looks exchanged between us, she said, "This Dvora was hardly in a position to question orders, no matter how repulsive and evil."

I nodded. "No, I imagine she wasn't. But I also imagine it would now be up to her Aryan lover to decide for himself whether to take risks to save her and, in the process, save himself."

Her stare was unwavering. "Do you think he would?" she asked with a shrug.

"Hard to say, since he's only found about her and the plot just now, but he'd be a poor specimen of a human being and a lover not to try. But I must ask," I forced myself to add, "how does this Dvora live with herself after what she's already done?"

She hesitated for an even longer moment, her lips still pressed together. "Easily, my love. Too easily. Terror and self-preservation are extremely powerful motivators and even more powerful rationalisations."

Is there a fine line separating self-preservation from betrayal? Was it a true case of an altruistic defence of family, or a monstrously narcissistic willingness to sacrifice others to save oneself? And there was something else, for which I already knew the answer but felt the need to ask anyway: "Why would her lover risk his safety by being with a Jewess in the first place?"

"A simple question," she chided grimly, "but not so simple an answer. Because of her assumed name and Aryan appearance, he wouldn't have known at first, and by the time he did, it might have been too late for his feelings to vanish or even diminish. And perhaps he isn't the sort of Nazi his position would suggest. But now, he should realise that the danger to him is no longer a matter of risk but of certainty."

One thought flapped and flickered noisily through my brain like the tail of a film reel: *In truth, just what "sort of Nazi" was I?* I shook my head. "All right, so, what now?"

She shrugged. "At least for tonight, give the words I've spoken a chance to register. And for right now, this minute? Let's continue our stroll, but in different directions, wouldn't you agree?"

I nodded reluctantly. "Would a parting kiss be inappropriate?"

"Do you think the word inappropriate even applies anymore?" she asked.

15 *November* 1939

I SPENT MUCH of the night after leaving Christiane agonising over her "fairy tale." Before we parted on that icy sidewalk in front of her apartment, she asked me why someone as ingenuous and coddled as I was in the "Führer's womb" would risk Himmler and Heydrich's terrible wrath, along with the euphoria they received from it.

I had no answer for her then, but now, as I dressed, I considered it. *Was it the electrifying thrill of risking everything on one throw of the racial dice? The misguided atonement for abandoning Adelsheimer? What?*

After last night, I had considerable information, but what had I learned? And more importantly, with all the big talk, what was I to do about her? About myself? But even without the skills that led from data to information to learning, I strove to make some meaning from the madness I'd encountered while speaking with her.

I desperately needed someone I could trust, but was that still Brückner? After all, he'd found Christiane (or should I now call her Dvora?) for me. So now, despite my suspicion, I needed to know how—and perhaps why—he found her and, more pressing, who else may have been involved in the finding.

❧

Before I could act on my resolve, Brückner arrived at my door to inform me that I was to be the projectionist again. "A meaningless and futile gesture, but you know, whatever 'Uncle Heinrich' wants, and all that."

"What does he want?" I asked in all honesty.

"What does he want? Just a guess, mind you," Brückner explained, "but I think he wants to end the Elser assassination attempt matter in the simplest way possible so he and his minions can continue the investigation clandestinely."

"But—"

"So, he sent Müller[12] to show the Führer a completed film of Elser's confession, which, in the Reichsführer's 'expert opinion,' proves the hapless bomber to be the sole culprit beyond any doubt. Himmler thinks he can impress the Führer with the ferocity of Elser's interrogation, but of all people, he should know better."

"You mean the Führer is convinced of a conspiracy, no matter what?"

Brückner smiled thinly. "That, of course, but something else no less important. In fact, Heinz, I'll make a wager with you. I'll bet you the Führer won't even look at the film."

"I have nothing to wager with."

"A gentleman's wager, then."

"All right, a gentleman's wager," I conceded, "but why would the Führer not wish to even see it?"

"Let's see who wins first, yes?"

I shrugged in agreement, and we set off to the Führer's quarters.

⁓

---

[12] SS General Heinrich Müller served as Chief of the Gestapo under Heydrich.

Seated for the screening were Müller, Himmler, Goebbels, Bormann, and Admiral Canaris. As Brückner had prognosticated, the Führer was conspicuously absent.

Oddly, as if the absence meant nothing, Müller had me run the film for the others. Why, I had no idea. It showed a physically and mentally shattered Elser, after days and nights of "vigorous interrogation," confessing through barely comprehensible squeaks and moans that he'd acted entirely alone, even in the making of the bomb. The Gestapo, clearly guided by police rigidity—and no little sadism—had set out to test Elser's declaration by providing him with all the necessary materials. With a hideously mangled mouth, he was able to mumble instructions to an SS engineer and construct an exact copy of the explosive device. Elser also admitted that his motive was a virulent hatred of the Führer and a determination to "put him out of the way for the good of the Reich."

Müller remained impassive, his eyes heavy-lidded, before, during, and after—the policeman right through. Himmler's face, as always, was blank, expressionless. Goebbels appeared vaguely saddened since, I imagined, without the Führer's imprimatur, the film and any story connected with it would never see the light of day. And even if it had, a lone assassin hardly possessed the shock value the Reichsminister craved. I had to wonder why he couldn't have coaxed Himmler into providing one. Since Bormann didn't have the Führer to impress with his enthusiasm and relief, he appeared merely bored. Canaris observed the film with patrician reserve, then, without a word, rose and withdrew. Appalled, I spent most of the time inspecting the projector mechanism, and when I chanced to gaze up once, all it did was revive my feelings of nausea and horror when I'd been compelled by Heydrich to witness the last of Adelsheimer.

❧

After the screening and the guests had left, I invited a more-than-willing Brückner for a stroll in the gardens.

"You don't have to say it, Wilhelm," I conceded. "You won."

"A hollow victory, my friend. Personally, I can live without Uncle Heinrich's entertainments; can you?"

"I'd been spared up to now," I told him with less than candour.

"We're a bloodthirsty lot, we Germans. All the film needed was the Riefenstahl touch, and our theatres would be packed to the rafters."

"Not with the Führer though," I ventured.

"No, not with the Führer," Brückner agreed, a sardonic edge to his words. "The Führer wants a conspiracy, whether there was one or not—so long as he's spared the gruesome details."

"From Goebbels's face, I'd say that he agrees."

Brückner laughed. "True enough, but I've seen the Führer sit through far worse. Remember the *Girl of the Golden West* last year?"[13]

"Unforgettably dreadful," I admitted. "I found myself concentrating on the projector noise."

"Well, unfortunately, I didn't have your proximity. But the Führer? He loved it. He told me afterwards that he, more than anyone, can appreciate how females are attracted to outlaws. No, quality is not an issue; it's more than that. An irony, if you will."

Brückner was being enigmatic again, a quality I both admired and detested. Whether ironic or not, I decided not to

---

[13] Mary Robbins is a beautiful young woman who owns a saloon. On the way to Monterey, her stagecoach is held up by the infamous masked bandit. While in Monterey, he dances, sings, and courts Mary, who falls in love with him.

indulge him, aside from the fact that I would never use that term with anyone or let anyone know I knew its intricate meaning. Instead, I chuckled with forced enthusiasm since the subject held little interest for me.

Then, with some mental palate-cleansing prattle, I got down to my business. It was an extreme risk, but I was out of my depth and needed some perspective. After telling him all that had transpired the previous night, the last thing I wanted was for it to resemble an interrogation, but as more and more of my story proceeded, the more it took on that aspect and the more frozen his expression became. It was like cross-examining a one-eyed ice sculpture.

"When did you know?" I finally asked him.

He shrugged. "Know what, my friend?"

There was so much. *Where to begin?* "For starters, that Christiane wasn't Christiane but a Jew named Dvora Hirsch. Not only a Jew, mind you, but a 'Catcher' of Jews for the Gestapo."

He slowly moved his head from side to side, then pursed his lips into a thin, grim line. "I didn't until now."

I discharged an involuntary laugh. "Then, my God, Wilhelm, I feel like that Oliver Hardy chap, who constantly complained to his unwitting partner: 'Well, here's another nice mess you've gotten me into.'"

The grim line was replaced by a troubled smile and nod. "I can't say I blame you, and I appreciate your attempt to make light of a grave situation."

"I didn't know I was doing that, but then you can imagine my astonishment at learning the truth. Of course, assuming that's all of it," which I didn't.

He laughed. "Then imagine my astonishment, since I'm the one who actively and visibly made your interest known. If the Gestapo's aim was to entrap you, they also succeeded in making me an accessory. Two for the price of one, as they say. Economy and efficiency: exquisitely depraved, even by Himmler's standards."

I nodded my admiration for Brückner's wit in such dire circumstances. I intended to end it there, but one even-more-nagging question remained in the queue: "Then, may I ask who told you about her as the ideal date for me?"

He took a deep breath and let it out slowly. "She did."

I CAN SAY to you now what I was too shaken and exhausted to tell you last night. Brückner hadn't finished with his response that Christiane herself had sought him out. He'd added that he accepted full responsibility for her duplicity and the potential catastrophe to me (as well as to him). He apologised most profusely—and, to me, convincingly—so, of course, I accepted his apology with no less sincerity. As to the why of it all, Brückner said he wouldn't rest until he discovered the answer, though he claimed to have a theory. However, when I pressed him, he said that, given the seriousness of the matter and the potentially disastrous implications, he wished to investigate first. With such a response, no further nagging on my part was either prudent or possible.

"Then," I said, "I'll ask you what I asked her: So, what now?"

"That should be a simple matter, my friend. At least she was good enough to warn you off—probably not without some substantial risk to herself. Regardless of my inquiries, I say consider yourself fortunate and move on. There are far more fish in the sea, as the saying goes, and, if I may add, far less fishy."

"I can't do that, Wilhelm."

He stopped. "I don't understand. Why on earth would you place yourself in such jeopardy and with so little to gain?"

What was "so little," I wanted to ask. I said nothing for a few moments, hating to recount my past to him—or to anyone, for that matter—but I wanted him to understand. "I'll tell you a true story. Being the only apprentice in a brickyard, all the thank-less, menial, filthy, dangerous jobs were invariably piled onto my shoulders. One day, the foreman told me to get my 'stupid, use-less ass,' as he put it, onto a rickety scaffold and deliver a load to a well-seasoned bricklayer who was leaning out of a fifth-floor window to cement some bricks into place as a sill. I loaded the platform, got aboard, and was raised level with the veteran. I was just about to transfer the bricks when I saw the old man's eyes roll upward, and he began to topple off the ledge. I was able to reach over, grab hold, and lug him onto my platform, causing the bricks to fall off and plummet into a clamorous dust storm of rubble below. When I finally got us down and the stricken man was taken away, the foreman, in front of all the other work-ers, began screaming at me, purple-faced, white-knuckled fists jammed into his waist. 'You fucking idiot!' he screamed. 'You salvaged a man who'll probably croak anyway, and in the pro-cess, wrecked a precious load of bricks! You're a goddamn fool, Linge! You know how many men can't wait to take that fucking geezer's place? Now you listen good and learn: Men are a penny a dozen, but bricks have real value, and don't you ever forget it!' I didn't—I quit that same day."

Brückner blew some air from his nose and nodded. "Yes," he said, "knowing you as I do, I would have expected no less. Personally, if I had your size and another eye, I would have sent that foreman to the hospital along with the old man. But that's me. However, I'm not all certain that joining the SS was a fitting alternative."

I couldn't imagine he meant my working for the Führer, but I could tell by his face that he enjoyed my discomfort and that I had no rejoinder.

"But you do make your point," he admitted. "She did take a considerable risk for you, so you feel you must now save her, if only from herself. The stuff of melodrama, I daresay, but potent nonetheless. You face no small dilemma, however. Should you suddenly stop seeing her, whoever set this plot in motion may believe something's wrong and trace the blame back to her. But should you continue to see her and refrain from consummation, the plotters will also know something's amiss, am I right? There's always a disposable prophylactic that only you dispose of so the happy couple achieves the benefit of sex without the burden of evidence. But on the other hand, without evidence, your Dvora loses her value, and you're back where you started. A textbook dilemma, my friend, no doubt."

"Between the Devil and the deep blue sea, then. So, what's to be done?" I asked in desperation.

We continued walking, passing innumerable checkpoints manned by shivering young SS sentries, clearly wondering why two men of our rank would be out strolling in the frigid air. None had the imprudence to ask for our papers, but it caused me to wonder how their superiors had accounted for Schlegl's passing.

"You have deep feelings for her," Brückner finally answered. "Ironically, it was my hope that such would be the case. And she clearly has the same feelings for you. This, too, was my hope. But now, as you say, we face a conundrum. Aside from her being a Jew (catcher or no catcher), which makes her future less than promising at best, clearly she is the centrepiece of a plot, the nature and extent of which is unknown to both you and me, and perhaps even to her, and which, in all probability, involves one or more of the most powerful officials in the Reich. So, to answer your question, if you're bound to err, at least do so on the side of sentiment. In other words, with utmost furtiveness, you some-how need to spirit her out of Germany to a place of safety—and let the bricks fall where they may."

Just then, a messenger ran up to us with a summons from the Führer, so I had no opportunity to ask Brückner how and where. But as I finish writing of this day, Brückner's analysis haunts me.

At the Führer's hasty direction, we left for the Berghof. I believe that he is so frustrated and disgruntled that he welcomes any activity, even physical, rather than sit in the Chancellery, as Goebbels told Brückner, "waiting for Godot." Since neither the Reichsminister nor Brückner explained what he meant, I must determine it for myself from the banned book the Führer lent me.

Dara joined us on our journey to stand by should the Führer need to dictate, in hopes that the occasion might arise. At luncheon, she told me of a young cousin of "impeccable Aryan purity" who would be "most eager to meet me." I could tell her nothing about my situation with "Christiane" (to the extent that I knew my situation), so I stalled while maintaining a plausible civility in the face of her well-intentioned matchmaking—and racial xenophobia.

I fear that Brückner may have been right: For me, the SS was no fit alternative to a brickyard.

This evening, the Führer summoned Göring, Hess, Keitel, Funk,[14] and Todt[15] to a meeting in the great hall. He had me hang a sign on the door saying, "Please do not disturb" so that Fräulein Braun and what the Führer called her "coterie of cacklers" would keep clear of the room that evening, for it was separated from the drawing room only by a curtain.

My predicament over "Christiane" still preoccupied me, and I was particularly glum, for reasons I've already explained, so I craved diversion. Fortunately, such is always possible when Göring is present, since his buffoonery relies not on words but on his mere presence.

Since he disdains cloakrooms as "undressing rooms" and feels that he appears considerably busier and more important in full regalia, he removed his enormous bemedaled coat, braid-encrusted cap, and field marshal's baton with a theatrical display of displeasure and threw them, willy-nilly, at the servants to a bumper-car tumult of grabbing as he passed. With great swinging strides, corpulent legs jammed into spurred, thigh-high Three Musketeers boots, he stormed into the hall to join the others as they waited.

I could tell that the Führer was absorbed in thought as he descended the short staircase; this I could see even as I followed. Then, as he approached the hall, he straightened his back and

---

[14] Walther Funk was a German economist and Nazi official who served as Reich Minister for Economic Affairs from 1938 to 1945.

[15] Fritz Todt was a German construction engineer and senior Nazi official who rose from Inspector General for German Roadways—where he directed the construction of the German Reichsautobahnen—to Reich Minister for Armaments and Ammunition, where he directed the entire wartime military economy. At the beginning of World War II, he initiated what Hitler named Organisation Todt, a military engineering company that supplied industry with forced labour and administered all construction of concentration camps during the late phase of Nazi Germany.

walked in with firm, quick steps. I ran ahead and announced the Führer, and all performed the customary obeisance. After greeting those present, the Führer walked them to the giant marble table in a geese-like V-formation of rank. Once there, they spread out round him, and he confirmed that Göring would take over running the entire war economy with full powers to secure the war's economic foundations. "His Corpulence," as Goebbels dubbed him behind his ample back, expressed high optimism about the state of supplies, especially armaments, while the others listened with varying degrees of masked indifference, as this development had been known to all for some time. But it was the Führer who generated all-consuming interest: *How would a gifted man of such indefatigable and ceaseless action contend any longer with such incomprehensible inertia on the part of France and Great Britain?* The Führer leaned with his entire weight on the table so that his fingers were splayed and bloodless.

"For once, Hermann," he began affably, "you have actually uttered an understatement. Our war industries, according to Speer and several military leaders of land, sea, and air, are in complete readiness for any task I set before them. I personally investigated this astounding claim and found it to be entirely accurate. To put it simply, gentlemen, our entire war machine is like a Thoroughbred racehorse, bridling at a starting gate that refuses to open.

"This situation, of course," he went on, "cannot continue in stasis without severe deterioration. If I learned nothing else from my experience with trench warfare, it was that the morale of our fighting men must be maintained at fever pitch and their bodies engaged in constant motion. And more than that, fate itself demands action. So, act we will. The French must come out and fight. We'll soon force those thumb-suckers out from behind their Maginot Line, eh, Keitel?"

The general laughed in a self-satisfied way. "That will mean a massive spring cleaning, my Führer."

"Yes, Keitel, and I'm just the chambermaid to do it," the Führer joked with utmost seriousness.

✂

On the way back to my quarters, despite all my efforts at avoidance, I chanced upon Fräulein Braun. To me, whether fact or fancy, she represents the most dangerous female in all the Reich since she's an intimate of the Führer yet appears to share no real intimacy with him, so she's an unknown quantity, perpetually frustrated. A part of me pities her, for she has a thankless role to play. She possesses no status as a wife (not least because of the Führer's own peculiarities) and, being a mistress, doesn't correspond with the successfully cultivated myth of the isolated Führer who sacrificed his personal life for the cause of the German people. By his own words, spoken often, he disdained any influence of a wife and family, and even his blood relations were obliged to stay away from him. The result? A ceaseless effort on her part to gain intimacy by proxy. In Berlin, evasion was relatively simple and efficient since the Führer kept her securely sequestered (not unlike what I'd read about a wife in an Arab household) in city apartments and isolated sections of the Chancellery. However, in the relative confines of the Berghof, Braun, when not being the playful, swim-suited nymph cavorting innocently with her sisters and lady friends, haunted the halls like a phantom, ruling her narrow domain like a needy consort, occupying a parallel universe.

Up to this point, any words exchanged between us had been perfunctory pleasantries, few in number and hastily spoken. However, a voice that generally radiated an almost frenetic merriment, frivolity, and mischievousness now assumed an ominous quality of anxiety and furtiveness as she took me by the elbow and guided me into one of the empty salon rooms, shut the door slowly and silently behind us, and locked it, all the time facing me. I wanted to race from the room but knew that tactic might create even more difficulties for me, so I stood there, waiting for her first move.

"I know this will appear unseemly, but—"

"How can I help you, Fräulein Braun?" I asked, attempting to steady my hands by placing them in my pockets.

"First," she said, "by calling me Eva, and second, by listening."

"But you have many friends who listen," I told her.

She smiled, paused for a long moment, then spoke very slowly, emphasising each word. "Yes," she replied with a lustrous, red-lipsticked smirk. "I know I have. But mostly other women, a bunch of dull, clucking hens who envy and gossip but know nothing. On the other hand, you appear to have no envy, gossip not at all, and know everything."

"Not so," I demurred. "I definitely don't 'know everything,' as you put it, Fräulein—ah—Eva. I really don't." I paused a moment to think, then, "And what if I did? What if I knew everything, as you say? It would mean nothing because I would merely know it as what I am—an unsophisticated, uneducated menial who understands little of anything he knows. What good would that be to anyone, not least of all you?" I hoped that what I'd said, or the way I'd said it, hadn't belied my persona.

A faint smile insinuated itself around the edges of her mouth. "Please sit," she offered, and I accepted, making sure to sit at a discreet distance beside her, so as not to seem as if I were leering straight at her. "Would you like some tea?" She nodded at a tea service perched on an ornate mahogany sideboard. Planned.

"Yes," I answered.

I got up to serve, but she waved me down, smiling charmingly.

"Please allow me. In here, now, you're not a menial but, I hope, an ally."

I shivered internally at the word and its implications. "Thank you" was all I said, and she rose with delicate athleticism, moved to the tea service, poured two cups, brought one over to my outstretched hand, and resumed her seat.

"I'm going to tell you some secrets, Heinz. Do you mind?"

"I'd rather you didn't... Eva."

She pouted theatrically. "Now please don't spoil my fun. I have so little."

What choice did I have? "All right," I capitulated.

"I envy you, Heinz. That's one secret right there."

"I don't understand." The truth.

"Ah, you compel me to explain my secret. Sly. All right, I envy you for having more intimacy with the Führer than I have." She raised her hand quickly, a traffic policeman's gesture. "Of course, I don't mean to imply that... you know... nothing sexual, you understand. It's just that you see him in many ways as a wife would: sick, well, clothed, naked, happy, sad, harried, restful, busy, leisurely, and all the situations in between. You see? Not even his oldest and closest associates have such access—even Bormann, who'd kill for it. Another secret." She winked impishly. "When I tell you that I've never seen the Führer naked, do I shock you? You won't answer that, I know, but it's there just the same. He keeps me, yes. In a golden cage. Closely guarded by Hoffmann and Bormann. Does the Führer keep you?"

She must have seen me begin to sweat and squirm, for she got up again, took my empty cup to the sideboard, filled it, sat down closer, and handed it to me slowly. "I keep a diary, you know. Another secret. Unfortunately, what I put down isn't worth the paper it's written on, for to me, nothing happens. I'm merely a decorative hamster, recounting my latest revolution on the wheel. On the other hand, everything happens round you, and yet, as the loyal servant, you write nothing, I wager. Yet I also wager that you could put down far more than the paper could handle. Is it not ironic, Heinz?"

I stifled a laugh. *Irony indeed!* I shrugged, desperate to leave quickly without being seen.

"I know this must be an embarrassment for you, but you can't know the torture he puts me through. Has he no regard for me at all?"

Was this a real question? How could she think I'd know the answer to it? "Of course he does. I know the Führer phones you regularly. The first time I asked him whether I should leave the room just as he began, he replied with a smile, 'Not to worry, Linge. I like to tease her, but she knows I also listen when she speaks, and I even make many decisions based on her advice.' There," I ventured, "a secret of my own for you." And a dangerous departure from my persona, I considered too late.

Her eyes had become shiny with moisture, and she tried to hide them by getting herself more tea. By the time she returned, the wetness had been replaced by redness. "I can't tell you how much I appreciate you telling me this, Heinz," she said. "Now it's my turn. You're friends with General Brückner, yes? Well, true or not, I have another secret for you—or maybe not so much a secret, but be that as it may. You should tell your friend that Bormann is determined to take his place with the Führer by any means necessary. And how do I know of such things? Even a hamster has ears. And how this may affect you personally, I leave to you."

Then she pushed herself up demurely, causing me to rise as well. "The dizzy blonde and the callow valet," she remarked with a hard laugh, taking my hand in hers, then releasing it. "Underestimation, though painful, does have its advantages. Please wait fifteen minutes before you leave; secret-keepers must also keep their distance." With that, she pivoted round with a charming swirl of her skirt, moved gracefully to the door, unlocked it, and left.

As I stood there for the agreed interval, I thought uneasily, *Not "secret-keepers," Fräulein Braun, but secret-sharers—a far more dangerous world of difference.*

WE ALL LEFT the Berghof in the Führerwagen to spend Christmas in the Rhineland, primarily to boost morale among the restless troops massed on the Rhine and the Belgian frontier. I could sense the high tension in all our party, not to mention the towns-folk, many of whom had family members in the Wehrmacht.

This morning, I witnessed an intense exchange between the Führer and his generals over the *sitzkrieg*.[16] As army commander-in-chief, von Brauchitsch stood before him, reciting once again, the degree of inactivity on the part of Britain and France in the face of our taking Poland. The others (including Brückner) sat at rigid attention with expressions ranging from moderate indifference to high indifference. The Führer sat so still, without blinking, he appeared comatose. *Was he really listening?* No one knew unless and until there was a response and not necessarily even then.

Unfortunately, the army commander didn't stop there. "My Führer," von Brauchitsch added, "given this state of affairs, we also must exercise caution. The German Army has just expended nearly all its available resources to mount the amazing *blitzkrieg* attack on Poland and badly needs a few months to regroup, refit, and resupply. Right now, our soldiers are simply not ready to leave Poland and abruptly turn westward to fight the French

---

[16] A war, or a phase of a war, in which there is little or no active warfare.

and British. And no less important, another drawn-out battle of attrition in France, like the one in the Great War, could easily unfold if they rush into things without adequate preparation."

While I already knew that the Führer agreed with von Brauchitsch's assessment of the French and British attitude, I also knew the Führer was hysterically opposed to von Brauchitsch's recommendations, though I hadn't come even close to realising how much.

The Führer stared down at his array of maps strewn across his desk, then, with agonising slowness, gazed up over his reading glasses at the commander-in-chief. "You have your final report, Brauchitsch?" he asked with eerie calm.

"Of course, my Führer." Von Brauchitsch raised his hand languidly behind himself for his adjutant to fill with a thick sheaf of papers. "Here." Von Brauchitsch held them forward for the Führer to take.

"Please, lay them on the floor," the Führer told him.

Squinted eyes filled the room, except von Brauchitsch's, who handed the papers back over his shoulder to his adjutant, again without looking at him, and the latter placed them gingerly on the floor.

"I am bitterly disappointed in you all," the Führer began, his tone hovering somewhere between rage and resignation, "and especially in you, Brauchitsch. It appears that once again, only I, a former meaningless corporal, learned anything from military service. Consider this, General. We are confronted with a listless, apathetic, unprepared enemy clearly intent on doing nothing, and you deduce, in mindless lockstep with your other inbred 'vons,' that, even so, this same enemy is both willing and able to thwart the greatest war machine since Caesar, led by a military genius even greater than Caesar. It's well beyond pity that my strategists are incapable of strategy. I ask you, is this gutlessness what I'm to expect from my top military leaders as I strive to fulfil the magisterial destiny of the Reich? *Well, is it?*" he shouted to utter silence and eyes cast down at the floor. "As I thought!" the Führer screamed, his fist hammering the desktop. "Then, all of you, get out of my sight, and don't even think of returning until you've proven yourselves worthy of the Reich and me!"

❦

Once they'd left, the Führer rose, went round his desk, straddled the papers, unzipped his fly, aimed his penis, and urinated on them. He then replaced his penis, motioned to me with a nod to zip up his fly, after which he moved back to his desk and farted himself down onto his seat.

Since joining the Führer's service, I'd overheard occasional reminiscences of the "Old Fighters" of the Führer having done similar things in the 1920s, when, as a struggling politician beset on all sides by anonymity, hostility, and worst of all, indifference, he'd been less than satisfied with a speech he'd composed or with written suggestions from advisers. However, this was the first instance I'd witnessed it since joining his service, so I waited anxiously for any remarks the Führer might wish to make by way of verbal elaboration. And waited.

"You know, Linge," he finally said, "I regret not having done that in front of that timorous military haemophiliac Brauchitsch and his pusillanimous cronies, but I suppose that we mustn't yet tarnish his sensitive sword with moisture, eh?" he joked, as though he thought I wouldn't understand, but I did. "But his time will come, as it will for all who lack the vision, resolve, and competence to win."

I ached to steal a few minutes with Brückner to prod him for progress on the "Christiane" matter, but the Führer was far from finished.

"The spineless French are insignificant," he said, absently drawing concentric circles round France on his map with his blue pencil. "Even the damn British," he grumbled, drawing a rectangle with his red pencil round the tiny island, "though they remain inert with indecision, not fear. Those damn fools in my military forget all too easily that the successes that have so far brought such glory and greatness to Germany—*and to them!*—have come from bold and audacious actions that seize opportunities by the throat and balls. And whose actions, I ask you, but—"

Just then, a loud buzzing from the Führer's desk console accompanied a flashing blue light. I'd never seen that particular light glow till that moment.

"Shall I come back later, my Führer?" I asked.

But he was too intent on getting to his phone and pressing the blue button to take notice. I could only hear the Führer's side of the conversation, so I understood nothing, save that it completely transformed the Führer's disposition, and for that, I was grateful.

"Go ahead," the Führer began.

[Pause, rising excitement.]

"Is Rahn certain? Are *you* certain?"

[Pause.]

"Ah, so, how long have you had it?"

[Spoken breathlessly, a pause.]

"Yes! YES!" he screamed, smashing his fist on the desktop again. "That would account for it! Yes! Too much coincidence, too little logic. And this is what even ONE can accomplish! And the other?"

[Longer pause.]

"I asked you about the other item."

[Irritation, pause, impatience stamped on the Führer's face.]

"Then, when and how do you propose we deal with it?"

[Shouting.]

"You, above all people, know what's at stake here! Nothing must be permitted to interfere!"

[Pause.]

"It had better!"

He slammed the receiver down on its cradle, took a few deep breaths, and turned to me.

"*Sitzkrieg*, indeed! In any event, we'd better dry out Brauchitsch's report," the Führer joked. "At least now I can justify my own forbearance, while laying the responsibility for it right at the feet of those medal-encrusted lily-livers. Discreetly, of course," he chuckled.

As I write this, I can only wonder how such experienced, decorated, highborn, and august military men felt, obliged as they were to give total loyalty and deference to someone they felt possessed none of those qualities but who possessed absolute power and, worse, successfully wielded it.

1940

3 January 1940

THE FÜHRER SPENT most of the morning lamenting the flamboyantly disgraceful behaviour of Bormann and Göring at last night's dinner. "It pains me to realise, Linge," he concluded, "that I have charged these characters with extraordinary responsibility to me and to the Reich. I must do something about their consumption of liquor, or soon, we'll all be back shouting slogans in beer halls with the police on our heels."

At the time, all I could think was that, unlike the Führer, Brückner would consider these "characters," especially Bormann, far more dangerous sober than they were besotted. Later, I wondered, not for the first time, how the Führer could come to absolute power, govern a nation, and wage war, with such a cadre of debauched and covetous inferiors.

This afternoon, the Führer introduced Krause's replacement to me. I'd heard that the fellow had been selected and sent over by Heydrich himself. I'd been running errands all morning, and when I returned in the early afternoon, I was surprised to learn that he'd already been seen by the Führer and approved for duty as second valet.

"Linge," the Führer announced as I entered his quarters, "I want you to meet Sturmführer[17] Junge."

He waved a languid arm over to a man with an athletic physique that could be detected even through his impeccably tailored uniform. His blond hair was so slicked down with pomade, it looked as if someone had painted the top of his head yellow. His face was recruiting-poster handsome, the skin of his angular face drawn back so tightly over his high cheekbones, I wondered if it was fastened behind his head with a zipper. Watching him standing at rigid and expressionless attention, I had the sensation that he only blinked on command.

The Führer's introduction acted like a sharp jerk on a puppet's strings, causing the fellow to slam his heels together stridently and shoot his arm out in a parade ground salute, which, because of the Führer, I returned with no less gusto.

"Since you'll be working closely together," he said to me, "you should go off with Junge here for a while and get acquainted. You can fill him in on his duties—and my peculiarities," he added with a snigger.

Junge dipped his head and snapped it back like one of those wooden Chinese drinking-bird toys. "Yes, my Führer," he declared with dutiful zeal, not looking at me. "We will get acquainted."

This was no Krause.

§

"Since we'll be working closely together, as the Führer said, I recommend that we begin by using first names." We were facing each other at a small table in an almost-vacant officers' mess.

---

[17] Lieutenant equivalent.

Junge pursed his thin lips. "I thank the colonel, but if it is all the same to him, I would prefer to exercise the formalities."

I shrugged, already sensing that any further sign of attempted familiarity would be met with all the warmth of statuary. "That's fine with me, provided you don't refer to me in the third person—ever again."

"May I ask who is this third person?"

I shook my head internally. "I'll make this simple. When we're speaking to each other, I'm Colonel, Herr Linge, even Heinz, should you weaken, but not the colonel, he, him, or his."

He nodded once. "As you wish. Colonel, then."

In one sense, I welcomed his apparent stolidity and lack of guile. But in another, I intended to take the apparent part with utmost seriousness. For someone with a carefully cultivated persona, I had an accompanying paranoia whispering to me that others may have one as well—perhaps even better than mine.

"I have heard much about you, Colonel," he said.

Since Brückner put in the request for Junge with the RSHA, I needed to ask him what he might know about this fellow before I committed further.

"Yes?" I asked Junge. "And just what have you heard?" I would reserve the when, where, and from whom for once I felt more secure. For now, what was enough.

"Oh," he answered quickly, "complimentary things only, I assure you, Colonel."

"Can you spare some particulars?" I ventured. If he required plodding, then we would plod.

"Only that while you have had little formal schooling, you have served the Führer with considerable insight and efficiency. I, too, have a meagre education in the formal sense but hope to make up for it as you have done."

"So, you see me as a mentor?"

He shrugged his well-muscled shoulders. "I was instructed to observe you with utmost care and attention."

I'll wager, I thought with some trepidation. "No need," I assured him. "You're fortunate that the Führer welcomes a variety of styles in those who serve him. I can tell you that the officer whose place you're taking was nothing like me and probably nothing like you."

"I certainly would not want to copy him. I was under the impression he had departed the Führer's service under something of a cloud."

If he didn't already know the facts, I certainly wouldn't provide them. "Well," I said, "you know how those things are."

Whatever he took "those things" to be, I left to him. I spent the next few minutes going over what I assumed would be his duties without advising him how to perform them, after which we saluted each other energetically, and I left.

THIS MORNING, I decided to cease using the lock on my door since the illusion of privacy cannot long withstand the reality of another key. The morons who monitor my quarters don't even bother to set things right after rummaging. If their aim is to demonstrate the futility of secrecy, I take considerable delight in their underestimation of me and the superficiality of their imaginations.

✍

I needed to speak with Brückner but couldn't locate him until late morning, when we both stood by while the Führer, Goebbels, von Ribbentrop, and Canaris discussed the results of a recent Gallup poll that asked Americans, "Which of these two things do you think it is more important for the United States to try to do—keep out of the war ourselves or help England win, even at the risk of getting into the war?"

"I love the Americans," the Führer said with a sardonic laugh. "Polls. They govern by polls! The fate of Weimar taught them nothing. You've been in America, Ribbentrop. Are these figures accurate, or are they frauds, designed to lull us into a false sense of security?"

"As you say, my Führer, I've visited America several times. I believe these figures to be accurate, that is, of course, to the extent that they are reliable."

"Double-talk, Ribbentrop," the Führer replied, his lips set in distaste. "One imaginary step above bullshit."

"My Führer," Goebbels stepped in, "I think that we can say the numbers indicate a significant isolationist sentiment amongst the Americans."

The Führer stared at Goebbels as if he were a visitor from a distant planet. "This, from my Minister of Propaganda?" he shouted.

"It's precisely that which informs my words," Goebbels rejoined with his usual external tranquillity. "America is not Germany. Most of what passes for information there is, to quote von Ribbentrop, 'accurate.' Their sources of information are far too independent to be the instrument for duplicity. Am I right, Admiral?"

The Führer's intelligence chief took a deep breath.

While Canaris ruminated with pursed lips, I seized the moment to glance furtively at Junge, who was, I believed, glancing furtively at me. In such matters, I resolved all suspicion—and the inevitable accusation of paranoia—in favour of certainty, so I wondered whether he noticed me noticing him noticing me. After the relative security of Krause's blatantly visible hostility, I foresaw years of tension and guardedness.

The admiral finally cleared his throat. "I think the key here, my Führer, is reliability. I don't, for a moment, question the accuracy or even the purpose of Gallup's numbers. The only caveat I would suggest is one of statistical proportion. Do eighty percent of Gallup's sample equal eighty percent of Americans? Samples are always problematic, in my estimation, and should be viewed with extreme caution."

The Führer shook his head. "So, what of any value am I to draw from all this?"

The group looked at each other, but it was Goebbels who finally spoke.

"My Führer," he said, "I would say that, at the very least, the poll illustrates a singular and perhaps even significant division amongst the Americans, unlike the British, who by proximity alone, not to mention treaty obligations, cannot brook such disunity."

The Führer sat back in his chair and nodded. "A reasonable assumption, Joseph." Then he turned to Canaris. "Admiral, can your people get me more reliable numbers?"

"I'll get on that immediately, my Führer," Canaris assured him, studiously avoiding the perils of a yes-or-no answer.

✥

After they left, the Führer dismissed Brückner and Junge with a languid flick of his hand.

He waved me to the chair that had supported Goebbels. "Did I appear interested enough?" he asked.

"I… don't follow, my Führer," I answered truthfully. "Interested in what?"

"All that twaddle about the poll."

"I'm sorry, my Führer," I said. "I wasn't paying attention."

"I don't blame you. Unfortunately, I actually know what they're going on about. I wish I could tell them that what Americans think or don't think occupies a very low rung on my ladder of priorities, but you know how sensitive those characters are." He began rapping the desktop with his fist and nodding. "Ah well," he murmured, presumably to himself, "soon, it won't matter what anyone thinks." Then his voice returned to me. "Now, Linge, what do you think of this new Junge chap?"

Dreading the question's inevitability, I'd prepared an all-purpose response. "He's no Krause, my Führer."

The Führer burst into wheezing laughter, and when it subsided, he asked, "You know, you sound just like poor old Dr. Bloch.
Are you sure you have no Jewish blood in you somewhere?"

Fortunately for me, the Führer was only joking. Himmler
wouldn't have been.

❧

I located Brückner in the Communications Centre, chatting with
the ever-plump Major Huber, the chief clerk, before picking up
his half of the Führer's mail.

I broke in with some prosaic levity as usual. "Say, Herr
Major, when are we going to get the mail delivered to us instead
of having to lug it ourselves all the way to the Führer's conference
room?"

Huber then subjected me to a slow, top-to-bottom once-over,
eyelids narrowed in mock suspicion. "You're unhappy with how I
run this department? Address all complaints to the Reichsführer,
my friend. I promise to visit you in Dachau."

Brückner and I chuckled.

"Not necessary, Huber," Brückner said. "I keep telling Linge
here that heavy lifting will prevent any more of his hair from falling out, but you know how kids are."

"Tell me about it. I have three, each one lazier than the other."

Brückner and I laughed at his plight, with me feigning
umbrage. "I never heard about heavy lifting and hair," I told
Brückner.

"Latest science," he joked, then turned to Huber. "Well,
Gottfried," he said, "always a pleasure chatting with you, but
Linge and I must be off." With that, he lifted his sack with a
theatrical grunt. "Your turn, baldy," he said to me, and with an
exaggerated sneer, I picked up my sack, and we both left without
saluting.

Once we reached the empty conference room and threw down our burdens, Brückner said, "That pig Huber could do with a little heavy lifting himself and not just when he gets out of a chair."

"I don't think he's as good-natured about his fat as I am about my hair."

"I believe you're right," he said with a snort, then, "Missing Krause yet?"

I shook my head and shrugged, then told him about my adventure on the train with Kempka.

"That's quite a story, Heinz," he said.

"I'd sure hate to make an enemy of that glorified cab driver."

"He's old-school Nazi," Brückner said. "They don't suffer obstacles well. You make the measure of Junge yet?"

"That's what I wanted to ask you about."

"Unfortunately, Heinz, to me, he's a blank. Well, not completely. He was personally selected by Heydrich for the post, so there's a cautionary tale."

"Cautionary tale? What's a—"

He pressed his lips together, spreading them in mock exasperation. "Heinz, lad, read something every now and then, and I won't have to teach school every time we talk. It means be careful round him. If his mission is to observe, bore him to death; if he's to report, give him nothing. I'll try to learn more, but until then, I recommend that you maintain a diplomatically professional distance. On the other hand, he's only a kid, the way you're not. Work him subtly, and maybe he'll give something away—that is, if there is something."

As always with Brückner, it was good advice, but now I was troubled by something else: Brückner's offhanded suffix to his sentence, "the way you're not."

5 *January 1940*

I AWOKE IN guardedly erotic spirits, for tonight would find me in another prophylactically protected assignation with the Jewess "Christiane." After breakfast, I thanked Brückner once again for securing a safe house for us, and once again, he told me that since I refused to give her up despite her "fairy tale," he considered it his obligation to "atone" for placing me in this perilous situation in the first place. I considered his theological explanation irregular but said nothing in the face of good fortune. Unfortunately, as Brückner reminded me needlessly, our protection was her peril, so it could not continue.

⤸

This preoccupied me, even while I attended the Führer, so I paid extra attention to tidying his desk, which looked as if a tornado had passed through it. In the process, I happened upon a crumpled wad of a telegram that fell into scraps when unfurled. Now they were a desperately wrinkled set of puzzle pieces. I set about restoring them to some semblance of their original state for a brief glance, and when I'd finished, all that I could make out was a message to Himmler from an Herr Weisthor, sent from a place I'd never heard of, called Montségur. Most of it was unreadable due to the violence laid upon it earlier, but some of it was intelligible:

"... regret... second mis... believe Füh... medium poss... proof not..."

Since it meant nothing to me, I returned it to its former crumpled state and tossed it with the rest of the bureaucratic flotsam and jetsam into the wastepaper container, then proceeded to polish his desktop as the Führer emerged from his toilette. I could tell by his pallor that he was enveloped by dreadful thoughts. Then, after dressing, he had me fetch Schroeder and Dara and told me that with Junge at hand, I wouldn't be needed until tomorrow.

⁓

Some trivial last-minute errands caused me to be late to the flat Brückner had secured for Dvora and me. She opened the door after my prearranged knock, wearing a long white satin robe secured with erotic tautness at the waist by a wide satin sash. At first, I didn't notice her face. I believe that we see what we expect to see, so as I looked up at her, it took a moment before I was stricken with the inability to breathe, as if a jagged stone had lodged itself in my windpipe. For the face I saw wasn't that of Dvora but of a giant grey rodent with an enormous hooknose—the wildly popular party mask of Streicher's cartoon "Jew" for sale in every department store in the Reich.

As she drew me in and shut the door, she peeled off the rubber horror and tossed it over her padded shoulder. "Don't have an attack, my love," she said with a low, malicious giggle. "A joke only. I merely wondered what you'd think about having a sexual liaison with a real Jew. Can it be that like most Aryans, you find nothing funny unless some poor clod's slipping on a banana peel or farting in a posh restaurant?"

I was speechless at her extravagant nonchalance about something that should be so monumentally abominable to her.

"Have you eaten, Heinzl?" she asked with no less casualness. "If not, I can make some *eintopf*.[18] Nothing swanky, mind you, but nourishing and easy to prepare."

Heinzl! How I hated that infantile sobriquet, but for the sake of her intent, I chose to bear it as an acceptable sign of affection. "No need," I replied. "I forced down some leftover vegetarian swill from the Führer's supper before coming here." I could tell by her initial greeting and her amazing eyes now that she wanted to tell me something, but I didn't know when. "But some… *Spätburgunder*[19] you called it? Now that might really hit the spot."

She smiled broadly, her first genuine one of the evening. "If only to take the taste away? I'm sure I can find some. Get comfortable, why don't you? I'll be right back. No mask this time."

After she disappeared into the kitchen, my routine began. I removed my uniform jacket and folded it neatly on the armchair along with my tie. I tugged off my boots and socks and laid them in front of the same chair, moved to the couch, sat down, and unbuttoned my shirt that was always so heavily starched, I felt as if it were made of celluloid. However, this time, I didn't unfasten my belt. Tonight, this wasn't the Dvora I thought I knew. Something was out of order, and I didn't think that sex was the solution.

She emerged holding two topped-off glasses of what I

---

[18] *Eintopf* is a traditional German stew that can consist of a great number of ingredients. Technically, the term refers to the method of cooking all the ingredients in one pot rather than to any specific recipe.

[19] *Spätburgunder* is to red wine what Riesling is to white wine: the cream of the crop.

assumed was the *Spätburgunder* I'd requested and handed me a glass without so much as spilling a drop, even when she sat down next to me. For someone in her situation, she had remarkable control.

After we'd engaged in some preliminary sips, she turned away, placed her glass on the side table, and turned back.

"Pity you've already eaten. I did so want to prove to you that I can cook more than one dish. Another time, perhaps; there's plenty of…" Her voice trailed off, then it returned, full strength. "You weren't offended by my little joke?" she asked, I thought, coyly.

"Not if you weren't," I lied.

"Sometimes, I find my situation unbearable. Humour helps me cope. You see that, don't you?"

The humour of a Bormann, I thought. *Unbearable? I imagine so do those poor, deluded Jews you catch for the Gestapo,* I wanted to say, but I waited for her next admission, if there was going to be one.

There wasn't. She just sat there, staring at my fastened belt, an expression of melancholy on her face.

"What's wrong, *schätzchen*?"[20] I finally asked. "Something's bothering you—more than usual, that is." She was hardly a simple soul.

She smiled, reached for her glass, and took a rather large sip. "Schätzchen?" she mocked gently. "I'm hardly that."

"I ask again: What's troubling you?" this time, adding some forced levity to ease the pill of revelation down her throat. "Might you be one of those women who take such pride in their cooking that a guest's lack of appetite is a personal affront?"

---

[20] Darling, honey, a term of endearment.

She forced a laugh. "Far from it," she said after another sip. "In fact, I never even boiled water until I was twenty-two. I'm quite certain that munching on Herr Hitler's leftovers would drain any appetite. No, I..." Her voice trailed off.

"No, you what?" I pursued.

She edged slightly away, just enough to guarantee distance without offending. "My... probation officer, as I call him, has issued a deadline for me to produce indictable results—or else. The 'or else,' I leave to your imagination. I can't toy with such an animal, since he's made you his personal project and has his police matron check me every morning for evidence. She delights in her task and is entirely thorough. I can barely walk after one of her examinations."

I had no immediate response. One of my more philosophical brick-mates once remarked (but not quite so elegantly) that a choice of evils is no choice. I disagreed with him then and no less now, for to me, even in a world of evil, a lesser one is always preferable. The only question for me was: *To what extent did this apply to Dvora?* As obscene and heinous as her actions towards her own people may have been, I nodded generously to commiserate with her and not to show concern about my own peril. I took another sip and motioned for her to resume her place next to me, which she did, but not before racing into the kitchen, filling her glass, and bringing out the bottle.

"I want to get really falling-down drunk and forget any of it ever happened," she said. "I've felt the same way many times, Heinzl, even as an adolescent. But I knew that when I sobered up, everything I thought I'd left behind would still be there— probably worse because of the neglect—because there's really no escape." She took a hefty swig, set down her glass, leaned towards me, and began unfastening my belt.

I stopped her hand. "Later, please," I urged softly. "We should talk first."

She regarded me in the most libidinous manner. "Well," she purred, "since you wish to remain uncomfortable, would you mind terribly if I didn't?" Without waiting for an answer, she loosened the sash on her dressing gown and lowered the upper portion just enough to reveal her beautiful nakedness from shoulders to waist, then slowly turned her back to me, lifted her shoulders, and gyrated them with feline nonchalance. "I would be even more comfy if you massaged me. While we talk, of course," she added coquettishly.

I could sense a sly smile. My hands moved gently over her back. I could feel the bones, the shoulder blades in particular, sharp and cleanly articulated under the skin. I could feel the warmth of her body.

"Harder," she demanded softly.

As I kneaded, she strained against me, as though trying to bore her entire body into mine. After a time, a rivulet of sweat edged down between her shoulders like a teardrop on a cheek, and a feeling of inevitability washed over me. Even so, I knew I had to act.

"I've been giving this situation considerable thought," I said, "and there seems to be only one solution—granted, not an ideal one for either of us—but the problem would be solved, and more than one problem at that."

"Hmmm?" she murmured. "A little harder, please. More on the left side. And just what is this solution, *liebchen*?" she asked cooly.

"Simple in theory at least." I kept massaging. "You must be spirited out of Germany to a safe harbour."

She shook her head vigorously. "Not possible, my love. They not only have me. They also have my parents and brother. If I were to disappear, I think you need little imagination to guess the consequences for my family. A bit more on the right, yes?"

So, that sour crone wasn't her mother. Thank God. Probably one tiny step up from a prison guard, a sentient apartment fixture, there to watch her, to evaluate her performances, to make certain she was both obedient and convincing.

"Where are they?"

"A little over a year ago, they were taken away in the middle of the night by some gutter-level Gestapo types. I didn't dare ask where at the time. I still don't. Lower, please."

With my free hand, I grabbed my glass and gulped down some more of the wine to give me at least some false courage. As an old cellmate once joked, "Better false teeth than no teeth." I had no way of knowing what I was about to say was a certainty, but I took the chance in any event. "I don't know how to say this diplomatically," I began tentatively, "but from what Brückner tells me, what will happen to your family will happen whether I get you to safety or not. No, I don't think there's much of a choice left for you—*for us*—at this point, don't you agree?"

She shimmied my hand away and manoeuvred herself round to face me. "This isn't fun anymore," she declared, not with a playful pout but with a cold-eyed stare. She rose quickly, causing her entire robe to separate and display complete frontal nakedness.

However, I sensed no eroticism on her part, and as for me, I was far too anxious to resolve the dilemma facing us to muster any of my own.

She quickly rewrapped herself and began pacing, more a glide than the Führer's speed skating. As she paced, she murmured, it seemed, more to herself than to me. "I was always considered exceptional, you know—in my home, at school. The most desired by males trolling the social waters, the most envied by other females who were obliged by their mediocrity to do their own trolling. Yes, in appearance, intellect, personality, always above the rest. 'Exceptional,' I was called by everyone." She halted abruptly, wheeled round to face me, her arms wrapped tightly across her midsection. "But never, Heinz, never exceptional as a Jew—and certainly never as a disgusting rodent, a vile disease, or a devastating threat to civilisation! And ironically, now, precisely as a Jew, I'm even more exceptional. I wonder what your boss, the greatest Jew-hater in history, would say if you told him we were lovers?"

My boss, the greatest Jew-hater in history? Oddly, I was stunned by her words, so I took a few silent moments since what she'd said cascaded through my brain like a large steel bearing in a pinball machine. Without doubt, that was the Führer's reputation. *But was it entirely accurate?* Of course I'd read *Mein Kampf*, listened to his countless speeches, heard his unremitting dinner lectures, overheard his generic conversations with Goebbels and Himmler, and his hysterical diatribes for the benefit of all who were pledged to keep the Führer's reputation of rabid antisemitism alive and flourishing.

But to me, all that was merely strategic talk and, therefore, suspect. I believe that his true feelings were represented by his Madagascar Plan and what he told me in private when lamenting his dismissal of Dr. Bloch: "I want you to know that I regret this action, Linge. In no small measure, I owe all I am and have to the Jews." Then he added, "But I confess to you that if what helped elevate me to absolute power and keeps me there requires that the flame of race prejudice be visibly burning, then so be it." He concluded with a phrase I recognised from a Grimm fairy tale: "'All magic comes with a price!'" Why would he want me to know that if he were truly the frothing anti-Semite his enemies claimed?

Given that, of what my "boss" would say to me about Dvora, I had little doubt and no fear. But what he would do might be quite another matter. To be frank, it was *her* boss, Heydrich, that terrified me. She answered to a character who would consider it a dismal day if he couldn't torture anyone. Now, it seemed that his day had arrived, and Dvora was both his instrument and his victim. And so, it seemed, was I. But as the bearing made its helter-skelter way down, I had to wonder if I was stunned or stung? Her words seemed neutral, but her tone was accusatory.

She stopped pacing and moved back to the sofa, crossed her long, slender legs down to her brightly painted toenails, all clearly visible through the forced slit in her robe, and parted her lips seductively. "Heinzl, my dear one," she murmured, "I know I can trust you. Don't ask me how or why. But can you trust me? With so much at stake, what are my options? And now I ask you: Do you know me well enough to have even the slightest grasp of how I deal with options?"

I certainly knew how she dealt with *one. But then, why did she relate her "fairy tale" to me of all people? What did that signify?* I knew nothing of loyalty before I joined the SS, save for literature, and after that, only what was drilled into me and the others by fanatics with their mindless, brutal doctrines. *But what did loyalty mean to Dvora? Survival? If so, why did she not withhold her "fairy tale," seduce me, have my... "evidence" collected, and from there, have me taken to Heydrich's cellar for one of his vigorous dental examinations? Yes,* I reflected, *if survival were her only motive force, why now relate their vicious plot against me and warn me off?* Her mental state and motives were clearly beyond my powers of analysis. *If I were to thank her and flee, what would be her fate and that of her family?* My perplexity was close to absolute. But out of all my confusion, something tangible pulled at my brain like a rubber band.

"All right," I answered her, "three things. First, I'm well warned, wouldn't you agree? And why I'm a target is for me to discover if I can. Second, it's certain that somehow, you must be placed in a situation in which no harm can come to you, regardless of your family, and also, not incidentally, in which you can do no harm to me." I also meant no further harm to Jews but had no idea why I felt this. "And finally, three: I think you need some time to consider what I said and make a decision, but not too long."

I rose, turned to the side away from her, and began dressing when I heard a sharp shattering of glass against the wall behind me. I swung round and saw the chunks and splinters of glass on the carpet and the splotchy red stain on the wall, bright, dripping tendrils radiating outward like a crimson sun. I turned back to her.

"Hey, what's this?" I shouted. "What did I say that angered you so?"

"Not you, stupid! I was throwing it at myself!" she shouted back.

"Then you have terrible aim," I replied, hoping that levity would cool her down. Her psychotic ambivalence was palpable.

She smiled ruefully. "The Gestapo never complained." Her hazel eyes shone dark with moisture, but no tears fell.

ANOTHER TURBULENT SLEEP followed by a vexatious headache. Last night's encounter caused my brain to dredge up Himmler's ten injunctions to "foster a responsible attitude towards selective breeding":

1. Remember that you are a German!
2. Remain pure in mind and spirit!
3. Keep your body pure!
4. If hereditarily fit, do not remain single!
5. Marry only for love!
6. Being a German, only choose a spouse of similar or related blood!
7. When choosing your spouse, inquire into his or her forebears!
8. Health is essential to outward beauty as well!
9. Seek a companion in marriage, not a playmate!
10. Hope for as many children as possible!

No, Dvora, I admitted to the mirror as I shaved, *I'm a far cry from the Reichsführer's ideal Nazi.* Fortunately, the Führerbuzzer ended any further useless ruminations.

When I arrived, the Führer was still in his private world of silent seething. Aside from his frustration over enemy inactivity, he'd been in a state of distressed melancholia since receiving that message I'd found mutilated on 3 January. I have no idea of its meaning or significance to him, now as then, but clearly, it was exceedingly unfavourable.

Today, as I stood before him, waiting for leave to tidy up, he stared down at his chaotic desktop and muttered a declaration, as if I'd suddenly become invisible, "For now, one will have to do." Then he lifted his head and glanced up at me. "Linge, have Brückner assemble my entire General Staff for a major briefing today. No excuses will be countenanced. Also, have him notify them that there will be no discussion. Now, hop to it."

11 January 1940

I WAS THANKFUL that this was a day of distractions for me and I could nudge Dvora aside for the moment. As I stood, wedged in a corner of the conference room, the Führer, surrounded by all his top officials—as well as Baur—was briefed by his military chief on the Mechelen Incident, in which a German aircraft with an officer on board carrying the plans for "Case Yellow"[21] crash-landed in neutral Belgium near Vucht, prompting an immediate crisis in the Low Countries as well as with the French and British authorities, whom the Belgians notified of their discovery. This time, it wasn't the Führer who was screaming, but Göring, who generally did little in meetings but fill his chair beyond its boundaries.

"Well, Admiral!" he shouted at Canaris. "You're the Führer's intelligence chief. Do you wish to add anything to the report I just received?" His face was beet red, his mouth twisted in rage, his massive frame trembling, causing his tunic-full of medals to clang like the bells in *The Hunchback of Notre Dame*.

The Führer sat at the head of the long conference table, utterly impassive.

"Nothing, Herr Reichsmarschall," the virtually unflappable

---

[21] In Fall Gelb—Case Yellow—German armoured units made a surprise push through the Ardennes and then along the Somme Valley, cutting off and surrounding the Allied forces that had advanced into Belgium to meet the expected German invasion.

admiral replied. "Perhaps, as chief of the Luftwaffe, you can ask General Baur to shed some light on the matter. I would imagine the Führer's personal pilot knows far more about the vagaries of aircraft than this poor sailor."

I was certain that the sophisticated Göring got the sarcasm but wisely chose to ignore it after glancing at the Führer and seeing no reaction. "Yes, of course," he agreed diplomatically, moderating his tone. "Perhaps Baur here can, as you say, 'shed some light' on something that could derail the Führer's finely tuned schedule."

What "finely tuned schedule" he was referring to, I couldn't say, since I was privy to no meeting at which any such schedule was discussed. All I knew was that Baur hated Göring, having referred to him one day in Kempka's office as a "thick-headed glutton" and "a pig who dresses like a peacock." Baur shot a quick glance at the Führer, who nodded his assent, so Baur related what turned out to be an event of spectacularly low comedy worthy of the Keystone Cops. I present only highlights here to amuse myself in the telling.

As Baur told it, the affair began with a mistake made by the aviator, Major Erich Hoenmanns. On the morning of 10 January, he had been flying from Loddenheide to Cologne when he lost his way, extensive low fogbanks obscuring his view of the landscape. In response, he changed course to the west, hoping to regain his bearings by reaching the Rhine. However, having already crossed over the frozen and indistinguishable river at the moment, he changed direction, leaving German territory and flying all the way to the River Meuse, the border between Belgium and the Netherlands, and ended up circling Vucht.

It was then, Baur said, that he appeared to have inadvertently cut off the fuel supply to the plane's engine by moving a lever inside the cockpit. The engine spluttered, then stopped, so

Hoenmanns was forced to land in a nearby field at about 1130 hours. The aircraft was severely damaged, in that both wings were sheared off when they hit two trees as he careened between them, and the heavy engine tore off the nose section.

"The plane was a write-off," Baur declared, "but Hoenmanns survived without so much as a scratch. That—"

"Now, gentlemen," Himmler interrupted, clutching some typed sheets as he took over the narrative, "had Hoenmanns been alone in the plane, nothing of great significance would likely have happened, apart from his internment for landing without permission in a neutral country. However, it so happened that he had a passenger, one Major Helmuth Reinberger, who was responsible for organising the formation that was to land paratroopers behind Belgian lines at Namur on the day of the coming attack. Hoenmanns was unaware that Reinberger would be carrying documents related to the attack plan on the Netherlands and Belgium, which on the day of the flight, was decreed by the Führer to take place a week later, on 17 January.

"Hoenmanns," Himmler continued, "only discovered that Reinberger was carrying secret documents when, after landing, they asked a farmhand where they were, to be told that they had unknowingly crossed Dutch territory and landed just inside Belgium. On hearing this, Reinberger panicked and rushed back to the plane to secure his yellow pigskin briefcase, crying that he had secret documents that he must destroy immediately. To let him do this, Hoenmanns, as a diversion, moved away from the plane. Reinberger first tried to set fire to the documents with his cigarette lighter, but it malfunctioned. He then ran to the farmhand, who gave him a single match. With this, Reinberger hid behind a thicket and piled the papers on the ground to burn them. But soon, two Belgian border guards arrived on bicycles. Seeing smoke coming from the bushes, Rubens rushed over to save the documents from being completely destroyed. Reinberger fled at first but allowed himself to be taken prisoner after two warning shots had been fired." At that, a round of involuntary nervous titters emerged from von Ribbentrop, Jodl, Dietrich,[22] Kaltenbrunner,[23] and Hewel. Göring and the rest, including the Führer, remained grimly silent.

"So then," Himmler continued, with no break in his book-keeper's monotone, "Hoenmanns and Reinberger were taken to the Belgian border guardhouse, where they were interrogated by Captain Arthur Rodrique, who placed the charred documents on a table. As a diversion once more, Hoenmanns asked the Belgian soldiers to let him use the toilet; Reinberger then tried to stuff the papers into a burning stove nearby. He succeeded but yelled with pain when lifting the extremely hot lid off the stove."

I could tell that many of the listeners were straining not to guffaw at this burlesque of errors.

"Startled by the scream," Himmler went on, "this Rodrique

---

[22] Prior to 1929, Josef Dietrich (also known as "Sepp") served as Adolf Hitler's chauffeur and bodyguard. He received rapid promotions in the SS following his participation in the extrajudicial executions of political opponents during the 1934 purge known as the Night of the Long Knives. Despite having no formal staff officer training, Dietrich, along with Paul Hausser, became the highest-ranking officer in the Waffen-SS, the paramilitary branch of the SS. Reaching the rank of Oberst-Gruppenführer (colonel-general), he commanded units up to army level during World War II.

[23] Ernst Kaltenbrunner, a general of the SS, was a committed anti-Semite. Under his command of the Gestapo, the persecution of Jews picked up pace as the process of extermination was expedited and the concentration of the Jews within the Reich itself and the occupied countries were to be liquidated as soon as possible. Kaltenbrunner stayed constantly informed of concentration camp activities, receiving periodic reports at his office in the RSHA. It was said that even Himmler feared him, as Kaltenbrunner was an intimidating figure, standing 1.94 metres (six-feet four-inches) tall, with facial scars and a volatile temper.

turned and snatched the papers from the fire, badly burning his hand in the process. The documents were now locked away in a separate room. The failure to burn them made Reinberger realise that he would surely be shot for letting the attack plan fall into the hands of the enemy. He decided to commit suicide and tried to grab Rodrique's revolver. When the infuriated captain knocked him down, Reinberger burst into tears, shouting, 'I wanted your revolver to kill myself!' and Hoenmanns added, 'You can't blame him. He's a regular officer. He's finished now.'

"Two hours later," Himmler concluded, "officers from the Belgian intelligence service arrived, bringing the papers to the attention of their superiors in the late afternoon."

All now turned their heads towards the Führer for a response, but Göring cut them off midturn.

"Gentlemen," he said, "farce aside, I believe we might consider the implications of the Belgians possessing our top-secret invasion plans of their own country and those bordering it."

That bit of sobriety managed to get everyone staring silently at each other until the Führer spoke.

"Hermann," he remarked through a narrow, moustache-lifting, beaver-like smile, "life is far too short to withhold levity from it. I've analysed the issue from all sides, and I can tell you with almost mathematical accuracy what the implications are: The Belgians and their Scandinavian neighbours will get into a dither and may even mobilise their puny forces; Britain and France will consider assisting them to gain a military presence in the area but will end up issuing their usual Shakespearean sound and fury, signifying nothing. As for us, we simply delay a bit beyond the dates mentioned in the documents. When they see that we've done nothing but create some clearly meaningless theoretical documents, they'll all breathe a collective sigh of relief, pull the blankets over their heads, and go back to sleep. Nothing of any consequence will change for them—or for us." His palms slapped the tabletop. "So there you have it, gentlemen."

I had no way of gauging the merits of the Führer's assessment even if I'd been interested in the bizarre business, but all round the table, the mood brightened dramatically: Göring's "bells" clanged with glee; Himmler actually stopped making notes; Goebbels gazed with near lover's ardour at the Führer; the generals nodded to each other approvingly, and even the face of Canaris, the cold realist, took on the aspect of begrudging assent.

❧

After they left, the Führer slowly shook his head. "Amazing, is it not? After all these years, Linge, and all the successes I've brought them, they still have so little faith in my judgement. Perhaps the next few months will teach them what the past sixteen years have failed to do."

"I hope so, my Führer," I answered with a perfunctory shrug. "Do you require me for anything further?" I asked, hoping he didn't, to provide me the opportunity to meet with Brückner and work on the Dvora dilemma since I realised that time was not on my side—or hers.

"As a matter of fact," he said, "I do."

"Of course, my Führer." Brückner would have to wait.

The Führer waved at two plush armchairs facing each other to the side of the great table and bade me sit in one, and he took the other. After easing himself back and taking a deep breath, he clasped his hands across his chest, tilted his head towards the ornate ceiling, and closed his eyes.

"No ceremony, Linge, you understand. Just two quite ordinary citizens of the Reich having a friendly conversation."

My eyes widened slightly. "If you say so, my Führer." Being in the Führer's service for so long, I learned that such offhanded expressions of ordinariness, egalitarianism, and camaraderie were merely his exercise of total control by covert means. The Führer was nobody's equal—and he knew it.

He pursed his lips. "Did you know that I've always admired explorers, whether they travel the external world or the inner reaches?"

I was taken aback. The Führer had never brought this up before.

"I never heard you speak of it, my Führer," I replied blandly, unsure of what he was driving at but certain that this was not simple chatter between two "ordinary citizens of the Reich."

"To me," he continued, "they are far more courageous than even the bravest soldier. You may ask why."

I didn't ask, because from experience, I knew it wasn't a solicitation.

"It's quite true, nonetheless," he said. "They're the most courageous because their enemies are both formidable and unknown." He crossed one leg languidly over the other, and I noticed that he wasn't wearing any shoes or socks. *That Junge is truly a dullard,* I told myself, vowing never to permit the clod to dress the Führer unless absolutely necessary.

"And it should be obvious to you by now," he went on, "that I'm such an explorer. And one of the things I like most to explore is the nature of those who serve me. For example, Linge, you've been with me for almost five years as a most important member of my family, and yet, is it not odd that I know virtually nothing about you? Quite perplexing—and also most challenging."

I shrugged, though the Führer couldn't see me. "There isn't anything to know, my Führer. I came from nothing."

"Humble and engaging as always, Linge, but that can hardly be the case," he countered. "There's always something if we probe hard enough and fearlessly enough—like true explorers."

He held his hands out, palms up. "Your childhood, for example, what sort of a childhood did you have?"

I began quaking inside. Even my lips began tingling. This question, if not the subject itself, was totally unexpected and even more unwanted. Why someone with the genius, majesty, responsibilities, and burdens of the Führer would be even remotely interested in someone like me, I had no possible idea. But regardless, I was obliged to deal with it.

"I had no childhood, my Führer," I told him.

Eyes still closed, he nibbled on his lower lip in thought, then nodded with some solemnity. "Yes, a pity, though Dr. Bloch wasn't a psychiatrist—and yet aren't all Jewish doctors psychiatrists?—Bloch told me that everyone needs a childhood or it affects them negatively all their lives."

I had nothing I intended to add, so I remained silent, waiting for the real meaning of his inquiry, since engaging in purely idle chatter was out of the question.

"No childhood at all?" he went on. "Not even a few toys?"

"None, I'm afraid, my Führer. Those come with childhood." *Too sophisticated a reply, I warned myself. Be careful of the Führer's wiles!*

"You know, as a boy," the Führer continued, "I had a box of paints and brushes—second-hand and incomplete, of course, but still quite usable. I would paint for hours, ignoring my meaningless schoolwork, pretending I was Michelangelo painting my own vision on the Sistine Chapel ceiling. Even adults—perhaps with the exception of Himmler—" he kidded, "also have their toys. Göring, for instance, the consummate child-man, considers everything a toy, even the Luftwaffe." The Führer suddenly lowered his voice conspiratorially. "And I will reveal to you, Linge, that I still possess a few toys from my youth. Mere trinkets really but, for some reason, still important to me."

"Yes, my Führer?" I responded with no little curiosity and apprehension, for I suspected the Führer was finally getting to the point of all this childhood talk.

"Two tiny metal tops. You know, the ones you spin until they lose momentum and drop. Mine had some peculiar designs on their sides. Quite peculiar, really. I suppose I kept them for luck. Silly superstition."

At the mention of metal tops, my insides froze, and my lips began to tingle, as if they were limbs just coming out of numbness. The Führer was certainly not reminiscing, or even benignly probing a member of his "family." I merely looked blandly at him. His head no longer tilted towards the ceiling with his eyes closed but aimed at me, his eyes fixed on mine like a sniper's scope.

"I still have one of those little tops, Linge. Unfortunately, I have no idea what happened to the second one. Would you like something to drink?"

Since he'd never asked that before, I was rendered dumbstruck. Mute, gaping, and immobile, I must have appeared like the village idiot in a trance, but the Führer must not have noticed—or chose to disregard it.

"Not thirsty, eh?" he asked with a solicitous stare. "No matter. In any event, as I told you, I still have one of them. I must have somehow mislaid the other. But for a superstitious fellow like me, only one is like not having any. So, Linge, in your many excursions round my quarters, have you perhaps come across such an item?"

"I asked you about the other item!" the Führer had shouted angrily over the phone. *Could this have been the item to which he was referring?* I had more than a little suspicion that it was the top, the dreidel I'd received mysteriously, then sent along with you to its secure location. I had to answer him, but what could I say now? What *should* I say now? A quote from Victor Hugo pushed its way to the front of my consciousness: "Blessed be Providence which has given to each his toy: the doll to the child, the child to the woman, the woman to the man, the man to the Devil!" I believe that for Hugo, man was the Devil's toy. Even more troubling was the reality of this "polite conversation between two quite ordinary citizens of the Reich"—no dimming or dousing of lights, no viewing myself from a disembodied distance, no hearing my voice utter things I couldn't possibly have known, no debilitating migraine. *What could I afford to reveal?*

"I've not encountered such a toy, my Führer," I finally answered. "Perhaps a housekeeper might have seen it or a guest or visitor may have—"

"That's all right, Linge," he halted me after a loud emission of breath. "My own fault for being careless, eh? It appears that your Führer can govern vast territories with ease but has difficulty managing his own quarters." He chuckled without mirth. "In any event, I appreciated our chat."

I took that as a dismissal and thanked him but walked somewhat slower than usual to the door, having made the educated guess that when having served up a chat with me, the Führer usually has a bit more chatting to do. So, when he spoke to my back, I was ready and turned round with studied innocence.

"Yes, my Führer?"

"I must say, pity about your lack of childhood. As to mine, should you happen upon that little top I mentioned, you'll bring it directly to me? Superstition or not, you can never have too much luck, can you?"

⁓

Once tentatively freed from the Führer's agenda-driven amiability, I began my search for Brückner. By design, I hadn't seen

Dvora for almost a week, but I knew that such intervals were courting mortal danger for us both. She was under pressure to incriminate me, and I was under pressure to get her safely out of the country. Clearly, something had to be done quickly to resolve the dilemma, but I was unable to see over the crest of it. Unfortunately, with Brückner racing about from ministry to ministry to coordinate the coming Scandinavian storm, I hadn't the opportunity to confer with my only confidant as well as the (I still believe) unwitting instigator of our current peril.

While searching, I bumped into von Ribbentrop, who had hung about after the meeting. He was intensely disliked by all but the Führer, which made him virtually invincible to his enemies. A man who, not unlike many others surrounding the Führer, employed arrogance to mask ignorance, he necessarily ran afoul of the others, principally Göring and Goebbels (especially Goebbels), whose pretensions at least possessed a fair basis in merit. I say "virtually invincible" because even he stood little chance with the Führer when all his top officials had a serious grievance, so he tried to stay out of their way as much as possible in his position.

"Ah, Linge," Ribbentrop said, "the Führer was in a rather playful mood, was he not?"

Of course, I had to stop and deal with what I knew to be a temperature-taking exercise. Being so close to the Führer daily, over the years, I'd gotten accustomed to receiving thinly veiled— and not so thinly veiled—inquiries about his mood and meaning from many of those about to see the Führer or having just seen him. Perfectly natural, I kept telling myself, but also potentially hazardous for me, so I made it strategically futile for them.

"I'm sorry, Herr Reich Minister," I said to allow myself some thinking room. "What did you say?"

The foreign minister always looked like an assistant bank

manager about to deny a loan. "I said that it seemed that the Führer was in one of his playful moods."

He wasn't saying; he was asking. "Playful, Herr Reich Minister?"

"Yes, Linge. You know. Playful. That is to say, tongue in cheek. All in all, a good mood despite the calamity."

"A calamity? What calamity, Herr Reich Minister?" I asked, my face a study in bafflement.

He pursed his thin lips as if he were actually thinking. "Yes, well, quite right. My apologies. How would you be expected to analyse anything, much less something as subtle as a mood?" With that, he turned without another word and strolled away.

Thank you, Herr Reich Minister, I thought as his figure receded. With him at least, I knew my persona remained intact.

ON MY WAY to the Communications Centre to collect the Führer's mail, I encountered Junge. Up to now, since Brückner had learned nothing of value about him—and also because of his admonition—I'd avoided all contact outside the Führer's quarters and hadn't spoken to Junge more than five times. Even then, I made sure to engage only in perfunctory prattle about the coordination of our activities according to the Führer's last-minute whims. But today, he attempted to draw me into conversation.

"It is unfortunate, Herr Colonel, that we have had so little time to get acquainted. You have been with the Führer for almost five years, and there is so much I wish to know."

Being similar in age and position, I was struck by Junge's formal and stilted speech, especially the complete absence of contractions. I was especially sensitive to this. Even more than poor grammar and worse spelling, it was a sure betrayal, not only of the fellow's poverty of education but of his avoidance of novels and dearth of active intellect as well. Gottfried Behrends, the noted linguist, wrote that "The human being thinks in words, and as such, the more words a human being knows, the more number and quality of thoughts he possesses." I considered this at the time, and not only did I concur, I even conjured up a corollary: The more intricate and variegated the word forms, the more intricate and variegated the thoughts. Of necessity, my persona has compelled me to reserve such matters to and for myself, but some force within me refused to succumb completely to the level of a linguistic clodhopper, and so, at least contractions. As for a sense of humour, it goes without saying.

"As you say, I've been with the Führer for almost five years, but there are still things about him even *I* don't know. Personally, I don't think anyone does. That's his mystery, his… his magic. Getting more acquainted with me would do nothing to—"

"No, no, Herr Colonel," he corrected, "I meant there are things I do not know about *you*."

I knew what he'd meant. I forced a laugh. "Herr Lieutenant, you flatter me, but I'm nobody. I dress him, clean up after him, and on occasion, make mistakes. I'm merely a valet—like you—no more, and there's nothing you can learn from me that I haven't already told you. Beyond the basics, to a great extent, both high and low, we all play it by ear."

His face assumed a patina of petulance. "My apologies, Herr Colonel. I was merely curious. I did not mean to give offence."

Over his shoulder, I spotted Brückner at one of the myriad security checkpoints, speaking intently with Kaltenbrunner.

I shrugged. "Herr Lieutenant, I have a reasonably thick skin, and you did nothing to offend. I'm just saying that I'm not the most promising subject for curiosity. Ask anyone." Which I suspected he would.

He nodded strangely, then heel-clicked, gave a "Heil Hitler!" with considerably more stridency than the occasion called for, pivoted, and moved off without giving me the opportunity to return the gesture.

∾

Once Junge left, I was in a quandary: approach Brückner now, while he was still with Kaltenbrunner, or wait—for God knows how long—to gratify my impatience. This time, impatience trumped prudence, and I ambled over to where they stood, almost as if I were on their level and my action held no attached implication.

"I hope I'm not interrupting something," I said for the sake of politeness. "I can come back."

Both turned their heads towards me, though Kaltenbrunner's was slightly swifter. "If you are, it's already too late, my friend," he replied with his customary sinister smirk.

I'd made a clumsy entrance, and now I was stuck in it and being pulled down, as if I'd lumbered into quicksand. To gain time, I studied Kaltenbrunner's elongated face with its little Führer moustache and deep duelling scars. His face resembled the back of a posthole shovel containing something vaguely akin to human features. He would have been considered ugly without all that, especially the scars, but with them, his gash gave him a ferocious quality that I was certain he employed for maximum advantage.

"I… merely wished to remind General Brückner of the mail awaiting the Führer's review."

Brückner's fair cheeks assumed a slight reddish hue, but I'd said it, and there was no turning back.

"Yes," he admitted with a sheepish tilt of his head. "I'd better get to it. Sorry if the whole burden fell on you."

But as he turned to leave, Kaltenbrunner remarked, "Yes, Willie. Do go about your business. I haven't yet had the pleasure of speaking with Linge here. I won't keep him long." Of course, he wasn't looking at me when he said it.

There was not much either of us could do, so Brückner clicked, saluted, and went on his way, leaving me with the man who, so the story went, had told someone, "Whenever I hear the word culture, I reach for my Browning."

"Now that the Führer has made the decisive move to extend the Reich, he must have you hopping, so I'll be brief," he said with feigned magnanimity. "I merely wish to give you General Heydrich's regards and his hope that your—how did he put it?—romance is proceeding satisfactorily."

Hearing that, I felt as if the blood in my veins had frozen and my back was drenched with sweat. My heart pounded in my ears so loudly that I was astounded Kaltenbrunner didn't also hear it. I can't fully articulate my degree of discomfort, engaging in such talk with a savage like Kaltenbrunner. And yet, I'd been desperate for a delaying tactic for Dvora and me, and suddenly, when Kaltenbrunner passed on Heydrich's "good wishes," one popped into my brain like a bingo ball.

"Please thank the general for me," I said, "but I must confess that all is not as I would wish."

Kaltenbrunner stretched his thin, bloodless lips into a frown. "No?" he exclaimed. "Pity. The general claimed to be eagerly awaiting a wedding announcement. He will be most disappointed."

I could imagine, I thought. *But why on earth would he wish me harm?* "May I confide in you, Herr Kaltenbrunner?"

"Of course," he assured me, heavy-lidded. "What you tell me stays with me."

"This is most embarrassing for me, and Christiane is most frustrated. Believe me, she's tried everything and more in her female's bag of tricks, I can assure you, but for some reason, I can't seem to, ah, rise to the occasion."

The pun had its intended effect, and it was a while before Kaltenbrunner could stop chortling and patting me on the back. "You, my friend," he said in his most comradely fashion, "are hardly alone. Even the most virile of us undergo such a condition from time to time. You should see that Morell chap. From what the Führer tells me, I'm confident the doctor can make a cricket bat out of a shoelace."

The imagery was considerably less than beguiling, but now it was my turn to chortle. I only hoped it sounded authentic. "A most inspired idea, Herr General!" I exclaimed. "With the Führer's permission, I'll ask to see him straight away. I thank you." I wasn't lying, for I had every intention of carrying my tactic further by speaking to the Führer about my carnal frustrations.

"It's nothing," he replied with faux humility. "Director Heydrich will also be pleased, I'm sure." He sported an expression residing somewhere between a sneer and a snicker—and one which fit Kaltenbrunner to perfection.

When I began in service, Brückner told me that the Führer generally knew what the people in his close circle did privately, but he never specifically asked anybody to spy and keep him updated. He would talk to this person or that person and ask conversationally what he did when not on duty, but he was opposed to gossip and would put a stop to any attempt to pass him information about third parties. Personal liaisons were only of interest if they concerned him directly or were intruding into the political realm. After so many years with him, I had no reason to doubt it, though he kept me constantly amazed at his degree of household knowledge.

I finally managed to track down Brückner, induced him outside, and related first, my chat with Junge.

"Well," he said, "since I've not been able to learn anything much about him, at this point, you may know more than I do."

"But what do I know, Wilhelm?"

"Good question," he said. "Unfortunately, *too good*, so I'd say that until we know more, should you dine with him, bring a long spoon."

Next, I told him about Kaltenbrunner, especially the part

about my "limp noodle," as the Führer would say of foreign leaders.

He smiled and congratulated me on my sacrificial cunning. "Extremely adroit, my friend. You're learning to navigate this rabbit warren of intrigue and betrayal with some considerable skill. Of course, this may not be a complete compliment. But a clever fellow like you must realise that all your efforts can be no more than a temporary expedient—not unlike wearing an adhesive bandage in the tropics. Have you considered Madame Kitty's?" His tone was not that of a jester.

"No," I replied. "Once I'd adopted impotence as my ploy, it seemed at odds for me to demonstrate any capability."

"Far be it for me to suggest otherwise," he countered, "but I'd venture that impotence would be a perfect explanation for visiting that place. They do all the work, and you can still see Christiane without much concern in the short run."

I merely nodded, mostly at the irony of him saying that since it was he who'd brought "Christiane" into my life to spare me from Kitty's. But he was right about my need to return. And he was also right about the short run. Of course, Dvora could continue her nefarious business with the few Jews left in Berlin. *But what about her business with me? When would she be called to account for her failure there?* "Have you learned anything about her assignment to snare me?" I finally asked.

He took a deep breath and let it out slowly. "Not yet, and that in itself is troublesome. Someone should know something. But I still have my feelers out."

Now why did that not comfort me?

IMPOTENCE, ALLIED WITH prophylaxis, continues to buy us time, but Dvora is coming under increasing pressure to produce "tangible results." Meanwhile, she claims she must at least be successful in her other activities, despite my disapproval. *Neither Brückner nor I have yet contrived a satisfactory solution, so under the circumstances, can I condemn her?* I also continue to avoid Junge as much as my situation allows.

Today, the American Undersecretary of State Sumter (sic) Wells visited the Führer to discuss his hopes for a lasting peace in Europe. The Führer curbed his indignation and resentment towards Roosevelt for sending the "cunning fox," as the former called Wells, but made it perfectly clear that they made their bed and now they must lie in it. After the meeting, he gathered his top leaders and gave them one of his lectures on statecraft while I rearranged books I'd already arranged.

"*My God!*" he exclaimed, "I've had dreams in which I was in charge of Germany at the last war's end, instead of those incestuous, spineless 'vons,' who considered it good sportsmanship to eviscerate the Reich. I've gotten to know these so-called 'world leaders' first-hand, and if I'd been in charge of negotiations, there would have been no Versailles, I can assure you. In fact—"

"Clearly, my Führer," Goebbels interrupted, seemingly in genuine distress, "but then, there would have been no need for a Nazi Party, and—"

"Joseph." The Führer smiled his moustache upward. "You

must learn to relax. I ask you: What is the Nazi Party, but the instrument through which I work my will and vision? The artist in me merely paints a scenario in which such an instrument would be unnecessary. And now," he continued, "I shall do whatever I think is right after the West rejects my proposals for a peaceful accord—which of course they will," he added, to raised arms and shouts of "Heil Hitler!"

I believe I could actually see moisture in Goebbels's eyes.

Then, as if to present a rich dessert after a bland meal, the Führer joked with them about the fact that while Wells was lunching with Ribbentrop the day before, the Führer had been busy signing the order for Operation Weserübung, the code name for his intended assault on Denmark and Norway and the opening operation of his Norwegian Campaign.

It appeared to me that when it came to statecraft, "Cunning Fox" Wells couldn't hold a candle to the Führer.

THIS MORNING, WHILE preparing the Führer for a strenuous day ahead—both for him and for me—I dared broach the subject of my "impotence."

"My Führer," I began, "I know that you have many important—"

"Linge," he interrupted, "you're going to give me that too-trivial-to-bother-me-with blather. Look here, if I can listen to the useless prattle of my ministers and generals, I can certainly make time for someone who actually serves me."

"Thank you, my Führer," I said, not a little relieved—and even overwhelmed. "It's a most sensitive matter."

The Führer pursed his lips. "Hmm, 'sensitive,' you say? Well, all right, Linge, you've sparked my curiosity. Just what is this 'sensitive matter'?"

I knew that to get the most from such a conversation, my recitation needed to be bashful, halting, and tentative. "My Führer, I am… I am… in need… I may require the… the services of—"

"Linge, Linge," the Führer interrupted my stammering as I hoped he would, "soon you'll start drooling, and this is a new carpet. Out with it!" he commanded with gentle good humour.

"You know of my… of Christiane, my Führer?"

He smiled indulgently. "I would be a poor parent if I didn't follow the amorous adventures of my children." He raised his hand, palm outward to prevent a response, followed by a sly grin. "Don't fret, Linge. I already know all about it. That tattler Kaltenbrunner couldn't wait to tell me. Fortunately, he'd told no one else, so I could swear him to absolute silence and save you from the gossipmongers." Suddenly, he reached his hand up to rest on my shoulder. "You know, you should have come to me as soon as this condition began. We can't allow a strapping young lad like yourself to agonise in silent frustration, can we?"

Since the question, like most of the Führer's questions, was rhetorical, I merely shrugged awkwardly and said nothing.

"I remember only too well how terrified I was in the trenches. So much so, I will admit to you, that whenever I got leave, I could do nothing but visit museums, if you catch my meaning." His moustache lifted slightly, and he removed his hand from my shoulder (which must have ached from the upward stretch).

I nodded energetically to show that I caught his meaning but would never intimate that anything short of hand-to-hand combat could sexually inhibit the Führer.

"It's a basic fact of nature, Linge. In a way, unfair, but nature is unconcerned with such matters. Man must work, and women must abide. You can see it even in fashion: Men dress for battle, and women dress for seduction. Can anyone seriously question this? In any event, I'll arrange for Morell to treat you. I'm confident that with his nostrums, he'll transform your boiled asparagus into a fresh cucumber faster than you can unfasten your trousers."

The Führer's herbivorous imagery countered any embarrassment I might have felt, and I was compelled to laugh.

"That's the spirit," he said with a wink. "Though I never needed such assistance—and now, well, you know my attitude—such a condition is not uncommon. Jews are the prime example. You ask why they have such small families despite their incessant breeding? This is the answer."

In truth, I never wondered about the sexual capabilities of Jews, but I nodded knowingly and enthusiastically.

"And now," he went on, "now that we're occupying a territory teeming with Slavs, I mean no insensitivity to you, but I wish our soldiers had your malady, at least in the short run. In any event," he concluded, "today I need Morell to prepare me for one of Hoffmann's endless photo sessions and, later, a meeting with one of Pacelli's papist whiners. But this evening, he's all yours. Soon, I predict, you'll be renting out your member by the hour." He delivered one of his comradely punches to my upper arm, moved to his desk, and phoned for the doctor.

I spent the entire evening waiting, but Morell never came. *Good,* I thought, since the situation was far more important than the solution, and the more drawn out, the better.

MORELL CALLED EARLY (for him) to tell me that he regretted not visiting me last night but that he would be by this evening. I took the opportunity afforded me by the Führer's total preoccupation with his war plans to bone up (no pun intended) on my "condition" and how it had been handled (again, no pun intended) in a pre-Morell world. I made a quick visit to the State Library, where I read that those methods most often consisted of dietary regimens and a salve of plant or animal origin. Included were the more psychically oriented remedies derived from contact with the perceived magical power of animal organs and artificially altered amulets. Other "remedies" read like a medical textbook and, thus incomprehensible, merely useless gibberish to an unlettered fellow like me.

However, even understanding little of what I found, my reading didn't fill me with confidence, but instead, great apprehension at the thought of being treated with such medieval craziness. I was hardly relieved by speculating that, knowing Morell, his methods might well be even more bizarre. Be that as it may, I was willing to undergo any treatment that would provide needed time to devise an escape plan for Dvora with minimal risk to me.

✑

As it turned out, my medical research was horribly incomplete.

"You know, Linge," Morell confided, "you're fortunate the Führer has enlisted me in the cause of true love. You wouldn't believe what passed for treatment before I came along. Why, would you believe that the Victorians actually implanted curved rods through the hole at the tip of the penis, and once these rods were inserted, a bulb at the end would be squeezed, pushing nitric acid into the bladder?"

To me, it seemed more like a technique that Heydrich would utilise with job applicants. However, since I knew Morell to have no discernible sense of humour, I was forced to believe him. I scrunched my face in horror.

"You might well wince, Linge," he continued, "but there's more. While not so, ah, rigorous as urethral rods, drinking large quantities of one's own urine has also been utilised widely. Even to this day."

My own sense of humour could withstand no more such tales. "Better than drinking someone else's, I suppose."

"Hmm, quite so," he answered with hooded eyes, making him resemble a frog more than ever. "Fortunately, I developed a true remedy, effective, painless, and not disgusting. For our soldiers, you understand, but it's done wonders for certain Chancellery personnel, so why not you, eh?"

"I'm most grateful, Doctor. What is this remedy?"

"Nothing for you to worry your poor layman's head over," he said. "A medicinal cocktail if you will. A perfect blend of ingredients that will, in short order, give you a third leg, so to say." He chuckled at his witticism.

"How short, Doctor?"

"You mean the treatments or the member?" he joked lamely.

"The treatments," I answered blandly.

"Well, my lad, as with all medications, much depends on the condition of the patient. I would have to perform a thorough examination to be accurate, but for a strapping young lad like you, not that long, I daresay. May I ask who this young lady is?"

Though he'd surely learned about her from the Führer, how much more should I tell this snoopy tattler? "Her name is Christiane," I said.

"And would she also be a menial?"

What was the relevance of that, save arrogance? I needed to put an end to any further prying. "She works for General Heydrich, Doctor. She never told me what she does. You might ask the general."

An uneasy laugh. "Truly a woman of mystery, then, and clearly the more attractive for all that, I'm sure." With that, he reached into his doctor's bag and removed a small rubber-topped bottle and a syringe. "I'll give you one of these to begin. By tonight, I'll have prepared my magic elixir for you to administer each day until the desired result is achieved."

My heart began pounding with such ferocity that I could swear Morell could hear it. I'd learned from Brandt[24] that despite the Führer's claim to have curbed any sexual drive for the sake of the nation, Morell was administering regular injections of testosterone and a concoction made from the semen and pros-tate glands of young bulls. I shuddered when I considered the horrific side effects of such a brew—and the even more horrific chances for swift results.

"Please, Doctor," I said, forcing a quaver into my voice, "I have this… terrible fear of needles. Is there some way your remedy could be given in powder form?"

---

[24] Karl Brandt was a German physician and SS officer. Trained as a surgeon, Brandt joined the Nazi Party in 1932 and became Adolf Hitler's escort doctor in August 1934. As a member of Hitler's inner circle at the Berghof, he was selected to administer the Aktion T4 euthanasia programme.

The frog's bladder lips pressed heavily against each other. "Not to worry. Fear of needles is not uncommon, so we physicians must have a variety of ingestion methods at our disposal. Fortunately, the Führer is not so disposed. In fact, I think he actually enjoys it. In any event, I'll cook up some powder, but you'll need to take the dosage twice a day since water invariably dilutes the potency."

"I'm most grateful," I said. "I'll follow your regimen to the letter."

"Ah, then you should see marked improvement quite soon, I'm certain."

"I can't wait," I said with the straightest of faces.

I RECEIVED MY first dose of Morell's "penis potion," as he called it. I hoped that the pipes beneath my toilet wouldn't be harmed when I flushed it down. Now the trick was to delay checkups.

For the first time, I overheard some speculative Chancellery gossip concerning the discovery of Schlegl's mutilated corpse. Some speculated that he'd been a victim of what minuscule resistance might still exist within Germany's borders. Others said that the arrogant debaucher had finally been given his comeuppance by a jealous husband or fiancé. And the rest placed the guilt on street hooligans who clearly had the treasonous temerity to brutally murder an SS officer without even robbing him.

As for me, having no reason to believe that anyone, save the architects of Schlegl's mission could possibly lay his fate at my door (and having nothing to connect me to his brutal demise beyond common sense), I went about my duties as if nothing had happened, albeit with a sense of profound unease, expecting the architects to "redraw their plans" at any time.

16 March 1940

FOREIGNERS WHO PRAISE—OR deride—the Germans' fondness for discipline and order should witness how preparation for the Führer's journeys is carried out. They would think they were visiting an Italian lunatic asylum. How the Führer ever gets to his destinations on time, is truly remarkable.

Today, we performed another exercise in pandemonium for a trip to a place on the Brenner Pass for a secret meeting between the Führer and Mussolini. The purpose: to forge a firm guarantee of cooperation in the "inevitable shooting war" (as Field Marshal Keitel put it) with Britain. France was not even worthy of mention. Brückner expressed to me his complete lack of surprise at the Soviet Union's exclusion from the meeting since, to the Führer, "all Stalin seems to want are the table scraps left over from German feasts."

After dinner, the Führer asked me to remain.

"Linge," he said with a chuckle, "I wouldn't normally ask this of you, but Morell is indisposed and the Duce is in extreme distress. Like our Hermann, he fancies himself a far more delicate specimen than he actually is. His vanity seems to require that he wear the boots of a far smaller man. Hence, he experiences great discomfort. I appreciate that you're not an English butler or… footman"—more chuckles—"but if you would salve his aching hooves with a bucket of hot water and salts, I believe that he would make you a general in his army. And believe me, his army could use you."

FROM WHERE I stood—literally—the meeting between the Führer and Mussolini was entirely cordial on both sides, since the conference consisted of the Führer's monologue, with Mussolini nodding approvingly at appropriate moments. Looking physically fit (with no small assistance from Morell), the Führer appeared less agitated than usual, making far fewer gestures and speaking in a relatively quiet tone. Mussolini listened to him with apparent interest and deference. He spoke little and confirmed his intention to move with Germany. The only caveat was his stated intention to reserve to himself the choice of the right moment.

According to Canaris, Mussolini truly believes that the Führer will think twice before he begins an offensive on land, but Brückner believes that Mussolini was engaging in a "breathtaking exhibition of wishful thinking."

A DEEP DEPRESSION kept me in my quarters most of the day. The Führer merely hoped that it wasn't a reaction to Morell's treatment of my "sexual affliction." I was able to assure him in all honesty that nothing could be further from the truth, and he seemed satisfied.

The American philosopher Ralph Waldo Emerson wrote: "Your genuine action will explain itself and will explain your other genuine actions. Your conformity explains nothing." I interpreted this to mean that if one really wanted to see someone's true character, one shouldn't listen to what he says, for talk is cheap and not necessarily accurate. Instead, observe what he does, for actions are a much clearer reflection of someone's character than anything he said. One would think that Emerson had laboured in the Chancellery.

While such a sentiment meant nothing to me before coming to work for the Führer, now, after Emerald and Katrin, two attempts on my life (at least of which I'm aware), Brückner's counsel, and now Dvora, I believe that Herr Emerson's aphorism requires an energetic revisiting. But not tonight, for the Führer has scheduled a screening of Hippler's *Campaign in Poland*, with me as projectionist.[25]

---

[25] *Feldzug in Polen (Campaign in Poland)* was a Nazi propaganda film released in 1940 depicting the 1939 invasion of Poland, directed by Fritz Hippler. The "Gleiwitz Incident," portrayed in the film, was part of Operation

Aside from the Führer, Junge, and me, attendance at the screening included Joseph and Magda Goebbels, Göring, Himmler, Brückner, Speer, Leni Riefenstahl, and of course, the film's producer, Fritz Hippler.

By Goebbels's instructions (and the Führer's acquiescence), I showed the Hippler film first. A sixty-nine-minute film, it depicted in graphic detail last year's invasion and conquest of Poland. Exquisitely photographed and edited, the film alleged that the Poles employed craven, heartless tactics in the war and characterised the defence of a besieged Warsaw as senseless and, thus, its complete destruction as necessary. At the conclusion, Hippler exhibited battered and demoralised Polish troops surrendering and being marched to the rear, while victorious German troops paraded through the ravaged city, viewed by a triumphant Führer, who saluted jubilant bystanders and resolute German troops.

Immediately after the film tail ceased its furious flapping, Goebbels ordered the lights switched on and asked the audience for their reactions. Most turned to the Führer, who nodded languid approval, causing an eruption of passionate acclaim, while Hippler beamed. Himmler merely sat stone-faced with his ever-present notebook and pencil, jotting down something

---

Himmler, run by the SS and SD to justify German aggression. It involved dressing Nazi concentration camp prisoners as Polish soldiers who apparently attacked a German radio station. The prisoners were then murdered by the SS/SD to make it appear as though they had been shot by heroic German defenders. Other aspects of Operation Himmler involved terrorist attacks on the Polish Railways and attacks by ethnic Germans on Polish property. French involvement was de-emphasised to cast Great Britain, in its attempt to encircle Germany, as the villain, in turn justifying the Nazi-Soviet pact. Polish provocations finally resulted in the blitzkrieg, led by Hitler.

I couldn't make out, and Riefenstahl tilted her head towards her lifted shoulder and pursed her lips in what I assumed to be either boredom, unconcealed rivalry, or a practised reaction to Göring's ogling.

Having already witnessed first-hand the aftermath of the Wehrmacht's rendering of a majestic and picturesque capital into a jagged horror of glowing rubble and putrid body parts, I marvelled at the cleansing powers of Hippler's cameras. I also marvelled at the quality of the filmmaker's lenses, always a German particularity, and vowed to obtain one for my own camera. I had no basis for assessing the quality of the actual filmmaking.

Boisterous plaudits having subsided into separate, hushed clusters of conversation, I began securing the film and projector. The Führer leaned over to speak with Riefenstahl, who sat to the Führer's left, while Hippler sat to his immediate right. Bored, I took my time with the projector and strained clandestinely to overhear them.

"I would like to know your opinion of Hippler's film," the Führer asked of Riefenstahl. "From a technical perspective, of course."

"Of course," she replied. "I will be happy to. But, my Führer, as a practitioner of the cinematic arts, I must say that a technical perspective cannot be separated from a film's purpose. Don't you agree, Herr Hippler?" she asked without leaning round to look at him.

The Führer swivelled his head to his right and assumed a faint smile. "Does she have a point, Dr. Hippler?"

It was then that I knew the Führer was toying with them, perhaps to fan the flames of jealousy for his own amusement, something that he'd done often with Göring and Goebbels, not to mention his military leaders. That seemed to be basic to his nature.

"As with architecture, my Führer," Hippler answered, "as I'm sure Herr Speer would confirm, purpose dictates design. My purpose, my mission, if you will, as directed by Reichsminister Goebbels, was to arouse German national pride through demonstration of German might. But there was another message for viewers abroad, to frighten the world into appeasement. I believe the effect on German audiences will be waves of sympathy and applause, and the effect on the rest will be the creation of second thoughts concerning any interference with your intentions. Unlike Fräulein Riefenstahl, I was not permitted the luxury of art for art's sake."

I could see a familiar twinkle form in the Führer's eyes as he turned back to Riefenstahl. "And do you concur with Dr. Hippler's assessment?"

She smiled beguilingly. "My Führer, if Hippler wishes to believe that I operated without restrictions in my *Triumph of the Will*, it is of course his privilege. I take it as a high compliment. Let me just say, my Führer, that to the artist, film has at least one of three purposes: to entertain, to enlighten, and to persuade. Now, to this humble moviemaker, if a film can do all three, it achieves the status of art. I believe that *Triumph* did just that. Can the good doctor say as much for what we just witnessed?"

By then, I'd grown weary of this game, so I put away the film and equipment and moved along the wall to a position near Goebbels and Himmler.

"Yes, a pity," Goebbels was saying, "that Hippler couldn't show your, ah, heroic pacification of the city, but you know, *'Mundus vult decipi, ergo decipiatur.'* That means—"

"I know what it means, Joseph," Himmler interrupted, his face its usual expressionless mask. "That people always want to hear agreeable things and events. There is no denying this, of course. Perhaps, then, we only differ on what is agreeable."

I sensed that Himmler, in his own peculiar way, was like the Führer, also pulling a leg. I couldn't possibly imagine that Himmler would have preferred a few scenes of what he called "pacification," the RSHA's inventive methods of procuring information and dealing with resistance—*his* idea of art.

As I STARED intently at my mirror image, all-too-vivid memories of last night engulfed me, bringing with them the foul-smelling detritus of guilt. Standing there beside the projector, I'd witnessed the savage destruction of cities and human beings, and all I did was vow to obtain a better camera lens. The scenes of slaughter had actually bored me. *So, to what place had all my years of self-education brought me?* Indifference.

Not that I could have done anything, then as now. And yet…

I cupped my hands and splashed some water on my face with a hard stinging slap. *A rebuke?* Perhaps Oscar Wilde said it best: "There is a luxury in self-reproach. When we blame ourselves, we feel that no one else has a right to blame us. It is the confession, not the priest, that gives us absolution." However, even if true—and I strongly suspected it was—I'd achieved no satisfaction from it and certainly no peace.

But as I dressed, Emerson's words again pushed to the front: "Your genuine action will explain itself and will explain your other genuine actions. Your conformity explains nothing." *Yes, conformity, another name for indifference?*

And finally, as I closed the door behind me, it was Voltaire that accompanied me to the Führer's rooms: "Every man is guilty of all the good he did not do."

"What did you think of the film?" the Führer asked me as I picked out a tie to accompany the shit-brown double-breasted suit I loathed. If clothes make the man, as the saying goes, the Führer was constructed for a uniform, and a suit—any suit—caused him to appear thickset, short... ordinary, which of course, was anything but the truth.

"I know you dislike this suit," he remarked, tuning into my thoughts as if I were a radio station. "I must agree with you, Linge, but too much of me in uniform makes certain types uncomfortable, especially industrialists and bankers, who constantly fear there's too much national socialism in National Socialism. African and South American potentates haven't the wits or sensitivity to recognise this, and well, Göring believes he has only to impress himself—which he always does. Enough of that. So, what did you think of Hippler's film?" He added, "considering Riefenstahl's remarks, of course."

Aside from the fact that I thought I'd been successfully furtive in my eavesdropping, what could I say? That I was bored by the film and even more so by the analysis of it? That I was greatly ashamed for having been so?

"My Führer," I began with a shrug, "I'm no fit judge of such things. If Fräulein Riefenstahl and Dr. Hippler are in disagreement, whether over form, content, or purpose, it is for you and you alone to judge its merits, not an ignorant menial who laughs at three clownish American idiots continually hitting each other over the head." It wasn't for anyone, even the Führer, to know that I found slapstick humour to be a contradiction in terms.

The Führer nodded slowly. "Yes, Linge, you're right of course. But ignoring the artistic aspects, do you think, even as a menial, as you like to call yourself, that it will both inspire the German masses and frighten our enemies?"

Cornered again. *What enemies? Was more insipid humility on my part even necessary, much less useful?* "I can't speak for our enemies, but it does appear that Germans love anything military—especially victory." I wanted to add, *No matter the carnage,* but most certainly did not.

The Führer laughed robustly. "Yes, yes, Linge. They do. And I must feed their love—that is, until I've made it no longer necessary."

I didn't understand that last part but kept silent, save for a yes-my-Führer nod. He appeared satisfied, so could I be less so?

1 April 1940

I WAS AWAKENED by Brückner, who proceeded to inform me that all my troubles were behind me since Himmler had prevailed upon the Führer to declare Dvora an "honorary Aryan."[26]

My jubilation was short-lived, however, once I'd shaken off enough of my grogginess to realise that it was April Fool's Day. Confronted, Brückner apologised profusely for the prank, knowing that a part of me still cared for her—at least for her welfare—but informed me that he hadn't thrown in the towel on finding a workable solution to my problem—and his own as well since, as he put it, "Our problems, romance aside, are not dissimilar."

"Perhaps we could volunteer for active service at the front and hide there," I suggested in poor riposte.

Brückner leaned over and pounded me on the shoulder with comradely regard, pursed his lips, and nodded slowly in mock thought. "Yes, Heinz, I think you've got it: a valet and an old man with one eye. The Wehrmacht would snatch us up in a minute. The enemy would take one look at us and laugh itself

---

[26] Honorary Aryan (*ehrenarier*) was an expression used in Nazi Germany to describe the unofficial status of persons who were not recognised as belonging to the Aryan race according to Nazi standards but were informally considered part of it. The prevailing explanation for why the Nazis conferred the status of "honorary Aryan" upon non-Nordic—or even less exclusively, non-Indo-Iranian/European peoples—is that the services of those peoples were deemed valuable to the German economy or war effort.

to death. Quite the strategist, my friend." The only jarring note in the otherwise well-meant buffoonery of April Fool's Day (and not a small one) was the brief typed message pushed under my door after Brückner left:

> *My Dearest Heinz. By now, I'm certain you are aware that "Christiane" is a mortal danger to you—and, consequently, no less to us. Though she is the poisonous remnant of a despised race, you wish to save her. The reason to us is obvious: You possess a perilously admirable chivalry— ironically in keeping with our hallowed Aryan traditions. However, I tell you that in this instance, you must consider your own safety above all things, so remove her from your sacred orbit round the Führer by any means necessary. With all my affection, K.*

8 April 1940

THE CHIEFS OF the Wehrmacht, finally chastened by the Führer into accepting the fact of war, still bridled at his decision to initially invade two insignificant countries like Denmark and Norway when that archenemy, France, should bear the initial brunt of Germany's overwhelming military might. Up to now, such "debates" invariably concluded with the Führer's face purple-red, his clenched, white-knuckled fists crashing down on his desktop, and his voice shrieking obscenities about the utter lack of imagination, audacity, and judgement among his military leaders.

Regarding these tiresome tirades, my mental radio had learned to turn itself off or switch stations, but no more. What Brückner told me on our last stroll persuaded me to listen to these increasingly frequent military briefings. By any normal standard, they would be irrelevant to someone in my meaningless and servile position. However, I've come to believe that at the very least, I'll become more and more proficient at a civilian's understanding of strategy, tactics, and the military perspective and add a practical component to the intellectual insularity of library reading rooms.

But today, the Führer was exceptionally mellow, one might even say serene or placid, so as I busied myself with his enormous military maps that lay scattered pell-mell across the conference table and floor, arranging by furling, unfurling, and furling again, I listened.

"Tomorrow," said the Führer, "will be a monumentally historic day for the Reich. Unfortunately, I'm sorry to say, many of you still believe that it will be not so momentous. Since you consistently fail to understand the inspiration guiding my military decisions, I will provide you with a simple metaphor and have done with it."

The Führer then eased himself back in his chair with exaggerated deliberation, I felt, to permit the gathered to stare wonderingly at each other. The Führer was always a master of suspense. He'd grouped his military and diplomatic leaders round his enormous oval table and, for five minutes, let them stew with anticipation.

Finally, he leaned forward, clasped his hands, and told them the story of the boiled frog. "Have any of you heard how one boils a frog?"

After a blank-faced moment, a chorus of "No, my Führer," followed.

"I assumed not," he chided gently. "You must learn that not all wisdom is found in military manuals and hunting magazines. The boiling frog is an anecdote describing a frog being boiled alive. The premise is that if a frog is placed in boiling water, it will jump out, but if it is placed in cold water that is slowly heated, it will not perceive the danger and will be cooked to death. And for you doubters, nineteenth-century experiments suggested that the underlying premise is correct, provided the heating is sufficiently gradual." He eased himself back again, allowing them to savour his "frog stew."

A whispered hubbub followed. If any of the gentlemen knew the anecdote, he was loath to admit it and spoil the Führer's lesson. I'd read about it years before, but it had no more meaning at the time than any other trivia my dustbin of a brain automatically stored.

The Führer chuckled. "Still baffled? All right, gentlemen, this ex-corporal will make it simple for you," he declared to the stunning array of bespoke suits, military braids, medals, and pre-eminent badges of rank sitting round him. "The boiling frog is a metaphor for the inability or unwillingness of people to react to threats that occur gradually. Regarding Denmark and Norway, these are but nibbles, which will illustrate our unwillingness to take larger bites. And when we finally begin devouring larger fare with gusto, it will come as a *fait accompli*, not a strategy."

Mixed metaphors aside, to this desultorily self-taught character, the Führer's game plan seemed eminently sound—even ingenious. When they'd all left with what I took to be varying degrees of disgruntlement, all the Führer said to me was "Well, Linge, until one of us locates the other one, we must now see what only one top can accomplish."

Despite my slowly increasing intellectual confidence, I'm still confounded by the Führer's reference and its relevance.

REMARKABLY, DURING THE very launching of Operation Weserübung, which for some reason plunged the entire Chancellery (with the sole exception of the Führer) into a frenzy of anticipation and patriotic fervour, I was able to pull Brückner outside just long enough to tell him about the note I'd received from Katrin and to solicit his advice. In any event, it was high time something was done about the Dvora situation, since I could stretch Morell's "miracle regimen" for just so long.

"Ah so." He pulled on his lower lip in thought. "It appears that at least one of those two stunning enigmas of yours isn't finished with you yet. Are you certain the note was from her?"

I shrugged half-heartedly. "I don't know, Wilhelm. Considering the K at the close and what Katrin had mentioned before about her activities at the RSHA—she certainly would be in a position to know all about it."

He nodded again, but this time, his face held a hint of melancholy. "All right, let's leave me and my regrettable, unwitting involvement out of this for the moment. In my view—one-eyed though it may be—these are the main questions we need to deal with: One"—he began ticking off each item with a moistened finger emerging from a closed fist—"considering where she works, is it a trap? Two, what is her motive for warning you? Three, if it's not a trap, have you made up your mind to help this Dvora? And four, if you have, how can it be done to ensure success and safety for you both?"

These were entirely legitimate and logical questions—but I had my own equally legitimate and logical question: *Was I capable of answering them?* I decided to take the path of least resistance. "This is all most overwhelming, I tell you, Wilhelm. At this point, since Dvora was your find, I'd be most grateful for any suggestions."

Brückner smiled and nodded. "Shifting the responsibility, eh? Being surrounded by the Party bigwigs has certainly schooled you well in the art of passing the buck."

As good as I felt I'd become, I still lacked the wits to tell a Brückner joke from a Brückner accusation, so I began stammering a quip-like response but never got to complete it, for he reached up quickly and held me fast by the shoulders. "Don't look so stricken, my friend. I'm just pulling your leg—not that you need to be any taller. You're perfectly right. I got you into this, and the very least I owe you is an effective escape route."

He released me, and I wiped my sweating brow with my tunic sleeve.

"Look, Heinz," he continued, "I'm an old soldier, though not nearly as prodigiously gifted as Ex-Corporal Hitler, so I always suspect a trap. And for someone who survived that memorable meal at Salon Kitty, you should too. But be that as it may, by the look on your face, I can tell that your heart has trumped your brain and you've made up your mind to help her, regardless." He quickly held up his hand, palm outward in a halting gesture. "Any denial is both needless and disingenuous. And anyway, I'm the last person to question the power of passion over prudence."

I'd heard things, but now seemed to be the moment. "You?"

His lips edged upward sardonically. "Of course me, Heinz. Do you think this eye patch is a battle ribbon? If so, it was bestowed on me by Sophie Storck, not von Hindenburg. It's hardly anything to take pride in. I was driving—and groping her, simultaneously—admittedly an activity for an adolescent or an idiot. I was neither, but there it was. A crash, and I received my 'medal.'"

"But—"

His face was set, solemn, one small shade short of grim. "I've disappointed you," he began. "Believe me, no more than myself. I've not told you this before because it's no great honour and was nobody's business but mine and Sophie's—and, unfortunately, the Führer's. He actually wanted me to marry Storck, the great chum of his Eva, but when I refused, he took it personally—as he takes everything—and our relationship was never the same. You know what a bourgeois bluenose the Führer is. But at least he kept the matter close to the vest, even when I started running around with Magda Quandt, who later married the esteemed Reichsminister Goebbels."

Close to the vest is right, I thought. Even I hadn't heard of his part in all this.

"As I said," he continued, "it was no one else's business. But gradually, our business has become others' business. Don't ask me how. The toothpaste was out of the tube, you might say, and there was no shoving it back in. So, why am I telling you this now? Because, my young friend, time is running out for me, no less than for your Dvora. That target I told you about, the one affixed to my back, is now within range of Bormann's sniper rifle, and I harbour no doubts about the bastard using it. So—"

"My God," I cut him off, "*your* life is in danger?"

The solemnity vanished, and he laughed lightly. "No, Heinz, I said that figuratively. You know what figuratively means?"

"Vaguely," I replied with the necessary ambiguity.

"Then you don't," he countered as I hoped he would. "It means that the slimy ape wouldn't dare to actually have me done in. No, he's content to manipulate the Führer into toppling me from my perch so he can take my place. So, if I'm to help you, it must be now, right now, and not a moment later. For friendship, I'll do my best to come up with a safe way to at least resolve the Dvora matter. But first, you need to speak with her, make her see the peril she's in and not merely the jeopardy she's put you in. If she confided in you, she must have had a reason. Find out what it is and work it to your advantage. And push aside K's note for the time being. Beyond that, you—"

"Ah, General, so now we'll finally see some action," interrupted Major Fashnauer, one in Göring's personal army of adjutants, as he manoeuvred round me and faced Brückner as if I were merely an inconveniently placed column. He was a small, insignificant figure with a large head, of which the forehead and eyes seemed by far the largest portion. His hair was as fine as spun glass and so blond it was almost white. A man of no determinate age but no longer young, of slight, wiry frame and ramrod posture.

"Action?" Brückner replied, eyebrow raised. "What action?"

Fashnauer blew some air from his slightly bent nose. "I meant to say Denmark and Norway, of course," he said almost derisively.

Brückner glared at the major with condescending indulgence, clearly lost on him. "I'm fairly certain you've said it. Now, Major, we need to flex our military muscle on far tougher adversaries, like Liechtenstein, don't you agree?"

"You know, Herr General," he said, ignoring Brückner's remark or not getting it, "that I intended to volunteer. To fight. But when I told the boss, he said no, and that was that."

"I will console you, Major. I'm certain the Reichsmarschall was merely trying to spare you the possible humiliation of being killed by a Dane," Brückner answered, straight-faced.

Again, no recognition registered in the major's expression. Either he was a complete dolt or a master of restraint. Perhaps he was both, but further analysis of someone so studiously ignoring me warranted no more of my time.

"When I mentioned the situation to Reichsleiter Bormann," he went on, "just in passing, you understand, he assured me that a man of my 'obvious martial talents,' as he called them, shouldn't be wasted performing trivial administrative drudgery. Of course, I agreed, then he told me that he would go over the Reichsmarschall's head to the Führer himself and get me into a fighting unit. Now I ask you, is that man a wizard or what?"

Brückner smiled indulgently. "So, has the wizard spoken with the Führer?"

"That's why I'm here. I have an appointment with the Reichsleiter. But considering his influence and assurances, I'm sure to receive positive news and be sent to the front in no time."

Brückner nodded with melodramatic solemnity. "Well, for your sake, Major, don't get your hopes too high. You're obviously aware of the relative strengths of the German, Danish, and Norwegian armies. The... battle may be over before you leave your meeting."

Fashnauer chuckled. "Unfortunately, you may be right. But not before the next one, eh? You know the Führer far better than anyone. Even the Reichsleiter, maybe. Do you seriously think that he will be content with some stupid Low Countries? And fellow Aryans at that? No, Herr General, there will be plenty of battles to come, against real enemies like those stinking Slavs, and I'll be in the thick of it, you bet." I could have sworn the major's chest expanded as he said it. "Thank God for the Reichsleiter," he added. "No one has more influence with the Führer than he does. Pity he spends most of his time at the Berghof."

"Yes," Brückner affirmed with dramatically pursed lips, "a pity indeed. When is your meeting?"

Fashnauer raised his arm, thrust it forward to uncover his

watch, glanced down, brought his arm down, then looked back at Brückner. "In a few minutes, Herr General. I should be going. I want to stop at the Communications Centre on my way. Latest news, you know."

With that, we all saluted, and he walked away. Goebbels's incessant radio broadcasts had us victorious even before any information arrived from the battle zone, and I was fairly certain that the major wanted to see if there were any battles left to fight. At no time did he ever look at me or even glance my way. I hated his guts but revelled in my sacred invisibility.

"*Speak of the Devil!*" I blurted, then lowered my voice when I noticed some heads turn.

Brückner shook his head slowly. "No doubt. You know, Fashnauer's transfer to active duty may be a blessing."

"How's that?"

"Maybe he'll be killed, and Bormann will have one less ally."

I laughed, but I knew Brückner was serious, despite the levity of his remark. "My God, can Bormann be that influential?"

Brückner scrunched his face to where he appeared squinty-eyed and bereft of teeth. "You'll see, my friend," he said before taking his leave. "Before you know it, after finishing me off, the most cunning and malignant brute in the Party will envelop our hapless Führer like a thick, poisonous fog until *he's* running the Reich. But first, my friend, we must see to your house."

So tonight, after arranging to meet her, I wrung my brain, straining to devise a way to "resolve the Dvora matter." But Brückner's reference to Bormann had shaken me so that I spent the entire night in numb incapacity until I spoke to you. At least it wasn't panic.

WHEN I ARRIVED at the Führer's quarters, Morell greeted me with a surgical mask over his face. Though he said nothing, I knew it was the Führer's latest and most extravagant effluvium, and by the stricken look on what I could see of the doctor's face, and the fact that instead of ushering me in, he waved me away, this latest episode was different in kind as well as in degree. To a substantial extent, I attributed it to Morell's chaos of curatives. On several occasions, I'd been told by the Führer's other physicians that medicinally, a state of critical mass can occur when all the "nostrums" begin to act as correctives, each working to counteract the side effects of one regimen with another, and so on until the patient implodes. *Was the Führer now in such a perilous state?* Even the tiny crack in the door was no match for the toxic cloud of stench that oozed through it, and with thanks to a god in which I didn't believe, I gratefully followed Morell's advice and fled to the safety of the main hall.

I sought out Brückner and advised him to avoid visiting the Führer until the masked Morell had the opportunity to finish up and the contaminated quarters could be sufficiently aired out for human habitation.

"Since you mentioned that time was crucial, have you come up with anything?" I asked once we were out of eavesdropper range.

He didn't answer for a moment, clearly struggling with something, so I waited. Whatever it was—fear for his own position, fear of something he didn't understand—his good instincts won out and quickly.

"There appear to be only two possibilities, and both carry a high risk, if they can be done at all." He spoke slowly and without any real conviction.

"Yes?" I nudged gently.

"Well, the first is to try to locate any Jewish underground group trying to smuggle their kind out of Germany and establish contact with them." He shrugged.

"And the second?" I nudged further.

"The second would be to do the same thing, but this time with Aryan anti-Nazi organisations."

"Hmm." I waited for the point of his tone.

"But I ruled both out."

"Why?" I asked him. "Both are promising, are they not?"

Brückner took a deep, noisy breath. "Can *you* think of any obstacles?"

The last thing in the world I wanted was a fucking test! "I have no idea," I answered in all my clueless honesty. "I know little about any pro-Jewish or anti-Nazi organised movements in Germany, though to hear Himmler constantly regale the Führer with an endless parade of horribles, I assumed there has to be some resistance, and quite an active one at that."

"Despite Himmler's hysteria," Brückner said, "there are no movements here that measure up to anything. The SS, SA, and Gestapo have seen to that. If you need proof, just look at that hapless idiot Elser. And if that's the case with Aryans, imagine the existence, much less the strength, of any organised Jewish underground. Even if there were such a thing, ridiculous as it may seem, can you possibly think they would jeopardise themselves to aid a Catcher? Frankly, I'm stumped."

Listening to this flung me headlong into a whirlpool of silent despair, and Brückner must have seen it on my face.

"It's really very simple. Take an outrageous risk and lose, you're a fool. Take an outrageous risk and win, you're a genius. Well, my friend, I daresay we're neither fools nor geniuses, so we're stuck with discovering a middle course, but to be frank, I'm at a loss to know what that is since Germany has never been a nation of middle courses. So, what's the upshot? If you're unhappy now, this will make you miserable, but it's unmistakable and unavoidable—and you already know it."

I shook my head. "Unhappy was before this conversation. Now I'm miserable. So, you might as well tell me because, despite the flattery, I don't already know what's unmistakable and unavoidable."

Brückner pursed his lips. "Really? All right, Heinz, then I'll give it to you without frills: It's you or her."

12 *April 1940*

IT'S YOU OR her. It's you or her, it's you or her! Brückner's declaration kept hammering my mind's ear. As I considered what might lie ahead, all the fearfulness in me counselled procrastination, but his irrefutable bluntness drove whatever survival instinct I'd carried with me from the treacherous Berlin streets of my youth and pushed me to do something. I still didn't know what, though I well understood what my friend urged upon me.

Awakening a semiconscious and unsuspecting Dvora, I arranged for us to meet for dinner at the Kaiserhof, a hide-in-plain-sight, politically sound, copulation-free venue. All the clamorous restaurant jabber I could make out centred on the Netherlands campaign: the laughable "contribution" of the British, the glory of the Reich, and the Führer's next inevitably doomed prey.

As usual, I arrived early, so bereft of strategy, I had the misfortune of having to endure the oppressive apprehension about what I would say and how Dvora would respond. Anticipating this, I invoked the Führer's name and my position and was instantly seated at a discreet remove from the patriotic din. For a moment, I even considered standing her up and letting the chips fall where they may. *But to what end?* Probably mine, I concluded, so I stayed, hoping that somehow, magically, the two of us would conjure some ingenious plan of escape.

The Führer, hardly the most ardent feminist, once remarked to me, "Women are the undisputed masters of visual artifice," and I ceaselessly wondered if that gift shaped their thinking—or the other way round. In any event, I always marvelled at the way naturally elegant women were able to put themselves together without assistance on the shortest notice, and Dvora was no exception.

She arrived precisely on time, attired in a stunning lavender dress cut in the current form-fitted style. Her appearance seemed straight from the fashion magazines I'd seen scattered about those areas of the Chancellery most frequented by females (that is to say, the secretaries and clerks). Despite the apparent preoccupation of the revellers, eyes turned as Dvora entered. Even the most race-obsessed would have gasped in disbelief. But then, they saw Christiane, Goebbels's Aryan goddess, not Dvora, Streicher's Jewish rodent.

"Don't bother," she joked disarmingly once I pushed in her chair and returned to my own. "I daresay, the entire room is aware. The tragic story of my life, wouldn't you agree?" The lavender brought out the grey and tan shades in her irises. In her presence, I felt like a comic version of an SS recruiting poster.

"It's not easy to be furtive in public with you."

She pursed her lips. "I see no need to be furtive, Heinzl, do you?"

"I have some news."

"So have I."

She looked and sounded the same, but something in her expression perplexed me. *What had happened in three days?* I quickly glanced down at my menu to buy time, knowing that tonight, I needed to see beyond Dvora's stunning face.

"You're hungry?" she asked. "I'm far too excited to eat."

I glanced up. "Too excited? About what?"

"No," she said impishly, her palm raised in a halting gesture. "Your news first."

"All right, my news then. I'm afraid to say that Morell has worked a miracle," I joked uneasily.

"Yes?"

"I'm cured."

Her eyebrows arched into apostrophes.

"Cured?"

"I can't stall Morell any further."

She lifted her shoulders slightly. "My love, what on earth is worrying you? We're two Germans in our prime, enjoying each other's company," she ventured blithely while stroking my calf with her pump. "Now, what can possibly be wrong with that?"

I was getting hard. I shook my head in bewilderment. "Please be serious," I entreated. "We've spoken of this many times. Once your handlers know the success of 'Morell's wonder cure,' they'll expect results again. Also, a recent development will make escape far more difficult."

She stared at me with a furrowed brow of incredulity, as if I were speaking in tongues. "Handlers? Results? Escape? My Heinzl, have you been indulging yourself before I arrived?"

I didn't know what to make of her words. *Was she playing a belated April Fool's prank? Had* she *done the indulging?* Devoid of any rational explanation, I tried again. "How long do you really think my feigned impotence will keep those characters at the RSHA content, once they learn of Morell's brilliant success? And they will learn of it, you can be sure. What I'm trying to say is that it's no longer safe for you—or for me. So, for both our sakes, you have to leave—and we'll try to get your family out too." That last part was not a lie, strictly speaking, but I couldn't vouch for its chances.

Just then, the waiter arrived, but she waved him away, then called him back. "I'll have a glass of Spirytus."

I'd heard of the notorious Polish Vodka from Kempka, who'd related that only one glass had him driving without the assistance of the steering wheel for several blocks until he ran into a cluster of trash cans, where he remained for the rest of the night in a veritable coma.

The waiter looked at me, then back at her. "Are you sure?" he asked solicitously. "If so, might I suggest a mixed—"

"If I wanted it mixed, I would have asked for it mixed," she said testily.

"My apologies, Fräulein. And the colonel?" he asked, quickly turning to me.

"Riesling. Very dry." I could imagine the waiter thinking that my choice of a mild wine was a good one since I would need to carry the lady home.

"You do like to live dangerously," I told her once the waiter had left.

"The drink? Yes. Not before. But now, with the Polacks getting what's coming to them, I believe I've developed a taste for it."

What was she going on about? "All right," I told her, "if you want to drink an explosive, fine, a choice. But you must leave Germany now. That's no longer a choice."

The drinks arrived with a smile for me and a glance of concern for Dvora. "I'll bring your menus," he said and left.

She took a wincing sip and gazed at me with an expression of incredulity. "But why should I leave? This is my home, no less than it is yours. We're both in love and blessed with serving the man at the very centre of world history." She tossed back the rest of her drink, this time without wincing.

Somehow, I had to pierce the veil of her delusion. "For me,

Dvora, yes. But no longer for you. Can't you see that? You of all people should see that. For Jews, those days are long gone."

"Jews? For Jews, yes," she said, her voice rising. "As it should be. But ours are just beginning. New days for me and for Germany." She waved at the waiter and ordered another.

Alarms were going off in my brain. "And just who are you?"

She took a smaller swallow and stared at me as if I'd just thrown my wine at a group sitting at an adjoining table. "Heinzl, dear one, I'm Christiane. I think by now, you'd know my name."

"But your family, they—"

"My family?" she blurted, her voice elevated again. "My family claim to be Germans, which, of course, they are. And do please stop calling me Dvora. That fool actually claims to be a Jew, which, unfortunately, she is. Can it be that the principal valet to our Führer is one of those Jew-lovers?"

I began shaking inside and hoped it didn't show. "In this case, I imagine I am" was all I could say, but even then, I knew it was the wrong answer.

"Then, for the moment, at least," she said, "I can only pity you. You're as doomed as they are—perhaps even more so since you have an Aryan's expectations." She downed her drink in one long gulp, like a Russian soldier in a Tolstoy novel.

I had no desire for my wine and even less to be there, but I needed to see it through. "I think we should order some food." I lifted the menu, motioning for the waiter.

"I'm too excited to eat," she said. "Have some Spirytus. It'll fix you right up."

"I don't need fixing," I told her. "Please hear me out. It's been made plain to me that I can no longer risk seeing you, and you can no longer risk not seeing me. There's the dilemma. It must be resolved, for both our sakes."

"I want another drink," she snarled petulantly, raising her arm.

"*No!*" I replied, far louder than I'd intended, causing a few preoccupied heads to swivel our way. I quickly lowered my voice and leaned forward. "Put your arm down. I don't want you to do any more of that, you understand me?"

She stared at me vacantly for a moment, then shifted into resentment. "Javohl… Herr… Obersturmbannführer!" she conceded, her hand forming a mock salute as it descended to the table with a thud.

Now it was my turn to signal the waiter, which I did, and ordered two cups of the strongest coffee they had. Neither of us said a word until the coffee arrived. I dropped a small ice cube into the first cup and ordered her to gulp it down, which she did, reluctantly, almost vomiting it up in the process. After the second, she seemed to have become a reasonable facsimile of how she'd been on arrival, but her sharp, resentful gaze had been replaced by a flat sullenness.

"Do you recall what we were talking about before the drink business?" I asked.

"Naturally. That's what 'the drink business' was all about," she declared snidely. "You were telling Christiane to forsake the Fatherland, yes?"

I noted that she'd shifted to the third person, and the wrong third person at that. It was not a good sign.

"It's not your home anymore," I said. "That's what I was telling you."

Her voice turned to dry ice. "Heinz, dearest," she said with no feeling, "I know her deluded lover thinks he's doing what's best for this Jewess, despite the vile illegality of it, when clearly what she needs is to be sent straightaway to a KZ where she and all her kind belong."

I desperately wanted to run out of there, but she reached over and grasped my arm and held it fast. "All right, I heard *your* news. Now, don't you want to hear *my news?*"

The waiter came by again, and I dismissed him before she could order another Spirytus.

"Your news?" I asked despondently. "Yes, of course. What is it?"

A broad smile formed on her lips, and she edged her shoulders forward and whispered, "The Führer has declared in no uncertain terms that the Jewish pestilence must be totally eradicated. You serve the Führer in your way, the best way you can, this I know. I serve the Führer my way, the best way *I* can. Tomorrow, dearest, I will accomplish my greatest achievement for him by delivering this… Dvora to my superiors, where she'll be properly dealt with, once and for all."

I had no words. She'd gone mad, and I could say nothing.

She removed her hand but not before bestowing a lover's pat. "See, *meine liebchen?* Even that vile Jewess knew you'd understand once I'd explained it properly. So now, let us celebrate the Führer's latest triumph."

I didn't think she meant herself, but I couldn't avoid the black humour of the calamity. *Where did that leave me?*

"But—" I started to say.

She cut me off with the answer. "And as for her traitorous lover," she said with hooded eyes and a malevolent sneer, "he'll join her."

❧

Terrified by what I'd heard, I had the unmistakable belief that there was no time to lose, so my first stop before retiring had to be Brückner, to whom I related the entire exchange.

"It's bad, isn't it?" I asked him rhetorically.

Instead of answering right away, he performed a slow, almost Asiatic, cigarette-lighting ritual. "Yes and no," he said, to my consternation.

"Wilhelm."

"I mean it," he said. "It could be bad, but to be frank, it changes nothing except our timetable and—"

"But she's insane, dangerously insane," I declared.

He took another red-glowing drag and nodded. "Yes, from your story, clearly she's dangerously unbalanced. But…"

"But what?" I insisted.

"Look, Heinz, I know you developed strong feelings for this woman, so it's not easy."

"After our meeting, I'm considerably less ardent, so I can take anything you have to say." This wasn't entirely true, but I needed to dig a gentle spur into Brückner.

"All right, Heinz. As before, this… schizophrenic must be taken to a place of safety—but now it's *your* safety, not hers. I'll be blunt. Your feigned impotence days are over, and you're dealing with an unstable, self-made Gentile Jewish zealot who now worships the Führer and probably considers herself more of a Nazi than Himmler. So, my friend, she must still vanish, but now and forever."

I knew what he meant, and I recoiled at the thought, despite her outrageous utterances. "But she might revert back to Dvora, and—" I heard the absurdity of my words and stopped myself.

Brückner removed the stub of his cigarette from its holder and ground it with his boot heel. "By her own words, time is not on our side. Her identities may be playing tennis with each other, but regardless of who wins, saving her is not even a dangerous luxury anymore; it's a suicide mission. In a sense, she—wittingly or not—gave you a few hours reprieve before betrayal."

"Then what?" I asked needlessly.

"She disappears completely. Tonight," he said simply, turned, and walked away, leaving me both relieved—and unclean.

13 *April 1940*

First Adelsheimer and now Dvora, I thought as I headed for the Führer's quarters: my small contribution to National Socialism—and a joyless jest.

The Führer's volcanic bowel movements had never caused me to feel gratitude until today, when supervising a housekeeping crew faced with the unspeakable aftermath allowed me to push aside all thoughts of Dvora and her fate.

[The rest of the entry was corrupted.]

IT'S THE FÜHRER'S fifty-first birthday, and as custom dictated, Goebbels delivered a birthday speech. All of Germany, including those of us at the Chancellery who'd heard it recited to the Führer earlier, were obliged to hear it. Standing at ease in the Führer's study, I pretended to listen with entranced attention, as were all those around me, save the Führer, who appeared preoccupied at his desk with something. I knew not what. Goebbels, of course, was the only absentee, since it was he orating to the nation (and the world, come to that) from his radio station.

I must confess that while I may have appeared rapt by Goebbels's eloquence, I was concentrated totally on Dvora—and my abject cowardice. I'd read that "flagellation," the beating or whipping of the skin by oneself, most often on the back and often drawing blood, as a bodily penance to show remorse for sin, was a widespread practice among some Catholics. Having no religion myself, I always considered such masochistic zealots to be completely insane. However, since my conversation with Brückner, I'd been doing just that: my brain whipping me bloody for not at least requesting details of her disappearance.

Knowing Brückner, I was certain he would do what had to be done about her, for he'd told me on many occasions that if anything "indecorous" needed to be done, it needed to be done by the only trustworthy party—oneself—or not at all. Partners, assistants, family, associates, hirelings? *Never!*

Did I still care for Dvora? I asked myself, probably as a form of penance I didn't even believe in, but she herself provided the answer: Dvora no longer existed—before, in her mind and, now, physically. But with all this mystery, intrigue, madness, and conspiracy surrounding the pitiful creature, two questions remained: *Why was someone so set on removing me from the Führer's service? And who was that someone?*

Thwarted in my rumination, I strived to concentrate on the oratory emanating from the massive radio receiver, but in my brain and against my will, the profound dissonance between the voice and the physical attributes stymied my attention. Appearance aside (an emaciated dwarf with pomaded hair that virtually glowed, a club foot, sunken, pockmarked cheeks, and a preference for body-encasing, double-breasted, shit-brown suits), Goebbels was truly a superb rhetorician. The Führer always acknowledged the value of Goebbels as a propagandist to his closest circle, where he often would not spare the blushes in being blunt.

The first part of Goebbels's speech was the usual rhapsodic slobbering over Germany's "battle for existence," the Führer's "godlike qualities," and his "historic role." On and on and on it went. All to be expected, of course, especially at the start of a war. The only purpose for me of these overripe and well-worn patriotic flourishes was a consideration of which high-flown phrases I would be forced to recount later to those Chancellery personnel who, for some reason beyond my understanding, ached to obtain my impression of the speech.

As I half listened, only one thing in his speech stood out as starkly as the sun suddenly appearing at night: certainly not the elaborate excoriation of the British—no surprise there—but the complete absence of any mention of France. *What could this obvious omission signify or portend?* That aside, I ached to ask Brückner details of Dvora's disappearance, though I already knew all I should need to know. *More flagellation!*

AT DINNER, HIMMLER, Goebbels, Göring, Speer, and [Martin] Bormann were the Führer's guests. Brückner and I were also present, but we both were fully aware that Brückner was standing sentinel while Bormann was a seated guest. Bormann was quickly gaining influence with the Führer, so it was clear that time was running out, and the imminent loss of my true friend and mentor depressed, saddened, and terrified me. Now, as I regarded him at the periphery of my vision, I wished he could have been my complete confidant as well, but the exigencies of my persona wouldn't permit such potentially treacherous transparency.

"My Führer," Himmler said with his usual non-blinking expressionlessness, his tiny moustache inert, "is it not a suitable time for you to provide some guidance on how we are to deal with even the slightest infractions of the populace we now rule, especially in Czechoslovakia, Poland, and those parts of the East not occupied by the Soviets?"

From the beginning, it was clear, even to me, that the East would be treated differently from the West, the former being not only occupied but also subject to the most exacting regulations and the most severe punishments for disobedience. Knowing Himmler as I did, I was certain that he had it spelled out in numbingly horrific particulars, but knowing the Führer as *he did*, needed it sanctioned in general, details be damned.

"Agreed, Heinrich," the Führer said, hands folded in front of him.

Himmler reached into his omnipresent attaché case, extracted a sizeable sheaf of typed papers, and placed them on his lap. "I have made meticulously precise notes covering each nation we subsume, and—"

"Subsume?" The Führer suddenly turned to me. "You know what subsume means, Linge?"

Once the shock of his unexpected attention wore off, I stammered, "N-No… my Führer, I have no idea."

"And I wouldn't have expected it." The Führer turned back to Himmler, who hadn't glanced at me once. "Now, if you would kindly indulge this poor semiliterate. I refer, of course, to myself."

Naturally, all laughed but Himmler. "My Führer, subsume means to entirely absorb," he replied slowly, as if he were addressing a kindergarten class of backward children, "and also those territories where we deem it safe enough to permit some small measure of home rule."

"You have my gratitude," the Führer said with no small touch of sarcasm. "Proceed." Then he rose, said good night to all, bade me stay, and withdrew, leaving some of us staring blankly at each other for a moment. But not all.

"As you know, gentlemen," Himmler continued as if the Führer had remained, "the most effective political weapon is terror. Cruelty commands respect. Men may hate us, but we don't ask for their love, only for their fear."

"Yes?" Goebbels, the man of words, asked while Göring yawned conspicuously, to Himmler's equally conspicuous disregard.

For my part, I wondered where the hatred or panic of the vanquished fit into Himmler's simple equation.

"Yes, Joseph," Himmler confirmed. "In addition, concerning the treatment of peoples of alien races in the East, we must acknowledge and cultivate as many individual ethnic groups as possible—that is, excepting the Poles and the Jews—also the Ukrainians, the white Russians, the Gorals, the Lemcos, and the Cashubos."

Who the hell were the Gorals, Lemcos, and Cashubos? I believed that only Himmler knew—and appeared to care. Brückner and I exchanged glances to signal that we knew Himmler, having received the Führer's tacit blessing, wasn't even close to finished—that he had a master plan ready for implementation, and that it didn't concern the Gorals, the Lemcos, or the Cashubos.

"This is all quite fascinating, Heinrich," Göring said blandly. "We're aware of your tireless efforts towards purity and order, and we, like the Führer, are most assured."

"Yes," Goebbels concurred, but with a caveat. "We can all agree that there's no questioning the value of fear in achieving order, but terror is quite another matter. We must be careful not to oversimplify and reduce all to one category. It seems to me that there are three kinds of people in areas we occupy: the willing collaborators who hope to profit by the occupation, the angry resisters who will make every effort to sabotage and undermine us, and finally, the waverers, who are uncertain whether they hope or hate, or perhaps harbour both sentiments. It seems to me that for the first, nothing need be done save to dole out just enough rewards to keep them hungry for more. The second— and even here, the matter is not so clear-cut—I agree that the leaders must be eradicated. I'd go that far, but the followers need not be, provided they're kept separate and confused. As for the third, one should never forget that maintaining order with the ambivalent is best done by manipulation, especially when those being manipulated are confident they are acting of their own free will. I ask you, Heinrich, is this not the most effective way to proceed?"

Again, Brückner and I swivelled our eyes towards each other, recognising Himmler's true purpose for all this detail, wherein the Devil usually resides. However, we also recognised that with a creature like Himmler, sometimes the Devil *is* the detail.

All the while Goebbels was lecturing, Himmler scratched out something in his little notebook. At the close, he shut it and slowly lifted his head to gaze up at Goebbels, then nodded a mild assent that I knew he didn't mean for one moment. I could sense the mockery behind the blank sterility of his rimless glasses. For such a creature, free will was no more than a pre-dawn roundup, some "cellar dentistry," a blood-drenched confession, and summary piano-wire execution. Dvora was a mere pathetic grain of sand in Himmler's malignant desert.

"A pity the Führer had to leave," Speer said to Himmler. "I'm certain that he would wish to know more about—"

Himmler cut him off. "Not so, Speer. As one who has known the Führer for seventeen years—and Hermann and Joseph can attest to this—I tell you that he is not a man of details. He's a man of vision, not specifics, a man of strategy, not tactics."

Vigorous nods of agreement by Göring and Goebbels followed.

"For example, I hadn't even begun to touch upon the critical Jewish Question, but the Führer would have no patience for such prosaic matters, content that in my hands, the Jews shall be dealt with in full accordance with his wishes." He began putting his papers back into his briefcase.

With that, the others rose and filed out, but not before Göring moved to where Himmler stood and patted him on the shoulder. "It's comforting to know that the security of the Reich is in such earnest and capable hands," he said with a slight upturn of his bladder lips.

THIS MORNING, I hastily summoned Morell once again to soothe the Führer's excruciatingly distressed bowels.

As Morell ministered, the Führer kept screaming, "It mustn't happen this way! The victory of the superior herd and blind luck! Nothing more proven, nothing transformed!"

All the while, Morell said nothing, merely injecting and massaging, treating his patient as one undergoing delirium. Of course, all political and military activity was suspended until the Führer was back to what passed for normality. Happily, I stood well outside, breathing from my mouth, tidally and infrequently, for the horrendous odours wafting from the commode were truly monstrous. That Morell must have been blessed with a prosthetic nose.

"Do not disturb him for any reason," Morell cautioned me with a head nurse's old-biddy severity. "He's… napping, and we don't wish to startle him. Just be there in case he topples to the floor." Then he snatched his jacket from my hands and left.

I went into the commode to discover the Führer of the Reich stark naked and asleep on the toilet, his chin nestled on his chest, breathing ponderously. When I moved closer, I could see his eyes fidgeting behind his lids like restless feet under a thin blanket. Then the Führer lifted his head and told me ever so nonchalantly to prepare for travel this very evening but, before that, to summon his top military, diplomatic, industrial, and political leaders and their most trusted adjutants for all-day conferences to, as he put it, "prepare them for the next step on the well-worn road on which nothing revolutionary will ever appear."

I had them summoned but left out the topic.

10 May 1940

THE ENTIRE MORNING was devoted to preparing for our departure. Up to now, Brückner had volunteered no information about Dvora, so I assumed that the bizarre and dangerous sentence had been provided its inevitable period. Being once burnt, I was also twice shy, so I determined to (temporarily, at least) abstain from any carnal contact. However, I must have appeared libidinously frantic, for even that shrew Schroeder told me of a girl, her niece, in fact, who, in her elegant phrasing, "might be able to ignore your infernal ignorance, menial position, and thinning thatch." Given those attributes, I found it difficult to imagine anyone, man or beast, could find me even remotely appealing. But be that as it may, since she wouldn't take even a maybe for an answer, I thanked her profusely, and she gave me her telephone number with extravagant reluctance. I had no intention of acting on it.

Travel preparations completed, I was squeezed into a saloon with Junge, Baur, a self-satisfied Schroeder, Dara, and Otto Dietrich, the Reich press chief, while Kempka drove the Führer, Brückner, and the latter's nemesis, Bormann. We were driven out of Berlin towards Staaken, leading us to assume that we would fly from the airport. That was not the case, for the car drove on past Staaken and eventually pulled into the forecourt of a small railway station, where the Führer's special train, the Führersonderzug Amerika, stood waiting. Apart from the Führer and his top brass, nobody below seemed to have a clue where we were supposed to be going. It was all quite mysterious.

❧

The mystery was solved when we arrived at Felsennest. Though built into a hill, the Führer's bunker is completely underground, so no trace of it can be seen from the surface, and a screen is set up to disguise the entrance. The Führer's rooms—bed and study—are furnished in campaign order. The bunker also serves as a home for Keitel and the adjutants Brückner, Schmundt, and Schaub as well as for me. Thirty or forty metres away is the mess with concrete walls, and two hundred metres further on, behind a copse, is a wooden meeting room, also disguised behind netting. Jodl lodges there. The area on the hill containing the three buildings is encircled with barbed wire and called Restricted Area I. The rest of the Führer's HQ is in the village at the bottom of the hill.

During lunch, all waxed jubilant over the phenomenal rapidity and efficiency of our forces as they cut through the Low Countries like a "sharp knife through soft butter," as General Field Marshal Keitel put it. Goebbels was somewhat more subdued since the "limp noodle" Chamberlain had been replaced by the "stammering old lion" Churchill. Lacking his usual conviction, the Reichsminister assured the Führer that it proved beyond doubt Britain's unreadiness to face a rearmed Germany. Vociferous agreements and congratulatory toasts occurred round the table, as if the well-informed guests hadn't been aware of the new prime minister's strident antipathy towards the Third Reich—and his resolve.

The Führer, visibly subdued, merely nodded occasionally

—and ambiguously—as he toyed listlessly with his unsightly vegetable concoction. When all the revellers had left and I was readying him for bed, he looked up at me.

"Are you aware, Linge," he remarked, "that Churchill had a near-death accident in 1931, when he was hit by an automobile in New York City? And are you also aware that I, too, was nearly killed by one the very same year?"

"I had no idea, my Führer," I said in real amazement. "The Reich is enormously fortunate."

The Führer's lips then assumed what I considered at the time to be a rueful smile. "Interesting how fragile is the fate of nations."

"I never thought of it like that before, my Führer."

"Well, perhaps you should," he said. "Clearly, my closest advisers don't think of it, at least in my presence. The what-ifs of history are both fascinating—and frustrating—but quite educational for all that. Had Churchill been killed, rather than seriously injured, Britain's most likely prime minister in June 1940, Lord Halifax, would most surely have ended the war once we conquered France, and we could then concentrate on the East." He puffed some air from his nostrils. "And had I succumbed to my own accident… well, what can I say?"

These what-ifs were too much for my underdeveloped analytical sense to ponder, and even if I possessed the competence, the implications were far too numerous and perplexing to pursue. *What if? What if Adolf Hitler the aspiring painter had achieved artistic prominence? What if the aspiring politician had been killed in the Munich beer hall or in prison? The contingencies could go on forever, and what would they matter?* "I'm certain," I finally replied, "that the Reich would declare a holiday to celebrate your victory over the automobile if it were well-known."

The Führer laughed heartily and farted mightily. "Never lose that sense of humour, Linge. I must remember to tell that to Kempka. He'll get a kick out of it."

⤐

At dinner, Kempka joked with his usual boorish abandon, "I'm allergic to vomit, so I hope you all brought your seasick pills."

Was he hinting that we were going to Norway, since the train was steaming north?

Oddly, instead of rebuking Kempka for his vulgarity at the table, the Führer added, addressing his comments to the ladies, "And if you're good, you might be able to bring home a sealskin as a trophy."

After much experience with the Führer, I didn't accept their unsuitable jests as a sign of anything, and I was proven right. After midnight—past Hanover—the train was suddenly switched to the westbound tracks, though this was only noticed by a few, like Brückner and me.

I WAS UP before dawn, reacting to a familiar catlike scratching at my compartment door, followed by an envelope sliding underneath—what I've come to call my "unofficial mail slot." The note inside read:

> *My Dearest Heinz, despite a deep concern that I might be both precipitate and impertinent, what your friend Brückner had to do to save you—and, in the saving, protect the Führer's master design—will secure unimaginable returns to us all. I say this: Regret is a powerfully destructive emotion, so I urge you to take all the time necessary to heal. With my affectionate regard, K.*

She wasn't on the train, so after reading, I sat on my cot for a while, shaking my head over the communications network at play around me and to what extent there was truly any privacy once something escaped from one's brain into the open air. I decided to ask Brückner about Dvora, despite his complete silence about her since the day he said that she would "disappear completely."

❧

Outside the Führer's quarters, the Chancellery was veritably exploding with excitement over the Panzer Corps XV and XIX breaking through the French forces at Sedan, thus allowing our military to completely bypass the formidable defences at the Maginot Line. Inside, however, all day, the Führer sat poker-faced, waiting for the latest reports. I could sense that his generals sitting round the conference table were considerably more rapt, but as usual with them, discipline trumped passion.

When the news of the breakthrough came via Brückner, the normally taciturn military commanders jumped to their feet, saluted the Führer, and applauded.

The Führer, still seated at his desk, gazed up at them with studied languidness and said in his snidest tone, "This surprises you, gentlemen? Your faith in me is truly overwhelming. It appears that Spain taught you nothing about trivial training exercises."

NEWS THAT OUR panzer corps crossed into Northern France just arrived. Naturally, there was jubilation in the Chancellery, but I couldn't help noticing that it was slightly subdued. I assumed it was because, after yesterday, the die had been cast and with such success that the spice of surprise had been diluted by ready expectation. The generals also remained low-key, but in their case, fretting that such effortless accomplishment was temporary at best and illusory at worst because the British—and even the Americans—might tip the balance the other way. This, of course, ensured the Führer's hysterical wrath.

"Are you, gentlemen," he screamed, "with over three hundred years of combined military experience, utterly incapable of accepting the fruits of brilliant planning and first-rate execution? You all remind me of the suitor who adroitly courts the woman of his dreams, proposes, then refuses to accept her 'yes' as an answer. She must be wrong, he says to himself, or crazy, or he accepts that she says 'yes' now but will bow out at the last moment. Outrageous! You have personally witnessed years of planning, analysis, hard work, and luck. In this poor, ignorant ex-corporal's opinion, these factors are what victories are made of. Too easy, you say? You think that more German casualties would suit you better? That perhaps endless, miserable, disastrous trench warfare would suit you better? No, gentlemen, I regret to say that you don't have three hundred years of experience. You have one year repeated three hundred times."

As always, after one of the Führer's purple-faced tirades, the traditionally stolid military brass were rendered even more stoic, not entirely unwise in the face of the Führer's implacable—and justifiable—egotism. Once his fury had subsided, the Führer blew air heavily from his nostrils and sank back into his austere war commander's "campaign chair," which he had me procure to replace his opulently plush executive "throne."

"Mark my words, gentlemen," he said, now icily calm, "there will be one unobstructed retreat after another by the half-hearted French and the astonished British until I own the damn place. And this, my friends, despite all your retrogressive pooh-poohing, timid nay-saying, and misguided predictions."

Once they'd gone after being properly rebuked, the Führer, still sitting, sighed. "Linge, what a sorry spectacle. But I tell you this: Even with only one top in my possession and the lily-livered whimpering of my military commanders, I shall prevail."

"Of that I have no doubts, my Führer." I had no reason to speak otherwise.

"But once I obtain both," he added, "I'll no longer need any of them." Then he crumpled up some dispatches, tossed them at his wastepaper basket—missing it, as usual—and waited until I successfully completed the deed.

GIVEN THE NEWS that the French and British forces were in full retreat, the Chancellery personnel, only a few days ago hysterical with exultation, appeared to settle into a confident nonchalance about our astonishing progress. This morning, the Führer informed his military leaders (now noticeably more sanguine) that "in the blink of an eye, France will surrender," and "that corpulent windbag Churchill had better remove his few demoralised troops out of the path of total annihilation without delay." I could tell from their faces that they wondered why he should wait for that. Even I wondered, until it occurred to me that the Führer had told me many times that he wished to keep Aryan England nonbelligerent if possible. Did that not occur to his generals?

To be frank, I never understood the Nazi mania for racial purity, considering that, based on my reading, ethnicity appeared to be far more important in the history of the world than race. Granted, Negroes had achieved little, but Asiatics had advanced civilisations while Caucasians were still wearing animal skins and fighting with clubs. And once ethnicity entered the picture, the disparities were even more striking. Any way one looked at it, Germans had always been prehistoric in the face of Greek, Indian, Arab, and Italian achievements. Not something I would tell Himmler, of course.

This evening, Goebbels, his wife, Magda, and Speer, accompanied by his latest conquest, the noted actress Kristina Söderbaum,[27] dropped by to watch *Abe Lincoln in Illinois*, another new American film. As with most, Goebbels had been able to obtain it from a thoroughly Jewish industry that wished to mollify the Führer and the Party, ostensibly to prevent further "unpleasantness" from their German brethren. As the Führer's projectionist by default, I was again given the honour.

Years before, I'd read a ponderously soporific biography about America's sixteenth president, but as I discovered, this movie covered only the prairie years when he was a shopkeeper and postmaster, a diffident candidate for the Illinois legislature, a sly but uninspired lawyer, a tragic lover who stood over his true sweetheart's grave, a failure who fled to the wilderness to search his soul, a man who then put his soul aside to marry a fanatically ambitious harridan, and with her incessant poking and prodding, accepted public life as a martyr to his beliefs. These were the years of doubt and denial, of relentless self-criticism, of a fiercely antagonistic marital relationship, of the empty triumph of winning an office he did not want, and that held no illusions for him. Short of not being an aristocrat, a man more dissimilar from the Führer could not, in my estimation, be imagined. But perhaps I hadn't the wits to see what a trained scholar like Goebbels and a pedant like Himmler would take for granted.

Once it was over, most sat round and discussed the film. I

---

[27] Söderbaum is frequently identified as the "most singularly representative of the Nazi ideal, as the quintessential Nazi star." As a beautiful Swedish blonde, Söderbaum had the baby-doll looks that epitomized the model Aryan woman. In fact, she had already played the role of the innocent Aryan in several feature films and was well-known to German audiences. Her youth and beauty made her a symbol of health and purity and thus an exemplary specimen of the Nazi ideal of womanhood. In several of her films, she had been imperilled by the threat of "*rassenschande*" (racial pollution).

noticed that every time Mrs. Lincoln was mentioned, eyes subtly swivelled to Magda, who stared blankly ahead as if she had no clue about the connexions being made. Goebbels declared that America was hardly unique, for "even in Germany, a man can rise from nothing to lead his country to victory in times of greatest peril." While saying this, he gazed steadily at the Führer with awe and pride, as did Magda, only far more so, to the point where Himmler and Speer were obliged to look discreetly elsewhere.

The Führer asked Söderbaum what she thought of the film, and she said that it was all right as far as it went, but that the Germans could have done a better job, and Leni Riefenstahl was the one to do it, with Söderbaum, of course, as the doomed first love—"with augmented screen time," she added coyly.

"But who, then, would play the shrewish wife?" Speer asked her, his tongue almost pushing through his cheek.

Without even a glance at Magda, she merely sat silently and let the implications speak for her.

Himmler, when pressed, remarked with bureaucratic blandness that the film had no meaning for him, that Lincoln's life up to his election was hardly as important—or as telling—as his time as a war president who declared martial law, had people arrested without trial, suspended the writ of habeas corpus (I vowed to discern the term's meaning), and initiated forced conscription. "When the time came, not unlike the Führer, this Lincoln did what needed to be done to preserve his country from disloyal radical elements that would have torn it asunder," he said with his usual lack of expression, but I was reasonably certain that no one doubted what he really meant. I also noted that the Reichsführer-SS, intent on a favourable comparison of America's sixteenth president to the Führer, made no mention of Lincoln's attitude towards Negroes.

However, not to be overshadowed, and despite the fact that

it was, like Himmler's observation, never mentioned in the film, Speer told Himmler that, though reasonably accurate, Lincoln also got the Emancipation Proclamation passed by a severely divided Congress, and that led to the freeing of all the Negro slaves in the reconstituted United States. Himmler merely lowered and raised his eyelids slowly while Goebbels pointed out that emancipation merely illustrated the weakness of both Lincoln and the American system of government. He explained that inferior races were born to their subservient roles, and that the Slavs and others like them would fulfil their destinies, as did the Negro under the rule of "Jim Crow" and the Ku Klux Klan, who understood the catastrophic dangers posed by the Black race and knew how to deal with them. I'd read about the Klan, but who was this "Crow," I wondered.

Heads bobbed assent all round, then looked to the Führer, who pursed his lips, nodded, glanced round the room, and said, "Remarkable likeness. I've actually seen photographs. If Lincoln had this Massey fellow as his body double, the incident at the theatre would have been labelled merely another failed attempt. My poor Weler's[28] no competition for him." He then rose and bade me follow him to his quarters, leaving the rest to their devices.

✍

As I was readying the Führer for bed, he asked me, "Linge, do you know where Madagascar is?"

I'd read of the place before, in my meaninglessly alphabetical expedition through the "M" volume of the encyclopaedia. It described Madagascar as an island in the Indian Ocean off the coast of Southeast Africa, comprising the main island of

---

[28] Gustav Weler was a doppelgänger of Adolf Hitler. He occasionally stood in for Hitler and was used as a political decoy for security reasons.

Madagascar, the fourth-largest island in the world, as well as numerous smaller peripheral islands. Over ninety percent of its wildlife is found nowhere else on Earth. Later, I occasionally heard the name mentioned, but usually in a bad joke about some godforsaken nowhere.

"No, my Führer," I told him.

The Führer clapped his hands and laughed, his tiny moustache bobbing up and down, all signs of his earlier weariness (which Brückner called "Himmler fatigue") apparently vanished. "Linge, Linge," he jested, "you must pursue your studies. Spend less time dusting my books and more time reading them. Madagascar is an island country in the Indian Ocean, off the coast of Southeast Africa, currently in French hands, but you know how that goes.

"At any rate, you cannot be unaware that from my first inept political rant to my prison-penned *Mein Kampf,* and all through the period of struggle to this very moment—and with no small amount of irony—the Jews have played a monumental role in elevating me to Führer and, with the assistance of the Party's relentlessly administered programme, keeping me here. Now, it's my wish to—how shall I say…?—repay the Jews, of course, without ruffling the feathers of my supporters, both high and low."

I was sure that Brückner the wit would have added that it was quite magnanimous of the Jews to render such valuable assistance—and without even being asked.

"The others know nothing of what I intend," the Führer said, "because I wish to gain your unlettered and unbiased reaction first."

This was hardly the first time the Führer had solicited my meagre opinion on things, both trivial and momentous. But even I knew that it was merely an autocrat's idiosyncrasy—that he actually wanted *his* opinion and for me merely to bear witness to his genius, as if he were alone, muttering his achievements to a piece of furniture. Why such a manifestly superior human being as the Führer required such a relationship consistently flummoxed me. But be that as it may, this role was a bountiful blessing. As I've said many a time to you, having the reputation of an ignorant object is an advantage, for then I'm not perceived as a threat to anyone. I always feel a deep shudder in my bowels at the thought of ever losing that persona.

"I'm honoured, my Führer," I said. "I'll do my—"

"It's nothing, Linge," he interrupted, and I felt the soothing warmth of custom wash over me. "You know how much I value your opinion." He propped himself up for me to arrange his pillows as a backrest and, as he resettled, let loose a blast of all-consuming foulness that almost singed my skin.

"Now, my friend, prepare yourself for a truly inspired and remarkable notion: namely, the immediate deportation of all the Jews of Europe to Madagascar, and before long, the rest of them, once our might and influence invariably and inevitably extend us well beyond Europe's borders. Mass deportation is hardly a new notion to me, for I've been considering the matter for some time. However, due to Himmler's incessant lobbying, I'd confined my thinking to the forbidding and barren wastelands in Eastern Europe and the like. However, just yesterday, as I was browsing through some random selections in my encyclopaedia, the entire course of my thinking altered absolutely to embrace something far more worthy of a leader with unlimited and uncommon vision."

The sheer nature and scope of the Führer's notion truly startled me. *All the Jews of Europe? When and how would he get access to them? And the rest?* There were millions upon millions. *How would he transport them there?*

"Now such a solution to the Jewish Question," he continued

with slightly less animation, "should be made one of the terms in the imminent surrender of France—of which there can be no doubt whatsoever. The resettled Jews, as a bonus for us, would be employed as hostages to ensure the future good behaviour of their racial comrades in America since Henry Ford, avid enthusiast and admirer though he may be, has little influence in racial matters, I'm afraid. Don't you agree?"

"I—"

"And an additional dividend," he interrupted as I'd expected, "would be the opportunity afforded Goebbels, Streicher, and the Party to trumpet the fact that such an… expatriation to a relative paradise like Madagascar would be of actual benefit to the Jews—unlike a Himmler-style deportation to some frozen wasteland or outright eradication—thus eliminating any possible adverse world criticism." He shrugged. "Not a Zionist's wet dream, perhaps, but infinitely more satisfactory than a KZ or Siberia." He chuckled roundly at his witticism, and another canon shot of flatulence filled the room.

Most certainly, this Madagascar the Führer described was a paradise compared to Siberia—actually, from what memoranda I'd come across and top Party officials I'd overheard, anything was. Despite tradition and position, I still sweated over the possibility that this time, the Führer might now truly wish an opinion from the likes of me on such a radical and prodigious undertaking. I needed time to think, and more importantly, to discuss the matter with Brückner. Unfortunately, I was bereft of such luxuries, so the only avenues open that might not generate rage or suspicion were a plausible postponement or an inane reply. "Yes, my Führer?" was as inane a postponement as I could summon up.

"I know what you're thinking," the Führer continued after a perfunctory nod. "You believe that I shouldn't thwart Himmler's mania to eliminate all Jews and their repugnant religion from the face of the Earth. While I have no such aspiration, to assuage him, I'll probably have to grant him and his 'Wolfhound' full security jurisdiction over the place, and soon, I'm afraid, the Jews may wish for Siberia. Such is the price of beneficence, eh, Linge?"

I moaned silently. I could have told him that his plan was genetically, if not logistically and economically, quite impossible. Miscegenation over the centuries alone would utterly defeat any such venture. That much insight I could claim but wouldn't. Instead, I was about to tell him that I knew nothing of such weighty and complex matters, but the Führer pre-empted me again.

"I sense your restraint, Linge," he said with breathtaking but understated accuracy. "But of course, your unwavering humility and natural discretion prevent you from raising the formidable issue of logistics." The Führer's narrow smile—almost a pucker— stung, as if he'd caught me in a blatant lie or cowardly omission.

"I will spare you from violating your modesty. As Göring has said many times, after all the years of intermarriage and crossbreeding, who is a Jew anymore? And even if we possessed a magical formula to determine such a thing, would we have the means to deal with such staggering numbers in a systematic and thorough way? The problem would exist, even with Siberia or anyplace else, for that matter. This, our friend Himmler, his cunning and relentless Heydrich, as well as all the resources of the entire Reich Security Services refuse to acknowledge. So, as always, it's left to me. I discussed the subject in the most general and hypothetical terms with Speer, and he assured me that if at least the obvious ones could be singled out, I could transport at least a million Jews per year. Of course, we would require the assistance of the British fleet, and these Jews would have to leave all valuables behind—if only to satisfy Göring and the rest of the looters. Some water, eh, Linge?"

I raced into his study and brought back a pitcher of water and a glass, poured the one into the other, and the Führer gulped it down with desert-parched vigour, then discharged an explosive belch.

"However," he continued with a sudden intensity in volume and feeling, "all this will soon be academic. When I secure the second item and you fulfil your role as medium, I'll be beyond everyone's reach, not just the Jews, Communists, British, Americans, and all my other enemies, but even my most ferociously adoring acolytes. Beyond all of them!" he shouted. "Beyond mortality! Beyond time itself!" His face had turned brilliant red, as if the hue had been waiting impatiently beneath his skin for just this opportunity to emerge. His eyes bulged from their sockets like a frog's. His fists pounded silently on the thick bedding beside him.

For me, this time, there were no dimmed lights, no feelings of disembodiment, no migraine, no one else in the room. But as had occurred many times before, these words were far too cryptic for me to attempt understanding, much less to venture a sensible response. Still, it did, for some reason—or even for some purpose—conjure up my pro forma interview with the Führer five years before, as well as my later hallucinations, visions, and blackouts, and finally, the crumpled telegram from Weisthor.

Too ignorant at the time, and not much more enlightened now, I asked myself once again: *What the hell was I involved in? And a no-less-important question: Why?*

As the Führer predicted, the "corpulent windbag," sensing a catastrophe in the making, ordered the preparation of vessels to evacuate the laughable "British Expeditionary Force" from Northern France, while Luftwaffe bombers hammer Allied defensive positions in and around the French port of Dunkirk.

⁓

"Now, how did I know I'd find you both here?" asked a familiar voice of menacing sleekness behind Brückner and me as we strolled in the Chancellery gardens. We stopped and turned to see General Heydrich smiling so broadly that his bright duelling scar widened into an elongated furrow. "I said to myself, 'Save for the Berghof, where else can two busy defenders of the Reich seek the bucolic?' And here you are."

He conveniently omitted Berlin's several parks, but of course, that was entirely beside his point.

"Yes, defending the Reich, as you well said, Reinhard," Brückner said for me. "Mustn't be too distant from the action, don't you agree?"

"I've just been with our glorious Führer," he said, as if the bucolic had ceased to amuse him. He was in the most celebratory of spirits. "First came Czechoslovakia, then Poland. The Netherlands are not so nether anymore. And here comes France, a malicious joke in the last war and now merely a joke." He shrugged his narrow shoulders. "But here I am, telling you things you already well know."

Entirely true, so I waited with Brückner for the real reason for this little "accidental" planned encounter since nothing that fiend ever did was spontaneous or random.

"You know," he continued, as I knew he would, "there are those who believe—and a few even dare utter under their breath—that the ease of the taking will dilute, if not entirely eliminate, our role. But we three know that to be utter rubbish, at best a political ingenue's ignorance of the exigencies of occupation. In point of fact, as we conquer, the RSHA will not only be necessary, it will be indispensable—and will blossom."

Only a Heydrich could coin the term "blossom" for night arrests, torture, piano wire hanging, beheading, flaying, "dentistry," and other SS-style mechanisms for establishing and maintaining order.

"Of that," Brückner said with an ambiguous nod, "I have no doubt whatsoever. I would even go so far as to—"

"Yes, Wilhelm," the vampire cut him off, ice-blue eyes hooded, "and there will be even more work to be done right here at home. Treason never sleeps, even in the heart of the Reich. One day, and mark my words, as the Führer would say, I believe there will be two Reich: the first, the principal one, will be governed by the Führer; and the second, less grand but no less necessary, will be governed by the Reichsführer-SS, the latter ensuring the former." His face was aimed at Brückner, but his eyes swivelled towards me. "And in such a system, there will be plenty of work for your Christiane, eh, Linge?"

Suddenly, I was fighting for breath, made even more difficult because I was also fighting not to reveal it. At that moment, I despised him with every cell in my body. I knew it was not merely a humanistic antipathy to his elemental sadism but a bone-deep loathing of his brutal arrogance. Immanuel Kant wrote that "arrogance is, as it were, a solicitation on the part of one seeking honour for followers, whom he thinks he is entitled to treat with contempt." While he could never have known the monster in front of me now, he was able to describe him utterly.

"Quite, Herr General," I replied blandly. A sudden ringing filled my ears, and I forced myself not to display even the slightest alarm. *But what did he suspect—or know?*

"Ah, but alas," he said through a mock pucker, "the lady appears to be as evanescent at play as she is at work." He stole a quick glance at Brückner, who, in Heydrich's arrogant estimation, would know what evanescent meant, but who merely shrugged. Then the general's eyes returned to me.

"You know, Linge," he continued, "it sounds absurd, but for a fleeting, farcical moment, we even considered that the two of you might have stolen off to parts unknown, let's say, to a well-chosen, clandestine love nest." He laughed thinly. "But then, you would never even think of abandoning the Führer, would you? Of course not. So, we immediately dismissed that ridiculous notion with a wink and a chuckle. But no need to fret," he assured me, crooked smile and all. "I'm reasonably confident she'll turn up, one way or another, and since your recent malady is a memory, your amorous adventures can resume. Well," he concluded, "mission accomplished, eh? Good to see you both again, and in such delightfully arcadian surroundings." With that, he click-saluted (as did we), pivoted gracefully on his gleaming metal toe-and-heel boot plates, and went on his way.

"Do you think he knows anything?" I asked Brückner with no little anxiety as we continued our saunter.

Brückner smiled as I shifted sides to be privy to his good eye.

"That we're still walking together in the Chancellery gardens speaks volumes about Heydrich's ignorance. And in any event, my anxious friend, there's no longer anything for him to know. Not a thing. Even his guesses would have to be embarrassingly fanciful."

Not entirely relieved, I told him of Katrin's note, asked him how she knew and Heydrich didn't, then what I should do.

Brückner nodded slowly, maintaining a casual, conversational stride. "Intriguing as always, but as with all things connected to these Katrin and Emerald of yours, we should no longer be surprised by their access, and therefore, their information. How and why, I have no idea, but my best instinctive guess is that if she meant you harm, you'd already be harmed. In any event, it's clear that her concern and beneficence have a purpose, and it might serve you well to discover what it is. But trust is quite another matter, so never fail to bring your wits with you."

And a long spoon, I told myself.

AFTER YESTERDAY'S STROLL with Brückner (and Heydrich), I spent most of the morning's pre-Führerbuzzer moments in turmoil. Many times, I'd heard Kempka boast of his prowess at "flipper," a silly electronic beer hall game in which points are scored by a player manipulating one or more steel balls on a playing field inside a glass-covered cabinet. The primary objective of the game, he says, is to score as many points as possible, which are earned when the ball strikes different targets. A drain is situated at the bottom of the playing field, partially protected by player-controlled plastic bats called flippers, thus the name. A game ends after all the balls fall into the drain. Secondary objectives are to maximise the time spent playing (by keeping the ball in play as long as possible).

In a sudden flash of awareness, it struck me that such a game had a real-world counterpart and that I was the steel ball being manipulated or "flipped" towards one target or another, of which, only the player or players knew. *And just who were the players? Himmler? Heydrich? Emerald? Katrin? Weisthor? Dvora? Any one of them, or all? Then who was the machine? The Führer?* I took an icy shower to turn away from the apparently futile and fruitless puzzle pieces, temporarily at least.

❧

In what the flummoxed generals called an "inexplicably stunning move," the Führer ordered his forces not to cross the Lens–Bethune–St. Omer–Gravelines line, thus allowing the retreating, mainly British, forces more time to reach the French coast. The Führer steadfastly refused to explain his reasons, and after being greeted with his forbidding facial expression, none dared ask.

After the generals filed out, shaking their collective heads, Himmler arrived to report that the final construction of his pride and joy, KZ Auschwitz-Birkenau, had been completed and that the camp, once in full operation, would "go a long way towards accomplishing your sacred racial mission."

The Führer merely asserted absently, "I'm quite confident, Heinrich, that you'll do whatever is necessary."

I assumed that the reply satisfied the Reichsführer-SS, though you'd never know by his expression, which was, as usual, utterly blank. As for me, I had no idea what Himmler was talking about, and I suspected that while the Führer presumably did, his expression seemed to indicate that it didn't really matter that much to him.

⌇

For the most part, the Führer has been in extremely positive spirits over his effortless victories, Churchill's elevation to Prime Minister notwithstanding. In fact, he was quite "thrilled," as Schroeder put it, over the events surrounding Dunkirk and ordered us all to travel there with him. However, when we arrived, I witnessed a wonder: Above and beyond the earlier "inexplicably stunning move," the Wehrmacht had been ordered to halt, to actually allow the British to evacuate. From what Brückner told me, the order to discontinue had been given personally by the Führer, despite the active dissent of Field Marshals von Rundstedt and von Kluge. Brückner (in a private conversation with me), believed this decision to be incomprehensible. I learned the Führer's version of the matter on the evening of 24 May, which, to me, was no more comprehensible.

I was readying the Führer for bed, not the simplest of tasks when he was held so fast in the grip of exhilaration. I was, at least, able to coax him into his bed, but when I turned to leave, he remarked, "Be glad you aren't a leader, my friend," he said, causing me to pivot quickly to face him.

"Yes, my Führer?" I replied.

"I know what all those fucking fossilised 'vons' think, now of course that my victories have miraculously summoned up their latter-day mettle: that this ex-corporal's a simpleton at best, and demented at worst, for allowing the British forces, ill-equipped, ill-prepared, and ill-led, off the proverbial hook when I could easily have destroyed them. They wouldn't say this to my face, of course, but you can wager that the whispers run rampant. Of course, they haven't the wherewithal to understand, much less appreciate, the incalculable extent and boldness of my vision and… special resources. So, I let them off the hook as well." He leaned to the side, aimed his posterior at the door, and farted mightily. "My answer, Linge, to them. Unmistakable and heartfelt, be in no doubt."

What possible response could I make to that?

He turned back to me. "Czechoslovakia is ours," he crowed. "Poland is ours. The Low Countries are ours, and now, even France is ours. Incidentally, it will pay dearly for its treatment of us after the last war. However, what these obdurate fogeys fail to realise is how much our British cousins, enemies for the present, will soon be absorbed into the greater Aryan Reich and will be so gladly, jubilantly even, with or without the blessing of that fatuous lump Churchill, for that stammering, cigar-sucking porker will no longer have meaning in the world I intend to create. So, let the others natter as much as they like. For them, it will be no more than pissing into a hurricane. Good night, Linge."

I merely added my congratulations regarding the humiliating defeat of France and agreed that the Führer was, as usual, right—that I was certainly glad I wasn't a leader (as if I ever could be). I said my own good night and left, closing the bedroom door behind me.

∽

On the way to my quarters, I bumped—literally—into an exhilarated Göring, who was entertaining his ass-kissing toadies with a story. He bade me join him in a way that made any refusal impolitic at best.

"You'll enjoy this, Linge, as will the Führer when I tell him," he predicted, and I dared not indicate, in any way, that I knew his stories to be invariably lacking any semblance of humour as well as being well-worn and squalid. "A few days ago," he started over, "I went into a tavern on the Rhine, and all the customers rose to their feet. The only ones who didn't were a couple of Catholic priests, so I showed them what for—I had them packed off to a concentration camp, and I gave orders for a pole to be set up there and one of my old caps to be put on top of it. Now, they have to walk past it every day and give it a National Socialist salute, so instead of Hail Mary, it's Heil Hitler."

Gut-busting laughter followed all round, not the least of which came from the medal-clanging Reichsmarschall himself.

"See, Linge?" he said, virtually breathless. "Imagine the reaction when I tell it to the Führer."

"I can imagine, Herr Reichsmarschall," I replied with well-concealed disgust, "since no one tells stories the way you do."

4 *June 1940*

I WAS JARRED awake by the sensation of a slight weight on my chest, only to discover a small envelope. Normally, I would have experienced a fearful concern over someone able to open a locked door, stroll over to where I lay, and deposit a message on my chest, all while I slept. And yet, I felt a peculiar calm, as if the incident was commonplace and I'd been expecting it. "Heinz," the elegant cursive began:

An elaboration of my last message. By now, you must be aware that there are those who recognise your powers and your indispensable role in the Führer's journey to the preternatural. They would stop at nothing to thwart him through you. Therefore, I must congratulate Brückner for his covert, decisive, and successful action concerning the Jewess who, despite her otherwise vital work for the Fatherland, was part of a nefarious scheme to bring down you and the Führer. I am not unaware of the powerful feelings you had for her since you were not conscious of her true origins. Please allow me to assist with the healing process. K.

In a postscript, she provided a telephone number, what to say when picked up, and a needless reminder to destroy the note.

As I sat on my toilet lid after flushing the ashes, my thoughts were forced back to those terrible times when I barely subsisted in hallways and alleys, a hungry, cold, ignorant, needy vagrant pilfering precious clothes and crumbs from those even needier: unemployed ex-soldiers, political castaways, mental defectives.

Some of the veterans were grotesquely wounded with faces I was barely able to observe without vomiting: empty eye-sockets, missing noses, torn and twisted mouths dripping pus and blood. In other words, all the post-war flotsam and jetsam. And I took from them. Even then, I was able to tell myself how easy it was for someone sufficiently motivated to talk himself into believing what he needed to believe, ignoring the obvious, lying to himself with a straight face, knowing what he'd done, but refusing to consider it. I didn't need Dvora to show this to me. Or Katrin.

IN THE LATE morning, the Führer and all his closest advisers, both civilian and military (save for Himmler, who I presumed was engaged in preparing his SS and Gestapo to deal with any paltry resistance the overwhelmed French might put up), sat round the enormous radio console, listening to a translation of Marshal Petain, announcing in a broadcast to the French people: "It is with a heavy heart that I tell you today that we must stop fighting." The French government called on the Germans for an armistice that would end the fighting.

Afterwards, came a thunder of huzzahs and applause for, as they put it, the Führer's "remarkable military acumen."

"So, now, I'm remarkable," he chided. "Before the crushing victory, not so remarkable, eh?" Then he raised a languid hand to mollify the early doubters. "That's quite all right, gentlemen," he said benignly. "Despite my steadfast predictions, as a former corporal, I expected little more from you than derisive scepticism. However, since this same former corporal has achieved the results you just heard for yourselves, perhaps now, you might wish to reconsider your views on the chain of command." After a theatrical pause, he laughed, generating contrite titters from the rest.

The Führer's loud slap on his desk silenced the group. "All right, we've had our little amusement, but now it's time for a matter both sober and momentous. I wish the French capitulation to take place at Compiegne, the exact spot where, twenty-two years earlier, we were obliged to sign the armistice ending the traitorous debacle of 1918. My intent, gentlemen, is simple and well warranted: I intend to disgrace the French and avenge the German defeat. To further deepen the humiliation, I will order the signing ceremony to take place in the very same railroad car that hosted the earlier surrender. To put it into the words of a mere corporal: I wish to take a shit on France's floor and have them wallow in it."

More huzzahs and applause, even from the "vons."

I noted that in all this talk of victory, rank, and humiliation, the Führer made no mention whatsoever of the British evacuation, nor did anyone bring it up. *Perhaps,* I joked to myself, *his lack of rancour towards Britain stemmed from his need to employ British ships to transport all of Europe's Jews to Madagascar.* I chose not to share my jest even with Brückner.

With Brückner's persistent encouragement, I succumbed to Schroeder's curious need to play cupid. However, military and political events were unfolding so rapidly, and in such numbers, that they precluded any serious social exertion. Romance would have to wait.

I SPENT MOST of the morning working with other menials as well as with secretaries and key officials to prepare the Führer for the momentous event ahead: the armistice signing between the Reich and France. All through the frantic goings-on, the Führer remained impassive, much like a mannequin being fitted out for an exhibition. Ultimately, he dismissed them with a languid wave. All but me. Once they'd left, he dropped his weight onto the campaign chair he'd ordered installed to, as he'd put it, "give my quarters a martial air." He motioned me to sit before him in a chair far plusher and more yielding. He leaned as far back as his chair would allow, clasped his hands behind his head, and gazed up at the railroad car's relatively low ceiling. He didn't speak for a moment, and it was clear to me that he was struggling with something.

"Since that infamous day in November 1918," he finally began murmuring, almost inaudibly, compelling me to lean forward, "I've been working towards this day." He sighed. "But now that it's at hand, while I must be seen to be ruthless and resolute, Linge, I tell you that I'm of two minds about this ceremony. On the one hand, the French must have their noses shoved into the shit of utter defeat. On the other hand, along with the Jews, I owe the French leaders plenty for my rise to power. As a result, I don't want the stench lingering longer than it takes to convince the French government that I mean business. But as to the rank and file, beyond the trappings, I have no wish to be vindictive. Even the rabid Himmler must allow that, like the Low Countries, prudent, watchful restraint is the key to the peaceful occupation of an Aryan possession. These aren't Slavs, after all. They're anything but combative by nature, and they do stand between us and the British. You see the dilemma facing me, eh?" He paused, his gaze still fixed on the ceiling.

As always, I had no sense that he was soliciting my opinion or suggestions. But the pause caused me to consider that a peace of reconciliation could only succeed with a peaceful, reconciliatory people. It seemed to me that if this insight fuelled the Führer's ambivalence, he was no less a genius in occupation than in nation building and warfare.

He lowered his head to face me. "It's all theatre anyway," he declared, "so, misgivings aside, I'll give them all a show." He shrugged, and I took that to be a dismissal until I started to get up.

"Well, Linge, what are you going to do about Schroeder the matchmaker?"

Where did he get the time, interest, and energy for such trivial matters? Even after five years, I could still be flummoxed by the Führer.

"I…"

"I know, but even with me, as you've seen, she's a woman requiring an exorbitant investment of patience and diplomacy. But she gets results, so we mustn't be too harsh in our judgements. Consider this: If the man's world is the state, his struggle, his readiness to devote his powers to the service of the state, the woman's is a smaller but no less important world—her husband, her family, her children, and her home. And yet, when a woman is willing to sacrifice this world to assist the man in his sacred task, we must exercise extraordinary indulgence, eh?"

As usual, what could I say? "Of course, my Führer."

"Good, so feel her out. You never know, you might finally get a truly worthy female—this time," he added cryptically.

✦

To heighten the "show," as the Führer had called it, he and his entourage arrived at Compiegne just moments before the ceremony. At 1518 hours, his personal flag was run up on a small standard near a great granite block standing some three feet above the ground. The Führer, followed by the others (including me), walked slowly over to it, stepped up, and read aloud the inscription engraved in great high letters on that block: "Here, on 11 November 1918, succumbed the criminal pride of the German Empire… vanquished by the free peoples which it tried to enslave."

Ignoring the others, I peeked furtively at the Führer's expression. Since entering the Führer's service, I'd witnessed a myriad of public and private faces before, during, and after the momentous episodes of his life, but never one so inflamed with the complex amalgam of scorn, rage, revenge, and triumph as I saw today. How he could constantly alter his appearance to match his strategy was, to me, always mystifying and awe-inspiring. I never saw a professional actor do it nearly as well from film to film. However, regardless of expression, after our "discussion," I knew that he only intended to make the French pay as a nation, unlike Himmler, who was setting in motion the machinery by which the French would pay as a people. *The two faces of Nazism,* I thought for the first time.

The Führer then stepped off the monument and contrived to make even this gesture a masterpiece of contempt. He glanced back at it, contemptuous, an anger both tangible and profound. He glanced slowly around the clearing, and suddenly, as though his face were not giving quite complete expression to his feelings, he threw his entire body into balance with his mood. He swiftly snapped his hands on his hips, arched his shoulders, planted his feet wide apart. To me, it seemed an exquisite gesture of defiance, of burning contempt for this place now and all that it stood for in the twenty-two years since it witnessed the humbling end of the German Empire.

At 1523 hours, the Führer and the other German leaders rose as the French entered the drawing room. The Führer gave his personal Nazi salute, arm raised languidly, elbow bent. Ribbentrop and Hess did the same. The Führer said not a single word to the French or to anybody else. He nodded to General Keitel at his side, who adjusted his papers. Normally, he fussed, but here, the occasion called for modification, and the Führer had briefed him well. Then the latter began to read the preamble to our armistice terms. The French sat there with faces of stone and appeared to listen intently. From what the Führer had told me this morning as I helped him dress, he had no intention of remaining very long, even for the reading of the armistice terms themselves.

So at 1542 hours, twelve minutes after the French arrived, the Führer stood, saluted again, then strode from the drawing room, followed by Göring, Brauchitsch, Raeder, Hess, Ribbentrop, and me. There were salutes but no handshakes, formality without feeling. The French remained at the green-topped table with Keitel, who read to them the detailed conditions of the armistice. I assumed that the Führer could not be seen to bother.

From my usual position behind, I accompanied the Führer, Speer, Brückner, Bormann, and Goebbels as they walked determinedly down the avenue towards the Alsace-Lorraine Monument, where our automobiles waited. As we passed the guard of honour, the German band began playing our two national anthems: "Deutschland, Deutschland Über Alles" and the "Horst Wessel Lied."

It was remarkable to me, a ceremony of such moment, over in a quarter of an hour—the summary execution of an entire political entity. And no less remarkable was seeing in the crowd of sideline onlookers Standartenführer Hausen, "Ziggy," the SS officer who'd proven so observant and generous regarding my "missing button," now so many years ago. As I passed, he waved a discreet hello with his eyebrows, and I returned it with no less discretion, wondering what he was doing here and how his life had fared since our last meeting.

BAUR TOUCHED DOWN at Le Bourget airfield, where three Mercedes saloons stood waiting. The Führer, as usual, sat in the front seat beside Kempka. Breker and I occupied the jump seats behind him, while Giesler[29] and Speer occupied the rear seats. Field grey uniforms had been provided for the civilians so they would blend into the martial ambience. As the Führer instructed, we drove through the extensive suburbs directly to the Opera, Charles Garnier's great neobaroque building. It was the Führer's favourite and the first thing he wanted to see. Colonel Seidel, assigned by the German Occupation Authority, waited at the entrance for us.

Up to the time of my employment by the Führer, I knew—and, to be frank, cared—nothing about art and architecture, having raced through the lifeless etchings reproduced in over-sized musty library volumes. However, from that point on, I became privy to interminable discussions by the Führer with various "Party-approved" artists and architects, especially the brilliant, urbane, and artistically gifted Speer, whom every cell in my body envied as everything I was not, save height. However, all this attention now being paid to paintings and buildings

---

[29] Paul Giesler, a trained architect, was, from 1924, a Nazi Party speaker, an SA leader, and an NSDAP district leader. Giesler was known for speaking out against higher education for women. During the Night of the Long Knives, he only narrowly missed being arrested and murdered.

provided me with a new interest that had my camera figuratively gasping for breath. Since I was running out of excuses to shoot in Berlin, I welcomed the additional opportunity to justify my "hobby."

When we were at last preparing to leave the building, the Führer whispered something to Giesler, who proceeded to pull a fifty-mark note from his wallet and went over to the attendant standing some distance away. Pleasantly but firmly, the man refused to take the money. The Führer tried a second time, this time sending Brückner over, but the man persisted in his refusal. He had only been doing his duty, he told Brückner.

Finally, the Führer had me make a note to send the money to the old man's address, turned to Brückner, and said, "I tell you truthfully, if the rest of the population exhibit the same attitude, the occupation will be a most pleasant and productive one." Once said, he turned and delivered to me a surreptitious wink.

The Führer had little reason to doubt it, for in addition to what he'd told me this morning, he'd mentioned on several occasions, "The French have no talent or stomach for war. They'll surrender in a minute once they believe that it might interfere with their dinner, mar a monument, or scratch a painting."

After the Opera, I accompanied the Führer, Speer, Brückner, Bormann, and Goebbels as they walked determinedly down the avenue towards the Alsace-Lorraine Memorial, where our automobiles were waiting. As we passed the guard of honour, the German band began playing the two national anthems again. I'd heard them so often that I was able to ignore them, but I was sure that the conquered French hadn't and couldn't. *And that was the point, wasn't it?*

By 0900 in the morning, we were back at the Chancellery. Our sightseeing tour of Paris was over, but the Führer's mind was still there.

"You know, Linge," he said as I helped him change uniforms, "when I was a young, struggling artist, I had a dream that one day, a painting of mine would hang in the Louvre. I hadn't a prayer, of course, but now, when I could actually have the whole fucking place to myself, I have nothing to hang there. Ironic." He sighed wistfully. "But that always seems to be the way of things. I must confess a certain admiration for the architecture, though. I tell you, Berlin will be made far more beautiful. In the past, I often considered whether we would have to bomb and bulldoze the place," he continued with great nonchalance, as if he were speaking of pruning hedges. "But when we're finished in Berlin, Paris will be a mere shadow. So, why bother to destroy it?"

Of course, he was speaking to himself, so I just stood there, waiting.

"Along those lines, Linge," he said, this time to me, "arrange for Speer to meet with me this evening." He sat silently for a few moments, appearing to study his splayed hands on his desktop. "At any rate, I have a hellish amount of paperwork to catch up on, so you're on your own till eighteen hundred hours. And no disturbances. Oh," he added as I made for the door, "make sure you speak with Schroeder. At least that'll stop her nagging."

His wish was fate's command, for on my way to collect the mail, I was accosted by Schroeder, her Wicked Witch of the West—face pinched in irritation, her voice ostentatiously low. "So?" she asked, her eyes narrowed.

I closed my eyes slowly, then opened them. "So what, Fräulein Schroeder?"

Her bloodless lips spread in exasperation. "All right, Herr Stud," she muttered menacingly, "I will tell you what. Since you clearly prefer the smelly sluts at Salon Kitty to decent girls, the least you could have done is tell me to mind my own business."

How she knew their smell, I had no intention of asking, but I had to agree that I'd deliberately disregarded the offer of her niece. After a dreadful incident during my bricklaying days, I'd adopted a rigid once-burnt-twice-shy policy towards blind dates.

I'd only been working in the brickyard for two weeks when the superintendent came up to me during my short lunch break and asked if I had "steady pussy," as he'd elegantly put it. When I told him I hadn't, he grinned, said he had the "hottest fuckin' tiger" for me, and all I had to do was drop my pants, show her my "whip," and she would be as "tame as a kitten." The imagery held little allure or accuracy, but I didn't want to offend someone who might thwart my advancement, so I took his information, telephoned, and arranged dinner at a modest but decent restaurant.

It was when I arrived at her flat and she opened the door that all the blood I possessed seemed to surge to my head, and I almost passed out. Her disfigurement was clearly the product of some grotesque violence, either before birth or by later catastrophe. I was virtually breathless with revulsion, and it took all the willpower I possessed to force down the bile and, at the same time, appear as if everything were normal. Facing her, I felt such a heat wave of horror, pity, and rage that it left me utterly bereft of words. Fortunately, she had fewer inhibitions.

"Bernhard didn't tell you," she slurred through one side of her mouth. "That was wrong, but please do not reproach him. He is merely a naughty child who likes to play pranks. Unfortunately, these pranks are oftentimes at someone else's expense. In this instance, yours. Now I shall shut the door, and we will pretend that none of this unpleasantness ever happened."

She began pushing the door towards me with her good arm—which I prevented from closing with my foot.

"Are you turning me away before we've even met?" I asked. "I'm quite a likeable fellow, once you know me."

"You needn't do this," she entreated. "I seldom venture out, as well you can imagine. If it matters, I think no less of you for being repelled."

Repelled! As an outcast myself, I had some vague idea of her existence, but no experience of mine, no matter how sordid or wretched, could come close to comparing with the daily horrors she must have endured.

"For years, I slept in filthy, stinking alleys, so I'm not easily repelled," I lied. "May I come in?"

Her small dark-brown eyes appeared to glisten with moisture. "Yes, of course," she said after staring at me for a long moment. "I just hope you cleaned up before coming here."

She was funny, something I imagined no one would take the time to notice once they'd seen her. Her flat was small but tidy, as if she'd worked hard to make at least something presentable. And as if she'd read my mind, after having me sit, she said, "As you can imagine, I eat at home a great deal, so I'm not the worst cook. Will you let me cook for you?"

I've never been, I think, the most sentimental person, but at that moment, I felt an overpowering shame for the expression I knew I must have displayed in the hallway, so I had no intention of running for my life, and neither did I intend to submit her to the gasps and gapes of a restaurant.

"I don't want to put you to any trouble." I hated the meaningless formality of the words.

"As you can also imagine," she replied, I felt, to dilute my discomfort. "I don't get many visitors, especially hungry ones. So, it would be my pleasure."

"And no less a pleasure for me," I said truthfully, still straining to ignore her deformities. It was difficult to understand her at first, but eventually, I adjusted to her distorted cadences. "And please call me Heinz."

She attempted a smile, but her face refused to cooperate. "You'll have to guess my moods, I suppose, but I'll be happy to call you Heinz if you call me Arabella. It means beautiful eagle, you know. You must admit, my parents had no small flair for irony. What does Heinz mean?"

I managed to smile. "Well, Arabella, I think it means 'ruler of the household' or something of the like. Since I've never had a household or ruled anything, irony certainly isn't lost on me either."

She nodded, I thought, approvingly at my attempt at wit. "There's a newspaper on the table. Make yourself comfortable with it while I fix us a small feast." With that, she twisted round awkwardly and began a serpentine trek to the kitchen, dragging one crooked, emaciated leg behind her.

The meal *was*, in fact, a small feast, during which we joked, recounted films we'd both seen in the safety of the dark, and shared half-guarded confidences. When we'd finished our after-dinner brandies, she showed me to the door.

Before I had a chance to say anything, she stared right through me. "I know that look only too well. You like me, and you wish to God I didn't have an appearance that elicited only pity or nausea. Unfortunately, God or no God, wishing hasn't made it so. I have no adequate words to express my gratitude for rising above your reflexes. I won't see you again, but please know that I thank you for an evening I'll always treasure."

The next day, when I had finally managed to corner the suddenly elusive Bernhard, I thanked him for providing me with "an evening I'll always treasure." In this, I was being only partially sardonic.

So you see, this was why I violated my no-blind-date rule only once, when I told Brückner I would meet "Christiane." But this was hardly a recommendation for accepting the advice of another would-be marriage broker. Then again, I had to work with the crone every day.

"My sincerest apologies, Fräulein Schroeder," I told her. "Please believe that all the while we were in France, your generosity was uppermost in my mind. But you must realise that my ability to act on it was severely limited. Now that we've returned, I'll get to it straightaway."

Schroeder's face remained in a state of belligerent scepticism, in counterpoint to her words. "Yes. What you say is reasonable. But," she threatened, "I'll be quite interested to learn how you fare."

"You'll be the first to know," I said, only too aware that she would be, whether I told her or not.

25 *June 1940*

ON MY WAY to track down Brückner for a strategy session, I was approached by Bormann the bull, encased in a virtual wrap-around, double-breasted, unadorned, shit-brown uniform that would make even Goebbels queasy.

"Just the man I seem to need," he said, his gravelly voice as heavily lidded as his eyes.

"What can I do for you, Herr Reichs—"

"It's awkward and unseemly for someone in my position, having to go through the likes of Brückner, and especially you, to get an appointment with the Führer, don't you think?"

He didn't really want to know my thoughts, for if he knew them, he would use his revolver on me. "Herr Reichsleiter, I'm hardly in a position to say. I accept things as they are."

"Ah, I see, a man of the moment. Good enough for a servant. Fortunately for the Reich, the Führer and I are men of the future."

The arrogant bastard! Then why was this creature who compares himself to the Führer asking me for entrée to him? "I envy you, Herr Reichsleiter," I said. "However, to your point, I wish I could be of assistance, but I'm reasonably certain that if the Führer wishes you to have direct access, he need only express it."

His bulbous lips spread into a malevolent smile. "He will, valet. Trust me, he will."

I'd always told myself to trust no one, but I trusted him then—and my insides shuddered.

By the onset of dusk, I managed to locate Brückner in the officers' mess. He appeared to be nattering over coffee with a colonel of the Wehrmacht. The colonel was a small, concise man in his middle years with commonplace features. His closely cropped brown hair was plentiful but beginning to reveal isolated strands of grey. The fibrous skin of his face and hands had acquired the premature web of intersecting lines and goggle-produced "racoon eyes" that one sees in those soldiers exposed to the sun for prolonged periods. Probably in Ethiopia and Spain. Now France. Brückner waved me over, bade me sit, and introduced me.

"Alfred, this is my friend and colleague Obersturmbannführer Heinz Linge. Heinz, this is Colonel Alfred Möller."

We both nodded amiably at each other.

"Heinz is val—"

"I know who he is," interrupted Möller. "Even in the field, your services for the Führer are well-known and highly regarded."

"I never realised that—" I started to reply, not a little confounded.

"Never underestimate the degree, range, and importance of gossip in a closed system," he said. Clearly, this was the sort of soldier Brückner would know. "You'd be surprised at what—"

"Hungry, Heinz?" Brückner cut him off. "You should both have something now so you can avoid the Führer's leftover baby food."

We all laughed at that.

"Yes, I think I will," Möller agreed. "I can't understand how the Führer keeps that swill down. Meat isn't the end-all, mind you, but nature has given us meat-eating teeth for a reason, am I right?"

"I believe that the Führer has determined to defy nature,"

Brückner said. "And not only with food, though the consequence is a ready supply of gas masks for us, and Morell's noxious nostrums."

Chuckles followed.

"Herr Colonel, do you think the fighting is truly over in France?" I asked.

"Alfred, please." He shrugged. "For the most part. The armistice is signed, our troops occupy the place, and the French are masters of pragmatic accommodation. Oh, there'll be the usual isolated pockets of foolhardy resistance by children, the aged, invalids, and the unemployed, meaning those with nothing to lose, including brains. But all that'll be quickly sorted out. And in any event, our role is only to take and secure. Soon the SS will arrive to… maintain, and we'll move on."

"To where?" I asked casually. In truth, I really didn't know.

Another shrug. "Well, Heinz, if you and Willie don't know, what chance do I have? My boss says England, but I don't think so. Rumour again. Personally, I think… well, better not to speculate at such an early date."

I was surprised by his hesitation after such candour, but I let it go since even Brückner didn't pursue the matter. Perhaps he already knew—or, like me, didn't care.

"Doesn't really matter, eh, Alfred?" Brückner said. "So long as there's action."

The Colonel smiled. "I suppose you're right. I'm a professional soldier, a warrior, and a warrior without a war is as useless as a doctor without a patient. And yet, I'll confess, a part of that doctor might wish that all were healthy, even at the expense of his vocation. It's no different for warriors, I think. Not all warriors, however. And after meeting Josef Mengele, definitely not all doctors."

I thought that events in France would allow me some time and space to discuss with Brückner what I should do about my matchmaker, but that was not to be, for now the Führer was preoccupied with Italy and made me a personal witness to his almost-comical misgivings.

The Italian ambassador had brought the Führer a letter from Mussolini informing him that Italy now desired an active role in the war.

The Führer, hardly amazed, reacted with typical sarcasm. "Now, when they see the flock swimming off, suddenly, there is haste to fleece it." He exhaled heavily. "I blame myself for this," he admitted to me as I watched him dress, stopwatch nestled in my hand. "My recommendation to the Duce not to enter the war until Italy was ready for it and the moment was opportune appears to have been bad counsel. Italians are only ready for battle after it's been won by others. And to think that the Duce repeatedly tells me that he intends a return to the glory of ancient Rome. Can you imagine, Linge, that Julius Caesar would hesitate for a moment to have his legions beat me to Paris?

"In March, I told the Duce that although I fully understood Italy's stance in the autumn of 1939, namely, that the Italian army lacked equipment to go to war, I would still welcome Italy's entry into the war as a show of unity if not strength. Of course, nothing resulted. Now, when everything is over and done with, Mussolini finally did what I had recommended he do at a time when he had not been sure how things would turn out for us." I handed him his tie. "Now, don't misunderstand me, Linge," he concluded. "I still admire the Duce, though exactly why eludes me, and I must confess that with an ally like Italy, we need no enemies."

I merely nodded a yes-my-Führer and said nothing. Since the relationship between the Führer and Mussolini was a mystery I had no way of solving, for me, discretion was the order of the day.

To the Führer's exasperation, between 10 June 1940, when Italy declared war on Britain and France, and 13 June, when our troops occupied Paris, the Italian "operation" was revealed at last: their plan was to do nothing. The Führer was visibly distraught. "These fucking Italians," he fumed half-heartedly, "still don't understand how you start a war in modern times. Nowadays after the declaration of war, you have to actually open fire. When I shouted at that idiot Ambassador Alfieri that nothing had happened after several days had passed, he said it was because of rain on the border with France. Rain!" he shouted. "If any of my generals came to me with that craziness, he'd leave without his head!" He paused a moment. "Understand me. I admire the Duce for several reasons, not the least of which is his astonishing ability to make Italians even remotely efficient, but he and the rest of the Italians know nothing about warfare." Then he added, cryptically and in suddenly hushed tones, "Fortunately, Linge, I believe that soon we'll not need the Italians, the Japanese, the fucking Soviets. Anyone. I'll be free of them all."

ANOTHER MIGRAINE KEPT me from my morning duties. Later, in the officers' mess, as I picked listlessly at a small late snack alone, I realised that a nothing like me was suddenly among those at the very centre of world history. Czechoslovakia had been taken. Austria had been attached. Poland, the Low Countries, and France had fallen. I thought back to our time in Compiegne, where I never saw the Führer so jubilant as he was on that day. Rapturous, he'd slapped his thigh and performed a little dance, but as he'd told me that morning, this was no more than political theatrics, merely to buy him "time to gather and employ forces that will render previous successes meaningless and future successes superfluous," whatever that meant.

Göring, on the other hand, slobbered with anticipation at the prospect of untold loot. Goebbels saw only the propaganda value of showing the world a well-treated, compliant, and cooperative former enemy, and Himmler was embedded with Heydrich, Kaltenbrunner, and Müller, busily constructing the bureaucratic machinery and logistics to accomplish his "sacred mission" of protecting the Reich and eradicating its enemies— all "in accordance with the Führer's wishes," of course.

⁓

My musings were interrupted by Kempka, who came up behind me, tapped me on the right shoulder, and when I looked right, he scurried to my left. Giving me his version of a sly, I-got-you wink, he plopped down across from me.

"Too bad you were sick this morning," he whispered needlessly. "Man, you really missed something."

"Have we attacked another country?" I joked.

"Nothing like that—yet. No, the Führer called me in to discuss the strategy for a little outing tonight, you know, like the one you came along on. When we finished, he let me take an emergency piss in his bathroom, and while I was finishing up but before flushing, I heard Junge come in and tell him some loony cock-and-bull story about you."

"Hmm. Really? Just what *was* this 'loony cock-and-bull story'?"

Kempka blew some air through his bushy-haired nostrils in derision. "Man, you'll love this. The kid told the Führer that he'd heard some shit about you fucking some Jewess."

"*I was?*" I exclaimed to demonstrate the proper innocent outrage, but I shook inside. "Did he put a name to this Jewess?"

"Not that I heard. But he said, real solemn now, that he hated to be the bearer of such news, but should the Führer wish to pursue the matter, he would do what he could to—how the fuck did he say? Oh, yeah—'shoot down such wicked gossip.' Say, you ain't fooling around with—"

"I didn't know there were any left in Berlin."

Kempka laughed. "Yeah, there's that, all right. Anyways, you should stick with my Black Book. Aryan pussy only. A personal guarantee from your Uncle Erich."

"What did the Führer say to Junge?"

Kempka pursed his lips. "Well, when I peeked out, I could see the Führer looked all puzzled. Then his face suddenly became all serious-like. He thanked Junge for being vigilant and told him that the matter was so sensitive that it must be handled on the highest level, meaning that he would personally put Himmler on the case without delay, and there was nothing more for Junge to do. But not to worry, Heinz. The Führer began chuckling after the rat shut the door behind him."

"Did the Führer say anything to you about it afterwards?"

"Nah. He just shook his head and told me not to mention it to you 'cause you'd just get needlessly upset. I said sure, but I figured you'd get a kick out of it, so that's why I told you. But don't run and tell him I told you, okay?"

I nodded in agreement and satisfaction. "So, that's that?"

He shrugged. "Well, probably, but then again, who the fuck knows around here?"

"Meaning what, Uncle Erich?"

"Well, I happened to run into Junge later, and he told me what he told the Führer and what the Führer told him but that he felt—what the hell did he say?—'duty bound to follow up.'"

So much for Brückner's "rumour."

SCHROEDER, APPARENTLY ON her way back from a mammoth dictating session with the Führer, burst into my breakfast with a copy of *The Eagle*.[30] She plopped it down in front of me, almost spilling my coffee.

"You of course read this?" she asked. "Is it not an understatement?"

"I must have missed this particular issue," I joked to someone for whom anything subtle went in one ear and out the same side. "Not to put too fine a point on it, but I seldom have cause to accuse military periodicals of understatement." I hoped that she would just accept my lame reply and leave it with me for later disposal, but she would have none of it.

"Well, Linge, thank God you have me to keep you abreast, or you'd know nothing of value." Her idea of a joke. "So, I will read it to you now." She'd been gazing at me in the strangest way in recent days and did so now, but I hadn't the competence, strength, or desire to interpret it. Mainly, since I hadn't followed up on her matchmaking attempt, I was just relieved that she hadn't come to browbeat me.

She retrieved her magazine with mock umbrage, as if I were a backward pupil who hadn't submitted his homework assignment, unfolded it with exaggerated care, and began reading

---

[30] *The Eagle* (*Der Adler*) was a biweekly Nazi propaganda magazine. From 1939 to 1944, 146 magazine issues were published in total.

aloud: "'For us Germans, the word "Dunkirk" will stand for all time as victory in the greatest battle of annihilation in history. But for the British and French who were there, it will remind them for the rest of their lives of a defeat that was heavier than any army had ever suffered before.'"

How she could consider that rhapsody to human destruction to be an understatement was something I had no desire to pursue. "It seems like a fairly accurate report," I answered, "though perhaps a bit softhearted, as you suggest. Would you be so good as to leave it with me for my scrapbook?"

She smiled with barely controlled antipathy. "I would like to see your scrapbook someday. Have you shown it to the Führer?"

I smiled. "Fräulein Schroeder, I hardly think that the Führer would be interested in my occasional clippings of strangers' accounts of his achievements, when he has himself, Dr. Goebbels, and Julius Streicher."

She placed the magazine down slowly and delicately like in a Japanese tea ceremony. "Her name is Klara," she said, her eyes now hooded.

Her real reason for our meeting. Perhaps I shouldn't have joked about the newspaper. *One day*, I chided myself, *the growing irrepressibility of my attempts at humour will get me into serious trouble.* "Klara?" I asked.

"A shame to lose your memory so young," she sniped. "Yes. Klara. You know, my niece. That Klara. You were to telephone her. You have, thus far, not done so."

Stall! "You're aware that I haven't been well, Fräulein Schroeder, and—"

Her clenched lips flattened and spread in aversion. "Aware? The entire Chancellery is aware of your... incapacity. But Dr. Morell has informed me that you are now quite as competent as you were before... however that was. But be that as it may, since you now have recovered your… capacity, do you or do you not have any intention of telephoning her? You should realise that I don't give out her name to just anyone. In truth, I wouldn't have given it to *you* had the Führer not insisted."

So much for doctor-patient confidentiality. *After Dvora, that's all I need,* I considered grimly, *a girlfriend with a direct family connexion to an intimate of the Führer and who roundly hates me.* Unfortunately, I was bereft of further stalling tactics. "Point taken; I'm well told."

Clearly dubious, she scrunched her crone's face into a reasonable facsimile of a prune. "All right. I'll take your word for now, but hear this," she warned, "Klara doesn't have my patience, so I'd get cracking if I were you."

"Consider it done." I hoped a positive interpretation of my ambiguity would mollify her.

"Herr Linge," she said, blank faced, "I'll consider it done when it's done."

So much for hope. "Yes, Fräulein Schroeder, I understand. Straight away."

Suddenly, she forced her mouth into a narrow grin, but enough to call unwanted attention to the lipstick-and-cigarette-carved vertical crevices lining her fuzzy upper lip, reminding me of a seismographic chart as well as providing me an equally unwanted glimpse of her crooked front teeth.

Thank you, my Führer, for Schroeder, I muttered to myself with bile once she'd gone. She was like the old advertising slogan for phonographs: "The gift that keeps on giving."

❧

Fortunately, Brückner and I managed a few moments of privacy in the gardens before attending an important meeting the

Führer had called to explain his decision regarding Dunkirk and Great Britain generally to his inner circle and selected generals.

"Arguably a matter of high comedy," Brückner said with a smile after I related my conversation with Schroeder.

"You find this situation comic?" I asked.

"Well, Heinz, what else would you call it? No sooner is the Dvora matter… resolved than your chum Schroeder finds someone no less hazardous to take her place."

"I'm glad you find this funny," I said, my face expressionless and with no reproof in my tone. "Between Schroeder and Junge, I have more enemies than Germany."

"My apologies. I'm afraid I have an aversion to seriousness—no small handicap in our line of work. But what's this Junge business? Something new?"

I told him what Kempka had told me.

"Hmm. Well, I wouldn't concern myself unduly at this point, my friend. If he really had anything, he would have presented it to Himmler before taking the risk of burdening the Führer."

I shook my head. "Then, what was he doing?"

"If I had to guess, I'd say he was testing the Führer's loyalty to you before chancing anything further. Only a guess, mind you, but to me, it makes sense. And you say that the Führer merely humoured him in response?"

"Assuming Kempka's retelling was accurate."

"In my opinion, while the chauffeur has many faults, driving and accuracy aren't among them. But to make certain, you should wait and see if the Führer brings any of this up, and if so, how."

"And if he does?"

Brückner nodded. "Yes, well, we might want to talk further

then. But it'll have to be quick and soon, for I need to tell you something."

An icy gust of apprehension scattered my thoughts, and all I could say was "Sounds serious."

"It is. I intended to wait, but your story just now, accurate or not, makes both my decision and the telling you of it more urgent." He stopped walking and faced the foliage. "This morning, I asked the Führer to transfer me to a Wehrmacht fighting unit."

Overcome, I also faced away into the gardens, not daring to see him. "But—"

"Why? Simple, my friend. I'm an old expert in handwriting analysis, and for some time, I've seen Bormann's devious and malign calligraphy on the wall getting larger and more legible."

I had no words for him.

"You know, my friend," he pressed on, "none of this should come as a surprise. As I've told you many times, it's rather burdensome to walk about with a target on your back. Even after the Storck debacle, it was different when the Bear was in permanent residence at the Berghof. But now, with him residing here? Well, all I can say is that now, here, under one roof, in a battle between myself and Bormann for the Führer's favour, there's no question who would emerge victorious. So I decided to strategically retreat before all exits were sealed—along with my fate.

"I'll put it another way," Brückner remarked, in the absence of my response. "This old warrior would prefer to be where the enemy is in front of him." Then, after a drawn-out pause, "Consider this, my dear friend: Assuming the Führer grants my request—and I have no reason to believe he won't—wherever I'm posted, I'll still be as close as the nearest secure phone and furtively delivered strip of microfilm. Not a walk in the park, so to say," he said, gesturing to the opulent gardens, "but still…"

"Then it is what it has to be," I conceded, bereft of greater profundity. And from that moment, both of us refused to look at one another. It wasn't to be a parting, and we knew it. It was to be a death, and we knew that too. I was numb with despair.

❧

The conference room chosen for the meeting was small, over-heated for late June, and crammed with military, political, and industrial bigwigs. Junge was there too. And Bormann. The Führer was in one of his professorial moods, which signified much give and little take. By the time Brückner and I arrived, he'd completed his lecture and had ceded the floor to General von Rundstedt.

"Some of you," he began, facing the others, "have questioned the decision to halt the Fourth Army, which General Kluger and I recommended and was endorsed wholeheartedly by the Führer himself. Of course, we could have annihilated the remaining British troops with little effort, but I would remind you that we fought in the last war and realised that like at the Marne in 1914, a sudden Allied counter-attack could well change the course of the whole war. In our eyes at the time, this risk still existed because the British and French still offered resistance in neighbouring areas. At the same time, we wished to give our armies time to rest, repair, and replenish after a thrust whose speed and distance had taken everyone by surprise, even us. An additional motive was to preserve the tanks for what we saw as their greater need, which was to destroy the French troops by moving south against them. And Reichsmarschall Göring had promised the Führer that the British troops would be bombed to bits from the air in any event. Of course, none of this would have occurred without the complete accord of the Führer."

The general reached for his glass of water, lifted it

regally—pinkie extended—to his mouth, and took a perfunctory sip, then placed the glass back and turned to the Führer, as did the others. "Have I covered the matter adequately, my Führer?"

"More than that, Rundstedt," he answered. "The decision was mine to make, and I stand by it. I believe we now have little to fear from a roundly chastened Britain. They've experienced a small sample of German might, and even for a fantasist like that fat, cigar-sucking Churchill, it should be enough—that is, until Göring here has his way with their puny air force. I predict that within a few months, Britain will lick its wounds, return to its senses, and reinstate a realist to the prime ministership. And perhaps even call for our friend[31] to be restored to the throne."

All eyes swivelled towards the resplendently corpulent air chief, who merely pressed his bladderlike lips into something resembling a grin. Then the eyes returned to the Führer. All save for Bormann, who, I could swear, stole a glance at Brückner and delivered a subtle victory wink.

---

[31] Hitler was referring to King Edward VIII, who abdicated on 11 December 1936 so he could marry the American divorcée Wallis Simpson. In October 1937, the Duke and Duchess of Windsor visited Hitler at Berchtesgaden, where Hitler had been vacationing since the 1920s. According to biographer Frances Donaldson in her book *Edward VIII*, the duke gave Hitler full Nazi salutes during this visit. While some say this trip was intended to garner support for Edward and his wife, the duke's actions spoke louder than any hypotheses. Shortly after the war, American diplomats uncovered four hundred tonnes of German diplomatic papers at Marburg Castle. Among these documents were details of the Nazi-devised plan "Operation Willi," where the Germans would gain control of Britain and overthrow the current monarchy, returning the duke to the throne. The Germans viewed the duke, perceived to be ambivalent about the war, as a better ally than his successor, King George VI. To get the duke on their side, German agents tried to manipulate the ostracised royal, even attempting to convince him that his brother, King George, was plotting to assassinate him. The documents were leaked to the British government, which tried—and failed—to suppress them.

"That is it, gentlemen. There will still be those who deny the resourcefulness of my strategy, but I have a far bigger fish to fry and must be prepared to throw it into the boiling oil without delay." This was all he said, and the group filed out silently, all that is, except for me, who was requested to remain behind.

Annihilate the British. Spare the British. Clobber the French. Bigger fish to fry. I couldn't have cared less about any of it. The meeting was worthless to me, so I didn't think about it. Instead, I thought about what Brückner had said. *But what was there to think about?* He'd done it, and that was that. *Did I think our situation would continue forever? In a word, yes!*

Don't walk in front of me… I may not follow. Don't walk behind me… I may not lead. Walk beside me… just be my friend. When I'd read that passage years ago it meant nothing, as most things I read at the time meant nothing. But with this particular passage, no longer, for now I realised that soon, *I'd* be walking alone. I will confess to you: at that moment, I hated Brückner for making me dependent on someone. But after a moment's reflection, I found that I hated myself instead for allowing myself to be dependent—willingly, even eagerly. Before Brückner, I was a hermetically sealed unit, needing no one, wanting no one. *But what would I do, now that the seal had been broken?* Aside from his occasional night adventures with Kempka, the Führer never appeared to depend on anyone, male or female—and he thrived. *But of course, that was the Führer, so how could an ordinary mortal (much less myself) hope to come within a light-year of his level of transcendence?* My brain was imploding.

After the rest had left, the Führer dropped heavily onto his tall, three-sided armchair, exposing himself only from the front. "Did you see them?" he asked, as usual, rhetorically. "Dunkirk is nothing, Linge. Less than nothing. They're all the same. No matter what I do, no matter how spectacular my achievements,

I'm still only a former corporal to them, only as good as my next error. And they consider my actions regarding Dunkirk to be just that.

"And yet," he continued, "I can't really blame them, since they couldn't possibly comprehend the full import of my strategy. A war commander must have imagination, audacity, and foresight. My strength lies in the fact that I can imagine the situations that the troops are called upon to face. And I can do that precisely because I've been an ordinary soldier myself. Thus, one acquires the rapid understanding of the appropriate steps to take in every kind of circumstance."

He'd said this countless times, so, what was he really telling me now that he wouldn't tell his highest-ranking subordinates?

"Even by their narrow, anachronistic, parade-ground standards," he continued, "these fools failed to grasp the simple fact that if we had destroyed the BEF, the empire would surely follow. As we neither wish to be, nor can be, its successor, I had to give them a chance to save their skins, territories, and whatever morale they still possessed. But as you know, even that motive was merely a politically diversionary tactic until I had in my actual possession the means for us to create my new world, the *real* Thousand-Year Reich—me, Linge," he shouted, "unrecognisable and invincible!"

I was completely out of my depth and just stood there, uneasily at ease.

Then he rose unsteadily, leaning over to prop himself on the tabletop with white-knuckled clenched fists. "I realise that I must sound obscure at best, deranged at worst. But I assure you that though, at this moment, you can't begin to see what I see, you are possessed of a unique sensibility. You can feel it in the deepest marrow of your bones, and as such, you will provide the means for me to cause the remarkable to occur."

Unique sensibility? A means for the remarkable to occur? What the Devil was he talking about? Morell again with his bizarre nostrums, I concluded. *He's poisoning the Führer! Driving him mad!* But since I could do nothing about it, I gladly obeyed the Führer's order and withdrew quickly, before he began speaking in tongues. Or I did.

My subordinate, Arnt, had to dress and prepare the Führer since, for most of the morning, I was held in the iron grip of the previous night's horror dream. Once again, I stood naked over my mother's mutilated body, but before last night, she'd always been merely screaming for me to kill her. This time, however, instead of the hideous screeching, she reached out with her skeletal arms covered in countless festering wounds and pulled me towards her with a force I could never have anticipated.

She whispered in my ear, "He who dares loses his footing for a while. He who dares not loses himself."

It was from the philosopher Søren Kierkegaard, a passage I'd read years after the dream's event, but could it have been my mother who spoke those words, a poor, ignorant, broken, desperate woman, a wretch who could have had no knowledge of Kierkegaard whatsoever? *What did it mean?* It plagued and perplexed me, and I could see, as never before, why the Führer was so reluctant to dismiss Dr. Bloch, his personal dream interpreter.

✒

This afternoon, I stood at ease, battered brain idling while the Führer entertained Himmler, Goebbels, von Ribbentrop, and von Rundstedt by repeating what he'd said to me about the qualities needed by a war commander, after which he added, "No offence intended, Rundstedt." To be frank, I was surprised, for it was the sort of pettiness I'd seldom seen the Führer employ—save on an enemy.

"None taken, my Führer," von Rundstedt replied without any vocal or facial expression.

I joked to myself that he had outdone even Himmler in that regard.

The Führer then rhapsodised about the news he'd just received that the British Royal Navy had destroyed the French fleet at an Algerian port. "You see?" he shouted, extending his hands outward, palms up. "Why should we attack the British, when they do our job for us? Those morons in the Admiralty just eliminated their opportunity to add to their battle fleet. Of course, I use this as only one example of how this ex-corporal can put to shame even the highest-ranking military men in the Reich. They all believed that Britain would be our most danger-ous foe and jeered behind my back at my naïveté. But today, I've demonstrated unmistakably that the stupid British are, despite themselves, virtually an ally. You see, gentlemen, how a true mil-itary leader must see beyond the obvious and create his strategy through inspiration, not by some hidebound military manual, obsolete even when written?"

Uniform and rank aside, I was as far removed from the military as a milkmaid, but even I wondered at the logic of the Führer's assessment. If the British couldn't have what was left of the French fleet, neither could Germany. I spent little time wondering why von Rundstedt had said nothing. Either he'd made the same assessment but dared not contradict the Führer's "insight," or he agreed with the Führer, so I was as naïve in mili-tary matters as I appeared to be in everything else. In either case, the entire issue was, to me, merely a welcome diversion.

∾

I didn't wish to speak to Brückner about the desolate and perilous future to which his decision to transfer would soon condemn
me. As for the rest of the world, I was happy to leave it in the
more-than-capable hands of the Führer. Consequently, I was sitting alone, drinking bitter coffee in the long, narrow, opulent
Marble Gallery. Unfortunately, solitude was an illusion.

"Hey, baldy, that your trash?" It was Rochus Misch, one
of the Führer's permanent bodyguards. A short, thick-necked,
solid, rough-and-tumble fellow, he had the coarse disposition
of a beer hall brawler and a nature so elemental that anything
one said was taken literally, if at all. Fortunately for me, over
the years, we'd arrived at an uneasy truce-like arrangement that
permitted some relatively harmless japes about our appearance,
humble origins, and lack of formal education.

"What trash, Quasimodo?"

At first his heavy eyelids narrowed, as if he actually knew
who the Hunchback of Notre Dame was, then he saw my smile.
"Yeah, uh, the scrunched-up paper at your big feet." He reached
down and brought it up with one hefty hand. "Maybe yours,
maybe not; might be important," he sneered, "and maybe just
shit, knowing you. Since you can't read so good, maybe I should
read it to you." He started to unravel it.

I made to grab it from him, but by then, he'd started reading it in his barely literate, halting, groping, word-by-word way.

"Uh, okay. 'My love'—hey, kid, it's from some pussy, or one
of your faggots—'I'm… desperate… to feel… your touch, to
be near you… again. Please… telephone me so we can be…
together. I will… wear that green dress you like so much to…
peel off me—as only you can, and well… afterwards, you know.'
There's some phone number written at the bottom." Then he
slapped the sheet on the table. "Shit, Linge!" he whooped. "Man,
you got some piece of ass crazy for you. Sure she don't look like

some mongrel? I can call her for you if you want—that is, if she don't speak Jew."

Where the letter came from and how it got to where Misch found it was beyond me, and explaining Emerald to Misch would be like explaining a Wittgenstein proposition to a simian. "Not everyone has your taste in women," I informed him, "or a free pass to where they work. Anyway, she's Aryan enough for me, so I'll muddle through on my own, thanks."

He shrugged. "Hey, okay, you hear this one? How did we conquer Poland so fast? We marched in backwards, and the Polacks thought we was leaving." He began cackling at the months-old joke known by all in the Chancellery. Grammar aside, at least it wasn't one of his excruciatingly vulgar sex jokes that made Kempka's sound like sermons.

"That's a good one," I said to humour the clod. "But since France just surrendered, you must have something juicy about the French?"

He nodded vigorously, his thick jowls bouncing up and down like balls tethered to a short rubber band. "Uh, you kidding? Listen to this one, okay? All right, now how many Frenchies does it take to shingle a roof? Three if you slice 'em thin enough." More self-satisfied guffaws followed.

I hadn't gotten that one at all. "That certainly captures the French," I answered, desperate to be rid of the brute. "Hey, didn't you say you were on your way somewhere?"

His eyes squinted in thought, and he scratched his chin, presumably for guidance. "I was just gonna go check my mail."

"You mean to tell me that you actually know people who can write?"

He jutted out his meagre lips. "Some. But since, aside from stuff like that shit on the table, you never get no mail, you can't say the same, huh?"

"You win," I conceded, just to be rid of his prole banter. "Go protect the Führer, eh?"

"From what, desert-dome? Nothing much up when the Führer's home."

"How about from you?"

Finally stumped, the dolt rose, saluted with all his fingers slightly bent, save the middle one, remaining up for my benefit, and marched off, leaving me with the note.

The migraine struck with a blitzkrieg the Wehrmacht would be proud of, and for a timeless time, pain, nausea, and a kaleidoscope of coloured lights blotted out my thoughts and my vision, but eventually, I pushed to the end. With trembling hands, I burned and flushed the shreds of the message, as I'd done with so many others since I'd begun my service at the Chancellery. But an internal voice whispered through the turbulence that somehow, this one was different.

5 *July 1940*

ONCE THE FÜHRER and I completed our morning ritual, he had me send for Dara and take the rest of the morning off, thus providing me an opportunity to contact Emerald and discover the true meaning behind her mysterious belated Valentine's Day message.

As usual, I sought out a relatively remote telephone kiosk and rang the number on the note.

One ring, a soft click, and the familiar melodious voice. "Hello, Heinz. I'm so glad you rang, and so quickly too. A good sign."

A good sign of what? I wondered but didn't ask.

"I imagine you're probably pressed," she continued, "so I'll not engage in meaningless pleasantries. Instead, I'll provide what my note couldn't. And if you allow me to do this without interruption, we'll have achieved economy, if nothing else. Agreed?"

Presumptuous and hardly in keeping with her note, but what could I do? "Agreed."

"Good. First, I would clear the table of some minor business. I must confess it troubled me that you neglected to save someone worth saving and, later, attempted to save someone unworthy of saving. Irony aside, and to place the most favourable interpretation on it, I assumed this to be merely a problem of sophistication, not of character. In this spirit, I reach out to you once more, not with a reproach but with an entreaty. A matter infinitely more momentous and graver than two lives, regardless of their relative worth, has come up. Your Führer has strived mightily to secure two objects that, in certain hands, can alter the world as we know it. Both in the same hands are essential. Selected individuals have been sent to retrieve them, but fortunately, not all answer blindly to the sender. Consequently, one of the objects came into my possession and, through me, to you. Make no mistake, the occult is no fantasy or myth, and the object is no toy or mere religious symbol. In the hands of the adept, it is a prodigious weapon, so whether or not you believe in such things, a demonic beast like Himmler and his insane instrument, Hitler, must forever be deprived of it. Heinz, only you can prevent a calamity of biblical proportions, so only in your possession and no one else's can it do no harm. Again, I assure you that more is at stake than you could possibly imagine. I'm quite confident that a gentleman with moral character, many secrets, and maturing enlightenment such as yourself knows of a place where the item can be safely sequestered. However, I would be criminally remiss if I didn't caution you that others with as much at stake may begin to speculate about its possessor. Finally, I implore you to take what I've just said with utmost seriousness—even if you believe that the things I've told you are insane ravings. Now you should go since I see a sizeable line forming behind you."

A click, and she was gone. It was like listening to a recorded message from a madhouse. Keeping the receiver to my ear, despite the incessant dial tone, I turned my head to see the resigned queue of uniforms I outranked and suits I terrified. I, too, was resigned and terrified. *How did she know about the queue?* I wanted to ask her what she would have done if I weren't the one who called, since I might not be the only one privy to the note, but I was sure she would say that she never assumed I would be and that anyone else would have reached a bogus clerk in a nonexistent bookstore or the like. *More important, where was the item she mentioned?* She spoke as if I might already have it, but if so, I was unaware of it. I replaced the receiver, swung open the door with haughty entitlement, and headed back to the Chancellery, shaking my head in perplexity.

AFTER GAGGING MY guts out in the sink, I knew it wasn't a dream of drowning that erupted me awake but something large stuck in my throat! With extreme, purple-faced labour, I spewed it out along with the residue of last night's dinner and pent-up phlegm. I couldn't bear to look at the filth, so I turned my head and fumbled with one hand until I found it in the drain.

Without looking, I had a fair idea of what it was but not how it ended up where it had. I never realised until now that I slept with my mouth open and that it had become just another slot under my door. How the deliverer got in and made his—or her—delivery was a mystery I knew I would never solve, so I devoted no time to it.

With a drunkard's theatrical caution, I moved back to my cot, eased myself down, took in a few deep, painful breaths, attained focus, and brought the object up to my face. Like the "toy" the Führer had told me about, it was a four-sided top with what I assumed were Hebrew characters embossed on each side. I'd seen ones like them before as a youth, in the homes of Jews who'd shown compassion and a "nosh" to a starving gentile street urchin by exposing him to alien cuisine and incomprehensible chants. But if Emerald is to be believed, this one is different in the extreme. If she is to be believed. *But do I believe it, or rather, is it believable?* Two quite different questions. Nietzsche wrote that "a casual stroll through the lunatic asylum shows that [belief] does not prove anything." On the other hand, Pascal wrote that "Belief is a wise wager. Granted that faith cannot be proved, what harm will come to you if you gamble on its truth and it proves false? If you gain, you gain all; if you lose, you lose nothing." As for Goethe, perhaps a middle ground: "Man is made by his belief. As he believes, so he is." Then to this I must ask: What am I made of?

I attempted to shove that conundrum aside by busying myself with preparing for the Führerbuzzer, but all it did was shove Emerald's words back at me: *The Führer, the "insane instrument" of a "demonic beast"? A Jewish religious toy that "can alter the world as we know it"? Was I supposed to believe, much less act on, such utter poppycock?* For a brief, unbalanced moment, I wondered how she'd known about Adelsheimer, Dvora, Himmler, the Führer, Brückner, and especially my history, but I forced myself to let it go, as I had done with all the other dangerously intimate fragments of knowledge about me she'd displayed since we first met on that fateful New Year's Eve. It also struck me that in referring to my assistance for Dvora, Brückner had claimed there was no more significant resistance within the Reich. And yet there was Emerald with her apparently unlimited access to me, as well as her desultory warnings, advice, and requests over the years. *So, was there an active resistance movement of which even Brückner was unaware, or was there merely Emerald?*

Jung wrote that "the pendulum of the mind oscillates between sense and nonsense, not between right and wrong." Since we met, Emerald had strived to poison my mind against the Führer: his evil nature, his depraved attitudes, his vicious acts, and now, his insanity in the service of another's diabolical intent. I refuse to believe any of this. I think I know the Führer as no one else, even Fräulein Braun, and I tell you that Emerald's Führer is certainly not mine. *And the craziness about the supernatural power*

of a toy? Was she insane? And yet, and yet… I had no idea what position Jung's pendulum assumed for me at that moment, but regardless of my belief or disbelief in Emerald's claims, whether sense or nonsense, against all I just said, I decided to do what she asked of me and send the top along with you.

I HAD THE morning off since the Führer was enveloped in a storm cloud of rage and refused to be tended to, even by me. He cancelled all his appointments and remained sequestered in his quarters with this mysterious chap Weisthor. Even Morell was forbidden to enter. From the hallway, not to mention his anteroom, all who passed could hear him screaming inscrutabilities at the top of his lungs. His screaming was so intense that I could only make out occasional phrases: "Catastrophic failure!" "Transformation aborted!" and the like. Whether this Weisthor was responding or hiding under the Führer's desk, I had no way of knowing, but for his sake, I hoped it was the latter.

All my attempts to avoid being alone with Brückner to condition myself to his absence were failing, for I seemed to lack the discipline or perhaps the desire even to accept it, much less endure it.

"When are you scheduled to leave?" I asked him as we hid in plain sight at a Café Schilling sidewalk table.

"Not for a while, if I'm any judge of bureaucracy," he said, "but soon, I should think. Bormann's not the most patient enemy."

I strained not to look as I felt, then strained not to look as if I were straining. "Do you know where?"

"Not yet. Of course, I'm hoping for Paris, but you never know the extent of Bormann's vindictiveness and reach. It wouldn't surprise me if I ended up running a KZ like Höss. Unfortunately, unlike Höss, I wasn't born to it."

"Perhaps you'll be sent to a fighting unit somewhere," I ventured in jest.

He snorted. "Possibly. I've heard that the Wehrmacht is desperate for old men with one eye. Decoys, I believe they're called."

I laughed heartily at this. "I think I'll miss your humour even more than your advice."

He reached up and patted me on my shoulder board. "Don't fret, Heinz. As I told you, I'll be no farther away than a telephone and that famously secret space below your door. And of course, we can visit each other from time to time. So, let's speak of other things, yes?"

"All right," I said, "then what about Schroeder? I can't keep putting her off."

"Ah, yes. Schroeder." He gave a resigned sigh and nodded. "You have me feeling as if I'm abandoning you to the real world. You take everything far too seriously, my friend. With all the real problems we face, I'd hoped you might have developed some perspective on the illusory ones. But I embarrass you," he said, watching my face blossom. "Well, be that as it may, I think I might have a solution. By all means, satisfy Schroeder, but nip it in the bud."

"Nip what in the bud?" I asked, befuddled once more by Brückner's serpentine manner of reaching his point.

"Make the first date your last. Show her your worst side, even if you must manufacture it. Then she'll run and tell her aunt that you were a horrible, nasty lout, which she already believes, and that will be that. You'll never see her again. Schroeder will blame you, which is natural with her and is your goal, after all, and never bother you again with unwanted matchmaking—or anything else, I daresay."

I nodded a vigorous assent. "Yes, Wilhelm, that's just the ticket."

"And one day, you'll figure such things out on your own, and I'll be just one more dead sage."

"Not dead," I answered shakily, "just retired."

"Even better for me," he said.

I WAS SUMMONED in the small hours to prepare the Führer for a "momentous day," as he called it. "Today, we teach the obstinate British a thing or two. Up to now, we've played military patty-cake," he said, clearly (to me at least) using the term to indicate a soft approach rather than referring to the actual conduct of the game, "but today, Linge, they'll face grown-ups."

He chortled at his comparison, I gave the expected "Of course, my Führer," and that was that, until "His Corpulence" arrived, medals clanging, bloated face florid with anticipation, and plopped with a grunt into an armchair that also grunted. I began dusting the immaculate bookshelves.

"Are all parts of 'Sea Lion' in place?" the Führer asked Göring.

"Of course, my Führer," he answered with exuberance. "We went over all this days ago, and nothing has changed, save for the impatience of my pilots."

"Impatience, you say? Like Thoroughbred horses at the starting gate, eh? Well, Hermann, today the gate opens, and the race begins. Coordinate with Jodl and Raeder."

"Yes, my Führer," Göring said. "Anything further?"

He started to pull his bulk up by his short, pudgy arms, when the Führer said, "And, Hermann, make it quick, eh? Britain can still come to its senses, so we must pummel them into seeing reason. We'll need their silence if not their support for what comes next."

Göring continued his bulky trip up to full height. "They won't know what hit them, my Führer," he proclaimed, saluted, and waddled out.

The Führer sat for a moment in silence, then, as I turned to face him, he said, "Won't know what hit them, eh, Linge?" He sighed loudly. "Hermann means well, but even after so many years, he still doesn't know me. I *want* the British to know what hit them," he announced in his oratorical voice, "and *who* hit them!"

Of course he did, I thought. In the Führer's mind, any "them" only had meaning to the extent that he was involved. A quote from Frederick the Great came to mind: "There are only two great men in the world. The other is the one I am with, but only while I am with him."

The Führer didn't have Frederick's portrait in his study for nothing.

THE FÜHRER HAD mellowed to the point where he was virtually placid. His toilette went quite smoothly, and he dressed with more than his usual methodical alacrity, beating his top record by four whole seconds. Once prepared, and not without some small pharmaceutical assistance from Morell, the Führer had a reasonably fruitful—if not exactly soundless and odourless—bowel movement and was ready to greet Himmler.

Against custom, and taking Brückner's advice to become "more involved in the processes round me," as he put it, when I was dismissed before the meeting commenced, I stood casually by the anteroom door, in plain view of a seemingly blind Herr Chinless, where I could hear the Reichsführer-SS assuring his chief that "One will most assuredly be retrieved," that "It was regrettable that the traitor Koch had managed to keep his own counsel despite General Heydrich's best efforts, but has been amply... rewarded for his foolish steadfastness," and that "So long as one is in your control and the key remains safe and close at hand, you might still be able to accomplish your sacred mission, even without the other."

After that, I was unable to hear more than the Führer's hideously shrieking response. "MIGHT STILL! MIGHT STILL! ARE YOU SO DIM, HEINRICH, AS TO CLAIM THAT I WOULD SETTLE FOR THE EQUIVALENT OF MOST OF ETERNITY! WHICH IS WHAT, HEINRICH? WHAT, EXACTLY!"

Because "Herr Chinless" (who appeared to be deaf as well) now glanced at me with hooded lids, I needed to leave before he slobbered any syllables about what I was doing standing by the door with my ear pressed to it.

Did Himmler cower and make a hasty withdrawal as I would have? Did he attempt to mollify with an acceptable interpretation of his obviously ill-chosen language? As for me, after reading Emerald's message, I had a reasonably good idea about what the "it" was. *But what and where was the "key"?* I only hoped that Brückner would be proud of my new "involvement."

❧

I arranged to apply Brückner's advice regarding Schroeder and her blasted niece tonight. Leaving a message at five in the afternoon with an older woman who'd answered, I told her in a voice laced with imperious incivility that I would be arriving at her door that very evening at six and that she'd better be ready. Rehearsing my archvillain's role several times before my bathroom mirror, I finally convinced myself that my performance would cause even Simon Legree to run for his life.

Unshaven, sweat-coated, attired in a carefully soiled uniform, and with what little hair I still had made greasy and dishevelled, I arrived at the floor that contained her flat, with utter disregard for our prearranged time, prepared to deliver a ruthless arsenal of insults. But when I rounded the corner and got to her door, it was already open. She stood there, and all Brückner's advice and my preparations made a beeline for the toilet.

It was as if she had floated off a movie screen and alighted in the doorway. I'd seen many female movie queens since beginning service: visiting for the Führer's pride and amusement, Hoffmann's photo opportunities, and Goebbels's advertisements. But none of them came close to what stared at me with a knitted brow: a cinema star's portrayal of a concerned love god-dess—tall, thin, and robust all at once, with a fascinating face that exuded character. Altogether, she was an amalgam of elegant wholesomeness that made Dvora seem just a better rendering of the dry ice queens at Salon Kitty.

Her knitted brow shifted to a look of alarm. "My God, were you in an accident on your way here? Shall I ring for a doctor?" Belying her über-Aryan appearance was her voice, which sounded as if it issued from an Eastern European with a stuffy nose.

I strained to make out her words, then shook my head to tell her a physician wasn't necessary.

"Aunt Christa told me I'd be amused by your appearance, but I'm not sure she meant this."

At least that was what I thought Klara said. I glanced down at my scuffed and mud-encrusted boots. "I'm… not always… like this," I stammered to the floor. Then I looked back up when there was no response. "I said that I'm not—"

"Please come in," she offered. "I should explain."

She moved aside, and I entered, mortified at my appearance since I'd already determined to jettison my original strategy.

With a gentle wave, she motioned me to a shabby couch, and I sat to the accompanying twang of a spring. "If you don't need a doctor, can I at least get you something to drink?"

I adjusted my backside between two faded-velvet hillocks. "Yes," I answered haltingly through a cough, still under the spell of her features, "whatever you have will be fine."

"I asked what would you like," she repeated.

"I said whatever you have."

"If you can stand my couch and my taste in drinks, you're marvellously easy to satisfy," she said with a dazzling smile. "I'll be right back." With subtle feminine grace, she turned and went into her kitchen through a swinging door.

I sat on that miserable sofa, struggling to be as easy to satisfy as she'd remarked. To be frank, I didn't know what to make of her. Between her appearance and her cloudy speech was a puzzling chasm I was determined to leap, despite her connexion to Schroeder—to whom she bore no discernible resemblance. Since she hadn't connected my appearance to my scheme, and I was sure I would adjust to her odd vocalisation, I was content to let the whole matter disappear.

Her living room was small and spare, with furniture that bore the same venerable tattiness as her sofa. On the dreary walls hung a few nondescript pastoral scenes and one portrait of the standing Führer, resplendent in his brown martial uniform, jodhpurs, boots, and cape, one hand in his pocket, the other holding his cap. All very Napoleonic; all very Knirr.[32]

I'd been present when Knirr was working on that very portrait, the Führer jesting that if he'd had the same recognition from the Vienna Academy of Fine Arts, he might be painting portraits instead of posing for them, and Knirr replying that Vienna's loss was the world's gain. The Führer merely nodded in sardonic agreement.

"I hope you like Riesling." Klara pushed her way out of the kitchen backwards, carrying a tray with two filled glasses and an ornate bottle. "I don't know much about wine, so I thought this would be safe."

I smiled. "You'd be astounded by the dangerous drinks I've had. It'll be nice to be safe for once."

She laughed lightly and, from her expression, more from politeness than understanding, as she set the tray down on the

---

[32] Heinrich Knirr was an Austrian-born German painter, reknowned for his genre scenes and portraits. He is best known for creating the official portrait of Adolf Hitler and is the only artist known to have painted Hitler from life.

side table, handed me a glass, took the other, and sat primly in the tired armchair before me. "I was quite concerned when I first saw you; are you sure you're all right?"

"Nothing to worry about," I assured her. "Just a friendly fracas at a beer hall. I probably should have rung you with an apology and set another time."

"Not at all," she said. "I'm just relieved you're all right, and…"

"And what?"

"I know I shouldn't say this, but I'm glad you didn't call."

While I was gratified hearing that, I suddenly became overwhelmingly self-conscious. I leaned over to put my drink on the table. "May I use your bathroom?"

When she said nothing, I leaned back to face her. "I must look like the victim of a Gestapo interrogation. May I use your bathroom to try cleaning up a bit?" The chasm was filling in.

"To me you look fine," she said, "but if you'll feel better, it's to your left down the hall. First door on the right."

When I finally emerged from the hallway, her back was to me.

"I'm not sure it's much of an improvement," I said, "but at least I'm cleaner."

When she didn't turn her head to face me, it confirmed what I'd only suspected. I sat on the sofa again, reached for my drink, and brought it back, this time without leaning over.

"Thank you," she said.

I knew what she meant, but I wanted her to say it. "You see," I told her. "I really must have looked awful."

A sad smile. "I was going to tell you as soon as you came in, but I was afraid you'd leave. I apologise for my cowardice at the door."

She'd said enough. "I'd guessed before I went to the bath-room, and I'm still here."

Her bright-blue eyes began to glisten. "Shall we drink to something?"

"Yes, by all means." I raised my glass. "To your Aunt Christa." I leaned forward, and our glasses clinked. I was sad that she couldn't hear it.

A NUMBING PARADE-REST morning for me since the Führer had suddenly determined to go beyond a mere air war and "crush" Great Britain, as he put it, and so spent the entire morning conferring with Luftwaffe Chief Göring, Grand Admiral Raeder, and the OKW Chief of Staff Jodl.

However, to my poor brain, despite the bombast, the Führer still appeared to be of two minds towards the British since he also told both military leaders that once the Luftwaffe had total control of the air and the British economy had been sufficiently weakened, an invasion would be a "last resort," should England stubbornly refuse to face reality.

Then he told Göring to issue an operational directive: to "destroy the RAF in such a sweeping and brutal fashion that the British will have no recourse but to capitulate. I would then be prepared to exercise the utmost magnanimity," the Führer told them. "Perhaps I'm softhearted—or softheaded," he stated in obvious jest, "but I still believe that one day, our two Aryan nations will stand together as allies."

Crush the British, spare the British, stand together, sit together, lie together, how should I react as Brückner's newly interested novice? I didn't know the British and the issues involved were for a genius like the Führer and his top military minds to comprehend, not a lowly, self-taught valet who had never seen war or even fired a gun. *What could someone like me think about that would have any meaning?* So I didn't think about it. Instead, as

I stood there, furtively shifting my weight from one numb foot to the other, I thought only about my marvellous evening with Klara—marvellous not just due to the collapse of my mean-spirited expectations. I had to confess a high jubilance over the turn of events.

However, when I considered thanking Schroeder, a troubling sensation enshrouded my joy like a coat of ugly paint, and several questions were visible underneath like an insistent pentimento: *Why did someone with such animus towards me take it on herself to be a matchmaker? Why didn't she tell me of Klara's condition? How did she know that once confronted with the fact of her disability, I would succumb to the "better angels" of my nature?* All these questions added up to one common denominator: *Had one Dvora been substituted by another?*

I needed time and privacy to consider all this and, I hoped, the opportunity to confer with Brückner, perhaps for the last time. So I was gratified when, finally, the Führer had done with Göring and Jodl and excused me till evening. But time seemed to be just beyond my reach, for after leaving, I careened into Kempka, who was answering the Führer's summons. Despite mutual apologies and comradely shoulder-smacking, my need to escape also appeared to bump into his need to chat.

"Just been gabbing with the boss?"

Why else would I be in the Führer's anteroom? Romancing Herr Chinless? "Not so you'd notice," I told him. "He was gabbing with Göring, Raeder, and von Below all morning. The RAF thing."

"Yeah, well, more than gabbing, too, you bet. Big stuff happening. But then there's always something big happening, now that he's finally on the move. Like an engine, you know: idle too long, and it overheats; go too slow, and it stalls."

He was beaming over his analogy and deserved some

confirmation. "Not a doubt in the world. Like an engine. Right on the money. Hey, Erich, I don't want to keep you. When you get the boss's call, you don't want to stall."

He pursed his lips, as if he had to actually think about it, then cackled. "Hey, that rhymes. But don't sweat it. I've kept him waiting before. He knows that when I have to be on schedule, there I am, and all gassed up." Then he tilted his head forward and cupped one hand round the corner of his mouth with theatrical stealth. "Hey, I'm hearing you don't need Baur's famous Black Book anymore. Come on, tell your old chum who she is and how she outranks his posh stable and Kitty's best."

That discussion was all I needed. *How did he even know the little he would know?* "Not outranked, Erich, just fewer miles and cheaper on upkeep," I joked back, hoping to settle the matter and move on. I failed.

"Well, who the fuck is this low-maintenance, almost-new cheapie?" he demanded jocularly. "You can tell your Uncle Erich. Your big-ass secret's safe with me."

Big secret. Safe with him. In my brain, I almost burst a gut over that one. "It's no secret, Uncle. Just a waitress. No big deal. Cute but scatterbrained, which is good. So I can keep up. Her name's Clotilde.[33]

He nodded with melodramatic solicitude. "Good for you, lad. If she's that cute, when you've had enough, toss her my way. For my book, you know. Her brain's unimportant."

"Consider it done." I gave a toothy smile of enthusiasm.

"Right," he said dismissively, as if even he'd gotten sick of the subject. "But if you're waiting for things to quiet down, you might as well go into one of them monasteries. History is being

---

[33] Meaning "famous battle" in Old High German.

made from here, and it don't look like the boss'll be done making it for some time to come. Just yesterday, the boss, Hans, and I were chatting it up about the poor fucking little RAF that'll have to face our Luftwaffe. He was so up about it, he told me that the destruction of the British air corps was only the beginning, a 'puny training exercise,' according to Göring. Not for me to ask where they were heading next, but you can bet… Hey, what am I saying? You wipe his arse; you'll know that before me. But I gotta tell you what Hans told me, that he was happy Göring don't intend to actually take a pilot's job, even in a 'puny training exercise,' 'cause with all that fat and those medals, his plane wouldn't even lift off."

Vulgarity aside, we both chortled at the obvious imagery, and I made another escape attempt. "Well, by now," I said, "the… boss has to be wondering what's keeping you, and I sure don't want to be the reason." Many of the Führer's "inner circle" referred to him as "the boss," affectionately, of course, but I would never resort to anything that colloquial and, to be frank, chummy. The Führer was many things to me, but never a chum—or a boss. But with this one lapse, perhaps my release was in sight.

"Yep, you're right," he admitted, "and when you're right, you're right." He gave me a farewell clap on the shoulder and went on his merry way.

You have to love Kempka.

AN UNEVENTFUL MORNING but for the reverberations from yesterday that led to hours of dictation to Schroeder and Dara. I must confess to becoming unnerved by the former's glances. I knew she was determined to elicit a report from me on Klara, but I was no less determined to put that off until I had spoken with Brückner. Unfortunately, she was so adept at her job that, even in the Führer's presence, she could stare at me while taking shorthand or typing, so I was subtly ecstatic when the Führer finally dismissed me.

Later, on my way to retrieve the Führer's mail, I observed Brückner having an animated conversation with Schaub, von Below,[34] and Peiper.[35] I knew I needed to wait for a more private moment with Brückner and was about to continue on, but von Below spotted me and motioned me over with a patronising wag of his hand. I quite enjoyed such brazenly instinctive displays

---

[34] Nicholaus von Below joined the German Air Force and became Hitler's Air Force military adjutant in 1937. Below's task was to serve as the link between Hitler and the Air Force leadership. Hitler generally disliked and was suspicious of soldiers with aristocratic backgrounds, but the clever Below was so unassuming and deferential to him that he became an exception.

[35] Joachim Peiper was a field officer in the Waffen-SS during World War II and served as the personal adjutant to Reichsführer-SS Heinrich Himmler between November 1940 and August 1941.

of class and intellectual snobbery, as they served to reinforce my cultivated image of a commoner with narrow competence and even narrower intellect. Schaub, an oaf who looked like a butcher's helper—and spoke like one—treated me as a flunky who, by my situation, had far too much access to the Führer—a Bormann without Bormann's ambition or intelligence. Peiper was a methodical nonentity whom I knew only as a favourite of Himmler (not entirely surprising). He accompanied his boss (or Heydrich) on all KZ inspections. He wasn't one to talk business, save for one time in 1938, when he related to Brückner, in my ignored presence, that he had witnessed the gassing of a resident of a psychiatric facility in Poland. He described the experience in a disturbingly detached, unadorned manner, only adding a personal note when he remarked, in the tone of an engineer describing a machine's exact tolerances, that gassing was a "wonderfully clean and efficient killing tool."

"You should join us, Linge," von Below said as I arrived, "unless you think you're perhaps too good for the likes of us?" A piss-poor jape but insulated from rejoinder.

"Herr von Below," I responded, "it was completely the opposite. I'm gratified even to be asked."

"No need to grovel, Linge," he said. "We all serve the Führer to the best of our abilities, do we not? In any case, the three of us were merely enjoying a comradely discussion about what I consider to be Churchill's rather puzzling attitude towards the Führer. Of course, you recall that in a speech to the Reichstag in early November 1938, the Führer attacked Churchill and others who had objected to the Munich Pact by name, describing them as 'warmongers.'"

The arrogant asshole was more generous with my memory than he knew, for I recalled every syllable. *Keep swatting me with your riding crop, you swine. I don't mind thinking back to the Führer's mock-chiding lecture to me about being "below the salt."*

"Ah yes, my friends, but in his reaction, now listen," Peiper added while unfolding a slip of paper with some scribble on it. "This same Churchill responded in the House of Commons, that if Great Britain were defeated in war, he hoped they would find a Hitler to lead them back to their 'rightful position among the nations.' So you can see why even the Führer is perplexed when it comes to that lunatic asylum."

Brückner managed a furtive glance at me, and I returned it, for we both knew there was a bit more to Churchill's speech, though only I would remember his exact words.

"This, unfortunately," Brückner said with the utmost discretion, lifting his shoulder towards his head and then down again, "may tell us more about Churchill's state of mind in 1938 than about the Führer's today. To me, it's reasonably certain that Churchill's views have altered somewhat and that the Führer, no less a master of realism and adjustment, has reluctantly accepted this and based his decision upon that acceptance."

The others gravely nodded their accord.

Only Peiper added that it was, to him, "a great pity that true Aryans like the British cannot seem to make common cause with Germany."

Again, grave nods of accord.

Common cause? I wondered. *What cause?*

Brückner must have sensed my discomfort, for he then excused us by wittily invoking the Führer's directive concerning the "critical importance of Chancellery mailmen." With me modestly seconding the motion, we set out, only diverting at the last moment for the gardens. We spoke as we walked for the sake of time and appearance. But before I had the opportunity to bring up my matter, Brückner ended my earlier wonderings.

"You know, Heinz," he said, "it's not as if those idiots hadn't read *Mein Kampf* or at least flipped through its pages. But you'd never know it, listening to them—or perhaps they didn't wish to recognise the obvious implications."

Obvious implications? I remembered every word from my SS training but understood little, couldn't have cared less, and never bothered to revisit it. "What implications, Wilhelm?"

"You too? Doesn't anyone actually read about the Führer's intentions? In that book—printed and sold round the world, I might add—he continually obsesses over only one enemy. He does so passionately, and believe me, it's not Britain or France. It certainly isn't those nothings like Czechoslovakia and Poland—or those laughable Low Countries," he added with a derisive snort. "It's not even the Jews, though God knows, you'd think so, to hear Himmler, Goebbels, and Heydrich tell it. They don't want to face the fact that the Führer's 'common cause' is the Soviet Union. Think about it, Heinz: a calculating, brutal, autocratic, paranoid megalomaniac at the helm, a nation of Slavs, and a loathsome, treacherous ideology. It even has Jews for Goebbels and the Two Hs to drool over. So, it doesn't take a genius to figure out the true threat."

The image of the Two Hs drooling was beyond my poor powers of imagination, but when he said that, all the bellicose rhetoric the Führer had been spewing in those private conversations I'd overheard through my five years of service but tucked away into the furthest recesses of my brain now elbowed its way onto centre stage. Genius or no genius, I cared nothing for this subject, preferring to leave such weighty matters to the Führer. I needed Brückner for only one thing, but I could see that I would have to humour him until he ran out of petrol.

"You think he will?"

"What?"

"Attack the Soviet Union?"

"I'd guess he's aching to, but they're an ally, so he's stymied. Thank God." He shook his head.

"'Thank God?' Why?"

"Think about it, Heinz. Think about it as if you were a military strategist. Considering the staggering amount of human cannon fodder Stalin can throw at us, not to mention the vast distances and inhospitable climate, we're far better off concentrating our energies west and south, not east, wouldn't you agree?"

"But do you think the Führer feels that way?"

"To be frank, I don't know what the Führer thinks. I don't believe anyone does. All I know is that I hope he doesn't take *Mein Kampf* as seriously as the rest of Germany."

"What you say makes sense. But if you feel so strongly about it, perhaps you should tell the Führer."

He laughed so hard that passersby turned their heads. Then he puffed some air from his nose. "As a parting gift? Heinz, do you think I would give bad news to the Führer? If I did, I'd quickly be wearing two patches. Believe me, the Führer already knows this but chooses to be the ostrich—and I won't be the one to pull his head from the sand. Let Göring, Himmler, and Goebbels risk their necks. But they won't, and Bormann even less, of that I can assure you."

I was compelled to agree, for I'd seen this about the Führer. Brückner was like an infallible barometer. He predicted a storm but knew that the Führer would still dress for the beach, certain of the sun. No rain would spoil his sunbathing. I nodded slowly with a mortician's solemnity, outdoing, I believed, even Schaub, von Below, and Peiper.

"I'm sure you're right," I admitted. "Russia holds no great allure for me." With that, I hoped to finally get my matter onto the table. "So, I say, why not aim our heads for the nearest sand dune and move on to another subject?"

Brückner nodded. "Anything in particular?" he asked with his I-already-know smirk.

"Well, I never had the opportunity to tell you about my evening with Schroeder's 'match.'"

Brückner's eye widened slightly. "True. I've been waiting to hear of your escapade with… ah…"

"Klara."

"Yes. Klara. I trust she was sufficiently impressed with your performance, so no more meddling from Schroeder."

"She's deaf," I blurted. I don't know why I said that first, because it didn't seem to matter when I was with her, and I certainly didn't wish her condition to define her. And yet I said it first.

Brückner's eye widened further. "Intriguing. I suppose Auntie omitted that fascinating fact when telling you about her."

"Actually," I admitted, "she omitted everything, merely saying that I should make up my own mind about her without prejudgement."

"Admirable," he replied, with a slight whiff of sarcasm that implied it was more clever than admirable. "Then I imagine that forced you to revise your script on the spot."

"More than that, Wilhelm. I found her to be lovely, humble, funny, interesting—and genuine. In fact, everything Schroeder isn't."

"Go on," he prodded, motioning forward with his head.

"I'd done all the physical preparations, arrived outrageously early, and had myself worked up into a virtual frenzy of mean-spiritedness, but—"

"You saw her beauty, discovered her infirmity, and became a balding puppy dog, am I right?"

"I'm no Heydrich, if that's what you mean."

Brückner erupted into laughter that took a few seconds to subside. "Yes," he choked out, still laughing, "you're no Heydrich. In fact, you're far too generous by half for your surroundings. What I like most about you may one day be your undoing."

"Should I tell the Führer?"

An odd look flitted across his face, then vanished along with any answer to my question. "I'm truly glad that your concerns about her were unfounded. My congratulations and best wishes. I mean it."

"Thank you, Wilhelm," I said, hoping my tone would counter the cliché. "I know you do."

"I assume she finds the same traits in you," he kidded, "except the lovely part of course. I wonder how *her* report to Schroeder will sound. Do I get to meet this prize before I go?"

"Of course," I exclaimed, not expecting his question. "I'll arrange for the three of us to meet, perhaps at a decent restaurant, to celebrate my good fortune."

"It will be my treat," he said, "since it's my good fortune as well."

AFTER SORTING THE Führer's mail, I spent most of the morning in idleness while the Führer dictated his next day's speech to Wolfin,[36] who had just returned from another extended sick leave. I was almost dizzy with relief that it wasn't Schroeder, as I would have had to plan an escape from the inevitable interrogation about my evening with Klara. I didn't know what, if anything, Schroeder had been told, but I desperately wanted a clean and clear separation between my discovery and its source.

I was present with the Führer and Wolf just long enough to catch the drift of his desire. After Brückner's schoolroom lecture about Stalin and the cost of a two-front war, I was not at all surprised that the Führer was prepared to settle for an arrangement which would give him complete control over Continental Europe, in return for which, he would acquiesce to Britain's overseas interests, with her Empire guaranteed by her Navy. His closing phrase was that he considered it "a last appeal to reason."

The Führer was so absorbed in his dictation that I could depart without any unwanted attention from Wolf and make an early journey to the Officers' Dining Room, where I sat at the

---

[36] Johanna Wolf, Hitler's senior secretary, was one of his oldest and longest-tenured secretaries. While he addressed his other secretaries formally as "Frau" or "Fräulein," he called her "Wölfin," meaning "she-wolf," because of his obsession with wolves and because of his affectionate regard for her unwavering loyalty, despite numerous debilitating illnesses that often kept her away for great lengths of time.

long rectangular table with only my thoughts. I still hadn't dealt with the Dvora matter, and rather than indulge in the pleasant fantasy that ignoring it would suffice, I resolved to discuss the situation with the Führer once he'd sorted out the British matter. I'd just started to consider how to arrange the dinner with Brückner and Klara when Heydrich came from behind and eased himself into the seat opposite me.

"You don't mind me joining you, Linge," Heydrich said.

Not a question, but I treated it as one. "Quite the contrary, General, I'm most honoured."

That infamous slit of a smile quickly appeared and vanished just as quickly. "You flatter me, Linge. No rank here, though; just two servants of the Reich having an unexpected chat."

I nodded exuberantly in assent, though I believed him not for an instant. I had nothing to say, so I waited for his reason to emerge in his own good time.

"I've just been with the Führer. It seems you've finally found some suitable female companionship. I congratulate you."

Schroeder must have told the Führer, and both had omitted to inform me. My brain felt like a brick being struck repeatedly by a chisel. I hoped he couldn't see the distress on my face. "Suitable, Herr General?" was all I could say to get him to elaborate. It was all I needed.

"Yes, suitable. It's not easy to be the romantic companion of someone in your exclusive position."

Was he referring to Klara innocently, or to Dvora not so innocently? "Hardly exclusive, Herr General," I corrected with gentle humility.

"Not so," Heydrich countered, "but I wouldn't expect you to agree. That's obviously what charmed the lady."

I noted that he'd sidestepped my question with his usual silky adroitness and, apparently, had no desire to pursue the matter.

"I just met her," I answered.

He smiled again, as if to let me know that he planned to let Dvora slip through the net. "Well, Linge, actually I wasn't here to see the Führer. That's my boss's job. I'm here to continue our investigation into the… disappearance of one of our security officers seconded to the Chancellery. Hauptsturmführer Horst Schlegl. I believe you knew him."

Knew him? That was months ago. Why was he mentioning it now, as if it had happened only days ago? And why was someone on his level investigating such a mundane matter? "Yes, we encountered each other on several occasions, mostly passing in the course of our duties, and we shared a few lunchtimes with some of his subordinates. That's the extent of it. We weren't friends, and I knew little about him outside the Chancellery." In my anxiety and the pounding in my skull, I probably said more than I should have done, so I resolved to be far less voluble.

"Yes, I know," Heydrich confirmed. "Actually, not a disappearance," he corrected himself, as I suspected he would. "It was treated as such at first, but then his body was discovered in an alleyway."

I tried to display shock but didn't feel particularly convincing, though Heydrich's expression hadn't changed. "What happ… what… how?" I stammered to reinforce my expression.

"He was beaten to death," he declared. "Roundly, I might add. Little of his face remained, and the rest of him didn't fare much better. Given Schlegl's girth and training, whoever did it was quite accomplished—or quite desperate."

The fiend always saves the best for last. "Well then," I ventured, "it could have been more than one assailant."

He took a deep breath and let it out slowly. "No, Linge, I don't think so. All the bruises were of a similar sort, and my instinct advises me that it was one very large and determined individual, judging by the clumsy ferocity of it. Unfortunately, it had been raining at the time, so blood and the like would have been diluted and washed away."

I didn't reply, waiting for his next gleaming boot to drop.

"But don't look so glum, my friend," the general said. "It's not as if he mattered—to you or to us. But he was SS, so we must investigate. In fact, we do have something—perhaps more. I believe it's safe to assume that the two combatants must have known each other. The men who discovered the body also found a collar patch that must have been torn off in the struggle. It couldn't have been the victim's, as he was wearing civilian attire. So, we know the perpetrator was a uniformed man. And not only that, an SS man, and a lieutenant colonel in the Führer's personal guard at that... like you, Linge." After a sadistically pregnant moment, he chuckled. "I jest, of course."

Of course. The other boot had dropped, and I strained to concentrate while the pounding in my skull and the nausea were joined by coloured lights that flashed round Heydrich's head like a halo made of shooting stars. Words were out of the question.

"You don't look at all well," Heydrich observed after a few moments. "You're picturing the incident, I can tell. I'm afraid that with your high degree of sensitivity, you'd make a poor policeman. We deal with such things every day—and many far worse than that."

After my guided tour of his cellar, I hardly needed reminding.

"Well, then, I'll take my leave." He started to rise but resettled himself. "Oh yes, not only the collar tab. I logically assumed that his entire uniform, not to mention his face, must have borne not a few marks of frenzied combat in the rain. So, we need only check to see if anyone with that untidy appearance returned to the Chancellery that night or later, question him with practised vigour, and we have our man." He smiled again, this time more broadly, displaying a slender line of perfect white teeth, and he rose slowly. "No need to stand." His palms waved me down. "Just two servants of the Führer having a friendly chat." With that, he donned his cap, saluted smartly, and walked away.

Returned to the Chancellery! What made him think the perpetrator worked there and not at SS Headquarters or any number of Gestapo facilities? I tried to go back to my plan for getting Brückner and Klara to meet, but my condition demanded that I return to my quarters and swill down the horrid-tasting concoction the Führer's witch doctor had prescribed. Planning of all sorts would have to wait.

I HAD LITTLE to do this morning except listen absently with Morell while the Führer practised his speech concerning his repeated heroic-but-futile attempts to get Great Britain to "see sense" before they were "crushed." I wanted to feel him out on the Dvora/Klara matter, but that was not possible. He'd awakened fatigued, with a painful throat, so he had Morell race in and inject him with something to pep him up and soothe the burning. *And it succeeded!* Still amazing to me, the physician always seemed to have something at his disposal to deal with any condition of which the Führer might complain. I daresay that even a hangnail would have had Morell instantly bring forth some curative elixir. While his other physicians harboured serious misgivings about many of the side effects (not merely his abrupt and severe mood swings), the Führer consistently swore by his "magician" and seemed to rely on him more and more on a daily (and sometimes even hourly) basis.

⊱

Though Brückner hadn't told me the date of his inevitable departure, save that it would be before the new year, I felt the calendar closing in on me like walls moving inexorably towards me in a narrow lift. As such, if he and Klara were ever to meet, it would have to be as soon as possible, so I decided to broach the subject with her this evening. Given her condition, ringing her was always awkward since I was obliged to leave messages with her neighbour, who would relay them and ring me back (or sometimes not). This time, it worked.

After that first night, I made certain to be absolutely punctual since she needed an unlocked door, and I didn't wish to leave it so any longer than necessary. I pushed it open, entered, locked it behind me, went to where she stood, kissed her, and sat down on her tattered sofa, but now she eased down next to me.

"I prepared something extra special for our fifth anniversary," she announced.

I shrugged, both with surprise and confusion. "Anniversary?"

"Yes," she confirmed. "This is our fifth assignation, so I thought to celebrate it. Was it wrong of me?"

"Assignation?" I said with a grim chuckle. "Nothing about us is secret. That's certain," I added, considering that no less than the Führer, Heydrich, and Baur had referred to it, and God knew who else was aware.

"I like the word assignation, even so," she answered. "It gives what we do an air of danger." She reached over and took my hand in hers. "More romantic, don't you think?"

Her hands were warm, and they quickly took away the chill I'd felt before arriving. "To me, romance is dangerous enough without labelling it, but we can call it anything you like if that makes you happy."

"I am happy, Heinz. I've never been so happy, and I want to share my happiness with the one who made me so. Now, let me tell you what I've prepared for us. At first, I wanted it to be a surprise, but a surprise won't make your mouth water like the names will: So, first, a thick lentil soup, then apple pancakes with apple sauce, followed by stuffed pork with potato dumplings, and finally, for dessert, my special apple cake. In your position, you must have dined at the finest restaurants, but I hope that tonight's fare will compare favourably."

She stared at me in such a way as if she were soliciting words of encouragement, but after her recitation, I was momentarily nonplussed by her need for my generosity.

"Klara," I said, "you give both my position and my palate far too much credit. There was a time when I ate from garbage cans, and now I watch the Führer consume things I would have discarded at my most ravenous. I tell you this not to denigrate your skills but to let you know that I welcome good food. I'm certain that yours will be memorable." Lame. Lame. But you know I've always been inept at issuing compliments. And also wary.

Her cuisine was exactly as she had described, and far better than my anticipation could conjure up. The way I devoured each course could leave no doubt in her mind that I delighted in the result of her labours. After dessert, she waved me into the parlour while she poured us an after-dinner drink.

We sat for a few moments in silence, digesting. I took the quiet time to formulate how to bring up Brückner and dinner at a restaurant. Up to now, we'd always stayed at her flat by her choice. I suspected the reason but didn't dare ask her. But with the matter now thrust upon me, I had little choice.

"Klara."

"Yes, Heinz."

"I've mentioned General Brückner to you."

"Yes," she replied. "Just the name, though."

"Well, he's my superior, my mentor, and most importantly, my dear friend. He'll be leaving the Führer's service soon, so now he's asked to meet you and to celebrate my good fortune by taking us out to dinner."

Her expression underwent a severe transformation, almost as if I'd placed her under arrest. She closed her eyes and said nothing, forcing me to say nothing in return. She remained that way for several seconds, making me wonder what I'd done wrong. Finally, she opened her eyes, but I could read great anxiety in them.

Was she that self-conscious about being in public?

"I would like very much to meet your friend," she said. "Invite him here, and I promise to prepare a dinner that will make what you just consumed seem like swill fit only for pigs."

I laughed at the imagery, but now I had to know. "That would be wonderful, but it was the general's express wish. He knows of your condition, if that's troubling you, and having only one eye, he couldn't care less about your hearing. Who gives a damn about what other restaurant patrons might think?"

She fixed a stare at me with an expression that seemed both sad and perplexed. "Heinz, my dear, how can you be so cavalier about something so serious? I'm certainly not sensitive about my condition and would gladly share the great outdoors with you—and your General Brückner—but there is too great a danger in this."

I shook my head in bewilderment. "Danger? What danger? It's merely dinner, not espionage. I don't understand."

Her eyelids became hooded. "Now you're toying with me!" she exclaimed, visibly distraught, before her eyelids resumed their original position, and she shrugged in resignation. "Can you truly be unaware? Since the Führer and the Nazis came to power, people with disabilities have been declared criminals by law and sentenced to sterilisation."

Then it all came to me in a flood of recollections about the Führer's meetings with his top jurists and, ultimately, the institution of health courts and other special tribunals to deal conclusively with infirmities. For some reason that escaped me, I hadn't made the association. I nodded gravely.

"I knew of it, but I didn't make the connection between that and you until you mentioned it." I only hoped my shame didn't show.

"Oh, Heinz, I don't mean to sound critical. There's no shame in it," she said, as if reading my mind. "You probably never met anyone like me before, so what you know has no…" She paused, searching for a word. "Anchor? But I live with it every day."

"Then how have you kept safe? Aside from avoiding restaurants, that is." A feeble joke.

"I mostly stay at home, and my good and decent neighbour buys me the necessities. Also, Aunt Christa does what she can to shield me from those who would gladly place me on the operating table."

"You mean the Führer probably knows?"

"She's never said, and I've never asked, but it stands to reason. Even if he knew and looked the other way, I would still need to stay out of sight, so as to cause no raised eyebrows."

"I completely understand," I said, "but I see a way to still have our celebration and keep you and your aunt from harm's way."

"Yes?" Dubiousness added a further complication to her deaf-speak.

"Tonsils," I told her. "You are silent because you recently had your tonsils removed. And with Brückner and me along, who at a restaurant would dare question this?"

"Oh, Heinz." She laughed. "This is why I… I'm so fond of you. You're such an innocent. Consider, my dear, wouldn't my complete silence at the table defeat the purpose of the dinner? Am I to chat with both of you through written notes passed from hand to hand? This would be comical at best and suspect at worst."

Why did all those who seemed to know about Klara without

my divulging anything (as well as the one person who did know after I told him) not warn me? Was I being set up again, as I'd been with Dvora? I pursed my lips in grim and embarrassed amusement. "No, Klara, you're right about that—and about my lack of sophistication."

"Leave the menu to me," she said, smiling. "When I'm done, both you and your general will crave *Kräuterlikör*." She tilted her head towards her bedroom. "And now perhaps, for something that requires no note passing?"

1 *August 1940*

FORTUNATELY, THERE WAS no early summons, as the Führer (with Morell's able assistance) had been dictating to Schroeder all through the night and into the wee hours, dressed in his pyjamas and robe. I arrived just as the visibly enervated secretary emerged from the Führer's study.

"I can't talk now," she informed me with a stern glance, as if I'd been begging for an audience. "Later," she declared and continued on her weary way.

Oddly, for someone who continuously demanded positive recognition from everyone, even the Führer, she hadn't asked me once about her success as matchmaker. I assumed she'd learned all she needed to know from Klara, including that first night's toast. She could wait, I decided easily; it was Brückner I needed to speak with.

When I entered, the Führer was slumped at his desk, the Lincoln green of the glass lampshade accentuating his sallow complexion and the bags under his eyes. He didn't look up as I made for the bathroom to arrange his badly needed toilette. When I came out, the Führer was mumbling to himself, but I could discern references to the "fucking stubborn British" and "forcing me to be ruthless."

Then he glanced up at me. "Get me Morell," he said weakly. "Big day ahead," he added by way of explanation, "I need to be at my best."

It was alarming, I thought, that the Führer's "best" appeared with increasing frequency to reside in Morell's syringe. I shuddered to think what would happen to the Reich—and to me—should Morell meet with a fatal accident, then chided myself for such unwarranted morbidity.

Once Morell departed, and the Führer had been pharmaceutically transformed into the sprightly and vigorous leader he needed to be, he took me by the elbow and led me to the portrait of Frederick.

"My military chiefs," he said, "especially Göring—for obvious reasons—assure me that my decision today will be decisive, providing the conditions for my complete domination of the continent. What do you think Old Freddie would say to that?"

I'd read what "Old Freddie" had said of conquest: "I begin by taking. I shall find scholars later to demonstrate my perfect right." However, since I was well accustomed to the Führer's rhetorical questions, this one only more rhetorical, I pursed my lips, as was my established custom, and nodded thoughtfully. For a few long moments, we stood gazing up in silence, then he turned to face me.

"So, how does it go with your Klara?" he asked with a slight moustache-ascending grin, as if he'd called me in to discuss her. "I trust she's at least an improvement over Baur's well-worn stable."

His question was just what I'd hoped for, yet on the asking, I felt a sharp pinch of dread. "I… I'm… entirely satisfied, my Führer," I answered awkwardly.

His moustache lowered, and a puzzled expression replaced it. "'Entirely satisfied,' you say? Hardly the words of someone smitten. You might just as well have been referring to a decent meal. Is it her deafness?"

"My Führer, as always, you've hit the mark. I've been at sixes and sevens about this, I will admit."

The Führer's head performed a metronomic dance. "Yes, I can understand your confusion and perplexity. But I will tell you something: Göring once said that he decides who is a Jew and who isn't. Typical Hermann, but on the whole, not unreasonable, considering our rather comprehensive and inflexible race laws—for which I'm primarily responsible, I must admit. But to be frank, I personally don't care who is or isn't a Jew. Becoming Führer with their able assistance ended the matter for me. Now, only Himmler and his race fanatics seem to care, so I leave the entire matter to them. But for those of us who bear the greatest responsibility for my well-being and that of the Reich, we must permit some play, not unlike a rubber band. Too taut, and it breaks, but just far enough, and… well, you see what I'm saying. To put it another way, if I care nothing about your dalliance with a crazy Jewess, what harm could follow with a deaf Aryan?"

"Yes, my Führer, of course I see, but I'm hardly in the exalted position you referred to. The Reichsmarschall is… well… the Reichsmarschall, after all, and I'm merely—"

His lips spread with mirth. "As I've told you many times, I consider you a much-valued family member and, soon, infinitely more. So, unless this woman's infirmity annoys you somehow, you have my blessing. But," he added, his voice dropping into a parody of a whisper, his head turning as if to see if anyone was listening in, "I will say that some discretion wouldn't do us a bit of harm."

AFTER SPENDING A fruitless morning of tension-filled waiting for the Luftwaffe's declaration of total victory over the RAF, the Führer cancelled his movie screening for the evening, citing no cause, but marked Weisthor and Himmler on his calendar for this evening—as usual, in the lightest pencil strokes for ease of erasure.

This time, Brückner sought me out to tell me that his transfer had been approved and that he would be leaving for Paris on 18 October. I'd been avoiding the inevitable, perhaps in hopes of waking up to find that I'd merely been in the grip of another terrible dream, but now I could ignore it no longer.

"What am I to do, Wilhelm," I asked him, "once you're gone?"

He shrugged and nodded. "I never told you this, Heinz, but in the last war, I had a very close friend. Dieter. We'd been classmates and joined up at the same time, 'full of piss and vinegar,' to quote a noted American author. We'd always shared the most intimate confidences concerning the most abstract aspects of philosophy, from the highs and lows of our romantic lives to our daily feelings about life and death in battle. So, you can appreciate that I was devastated when his head was sheared off by an enemy's sabre right in front of me."

I let out a deep, troubled breath. "My apologies for even daring to compare my feeble situation with what you experienced."

"No apologies necessary, Heinz. I only brought it up to demonstrate to you the difference between one sort of parting and another—no pun intended."

I couldn't help laughing at his show of wit, no matter how macabre.

"You're behaving," he continued, "as if there can no longer be any contact between us, when quite the opposite is the case. In Paris, I'm far from prying eyes and ears but no further from you than the closest secure telephone. And of course, the situation is no different for you. No longer will we have to constantly—and conspicuously—wander the Chancellery gardens like Canterville Ghosts."

"You make it sound as if it's a blessing for both of us that you were exiled."

Brückner chuckled. "Yes, that's the ticket. We should see it as something that causes celebration, not mourning."

Should I tell Brückner about Heydrich's "impromptu" visit—which would also involve me telling him about Schlegl? "How do you think you'll like Paris?" I asked instead.

After a shrug, he said, "Aside from our grand tour with the Führer, I was in Paris once before with a young lady. Only for a few days in the mid-'20s, but they were enough. I remember her asking me when we got back to Germany, 'What's the difference between a Frenchman and a bucket of crap?' When I asked her what, she answered, 'The bucket.' A complete romantic otherwise, the lady was one of the few people not beguiled by the 'City of Light.'"

His story called to mind what Kempka was announcing to all within earshot after the fall of France: "How do you kill a Frenchman? Slam the toilet seat down when he's getting a drink."

∾

With no warning or explanation, I was summoned back to the Führer's study at midnight. As I entered and shut the door behind me, the Führer, seated at his desk, motioned with a wave of his hand to his beautifully inlaid liquor cabinet and bade me pour a glass of Riesling for myself, then he waved me over to an armchair facing him. It was the first time the Führer had ever offered me liquor.

"I hear you're now a Riesling man," the Führer said, once I'd eased into the chair's warm plushness.

"Only socially, my Führer." I didn't bother to ask how he knew of Klara's influence. "Are you not partaking as well?"

"You know with me—only desultorily, and nothing at all for a while. Morell ordered me to temporarily lay off wine for my poor stomach's sake. If that fucking Pope had my stomach, he'd have to resign." He laughed at his joke as if someone else had told it to him. "But don't let my abstinence stop you. Drink up, eh?"

I couldn't imagine that he'd brought me here for a friendly drink, so in the interim, I took a substantial sip. It was considerably stronger and more bitter than Klara's, but I managed to keep my wince to myself.

"Good stuff, eh?" he said. "Göring gets it for me. Knowing our Hermann, probably plundered from a *real* oenophile. In any event, I wanted…"

The Führer's Riesling was also infinitely more powerful than Klara's, so as I strained to hear his words, I could actually see the letters (as if typed) drifting lazily into a void and disappearing before I could understand them.

"My Führer?" I asked, with what lucidity I still possessed, now that my words were also visibly retreating. "May I use your bathroom?" I knew I would pass out if the Führer refused.

The Führer's face became a study in solicitation. "Not to

worry, Linge. Just relax, and you'll be as good as new after a brief nap."

These were the last words I heard before closing my eyes and drifting into that same nothingness.

✍

"Come back," the Führer command gently. "Open your eyes."

Come back? From where? How long had I been away? And the most important question I've never been able to answer accurately: *Even with my eyes open, was I now awake?* For I was no longer sitting before the Führer's desk but standing at rigid attention in a pitch-black space, in the very centre of a circle of armchairs, where, in separate pools of directed light, sat Weisthor, Himmler, Katrin, the Führer, and the small blond man I'd seen in that Munich church catacomb in 1938. One chair was vacant. There must have been more, for I could hear indistinct murmurs emanating from the surrounding blackness. All those seated were completely naked, save for Himmler, who wore full SS uniform (even to the cap), sitting with his blank stare and ubiquitous little notebook and pencil perched on his lap.

"Please do make yourself comfortable, Heinz," Katrin said, her breathy voice like thick whipped cream. "You're among friends."

"Must I undress?" I asked, partially surrendering to my surroundings.

"Only if you wish to," she answered.

"Thank you," I replied. "I prefer to remain in uniform."

"Pity," she said, with a slight pout in her voice, then pointed to the only empty chair—to the immediate right of the Führer and directly across from her.

I sat. After what seemed like an hour of absolute silence, I heard the clearing of a throat.

"Herr Linge," Weisthor said, "I asked you this once before,

and now I ask you again: are you able to exercise volition in your dreams?"

It was his question from our meeting at Madame Kitty's—just before I was poisoned. Naturally, I remembered my persona's answer.

"Volition?"

"My apologies, I overlooked that." Weisthor kept his eyes fixed on me. "I thought I'd explained it then. I'll rephrase the question: when you dream, are you able to exercise control over what you or others do?"

"Also," the blond man added, "control or no, in your dreams, is there ever a small metal object—like a child's top?"

I squinted with my left eye and swivelled the other upwards to simulate thought. "I never remember my dreams, so I can't really answer either question." It was my answer, now as then, and now I had even less reason to change it.

All heads turned to the door as Klara entered, and all the men, save for Himmler, stood, went to her, and kissed her extended hands.

"You make me wish I had more than two," she remarked through her distorted speech and an icy smile. She, too, was naked, and I felt a slight stirring.

Weisthor escorted her by the elbow to a chair that had suddenly appeared in the centre of the circle, directly facing me, then returned to his seat along with the others.

"Now, Fräulein Klara, have you anything to say?" Weisthor asked.

When she didn't respond, Weisthor cleared his throat again and leaned over to face her. "My apologies. I'd forgotten. Do you have anything to say to Herr Linge?" Then he leaned back.

"Hello, Heinz," she began. "Well, you've finally coaxed me out of my flat." Her voice had warmed several degrees.

"I had nothing to do with it," I answered, "but of course, I'm pleased to see you."

"Not so," she said, the temperature dropping again. "I thought we'd promised each other complete honesty, and yet you haven't been that with me."

"I… don't understand," I stumbled, flummoxed only because I didn't understand how she could know such a thing. "What do you mean?"

"You've never confided your dreams."

I had no idea why I wasn't upset or even moved by what was occurring, even by Klara's public nakedness. "You never asked me about my dreams," I told her with complete accuracy, "and I never asked you about yours."

She nodded and smiled with beguiling charm. "Well then, my love, what better time to tell me than now, here?"

Now? Here? What better time? Was she demented? I should divulge my most private, my most intimate subconscious moments to a collection of naked people: my boss, a woman I've known for less than a month, and two strangers—and all accompanied by a taciturn monster in full dress and a notebook?

"I wish I could, Klara," I finally said, "but as I said before you arrived, I have a terrible memory, and the rare dreams I have are no exception. I never asked you about your dreams because I have no interest in them, and I've never kept anything from you that you've asked me about—that is, anything that would stick in my head." A blatant lie I hoped would end the matter once and for all.

Klara turned to Himmler. "I believe him, Herr Reichsführer. Don't you?"

"Belief is for theologians. I deal in facts, and so far, you've uncovered none. There are those who believe that Herr Linge knows more about this top business than he's letting on. Belief again. I, for one, have no facts and, therefore, no reason to make such a judgement." Then he turned to the Führer. "However, as you know, we have ample methods of verifying or discrediting such beliefs. Do I have your authorisation?"

I knew what the fiend meant, so I glanced at the Führer, who, by his expression, appeared to be weighing the benefits and burdens of his answer.

"Not yet, Heinrich," he said.

"Then I'm sorry to have to tell you, my Führer, that until you permit me to accrue more facts—that is to say, facts that will unquestionably secure you the other item—I'm afraid the one you now possess will have to suffice."

Then the Führer, eerily calm, rose, bringing all of us up with him. "You may all leave, save for Linge here."

Once they'd gone, I noticed that not only had the circle of chairs vanished but so had the liquor cabinet. The Führer, suddenly looking enervated and despondent, said only, "Since I needn't worry about you remembering any of this, after preparing me for bed, you may resume your nap."

Was any of that real? I asked myself after returning to my quarters, but despite much thought, I still had no answer. Whether dream, hallucination, or hypnotic trance, I went away from that episode, real or not, with at least one thing I sensed to be true: for some, the little metal top that Emerald bade me secrete away possessed great value.

But what kind, was another matter.

3 *September 1940*

THE FÜHRER STILL writhes noisily on pins and needles of impatience, waiting for Göring to finally announce his Luftwaffe's triumph. With no announcement forthcoming, the Führer has had to postpone the invasion once more. Since he didn't require my presence at his screaming session on the phone—or even notice it—I had no need to sneak out.

Knowing that only a few grains of sand remained in Brückner's Chancellery hourglass drove me to hoard his company as often as propriety and responsibilities allowed. Evenings were out of the question since Klara had progressed in my consciousness from luxury to necessity—that is, once she'd convinced me, with appropriate and noisy hilarity, that she had never appeared naked in the Führer's study. We also decided to curtail our garden strolls, for as Brückner the wit put it, "There comes a point where hiding in plain sight is no longer hiding because the sight has become far too plain." Which left only lunchtime.

Today, we decided on the delicatessen in KaDeWe.[37] As we

---

[37] The Kaufhaus des Westens ("Department Store of the West"), usually abbreviated as KaDeWe, is a department store in Berlin. By 1926, it was the largest department store (retail and restaurants) in Europe, with a turnover of 128 million Reichsmarks and eighteen thousand employees. In 1931, two floors were added to the original five. In 1929, the Great Depression, followed by the 1933 Nazi takeover, meant that the Jewish owners were forced to sell their shares. Georg Karg was selected by the Nazis to manage KaDeWe, and an eleven-million-Reichsmark loan from the Ministry for Trade and Commerce soon followed.

sat regarding the throngs of package-laden shoppers waiting to spend even more on food, it occurred to me that much had changed for the better since the Führer had taken power, for on their faces, I could see pride and plenty instead of despondency and want. *But how long would such satisfaction endure under wartime conditions?* I asked myself. I must have asked myself aloud, for Brückner answered me.

"Longer than you might think. The Führer knows his history, and he won't make the mistake his predecessors made during the last war."

"What mistake?"

He smiled. "Sometimes, I forget how young you really are. Domestic unrest, my friend. Privation and fear, crime, strikes, and riots. Just a few of the many things he believes led to our capitulation. And he's not far wrong. So, you can bet he won't permit anything to burden the people at home until he absolutely must. And 'must' is fairly far off. Even with the British blockade, we have all we need from the territories we've… appropriated. And what they don't supply, the Soviets do."

As Brückner spoke, it brought back memories of innumerable conversations the Führer had with Goebbels and the industrial leaders about the need to ensure peace at home to wage war everywhere else.

"Speaking of territories we've appropriated," I said, "very soon you'll be in a position to send us the best that France has to offer."

He laughed. "Not if Göring gets there first. Do you know that woman?"

"What woman? Where?"

"Off to your left, the chic woman aiming like a guided missile right for our table."

I turned to see, and there she was, exactly the same as when she'd returned my button to me on the first day of 1939, even to the small, jewel-encrusted red-black-and-white enamel Nazi Party pin on her lapel. We both stood as she came upon us, and I introduced her to Brückner.

She nodded and extended a gloved hand. "I'm so pleased to finally meet the fabled chief adjutant to the Führer." Her voice seemed, to me, to hold a touch of irony.

Brückner took her hand, wagged it once, and returned it to her. "Fabled is the word, Frau Höss. The reality is far more mundane."

She smiled at that. "Perhaps. May I join you two?"

Brückner, as senior, responded. "Of course, Frau Höss. Can we get you some refreshment?"

"A glass of *schankbier* will be fine. Thank you."

Brückner pulled out a chair for her. She nodded and sat down, and Brückner returned. Then he and I both sat, and Brückner called the waiter over, ordering a glass for himself and me as well.

"I've heard much about your husband," he said. "Please convey my best wishes to him in his new assignment."

A thin smile. "Thank you, General, but I'm afraid that even with his promotion, he's no more than a glorified hotel manager." She hadn't changed, still the adoring wife.

"Hotel?" I asked with raised eyebrows. "But I heard that Auschwitz is the largest and most complex KZ we have, and are likely to have." Actually, overheard would have been more accurate, for I was hardly involved in Himmler's intermittent and superficial reports to the Führer.

"It's in Poland" was all she said.

"Anyway," Brückner said, "please wish him well for me."

"I will, General; I know he'll be honoured."

"General Brückner will soon be joining the Wehrmacht in Paris," I offered without thinking.

Her face lit up as if electrified. "Ooh la la!" she exclaimed. "Paris. Now that's a posting. Even the stinking Frenchies are better than the stinking Polacks. That is, once the French deal with their Jews."

"Knowing the French as I do," Brückner replied, "your wish will be their command."

⌘

Once Brückner cleverly deduced that her formidable lung power was marshalled entirely in the service of thoroughly diminishing her husband while extolling the racial virtues of Nazism—a seeming contradiction in light of what I'd heard about the prime purpose of Auschwitz—we could wait her out by sitting silently until her speech ended. Having no other reason to remain, she scribbled something on a calling card and handed it to me, bade us a hearty salute and farewell, and left to continue her shopping.

"Quite a character," Brückner observed. "Her type's what kept me from marrying."

"She's just a better-looking Dara, it seems to me," I added with a tinge of unintended bitterness.

"Far better," he corrected. "But about his new assignment, I think I have to grudgingly agree," he confessed. "Running a KZ? Not a 'glorified hotel manager' so much as a lofty prison warden, I'd say—but I'd never tell her that. She's ashamed enough of him without our rubbing his nose into shit instead of mud." His mock smile suddenly changed to a mock frown. "I see you didn't eat anything," Brückner chided, "and you never know. This could be our last meal together for quite a while."

"That's why," I told him. "One of the many times I was a guest of the Berlin jails, I had a cellmate, a real pro, who told me of a fellow he'd met who had once been sentenced to death, and the night before his execution, he was asked what he wished for his last meal—he could have anything he wanted—and you know what he said?"

He shrugged.

"Nothing, Wilhelm," I said, "he wanted nothing. When asked how this could possibly be, the condemned man said that knowing he would be dead by dinnertime the next day defeated whatever appetite he might have had."

"And you associate yourself with that condemned man?" He frowned.

"To some extent." I gave a tentative shrug, part of me knowing I'd given away far too much.

He nodded in such a way as if he'd been thinking about that very thing, then signalled for the waiter. "Well then, time to get back to serving the Reich, eh?"

When I returned to my quarters, I took out the card and squinted at the scrawl. It was a request to visit her before she returned to Poland a week from now. She'd put down a room number at the Adlon but had omitted her name, signing merely "Heil Hitler." Chuckling as I went into the bathroom to tear and toss the card, I saw the note taped to the toilet lid. In large block letters it said:

PLEASE, HEINZ, BEFORE YOU ONCE AGAIN TAKE
THE PATH OF NO RESISTANCE, YOU SHOULD
SEE HEDWIG. YOU REALLY SHOULD. E.

For an hour this morning, I pressed myself into a corner as the Führer aimed a shrieking fusillade of invective at Göring for continuing to bomb British airfields when Berlin itself had been hit. The hysterical diatribe ended only when the Führer ripped the phone from its moorings and flung it at an enormous, suspended military map, tearing right through. I sidled along the wall, stole into the anteroom, and had Herr Chinless summon Morell to come at once, which he did. After several injections, peace returned, and once another telephone was installed, the Führer had me connect him again with Göring.

"This is entirely unacceptable, Hermann!" he declared loudly but with infinitely more calm. "I'm at the end of my rope with you and your meaningless promises. You target their airfields, and they still batter down our planes. You boasted that no enemy planes could break through the outer and inner rings of our antiaircraft defence, and what happens? They bomb Berlin. *Berlin!* And you're still with their airfields. Now I directly order: Today, and not one day later, I want London smashed with such sustained force that Churchill will weep bitter tears over the devastation, you understand me?"

Then he slammed the receiver down before a response could be given and turned to me. "There are times, Linge, when I regret having selected that flamboyant dirigible to command my Luftwaffe. He's no more fit for that than you would be for Führer, meaning no disrespect to you, of course."

Clearly, silence was the only suitable response.

"I tell my people," he continued, "that I'm proud of their discipline and that their reward will be to teach the British the price of their piracy by pulverising their cities into vapour, and now I'm being made to look the fool. That bloated clown had better not disappoint me this time."

The Führer was still talking to himself, so I waited until he dismissed me with an errand. In any event, I'd been paying scant attention, for my active mind was preoccupied with Frau Höss and her card. Emerald's note had caused me to succumb to curiosity, so earlier in the morning, I had cancelled my evening with Klara (citing late-night duties) and arranged another time to meet.

❧

After the morning's fracas, all I sought in the officers' mess was a tranquil—and private—lunch, but any hope I had of that vanished with the arrival of Kempka and Baur, who took the empty chairs in front that I'd tilted to prevent just that. By the stricken looks on their faces, I jettisoned all expectation of the usual chitchat.

It was Kempka who spoke first, but not before he turned his head slightly from side to side, then leaned forward. "He's fucking crazy, Heinz," he whispered, as if he intended to leave the context to my imagination.

"Who's crazy?" I replied. "We work in the Chancellery, so you'll need to narrow it down."

"Heydrich," Baur answered, also in a whisper.

I shrugged. "What else is new, Erich? That there are high and low tides?"

"You wouldn't joke like that," Kempka advised, "not if you heard what I heard."

"But I haven't heard, so a joke is all I'm capable of."

"Heydrich's plan," Baur said. "Kempka here got it from Brandt."[38]

"Himmler's Brandt?"

"No, Churchill's Brandt," Kempka said with no little sarcasm. "Of course Himmler's Brandt."

I was too battered and enervated from the morning to play further with these two. "All right then, Himmler's Brandt. What plan?"

"To drop captured British soldiers and Jews on London," Baur said.

I shook my head. "Are you serious?"

"Instead, you should ask if Heydrich's serious," Kempka answered. "If it's insane enough and barbaric enough, he just might be. Brandt was there when Heydrich brought it up to Himmler. Heydrich told Himmler that such a move would not only repay the British for daring to bomb Berlin, it would also sufficiently demoralise Churchill into begging for an armistice. He told Himmler with, you know, that fucking grin of his, that it would also save lives since the only victims would be the Jews, the British prisoners, and anyone they happened to land on."

I knew that Heydrich was capable of such a grotesque stunt, but I couldn't imagine even Himmler taking it seriously.

"What did Himmler say?" I asked.

"Well, according to Brandt, Himmler said, and I quote, 'The idea has a nice poetic ring to it, but unfortunately, the Führer would have a fit if he found out, and he certainly would from Liver Lips.'"

---

[38] A member of Hitler's inner circle at the Berghof, physician Karl Brandt was selected to administer the Aktion T4 euthanasia program.

That was one of the many pet names Himmler had for Göring.

"All right," I said, "just some more crazy shit tossed into the toilet and flushed away. Then what's the problem?" I knew the answer as I asked the question, but by then, it was too late, and I was forced to hear it from someone else.

"That's easy, lad," Baur answered. "What about some more crazy shit he *can* keep from the Führer?"

⌒

I'd visited the Adlon's many restaurants several times over the years but never an actual hotel room. When Frau Höss swung open the door, I couldn't help but gape at the magisterial opulence beyond her. The room was even larger than the Führer's enormous study and far more splendidly appointed, from the thick Persian rugs, silk wallpaper, and velvet drapes to the inlaid dining table, satin-covered chairs and sofa, and the king-sized canopied bed, the last of which she appeared ready for, since she was encased in a shimmering silver satin dressing gown. She stepped aside just far enough to force me to brush past her as she shut the door.

"You know, this room was once occupied by Henry Ford," she remarked, obviously noticing my expression. "Now he's afraid to come, I hear, because of what his customers might think. What a people," she stated sourly.

I couldn't imagine such a spartan character like Ford, as he was reputed to be, feeling comfortable in such extravagantly feminine surroundings.

"Please sit down," she offered, pointing to one of the over-stuffed chairs. "I had them bring up some excellent brandy. The decanter is of the finest crystal, the snifters too," she touted, as if attempting to sell them. "And since we are already acquainted,

I'll call you Heinz, and you can call me Hedwig." She removed the crystal stopper from the bottle, poured two glasses, and handed me one. "Now, what shall we toast?" She raised her glass.

Considering what I took to be the subtext in Emerald's note, I asked Hedwig to propose it.

"All right." A smile brightened her handsome face. "To your upcoming visit."

"Upcoming?" My forehead creased with confusion. "But I'm already here."

"Not that visit, Herr Comedian." She laughed. "The one I'm *going* to invite you to. I'd like very much for you to meet my husband. A born bureaucrat, he's very proud of his camp, you know, and I'm certain he'll wish to give you the most marvellous guided tour."

I had no desire to visit a prison, so I stalled in hopes of a sudden inspiration. "Your husband doesn't know of this," I ventured.

She pursed her lips and put down her drink. "Well, not quite yet, but I'll begin coaxing him when I return."

"So, it's you who wish me to visit and not your husband. Why?"

Her face became all sly smile. "Can't you guess?" She raised her glass again. "Well, in that case, I'll demonstrate it to you in… unmistakable terms—that is, once we've toasted a few times and I've shown you round my camp right here." In case I missed her meaning, she tilted her head towards the canopied bed.

ANOTHER RAF RAID on Berlin caused little damage to anything but the Führer's disposition. However, he finally coerced Göring into targeting British cities instead of air bases. Baur confided that such a strategy would merely harden and enrage the enemy while providing the RAF with the opportunity to breathe and regroup, but that neither Göring nor his generals—or his personal pilot—would tell this to the Führer. Baur hoped that I might influence him in some way. I agreed, though I had no intention of complying, for even the thought that I might sway the Führer was fanciful to the point of madness.

There was so much that none of those with whom the Führer surrounded himself dared tell him. I shook my head at this state of affairs. *How the Devil could he make informed decisions?* And yet he did, invariably and infallibly. Perhaps that was the true magic of genius. When Goebbels had screened *The Petrified Forest* three years ago, all I could focus on afterwards was the exchange between the starry-eyed girl and the doomed poet. When she told him, "That means you've got brains," the poet replied, "Hmmm. Yes. Brains without purpose, noise without sound, shape without substance." On the most generous reflection, that might also be me—at my best—now as then. *And Baur would have me counsel the Führer?*

I remained perplexed by Brückner appearing to do everything he could to avoid me. Even in the Führer's presence, he made sure to look everywhere but at me, and once dismissed, he fled as if I were Javert and he, Jean Valjean. *What did I do?*

I've heard nothing from Frau Höss—Hedwig—since that intriguing night at the Adlon. It's a source of great comfort that I'll be spared both having to visit a place of such awfulness as well as needing to ask leave of the Führer to do it, even if that comfort is only temporary.

WE ARRIVED BACK in Berlin from the Brenner Pass, where the Führer met with Mussolini to discuss the latter's desire to invade Greece, arguing that such a move would make it a victory for Germany, not Italy. As I stood by, I could tell that the Führer was unmoved by such a well-worn sales tactic but, once again, was forced by personal regard to humour the Duce.

"Your plan has substantial merit," he told Mussolini with a straight face, "but I promised my generals that I would only support an invasion of Greece after the defeat of the British in Egypt. You can see how awkward it would be for me now to override them after making such a pledge."

With that, Mussolini nodded his shiny dome, visibly disappointed but fully accepting of the Führer's diplomatic intransigence.

On our way back to Berlin, the Führer took me aside and smiled. "Linge, I ask you: how can one not like the Duce?" He shook his head. "But even you can see that the man has no strategic sense whatsoever. As an ally, he's the proverbial bull in a china shop—and the china is Germany." He loved that quip so much, his tiny moustache twitched with merriment. All chuckled out, he moved to his new telephone console, pressed the intercom button, told Herr Chinless to summon Schroeder, then looked back at me.

"I don't know about you, but your love life has certainly been a tonic for Schroeder."

"I'm glad, my Führer," I told him honestly, since her visible hostility towards me had been unnerving and unremitting. "Klara is a pure delight, and—"

"Good, good," he interrupted, uninterested in any embellishments from me. "Schroeder makes more errors now, but she smiles more. This is one of the reasons I told Himmler that he shouldn't be too ardent in his cleansing of the Reich, for even the deaf have their uses."

Trying to picture Himmler ardent was *my* moment of merriment.

TODAY, I LEARNED why Brückner had been dodging me for so long. When I arrived at the Communications Centre this morning, I discovered a note in his precise handwriting:

> *My Dear Heinz. When you finish this, you may well consider my recent behaviour both inscrutable and unforgivable, and I could hardly blame you, but I hope that one day you will understand and so allow me some measure of grace. Until you told me your jailhouse anecdote about the "last meal," I felt comfortable leaving in the normal course of things, but once told, that is no longer possible. I now see that to someone so emotionally embryonic, I may have become more of a focus of dependency than a person. Of course, I accepted the responsibility of such a role without complaint, for I enjoyed it, so I made myself insensitive to what transpires when the enabler suddenly vanishes. However, with my departure imminent, I felt another responsibility: to provide the opportunity to recognise that you are more than capable of functioning on your own resources, relying on nothing but your raw intelligence and informed instincts. And given the times, you will sorely need them. Your good and constant friend, Wilhelm.*

As usual, Brückner was right, but it took most of the day to vent my rage (without being seen) at what I initially felt was the note's condescension. It took the evening for me to accept the fact that everything Brückner had said was true. As I sat on my cot in resigned despair, Charlotte Brontë's words from *Jane Eyre* came to me: "I care for myself. The more solitary, the more friendless, the more unsustained I am, the more I will respect myself." And yet, given the unknown perils I would now have to face alone, I muttered, "Easily said, Charlotte. Easily said."

THOUGH I HAD no stomach for breakfast, I felt the need to camouflage any last traces of abandonment and isolation in the relative anonymity of a crowd. Regrettably, while a crowd is concealment, the man directly across from you is a companion, so I compensated by studying my oatmeal as if transfixed by its vapid colour.

"Pardon me, Colonel, would you have the accurate time?"

I glanced up at the collar tabs of a young SS major.

"What?"

"My apologies for disturbing your thoughts, Herr Colonel, but may I know the time? My watch has stopped, and I don't wish to be late on my first day."

"I understand; 'Time and tide wait for no man,'" I quipped feebly, still in the throes of Brückner's absence. I jerked my arm forward and consulted my watch.

"Tide?" he asked, furrowing his brow. "Not necessary. I need only know the time."

I could see that any attempt at wit, no matter how feeble, would be defeated by his artlessness. "Pay it no mind," I said, now feeling it was both safe and accurate to respond that way. "It's precisely eleven thirty-three."

"Of course, Herr Colonel," he said. "Thank you. It seems that I have some time."

And some tide, I wanted to reply but needed no further displays of density. I nodded and resumed my close inspection of the oatmeal still occupying my bowl.

"Herr Colonel."

I glanced up again, this time more slowly.

"Yes, Major?"

"Again, I apologise for disturbing you, but might you be acquainted with an officer named Wilhelm Brückner?"

My throat constricted. *Who was this fellow?* "I knew the general," I told him with a flatness of tone worthy of Himmler. "He was chief adjutant to the Führer, but he's now in the Wehrmacht stationed in Paris."

"May I ask the colonel what he was like?"

"May I ask the major why he asks?"

The convolution of my question must have flummoxed him temporarily, for he just stared at me. "I… I'm attempting to find out all I can so I can become a worthy successor."

The next few seconds were taken up by me straining to remain calm. *This young clod, a successor to Brückner? This relative adolescent, promoted over the veteran adjutant Schaub?* The few seconds after that were given over to considering the proper response. Comparing him to Brückner would be like comparing a child's toy balloon to the Hindenburg. And yet, here sat his successor, my superior—whom I outranked. Brückner once told me that there were too few coincidences to permit assumptions. *So, was this happenstance or design?*

"Are you all right, Colonel?" he finally asked, clearly struck by my hesitation.

"I'm fine, Major," I responded, perhaps a bit quicker than I'd intended. "I was merely attempting to do full justice to your question. General Brückner was quite… may I ask your age?"

He smiled, a sloping slit not unlike Heydrich's. "I'm twenty-three."

Christ! I exclaimed to myself. He was even younger than I had been when I'd joined the Führer's service.

"Well, Major," I said, "the general is fifty-six, and you're twenty-three, so obviously, the Führer sees in you something quite different from what he saw in Brückner. That is to say, the general was—how shall I put it?—all he was, if you get my meaning. You, on the other hand, are pure potential. These are not competing values."

His eyes narrowed in perplexity. "I'm afraid you've lost me, Colonel. I'm much embarrassed by this, but I must confess to you that despite my rank and position, I've had only a high school education."

I had far less, I wanted to tell him, but he might just be better than I was at diffidence. "Well, Major," I said, "that just goes to prove what I told you: obviously, the Führer sees something in you that goes beyond mere education."

Before he could answer with some inane scrap of flattery, I asked him his name.

"Otto Günsche," he said, accompanied by an ambiguous shrug. "And yours, if I may ask?"

"You may." I forced a smile as warm as my suspicions would allow. "Linge. Heinz Linge."

"You're Heinz Linge!" he exclaimed, his eyes bulging with astonishment, as if I'd seemed unsure of my own identity. "And you just happen to be sitting right in front of me. I tell you"—he laughed—"a coincidence to remember."

As with Junge, I believed not for one moment that this was a coincidence, and an icy wind began gusting through my insides.

"Yes, isn't it?" I replied blandly. "The Chancellery's full of those."

❧

It was when I'd unthinkingly set out to confer with Brückner about this intriguing encounter that I halted mid-stride, finally forced to concede with finality that my mentor, friend, and confidant, was truly gone.

This morning, the major and I stood at ease on either side of the door as the Führer listened to Himmler with what I could see was growing impatience.

"You are well aware, my Führer," Himmler said, "that I seldom meddle in foreign policy matters, but I believe the seriousness of recent events merits comment."

The Führer pressed his lips together and flattened them at the sides. "So comment, Heinrich."

Without looking, Himmler reached down, lifted a sheaf of papers from his attaché case on the floor beside him, and began reciting, "Since 1939, the Soviets have annexed a sizeable portion of our Poland, annexed Estonia, Latvia, and Lithuania, as well as Bessarabia and Northern Bukovina. They have also taken from Finland the Karelian Isthmus, the land bridge that gives access to Leningrad, and soon, I daresay, they'll take Finland itself. Moreover—"

The Führer, instead of demonstrating his usual shrieking and table-thwacking, raised his hands in a facsimile of surrender. "Heinrich," he said, almost grinning, "no more recitation, please. You must realise that I am no less aware than you of these paltry nibbles. You must also—"

"With respect, my Führer," he dared to interrupt, "I do not consider these 'nibbles,' as you call them, to be 'paltry.'"

Again, flouting tradition, the Führer raised his hands palms outward once more. "Heinrich, Heinrich," he said in his most ostentatiously indulgent tone. "As you well know, I'm currently engaged in a life-and-death struggle with the British. In this regard, prodding Hermann to finally bomb targets with some strategic meaning is more important than gratifying Stalin's need for more Jews, Slavs, and a few Eskimos."

At that, the major audibly stifled a guffaw, but I stared straight ahead while the Führer turned to him, then back to Himmler, whose head and all its features also hadn't moved.

"My Führer," Himmler continued against custom, "if I may say, these 'nibbles' you deride—and justifiably so—are, in my view, but the tip of a very treacherous iceberg. Once Comrade Stalin feels emboldened enough by our acquiescence, I fear he will seek bigger morsels."

I wondered if the major had any idea what was transpiring. I was reasonably confident after our introductory encounter that, while he just might be dimly aware of the relatively trivial political issues, he was utterly unmindful of the far more important immediate psychological ones. "Informed instinct," Brückner had called it.

The Führer closed his eyes slowly and opened them again—a certain sign of laboured forbearance. "Heinrich, we've known each other a long time. Up to now, you have expressed total faith and confidence in my judgement, and that faith and confidence have been amply justified, have they not?"

"Of course, my Führer," Himmler replied.

If he were thoroughly chastened, it never showed on his face, nor did anything else, so I knew that the Führer would have to nail down his coffin of doubt—which he did.

"So, when did you decide that I ceased to merit them?"

There was total silence while the Führer waited for Himmler's predestined surrender.

"Yes, my Führer," the Reichsführer conceded, "of course you always know best."

The Führer's moustache lifted slightly, his most ardent *beau geste* to the momentarily misguided.

"So, you're content to leave such policy appraisals to me?" As always, it was not a question.

❦

After Himmler left, I began tidying up while the Führer signed some papers and the major continued to stand at attention by the door as if he were a mannequin placed there.

"Linge," the Führer finally said as he handed me the signed sheets, "have you had the opportunity to meet Günsche here, Brückner's replacement?"

"Yes, my Führer, I met him yesterday. A 'coincidence to remember,'" I said without turning my head. "He happened to be sitting right in front of me at breakfast."

"Günsche," he called. "Come here."

The major shouted, "Yes, my Führer!" and marched over to stand beside me.

"No ceremony needed when we're alone, Günsche," he informed the major. "I get more than enough of that at rallies and parades." He chuckled lightly at that, which Günsche apparently didn't interpret as licence, for he made no response and remained at attention.

"Linge," the Führer said, "please inform the major that when I said no ceremony, that meant he could at least stand at ease."

I complied, and he shifted with exuberance to his new position as if he were being reviewed by the Führer on a parade ground. I always considered myself to be of above-average height, but standing beside Günsche made me feel like a Lilliputian. He stood at least six foot six, I guessed, for I would never ask him (being content to leave such personal matters to the Führer, who never exhibited any hesitation).

"You're quite the giant," the Führer remarked. "I'm astonished that Himmler allowed you to escape his clutches."

"Yes, my Führer," he answered, apropos of what, I had no idea.

The Führer began to look uncomfortable, so I knew it wouldn't be long.

"All right, Günsche," he said. "Why don't you go to the Communications Centre and get familiar with its workings? I'll send Linge over presently to go over the allocation of mail duties with you."

As I expected, Günsche snapped back to attention, clicked, saluted crisply—and noisily—pivoted, and marched out.

The Führer shook his head. "You know, Linge, I tell only you, I'm beginning to miss Brückner."

Now *you say it*, I considered grimly.

"He's young, my Führer," I said.

"So were you, Linge."

"Perhaps he's uneasy because your chief valet is a lieutenant colonel and your chief adjutant is a major."

"Hmmm, this could be, but I think that this is more awkward for you even, than for him. Would you feel better if I promoted him to full colonel? Or general, like Brückner?" When I didn't respond, the Führer laughed. "Take heart, Linge, for in ways that are, to me, more critical and momentous than collar tabs, you do outrank him handily. Now, be a good lad, and do what you can to train him in sorting my mail. And tonight, you'll be showing *Pinocchio*. Goebbels is a miracle worker. Brand new, the Americans haven't even seen it yet."

As I was leaving, he halted me at the door.

"Oh yes," the Führer added, as if he'd forgotten and it had

just now occurred to him—a tactic honed to perfection by Heydrich but, I felt, fairly benign in the Führer's hands. "I took the liberty of inviting your latest paramour, Klara, to the screening. Considering her affliction, I assumed that she doesn't go often to the cinema, so an opportunity to see a film containing subtitles, also courtesy of Disney, will be welcome. That is, if you don't mind her company, of course." His moustache didn't even have to lift for me to recognise the impish largesse.

"I… I don't know… what to say, my Führer," I stammered.

"No need to say anything, Linge," he assured me. "I only hope that Himmler doesn't have her arrested during the screening."

We both chuckled at that, though my chuckle was considerably darker. I kept my curiosity about how Goebbels had arranged for subtitles to myself.

⚜

Guests present at the screening were Goebbels and his wife, Magda; Himmler; Speer; Riefenstahl; von Ribbentrop—and Klara. Junge was there to serve refreshments, and Günsche, I assumed, to ensure by size alone that there would be no sneaking in by anyone not expressly invited. To witness the teensy Junge and the colossal Günsche beside one another was, to me, more amusing than any Disney cartoon could possibly be.

As usual, when it was over, the Führer asked the assembled what they thought of it before ignoring their opinions and providing conclusive insights. And I knew that, as usual, each would opine according to his or her nature. In point of fact, I knew what they would say before they said it, so knowing, I was suddenly struck by the disquieting thought that people, aside from the Führer, were so predictable, even these exalted leaders of the Reich. *What would happen*, I reflected, *were the public to overhear such triteness and vapidity, such infantile pedestrian nonsense from those they worshipped and followed blindly?* I was forced to conclude that such dignitaries must be infinitely more brilliant in their jobs than in their private lives—that they must live a truly hermetically sealed, compartmentalised existence.

Riefenstahl was first since the rest didn't appear eager to volunteer, and her hubris could always fill any empty space, regardless of size.

"My Führer." She shrugged. "While the film displays considerable technical proficiency, it unfortunately lacks soul, something that German cartoonists can provide in their sleep, of course."

Of course, I laughed to myself, *but only under her personal supervision.*

Von Ribbentrop asked to be excused for the moment, as he had no opinion—*Save for the Führer's,* I thought with an internal head shake. After learning of it, he would most certainly have one.

Speer felt that it was "well drawn and mildly entertaining, up to a point, but," he added, "it illustrates, unmistakably, the simplistic nature of the Americans and their bourgeois morality."

Ever the arrogant snob.

Magda Goebbels then declared, "Cartoons are for children, my Führer, so von Schirach and my husband are far more qualified than I to determine its political value, both for children like mine and for our nation's youth generally. And of course, the characters *are* Italian."

What she meant by her last reference, I possessed no clue, though I safely assumed it wasn't a compliment.

Then her husband felt free to speak. "For Americans, it seems, all one need do is condition those who stray from the straight and narrow to correct aberrant behaviour. In this regard, they are not unlike the Germans."

Then it was Himmler's turn at bat. "My Führer, it's a cartoon, after all," he said blankly. "If I'm to express an opinion, it would only concern Pinocchio's nose and how simple my job would be if each perpetrator's lie would cause the liar's nose to elongate."

But not nearly as much fun, I wanted to tell the group.

The Führer then asked Klara her opinion, and all heads but Riefenstahl's and Magda's swivelled towards her. For my part, I shut my eyes and prayed.

"My Führer," she answered in her "deaf-speak" accent, "I must confess that I was too grateful for the captions to pay much attention to the story."

Heads shook, eyebrows knitted, and I smiled. She was as clever as she was discreet.

Finally, all turned their heads towards the Führer, who held up a sheet of unlined paper containing what I considered to be a competent rendering of *Pinocchio*.

"As a struggling artist," he said to all with a tone of mockery, "I couldn't get a crust of stale bread for my paintings." Then he put down the cartoon, signed his name at the bottom, and held it up again. "I wonder how much I could get for this puerile trifle today."

Head-bobbing laughs followed all round, save for Klara, who hadn't turned to read his lips.

15 November 1940

TUNING OUT A solitary rant by the Führer to no one in particular over Stalin's visit on 12 November, in which the latter expressed more than a passing interest in Finland, Bulgaria, Romania, the Dardanelles, and the Bosporus, I spent most of the day mentally squirming with eagerness to see Klara and, among other things, to get her estimation of the previous evening. Also—perhaps something perverse in me—I wished to do the same with my new "superior," Günsche, and since I was at work, the latter would have to come first.

After we finished dividing the mail but prior to sorting and distributing it, I invited him for some coffee in the officers' mess, always conscious of the political ambiguity of our respective military ranks.

"Well, Major, what did you think of the film?" I asked once we were seated closely at right angles to each other.

I chuckled to myself, as he closed his left eye and raised the other in an attitude of deep deliberation, as if I'd asked him to critique a proposition by Wittgenstein rather than a cartoon by Disney. Finally, after several agonisingly cogitative moments, the Führer's chief adjutant and Brückner's successor was ready to tackle the complexities of *Pinocchio*.

"Well, Colonel—" he began, but before he could continue, I interrupted.

"Might it not be preferable for two gentlemen who work

so closely together for the Führer to use a less formal mode of address?"

Günsche nodded vigorously. "Yes, yes, I see your point. What would you suggest?"

I smiled to myself. "Let's make it simple. Heinz and Otto? How would that be?"

More vigorous nods. "Great!" he exclaimed. "Shall we start now?"

"Now that's an astute suggestion." I hoped that by his beaming expression, he hadn't spotted the metaphorical tongue pushing out my cheek.

After listening with gnashed teeth to Otto's mental dissection of the film, all I could think of was a maxim I'd read long ago: "The difference between stupidity and genius is that genius has its limits."

✖

I never made it to Klara's. When I returned to my quarters to change, I discovered that my door had been replaced with one that provided so little space at the bottom that it scraped the linoleum audibly when I opened it. One didn't have to be Brückner to realise that someone had decided to seal up my "clandestine mail slot," which I'd long abandoned. And without much deliberation, I felt I knew who that someone was. I also knew that it wouldn't be long before the perpetrator would need to personally, and ever so subtly, shove his savvy in my face.

THOREAU WROTE, "THE path of least resistance leads to crooked rivers and crooked men." Universally true or not, I felt that the least resistance was with my new "superior." I waited until our morning duties were completed, and just before we were about to go our separate ways, I steered him into an alcove for a brief, friendly chat.

"So, Otto," I began on a tangent, "I can see that you've adjusted quickly to the Führer's personal style?"

"Well, the Führer makes it easy." He nodded. "He makes so few demands that I really feel as if things could get done without me."

Of course, they could—and did, but I had no intention of telling Otto that the reason was his stupidity and incompetence, which drove the Führer to bestow most of Günsche's duties on me.

"That's the Führer for you," I said with an indulgent smile. "Brückner used to say that it was as if he were on a perpetual vacation, getting free money for nothing." I paused a moment. "So then, Otto," I said, finally getting to my point, "what does the Führer have you doing besides the mail?"

He pursed his lips in thought over that one. "Well, honestly, the only thing I did all yesterday morning was to have a new door installed for your quarters. Better now, eh?"

Bormann wasted no time. *Better than what?* I wanted to ask, but I said, "Words can't express my gratitude, Otto."

Günsche smiled cheerfully. "That's great! No more drafts, eh? Now you'll sleep better, I bet."

"Good of you to concern yourself with my slumbers," I said.

"Oh, no need to thank me," he said. "I had no idea you had a defective door."

"Really?" My face brimmed with cherubic innocence. "Then I must thank the Führer."

He shook his head. "Not the Führer, Heinz," he corrected, as I'd hoped.

"Who then?" I asked with the barest touch of incipient confusion.

"Reichsleiter Bormann."

A feverish heat enveloped my face, and I struggled to compensate with an expression of mundane nonchalance. "Really. I thought Bormann was sequestered at the Berghof."

"Sequestered?"

Careful, I warned myself. *This puerile lout is definitely not Brückner.* "Sorry." I gave a slight shrug. "I meant headquartered."

"Not anymore," he corrected. "He's here now."

"Permanently?"

"No idea, but the man really knows how to take charge."

"How do you mean?"

Furrowed forehead again. "What do you mean, how do I mean?"

"An example," I instructed the clod.

A swivelled eye again. "Uh, well… everything, you know."

"One example of 'everything' will go a long way."

"Well, your door, I suppose, for an example."

"Nothing too small for the Reichsleiter, it seems."

"Well, that's what I meant. You know, I don't think he ever sleeps."

I assumed that any more questions would put even this

character on alert, so I decided to exit gracefully. "Then, I suppose he doesn't care whether he has a defective door or not." I left Günsche with his mouth still open.

IN A LATE-MORNING conference with a cherubic Göring, an elegant Speer, and an impassive Himmler, the Führer was virtually delirious with glee over the former's report of massive bombing raids on Liverpool on 29 November, on Southampton on 30 November and 1 December, Bristol on the second, and yesterday, Birmingham.

"This is special news!" the Führer shouted as he jumped up and slapped his thigh in triumph. "This might even force that stuttering whale Churchill onto a diet—no offence, Hermann."

"A diet of humble pie, perhaps," Göring ventured with a laugh, "and no offence taken, my Führer."

"It's good that you have such a thick skin, Hermann—and so much of it," the Führer jested, as if it were a schoolyard test of Göring's tolerance, but all he received in response was, "That's a good one, my Führer," before Göring let it go, as all knew he would.

While they continued to laugh and joke about the destruction of British cities and their civilian inhabitants, I stole a glance at Günsche. With his light-blond hair slicked back, blue eyes, long narrow face, broad shoulders, and athletic physique, he resembled nothing less than a young, taller Heydrich—save for the former's expression of mindless innocence, an expression I prayed represented his true self and not a carefully constructed persona.

"So, Heinrich, what do you think of all this?" the Führer asked Himmler once the merriment had subsided.

All eyes turned to the taciturn security chief.

"If you're referring to our previous discussion, my Führer," he said, "I never for one moment doubted the wisdom of your strategy—"

"Be that as it may, at least now you can see that—"

"However," Himmler interjected, "I also never doubted, for one moment, Comrade Stalin's territorial resolve."

Damnation by faint praise, I thought, leaving me with the fleeting sensation that Himmler feared the Soviets far more than he feared the Führer.

"You've been extremely quiet, Speer," the Führer observed, and eyes shifted from Himmler to the dapper architect. "Are you lost in thought?"

"Incisive, as always, my Führer," he replied. "I was just thinking about how your strategy, while brilliant and perhaps even pivotal, will deprive the world of many irreplaceable structures."

The Führer smiled broadly. "You disappoint me, Albert. Here I go to all the trouble of providing you with untold opportunities to display your architectural genius to the world, not merely to Germany, and you lament the loss of some unimaginative piles of brick, wood, and plaster. I knew, even as a student, that art must not wallow in sentimentality. This is precisely why there are no female artists or architects. Surely you must recognise this universal truth."

Speer's eyelids fluttered for a second, then focused again. "Of course, my Führer. You're quite right as always; I must learn to overcome my unmanly mawkishness."

The Führer smiled again, this time with more indulgence. "No need to fret, Albert. Whenever you falter, I'll be there to steady you."

For a moment, I wondered why Bormann the door replacer wasn't present, but that passed, being supplanted by Brückner's warning that the Reichsleiter was an Iago (Othello's conniving underling, who constantly schemes, plots, and manipulates behind a curtain of anonymity and indefatigable efficiency). It suddenly became clear to me that, whether dependent or not, I needed to confer with my old mentor as quickly and naturally as possible.

MOST OF THE morning on the day I designated, for myself, as "Operation Willie," the Führer was in conference with Field Marshals Keitel and von Rundstedt as well as Admiral Canaris, concerning events in Egypt involving the hapless Italians. The Führer was clearly distraught. Nevertheless, since I was concentrating most of my mental energy on my strategic approach to Klara and then to the Führer about my door, I can relate only occasional sketches and snatches here.

"I'm well aware, Keitel," the Führer said, "that it's that idiotic system of… dare I say… government under which the poor Duce must operate. Having to share political and military power with that moronic antique in uniform! Can you picture me having to continually share power with Hindenburg? Well, can you?"

"No, my Führer," the three soldiers replied virtually in unison.

"Of course not," the Führer echoed derisively. "And yet… and yet, the Duce must, or he loses the support of the people. So, he has a Hobson's choice before him."

To me, with what little concentration I could muster, it seemed more like choosing the lesser of two evils, but I would never presume to second-guess the Führer's choice of idioms.

"And now, Canaris," he continued, turning to his intelligence chief, "since the British seem to have had the time between bombings to break the Italians' so-called secret military code, what's left for him? Hmm?" he shouted, then turned back to his field marshals.

Von Rundstedt replied first. "My Führer, given the lamentable situation in Greece that may well force—I mean, cause—you to intervene, any support you give to the Duce in Egypt could be the proverbial straw."

"Yes, my Führer," Keitel added, perhaps emboldened by von Rundstedt's blatant demonstration of pluck. "What if he decides next to invade Brazil? I mention the ludicrous because I fear for our own aspirations if we're to endlessly follow his failures."

The Führer's eyes became hooded, and he gripped the sides of his desk with white-knuckled hands—two gestures seemingly at odds with one another—but said nothing, I presumed, to allow the implications of their misguided audacity to sink in unmistakably. And as usual with the Führer, it worked. I laughed to myself. So many visitors to the Chancellery and even employees who hadn't the benefit of close, daily association with the Führer saw only what they would describe as "rug chewing," meaning hysterical, purple-faced screaming.

I, of course, knew better. As the Führer explained to me not long after I began my service, "I'm not magic. It's the old story of the blind men who touch an elephant to learn what it's like, but by feeling a different part—such as the side or the tusk—when they finally compare notes, they find that they are all in complete disagreement. Do you seriously think I would have risen this high from nothing if all I did was bellow and fume? Do you seriously think that I was able to defeat my enemies and enchant my friends through hysterical ranting? What these puny minds all fail to grasp is that a born leader must possess a comprehensive repertoire of responses to events and people, all finely calibrated for maximum effectiveness. Here's a lesson for you, Linge: never allow either your friends or your enemies to anticipate you."

At the time, I performed a perfect yes-my-Führer-thank-you, but I'd already learned that lesson on my first day with him. I would certainly need it today.

The Führer didn't have to wait long for von Rundstedt, Keitel, and Canaris to come to their political senses.

"My Führer," Keitel said, "as I've reconsidered the matter, I must confess that my first reaction was somewhat precipitate. The Duce is a good friend and valuable ally of the Reich in a world growing increasingly hostile to our aims. Moreover, our presence in Greece and Egypt takes nothing away from your incisive British strategy. Perhaps it might even compel them to divide their forces, leaving their isolated island more vulnerable."

"I'm compelled to agree, my Führer," von Rundstedt followed with breathtaking ambiguity. "Such action against such paltry adversaries will provide additional territory, labour, and raw materials with minimal sacrifice. We're not Italians, after all."

The Führer smiled, then slowly released his grip and clasped his hands.

"And what of you, Admiral?" he asked Canaris with his warmest intonation.

"I must agree with the field marshals, my Führer," he said, following von Rundstedt's lead. "For my part, I place the blame at the feet of the Duce's cryptographers, who are unworthy of their leader's vision. Perhaps you might suggest to him that he would profit from having our own cipher experts consult and advise."

"Then it's settled, gentlemen," the Führer declared. "When the time is right, I'll inform you, and we'll go in and pull the

Duce's fat from the fire. We'll have gained more than his gratitude, I can assure you."

He stood, signalling the meeting's adjournment, and they left, I imagined, properly chastened if not warned.

৯

"The fools still don't know me," the Führer declared as he resumed his seat. "Sit down, Linge," he directed with a wave. "Let's have a chat."

I sat, not knowing what to expect but grateful for the informality I would need for my plan.

"I'm not insensitive," he began, "to the added burdens placed on you since Günsche came on board. He seems to be a nice young chap, not unlike you when you first joined my service, only more hair and height."

I chuckled at that, grateful he'd not seen more.

"As I told you, he's definitely no Brückner, but I learned long ago that you want clever men to advise you, not live with you. It's no different with clever women," he added, "intending no disrespect to Fräulein Braun, of course."

Then I thought, *Where the Devil did Bormann fit into the Führer's scheme of things?* Then I found out.

"Be that as it may, with Bormann here, assiduous nonentity that he is, things have settled down to the point where I can spare you for a while and let Junge think I've replaced you with him—a little harmless joke, eh? So take a vacation. If you wish to motor somewhere, Kempka can spare a saloon. If you wish to fly, I'll make Baur available. And take your Klara with you. Attractive young woman. Personally, I require a companion who can hear me, but I can see the attraction for you quiet types."

"I'm overwhelmed, my Führer," I replied in all truth. "I was just about to request some time off."

The Führer nodded. "Well then, Linge, I come not only to the Duce's rescue but to yours as well."

As I made for Klara's flat, I had to say that the Führer was dead wrong about one thing at least: he *is* magic.

⤳

Since I had doorbell-activated blinking red lights installed, I no longer needed to have Klara waiting by her open door ahead of my arrival, but I still had to phone ahead, employing the good offices of her cooperative neighbour.

"Have you ever been to Paris?" I asked her after dinner.

The two of us were nestled on her sofa, brandishing our brandies to a popular tune on her radio that only I could hear. She was wearing the satin negligee I'd gotten her, and I'd removed my tunic and boots. I felt quite the *bon vivant*, a sensation perfect for my purpose.

She laughed. "You'll think me hopelessly provincial, but I've never been out of Berlin. Why do you ask?"

"The Führer granted me some leave, and I thought we might enjoy a complete change of scene. Like Paris, for instance."

"You were in Paris, weren't you?"

"For a short time, yes, but it was all business, trotting after the Führer, whose only purpose was to briefly savour his historic revenge and quickly tour some buildings and monuments—hardly recreation for me. But in the process, I happened to learn of several enjoyable possibilities that—"

"May I be candid?" she asked.

"What a question to ask me by now," I answered in mock umbrage. "Of course you can be candid. In fact, you must be candid."

She smiled. "Must, eh? Then yes, Herr Colonel, candid I shall be. It's all the damn uniforms round me. Everywhere.

Berlin is like an enormous, beautifully appointed military base. I stay home, not because of my condition but to avoid the vast ocean of uniforms that surround me wherever I go."

"But I wear a uniform," I said, "and—"

"Yes. You demanded candour, my dear," she cut in with a sweetness in her voice I felt she didn't mean. "I was going to discuss that very fact eventually, but I'm grateful to you for forcing the issue."

Forcing the issue? When? How? I shook my head in confusion. "But I don't understand. What's the problem for you with uniforms? And what does that have to do with our visiting Paris?"

"*You don't know?*" Her voice raised slightly. "You, a lieutenant colonel of the SS, don't know the significance of a uniform? Well, my love, clearly you've been cocooned in the Chancellery far too long, so I shall enlighten you: In the Reich, a uniform has become the triumph of anonymity in the mindless service of evil. They all bear the stink of horror, death, and putrefaction. And Paris, where you would have us frolic innocently, is now no better than Berlin. Or Rome. Or Warsaw. Or Tokyo. Or Madrid. Or…but then again…"

Klara poured me another brandy.

"It does sound wonderful, Heinz," she said, back in her normal voice. "I've read so much about it. Understanding no French," she kidded, "my deafness will finally not be a problem. And you even have a friend there, so he can show us the best of Paris. When can we go?"

For a moment, it struck me that I was violating the independence that Brückner wanted me to develop, but I rationalised it away with a salute to coincidence.

"It depends. Plane or auto?"

"No train?"

"If we're going to be leisurely, wouldn't we rather spend our time there than in travelling?"

"You're right; plane, then, so we can reserve our leisure for recreation, hmm?" She finished the rest of her brandy and nodded towards her bedroom. "And speaking of recreation…"

CIRCUMSTANCES AND EVENTS afforded me no opportunity to write you until now, so I compress the previous three days into this one entry.

DAY ONE:

Baur—aided and abetted by surprisingly excellent December weather and a temporary absence of the RAF—delivered us to Paris in record time. He departed just as quickly but not before turning away from Klara and whispering in my ear needlessly, "She's quite a dish for… well, you know. If you ever split up, you let your uncle Hans know, right? You may not believe it, but with the laws being the way they are now, there's one hell of a market for a good-looking deafie who's protected. Dumb as well would be even better, but you know…" His shoulders performed a what-can-you-do shrug.

Quite the gentleman, this steaming pile of aeronautical shit! "You'll be the first to know, Uncle," I assured him. "But you have to cut me in on the profits."

"Hey, I never thought otherwise. Göring and I are the only ones who appreciate the socialism part of National Socialism. Share and share alike, I say. But now I must go." He saluted me, turned, waved a wishful goodbye to Klara, and returned to his plane while we headed for the crammed terminal.

"He was talking about me, wasn't he?" she asked as we walked.

"He was telling me how valuable you are."

"Valuable? That compliment's a new one to me."

"Not new in Baur's world," I said. "Anyway, let's see if my pass can cut through the crowd."

෪

My pass held more than enough authority to make the German officials deferential and the French officials servile. Since Brückner was now in the Wehrmacht, I rang the Majestic Hotel on Avenue Kléber, which housed the German military high command. There, I was told that "Colonel Brückner" had been seconded as adjutant to General Otto von Stülpnagel, commandant of Paris, and was headquartered at the Hotel Meurice on the rue de Rivoli.

To avoid anyone connecting the dots of my intent, I decided to contact him once we arrived, rather than in advance of our coming.

"Good God!" Brückner shouted merrily, "Heinz! Where are you calling from?"

"The hotel lobby," I answered. "It's like the Adlon, only grander."

"Yes," he said, "the French are as good at preserving their finery as they are at surrendering them since both involve the same considerations."

"Klara's with me."

"Well done, Heinz." Then a slight hesitation. "Say, don't bother to come up. I'll meet you both in the restaurant. You can't miss it."

෪

As usual, Brückner was right. Whatever ability to describe that I might claim was defeated by the restaurant's prodigious opulence, for only a poet or Speer could begin to do it justice. We were, of course, early, but between my pass and Brückner's name, we were seated at a table fit for royalty. Klara did her best to appear dispassionate, but the glow in her eyes as she gazed round the vast elegance signalled nothing less than wonder.

In one sense, the dining room might as well have been in the Adlon, for all the high-level German uniforms surrounding us. It made me think of Klara's emotional reservations in her parlour.

"You shouldn't have waited," Brückner said cheerfully as he arrived at our table.

I rose to greet him, saluted, shook his hand with vigour, and reintroduced him to Klara, who didn't seem to know what to do, but Brückner reached down, took her hand, moved it gently towards him, kissed it, moved it back, and we both sat.

"Are there any French here?" I joked, having looked around and seen virtually the same faces I'd seen at the Adlon.

"Fewer and fewer as the days go by." He shook his head. Brückner hadn't changed one bit, save for the grey Wehrmacht uniform and the collar tabs of a full colonel. "Most fled, and aside from top-level collaborators who are here more or less permanently, Paris is the primary destination for the rest and recreation of our soldiers, each one being promised one visit to Paris. Not to places like this, of course, but go out into the street, and you might as well be in Munich."

Klara and I laughed at that.

"I told you the colonel here was quite the comedian," I said to her.

"Unfortunately, Klara," Brückner said with a mock frown, "without your Heinz here, I have a rather limited audience."

She smiled but said nothing. I could sense the tension wash over her features, the uniforms probably.

A liveried waiter appeared at our table, appropriately efficient and obsequious, and we had Brückner order for us, which he was glad to do. Our drinks arrived almost immediately, making it clear to me that Brückner was an important habitué.

"I'm a good tipper," Brückner offered.

I smiled at his always-witty humility and missed him even more, something he would have disdained.

A gourmand's feast arrived not much later, and we lit into it with gusto.

"If it's not an imposition," I said when we'd finished, "we were hoping for a personally guided tour. Perhaps where we can see some actual French people."

"I can do that easily," he said. "We'd only need to tour Gestapo Headquarters."

"You joke," I said, not a little startled.

"I joke," he replied. "I'd be delighted to. The nightclubs are especially French since most of the native entertainers chose to remain rather than suffer the inconvenience of anonymity elsewhere. The best show in town seems to be *Bonjour Paris*, with that obnoxious warbling crooner Maurice Chevalier. Packed every night. Without reservations, it'll take a pass from Stülpnagel himself—which I can get, of course—if you'd like to go this evening."

"Well, Wilhelm," I said, "that would be wonderful, but I'm afraid the magic of Chevalier would be lost on Klara."

Brückner chuckled affably. "Of course. Clumsy of me. I'll tell you what: I'll take some emergency leave and show you both the daytime sights. How'd that be?"

"Much more practical." I winked at Klara, who smiled back.

There seemed to be the beginnings of a commotion across

the room. Two leather-greatcoated behemoths whispered down to a man sitting alone in a smartly tailored pinstripe, poking him repeatedly while people at surrounding tables were engaged in an intense inspection of their food.

"What's all that about?" I asked Brückner.

"Just what it looks like," he said. "Soon he'll be gone, and the rest can raise their heads and resume eating."

As he'd predicted, within seconds, the man rose to be escorted from the room, allowing the other patrons to look at each other as if nothing had transpired.

"I'm afraid I need to visit the powder room." Klara stood, causing Brückner and me to follow suit.

"Do you know where it is?" Brückner asked.

"Thank you, Colonel, but I can find my way in a hotel." Then she turned and headed for the lobby.

We sat down. "What was that about?" I asked absently.

Brückner smiled. "Either digestion or discretion, I'd guess. Anyway, I'm so glad you chose to visit Paris. A little notice, and I'd have concocted a decent itinerary. But why do I get the feeling that this is how you wanted it?"

"You know me too well. It is."

"Ah yes." Brückner nodded. "Well then, we should probably do some business before Klara returns. You didn't come all the way to Paris to be entertained by Chevalier. How are you faring under the new management?"

I paused a moment before answering. "I really don't know, Wilhelm. That's what I need to ask you."

"Happily, I'm well out of all that," he said. "But not entirely. You know, I actually thought that by joining the Wehrmacht, I'd see some action. But it seems the high command need an adroit bureaucrat, late of the Führer's 'inner circle,' more than they need an ancient warrior with one eye. Crazy, isn't it?"

I laughed. "The war doesn't know what it's missing."

"So, what do you need from this adroit bureaucrat?"

"Access to you. I know"—I raised my hands, palms up—"it's despite your desire for my independence, but there are times and there are times, as Kempka would say. I have no one at the Chancellery I can truly confide in, and you did tell me you'd be just a phone call away."

"Absolutely, for what it's worth. But not just any 'phone call.' All right, here's how it must go: write down this number."

"I'll remember it."

"Really?" he exclaimed, wide-eyed. "You've improved. I always felt you had to write down your own name and check on it from time to time for accurate reference." He recited the telephone number. "Now, you can ring this at any time, day or night, to leave a message that must include a number from a public phone and precisely when I can ring you back. But I can give you some quick and dirty right now." He lowered his voice to a whisper. "Don't worry yourself about Günsche. He's a mindless mediocrity with the physique of a Roman statue and the intellect to match. However, this is certainly not the case with Bormann, regardless of his physique. The grasping swine managed to rid himself of me, but it won't be so easy with you. Nevertheless, he wants the Führer all to himself and will use any means necessary to shut you out of all but the most menial and distant duties. His ideal replacement for you would be Junge. You already know a lot more than you did about that conniver, so watch out for him. And whatever happens, Heinz, you must know by now that the Führer holds you in special regard. Stay close to him. Never be away from his side for long—and hope that his regard endures, despite Bormann's best efforts to unseat you."

Just then, Klara returned, lovely as ever, but her face wore an inexplicable pallor. "Please don't get up." She eased onto her chair.

"Are you not well?" Brückner asked solicitously.

"Thank you for your concern, Colonel, but—"

"Call me Wilhelm. Please."

"It must have been a delayed reaction to the flight... Wilhelm. I'd never been in an aeroplane before."

Brückner looked at me. "Baur still showing off?" Then back to Klara. "You should know that your pilot has consistently boasted that he could defeat the entire RAF by himself if Göring would only let him get drunk before takeoff. Isn't that right, Heinz?"

I smiled. "I don't really think that Baur would bother with Göring's permission."

Brückner smiled.

"I'm sure that with a small nap, I'll be as good as new," she promised—unconvincingly, I thought.

In front of my friend and confidant, I felt no hesitation in sounding her out, though I suddenly thought I knew the source of the problem. "Was it the incident over there a while ago?" I asked with a slight tilt of my head in that direction.

She sat silent for a few moments while Brückner and I waited.

"The man was deaf," she finally said, no expression apparent in her voice, only in her eyes. "They were taking away a deaf man."

"How do you know this?" Brückner asked, though I believed I knew the answer.

"I could read their lips," was all she said.

As she spoke these simple words, I thought back to a conversation a year ago that Himmler had with the Führer about the 1933 law to prevent, by sterilisation, the "unfit" (including the blind, the manically depressed, the physically malformed, promiscuous women—and the deaf) from having children and the 1935 law in which doctors were given the legal right to terminate pregnancies by force if an inherited genetic condition such as deafness was suspected. Abortions were carried out as late as six months into the pregnancy. The Reichsführer had been lobbying for all adult "defectives" to be euthanised without exception.

The Führer had indulged him with soothing words, but after Himmler had left, presumably satisfied, the Führer had said to me with his customary faint damnation by even fainter praise, "Heinrich has many fine qualities, but flexibility and moderation, I'm afraid, are not among them. You know, Linge, I was such a poor and inattentive student, my teachers almost put me in a class for backward children. If that had happened today, where would I be?"

I'd wanted to say, *On a table, waiting for the scalpel.* But of course, I'd said nothing. I would say even less now.

Neither Klara nor I could say with certainty that the man had been arrested for deafness, and it being Paris and, so far, still beyond Himmler's reach, it probably wasn't, but the mere fact of his deafness was enough for Klara to make the connexion.

"Well then," Brückner said to break the grim silence that followed Klara's declaration, "I must get back to my vital war work. Of course, you'll stay at the Meurice; it's all been arranged. And tomorrow, I'll show you as much of a Frenchman's Paris as is possible nowadays." He stood and took Klara's hand again, only gently pumping it this time. "It was a pleasure meeting you," he said. "I do hope that little unpleasantness didn't spoil your trip." Then, without waiting for a response, he turned to me. "Wonderful seeing you again, Heinz. Tomorrow, then."

"Did he actually say 'unpleasantness'?" Klara asked once Brückner could no longer be seen.

"He's very sophisticated," I answered obliquely, leaving any-thing further to hover unspoken in the space between us.

DAY TWO:

By the time we finished breakfast, compliments of Brückner, Klara had recovered sufficiently and claimed to be looking for-ward to seeing the sights, if not the sounds, of Paris.

As he'd promised, a car and driver waited for us when we exited the hotel, where a short, portly gentleman encased in an impeccably bespoke, double-breasted pin-striped suit stood by the open passenger-side door, waving at us.

"My name is Bedaux, Charles Bedaux," he informed us in decent German seasoned with a blend of several nondescript foreign accents. "Colonel Brückner sends his regrets that he has been detained, but he prevailed upon me to act as proxy until he can join you, and of course, I was only too happy to oblige."

Of course he was. I'd heard the name as early as 1937 but had no picture of him until now. At that time, Goebbels was telling the Führer that Bedaux was what he derisively called a "businessman-cum-go-between-cum-raconteur."   According to Goebbels, the wealthy, French-born American had recently purchased the sixteenth-century Château de Candé in France, where he lived with his American second wife, Fern. On 3 June 1937, they hosted the wedding of Wallis Simpson and Prince Edward, Duke of Windsor, at the château.

Goebbels claimed that such a type could be useful. As he put it, "My Führer, the man is like a needy canine: Hold up a bone, and he'll sit up and beg. Give it to him, and he'll follow you any-where." So, Goebbels arranged the royal couple's honeymoon in Germany, where they would meet publicly with the Führer and make it known that this largesse was all due to the "influence" of Charles Bedaux.

But not all had gone well for the canine. The next stage of the happy royal couple's trip, the United States, had to be called off due to labour union, press, and public outrage at Bedaux's involvement, and he'd been quickly demonised as a fascist in all media outside Germany. Bedaux had soon suffered what was undoubtedly a nervous breakdown but had been diagnosed diplomatically as arterial thrombosis. He'd spent months convalescing in a Bavarian hospital, where his only visitor was his wife (and Goebbels, who still harboured hopes of someday using his important connexions).

The day seemed to come for both when we occupied Paris. No fool, Bedaux had scurried to become acquainted with leading Nazi and Vichy figures, and it had paid off, in the form of an appointment as an economic adviser to Vichy and the Reich, reporting directly to Brückner.

❧

I won't bore you with tour-book descriptions, but clearly, informed guiding was one of Bedaux's strong suits. Within one day, he ushered us to the Eiffel Tower, Notre Dame Cathedral, the Louvre, the Arc de Triomphe, the Champs-Élysées, Montmartre, and Sacré-Cœur. And after that whirlwind expedition, he still managed to arrange for us to enjoy a lavish dinner at the illustrious Maxim's.

However, as gifted a guide as he was, I was concerned about Bedaux's health, for in a full day of being out and about in the December chill, he was continually drenched in perspiration, even during dinner. Klara and I were concerned that he'd done his best for Brückner—and us—at the cost of his well-being. I told him so as we finished our *crème brûlées*.

"I'm most appreciative of your consideration, Herr Linge," he said, still sweating, "but truly, I'm absolutely in the pink."

The pink I could testify to, since his face appeared constantly flushed. "Yes, well, I'm glad to hear it," I replied as convincingly as I could. "We were concerned that Colonel Brückner might have prevailed upon you without considering your health."

He shook his head vigorously, spraying beads of sweat left and right. "There was nothing for him to consider, I assure you. And as you must know, the colonel can be very persuasive."

I noticed that Bedaux had the habit of saying two opposing things in a sentence with equal conviction, presumably an asset in business, no less than in politics.

"In that case"—I glanced at Klara, then back at Bedaux—"the matter is closed. I'll make a point of ringing Brückner to tell him what a gracious and splendid guide you've been to Klara and me."

The portly ball of dampness shot out his hand with such velocity that at first, I thought he was saluting me. "Please, do not do that, Herr Linge," he entreated. "It was my sincere pleasure, so I'd rather tell him myself. I pride myself on… how shall I say it?… 'modesty' is too self-righteous a word. Perhaps, 'unpretentiousness'? If the two of you enjoyed yourselves, that is reward enough."

"Well," I volunteered, "we'll leave it at—"

"On the other hand," he interrupted with a shrug, "if you might put in a few carefully chosen words of moderate approval with Reichsleiter Bormann?"

At that, alarm bells began clanging in my brain, and I struggled to remain insipidly—and ignorantly—grateful. "Of course, Herr Bedaux. I'll be more than happy to speak with him, though," I added for effect, "I report directly to the Führer."

His hand started to shoot up again but only made it halfway

before dropping. "Oh no-no-no," he sputtered. "Please don't even consider burdening the Führer with such trivia. A word to the Reichsleiter will be more than sufficient." He raised his hand once again, but this time slowly and higher, to signal the waiter.

DAY THREE:

I hadn't intended to contact Brückner until Klara and I arrived back in Berlin, but the previous night's dinner conversation caused me no little anxiety, so I rang him at his office before Bedaux came to collect us for more sightseeing.

"I didn't expect to hear from you so soon, my friend. So, tell me," Brückner asked effusively, "how do you and Klara like our Paris?"

"'Our' is the right word," I answered. "There were so many Germans, uniformed and otherwise, that the city looked as if the Führer had it dismantled and put up in Berlin as an exhibit."

Brückner broke into laughter on the other end. "I understand your point, Heinz. To be frank, it's so Germanised here that the only thing I still miss about the Fatherland is you."

It was far too generous a compliment for a response, so I made certain he could hear my laugh before I went on. "We visited so many monuments and neighbourhoods, I think I could apply for a taxi licence."

More laughter.

"I'm sorry I couldn't have been your guide, but I trust the hotel had a decent one on hand."

It was a perfect opening. "The hotel? But Monsieur Bedaux told us that you'd prevailed upon him to—"

"*Bedaux* took you round the city?"

"Yes, and quite a guide at that."

A few beats of silence followed, then Brückner returned with a completely different tone.

"I prevailed upon him? Is that what he said? Intriguing."

"How so?"

"Well, somehow he heard you were coming and literally begged me to allow him to be your guide. I gave him an unequivocal no. In my world, that's intriguing—and highly troubling."

No less to me, I thought with a shudder.

"You're calling from your room?" he asked.

"Yes, we were going out again with Bedaux to see the few leftovers."

"Now this is vital, Heinz," he cautioned, and I stiffened. "Put him off. Claim illness—yours or Klara's or both, it doesn't matter—sour tummy from too-rich food or something equally plausible. Then call Baur. Have him get you back to the Führer without delay and stay as close to him as you can without rousing suspicion."

"Of course, but why the rush?" I asked, trying not to sound as alarmed as he seemed.

"Have you ever heard of Thomas Cromwell? Probably not, but you need to," he answered with more than his customary obliqueness, then he rang off.

Bedaux rang me from the lobby not long after I had spoken to Brückner.

"Such a great pity your charming lady friend is indisposed." Oily solicitude oozed from his lips. "And I had such a splendid day planned for you both. Ah well." He sighed. "As the French say, *c'est la vie.*"

"What?" I asked in my most ingenuous tone.

"C'est la vie. It means 'such is life.'"

"No doubt about it."

"Well then, when she's feeling better, you only have to contact me here, and we'll make up for lost time, eh?"

"Of course, Monsieur Bedaux, that is, if time permits."

"That goes without saying," he said, then added what I thought he would, "but if it doesn't permit, please convey my best regards to Herr Bormann. I know he'll be pleased to hear that I was of some small service."

"Consider it done," I replied with syrupy sincerity and replaced the receiver, wondering just who was the intended recipient of the small service.

⁕

Next came Baur, who was agreeable but somewhat flummoxed.

"My God, man," he exclaimed, "if the Führer gave me an open-ended vacation, he might forget who I am by the time I decided to come back."

"Well, Hans, I'll tell you, if Klara hadn't gotten sick, the Führer might have needed his memory refreshed about me too."

"I'm sure she's entirely worth it," he said. "Okay. I'll talk to the Führer, and if I'm not needed, I'll get right over to collect you—RAF fuckers willing, of course. I'll let you know the when of it as soon as I can."

After my conversation with Brückner, I knew I needed to exercise caution. "Good of you, Hans. But please do me one favour, eh?"

"What?"

"Speak to the Führer about this without Bormann there."

A few beats of silence put me on alert.

"I'll try, but it won't be a piece of cake. That character is always with him, or real close by."

"Thanks, Hans. I'm sure you'll do your best."

"I'll call you as soon as I know something."

❧

While waiting for Baur's call, I busied myself with the mighty task of trying to entertain a disappointed Klara, but my thoughts were elsewhere—poring over every word I'd read about this Cromwell in an attempt to uncover what Brückner claimed was a connexion between him and Bormann.

WE ARRIVED BACK in Berlin this morning, and after depositing Klara at her flat, I went directly to the Chancellery. As usual, Brückner was right about the need for my speedy return, for when I arrived, I was informed at the entrance that, by a directive from Reichsleiter Bormann, all Chancellery personnel, regardless of position, rank, or familiarity, would have to show "full and proper identification" at each security checkpoint.

Since, from the day of my hiring, I'd always been passed through as a matter of routine, I would have been greatly irritated by such a ridiculous precaution. However, after a thorough mental review of what I'd read about Thomas Cromwell and his indefatigably manipulative relationship with King Henry VIII, I attributed this ugly development not to a genuine need or desire to protect the Führer, but to unmistakably illustrate to all that Bormann was in charge—not only of the Chancellery, but of the Führer himself.

This was amply confirmed when I'd reached the innermost checkpoint and Chief Security Officer Colonel Heinrichs confided in me that no one saw the Führer without going through the Reichsleiter. To spare Heinrich any reprisal for his generosity, I allowed him to eye me up and down, check the signature on my pass, and have me empty my pockets into the tray for inspection. Afterwards, I saluted smartly and continued on my way.

When I got to the Führer's outer office, which had once been the personal and sole preserve of Herr Chinless, Günsche—who now sat at a desk directly across from him—rose quickly and, without a word, took my elbow and walked me back into the hallway.

"We didn't expect you back so soon," he said, after an audible deep breath.

"Oh, did I spoil your surprise birthday party for me?" I joked, hoping it wasn't too esoteric for this *dummkopf.*

But I could see it was, as narrowed eyelids and a furrowed brow greeted my words.

"Your birthday? Is it? No," he said, "there's no surprise party. We just thought you'd want to take a longer vacation. I know I would. In fact—"

"Why are we in the hall?" I asked, hoping to cut off any further inane bullshit and expecting no intelligent elucidation. "If it's not vital, I need to check in with the Führer and let him know that I'm back and ready for action." A light touch, whenever possible.

He pursed his lips. "Sure," he said, just short of a stammer. "Check in. A few changes have occurred since you left, and… well, we can go over them after you see the Führer. Plenty of time, eh?"

"Will I need to show you my identification first?" This time, I wasn't joking.

He laughed uneasily. "I get it. You've already seen one change. But all that can wait. By the way, Junge is in with the Führer, so just a heads-up, eh?"

"I'm well advised, Otto. Thanks." Then I turned without saluting and re-entered the anteroom, passing Herr Chinless, who merely shrugged, and entered the Führer's quarters without knocking. Junge was indeed there, standing at ease in a corner, but Günsche had failed to mention that Bormann was also there, along with Goebbels and von Rundstedt. I sidled into another corner, observed only by Junge, whose eyes met mine before they swivelled back to the Führer.

The Führer was still wearing his bathrobe and, I assumed, his slippers as well.

"Well, Herr… Reichsminister," von Rundstedt said with his patrician's supercilious drawl, "after the Duce's stunningly humiliating debacle in Egypt, is the Führer to assist him once again, at the risk of looking like a pushover to the world?"

Goebbels paused, presumably to allow the heat—namely his own—to dissipate, then shook his head. "No, Herr Field Marshal, I'm never fond of throwing good money after bad, as it were. No less than you, my concern is how the Führer will look to the world—and to the Italian people, for that matter—should he forsake his staunchest ally at a time of crisis."

"That's all well and good, Herr—"

"Gentlemen, gentlemen," the Führer intervened, not smiling but clearly enjoying himself. Making these faits accomplis appear as inspiration seemed to act like a colonic on his mood. "You, Field Marshal, never cease to make me nostalgic about my days as an art student in Vienna," he said, causing von Rundstedt to wrinkle his forehead, while Goebbels's face glowed knowingly.

I also knew what the Führer meant, but even if the reference had been explained to von Rundstedt, he would have yawned internally.

"I'll deal with your point first. I think that my appearing as a—how did you put it?—ah yes, 'pushover to the world' might be offset slightly by my record in the Rhineland, Sudetenland, Austria, Czechoslovakia, Poland, the Low Countries, France, North Africa, and soon, not-so-Great Britain, not counting the Reich. Don't you agree?"

It wasn't a question, and all present (including Junge, by now) knew it.

While everyone waited for the Führer to savour his litany of triumphs, I sneaked a peek at Bormann, who was busily scribbling notes—for what purpose, I had no clue, since the Führer generally disdained the idea of anyone taking minutes of his meetings, conferences, or telephone conversations. The more I thought about it, the more I marvelled at Brückner's choice of historical linkages. Like Cromwell, the blacksmith's son, Bormann, the offspring of a postal worker, had risen through inexhaustible energy, iron will, ambition, stealth, and cunning. And like Cromwell, Bormann had to practise an exorbitant self-restraint to negotiate within the Führer's inner circle, a mortal minefield of boundless ego, ruthlessness, territoriality, and suspicion, where any carelessness or audacity could have catastrophic consequences. He was a triumph of underestimation. Not unlike the Führer. Or me. There was no doubt: this man with the plane-smooth face and rotund body of a porker was truly dangerous.

"For the present, I must agree with Joseph," the Führer continued. "As you well know, I always favour striking while the iron is hot. But in all cases, gentlemen, I must rely on my unmatched skill at gauging an iron's temperature." He smiled thinly, clearly pleased with his boastful exploitation of the phrase. "So I will again come to the aid of my hapless ally—but in my own good time. A bit of watchful waiting, and with scant effort, my troops will achieve in days what the Duce couldn't achieve in months. Then I can add one more conquest to the list I just presented to you. The Reich shall control the Adriatic—something that should appeal to you, von Rundstedt. I shall also show the world—whose opinion of me you and Joseph consider so crucial—that while I support my friends, cries for help will no longer be answered with precipitous philanthropy. Now, does that not satisfy you both?"

This master of men was also a master of timing. Before the

room exploded with the inevitable huzzahs, the Führer raised his hand again. "I would only add this." He turned his head to me, then back again. "What I have planned for that world you both say is so interested, I cannot divulge now, but mark my words: that world will soon have more on its mind than my reputation."

After Goebbels and von Rundstedt exchanged head-scratching glances, they rose as one and saluted with verve, leaving Bormann scribbling on his pad, Junge glaring at me, and the Führer saying to Bormann and Junge, "Thank you, gentlemen. Now please leave me with Linge."

❧

"All right, so tell me," he asked as I helped him dress, "how did you and your lady friend like Paris?"

"She liked it without reservation," I answered with measured candour, guessing from his question that the Führer already had a full report of our movements, "except for some unpleasantness at dinner on our first evening. For me, it was like Berlin being visited by a few French tourists."

A chuckle caused his moustache to bob up and down. "Well, my young friend, I could have told you that. That's why I came for the surrender and went like a mighty gust of wind. Soon, mark my words, there will be nowhere to escape the Reich, so you might as well stay here."

I nodded. "I'm sure you're right, my Führer, since I only wanted a change of scene and some active relaxation."

"Active relaxation? A nice turn of phrase. You know, I don't think you realise how much you've grown in sophistication since coming to work for me. You see, a brickyard is no place for the likes of you."

"My old foreman would have agreed with you, my Führer."

The Führer grinned. "Well, I'm damn glad to have you

back," he said with a nod. "I don't dislike Junge; don't misunderstand me. But to be frank, I'm happier when he's not around. Bormann likes him, but in the things that really matter, he's no fit substitute for you."

What he meant, I had no intention of pursuing. Nor did I propose to bring up the matter of Bormann, since experience with the Führer had taught me that he would reveal what he wanted, as he did with all things (including Greece)—in his own way and in his own time.

"A few changes have occurred since you went away. That Bormann is remarkable. I thought *I* was industrious, but that man is a perpetual-motion machine. He's running the Chancellery the way he ran the Berghof…"

Yes, my Führer, I wanted to say, *like a KZ.* I didn't, of course, but I needed to say something, if only to confirm or deny Brückner's characterisation.

"Brückner would have used his dagger on Bormann," the Führer continued. "That giant simpleton Günsche, well, that's another story. But none of this need affect you."

"I'm glad, my Führer," I told him now that the subject was open. "I expected you to ask for my identification."

He smacked his thigh. "My 'lending library' has done you a world of good. You're becoming a regular jester. Bormann calls those extra checkpoints 'my moat,' but to the rest, it must seem like a series of offensive roadblocks."

"Well, my Führer, I would say… inconvenient roadblocks."

"Of course you would because, at bottom, you're a gentleman. But in any event, you'll be spared any of that inconvenience. I've given explicit and strict instructions that you're to have the absolute freedom of the Chancellery, answering to no one but me. Happy now?"

"The better to serve you, my Führer," I answered, perhaps a bit too ceremoniously.

"It's nothing," he said with his usual equanimity. "To be frank, I'm not entirely unselfish. That Bormann, able man that he is, is rather too puffed up by half. Seeing you frolic round here with impunity will be just the thing to cut him down a size or two."

Somehow, I doubted that, but I still felt a great relief that Reichsleiter Bormann wasn't entirely Cromwell—at least not yet.

I HAD TO wait for the Führer's toilette until he'd assured the high command once again that the increasingly unfortunate events in Greece would be remedied once he determined it was a propitious time for him to act. After ringing off and submitting to his dressing regimen, he asked me to send for Schroeder, which I did. While he waited, he decided to ruminate audibly.

"I don't blame von Rundstedt," he began, "despite—or perhaps due to—his pedigree and exalted rank, he can't be expected to understand and, therefore, appreciate inspiration. But thankfully, that pedigree and rank demand that he follow orders, so he's relatively harmless. You know, Linge," he continued as he eased down slowly and fragrantly onto his desk chair. "People believe that the physically disabled are simpletons, when it's just the opposite. I know the Party's position since I helped to create it, but that's quite another matter. Don't you agree?"

As usual, I took his question to be rhetorical and waited, but that didn't stop me from wondering where this provocative non sequitur was going, especially in light of my relationship with Klara.

"Personally," he continued, "I've always believed that the disabled compensate by being clever and devious. They understand how they're perceived and employ it to their advantage. *That* would be my reason for euthanising them, not Himmler's genetics." Then he reached for his spectacles and began riffling through a sheaf of papers.

I took that as a dismissal until, at the door, I heard the

Führer say, "Oh yes, Linge, you may bring your lady friend to our New Year's celebration."

I turned round. "Thank you, my Führer. I'm certain she'll be delighted and honoured." Then I left, not a little distressed.

∾

Knowing that once the Führer was sequestered with Schroeder, I had ample time to run a suddenly important errand. I raced from the Chancellery to a public restaurant telephone, rang Brückner, left the number with his aide, and waited with the receiver pressed to my ear and the switch hook depressed. Five long minutes later, the phone rang, and Brückner came on the line—yes, I'm aware, another violation of independence, but this is all new to me, and if Brückner is willing…

"A bit early to wish me a happy new year, isn't it?"

I forced a laugh. "I assumed that any later, you'd be celebrating."

"That was good thinking on your part. All right, now what's the trouble?"

"I don't know how to tell you."

"Difficult to help then." He lowered his voice to a breathy whisper. "I can only guess. Could it be the Bormann curse?"

"What's the Bormann curse?"

"Bormann."

I didn't need to force that laugh. "No, no," I assured him, "though you were right. He's trying his best to be the Führer's Cromwell, and I can only hope he achieves the same end, quickly.[39] But so far, though the brute's assumed a great deal of stifling

---

[39] Cromwell was arraigned under a bill of attainder and executed for treason and heresy on Tower Hill on 28 July 1540. The king later expressed regret over the loss of his chief minister.

domestic control, the Führer's still not completely in thrall to him, at least where I'm concerned, so no, that's not it. It's Klara." I then related the Führer's peculiar discussion about the disabled and, in the same breath, his having me invite her to the New Year's celebration. "What should I make of that?"

During a prolonged pause, I could hear him empty his office of all but himself, then he got back on the line. "I don't know what to make of it, Heinz. On the one hand, she's Schroeder's niece and the Führer has always encouraged your seeing her, regardless of her condition. On the other hand, you know that the Führer enjoys making people feel secure and then pulling the rug out from under their complacency. It's ingrained in his makeup, I'm convinced, and has served him well. But in my view, this latest incident signifies nothing particularly sinister in your case since your relationship with him appears to be more like son to father than employee to employer."

It was my turn to pause while I considered Brückner's words. The Führer, in my experience, never said anything casually, despite the apparent insouciance of his words or tone of voice. Even if the purpose was obscure, he always had one.

"Yes," I conceded, "what you say makes sense. I can't put my finger on it, but it was the way he expressed his attitude towards the disabled in general more than the specific invitation. Could he have been hinting at something?"

A sizeable line of anxious and irritated voices had formed behind me.

"I don't know, Heinz," Brückner replied. "I really don't. Of course, with the Führer, anything's possible. But the only thing I can make out from what you've said is that if Klara wasn't the subject of the Führer's remarks, who was?"

A sudden chill coursed through me. "I haven't a clue, Wilhelm."

"Well, my friend, perhaps you'll find out something at the Führer's celebration. In any event, I wish you a most happy—and safe—new year." He rang off.

31 *December 1940*

I NEGOTIATED ALL the Führer's New Year's Eve rituals with practised numbness. Except for the last, when those for specific participants gave way to the one for the Chancellery masses. It was here I would finally be reunited with Klara and, perhaps, secure the information Brückner had alluded to.

The Führer, who circulated to make sure he hadn't slighted anyone, was followed on his heels by Bormann and Günsche and, as such, whether by design or by happenstance, this guaranteed my studied avoidance. Instead, Klara and I wandered among the lower-rung hired help. It was while we were with Baur, who was recounting some hair-raising tales of his aeronautical prowess, that I heard a familiar voice behind me.

"Hey, Hans," Kempka slurred, empty champagne glass in hand, "you gonna hog these two?" Without waiting for an answer, he turned to Klara. "Hap… Happy New Year. Hey, I… heard a lot about you. Can, uh, you really read… lips like Linge here said?" He was already two sheets to the wind, and well on his way to a third.

"If they face me," she replied impassively. "They don't always, especially if they know I can."

"That's okay," Kempka said with a lush's lascivious smile. "Hey, you don't have to worry about me facing you." Then he chuckled, turned his head towards me, and cupped his hand over his mouth. "Not bad, kid. Except for her talking funny, she'd be… well… too bad some of the best broads got some physical or mental shit. You pro'lly got the only one tha' got away."

He and Baur were perfect for each other. Before I could suggest to the drunken boor that it might be ungracious to exclude Klara right in front of her, he moved his hand away.

"Lucky dog," he said, then wandered woozily back into the raucous crowd.

I turned to apologise to Klara, but she was well ahead of me, chuckling.

"He may be a great chauffeur, but he's a terrible confidant. No need to apologise for him, Heinz." She shrugged. "Not all men are gentlemen like Colonel Brückner—and you."

I could add nothing to that, so I, too, shrugged, took her gently by the arm, and guided her towards Schroeder, who was making her way towards us.

For Klara, she had hugs and kisses; for me, a perfunctory head tilt. "It's early, I know, but in case I don't see you later, I wish you both a most Happy New Year."

"Thank you, Fräulein Schroeder," I said, "and the same to you."

Klara followed suit.

"And how is my favourite niece?"

"You have only one niece," Klara said.

"Then definitely my favourite, eh?" she rejoined with a thin cackle. "I'm sorry I've not spoken with you in a while!" she hollered over the festive clamour. "But between Great Britain and this Greek nonsense, the Führer has me hopping. I'm amazed my poor hands aren't in slings."

She spoke as if she expected Klara to know what she was talking about, and by her niece's blank stare, I could see that she didn't.

"But I can tell you, my dear, that all my slaving paid off."

She paused for Klara's curiosity, but when there was no response, she continued. "Anyway, I managed a miracle," she announced with a sly smile. "The Führer was so pleased with my poor efforts that I managed to persuade him to let you move in with me."

Klara's face assumed the expression of someone who'd just been told she'd contracted a fatal disease.

"What… what did you say?" she stammered. "Move in?"

"You read me right." A Schroeder joke. "The Führer told me just this morning that he'd have Reichsleiter Bormann secure me larger quarters to accommodate us both, so now you won't have to be all alone in case of an emergency."

Klara shook her head so violently that her hair whipped her in the face. "No, Aunt Christa!" she yelled, making her peculiar "accent" even harder to understand. "I can't possibly allow you to do that." Then she cooled down slightly. "I'm fine by myself. Really. My neighbours look out for me, and Heinz fixed up some lights so I know when someone's at the door. I won't put you to such bother."

Schroeder smiled indulgently, as if Klara were as impaired in her brain as she was in her hearing. "It's no bother." Her face softened a little. "Look, my dear, if you're concerned for me, I can assure you that I would welcome the company, and"—she closed one eye with the awkwardness of one who winks seldom, if ever—"just think how accessible you'll be for Herr Linge."

"I can't let you do this," Klara declared, her face now beet red. "I won't, and that's all I have to say on the matter." She turned her head away, as if to say, "Your lips may move, but I refuse to read them."

Schroeder's ungainly attempt at cleverness having fallen on deaf ears (pun intended), she turned to me. "Herr Linge, I appeal to you. What do you think?"

Before I could tell her in the most diplomatic terms I could rally that it was as preposterous as the Führer's Madagascar scheme and to fuck off, Klara turned back and told her aunt in no uncertain terms, "I do appreciate your concern, but I have no intention of moving. None whatsoever." She then took my arm more tightly than was her custom. "I'm feeling unwell, Heinz. Please, may we get some fresh air?"

Though it was not unseasonably cold for late December, I hardly relished the thought of standing—or even walking—in thirty-degree weather. And yet, I knew by the uncompromising look on Klara's face that her words bore no civil relationship to a request and would countenance no equivocation from me.

"I think I need to get Klara home," I informed Fräulein Schroeder, who'd suddenly turned colder than the outdoors.

"Well then," she began, her tone a study in menace, "I can see that my generous and well-meaning efforts, not to mention the Führer's, have been greeted with selfish ingratitude. It will not be spoken of again. But if I were you," she added, her tone barely short of Gestapo caution, "for Klara's sake if not for your own, I would do everything in my power not to place my unique position in jeopardy. You understand me?"

By Klara's face, I could tell that *she* did. I tried my best to show that I didn't.

The roar of revellers followed us out to the Chancellery steps like thunderclaps, but the frigid air seemed to act like a tonic on Klara's disposition. She even smiled. Since it was too awkward and inefficient to converse while walking abreast, I suggested we go to her flat, but she said she preferred a restaurant. I didn't ask her why. After a few arctic blocks, we chanced on a basement beer hall and went in.

The clamour in the cavern-like chamber was almost impenetrable, and my first thought was that the only one unaffected by it was Klara, which was confirmed when I whisked my hands to my battered ears and she smiled mischievously and shrugged. Gazing round, I saw a typical cross-section of Teutonic faces, flushed red with inebriation and revelry, and a regiment of beer steins crashing down on wooden tables in awkward step with the raucous gemütlich singalongs. I peered through the foul fog of cigarette and cigar smoke to see that there were no empty tables. However, from long familiarity with such trivial obstructions, I searched for a rear table accommodating SS men of lesser rank, moved over, displayed my identification, and relieved them from further merrymaking—but not before hinting at a miserable death if they were ever to grouse to their superiors.

Once we were seated and served, I hoped she would confide in me if I let her reveal it at her own pace—within limits, of course.

"I'm sorry I forced you out into the cold." She took a gingerly sip of her *Glühwein*.[40]

I smiled, straining to hear and speak over the singing, banging, and shouting. "You didn't force me," I assured her with an awkward touch of wit. "Being out in the cold is a natural state for me, and anyway, it was getting far too warm where we were."

"Yes," she said, "for me too."

"I could tell. You realise I have to deal with your aunt almost every day."

She took another sip, less gingerly this time. "I'd rather deal with her as a valet than as a niece." It was no longer an

---

[40] Glühwein (roughly translated as "glowing-wine," referring to the temperature to which the wine is heated) is popular in German-speaking countries and the Alsace region of France. It is a traditional beverage offered during the Christmas holidays. Glühwein is usually prepared from red wine, heated, and spiced with cinnamon sticks, cloves, star anise, citrus, sugar, and, at times, vanilla pods. It is sometimes drunk *mit Schuss* (with a shot), meaning that rum or some other liquor has been added.

amorphous predilection but a clear and distinct disposition with definable features.

Unlike Kempka, Baur, the Party, and the Führer, I truly adored intelligent women—and feared them in equal measure, so I understood the men's preference without sharing it. I nodded in knowing assent and downed my drink.

"Please don't misunderstand me," she added quickly. "I… I'm fond of my aunt. It's just that she gets far too protective at times."

I smiled duplicitously. "I'm no expert, but she didn't sound terribly protective to me."

With that, I hoped to prod her into a confession, but instead, she shut down, so I ordered another round for us, and we sat silently for a time.

Finally, her vacant expression shifted to one of apprehension. "What is it you want me to say, Heinz?"

"Nothing you don't want to say," I lied, but my face wasn't as cloaked as I'd hoped, for she set down her glass and rotated her hands, palms up.

"I don't know what you want me to tell you."

Since she'd moved the curtains partially aside, I felt less reluctant to draw them the rest of the way. "I think you do," I countered. "Just what was behind your aunt's threat—and it was a threat. It's difficult to work for the Führer and not recognise one."

The refills arrived, and she took a more substantial sip, causing me to prod even harder before she became incapable of lucidity.

"Klara, please," I entreated. "You must know how I feel about you. I want to help, if you'll permit me."

"I know you do," she said, "but unfortunately, in arranging for us to meet, Aunt Christa did her job better than she knew.

You must know that my feelings for you are no different from yours for me, and because of that, I wish the same safety for you, so I'm afraid that our mutual feelings now place us at odds."

I emptied my glass and shook my head. Somehow, I had to get beyond useless debate and its inevitable tit-for-tat logjam. I needed to devise a transcendent strategy, and fortunately, once my brain had moved in that direction, one came. It wasn't bereft of risk, and the temptation to overpower her with clever cunning was great, but I knew that for my own safety, I had to seem as close to the person she believed me to be as possible.

"I don't have any grand words, Klara," I began, "but you have no need to be afraid for me. "You saw how we got this table? It's more than power. Power makes a strong case, but absolute power doesn't need to make any case at all. What I mean is that, for reasons I can't explain, as the Führer's valet, I appear to have a special—I don't know—immunity? You, on the other hand, even with such an influential relative in the Chancellery, have no such immunity—that was abundantly clear tonight. Now, I promise you, on our bond of affection, that nothing you tell me will alter that. It might even strengthen it. So please, Klara, let's begin the new year with an even stronger bond." Without waiting for a response, I asked, "So, what was your aunt's threat all about?"

I let her consider this as I ordered another round from the visibly spent waiter, who looked as if he could sleep right through to the next New Year's Eve. Once our drinks arrived, I shrugged a "Well?" to her and waited.

After a time, with an expression I interpreted as an incongruous mixture of anxiety and relief, she told me her story. "You knew very little about me before we met, Heinz, and you know little more now, so I'll enlighten you and hope for the best. I'll make it quick and dirty. While my father, who was killed in the last war, had normal hearing, my mother was congenitally deaf. I also had a brother, younger than I, a beautiful boy with intelligence and heart. Also deaf. Once the euthanasia laws were passed, the three of us lived in constant fear. Then, one night, late, the landlady let the Gestapo into our flat, and my mother and brother were taken away, leaving only me. I only survived because I hid on the ledge outside our back window. Afterwards, terrified, with nowhere else to go, I ran to Aunt Christa, my father's sister, for help. She coolly informed me that arrangements had already been made that I would be spared, but she could do nothing about my mother and brother. When I asked her why, she said simply, dispassionately, and cryptically, 'You, at least, can be useful.'"

Vintage Schroeder. I didn't get the chance to pursue the matter, for just then, the massive, extravagantly ornamented cuckoo clock struck midnight, and the already cacophonous beer hall erupted with rowdy cheers, indiscriminate embraces, songs, and drunken toasts. Needing to return to the Chancellery, I paid the bill, and we left into the frigid street, where I hailed a taxi for her. We exchanged quick, half-hearted smiles and kisses before she departed. Nothing had been resolved. A new year had arrived, but I felt no joy, no hopefulness. I'd lost the comradely companionship of Brückner and gained the hovering hatred of Bormann. My Klara was in harm's way. Nightmares, migraines, and hallucinations still tormented me. No sense of completion. Nothing affirmed. Nothing justified. And too little clarity.

1941

PERPLEXED AND UNSTEADY from last night's "festivities," and conscious of it, I went mindlessly but convincingly through the motions of the Führer's toilette. I'd been with him now for almost six years, and I still marvelled at his ability to undergo the enervating ordeal of three New Year's Eve festivities, then arise as if he'd slept through them all. *Perhaps,* I thought, *he had.* But this morning, he was especially vigorous and chipper, a condition I attributed not to slumber but to Morell's medicinal ministrations, a notion not without a disquieting foundation.

He dressed quickly, even beating his previous Morell-enhanced score, then immediately went to his desk and, in typical Führer fashion, telephoned Göring to congratulate him on yesterday's belated "Christmas present" for the British. At the same time, he reminded Göring that such a success was due to his "failure to prevent raids on Berlin and to gain air supremacy for an invasion" and that many more such "presents" would demand delivery to even begin compensating for that failure. In the few moments I left my own thoughts to actively listen, I noted that despite the harsh words, the Führer seemed little perturbed by "Göring's premature ejaculation," as Baur privately called the Reichsmarschall's boast that he would eradicate the RAF. I had no idea why the Führer was so blasé.

Then, with a flourish, the Führer swept his topsy-turvy desk clean for me and the housekeeping staff to deal with later, waved me to a chair, and stared at me for a long moment.

"So, Linge," he finally said, "you and your lady friend made a run for it last night." He laughed. "Not that I blame you. I'd do the same if I could, but Bormann would send a search party for me. He almost sent one for you, but I told him to respect young love, so he made a face but relented."

Cromwell.

"We hadn't intended to leave so early, my Führer," I explained needlessly, "but Klara was feeling poorly, and—"

"Well," the Führer interrupted, "if it was that, you should have told me, and I'd have had Morell tend to her. That ugly magician could probably even restore her hearing." A chuckle.

"It's not possible, my Führer," I countered gingerly. "I'm afraid she's never had hearing. She's been—"

"Don't make plans for the evening," he interrupted again, done with the subject and, I could sense, with finality. "I'll want you at hand."

⁓

First, I phoned Klara's neighbour to have her deliver my regrets that the Führer's needs superseded our evening plans. Then, at the Communications Centre, I ran into Günsche, who informed me that I would no longer be "burdened" with the Führer's mail since, "well, the Reichsleiter assigned that routine job to members of his own staff."

"You mean yourself," I suggested matter-of-factly.

"Well… I suppose so," he admitted with a stupid grin and a tilt of his massive shoulder. "But the Führer has no objection, and anyway, who gives a shit who sorts mail, right?"

"Clearly the Reichsleiter does," I tossed out, my face far more innocent than my words or intent.

He laughed as stupidly as he grinned. "Well, you got me

there. Still, so what, right? Bormann, the Führer, it makes no difference, eh?"

It should and it does, I wanted to say. "True," I said. "One letter carrier's about the same as any other. Am I permitted to collect my own mail?"

A look of primal confusion spread over his ordinarily blank features, and another stupid laugh followed. "Well, uh, sure. It's yours, after all, right?"

"Right. Anything else?"

Another expression suddenly appeared on his face that suggested a war between bringing up something more controversial and remaining tactfully silent. I assumed he couldn't even spell tact, much less use it, so I waited for the revelation.

"Well," he began, "I... I wasn't going to bring it up, you know, but as long as we're chatting here friendly-like, it's... well... your door again."

"What about it, Otto?" I asked, knowing full well what the stammering fool would say.

"You... uh, know how we replaced the broken one with a new one. Well... it seems like you have your old door back."

I was waiting for this and had my response prepared. "I *liked* my old door, so I had it put back. To be frank, I'm used to the draft and the outside noise, and I sleep better that way. But thanks for asking." Then I saluted smartly and left before the idiot could react. As I strolled to the lunchroom, I wondered about the extent of the immunity I'd bragged about to Klara.

⚘

After checking my mail, unconcerned about its popularity, I returned to my quarters and glanced at the note I'd received from Hedwig Höss, "cordially" inviting me (in her husband's name, of course) to visit his KZ in Oświęcim[41] for a few days. Of course, I was most welcome to stay with them, but she suggested ever so coyly that I'd surely be more "comfortable" in a nearby hotel, which she named "in passing." She concluded with "*Répondez s'il vous plaît.*" I understood little French, but I'd seen enough formal invitations at the Chancellery to know it meant "reply if you please." But I also understood Frau Höss and knew that the "if you please" meant I was expected to respond. So, after flushing the note, I took some moments to sort out the response she'd obliged me to give.

I must confess that my interest in visiting a KZ was non-existent at best, and one in Poland even more so. I'd "visited" enough jails in my time on the streets. But I also must confess that when it came to a jail as extraordinary as a KZ, I harboured a disturbing degree of masochistic curiosity—not least as to why she was so eager to have me visit. So, I decided to "*Répondez*" positively—but not before checking with the Führer and doing a bit of research.

❧

I took a chance and proceeded to the Führer's quarters in advance of his summons, despite a sour antechamber glare from Günsche.

"Good, Linge," the Führer said effusively from his bathroom. "I was just about to buzz. Here, help me with these damn cufflinks, will you?"

He stood with his arms outstretched, his cuffs hanging open. I went to the sink, picked up two enamel cufflinks with

---

[41] Oświęcim is a town in Lesser Poland situated fifty kilometres (thirty-one miles) west of Kraków, near the confluence of the Vistula and Soła Rivers. Auschwitz, in German.

the swastika emblazoned in black on a white circle with a red background, and was able to fasten them despite his shaking hands. This was nothing unusual, and I knew better than to inquire. Morell usually kept this condition in check (among many others), but the good doctor was nowhere in sight. Nor was anyone else, so I spoke up.

"My Führer, may I have a word?"

He pursed his lips and sat down on the lidded toilet bowl. "Go ahead."

"I've been invited to visit a KZ, my Führer, and I wanted your opinion."

He tilted his head slightly, lips still pursed, then asked, "And who made this offer?"

"The wife of Commandant Rudolf Höss. She—"

"Ah, the wife," he murmured with a sly wink in his voice. "And do you intend to tell your lady friend about this invitation?"

I smiled sheepishly. "It's not like that at all, my Führer. She's speaking for her husband; it's his invitation."

The Führer nodded dubiously. "Of course, Linge, of course. I'm nothing if not a man of the world. Where is this KZ?"

"Poland, my Führer." I must admit some surprise that he hadn't put Höss and Poland together. *Just what did he know about the KZs?*

"You really wish to visit one of those ghastly places?" he asked.

"I… was curious, my Führer."

He shrugged. "All right then. If you must, I'll smooth the way for you with Himmler so you'll actually go as a visitor and not as a 'guest,' eh?" He smiled.

I smiled back. "I'm most grateful, my Führer," I said sincerely.

"When do you plan on leaving?"

"I need to reply to Frau Höss, but I was thinking next week, if that's convenient for you, only for two days at most."

He nodded. "All right then. I'll tell Günsche to have Junge replace you." He fastened his reading spectacles, bent his neck, looked down intently, and began shuffling some papers round as if searching for a particular item—a dismissive task I'd seen him perform often when he decided that no further talk was warranted or desired.

However, when I made to go to his bathroom to tidy up before his visitors arrived, he raised his head and gazed over his glasses.

"That wife of Höss's must be quite something," he said to my retreating figure, turning me instantly round. "You couldn't get me to a KZ at gunpoint. You can't imagine how many times Himmler has nagged me to admire his handiwork."

I could imagine.

2 *January 1941*

Before beginning my Führer routine, I telephoned RSHA headquarters and asked for Siegfried Hausen. I hadn't spoken to Heydrich's KZ liaison in years and had no idea where he was or what he was doing at present, save for being one among a throng in a Paris crowd, but I had to begin somewhere. I was connected to the office of a Lieutenant Colonel Eichmann.

"This is Eichmann," a curt voice answered. "Please, state your business."

"My name is Heinz Linge," I said, "principal valet to the Führer. I'm attempting to locate Major Siegfried Hausen. Would you happen to know where I can reach him?"

After a long pause, "May I know how you're acquainted?"

"Of course," I responded equably. "He once assisted me in a delicate matter."

"And what exactly was this assistance?"

My brain went on alert. "Nothing important, Herr Colonel. It mattered to me a great deal at the time but was trivial in retrospect, nothing that needs recounting."

"I would prefer to be the judge of that."

"I'm sure you would prefer." I was growing increasingly irritated by the prick's frosty, inquisitorial officiousness. *Who did this offensive bureaucrat think he was?* Clearly, he needed a lesson in manners. "At the Führer's suggestion," I lied, "I attempted to phone General Heydrich directly, but the idiot at the switchboard mistakenly put me through to you."

A slight pause greeted my words, as I expected, and I waited silently while the swine recalculated.

"No need to disturb the general," he finally said, still frosty but more cooperative. "Perhaps I can provide the information you're seeking. I'll be right back."

I could hear him speaking on an inter-office telephone but couldn't make out any words. Then he came back to me.

"Colonel Linge?"

"Still here."

"He's currently in Buchenwald."

"Where?"

"It's not a 'where,' Colonel. It's an 'it'—a KZ."

That made sense, though I'd never heard of it. *But why did he say "in" instead of "at"?* "All right, Colonel," I asked with no little annoyance in my voice, "then where is the 'it'?"

"It's near Weimar, on the Etter—"

"I know where Weimar is, Colonel. I just didn't know there was a KZ there."

"Really?" he said with a touch of acid. "Well, it's just possible that in your… position, you didn't need to know."

"Thank you, Colonel," I said briskly and rang off.

Next, I placed a call to Buchenwald KZ, gave my name, rank, and position to the commandant, an SS Lieutenant Colonel Koch, and asked to speak with Siegfried Hausen, a question that elicited first a pregnant pause, then loud laughter.

"Is this some sort of joke?" Koch eventually asked, almost breathless. "Who did you say you were?"

I repeated what I'd told Eichmann, but this time with greater emphasis on the Führer portion, and the laughter stopped.

"All right, Colonel Linge," he said with newfound sobriety. "I understand, but I think *you* may not understand. There are procedures, you know, even for you. We can't just put political prisoners on the phone for chats."

The impact of his words knocked the wind from my lungs, and I fought to concentrate. *Hausen, once a KZ liaison, now a prisoner in a KZ!* Eventually, straining to consider the bizarre irony of it restored to me a semblance of vocal normality.

"No, Commandant," I said slowly. "I fully understand. May I ask what the prisoner did?"

"You may ask, but the answer must come from RSHA Headquarters, not from me."

"Are you permitted to make an educated guess?"

"You have wit, Colonel," he remarked. "Most of our political prisoners are here for disloyal acts committed against the Reich. The specifics are withheld from us. Your Hausen could well be one of them, but for details, you'll have to contact Colonel Eichmann—he knows them all."

The bastards have me on a bureaucratic hamster wheel. *Got to jump off!* "I'm inquiring for the Führer, Commandant," I prevaricated blatantly, praying it would short-circuit any need for confirmation. "Must I report failure to him?"

"May I ask why you wish to speak with the prisoner?"

It worked; now it was my turn. "You may ask, but the answer must come from the Führer, not from me."

A long pause followed, so long that I thought we'd been disconnected. Then he came back on.

"No need for that, Colonel," he said. "It appears I do have some information. Hausen was convicted of being an integral part of a conspiracy to sabotage Reich property."

This didn't sound like Ziggy at all. "Sabotage of Reich property? What Reich property?"

"It says on the form that he helped plan the physical destruction of our newest and most important KZ."

"Which is?"

"Auschwitz."

⁊

After the stunning news from Koch, the rest of my morning passed in a viscous haze of bewilderment, a condition I prayed the Führer wouldn't notice. Siegfried—"Ziggy"—a man who'd provided such a kind and thoughtful service to a total stranger, a high-ranking, responsible officer who once provided KZ reports directly to Heydrich. This same man was now nothing more than reviled scum, an inmate of the very sort of place he'd attempted to destroy. And yet, I had to confess that I knew little about him, save for his one kindness to me and his humour. I had the overpowering sensation that had he been posted to the Chancellery instead of the RSHA, he might well have become another Brückner to me. *How then could such a man be a saboteur, a traitor?* And yet, there it was. And of all the KZs in all the places we controlled, Auschwitz, the very one I'd decided to visit. The coincidence was truly breathtaking. *And it had to be a coincidence, hadn't it? And yet, what would Jung have said?* So many "and-yets" that my brain was reeling.

⁊

By lunchtime, since the Führer had no further use for me, I hurried to the Communications Centre and dispatched a note to Frau Höss, cordially accepting her "husband's" generous offer and saying that I would be arriving on Sunday of the following week, if that was convenient. Once done, I went to the officers' mess to see if I could locate Baur. He was there, all right, entertaining some security officials with more fanciful tales of aeronautical adventures with the Führer. There happened to be an empty chair across from him, and I grabbed it just as another officer arrived with a loaded tray (and a scowl, since I'd brought no food). I hoped Baur would finish quickly so I could have him to myself, but he'd shifted seamlessly from the Führer to his heroic feats in the Great War, service that, in his telling, made him out to be even more fearless and gallant than Göring, or even the legendary Red Baron. Of course, I knew all these derring-do stories to be pure poppycock—and he knew that I knew—but he also knew that I would never contradict him in public.

To get him to leave ahead of his audience, I gently kicked him twice under the table, all part of a signal code we'd developed to avoid social awkwardness. He returned it with a bit more vigour, and we were set.

He ended his lecture with a quaintly phrased prediction. "Well, gentlemen, I'm afraid that duty calls, but I leave you with this: What I told you will shortly pass into the always-sunny land of nostalgia. The Führer has told me, and these are his exact words as best I remember them: 'Baur, quite soon, and you mark my words, all the aeroplanes now flying will be fit only for junk-yards, their propellers sold for scrap'—or something like that." Then he rose with an exchange of salutes and departed.

I followed suit after a discreet period and met the pilot in the gardens where Brückner and I used to stroll so often.

"So, Shiny Dome," Baur japed with his usual well-meant coarseness, "what's all the secrecy for? Another trip to Paris, this time under the Führer's radar beam?"

I laughed uneasily, since I knew that "the Führer's radar beam" meant Bormann. Baur had complained bitterly to me and Kempka that the Reichsleiter now felt it necessary to personally conduct a detailed inspection of his plane prior to every flight that carried the Führer—"as if I don't, the fucking prick."

"No, Hans," I assured him, "not this time. One trip to Paris was more than enough. Gaudy monuments and Germans—that I can get here. No, what I wanted to ask is whether you knew anything about this new KZ in Poland. I think it's called… uh, Aus-something."

Baur nibbled his lower lip in thought, then shook his head. "You probably mean Auschwitz. I don't know a hell of a lot," he admitted, "except that it's Himmler's pride and joy. The Führer never mentioned it, that is, assuming he even knows. KZs are in the Reichsführer's bailiwick, and you know that character keeps such shit in-house, you might say. Well, actually," he suddenly qualified, "Göring might have an inkling, but you know how he likes to maintain a safe distance from unpleasantness—like the Führer."

What Baur said made sense since it fit what I knew of the Führer, Himmler, and Göring. What struck me as he spoke was just how few people I knew, since joining the Führer's service, in whom I could confide. *When I eliminated Brückner, who was left?* Not Baur or Kempka, none of the women I'd chanced to meet, not even Klara. *And yet, was it any different before?* It appeared, on reflection, that aside from books—and you, of course—there was no one. Early on, Brückner had cautioned me to trust no one, but he needn't have bothered.

"Why do you want to know?" Baur asked, a perfectly legitimate question, and one I could answer.

"I received an invitation to visit, and I wanted to know something about it so I won't appear entirely ignorant when I get there. By the way, did you know of any plot to sabotage it?"

He laughed so loudly that heads turned to the racket. *"Sabotage Auschwitz?* Man, anyone fool enough to try something like that would have to be way beyond certifiable. You know, those places are guarded like the Führer. Considering Himmler, maybe even more so. And with Auschwitz? Even more than that."

Again, what he said made sense; Baur was always eminently sensible. If even the relatively innocuous pilot hadn't heard offhanded scuttlebutt, "those places," as he put it, were truly formidable, well-guarded—and mysterious.

Now, there was only one more possible avenue left to me, but that would have to wait until tomorrow, since I needed to prepare the Führer for dinner with some mucky-muck business types, and I'd told Klara I would come over afterwards.

❧

At midnight, I awoke with a jolt in Klara's bed, bug-eyed, alone, naked, and sopping with sweat, the blanket and sheets on the floor, the sole pillow gashed and bleeding feathers. I sat for a moment, then got up, wrapped one of the sheets round me, and began a search for Klara. For a moment, I forgot her condition and began calling her name, then I came to my senses and went silently from room to room—all empty, except for me. Klara seemed to have vanished. Confused and frustrated, I moved to the closet to gather up my uniform, and that was when I found her curled up on the floor, also naked, cowering, her arm raised in a defensive gesture.

"Please don't hurt me!" she cried.

Startled, I stepped back. "Hurt you? What are you talking—"

"You tried to kill me!" she screamed, her eyes wide with fright. "You were leaning over me with a pillow in your hands. You kept saying it was all right, it was all right, that 'he'll never do that again,' then you put your pillow over my face and pressed down hard so I couldn't breathe."

"I don't... I... never..." I stammered. "You must have had a bad—"

"I wasn't dreaming!" she shouted, now angry. "It was like you'd gone crazy, like you were somebody else!"

"Whatever it was, it's over now." I reached down for her hand. "Please. It's all over."

After a tentative stare, she uncoiled her body and allowed me to take her hand. I pulled her up with utmost gentleness from the floor and led her back to the bed. I grabbed a handful of the blanket and settled it over her.

"I don't know how long you held the pillow on my face, but I must have been hysterical with panic because I was able to shove you and the pillow aside and run from the bed to where you found me."

An incubus had clawed its way to the surface and ravaged the landscape. "I must have had one of my nightmares," I mumbled lamely into a lie. "The Führer's personal doctor has been treating me, and—"

"A nightmare to you, maybe." She shook her head excitedly. "But to me, it was all too real. You mean to say you have no memory of what you tried to do to me?"

I took a deep, shuddering breath. "Yes," I admitted, "I remember, but to me, it was in my dream—and it wasn't you."

"Well, I hate to disabuse you, but it *was me!*" she replied vociferously, reaching down, grabbing the broken, depleted pillow, and shaking it in my face.

I nodded with resignation. "Let me get you a drink," I said, if only to get away from her accusatory stare and allow her sufficient time to calm down.

She bit her lower lip and shrugged, gestures I interpreted as agreement, regardless of her actual intent. When I returned with two brandies, she'd changed into her robe and sat on the bed's edge, her head down. I tapped her lightly on the shoulder, and when she raised her head, I handed her the snifter, which she took with a reluctant smile.

"You look silly," she said, "standing there naked with a

brandy snifter in your hand. It's not as alluring as you might think." Then she threw the pillow at me.

Perhaps she'd gotten over the horror—but I hadn't.

THE FÜHRER INTENDED to be sequestered with Goebbels and Dara until his speech to prepare the nation for an imminent invasion of Greece and North Africa met his perfectionist's satisfaction, so I raced from the Chancellery and found a sufficiently hidden-in-plain-sight telephone kiosk. I entered the stifling booth, dialled the number Brückner had given me, held the cradle down surreptitiously, and pretended to speak as I waited for the ring-back. I hoped it would be soon, since an impatient queue was forming rapidly.

Ten anxious minutes later, Brückner rang, and I turned my back to the unhappy crowd.

"Happy New Year, my friend!" he shouted over the static, then the connexion improved.

"And a Happy New Year to you, too, Wilhelm. Did you have a pleasant holiday? Did you—"

"Heinz," he interrupted. "I may be over a thousand kilometres away, but I'm still Brückner. So, enough with the pleasantries, eh? What can I do for you?"

He dismissed my overture with such gentleness in his voice that, without any embarrassment, I immediately told him about Klara and Schroeder, Hedwig, the invitation, and my misadventures with Eichmann and Koch.

"I need your advice, Wilhelm." I began to hear noisy muttering behind me and light laughter on the other end of the line.

"Why do you laugh?" I asked, secretly guessing his answer.

"Your life is quite an excess of entanglements," he said. "Nothing changes, I suppose—for some people, at least. I feel for you, Heinz, I really do. I'm beginning to think I was precipitate in urging independence. Fortunately, I was able to escape from that cesspool of intrigue to the relative safety and simplicity of military-occupation bureaucracy. Boring? Yes. Routine? Yes. Trivial? Yes. But out of harm's way? Also yes. Be that as it may, let's take an imaginary stroll around the Chancellery gardens and see what we can come up with, eh?"

"Just the ticket," I answered gratefully. But I needed time to hear Brückner's ideas and suggestions, and the surly queue was becoming burdensome. "Please hold for a moment," I asked Brückner. Then I turned round, swung open the door, brandished my identity card and announced with cold, theatrical authority, "Now, listen to me. I am speaking directly with the Führer. I don't know how long we will be, and since he wishes the two of us to enjoy complete privacy, you are to disperse immediately and indefinitely." I held up the receiver with my other hand. "You may complain directly to him if you so wish." Within seconds, I was entirely alone. So much for hiding in plain sight—or otherwise. "I'm back," I told Brückner. "I had to—"

He laughed. "I heard you. Impressive, but it's fortunate that no one took you up on your challenge since I haven't the Führer's operatic lung power. All right," he shifted, "now we move to the problems at hand. While you were taming the crowd, I had a chance to chew over what you told me, and I believe there may be a common denominator—you do know what a common denominator is, yes?"

I'd learned of it years before while plodding alone through a mathematics textbook. "No idea," I said.

"Pity you can't go back and get an education. It's a common term in mathematics, but it has applications in other areas as well. For example, our friends in the Gestapo employ it when they attempt to determine whether apparently separate offences might have enough common factors to justify combining them in an investigation. You understand?"

"I… think so, but I don't see—"

"You will," he assured me. "You just have to be a little patient. I asked myself whether any or all of your apparently separate situations share certain elements, in other words, common denominators."

"And you came up with what?"

"At the moment, I'm not quite sure, but if I'm right, there's little that you or I can do from within. I need to deliberate further. When I have an answer, you'll know."

"But I told Höss's wife I'd be coming. Should I—"

"You should go," he said. "At the very least, you'll make Frau Höss happy and get an education in the Party's penal practices in the bargain, so where's the harm? And by the time you return, I may have some news. Now, let someone else get at that phone."

THE FÜHRER SPENT the early morning with von Ribbentrop and Admirals Dönitz, Raeder, and Canaris, concerning a Japanese memorandum the latter had just secured.[42] To justify my unseen presence, I reordered the Führer's books (from alphabetical to colour-coded) while Günsche stood rigidly at ease in a corner.

The Führer sat at his desk in his bathrobe. "Well, gentle-men," he asked his admirals, "is this titbit of Canaris's worth bothering about or is it Asiatic opium-pipe dreaming?" A toothy grin followed.

"My Führer," Dönitz answered, "the memorandum has value for us, only if such a Japanese attack were feasible. I happen to regard Yamamoto's proposal as fanciful at best. Their navy is serviceable but hardly capable of attacking Pearl Harbor."

"And what of you, Raeder?" the Führer asked.

"My views are well known to you. Our navy is fully engaged in fighting the British. Consequently, anything that might… distract them, and at the same time keep a potential ally of theirs occupied, would be welcome. As to their choice of Pearl Harbor, I agree with my colleague that it touches not a little of the fanciful, requiring a degree of inspired audacity that only you possess.

---

[42] Japanese Admiral Isoroku Yamamoto presented Minister of the Navy Koshirō Oikawa with his ideas for a war against the United States in a memorandum. Yamamoto proposed a crippling first strike on American forces in the first few hours of the war, something that could best be accomplished by an air attack on the U.S. fleet at Pearl Harbor.

On the other hand, an attack in the Philippines would not be out of the question."

It was hardly a surprise that the admiral's reference to the Führer's "inspired audacity" met with a languorous nod of approval and a wan smile.

Then the Führer asked von Ribbentrop for his view of the matter, but by then, I'd wearied of Japan and stopped listening. I knew that when it came to allies, the Führer had only a passing interest in what he called "the yellow diversion," by which he meant that so long as they kept the Russians too occupied to behave as a gluttonous rival or pose any military threat, he was content to leave the Japanese alone. And now, with their ridiculous reference to Pearl Harbor…

Like the Führer, I had far more important things to preoccupy me. Only four days before I was to leave for Poland, and still no word from Brückner. Without his information and insights, I dreaded the trip the way a blind man dreads disorientation.

And no less disquieting: I still hadn't confirmed my leave with the Führer.

⁓

Once the group had left and just before Bormann arrived to hover, I made my move while the Führer shaved, only holding off until he completed the critically delicate task of ensuring the longevity of his illustrious little moustache for one more day.

"My Führer," I began as he tilted his head back and the safety razor glided round his neck like an ice skater, "I have something to ask you."

"All right, Linge," he said without breaking his rhythm. "What is it?"

"I've accepted the invitation to visit the KZ at Auschwitz, and—"

"Hand me my wrinkled meeting-with-a-prelate tie, would you?" he interrupted. "That ridiculous cadaver in the Vatican is still nagging me to go easy on his flock, and of all people, he sends a patrician enemy of National Socialism to persuade me."[43]

I retrieved the tie and laid it over the heated towel rail. "As I was saying, my Führer," I pressed on, "I was invited—"

He plunked his razor into the murky sink water. "Arrange your leave with Junge, and on your way out, ask Günsche to get Bormann and Dara. I don't wish to be alone with that papist idiot without witnesses."

"Of course, my Führer," I said, and that was that.

I knew from long experience that when the Führer didn't wish to discuss—or even hear about—something, he would change the subject abruptly, and any attempt to raise it again would meet the same fate—or worse. For the wise, there would be no third try.

Wittgenstein wrote, "Someone who knows too much finds it hard not to lie." To this I would only add that someone who does not understand what he knows finds it even harder. Without having heard back from Brückner, I intended to lie to Klara, and I didn't even know why.

"I'll need to be away for a few days next week," I told her when she came back from removing the dinner dishes.

---

[43] Clemens Augustinus Emmanuel Joseph Pius Anthonius Hubertus Marie Graf von Galen, better known as Clemens August Graf von Galen, was a German count, bishop of Münster, and cardinal of the Roman Catholic Church. During World War II, Galen led Catholic protests against Nazi euthanasia and denounced Gestapo lawlessness and the persecution of the church.

Her eyes widened as she sat down. "Oh? Really? Where to? Can I come with you?"

I shook my head. "It's for the Führer. Confidential. I can't tell you, and I'm to go alone."

The colour drained from her cheeks, and her eyelids shuttered to a dubious squint. "You're going away by yourself, and you can't tell me why or where? You're a valet, not a spy. That's crazy."

"You're right, Klara," I said. "You're right. I thought it was crazy… well, not that, but at least odd when he told me." I shrugged. "With the Führer, though, one can guess endlessly as to the why of things, but one can never ask."

After a few agonising moments for me, she shrugged, her stare cool, and held out her hands, rotating them to palms up. "Yes, of course, if the mysterious Führer commands. When do you leave?"

"My train leaves Saturday morning, and I've been told that the journey on this particular train is between ten and twelve hours. I'm not looking forward to it, believe me."

Some colour returned, and she smiled mischievously. "Well, if you took me along, we could get a sleeping compartment, and I could make those hours fly by. No pillows, though." She must have sensed something because she quickly held up her hand. "Just kidding, love, just kidding. Don't get excited. Perhaps, instead, you can doze off in your uncomfortable aisle seat all the way—dreaming about the Führer."

"I knew you'd come up with the perfect alternative," I kidded back through a short bout of forced laughing and coughing that stopped when her expression suddenly turned serious.

"Well, my love, since you're leaving so soon, don't you think we should discuss right now what's to be done about Aunt Christa?"

I wanted to wait until Brückner contacted me, but I could see from her face that the matter was a Damocles sword poised directly over her, so I needed to radically adjust to the situation. I took a deep breath and let it out slowly.

"When does she expect you to move?"

"She said 'right away,' and knowing her as I do, it means right away."

The philosopher Virchow wrote: "Once you tell the truth, you're trapped within its finite boundaries, but a lie is infinite."

I pressed my lips together in consideration of the infinite. "All right," I finally said, "then until we have a plan, we need to delay her, yes? Can you be ready to leave with me on Saturday?"

In the adrenaline rush of urgent improvisation, I'd taken no account of Frau Höss—my devious brain had apparently shoved it aside for later reckoning.

Her face suddenly took on a glow, and she smiled broadly. "I'm ready *now*," she joked, "but not to worry; of course I can be ready."

"Good," I said. "I'll collect you on my way to the station. I'll tell your aunt that we're going on a little romantic vacation during which I'll try coaxing you into moving to the Chancellery. That should hold her at bay, at least until we return with a longer-term solution."

"Brilliant!" she whooped. "But what about the Führer?"

"Well," I explained feebly, "the way I see it, even the Führer can't know everything about everything, so this will be just one more infinitesimal fragment of that everything. With luck, it should get lost in the crowd, at least temporarily."

"In that case," she murmured, her eyelids fluttering coquettishly, "you might get us that sleeping compartment."

THIS MORNING, WHEN I arranged with Günsche to have Junge fill in during my absence, he appeared uncommonly chipper, even for him—the cause, he wasted no time in telling me.

"I sure owe you one, Heinz."

"How so?"

He shook his head slowly. "Because with you gone for a while, I don't have to listen to Junge whine to me about not having anything to do."

I forced a chuckle. "I won't be gone all that long."

"I'll take whatever I can get."

I didn't do it for you, I wanted to tell him. "Anytime, Otto. Always happy to help." I also didn't tell him that I dreaded leaving the door ajar for Bormann and Junge to snake through. Since Brückner's warning, I'd been staying closer to the Führer than his moustache, but with my imminent absence, the old adage "A chain is no stronger than its weakest link" began haunting me. To be frank, even before the Führerbuzzer sounded, I was giving serious consideration to cancelling the trip, regardless of the consequences for Klara. Then a note slipped under my recently reattached original door, stopping me in my tracks.

Heinz, you must keep your appointment, but first, telephone this number to acquire the information I couldn't supply. Take care, my friend.

It was unsigned, but I knew the sender.

I braved the frigid aftermath of a savage snowstorm to locate just the right kiosk. With fingers almost numb with cold despite my fur-lined gloves, I fumbled through the numbers with the strange-looking prefix, and a male voice came on the line after the twentieth ring.

"Please remain on the line, Herr Linge," the cultivated voice said with what I knew to be a Swiss-German accent, though from the telephone exchange letters and numerals, it couldn't be Switzerland. "She'll be with you shortly."

Fortunately, no queue had yet formed, so I waited without concern, save for the cold and the identity of the lady who would be with me shortly.

"Hello, Heinz," the voice said, and instantly, it brought me back to that night at the Adlon when I first met the Jewish journalist. I hadn't seen or even heard about her since her situation had become so precarious that one or more of her "associates and friends in high places," as she'd put it, had to spirit her out of Germany.

"Frau Bella" was all I could say.

"Yes. Frau Bella. Despite everything." Her voice held no levity, and the line had a scratchy quality.

"It's hard to hear," I said. "Where are you?"

"I live now in New York City. That's where you called."

"I'm… so glad to know that you're all right."

"I'm in one piece," she said. "I'll be all right when your boss and his cronies are not."

There was the wit, but where was the warmth I'd experienced at the Adlon? I began to wonder whether I should continue or ring off. I decided to try once more. "Are you still a journalist?"

"Not officially. Officially, I'm a secretary—actually, more a typist. But occasionally, I contribute, despite my exile. I can still boast some associates—even friends—in high places." A long pause followed, then, "Be that as it may, your friend Brückner tells me that you may need some dots connected?"

Clearly, the time for banter had long passed, that is, if it had ever existed. And I was freezing in the bargain. "Did he provide any details?"

"I don't know if they're details, but he did mention the elevation of Bormann, the hiring of Junge, the arrest of Hausen, and your invitation to visit Auschwitz. He asked me the possible significance of each and whether there could be any possible connexions among these seemingly disparate particulars."

"Brückner called them common denominators."

"Yes. But before we go any further, is there not another question you have for me?"

"Should there be?"

"That's not the question I had in mind."

"Is this a test?" I asked her, suddenly annoyed.

"Yes, Heinz, it is. I need to know if you're the same person I met at the Adlon."

"Would Brückner ask you to help anyone else? I can't show you my papers over the telephone." Annoyance was turning quickly to indignation. "All right, I'll indulge you." My brain travelled back to that evening when she'd felt comfortable telling me about Katrin. What had struck me most about our conversation then was the way she prefaced the information she'd generously come to furnish:

"Actually, I was hoping you'd give up your search. I know you're not like the others, so [Katrin] can only be misery for us."

"'Us?'"

"Yes, us. You and me—and all the others. The innocent, the vulnerable, the victims."

"And in your mind, I fit one of these categories?"

"You fit all of them."

"I don't understand you."

"You will, I hope, before it's too late. Some already know. Some must be shown."

"You want to know whether I'm still the innocent, the vulnerable, and the victim you said I was that night?"

"Good memory. Yes," she replied, "that's precisely what I want to know."

"All I can tell you is that Brückner must think so, or he wouldn't have contacted you. As for me, I must think I am, or I wouldn't feel the need for your information. Why he thought that you of all people would know anything now is a matter I'll take up with him later, but if your information is useful, I'll drink a zombie in your honour. Will that suit you?"

I pulled the receiver from my ear, ready to slam it down and get out, when I heard light laughter on the other end, and as her voice returned, her ice had melted.

"Well, Heinz, if my information should prove useful, I'll join you in that drink, even though four thousand miles separate us. All right, let's proceed. First, in my informed opinion, all the pieces Brückner listed are part of the same puzzle. To the naked—or shall I say, innocent?—eye, these pieces are distinct, but in fact, there is a connexion, what you said Brückner called a 'common denominator.'"

"And?"

"It's you."

The veins in my temples inflated and began throbbing. "But how can—"

"The how, my friend, is both irrelevant and a distraction. A far more important question is why?"

I held my palm over the mouthpiece while I took some deep, cloudy breaths, then removed it. "All right, then, why?"

"Your boss knows the answer to that. Himmler knows the answer to that. Katrin and her associates know it too. All I'll say is that a few more pieces are still needed to fill in the entire picture."

"Is that all you—"

"Far from it, Heinz," she said, cutting me off. "You accepted Frau Höss's invitation to hell. Consider your reason, then go."

"I will," I assured her, "but who is your source for these pieces?" I asked.

A dial tone greeted my curiosity.

T̶ʜᴇ ꜰɪʀꜱᴛ ᴅᴀʏ, 11 January:

Klara and I almost collapsed with giddy relief when we entered our heated railroad compartment.

That morning, I'd been informed by Captain Dressler, the officer in charge of providing the Führer with daily weather reports, that I was "indeed fortunate to be getting out of Berlin for a while since January, I'm afraid, will prove to be the coldest month in Berlin in a century."

However, when I told him that I was leaving Berlin for Poland, he laughed his way to a coughing fit. Yesterday's snowstorm had been so ferocious that up until the last moment, we harboured serious doubts that our train would be given the go-ahead. But luckily, due to the exertions of certain influential industrialists with the same destination, German assiduity and efficiency prevailed, and we clanked off through wheezing billows of smoke. Now, I could shift my concern from the journey to how I would explain Klara to Frau Höss.

✺

As our train clattered, screeched, and hissed into the small railroad terminal, I palmed a small, clear circle on the frosted window to peer out and, seeing only a swirl of white, thought to myself that anyone who complained about Germany's winters had never visited Poland. When I'd mentioned to Kempka that

Klara and I were heading there, after asking about my sanity, he warned me to dress for weather "colder than a witch's tit," as he poetically put it. I didn't dare ask him to explain how he knew this, but I had to admire his imagery as we stepped down to the ice-encrusted station platform. I had trouble imagining why someone with a witch's power would suffer such breasts, but the thought froze along with the rest of me. One look at Klara's brave bluish face and frosted eyelashes caused me to quickly grasp her shuddering body and press her tightly to me. We made our cautious way down the icy platform to the station office to telephone for a taxi.

We were deposited at the hotel that Höss had booked for me. Perhaps I'd grown too posh for my own good. Having become accustomed to hotels like the Adlon and the Meurice, I was totally unprepared for the Wielki, a shit-brown rectangle jammed between an ethnically flamboyant restaurant and a tailor shop. The hotel reminded me of those shabby, disreputable hospices that littered Berlin's once-notorious red-light district. In fact, to me, it almost seemed to flaunt its nondescript homeliness in defiance of its ostentatious neighbours.

The street was devoid of all life—no SS or Wehrmacht, no pedestrians or automobiles, save for an unoccupied Mercedes saloon stationed incongruously before the nondescript entrance. I couldn't afford to consider the operator to be anyone but Frau Höss waiting eagerly for me in the lobby. My empty stomach heaved with my sudden recognition that the moment of truth had arrived. However, when I clumsily related to Klara the circumstances surrounding my invitation, she merely smiled slyly, told me that I'd better behave, agreed to wait in the restaurant while I checked in, and said she would come later and get a separate room for appearance's sake. I was overwhelmed with gratitude and relief by her trust and discretion.

As I entered, the desk clerk, a chunky mouse-looking man in a shabby, ill-fitting double-breasted suit, tattered dress shirt, no tie, and an incongruous beret, shot up and shouted the Führer salute in a heavy Polish dialect. I returned the salute, motioned him back to his chair with an up-down wag of my hand, and saw her from the periphery of my vision. Hedwig sat primly on a well-worn sofa in a ragged little foyer—more a cramped alcove—to the side of the desk clerk's counter. She looked the same as I'd remembered: slim, severe, attractive. Heat without warmth. I put down my one suitcase and moved to her outstretched hand, touched my lips to it, and sat on the rickety armchair in front of her.

"Welcome to what used to be Poland," she said in a half-mocking tone as she waved her hand round the dilapidated lobby.

I smiled. "I've been to Poland before," I said with no mockery. "Just when it was becoming a 'used to be'—with the Führer in September of last year. In the Führerwagen, though. Nothing so fine as this."

She chuckled lightly, then her voice turned earnest. "I'm so glad you came, Heinz. I wished to welcome you personally. Rudi wanted you to come directly to our home from the station, but I convinced him that after such a journey, you needed to, well, freshen up first." Her lips curled up at the sides. "Perhaps I can help?"

That's all I needed with Klara waiting to check in. "That's more than generous of you," I said, "but I have the beginnings of a migraine; I get them from time to time. What I really need is a few hours of medicated sleep, and I'll be right as rain by tonight."

"Ah, a migraine." Her vocal shade hovered somewhere between sarcasm and solicitation. "I must remember to use that to fend off Rudi's desultory ardour."

I had no safe response to give, save for a subtle squint of pain.

"My apologies, Heinz." Her face suddenly became drawn with concern. "I made a bad joke. Of course, do what you must." She reached into her pocketbook, extracted a small calling card from a silver case, and handed it to me. "When you've recovered, ring that number. You'll be collected and delivered within thirty minutes. I have a special meal planned in your honour."

"But I thought my coming was your husband's idea."

A shrug and wink. "It was, once I gave it to him."

I smiled weakly, in keeping with my sudden migraine. "That's so very kind of you. I'm certain I'll be myself by evening."

We both stood, and again, I kissed her upraised hand. Then she left, only slowing slightly at the door to raise her hand and wiggle her fingers at me without looking back. Once I knew Hedwig was out of range, I slipped next door and told Klara it was all right to check in.

"But what am I to do while you're at the Hösses'?" She smiled sadly.

"See the sights," I joked.

"Here?" she replied. "In this bleak nothingness?"

I took her gently by the shoulders and brought her closer. "I'll admit, it's not exactly Berlin or Paris, but it's only for part of one evening. While I'm gone, imagine the same evening with your aunt, and that'll keep you busy—and grateful—until I return."

She just winced and nodded.

At 1900 hours, I dialled the number on Hedwig's card, and a man answered.

"Fritzch." Impersonal, officious.

"Herr Fritzch, I was told to telephone this—"

"Wait in front of your hotel." He rang off.

❧

The highway (if one could call it that) ran for less than a mile along a well-maintained railroad track before becoming a short dirt road that snaked round to the Höss's villa. If not for the bone-cracking cold, I could easily have walked. I exited the car, moved carefully up the icy walk to the door, and twisted the brass bell knob. A cadaverous creature in grey-striped pyjamas on which a yellow Star of David was sewn greeted me with a deep, painful bow. Then he turned and shuffled unsteadily as he led me into a large formal dining room, where stood Hedwig, Lieutenant Colonel Höss (a small compact man with close-cropped hair and a baby face), and beside him, an even smaller, nondescript blond man in the uniform of an SS captain. After we all saluted each other in the Führer's name, Hedwig introduced me to her husband and the captain, his adjutant, Karl Fritzch, then bade us sit at the opulently set table on which each item seemed to have been arranged with geometric precision. Höss was at the head of the table, Hedwig to his immediate right, Fritzch beside her, and I was positioned to Höss's immediate left, directly across from Hedwig and Fritzch. On the floor next to Höss, an empty dog bowl rested, but I saw no dog.

"Have you seen action?" Höss asked me once Herr Pyjamas served our soup course.

"You mean military action?"

"What other kind of action is there?" he asked with a curious grin.

His tone was matter-of-fact, even pleasant, but I detected an undercurrent of aversion. "I'm afraid not, Herr—"

"Rudolf, please. Formality is hardly necessary here."

"All right… Rudolf. I was about to say that I was too young for the last war, and well, now all my action is confined to the Führer's household."

Höss chuckled. "Pity." He grimaced sadly. "War is in my blood, you might say. When the last war broke out, I served briefly in a military hospital, then, at fourteen, I was admitted to my father's and grandfather's old regiment. One year later, I fought with the Ottoman Sixth Army. While stationed in Turkey, I rose to the rank of sergeant, and at only seventeen, I was the youngest noncommissioned officer in the entire army. Wounded three times and a victim of malaria, I was awarded the Gallipoli Star, the Iron Cross first and second class, and several other decorations I wouldn't bother mentioning."

I could see Hedwig's eyes yawning, though her mouth remained closed and her gaze, attentive.

"That's quite admirable," I said with some feeling, actually impressed. "Unfortunately—"

"And yet," he interrupted, "we hold the same rank. Is that not curious?"

I was right about his hostility and needed to nip it in the bud. "Well, Rudolf," I risked, "as you know, there are military ranks and political ranks, and unfortunately, they both sound the same."

Both Höss and Fritzsch smiled thinly, and Hedwig chuckled.

"Now, Rudi, you see that what General Heydrich told you about Heinz is true," she said. "It's time for the main course, gentlemen," she purred, nodding at the doorway, and Herr Pyjamas began slowly moving a heavily laden cart on rollers towards us, taking deep wheezing breaths every few steps.

Once served, Fritzsch also nodded. "You need to speed up, Meyer," he said to the scarecrow, whose head was down, facing the floor. "With you, every meal becomes the next one. You get me?"

Without looking up, he said, "Yes, Your Honour."

"That's the ticket, Meyer. You don't mind me calling you Meyer, do you?"

Still without looking up, he said, "I am whatever you call me, Your Honour."

"Even a stinking, filthy rat kike?"

"Yes, Your Honour."

Then Fritzch glanced at me. "You see what we who toil in the provinces must contend with? The Führer has you. Göring has Lisakofsky. The Reichsführer has Möller. Goebbels has Grundig, and we have… *this!*" A snarl of disgust twisted the captain's lips.

I merely nodded, not wishing to enter the boxing ring the captain seemed to be constructing. "Well, if this Meyer is so terrible, why not employ a Pole?"

At that, the three burst into boisterous laughter.

"I heard you have a keen sense of humour," Höss said, almost breathless with merriment, "but this is truly priceless."

Where had he heard that? I wondered.

I'd also begun to wonder why my host had said nothing up to now, when he explained, "We tried out a few Polacks, but they were too stupid to understand my orders, much less possess the ability to carry them out."

"Kikes are much better, aren't they, Meyer?" Fritzch asked the shaking scarecrow.

"If you say so, Your Honour." He stood at rigidly painful attention by the sideboard but still stared intently at the floor.

"Good for you, Meyer. Yes, I say so. If you want efficient service, go for intelligence over brawn every time. And who better at intelligence than a Jew. Am I right, Meyer?"

"If you say so, Your Honour."

"Don't be modest, Meyer. You are superior to a Polack. Am I right?"

"Everyone is, Your Honour."

Raucous laughter.

"You see? Intelligence." Höss fixed his stare back at me. "I've been told that you serve the Führer so well you, too, must be intelligent."

I didn't know Höss's game, but I refused to be toyed with. "I'm merely an unschooled orphan child of the streets, hallways, and back alleys, Rudolf, and not all that intelligent. For the simple tasks the Führer gives me, I certainly needn't be a Jew."

Höss stretched his thin lips into a begrudging smile. "You see, Meyer?" he asked, his gaze never leaving my face. "Aryans also have a sense of humour."

"If you say so, Your Honour."

"Well, Hedy," Höss turned, for the first time, to his wife. "I must say that the dinner was truly superlative. Is that not so, gentlemen?"

"Hear, hear!" Fritzch and I shouted with vigorous nods.

Hedy dipped her head with theatrical modesty then raised it again.

"Well, all right," Fritzch said, "now a reward for our dog for his unwavering loyalty."

I gazed round but still saw no animal.

"Dog!" he shouted.

Meyer fled his post, shuffled to the small bowl, and knelt awkwardly on all fours, his gnarled hands splayed and pressed on either side of it. Unable even to hold up his meagre weight, his bony arms collapsed, and his face fell flat into the bowl.

"Lift your fucking head, dog!" Fritzch shouted. "Or perhaps you're not hungry, eh? Are you hungry, dog?"

With what appeared supreme exertion, the Jew managed to use his skeletal arms to raise himself just high enough that his head hovered precariously to the side of the bowl. At that, Höss and

Fritzch slid their bones and cut-off fat and gristle onto Hedwig's plate. She leaned over and slopped the contents into the dish.

"And what of you, Heinz?" Fritzch gazed down at my plate. "Have you no appreciation for a job well done?" Again that stare.

Was this for my benefit or a typical evening's entertainment? Regardless, I needed to act, but when I leaned over to dump my scraps, Fritzch moved his boot out and kicked over the dish, spilling the contents onto the rug.

"You clumsy fucking kike!" Fritzch shouted, then slammed the toe of his boot into the "dog's" rib cage, sending the poor man rolling in agony, gripping his sides, unable to make a sound. Fritzch then turned his head towards the kitchen door. "Meyer!" he yelled, and another skeletal man in grey-striped pyjamas shuffled in, also with his head down. "Meyer"—Fritzch tilted his head towards the scattered scraps—"just look at that mess. Do a good job of cleaning it up, and I might let you have it. But first, take out the garbage."

"Yes, Your Honour," the second Meyer muttered, still looking down.

He moved to where the first Meyer lay, holding his sides and moaning. Blood and something viscous and vaguely brownish-yellow oozed from his ears, nose, and mouth. The second Meyer bent over, grabbed the poor fellow's collar with both hands, and dragged him slowly backwards out through the door, then returned.

"Good job, Meyer," Fritzch said, eyes hooded. "Now, lick up every drop of that muck, put the scraps back in the dish, and take it out. You'll have worked up quite an appetite by then."

I turned to see Hedwig and her husband nod approvingly. All I could think of was Heydrich's cellar and felt the urge to vomit, but the thought of Fritzch ordering "Meyer" to lick it up caused my throat to force back the searing bile.

Once the floor had been cleared off and the second Meyer had left, I asked, "Two Meyers?"

Fritzch answered, "Currently, the camp has over one hundred kikes—all Meyers. Simpler than bothering to remember each kike's name. But soon, if the Reichsführer has his way, we'll have hundreds of thousands, and after Dirlewanger deals with them, there'll be just one colossal pit named Meyer."[44]

⁓

As we drank our brandies and coffee, Höss said to me, "Look, Heinz, that sty of a hotel isn't even fit for Polacks, much less an SS officer. You must stay with us. Hedwig insists, and you wouldn't refuse her hospitality now, would you?" An odd stare followed. "Tomorrow, I'll give you a personally guided tour of the camp. Now, how does that sound?"

Like a defective lift, my already-knotted stomach dropped several floors. While his offer saved me from Hedwig's unwanted amours, it would do nothing to dilute Klara's wrath.

"I couldn't ask for more." I forced a smile of gratitude, all the while trying to conjure up a strategy. "However, the Führer asked me to phone him tonight about a private matter. I was going to do it from the hotel. May I do it from here since I'm staying?"

---

[44] Oskar Dirlewanger (26 September 1895–7 June 1945) was a German military officer and war criminal who founded and commanded the Nazi SS penal unit "Dirlewanger" during World War II. His name is closely linked to some of the worst crimes of the war. He died after World War II while in Allied custody, reportedly beaten to death by his guards, though lack of evidence has led to theories of him escaping. Dirlewanger is invariably described as an extremely cruel person by historians and researchers such as Timothy Snyder and Chris Bishop, and as a "psychopathic killer and child molester," "violently sadistic," "an expert in extermination and a devotee of sadism and necrophilia," and "a sadist and necrophiliac." As one account states, "In all the theatres of the Second World War, few could compete in savagery with Dirlewanger."

Höss nodded energetically. "Of course, anything for you and the Führer. There's a telephone in my study. Meyer's waiting in the hallway. He'll escort you."

"You trust him that much?"

"I don't rely on trust, Heinz. I caught a previous Meyer trying to sneak some food from our pantry, so I had Fritzch chop off his hands—in front of our current Meyer. Even a kike can decipher an Aryan message."

Not surprisingly, "Meyer" was a model of terrified efficiency as he shuffled me to Höss's study, the walls of which were studded with photographs of the Führer, Himmler, Heydrich, Göring, Kaltenbrunner, Hedwig, and their five admittedly beautiful children. After making sure the study door was locked, I checked for a party line. Hearing nothing but a dial tone, I rang the hotel and had the multilingual desk clerk deliver a message from "Baldy" telling her that I missed her terribly but my hosts, believing me alone, had coerced me into staying overnight and taking me on a guided tour the next day. I told her of my desolation and promised on no uncertain terms that I would be with her immediately afterwards and that we would make up for lost time and then some. I wanted to tell her how much I despised the Hösses and Fritzch, but such sentiments couldn't be transmitted second-hand, or perhaps at all.

Flailing from side to side in the guest-quarters bed, trapped between nerve-shredding insomnia and the probability of a nightmare in which I re-experienced dinner, I failed to react when my door squeaked open and closed. A silent shadow approached and knelt beside my ear.

"Better to whisper, I think." The voice was Hedwig's, like two pieces of velvet rubbing together.

Startled, I grabbed for the cord on the table lamp, but her hand stopped mine.

"Also better in the dark."

"What is?"

"Guess." She moved round the bed, slid under the covers, and I felt her turn on her side towards me. "You were asleep?"

"No," I answered. "I wasn't asleep. Upset stomach; I'm not used to such rich food."

"Ah yes, the Führer's regimen. I thought perhaps it was the service."

"Now that you mention it, I was wondering how Herr Fritzch arrives at just the right tip."

"Not always so," she said. "For Jews, sometimes, he over-pays. That troubles you?"

Careful! "Not sleeping troubles me. I want to be fresh for the tour."

The protesting mattress springs told me that she'd turned onto her back.

"Won't you be missed?" I asked her.

"Rudi knows where I am."

"Then why are we whispering?"

"Well, Heinz, there's knowing, and then there's knowing."

I had no response to give.

"However, tonight, Rudi is in no danger of becoming a cuckold," she said, "in case that was distressing you."

"Becoming what?" I asked, true to my persona.

"Even for a valet, a good dictionary wouldn't do you a bit of harm," she whispered after a low, breathy chuckle. "A cuckold is the husband of an adulteress."

"All right," I said as matter-of-factly as possible in an attempt to mask my perplexity, "if your husband's safe, even though you're lying under the covers next to me, please forgive a little curiosity on my part as to just why you invited me here."

A pause, then, "Frau Bella told me you were droll, with an intelligence and sophistication far exceeding your years and education. For a moment I was concerned that perhaps she'd misjudged, but now I suspect that she may have underestimated."

A raw chill shot through my bowels. Some puzzle pieces were beginning to edge into place, but far more still lay scattered meaninglessly in the box, a few even upside down. Now I knew a little of why Bella had pressed me to accept Hedwig's invitation, but not nearly all, I was certain. And there was also the matter of Brückner's involvement.

"I don't mind compliments," I told her, "but I'm not a little ashamed of myself for being so easily led—and misled. And you still haven't answered my question: why was I manipulated into coming here?"

More sheet rustling as she returned to her side. "We need you to witness the real meaning and purpose of the man you serve, through those he's selected to carry out his will—not the least, you."

We again! And me! "All right, I give up on the why me," I told her, "but I'd appreciate some idea of why now."

A pause, then, "You mean this minute? In your bed? Well, ideally, I would speak with you after the tour, but ideally won't be possible, since you may not be alone before you and your lady friend get on your train back to Berlin."

How the hell did she know about Klara? "All right then." I sighed wearily—and warily. "Tell me what you need to say."

More rustling, then, "What you witnessed at dinner tonight is every night, sometimes even more so. But I wonder if you really understood what you saw."

"What was there to understand, beyond power having corrupted once again? Somebody told me that once, and I even understood it."

There was a short pause. "That's the simple part, a cliché really, and of course, like most clichés, it's also true. But within that cliché is a far more insidious truth. I'll wager that in the future, should you remember our dinner at all, you'll remember Fritzch, for the Fritzches are only too visible, and so, memorable. I'll also wager that if pressed to remember my husband, you would draw a blank, for the relatively numerous barbaric brutes are seen and remembered, while those few who are infinitely more destructive are not. This, Heinz, is the true horror facing the Reich."

"Now I don't understand," I said, suddenly intrigued.

"I know you don't, so I'll explain it to you. It may not be readily apparent, but the Fritzches, the Heydrichs, though underneath are evil and grotesque, they are also men with imagination, ideas, feelings, plans, hopes, dreams, loves, hates. They are not the real danger. No, Heinz, the true enemy are the faceless men, fastidious men, efficient men, compliant men, obedient men, men without thought or feeling. To such men, everything, including mass murder, is a problem of engineering, mechanics, not morality."

"You're the wife of a KZ commandant." I challenged. "You can say these things?"

"As the wife of a KZ commandant, I'm uniquely qualified to say these things."

"You sound like a woman I met long ago, one who spoke the same way. She even tried to have me—"

"Do the unthinkable," she interrupted. "Yes, I know—the lady in green. Pity. Though highly gifted and well-meaning, she was far too eager and far too precipitate. At the time, you hadn't experienced enough, and there was nothing to demonstrate that might have moved you."

"But now is the right time," I said, in a manner containing no little sarcasm.

"Not now, Heinz," she said straight on, as if she hadn't sensed the mockery. "Tomorrow. And
I'm afraid, if that isn't the right time, it may be too late."

"Too late? Too late for what?"

"To save what remains of the German soul."

"Please, Hedwig, save the German soul? Such apocalyptic melodramatics are ridiculous," I exclaimed, temporarily and dangerously deviating from persona. "And I'm the one to save it? Even more ridiculous. I'm nobody. Less than nobody."

Her hand began to caress my face with her cool, silky skin, like a scarf gliding slowly down my cheek.

"Apocalyptic melodramatics? Well then, Herr Less-Than-Nobody," she said, "perhaps even after all you've experienced, it still hasn't dawned on you, but it should. Think, Heinz!" she commanded, her whisper strident. "How many seemingly bizarre and inexplicable episodes must you experience, how many exercises of extraordinary capabilities must you perform, before you recognise and accept the truth? At long last, employ that remarkable brain of yours to realise that you're as far from a nobody as anyone can be. And I tell you this: even if *you* still don't know, Himmler knows, Goebbels knows, Göring knows, and most importantly, the Führer knows. Can you be totally oblivious to the fact that, since you arrived at the Chancellery, you've enjoyed an extraordinary position—and with more than ample evidence to support it? And even in the negative, have there not been enough attempts on your life to convince you of your inestimable value, both to them… and to us?"

As she spoke, a conclusion I'd dismissed and shut away

forced its way into my consciousness: *I believed her!* But it was belief bereft of implication. "All right," I told her, still battered by her words and, even more, my acceptance of them, "if all that you say is true, manipulation or no manipulation, what now?"

She drew her hand away. "Let's see what tomorrow brings, yes? Until then, perhaps now you'll have more pleasant dreams."

"I wasn't dreaming," I protested, but I could sense a smile on her lips I couldn't see.

"Yes, you were, Heinz," she rejoined gently. "You still are."

"How can you say that? We were just speaking about—"

"Yes, we were. Don't you exercise control in your dreams?"

"This is insane!" I shouted, in total disregard of her earlier admonition. "And I'll prove it to you!" With that, I reached over and jerked on the lamp cord, but save for me, sitting bolt upright and dripping sweat, the bed was empty.

The second day, 12 January:

I had no time to ruminate over my bedtime adventure, since at 0400, an almost inaudible knock on my door brought in another "Meyer," hobbling slowly and painfully towards me and pushing a breakfast trolley.

"Thank you," I said.

But when he merely bowed again, I asked him why he came so early. He lifted a bony finger to his mouth.

"You have laryngitis?" I asked.

He shook his head and pointed again to his mouth. If he had some communicable disease, I needed to know before making use of the cart, so I eased myself out of bed, went over to my uniform tunic, took out a small notepad and pencil, and extended them towards him. "If not laryngitis, what?"

I'd seen stricken looks before, but nothing like this. He

shook his head violently and fled into a corner, cowering there as if facing a rabid dog. I put the pad and pencil down, held up my hands, palms outward, walked over, and raised him up. It was like lifting a rag doll.

"Don't be afraid," I told him with my most sincere expression and voice. "I mean you no harm. Please tell me what's the matter with you." I picked up the writing materials and held them out again.

This time, he took them with agonising hesitation and began writing. When he'd finally finished, he handed them back gingerly and shrugged. I had to strain to read his shaky abbreviated scrawl. *Your Honour,* it said, *first day when come, ask something guard. Assist Commandant hear, tell never speak until told. Then escort to medical barracks orderly, no anaesthetic, cut out tongue.* His sunken, bloodshot eyes were moist.

I was too shaken to respond, short of a mumbled "thank you" and "please sit," which he did—on the very edge of the bed.

When I'd finally composed myself sufficiently, I asked him how long he'd been in the camp. He held up three gnarled fingers. Since the camp was relatively new, I assumed he meant three weeks. I sat down next to him and handed back the pad and pencil. "Nothing you write will leave this room; you have my solemn word as an SS officer."

I could have sworn that the poor soul was attempting a laugh, but it merely emerged as a distorted, phlegmy gargle.

"I understand," I told the wretch. I couldn't stop seeing the devastated Adelsheimer, pointing an empty, rebuking sleeve at me. "They're giving me an official tour today; what will I see?"

He stared at me with judgemental intensity for a few moments, then pursed his bloody, swollen lips and motioned tentatively for the pad and pencil. I handed it to him, and he scribbled some more, passed it back, and I held it up: *See future Germany. Land of dead, rule by murderers.*

I began trembling inwardly. First Brückner, then Bella and Hedwig (dream or no dream), and now this "Meyer." *More manipulation?* But before I could question him further, he scrawled some more.

Comrade try find, now here, it read.

"You mean Siegfried Hausen?"

Only number, he scratched, his forearm stretched out, and I saw a line of blue tattooed numerals.

Hearing that, I felt an involuntary twitch of my jaw muscles. "How do you know he's a comrade?"

Tell me when know I come to you.

"When was that?"

Three day. Transfer week before you come. No coincidence, no accident. They want you see. Warning.

"See what? What do you mean?" I edged closer to watch what he wrote.

He seemed not to notice. Then he glanced over at the food cart. My eyes followed his, and he turned to me, nodded back at the trolley, then printed carefully: *DON'T EAT.*

❧

At precisely 0500, ten miserable minutes after "Room Service" departed, there was another knock, this one far more audible. It was Fritzch, who scanned me up and down like a searchlight.

"Ah, good, Colonel," he said, "you're ready. Herr Höss is quite the stickler for punctuality."

"So is the Führer," I lied, if only to temper his arrogance.

"I regret that the Commandant cannot join us. He has an important meeting this morning with Colonel Eichmann of General Heydrich's staff and some important men of finance and industry. Should the meeting be a short one, he may join us later. In any case, you'll be in good hands with me since I know the camp and especially its… guests far better than he does." Clearly, his arrogance was impervious to tempering. "You'll have quite an instructive experience to report, I think."

"No report is involved, Major," I corrected. "This is entirely a private visit."

His eyes narrowed, then slowly recovered. "My error, Colonel. Well then, shall we begin?"

As we exited the Commandant's house, the fierce Polish winter hit me again like a hammer made of ice. Shivering on the porch in a greatcoat and muffler, all I could see in front of me was a vast, snow-encrusted forest, a deceptively bucolic setting out of a fairy tale. It was only when we moved round to the back, frost pouring from our noses and mouths, that I saw the watchtowers, floodlights, and hooked fence posts to which electrified wire was attached, extending as far as the eye could see. A double set of railroad tracks ran straight into the camp through the main gate. Set in the gate's wrought iron were the words: Work Makes You Free.

Before I had an opportunity to inquire, Fritzch volunteered, "The Commandant has a playful flair for irony, don't you agree?"

Not understanding what he meant at the time, I merely said, "Irony is undervalued," which seemed to satisfy him. After negotiating three separate, heavily guarded, caged checkpoints, we finally entered the camp proper, where I was confronted with endless lines of barely alive, frost-belching skeletons in striped pyjamas shuffling at a jog-trot and lugging burlap sacks that appeared to be far heavier than they were.

Beside them trotted booted and greatcoated guards,

shouting, "Left RIGHT! Left RIGHT!" Each arm barely controlled a vicious German shepherd that snarled, bellowed, leapt, and strained at its leash. It was a hideous chaos of screams: the screams of the guards, the screams of the dogs, the screams of the prisoners. How I hadn't heard all this horrible racket from the house remains a mystery to me.

Construction work was in evidence everywhere. The air had been heavy with varied sounds: whistles, beams being unloaded, the huff of engines, and giant mixers sloshing concrete down endless chutes. Snow-swirled mud, like mountains of Rocky Road ice cream, sat beside enormous craters from which the substance originated.

"What are they all doing?" I asked.

"Right now? These vermin you see have been set to the sacred task of building and expanding the camp. That is to say, levelling the ground, erecting new blocks and buildings, laying roads, and digging drainage ditches."

"Then, practically speaking, Major," I asked, after witnessing a long line of naked bluish skeletons, some standing rigidly, some hopping clumsily, and some sprawled on patches of snow, sticklike limbs akimbo, blood oozing into the pristine whiteness, "shouldn't the workers be provided with warmer clothes?"

Fritzch laughed a cloud of frost. "These particular vermin are malingerers and so are unfit to wear uniforms like the others. In any event, you saw the sign as we entered. It should really read, 'Work not only makes you free, it also makes you warm.'"

I had no desire to comment on the bastard's lame attempt at humour, and we continued on until we came to a small, fenced-off pigsty in the centre of the compound, where, instead of pigs, sat two small wooden boats, one atop the other, making it resemble a giant walnut.

"What's that?" I asked.

"Ah," Fritzch replied, "it intrigues you? It's a little present General Heydrich brought us on his last inspection—to make examples of the particularly troublesome. The prisoner is placed between the two boats and secured with head, hands, and feet protruding. He is then force-fed a large amount of milk and honey until he develops severe diarrhoea. The mixture of milk and honey is also rubbed on the exposed parts of his body, attracting flies, wasps, and other insects—especially effective in summer, I'm told. Of course, shit slowly accumulates within the container, attracting even more flies, which eat and breed within his or her exposed and increasingly gangrenous flesh. The person is repeatedly fed each day to keep him alive for several days or even weeks. As you can see, no one's in it at present, for it's quite the tonic for the rest of the filth who are marched by it each day to witness. It was devised especially for Jews, the general told us. He calls it 'The Land of Milk and Honey.' *He's* quite the ironist too."

I strained to block his words from my ears, but something in my brain compelled me to hear every one. "Yes, Major. I've had occasion to experience the general's irony first-hand. Shall we continue?"

On our way to check out the barracks, I spotted a loose German shepherd gnawing noisily on what looked, on closer inspection, to have once been a human arm.

Fritzch must have seen me cringe, for he patted me on the shoulder indulgently. "Under Commandant Höss's rational management, this camp is the standard for German efficiency. Nothing is wasted. The dogs must be fed, after all. The dogs on top, Jews, Poles, traitors, and defectives at the bottom. An enlightened food chain, wouldn't you agree?"

"Saves on leashes, too," was all I could say.

"Exactly so. It seems you possess a wry sense of humour we hadn't anticipated."

"It isn't the sort of characteristic one lists on a job application."

"To work here," he replied, "it should be mandatory."

He chuckled at his quick display of wit, and we proceeded to the barracks area.

The length, if not the width and height, of a private-aeroplane hangar, each barracks was constructed of old brick, where, according to Fritzch, several hundred three-tier wooden bunk beds were installed for triple that number of prisoners. When I stupidly asked Fritzch how this worked, he answered as I should have assumed, "Our model is a simple and effective one, the sandwich."

We passed several such buildings before arriving at the one I presumed served his purpose.

At the door, Fritzch took out two cigarettes from his silver case, broke them in two, and handed a set to me. "Stick these up your nose."

I thought this eccentric until we entered, and the horrendous stench assailed me like a hammer made of summer shit. I quickly inserted the cigarettes as advised. I would have been even more disgusted, had I not had years of experience with the Führer's bowels.

I knew it had to be illusory, but it felt colder in the barracks than it was outside. The cavernous space appeared uninhabited, but for two "skeletons" crouched on a filthy, rotting plank floor, scrubbing it with toothbrushes. When they saw us, they struggled up to a sickly form of attention.

"Isn't it amazing, Colonel?" Fritzch turned his head to me. "Traitorous bankers, industrialists, and professors undermining the Reich one day, patriotic janitors serving the Reich the next. Versatile, these Jews, eh?" He turned back to the quaking wretches, fixing his stare on one of them. "Isn't that true, Meyer?"

"Y-yes, Your Honour," he stammered, eyelids fluttering nervously. Several sores festered on his cadaverous face. His eyes bulged, flaming with fever, but I could also detect a contradictory mixture of wariness and resignation. No fear, though, and long past despair.

"You seem unsure, Meyer." Fritzch's eyelids narrowed with menace. "Are you unsure?"

"No, no, Your Honour," he said, shaking violently with cold. "I am as you say, versatile."

"May we continue the tour?" I asked in earnest, wishing to at least end our part in the poor prisoner's misery. "I'm sure there's more—"

"In a moment, if you please, Colonel." Fritzch jerked his head towards me. "This *is* more, and it will also prove instructive." He snapped back to the prisoner. "Versatile, you say? Now, who makes those decisions, Meyer? You?"

The prisoner helplessly shrugged his bony shoulders. "Your Honour makes those decisions."

Fritzch's thin lips formed a crooked smile. "All right then, Meyer, and here's how we prove your versatility to the colonel here as well as the efficiency of our Aryan discipline. A role-play, yes? You were a janitor; now I've promoted you to sentry, and that Meyer beside you is attempting to escape." He unhooked the flap of his holster, removed his revolver. "Here, take it and do your duty."

"This isn't necessary," I told Fritzch, in a panic I didn't show. "I'll take your word for it."

"You would thwart this Jew's ambition?" he asked rhetorically, his eyes still fixed on the prisoner. "Well, Meyer, are you going to perform this simple task, or shall I promote your Jew partner instead?" He swung his hand with the revolver towards the other emaciated, shivering creature.

"Look," I said in a silly jest I hoped would shift the focus, "the floor's filthy. At least wait until they finish scrubbing."

But he was so swallowed up by his game, it was as if I'd disappeared. "Now which one of you vermin will accept the promotion?" he asked the hapless Jews while swinging the gun barrel from one to the other. "Or shall I make the choice? I'll count to three. One, two—"

"Major," I interrupted sharply, "as your guest and, not incidentally, as one who outranks you, I insist we continue our tour, not re-enact last night's dinner entertainment. Am I clear?" Though I knew that at best, I was merely postponing Fritzch's fiendish amusement, I had to do something, whether it was because I needed to atone for Adelsheimer, or because of last night's "dream" or… because of some reason of which I was unaware.

After a few pregnant moments, Fritzch shook his head, as if he were coming to after being knocked unconscious. Slowly, he put his revolver back in its holster and turned towards me. He stared at me with an ambiguous expression for several seconds, then smiled no less ambiguously. "Please forgive me, Colonel," he said with icy menace. "For a moment, I'd forgotten just how high a menial can rise in the Führer's household."

And how mighty, I'm certain he ached to add.

"The Führer is very generous," I told him. "Shall we go?"

"Of course, Colonel," he said, with his usual insolent emphasis on the rank. Then he turned back to the prisoners, his eyes slits. "By tonight, my Jew friends, I want this floor shining like a mirror, or tomorrow, you'll be polishing it with your tongues. Now get to it!" he shouted.

They produced a weak "Yes, Your Honour!" and "Heil Hitler!" before shambling back to the floor and resuming their Sisyphean task.

Fritzch then turned to me. "The rest of the tour, yes. But before we leave here, there's one more attraction we couldn't permit you to miss." He aimed his index finger down one of the long corridors between the rows of bunks.

The aisle was so narrow, we had to edge our way along to get to the other end. When we finally arrived, we stood before a metal chest the size of a small trunk, with several tiny perforations running in a straight line along the padlocked lid.

"We couldn't call this a complete tour," he declared, "without showing you the camp's Magical Ventriloquist's Dummy."

"You have a ventriloquist here as well?"

Fritzch grinned malevolently. "With this particular dummy, no ventriloquist is needed—that's the magical part. Permit me to demonstrate." He extracted a cramped set of keys from his trousers, made his way through each one with theatrically conspicuous care, and, finally finding the right one, removed the lock, then raised the lid.

My early morning "Room Service" was accurate. It took all the strength I possessed not to vomit. Inside was once a human being in an SS colonel's uniform. I couldn't imagine how many bones they had to break to fit Siegfried, my Ziggy, into the chest, facing up with his legs bent back in sections and forced over his shoulders. A form-fitting coffin for the barely alive.

"All right, dummy," Fritzch commanded, "tell the colonel how you like it here in our KZ."

Since only one eye remained, it stared up at us vacantly, then his torn, toothless mouth opened, but only a muffled moan emerged.

"Is that all you have to say, dummy?" he taunted. "Nothing pithy for our honoured guest?"

More guttural moaning.

"My apologies, Colonel," he said, "our dummy seems not so magical today."

"Another gift from General Heydrich?" I quipped, to keep from tearing out his fucking throat. I knew what had to be done, but wondered if I had the courage and skill to do it. *Ziggy would do it for me,* I told myself. Just another favour for a needy stranger, just another button.

"May I play with your magical puppet?" I asked the monster.

"Of course," he responded with malignant equanimity. "That's what puppets are for—especially traitorous ones."

It had to be quick. Years before, I'd read in a forensic medicine textbook that severing the brain stem was the most efficient method of killing with dispatch and, though difficult to pinpoint in a fight, would theoretically result in nearly instantaneous death if done correctly. There would be no fight.

"Thank you, Major." I leaned over and down and whipped out my SS dagger in one movement. Reaching between Ziggy's feet, I forced his head forward by the hair and severed the stem. After some involuntary twitching, it was over. Then I stood upright. "This shouldn't inconvenience you too much," I assured him with my best SS grin, though I convulsed inside. "One traitor rewarded. I'm quite certain you can acquire another puppet, perhaps one even more magical."

I couldn't precisely interpret Fritzch's expression, but I knew it wasn't happiness. After a few moments of glaring helplessly at me, he shrugged. "You can count on it, Colonel." Then, "You haven't yet seen our medical facilities." Forced matter-of-factness oozed from his mouth like pus. "Unfortunately, we haven't yet received our permanent medical director, but since you've seen everything else of interest, we can make it our last stop."

I nodded my assent, and we pushed off. Relieved in some infinitesimal measure, I'd repaid Ziggy for his generosity. It was just another button to him, but a career to me.[45]

---

[45] For the incident mentioned, see Volume One.

When we returned to the house, I had to spend some moments with Höss, who merely asked me if I enjoyed my tour.

I told him, "It was most educational and stimulating, Herr Colonel. I have no words to express my gratitude."

Höss glanced towards Fritzch, who seemed somewhat dour, then back to me. "Words are unnecessary. It was our great pleasure." Then he added, "Not a request, mind you, but should you have the opportunity to mention your visit to the Führer and the humble strides we're making, well… you know how that is."

I looked at Fritzch, then at Höss. "I can personally guarantee, Colonel, that I will make the subject my first order of business. Please give my sincerest regards to your wife and convey my regrets that I couldn't tell her in person. Now, if you'll oblige me, all I require is transport to the railway depot."

Once there, I waited until my ride left, then, with justifiable caution, skulked back to the hotel and discovered that, according to the clerk behind the counter, no one named Klara Schroeder was staying at the hotel.

"All right," I told him, "she may have used another name. Perhaps Linge?"

He glanced down at the register. "That is *your* name, Herr Colonel."

I pursed my lips, not wishing to show concern. "Yes, I know that's my name. Are other women staying here?"

He put his index finger to his lips in thought. "Ah, Colonel, of course there are women staying here. But which one?" he asked with a shrug of helplessness.

"I'll assist you," I said, jettisoning all caution and still reeling from my tour of hell. "She's deaf. Shouldn't be too many of those at your hotel, I'd wager."

A pause, then another finger to his lips and a shrug. His gaze returned to the register, then back to me. "My apologies, Colonel. A Klara Linge did check in, but it appears she also later checked out."

"Appears?" I asked him. "Appears? Are you saying you don't remember something that recent?"

The clerk shrugged. "It happened when I was off duty and the night clerk was here."

"Show me your register," I demanded.

He turned the large vertical ledger round and slid it across to me. I could see his hand tremble slightly. I looked for the last entry and found that a Klara Linge had indeed checked out—at 0345 in the morning. I could hardly concentrate for the sudden trepidation churning my bowels. Something was wrong, but it had no tangible form.

"Was she alone?" I asked him.

Another helpless shrug. "As I told you, Colonel, I wasn't on duty then. The night clerk comes in at six, and of course, you can ask him then."

He began fiddling with items on his desk, so I handed back the register to steady him.

My brain was in turmoil, and sweat coursed down my back despite the lobby's chill. "We'll see," I told him, and left, having no intention of waiting till six only to get more shrugs. As I walked back to the station, I attempted to humour myself with the far less disturbing thought that Klara had become so cross with me for ruining her vacation, she'd actually taken the night-train back home. *But what then of the clerk and his register? Oh three forty-five?* Something was wrong, but I had no way to interpret it, and so, riding the train home with no companion save my reflection in the window, I forced all my concentration onto the KZ, but even that was distorted by the hailstorm of circumstances surrounding my visit.

"Room Service Meyer" had warned me that Ziggy's transfer was "no coincidence; no accident." Since I believed him, I had to conclude that neither was Hedwig's invitation, Brückner's putting me onto Bella, or Bella's urging me to accept Hedwig's invitation, or the "comedy team" of Höss and Fritzch's dinner frolics, my "dream," and… Ziggy. The only thing not orchestrated—or certain—was whether I would accept the invitation. And yet…

In *Synchronicity: An Acausal Connecting Principle*, Jung asked how we are to recognise causal combinations of events, since it is not possible to examine all chance happenings for their causality? He answered that acausal events may be expected where, on closer reflection, a causal connection appears not to be conceivable. I'd had no understanding of it when I'd come across it years before, but suddenly, the dawn of comprehension was breaking, so to say. Perhaps they all knew I would follow the breadcrumbs they'd strewn in my path. However, even though I could imagine a confluence of circumstance, I couldn't detect a consistency of motive, and that was confounding and not a little terrifying.

But despite my turmoil and confusion, by the time my train arrived in Berlin, I knew for certain that the first thing I needed to do was inform the Führer in the most graphic detail about how others, high and low, were interpreting and carrying out his vision. It was too late for Ziggy and probably all the condemned "Meyers" I'd encountered, but once apprised, the Führer would immediately put a stop to the abominations perpetrated in his name. Of that, I was certain. And once accomplished, I intended to do everything I could to contact an obviously irate Klara and make it up to her. But considering the circumstances of her disappearance, of that, I was far less certain.

OUTWARDLY, LITTLE HAD changed at the Chancellery, but I was struck immediately by an odd ambience of extreme insularity, as if all sense of life outside the walls had vanished. I'd only been away for two days, but as I made my way to the Führer's quarters, I was greeted as if I'd returned to Christendom with the Holy Grail. Slaps on shoulders, pumping of hands, effusive compliments—and one furtive and heartfelt refrain connecting all the gestures: *My God, Linge, it's so good to have you standing between us and the Bear again*—the "Bear" being Bormann. Clearly, as with my Paris trip, the Reichsleiter had wasted no time in imposing his will on all those too vulnerable to resist.

Entering the Führer's antechamber, I spotted Günsche looming over his desk, but there was no sign of Herr Chinless. As I made for the Führer's door, I heard the giant's surprisingly high voice simper behind me.

"Hey, good to have you back, Heinz," he said, one narrow notch above the perfunctory, "but don't go in there just yet, eh? The boss is huddled with Goebbels and Schroeder and told me not to disturb him."

I reached for the knob and turned it. "Then don't," I replied without turning round, and went in.

The Führer sat at his desk, absently moving papers about like a planchette on a Ouija board while Schroeder sat primly in her small, straight-back chair, stenographic pad and pencil at the ready but nothing written. The Reichsminister was at one of the enormous pull-down military maps, studying it intently. As usual, no one appeared to take notice of me going directly to the bathroom and tidying up the smelly shambles of a two-day absence. All was silent until Goebbels spoke.

"My Führer, there's plenty of time, almost a fortnight before you deliver your speech. We should wait for developments."

"Developments?" the Führer shouted, "DEVELOPMENTS? I'll give you developments! Britain is still able to thwart me. North Africa is touch and go, and even that clod Boris,[46] that two-bit Slavic nonentity, defies me. I seem to be the Führer only in this room!"

Despite my dour apprehension, I had to stifle a laugh. Even in the Führer's rages, seriousness of substance couldn't fully drown out a levity of style—the mark of a high order of intelligence, I'd read. I knew little of Bulgaria and cared even less. I only hoped his temper—and his humour—would mellow enough for me to convey my alarm over the revelations of the last two days.

"Look, Joseph," the Führer said, his voice suddenly tranquil, "I shouldn't have to tell you, of all people. If I'm to deliver a rousing address on the thirtieth, I must have something to rouse with, at least something more than empty shouting and gesticulation. That I leave to the Duce. The Italians dote on display, but Germans require results. Since I still lack the capability to totally control events, I rely on you to conjure up something I can recite to Schroeder here, that will…"

---

[46] Boris III was Tsar of Bulgaria from 1918 until his death. When Adolf Hitler rose to power, he tried to win Boris's allegiance. In the summer of 1940, after a year of war, Hitler hosted diplomatic talks between Bulgaria and Romania in Vienna, after which, on 7 September, an agreement was signed for the return of South Dobruja to Bulgaria. The Bulgarian nation rejoiced. Boris was more reticent when Hitler asked to join the Axis powers.

The Führer's words caused my brain to play out a fantasy in which I strode in and interrupted the discussion: *"So you wish to have something to rouse the German people? Well, my Führer, I have something for you that will turn the Reich on its ear. I've just returned from a place that, if they knew, might rouse your people, a place you would never visit—or even wish to hear about."*

What shape would his rage take then? I wondered. *And how much mirth would accompany it?*

"… turn the Reich on its ear. A week should give you enough time, eh, Doctor?"

I assumed that the Führer waved them out, for I could hear salutes from Goebbels and Schroeder and a door close.

"Linge, stop fussing and join me."

When I rushed in, he nodded to the chair that once held Goebbels, and I sat, loaded for bear but bereft of when and how to bring up the matter.

He hunched forward, his elbows planted on his desktop, his palms supporting his cheeks. "I don't know what's wrong with Goebbels. The man's legendary creativity seems to have abandoned him, and what remains is banality and timorous sycophancy. Of course, blind obedience has its place, but I can get that from Bormann and such like. You and Speer seem to be the only people round me who I can still rely on for an honest opinion that makes sense."

Me! How could he possibly mean me? And in the same regard as an urbane prodigy like Speer? What could I have possibly done to merit such fulsome praise? Thankfully, since I'd heard nothing that seemed to require a response, I just sat there, considering that perhaps with such an opinion, the Führer would be more receptive to my report than I'd thought.

"You know, Linge," he continued, "when I was a young man, everyone I encountered seemed to feel qualified to lecture me on anything and everything in the most rigid, pompous, wrongheaded, and simplistic terms, as if I were the village idiot. I got so sick of their mindless arrogance and presumptuousness, I spent most of my early life striving to reach a position where I alone did the lecturing, allowing me to focus my unique intellect and imagination on the destruction and creation of worlds. Unfortunately, as you've seen only too often, such a situation can lead to isolation, for day and night, all I get is 'Yes, my Führer,' 'No, my Führer,' 'Whatever you say, my Führer.'"

A lecture about lecturing! Only the Führer could execute it so effectively. But now I needed him to listen as well, listen as never before, and listen to what he said he craved: "an honest opinion that makes sense." *How effective would the Führer be at that?* I wondered.

He sat back, his head against his seat back, tilted up at the ceiling, eyes shut, hands clasped on his stomach, a mask of serenity, not unlike statues of Buddha I'd seen in a book of engravings. But I knew, unlike Buddha, beneath that veneer, the Führer was anything but serene. Then his head righted itself, his eyes opened, and he fixed his gaze on me.

"You don't look at all rested, Linge. Perhaps you should take your next vacation in the Chancellery. You'd be surprised how many do just that." He chuckled. "But I know your trouble. You must learn to relax. Bormann never relaxes, but that's Bormann. A perpetual-motion engine, the man thrives on relentless bustle. You, unlike our esteemed Reichsleiter, are human and so must cast off your burdens, even for a short time, am I right?" His eyes seemed to shine with mischievous merriment.

This was the moment, I concluded, but I knew I needed to be articulate yet true to persona, earnest but not ardent, cogent without being demanding—a ridiculously perilous balancing act for a nothing like me.

"As always, my Führer," I said, attempting to employ his irony as a way in. "I *should have* vacationed in the Chancellery. Unfortunately, instead, as you know, I accepted an invitation to visit a KZ in Poland, and I need to tell you—"

"By the way, Linge," he cut in, "speaking of KZs, tonight, you'll be showing one of Goebbels's American movies. He's still adept at that. I think it's called *Escape*—about a German-American who discovers his mother is in a KZ and tries desperately to free her. He says it's hilarious, though it isn't a comedy. Personally, I think the real comedy will be watching to see whether Himmler's equally amused. In any event, I'll want you to run the projector since that lunkhead Arnt couldn't even put on a belt without instructions."

A KZ film! My nerve endings sparked with excitement. A coincidence? Truly, Jung was a wizard! It was not only the moment. It was another example of synchronicity. "Of course, my Führer," I told him, trying not to show my excitement over such a fortuitous development. "I guarantee it'll go off without a hitch."

The Führer nodded. "Naturally, that's why I want you."

"Thank you, my Führer, but as I was about to say about my invitation to the—"

"Oh yes," he interrupted again, "I forgot to add that I won't be attending the screening, so don't wait for me before showing it." Then his eyes widened slightly. "Are you all right?" he asked—and with no little justification, since his announcement had rendered me dumbstruck.

"I'm fine," I assured him. "I was just surprised that you won't be—"

"Hilarious or not, I have no interest whatever in KZs. That's Himmler's hobby, not mine. I have far more important things to occupy me."

"B-but," I stammered, "I need to tell you about my—"

The Führer waved it away with a sweep of his hand, a gesture I well knew would brook no alternatives. "Not to worry. Plenty of time to regale me with your adventures. Now, I must meet with some fat-cat industrialists who managed somehow to bypass Speer and seem to require my approval with some major transport mess. You'd think that making these humdrum logistical decisions would be second nature to the so-called leaders of industry. At least, that's what I thought years ago when trying desperately to gain their financial support for me and the Party. But the sad truth is that they can't even wipe their own behinds without checking with me first. So leave me to that while you go and check my mail, eh, no matter what that brainless hulk Günsche told you. Yesterday, I got letters meant for the naval adjutant and a nurse."

A small, moustache-lifting smile sent me on my way, completely frustrated. *Somehow,* I said to myself with an urgent and weighty resolve, *the Führer has to be told—and soon.*

Since Klara had been pushed to the front of the queue, on my way back from the Mail Centre, I intended to make a quick stop to telephone her neighbour and arrange a date for the following evening, when I could apologise profusely and perhaps learn why she left without a word. But I happened upon Kempka and Baur, who cajoled me into having a late lunch with them first.

The lunchroom was noisy and bustling, but through rank and recognition, we managed to force our way over a score of others to a table just being vacated.

Once served, Kempka shook his head. "You look like shit, Heinz," he garbled, shoving sauerbraten, potato dumplings, and applesauce into his mouth as if stoking an empty furnace. "Even more than usual," he added for comradeship's sake. "That must have been some fucking vacation."

Even without knowing it, the chauffeur's flair for under-statement hadn't failed him. "I wish it *had* been fucking," I complained, "but I'm afraid it was only too abstemious for my own good." I blurted it out so quickly and heedlessly that there was no way to force the toothpaste of elocution back into the tube.

Kempka narrowed his mouth in confusion, causing some errant strands of sauerkraut to jut out like weeds, then he sucked them back in and resumed chewing. "Abste-*what?* Well? Shit! You can't leave us hanging. You were with this Klara dame, yes?"

It had gone right past him into the ether. Thank God for Kempka's ignorant denseness. *But what of Baur?*

"Abstain's what he said," Baur threw at the chauffeur. "But don't you fret about it. They say the deaf make up for it by using, ah, other parts of them. I never figured thighs, but—"

"I hardly had any time with Klara," I admitted, hesitant to convey more but trapped by my momentum, as if I needed to tell someone to test my story before briefing the Führer. "I'd accepted an invitation from the wife of the commandant of the KZ at Auschwitz, and—"

Two sets of eyes widened.

"You took your girlfriend on vacation to a fucking KZ?" Kempka exclaimed and, in the process, spat out some partially chewed chunks of sauerbraten. "And of all the KZs, *that one?*"

I shrugged. "I didn't choose a KZ, that one or any other," I explained, as if I were on trial. "As I said, it was by personal invitation of the commandant. Klara stayed at the hotel while I went on a guided tour. I'd intended only—"

"Shit." Baur shook his head. "That's one fucking invitation I would have begged off. I'll tell you something. Just before they started construction of the place, the boss asked me to fly Göring, Himmler, and Heydrich to the Berghof to meet with

Höss about something or other, and all the Two H's could talk about on the flight was how their—what did they call the fucking place?—the 'last solution,' or something like that. 'One day'—and these were his words, or at least close enough—'it would become the model for all such sewage-processing plants.' Anyway, I think that's what he said. Whatever the case, not the ideal vacation spot."

Nothing Baur said contradicted my experience, but to speak with conviction to the Führer, I needed to know more—but not look as if I needed to know more.

"It definitely fell short," I told them with a straight face. "No doubt about it. It was quite an education, I can—"

I was cut off by Kempka, who barked, "Hey, Baur, look who I just spotted." He aimed his thumb at a rangy middle-aged SS officer, impeccably uniformed, pallid of face and topped with a dense brush of platinum-blond hair glistening with pomade, who appeared just about to leave.

"Yeah, Weber," Baur confirmed, "your lucky day, Heinz. Weber's high up on Eichmann's staff, so if anybody knows about your vacation spot, he does."

With that, Kempka waved the major over with no little ostentation. He introduced Weber to me and dragooned him into joining us. "You won't believe this," Kempka informed the major, once the salutes and introductions concluded, "but Linge here just came back from, uh, vacationing at your latest KZ, you know, the one at Auschwitz."

Weber fixed me with a gaze of incredulity. "Vacationing, Colonel? An odd choice of locales, I would think."

"I was invited by Colonel and Frau Höss," I told him, "and I had no idea what the place was like."

The major smiled, more a smear than a gesture. "And do you now?"

"I have some idea," I replied, "but how much information can a one-day tour provide?"

The major shrugged. "It depends on the guide."

"Major Fritzch."

He nodded. "Well then, you had the deluxe treatment. Even Colonel Eichmann couldn't provide better. Whatever Fritzch showed you need only be magnified exponentially to give you the full picture. But realise, what you saw was only the barest of beginnings."

I scrunched my face into a compressed mask of ignorance, hoping it would motivate Weber into providing more detail. "Expo…?" I stumbled and shrugged.

"He's just a kid," Baur explained. "Be nice. He's trying to learn."

Weber stood. There was a small show of teeth, a thin white line, the kind sported by those who never smile. "Perhaps another time," he suggested, with cordial finality in his tone. "Now, if you'll excuse me, gentlemen, I'm due at headquarters. Good meeting you, Colonel." He saluted us, turned, and strode away.

All three of us stared at each other for a few moments with quizzical expressions.

"Not exactly a fountain of information, that Weber," I told them. "It seems that you, Hans, are still the reigning champion of chat."

"Not too big of a surprise," Kempka told Baur, then turned to me. "Himmler always keeps the good shit to himself. You'd think if the place was as great as Weber says, Goebbels couldn't wait to advertise the fucking thing all round the Reich, and the boss and Hoffmann would arrange some special photo shoot there. Maybe even get that swellhead bitch Riefenstahl to make a movie about it."

Both laughed heartily at that last notion.

Once free of Kempka and Baur, I rushed to my quarters to call Klara's neighbour and arrange to come over after completing my projectionist chores. My migraine returned with ferocity when her neighbour informed me that she hadn't come home and so had assumed she was still with me on our "vacation." My brain was in a frenzy of pain and confusion—and something else, much worse, for which I yet had no name.

14 January 1941

AFTER SEEING TO the Führer, I raced over to Klara's flat and had her neighbour let me in. I checked every centimetre but found it the same in every detail as when we'd left for Poland. When I returned to the Chancellery in a state of severe anxiety, a note was waiting for me in the Communications Centre. It was from a man urging me to meet him at an address I knew to be on a relatively secluded side street near the Chancellery. The time was unimportant, so long as it was that day, and that I should wait by the telephone, appearing to use it. Since it was signed "L. J. Silver,"[47] I knew who'd sent it, although how he knew I would catch the reference was most puzzling. But I was too surprised and elated to concern myself with relative trifles.

Before that, however, I sought out Schroeder. Since she was so eager to have her niece move in with her, the harridan might have some knowledge of her whereabouts. She was alone in the secretaries' office, her back to the door, typing some letters Wolf was once again too sick to complete, so I knew I would be greeted with irascibility at best.

"Good morning, Fräulein Schroeder. I'm—"

"Yes?" she said curtly without turning her head.

---

[47] Long John Silver is a fictional character and the main antagonist in the novel *Treasure Island* (1883) by Robert Louis Stevenson. The most colourful and complex character in the book, he continues to appear in popular culture, especially because of his parrot, peg leg, and eye patch.

"I'm… back," I answered lamely, "and—"

"I knew that yesterday," she retorted, "and you confirmed it just now. What do you want?"

"It's about Klara," I told her. "Might you know where—"

"Where? You were with her—and you didn't see fit to tell me where you were going," she said quickly, a bit too quickly. "So how would I know where she is?"

"She was with me in Poland," I told her, "but then later, I couldn't locate her. I still can't."

"Locate? What later? And Poland of all places? What the Devil were the two of you doing there?"

Something had seeped into her usual scowl and growl, but I couldn't place it. I related the story of the invitation, my departure with Klara, and my return without her—carefully omitting my KZ tour. When I finished, she was breathing noisily, and her face had reddened.

"Since you and I know nothing, why are you bothering me with this?" she spat out, exhibiting far more vituperation than was warranted.

"Fräulein Schroeder," I said, "I just thought she might have contacted you before she contacted me. Clearly, I was mistaken."

With that, some of the heat dissipated, and she smooshed her lips in her familiar grimace of antipathy. "Clearly," she confirmed with no little nastiness. "Had the two of you quarrelled?"

"No," I said, not really a lie but certainly not entirely accurate.

"Now you see why I… prevailed on her to come and stay here with me."

Prevailed? I thought. It was nothing short of a command and a threat, and we both knew it.

"You tried her flat?"

"Of course," I said. "There was no sign she'd returned to it."

"Then, for all you know, she could still be in that cesspool that is Poland."

"Anything's possible," I admitted. "All I can do now is assure you that I'll do everything in my power to locate her. In fact, after I tell my story to the Führer, I'm certain that he'll place all the considerable resources of the Reich to assist us."

Suddenly, her coarse features softened slightly and returned to their usual powder-augmented pallor. "All this fuss and bother. The Führer has far too much on his plate to get embroiled in a servant's domestic problems. If you want my opinion, I think you two had a lover's spat and she's off sulking somewhere. This is what women do, Linge, even deaf ones. I tell you, when she's good and ready, she'll contact you and maybe even contact her poor, devoted auntie. Give it some time before going off half-cocked, yes?"

To end any further opining, I agreed to wait, then took my leave, but her entire demeanour troubled me. *Where was the "poor, devoted auntie's" anxiety over the whereabouts of her only niece—an impaired niece at that—who had no other family? Where was the dread?* All this was most unnatural, even for Schroeder.

✧

After leaving the Führer to suffer some hapless papal delegates who'd come to complain one more fruitless time about Göring's voracious church-property confiscations, I left the Chancellery and made for the address I'd been provided. It turned out to be another basement beer hall, a reputedly rowdy establishment. As I entered, I was instantly invaded by a gust of heat, the stink of limburger, stale beer, sodden sawdust, and of course, the convivial thunder of chatter, singing, beer-stein banging, and bellowing laughter.

Smoke hung heavy in the large, open space as I made my

way to a gap at a long trestle table and ordered a beer I had no intention of drinking. When the drink arrived, I shouted to the waiter, asking where the telephone was located. He pointed to a corridor beyond a row of beaded curtains, and I headed for it as quickly as I could, hoping to temper the roar, even a little. When I located the instrument and lifted the receiver, depressed the cradle, and pretended to speak to someone, as instructed, my heart pounded in my ears as I waited.

"Ahoy," a familiar voice greeted behind me, imitating a pirate's growl.

I spun round.

"Still the glabrous giant, I see," kidded Brückner.

Perhaps I should have been offended by his arrogance implicit in his use of language he would never expect my persona to know. But at the time, I was more concerned with the reason for his visit, and it *was* Brückner, after all. And yet…

"I got the giant part!" I hollered, by way of limp rejoinder, and replaced the receiver, wincing from the din. "It's so good to see you again."

"Same here!" he hollered back, his hands cupped round his mouth for added volume. "This place is a bit too gemütlich, don't you agree? How about a brisk stroll? Old times and all that."

⁂

In the mid-January chill, I could watch the breath pour from our noses and mouths as we walked, but I felt no cold—or any other sensation, save for curiosity. *Why had Brückner come all the way to Berlin from Paris to see me when a telephone would have done?* And so clandestinely. Of course I needed to speak with him, but it seemed as if he also needed to speak with me, even though he said nothing as we traversed several streets. I decided to take the plunge with some small talk.

"So, Wilhelm, are you as popular with the Parisian ladies as you were with the Berliners? I've heard a lot about the charms of the French female."

He turned his head towards me. "Charms? Well, Heinz, there appear to be two kinds of Parisian women: those who run with the resistance, and those who run with the occupiers. The former frighten me, and the latter offend me. So much for 'Gay Paree.'"

I laughed a cloud of frosty breath, and Brückner smiled.

"I'm sure you're wondering why I arranged this theatrically elaborate scenario. But before I explain, I'd like to hear of your recent exploits. And spare no details."

After a moment's reflection, I nodded, and with what I considered to be a heroic feat of dispassionate candour, I related the events in all their miserable minutiae since Schroeder had "asked" Klara to move in with her, including our trip to Auschwitz, our awkward hotel arrangement, my dinner, night and early morning visitations, my horrific tour, Klara's disappearance, my attempt to relate it all to the Führer, my morning's encounter with Schroeder, and finally, my conversation with Baur, Kempka, and Weber. All the while, Brückner stared straight ahead as if he were travelling alone. For some reason unknown to me, I left out my "encounter" with Ziggy.

"Wilhelm?" I asked, after a time.

More silence. Then, without warning, he turned to me and nodded. "Yes, let's find a decent and considerably more tranquil eatery. After all you've been through, you must be hungry."

❧

It was a long, cold, silent trek to Zillemarkt, just half a block from the S-Bahn station and a world away from the convivial cacophony of the other establishment. Brückner and I headed to a small, empty booth up a couple of stairs and positioned ourselves to face the entrance. Brückner ordered the strongest Schnapps for both of us. I didn't question his choice or his motive, but even after two rounds, we remained sombre, sober, and silent, until the third.

"What's really wrong, Heinz?" he asked.

I didn't know how to respond, so I didn't.

"You've given me quite an earful," Brückner remarked. "It's only natural that you'd be distressed."

"I'm… perfectly fine," I told him, though I knew I wasn't and was clearly incapable of hiding it from him.

"Of course," Brückner said, "your voice says fine, but your face says not so fine. Finish your drink so your face can catch up with your voice, eh?"

I did as Brückner commanded, but it did little to alleviate the overwhelming melancholy that had overcome me when I told him of Auschwitz. When I just shook my head, Brückner tossed back his schnapps and smiled.

"You've been through a great deal, my friend," he said. "More than you realise. And I daresay, for far longer."

All I could do was shrug with confusion and turn up the palms of my hands to plead for clarification.

Then Brückner lowered his voice. "I'm going to tell you some things you won't wish to hear and, once heard, won't wish to believe. But the chance must be taken because"—his eye moved towards the entrance—"I'm convinced that time is running out, so I'll get right to the business at hand. Here and now, Heinz, I must somehow rid you of whatever blissful obliviousness you've managed to retain after six years with the Führer. Karl Marx said that 'history repeats itself, the first time as tragedy, the second time as farce.' Well, Heinz, the Führer has stood that clever aphorism on its head; that is to say, the Führer has caused the first repetition of history to be a farce and the second, a tragedy. And, my friend, I believe that you've just arrived at the very beginning of that second repetition."

A farce? The Führer's rise to power a farce? His plans and actions a farce? The war a farce? Our dominant position in Europe a farce? How could Brückner, of all people, say this? My eyes widened in astonishment. I couldn't believe what I was hearing, so I assumed I lacked proper understanding, rather than presume anything sinister or subversive on Brückner's part. But before I could express my stupefaction, he lifted his hand slightly from the table and, palm turned down, gave a lower-your-voice gesture, then smiled benignly.

"Heinz, listen to me," he said. "I've been intimately involved with the Führer almost from the beginning of the movement. From nineteen hundred-thirty onwards, as adjutant, I was privy to virtually every one of the Führer's megalomaniacal rants and was present at every meeting, not the least of which were those when he gave completely free rein to that psychotic monstrosity Himmler, not merely to secure the Reich from its enemies but also to define who they were and how they should be dealt with. After which, as always, the Führer mentally washed his hands. I ask you, could Heydrich, Eichmann, and Höss be far behind? To put it bluntly, I believe I'm reasonably qualified to know what a farce is, what a tragedy is, and in which order they occur."

By then, all effects of the schnapps had vanished, and the melancholy I'd felt had turned to apprehension and suspicion. Too many improbable things had coalesced: an aggregate of seemingly unrelated circumstances that Brückner had cobbled together and called a "lowest common denominator" and I called synchronicity. A belladonna by any other name.

"All right, Wilhelm," I conceded for the sake of argument, "I'm at the very beginning of a tragedy. But—and this is what

I need you to explain to me—what do you consider to be the tragedy, and what can I and my experiences possibly have to do with it? I'm an ignorant menial who might well have been a journeyman bricklayer by now if I hadn't walked off the job and had the miraculous good fortune to be selected to serve the Führer." *I heard myself say it, but did I really believe it?* From the beginning of my service to the Führer, I'd felt myself being pulled down into something dark and recondite, but never so much as now, believing myself manipulated by almost everyone, for purposes of which I had no understanding. Up to now, I'd exempted Brückner, but after what he'd just said about the Führer and the Party, not to mention his connexion to Bella Fromm, I wondered whether such an exemption was still wise or even possible.

"Supposedly," I went on, "until now, you hadn't known anything of what I just related, and yet, after listening to you, I can't believe that what I told you was unexpected, or you and Bella wouldn't have encouraged me to go. On our stroll, you said that if I related my experiences, you'd tell me why you came all this way to see me at this particular moment and with such furtiveness. If I'm to be manipulated, Wilhelm, I'd at least like to be in on it." I held out my hands, palms up in a gesture of supplication and Brückner nodded.

"All right, Herr 'Ignorant Menial.'" He nudged his plate aside, food untouched. "You used the term'miraculous' for your situation. Have you ever considered just how miraculous?"

I remained silent, for I had no idea where he was going.

"I'll assist you," he offered. "Dig into your memory as best you can, and consider all the anomalies in your life, both in kind and in number, since entering the Führer's household, then tell me what you discovered. Meanwhile, also dig into your sauerbraten. Food for thought, eh?" he joked, then slid his own plate back and began carving.

Consider the anomalies in my life? Easily asked, I moaned to myself. With my memory, the digging alone could occupy me endlessly. *Theoretically, anomalies should narrow my research, but how would I recognise one, since I had no context but my own experience? What* were *the anomalies? My job interview that wasn't an interview? The ethereally enigmatic Emerald and Katrin with their conflicting agendas? Meeting Bella? Courting "Christiane"? Weisthor and Rahn? Recurrent hallucinations, visions, migraines, nightmares, and blackouts? Two attempts on my life (that I knew of)? My invitation to visit Auschwitz with the encouragement of Brückner and Bella, and my encounters with Höss, Hedwig, Fritzch, the "Meyers"—and Ziggy? And finally, the disappearance of Klara?* As I considered each one, then in the aggregate, I was forced to conclude that my life deviated exponentially from what I knew of other valets in the Chancellery, other households, and even in literature. *But what could I say of them to Brückner?*

"Well?" he prompted, accurately reading the perplexity in my expression.

"Yes, Wilhelm," I admitted, "miraculous or not, there has been much of the inexplicable in my life since coming to work for the Führer, but how can I explain the inexplicable?"

Brückner chuckled lightly. "The way you put it, you can't. I'll try, but you must smile and laugh a little at times so the other patrons witness only a congenial conversation. I'll kick you gently under the table if I see you getting too sombre." Then he tried out his tactic, startling me. "If you weren't prepared for the Führer," he joked, "you're even less prepared for the stage."

I laughed at that, and he said, "Right, there you go. As I said before, I need you to listen to me and try to keep an open mind—not an easy or pleasant balancing act. You have been manipulated. By everyone. And I imagine that you believe this undeniable fact to be the common denominator I referred to, but you'd be wrong. The American humourist Mark Twain said that 'The two most important days in your life are the day you are born and the day you find out why.' Today, my friend, you find out why. *You*, Heinz Linge, are the common denominator, the very centre of all that's happened and may yet happen. It's—"

"But the Führer," I interrupted with no little stridency, "he—"

"Please lower your voice, smile, and listen," Brückner commanded, his whisper suddenly sharp and hard like the blade of a knife. "Lies are innumerable, but there's only one truth. You wanted to know, and now is the time to learn. You've seen it, you've even experienced it, but I doubt whether you've ever analysed it. You see, Heinz, the German character holds a primal deformity: a desperate need for order at any price, and at the same time, an atavistic hunger for dominance. Early on, the Führer recognised this coexisting contradiction—and the promise it held for anyone who possessed the formula for synthesising those opposing elements—and possessed the genius to embody it, employ it, and ultimately, to transcend it. However, the men he chose to assist him in achieving it had nothing in common with him, save for ambition and hate. These were sadistic men, cynical, avaricious, brutal, and dangerous. The Führer, on the other hand, is a mystic, and so, in his own way, is guileless, harbouring no fixed doctrine or ideology. His worldview exists beyond good and evil, and the purity of that, as interpreted and executed by lesser beings, makes him more dangerous than all of them combined.

"There are those who have persuaded the Führer that a certain metal object, disguised as a child's top, contains the metaphysical means to transcend peoples and nations and, achieve in an instant, a position of complete dominion over all things physical and spiritual. They have also persuaded him that such a means cannot be harnessed and exploited, except through a predestined medium. Master politician? Hypnotic orator? Superb strategist? Of course, the Führer is all that. But at bottom, he fancies himself a magician, a conjurer who only requires a human magic wand. That wand, I'm afraid, is you.

"I see by your expression that to you, all this sounds bizarre and fanciful, if not utterly preposterous, like a lost fable by the Brothers Grimm, and I can hardly blame you. If it were only that simple—and that benign. On the contrary, I've become convinced of the truth of it—and the potential catastrophe it portends. You must admit that as bizarre and incredible as all this must sound, it goes a long way towards making sense of all the apparent anomalies I asked you to consider."

Our waiter, probably seeing us still remaining after the bill was paid, came over to ask whether we wanted anything further. Brückner waved him away, then turned back to me. "You've been very patient and indulgent. Have you any response?"

I'd heard every word but from a place outside myself, hovering about. Even at such a distance, I could hear my heart thumping in my chest, neck, temples, and ears. All around me, people and objects were losing cohesion, parts of them beginning to float. Suddenly, I began to shudder violently, and when I gazed down at myself, Brückner was shaking my arm, and I returned.

"Are you all right, Heinz?" Brückner asked, his face pinched with concern. "You seemed to be in some sort of trance, and I couldn't get you out of it."

I shook my head, not so much to clear it, as to prepare Brückner for my lie. "Just one of my migraines, I'm afraid."

Brückner pursed his lips. "I'm relieved." He appeared genuinely relieved, perhaps more that I'd heard his words than that I was feeling better—a sign of my burgeoning paranoia. "I was afraid that I may have strained your sense of reality beyond the breaking point, and I wouldn't blame you for considering me quite the fantasist. I sometimes forget that you still haven't the sophistication and language that formal education and maturity would normally produce, and for that, I apologise. That aside, from what you did understand, have you any thoughts about what I've told you?" His face seemed to blossom with expectancy.

Thoughts? Brückner wants my thoughts? How can I have any thoughts after what he just told me? He might just as well have told me that he's actually the king of Spain—or rather, that *I am!*[48]

Was any of this real, or was I still hallucinating in Höss's guest room? "What can I say, Wilhelm? I'm certain you believe what you're saying. But that doesn't mean—"

"More important than whether I believe, Heinz," he interrupted, "or even whether you believe, is the absolute certainty that others believe, some of whom would assist the Führer in destroying all we are and know and some who would unhesitatingly prevent this by eliminating you by any means necessary if they can't convince you to—"

"Kill the Führer?" I ventured with no little sarcasm.

"No, my friend," he demurred gently. "They know you better than that. In point of fact, they would be content merely to know that you will exert all your incomparable influence to prevent the Führer and his malignant functionaries from achieving their unthinkable goal."

"Incomparable influence?" I exclaimed, as stridently as a

---

[48] In a section of Nikolai Gogol's *Diary of a Madman* (1835), the protagonist, a deranged government clerk, believes he is the King of Spain. However, he claims that he wishes to be treated like an ordinary person, and so he goes among the people in the disguise of a government clerk, and later, boasts that his disguise worked because no one recognised him.

whisper would allow. "My God, Wilhelm! What are you talking about? You of all people know my function. I wipe the Führer's behind, and it's rather difficult to influence him from that position." It was a reflex borne of habit. Did I really believe what I was saying? Once again, I thought back to that screening of *The Petrified Forest*, where the doomed poet said, "Brains without purpose, noise without sound, shape without substance." *Was that how I saw myself? And more importantly, was that me?*

Brückner smiled and nodded a begrudging appreciation. "Yes, the revolting image you present is hardly encouraging, and I don't fault you for making light of a potentially precarious and catastrophic situation. But you must believe that the experiences you labelled manipulations are, in fact, also dire warnings— Auschwitz being only the most recent and extreme example, even more so than the attempts on your life." Brückner gazed down at the tablecloth, then back up to me. "Time is running out, my friend. To pierce the heart of the matter, is there anything I can do or say that will at least persuade you to consider what I've said as a probability, rather than merely a preposterous possibility and, if so, do all you can through your singular position to thwart the Führer's fiendish objective?"

Before I could answer, Brückner's eye moved towards the entrance, and for a moment, my eyes joined his, and I saw her: indeterminate age, broad shoulders, tall frame, horselike face, hair tortured into an ascending row of tiny salt-and-pepper braids, leather greatcoat, clodhopper shoes, and shabby shopping bag—a laughably cinematic parody of a female Gestapo agent. Pushing aside a young, brawny man in a Wehrmacht uniform as he leaned painfully on a cane, she proceeded to a table so close to our booth that she might as well have joined us, then placed her bag on the floor, but not before removing a copy of

Volkischer Beobachter and beginning a clumsy pretence of reading it.

Brückner's eye returned to me and must have read my thoughts again. "I only wish we had the luxury of such types," he joked in an even lower voice, perhaps to reassure me and to show us both having a pleasant laugh in an innocuous conversation. But in typical Brücknerian fashion, he took it back. "Unfortunately, she's only here to draw our attention. Don't look!" he directed under his breath. "It's the boy, not the hag, and someone, I daresay, who, even with his prop crutch, could give Jesse Owens a run for his money."

I know I just sat there, stunned into a silence I knew Brückner would not tolerate for long. All he'd said made terrible sense once one's disbelief was suspended. I tried with all my might to suspend it, but I was only partially successful.

Brückner's lips formed a broad smile I assumed was for the benefit of our watcher and, after a pause that could have given birth to triplets, said simply, "She's dead." His eye stared at me without blinking.

"Dead? Who's dead?" I knew what he was going to say.

"Klara."

When I sat there staring past him, as if in a coma, Brückner added, "From what Bella's source inside the RSHA told her, she's been euthanised. A message, perhaps."

There's knowing and there's knowing, Hedwig had said. But even knowing, my brain felt as if a blacksmith had attacked it with the full force of his hammer, anvil, and chisel, and my face burned as if this had taken place in a forge in hell.

"Laugh energetically," Brückner commanded softly. "I just told you a great joke, so remove that stricken look, crinkle your eyes, and laugh. Then use my handkerchief to wipe your eyes from all the merriment."

He reached into his inside tunic pocket, extracted a perfectly starched and folded handkerchief, and handed it across to me. "Here, blow your nose and drink up."

I tried my best, but in the effort, I must have looked and sounded deranged. How Brückner always managed to remain composed never failed to impress and confound me.

"All right, Heinz," he cautioned, "you can stop laughing. Nothing's that hilarious." He was silent for a few moments as he gazed at me. "I know you're devastated, my friend. I would be too. But this is the world we've helped create. The question you have before you now is whether you will be content to stand at mute attention while that world creates even greater horrors, some beyond description. But I'll leave you to ponder that. Our more immediate situation is dealing with the young chap over there. He saw us together, and he must not be permitted to report it, despite our manufactured levity. When we leave to go our separate ways, he can't follow us both, so he must choose. During your wayward youth, I imagine you've had your share of altercations, but have you ever killed anyone?"

"No," I lied.

"I'm afraid it must come to that. And since young men tend to be impatient, it's time to go. Please consider what I've told you with great care."

I'd heard Brückner, but I was thinking of Ziggy, Adelsheimer, the "Meyers," and now, Klara.

"I hope he follows *me*," I said.

AFTER TAKING OUT Brückner's news on the follower and cleaning up in a nearby hotel lavatory, I spent most of the time between nightmare and Führerbuzzer slumped on the toilet after a bout of violent vomiting that managed to excise all the food and drink I'd consumed with Brückner, but not his terrible revelation that my brain already knew: "She's dead."

In my tormented dream, as Brückner told me of Klara's extermination, the Führer's vision, his followers' mission, my function, and "perhaps a message," my concentration was split between his words and the suddenly mutating dining room. The gemütlich, Alpinesque eatery gradually reconstituted itself into the swirling, absinthe-and-madness-spawned hallucination of van Gogh's *Night Café*, a painting of degradation, decay, and depression that I'd glimpsed only once in an oversized volume of reproductions. Now, as my brain inhabited that café, I heard a voice uttering what I took to be the tortured painter's own description: "I have tried to express the idea that the café is a place where one can ruin oneself, go mad, or commit a crime," all of which filled the space in my brain between the restaurant and Brückner's narrative, one easing out the other. Brückner had vanished, and before me was the man in the painting, standing casually in his white suit by the pool table in the centre. Unlike the painting, his face possessed no features, save for piercing blue eyes that gazed intently at me. Klara was splayed naked on the pool table, encased in a viscous membrane of untended festering sores and bruises, all glistening with swirls of blood and pus, rendered as only van Gogh—and my reality—could.

And this time, I did nothing but stare blankly at him, like a moron, while she writhed and moaned.

A place where one can ruin oneself, go mad, or commit a crime.

The Führer's summons arrived just before I could put a name to that place. *Was it a reprieve or an omen?*

❧

Keeping composure was the major task of the day. The Führer, looking more rested and cheerful than I'd seen him in days, had me race him silently through his morning toilette since he said he needed to dictate some urgent correspondence to Wolf, as he put it, "Before the poor creature falls prey to some malady again." I always wondered why the Führer never sicced Morell on her, but I would never ask. On my way out, I saw her standing and chatting with the seated Günsche (so they would be almost the same height). About what, considering him, I couldn't imagine. Since she was usually away on what seemed to me to be the most generous sick-leave arrangement in history, I went over to welcome her back.

"Yes, Herr Linge?" Günsche asked, rising and greeting me with more-than-usual formality, probably for Wolf's sake. "You need to—"

"I have no needs, Herr Günsche," I cut him off with equal formality and turned to her. "I merely wanted to welcome back Fräulein Wolf."

She nodded. "I trust the Führer is well."

"He's quite well and anxious to dictate. I'm just glad to see you well."

She was still as horsefaced as ever, resembling more a cinema matron in a women's prison than the senior secretary to the Führer.

"Thank you," she replied with what, for her, passed as a sincere smile. "Of course I'm still not fully recovered, you understand, but when the Führer needs me, I'm here."

A perfect opening. "Naturally, naturally," I replied. "But—" I began to ask, when Günsche interrupted.

"I'm sorry, Herr Linge, but the Führer is wait—"

"I was about to say, Fräulein Wolf"—I cut him off without turning to him—"that with your health still… delicate, could not Fräulein Schroeder do the honours?"

"Don't I wish?" she grumbled plaintively, replete with shrug and head tilt. "But unfortunately, she's out on bereavement, and—"

"I'm afraid the Führer is wait—" Günsche tried again.

"Bereavement, you say?" I continued. *Fuck Günsche and his lame declarations.*

"It seems that a close relation recently passed away," she explained, "and she must attend to the formalities." She stole a glance at Günsche, who tapped his enormous booted foot on the linoleum with theatrical impatience, then looked back at me. "Now, if you'll excuse me."

Passed away. "Of course, Fräulein Wolf," I said. "Mustn't keep the Führer waiting."

She nodded. Günsche sat back down, pressed a buzzer on his desk, and Wolf went in.

"You can breathe now, Otto," I kidded the oaf and left him staring at my back.

❧

Since the Führer's sudden reanimation placed me at loose ends, Günsche was useless for the present (not counting his uselessness at all other times), and Schroeder was scurrying round, attending to her grief (either authentically or for appearances), I began searching for anyone who might shed light on Klara's fate. I went first to the central garage, where I discovered Kempka busily chewing out a mechanic.

"Your shift?" he screamed. "Your shift, you say? You have a shift when I have a shift! When the Führer calls me, that's my shift, and when I call you, that's yours. You hear me, you lazy fuck?"

Does he hear Kempka? It would be a joke otherwise, but from the fierceness of Kempka's onslaught, the poor mechanic could only stand there quaking, drool coursing down his florid face, while his compatriots now paid obsessive attention to their tasks. I stood just out of visual range, waiting for the relentless bombardment to end, which it did when Kempka screamed, "Now get the fuck out of here, you steaming pile of shit!"

The mechanic turned and sped off like an Olympic sprinter.

"Another day at the office?" I kidded Kempka as I entered and shut the door behind me.

With an index finger pressed against one nostril, he expelled some snot from the other, shrugged, then flopped his tiny bulk onto his poor, beleaguered roller chair.

"You can joke, my young friend," he said, wiping his nose with the sleeve of his once-white, now-filthy coveralls, "but wait until you have to supervise; you'll get serious pretty quick, you can bet."

Ease the crude hothead into information-mode gently, I cautioned myself. "Well then, I'm happy that for me, a career in supervision is not in the cards," I told him. "Arnt is away all the time physically, and Junge is away all the time mentally. I don't dare issue commands to the clod Günsche, who's not only my superior but could eat me for breakfast, and the Führer seldom dances to my tune."

The chauffeur started to fall backwards with laughter, then righted himself with a jolt, just in time. "God damn, that's rich, Heinz! The Führer dancing to your tune. Or anyone's for that matter. I've seen him dance all right, but only to his own tune. You know, last night, just before I had to drive him, Blaschke[49] met us at the door and told him this one: 'What's the difference between Churchill and Hitler? One takes a weekend in the country while the other takes a country in a weekend.' With the war going nowhere right now, the idiot-ass dentist was not a master of timing. The Führer, no expression, just said, 'You should tell that one to Churchill,' then turned, and we left."

"Left at night?"

He shrugged. "Yeah, like a bunch of other times. Like that time you went along with us. Remember?"

"Not really," I lied.

"I'll tell you, my son, even those of us who serve the boss every day sometimes forget that, despite his superhuman energy and genius, he's still a human being, so he's gotta have diversions, relaxation, and recreation—like we all do, eh?" A wink followed.

"Nothing could be truer," I answered instead, "and it must have worked like a charm, for the Führer was in fine and energetic spirits this morning. Couldn't wait to dictate to Wolf," I added, as a tentative toe in the doorjamb.

He chuckled through a crooked smile. "You mean the ugly crone's actually real? I was beginning to think she was some mythical character, kinda like a… you know, one of them church statues that—"

"Gargoyle," I assisted, with little risk. "Yeah, well, her face can give that impression. Actually, I was surprised Schroeder was

---

[49] Hugo Blaschke was Hitler's personal dentist.

out, since she never takes a vacation or even gets an ingrown toenail, but yes, Wolf actually came in." I made certain that the notoriously insensitive Kempka couldn't miss me biting my quivering lower lip as I hesitated. "Then Wolf… told me why."

Kempka's expression of jocularity descended into one of gravity. "Hey, I'm real sorry, pal." He'd become visibly ill at ease and leaned forward, causing a massive squeak of his chair springs. "Yeah, I heard about it. Nothing official, mind you, but I get around."

Of course you do. I said nothing but was confident that my vacant Little Orphan Annie stare was interpreted correctly.

"Damn shame about that, but hey, you got to admit that she was living on borrowed time. I just drive a car, but these eugenics guys are de—uh… real serious about this shit." Kempka was about to say *dead* serious, but even he had some tact.

I nodded solemnly. "Doubtless, but I thought Klara had the Führer's protection from the RSHA and the Aktion-T4 guys through Schroeder's relationship with him."

Kempka shrugged again. "Look, I don't have to tell you that the Führer stands by his word, especially with people like us—his family, you might say. If Schroeder got him to give this Klara of hers some special treatment, that's that. Period. So you got me there. Maybe the Führer didn't know."

Because Schroeder didn't tell him? I wanted to ask but thought better of further stirring the pot.

I agreed with funereal solemnity, told him I would check with Schroeder when she returned, and started to leave, when Kempka called after me, "If anything changed, Heinz, it's because Schroeder—or something else—changed, not the Führer."

Kempka was a notorious tall-tale-teller, but in this, I believed every syllable.

Since he was in the presence of the Führer almost every day, I wondered what Baur might have to say, so I visited him next. Between sincere condolences and offers of any occupant of his Black Book as compensation, he provided information, such as it was, that differed not at all from Kempka's, save that he attempted to soothe my misery with Baur humour. "Hey, but you gotta admire those scientists," he joked. "If they get rid of enough defectives, soon everybody in the Reich will be perfect, just like Goebbels and Himmler."

I ground my teeth as I reflected on that tired old gag: "What must an Aryan look like? Slim like Göring, blond like the Führer, and tall like Goebbels." He'd omitted handsome like Morell.

For the first time, I stopped by the doctor's quarters, his sanctum when not attending the Führer or being loaned out to top-tier hypochondriacs and hedonists. I've mentioned this before, that Morell was not popular with the Führer's entourage, who constantly complained about the doctor's offensive table manners, wretched hygiene, and pernicious body odour.

But to this, the Führer invariably responded, "I do not employ him for his fragrance but to look after my health, which he does splendidly." Of course, the Führer had the luxury of a more overpowering stench.

After knocking several times and being met with strident, unintelligible snarls, I tried the door and, finding it unlocked, entered, where Morell's ghastly reputation pummelled me with renewed ferocity. It was all I could do to keep from rushing my handkerchief to my nose and mouth to prevent the deep, penetrating reek of faeces, urine, vomit, decay, stale sweat, and something I found unnameable from engulfing me. It would take an army of gas-masked maids entering under threat of miserable death to cleanse and fumigate this horror. And yet—and perhaps this is a form of perversity on my part—there was a certain extravagance, even a delirium to the degree of foulness enveloping me in the windowless room. After years with the Führer's bowels, my shift to tidal mouth-breathing was automatic and swift.

Morell was sprawled in a plush, wine-coloured oversized armchair, his eyes glazed, yellowish drool coursing down his bloated, unshaven, pockmarked cheeks. How the disgusting creature before me could be the medical miracle worker permanently on call for the Führer was a mystery beyond my powers of analysis.

"Dr. Morell?" I called several times, and when there was no response, with a shudder, I moved over to the chair, leaned over, clutched his shoulders, and shook him vigorously. "Dr. Morell!" I shouted, "the Führer needs you immediately!" then quickly released him and backed away out of immediate range.

As if animated by the sort of electric shock I'd witnessed only in horror films, Morell jerked upright, assembled his akimbo appendages, reached down with a groan, lifted a soiled cloth from the sticky linoleum floor, mopped his florid face, and gazed up at me. "The Führer? Yes. All right. You can go now, Linge," he croaked. "Tell the Führer I'll be there straight away." He started to rise.

Aside from his breakneck recuperation, he appeared to possess no self-consciousness about his condition, disgusting surroundings, and appearance—and I was caught in a blatant lie.

"I… I'm happy to say… that there's no need, Herr Doctor," I told him. "The Führer didn't really send me."

His bloodshot eyes narrowed menacingly, and he sank back into his chair. "No? No, you say? Then what's this all about, Linge? You invade my quarters uninvited, manhandle me, and top it off with a flagrant prevarication."

"I… I can explain, if you'll permit me."

There was a long pause, then, "All right, I'll permit you. Go ahead, but you'd better be quick about it."

I took a deep breath through my mouth. "It's like this," I began. "I tried knocking, but there was no answer. I was about to leave, when I heard some dreadful noises, became alarmed, tried the door, found it unlocked, and went in. When I saw you in that chair, looking and acting… unresponsive, I became quite alarmed. I thought you might have sunk into a coma or worse, so I said something I knew would either rouse you or give me cause to send for immediate assistance."

Eyes still narrowed, Morell asked, "Noises? What noises?"

"I can't really explain them," I answered with somewhat twisted truth. "But there was something, I swear. I was terrified that… I can't say it."

The doctor nodded me to silence with extravagant indulgence. "You understand, Linge, that normally, I would report such an outrageous intrusion and cock-and-bull story directly to the Führer." Then, after a long pause for effect, he said, "However, for the sake of maintaining harmony within the Führer's household and to spare someone so intellectually barren and emotionally delicate from unpleasantness, I will assume that you did it out of a genuine regard for me and, of course," he added, "being in the throes of your recent loss."

I sighed with more than relief since he'd brought up the real subject of my visit without me creating suspicion through any awkward prompting. "I can't tell you how grateful I am, Doctor. You're as understanding a human being as you are a medical wizard." I could see the ugly megalomaniac wilt under the warm bath of praise.

"It's nothing," he tossed off with clumsy magnanimity and the metronomic movements of his outsized head.

"I was, of course, devastated."

"Of course. The Führer has told me of your relationship—despite her problematic disability, of course."

"You mean the Führer knows what happened?" I asked, my eyes widening.

"Of course not!" he shouted, then winced with pain at the exertion. "No, only of your relationship. I know that giant idiot Günsche tried to tell him, but the Führer threw him out, and I don't know of anyone else stupid enough to do something so unthinkable as telling that sort of thing to the Führer. I was in the antechamber when Fräulein Schroeder received the news. She turned white and was speechless, naturally. I asked Günsche what the matter was, and he whispered the full story to me—my being a physician, of course."

"Of course," I echoed.

"I offered to give her something, but she was too distraught even to listen. She began shaking, sobbing, and rushed from the room."

"The full story?" I enquired with as much subtlety and calm in my demeanour as I could rally. "And to her aunt?"

He pursed his bloodless lips thoughtfully. "I hesitate to do this. For your own sensitivity, I think it's sufficient for you to know that the woman experienced no pain. At least according to Günsche. And I know enough about the techniques of euthanasia to believe him."

No, you hideous swine, the pain experienced was mine. "By 'entire story,' Doctor," I corrected, "I wasn't thinking of method. I meant the circumstances surrounding her taking. I mean, since she had what I thought was immunity through Fräulein Schroeder and especially through the Führer, what could possibly have gone wrong?"

Morell nodded, his vaguely purplish bottom lip distended. "Ah yes, that would be your concern. Unfortunately, that I don't know. Günsche might know but perhaps didn't see the relevance of telling me. Perhaps Fräulein Schroeder knows, but you'll have to wait and ask her when she returns. Anyone else? I have no idea. I'm sorry to disappoint you."

I thought of asking him where he thought Günsche even got the relevant information he'd imparted, but I felt I was in danger of overstaying my limited welcome. I would have to deal with Günsche and Schroeder myself somehow, and without alerting them.

"Thank you, Herr Doctor," I said. "Again, my apologies for—"

Morell lifted his pudgy arms and turned the palms of his hands up in theatrical benevolence. "It's nothing, the least I could do. But you shouldn't grieve for long, if I may say so. There are plenty of suitable females. At your age, you'll find another soulmate soon enough, and as a patriot, consider this: through programmes like Aktion T4, the health of the Reich is now far better off, am I right?"

Everything in me struggled against the incitement to tear out his fat, rut-ringed throat with my teeth. "I have no words to express my gratitude. What you've just told me will never be far from my mind," I assured him and quickly exited the poisonous cloud.

As I raced back to my quarters to allow a scalding shower to plane off the corruption, it struck me that in all probability, of all save those who ordered and arranged the taking, Brückner knew the "full story" and had probably planned to tell me at the restaurant before our late, unlamented watcher had interfered. *No one will interfere next time, I vowed—and the next time will be soon.*

SCHROEDER RETURNED LAST night, and when the Führerbuzzer jarred me awake, I had every intention of somehow getting her alone and willing to fill in more blanks surrounding Klara's fate before turning to Brückner. Unfortunately, my every intention was no match for the current impact of that bombastic clown Mussolini's ill-conceived invasion of Greece the previous October and the colossal Italian military incompetence in North Africa. Waiting for the Führer to finish so I could follow Schroeder out, I bent over, gathering, adjusting, and rearranging his enormous and unwieldy war maps, all the while straining to avoid staring at her as she converted the Führer's rapid-fire message to Mussolini into stenographic scribbles. The Führer, as usual, paced as he dictated, but this morning his gait was especially strident, his tone even more so, his dictating so protracted that I felt the necessity to sidle from the room to the relative peace and quiet of the bustling Communications Centre to collect the mail.

When I entered, I spotted Günsche and Schaub but too late to avoid them.

"The boss still fuming?" Günsche asked, losing no time adopting the out-of-earshot, *parole argot* for the Führer.

"About what?"

"Shit, Heinz!" he exclaimed. "You were in there the whole time. The Italian mess."

"I'm afraid I wasn't listening," I lied. "Above my station. But not above yours. What 'Italian mess'?"

The dull giant paused and stared blankly at me. "Beats me, Heinz. I'm not that great with foreign affairs. I asked Bormann, but he snapped at me, then said to ask you since—uh, how did he say?—'the Führer… appears to have more confidence in an ignorant nothing of a valet'—sorry about that—'than in'… I don't remember the exact word he used to describe himself, but you get the idea."

"Of course I do. An 'ignorant nothing valet' can get an idea every now and then, even if he can't have one." I refrained from giving him *my* exact word for Bormann.

He stared at me quizzically, as I would expect, and I was sure that Schaub would be of even less assistance.

"Hey, maybe Engel knows," Günsche speculated, tilting his head towards a fair-haired, middle-aged man of medium height, grand, raw-boned, and craggy, attired in the splendid grey-and-red uniform of a Wehrmacht general. It was Gerhard Engel, the Führer's new Army Adjutant, speaking to one of the clerks.

"General," Günsche called, "would you be so good as to join us for a moment?"

Engel turned his head to where we stood and paused a moment, I thought, to subtly register haughty disapproval at being so addressed by an underling from a distance while being otherwise occupied. Then he nodded, spoke a few more words to the clerk, pivoted, and came over as we stood to greet him.

His eyes were pale and ringed, his expression concerned, but he carried himself erect and with an air of justified importance. He was, clearly, a man who knew who he was and never, for a moment, forgot it. I was convinced that he also knew who we were. The only question for me was the extent of what he knew, for, to a cavalier like that, rank aside, we couldn't have been more than the Führer's human furniture.

"What can I do for you, gentlemen?" he asked after clicking and saluting smartly, then lowering himself into a chair beside me.

Apparently caught off guard by the general's gracious manner, Günsche merely shrugged.

Engel smiled broadly, clearly accustomed to such responses. "Surely, you had something in mind when you called me over, yes?"

"Yes... yes," Günsche finally stammered, "we were wondering if maybe you can tell us what this Italian business is all about."

Schaub and I nodded.

Engel smiled again. "I'll give you the quick-and-dirty version. Italian business is right. Unfortunately for us, it's business as usual. Mussolini, in his usual cocksure manner, was determined to match the Führer's record by unilaterally subjugating Greece. Well, we know how that turned out."

At least *I* knew from overhearing the Führer's exasperated discussions with his military leaders in the fall of last year. Without a word to the Führer, Mussolini began sending two hundred thousand troops into Greece from his puppet state, Albania, expecting a speedy and overwhelming victory. Mussolini's attack was poorly planned, however, and the Greeks, though lacking mechanised equipment and possessing an obsolete air force, turned on the invaders and, by mid-November, expelled them and even penetrated into Albania.

"Now, as the Führer put it, 'the Duce has the temerity to ask me to, once again, pull his chestnuts from the fire.' And if that weren't enough," Engel went on, "Mussolini insisted that as a matter of national pride, Italy needed to create a Mediterranean sphere of influence on its own or risk becoming a mere 'junior' partner. And so he ventured in. But as any experienced military man could have predicted, despite expansion into parts of East Africa and Egypt, the Duce's forces proved no match for the Brits in the long run, and their troops pushed the Italians westward, inflicting extraordinary losses. And so, gentlemen, since Britain threatened to push the Italians out of Libya altogether and break through to Tunisia, Mussolini—no mean swallower, if you've seen him—swallowed his pride and asked the Führer for assistance.

"The Führer reluctantly agreed," he continued, "though it would mean the first direct German-British encounter in the Mediterranean—but stipulated that this would happen only if Mussolini stopped the Italians' retreat and kept the British out of Tripoli, the Libyan capital. Mussolini agreed, but the Italians continued to be overwhelmed, and in three months, twenty thousand men were wounded or killed and a hundred thirty thousand were taken prisoner, forcing the Führer's hand. That's the 'Italian business,' in a chestnut shell, so to say. Anything else, gentlemen?" Engel enquired, and when we all shook our heads no, he rose. "Then, I bid you all a good day." He snapped a military salute and moved back to the clerk.

Short of massaging Mussolini's aching feet, I cared nothing about Italy and even less so now. But as I listened to Engel, one thing gnawed at me: *how could the Führer, who listened to continual costly and embarrassing tales of woe from Mussolini, be the same Führer who threw Günsche out when he tried to bring up Klara or evaded me when I mentioned my visit to Auschwitz?*

"The poor Führer," the humourless Schaub remarked. "Like he didn't have enough to deal with, eh?"

Günsche nodded solemnly to this insight, told me that the Führer wanted to meet with him, Schaub, and me before dinner, and then the two of them walked away, bosom brothers in mindless ineptitude. As I also made to leave, I was startled when General Engel called out to me to join him in the hallway.

"I imagine you're happy to be well rid of those two idiots, Linge," he said as he took my elbow and manoeuvred me to a relatively secluded space between the wall and a wide column.

His overture caused my stomach to lurch, and I couldn't find the right words to reply.

"To be frank, I don't know how you do it," he added.

I must have started to gape, because Engel placed his hand firmly on my forearm and urged me to relax. "I come in peace," he said softly, his hand spread across the sparser left side of his bemedaled chest. "And I bring greetings from a mutual friend in Paris."

I compelled myself to calm down. "You… know Gen—ah—Colonel Brückner?" I asked stupidly, temporarily bereft of a more apt response.

"I know him well," Engel said. "I have for quite a long time. And he's always spoken of you with the highest regard. Like a younger brother, I think he said."

In all the time I've known Brückner, not once had he mentioned Engel. "May I ask how you know him?"

"We met through a mutual acquaintance who felt that we had much in common. It turned out to be true—even more so now that he's sensibly traded in his black uniform for a grey one, no offence intended."

His demeanour was soothing, his words reassuring, yet I was little soothed or reassured.

"I miss him," I admitted safely. "As you said, we were quite close. I miss his ready humour and counsel."

Engel nodded solemnly. "I know he misses you too. He's mentioned it often. In fact, he said as much when I saw him yesterday."

"In Paris?"

"Yes. He asked me to tell you how much he regretted having to cut short your last meeting, and that he hoped you had a—how did he put it—'safe and successful return to the Chancellery.'"

Again, there was that lurch in my gut, but this time, I resolved to ignore it and risk it. "Please, Herr General, be good enough to tell him that my trip was not particularly safe but was successful. Did he say anything else?"

Suddenly, Engel's face went hard, and what little colour there was in it all but vanished. "In point of fact," he said, first glancing to the left and right, emotion draining from his voice, "he did. Would you like to hear it?"

I could tell by the steeliness in his stare that the question was not rhetorical. He was sounding me out. "If you still come in peace," I answered with what I hoped was just enough levity to smooth the way.

"Of course," he answered, "and to the best of my ability, I'll tell it to you the way he told it to me since he needs you to respond to me the way you'd respond to him."

As he began to speak, it happened again, as if the cells of my brain started to melt like candle wax. His voice faded into silence, like someone turning down the volume knob on a radio, and when it returned to a whisper, it was no longer Engel speaking Brückner's words in the Chancellery hallway but Hedwig Höss speaking to me in whispered bedside conversation the night before my Auschwitz tour, the night Klara was taken away to her doom. As I told you, at the time, I'd hardly listened, fearing I was experiencing just one more hallucination; I wasn't even sure she'd actually been in my room. But this time, through Engel—though doubting his existence as well—I listened. Even though it was Hedwig's voice, I saw Engel's face, and not a muscle had moved on it all the while. I felt suspended in a terrible darkness, without any sense of time or place.

"Linge?" I could now hear his voice calling to me through the void. "Are you all right?"

"I… I… was… I—"

"Please act natural, Linge. No attention, you understand."

"I… am acting natural, General," I faltered, a tinge of uncertainty creeping in.

"Ah, I see. You consider it natural to repeat over and over in a raised voice, 'Fastidious men, fastidious men,' with your eyes closed and shaking your head violently," he suggested wryly—like Brückner would have done. The same stare.

"I… I didn't realise," I said, feeling the heat of humiliation in my face. "I… don't understand it. Without any intent on my part, I was no longer with you but with Frau Höss, the wife of—"

"I know who she is." He paused for a moment. "You say you were with her just now?"

I needed to explain but was too flummoxed to answer in a straight line. "No… Herr General, I was with you, but… but you'd become Frau—no, I didn't mean that. You were you… but… I'm certain she wasn't real, then…" My voice faded into the space between us.

"Intriguing." Engel scratched his chin. "Your relationship with reality is even more complicated than we'd imagined. In any event, I can assure you that I'm not Frau Höss, but I can also assure you that she's quite real—and quite dedicated."

"I was experiencing her dedication while Klara was being taken away. I wonder if she knew."

"Klara? You mean that notorious enemy of the Reich who stood between the perfect Aryan Valhalla and the genetic abyss? *That Klara?*"

Whether Engel had mastered Brückner's sarcasm or came by it naturally, I had no idea, but I found it unnerving.

"Brückner already spoke to you about it. Normally, he would have suggested that you take the matter up with the Führer, but the Führer is anything but normal. The horse had already escaped, so to say, and by now, you must know better than to take anything up with him that might, in any way, upset his impenetrable denial of reality and consequence."

"Is this what Brückner was going to tell me in the restaurant?" I asked.

He shrugged, then exhaled deeply, more than a sigh. "That, to be sure, but far more," he said. "He claimed to have known you long enough to anticipate all the excuses you might make for…" His voice trailed off, as if he were searching for a word to describe my typical reaction to anything but couldn't locate it, so I assisted him.

"Passivity?"

He stared intently, letting a mixture of satisfaction and concern collect visibly in the seams of his face. Appraisals of character. "Yes. That's the exact word Brückner used. He said that its lure for you is that it allows one to elude the pressure of procrastination and the dangers of decision."

"Sounds like Brückner," I said. "And like all of Brückner's judgement of character, he hit the bullseye."

"Yes, he usually does. But there's more. He also said that you protect that passivity with a moat of morality, and so—"

"Alliteration aside," I risked, "I don't understand you."

"You don't? Brückner swore that you would. He said that you've chosen to operate on the principle that if you 'think no harm,' 'say no harm,' and 'do no harm,' your moral quotient is more than sufficient. Now, don't misunderstand me, for many decent and good people, it is. To Brückner, me, and many more, however, it's no more than a thinly disguised rationale for inaction. And given the situation we face, it's by far not enough. I daresay, it shouldn't be enough for the man who chose to make a disabled woman's life of isolation and misery a little better, if only for one evening; who chose a fellow bricklayer over a palette of bricks, then quit his job over a foreman's misanthropic venality; who chose to repay his friend for his kindness over a purloined button, and lost a loved one to euthanasia.

"In the way of things, your history could have led to insanity, gangsterism, zealotry, and self-obsessed sadistic hatred and lust. In other words, the *real* SS. But it didn't. None of that happened. Have you ever wondered why? I ask you, Linge, have your experiences, just in the past year alone, not shown you unmistakably that there are times when inaction is action, just as there are times when no decision is a decision? And though it pains me to say this, in a sense, it could be argued that *you* were the immediate cause of Klara's death." He held up his hand in a conciliatory gesture. "Consider this: If you hadn't courted her, hadn't any connexion with her, she might still be alive. So perhaps what occurred was intended as a message, a warning."

My history? We? Klara would be alive if not for me? A feeling of black exhaustion crawled over me. I tried to compose myself, but the difficulty must have shown.

"I regret having to put it this way," Engel continued when I remained silent, "but there is little time left. There can be no doubt concerning the Führer's true intent, despite all the easy victories and even more to come. He possesses one of the implements, and…" He stopped speaking for a moment; it was clear that he was struggling with something and, having resolved it, resumed. "There is always the possibility that he can secure the other. But even without both, he believes that through you, he can inflict incalculable, unobstructed abominations and horrors on the world. And he desperately wishes to do so. At any cost. And he cares not one whit how it's accomplished, so long as he is kept unaware of the process. Without more, your visit to Auschwitz and its aftermath should have erased all doubt." There was a pause—just enough for him to take a deep breath. "The Führer shields himself behind his hysterical hyperboles and bliss-ful ignorance of what those who share his beliefs are only too happy to execute, destroying everything in their path, that is, until, through magical means, he renders all that superfluous."

Magical means? Is Engel insane, or am I? Or are we both per-forming a demented play for the equally mad Marquis de Sade?[50]

"What I'm trying to get through to you is that while the Führer drones on and on about his destiny, it's your destiny he's depending on to reach it. He must be stopped. By you. By any means necessary."

I tried to focus on Engel's words, but all I could hear was Klara's wonderfully tortured deaf-speak countering some pom-posity of mine with a witty comeuppance. Something there, in that, a glimpse, some long-buried hint that made me sense that what Engel was telling me was somehow true, no matter how insane and treacherous it sounded.

"I must confess that you're not the first, Herr General," I said with a grim nod. "Some years ago, a woman who called herself Emerald actually tried to persuade me to assassinate the

---

[50] After intervention by his family, the Marquis de Sade, the man for whom sadism is named, was declared insane in 1803 and transferred to the Charenton Asylum. The director of the institution allowed and encouraged him to stage several of his plays, with the inmates as actors, to be viewed by the Parisian public.

Führer. Do you believe it? But another woman, her name was Katrin—"

Engel cut me off, an amused smile spreading across his face. "My belief isn't important, but what if I were to tell you, Herr Hamlet, that there were no Emerald and Katrin, that they never existed but were merely two sides in a war within your mind? Would you believe me?"

We exchanged glances.

Given my experience, such craziness made perfect sense, but I felt in no position to admit this to him. "Is there anything else, Herr General?" I asked instead.

He took what seemed a long time, apparently considering his response, and when he made it, his voice held a slight edge of concern. "From me, only that you know all you need to know. It's now in your hands and only yours. If you decide to act, I wouldn't presume to tell you how, but act you must—strategically and quickly. From Brückner? I think he would tell you that not many people can say they saved the world from the apocalypse and not be branded a defective. You're lucky, he would add, for you know only too well what befalls defectives in the Reich."

My face went slack, and I stood there, numb to all the regimented bustle surrounding me. *Emerald and Katrin—illusions, fantasies? Then what of Hedwig, Bella, and Klara? The brickyard? The interview? Was Engel real? Or were they all part of that "war" Engel spoke of? What then was real? Was I, in actuality, principal valet to the Führer of Germany, or instead a wretched, unemployed prole, alone, huddled and hungry in a rainswept doorway in a feverish delirium, imagining all this? What really existed outside my brain? Or inside?*

I laughed, a faint, embarrassed sound deep in my throat. Sensing that my resolve, my fear, my constraint, my dubiousness, were being forced away like a bulldozer moving seemingly intractable mountains of earth, I attempted one last feeble gesture of resistance. "What if, right now, what I am, who I am, where I am, all of it, is a dream? That I'm dreaming all this."

Engel shrugged, the tiny laugh lines round his eyes crinkling. "Linge, Linge." He sighed. "Brückner said you might respond this way, so he gave me this piece of wisdom to pass on to you: Whether a dream or reality, it brought you to this moment, here, with me. And even if it is all a dream—a nightmare, really—do you exercise any volition in it?"

Again, that question! I'd never understood the reason for it, and up to this moment, I'd been able to evade it. But now I felt the necessity of finally answering. "I don't know, General. I never tried."

Engel nodded gravely. "Well then, Linge, I would try if I were you. I would try very hard." Then he told me he would give my regards to Brückner, saluted smartly, turned, and made his way down the vast hallway to… who knew where?

As I stared at Engel's retreating figure, an aphorism by Nietzsche occurred to me: "He who has a why to live can bear almost any how."

I spent most of the morning performing my duties by rote, hoping that no one, especially the Führer, took notice of my insensibility. However, in the early afternoon, Günsche, Schaub, and I were informed that we would be assisting at dinner, and later, while I was projecting a new film for select guests, the other two would be helping prepare for our rail journey to the Berghof.

"Gentlemen," the Führer declared, "this is to be—" he paused, then resumed, "not a top secret meeting, or even a secret meeting," he elucidated, "but it is a confidential meeting, mainly because the proud Duce doesn't wish to be seen begging me for assistance again. I mention this because I respect his wishes, and so I want as few people as possible to know about this meeting. Only those absolutely essential to the event, you understand."

I could sense Günsche's panic. He hadn't a clue whom to place on the need-to-know list—something Brückner, even in his sleep, would already have anticipated and arranged. Schaub, as usual, in his stolid, humourless way, cared nothing about such matters, since he was able to rely solely on my learned mastery of procedure, so he fled the scene for the officers' mess. Before I, too, left, I reached up, patted Günsche on his shoulder board, and told him I'd prepare a list of essential personnel and give it to him before dinner.

"I don't know what I'd do without you, Heinz," he gushed. "Otherwise, I'd have to ask the Reichsleiter, and you know what that means."

Of course I knew what that meant, though the giant didn't: Bormann would make a pretence of reprimanding Günsche but secretly delight that he was surrounded by needy, incompetent underlings who would rely on him exclusively and, thus, be no threat.

"My pleasure, Otto," I said. "Needn't disturb the Reichsleiter if it isn't necessary, eh? But don't tell him I helped, okay?" I thoroughly enjoyed that one.

He made a wipe-his-brow gesture with his sleeve. "You bet I won't, and that's a promise," he assured me, and I believed him—to the extent he could keep his big, stupid mouth shut when rattled or caught unawares.

❧

I wasn't granted even a moment to process my encounter with General Engel, which I felt was all to the good since, in my current condition, any contemplation would have merely terrified and confounded me. What I needed was a satisfactory resolution or successful escape.

❧

As I was finishing supervising the dinner table setup, the guests entered, led by the Führer, who, as usual, had arranged the seating to suit some impish agenda of his. With the Führer at the head, he placed Eva Braun to his right, presumably to avoid her pouting in the bedroom later. To his left, he sat Heidemarie Hatheyer, a wholesomely appealing woman I'd seen only in films up to then. At the foot of the table, he positioned Magda Goebbels, presumably to provide her with an unobstructed, masochistic view of Braun and Hatheyer, while he seated her husband at the foot so Magda had an unobstructed, masochistic view of her husband gazing lasciviously at his latest protégé. *But who was I to second-guess the Führer's intentions?* And yet, now I needed to do just that, but not for such adolescent hijinks. The rest of the seats were occupied (it seemed, with no particular rank or order in mind) by Deputy Führer Hess, Himmler, von Ribbentrop, Field Marshal Keitel,[51] Goebbels, Morell, and Bormann. The headwaiter and I stood at ease behind the Führer in case of unanticipated need. My only question was why Morell, since he'd never been invited before.

Normally, my brain would have tuned to another station during such trivial table talk, but after Hedwig and Engel, real or imagined, I forced myself to listen instead of mindlessly recording.

The Führer was in the middle of a discourse on a visit to Italy. "Perhaps the Duce came on the scene a year or two too early with his revolution," he was saying. "He probably should have let the Reds have their way for a bit first. They'd have exterminated the aristocracy, and the Duce would have become head of a republic instead of a ridiculous monarchy. Thus, the abscess would have been lanced."

"Incisive as always, my Führer, but despite the monarchy, the Duce appears to be well-liked," interrupted the sycophantic lout Ribbentrop, with one of his usual innocuous responses to the Führer's rhapsodic tendencies. No one at the table even bothered to glance his way.

"'Well-liked?' Ribbentrop," the Führer corrected, "in Florence, I was alone with the Duce, and I read in the eyes of the population the respect, devotion, and burning love for him. The common people gazed at him as though they'd have liked

---

[51] Chief of the high command of the Armed Forces from 1938 until the end of the war.

to eat him. If that's being well-liked, I wouldn't mind some of that here."

All round the table exploded into huzzahs of laughter.

"If he merely had external enemies to contend with, my Führer," Keitel started, "things—"

"Yes, there's also a third power," the Führer interrupted. "The Vatican. You may have heard of it."

More laughter.

"Despite their incessant meddling, I've managed to neutralise most of that nonsense here, but in Italy, sitting in the very shadow of the Papacy, what can Mussolini do? And yet, he succeeds for the most part despite the incompetent obstructionism of King and Church. Oh, I know there are those who, behind my back, ridicule me for my support of the Duce, but I tell you, I hold him in the highest esteem because I regard him as an incomparable statesman. On the ruins of a ravished Italy, he succeeded in building a new Aryan State, which is a rallying point for the whole of his people. The struggles of the Fascists bear a close resemblance to our own struggles. And they began even earlier, I might add."

"Such a successful comradeship, my Führer," Hess interjected, "was clearly meant to be. It came to me in a vision, years before you'd ever met, and the improbability of such a fraternal union speaks for itself."

I took note of something I hadn't noticed before. Bormann was making his usual copious dinner transcription of all the speakers (even von Ribbentrop), but when it came to Hess, Bormann's pencil suddenly became inert. Having no context, I filed it away and returned with reluctance to Mussolini. My brain yawned with boredom since I'd heard all this Führer slobbering over Mussolini so many times. I'd begun to wonder whether he was actually attempting to talk himself into what he was saying, rather than actually meaning it.

I intended to sidle out to set up the projector, when the Führer remarked, "And aside from all his other admirable qualities, the Duce is one of the people who, like me, appreciates the full measure of the Bolshevik menace. He told me himself that he has no illusions as to the fate of Europe, should Stalin turn his insatiable Asiatic eyes on the West. I have even fewer illusions."

That, I didn't file away.

After the Führer had wearied of his panegyric to Mussolini, a few moments elapsed, providing assorted private cluster conversations until von Ribbentrop, in a voice raised above the rest, asked Goebbels, "Joseph, about our cinematic treat for tonight, could it possibly be something with our stunning visitor here?"

He tilted his head towards Fräulein Hatheyer, who smiled with a practised beguiling shyness, causing all heads but the Führer's to turn towards Goebbels.

"Your instinct for the obvious hasn't failed you, Joachim," Goebbels kidded. "Yes, tonight we're screening her latest film for the Führer, *I Accuse*. Her studio is enormously pleased with it, and I, even more so. My ministry is arranging gala openings throughout the Reich."

"Can you tell us a little something about it, Fräulein Hatheyer?" Magda asked with no expression animating her features of chiselled ice. "A teaser, perhaps. My husband is notoriously reticent about his... affairs."

All joined her curiosity, save for Hess, who seemed to be in deep meditation, and Morell, who was unsuccessfully stifling a titter.

The actress lifted her well-padded shoulders in a casually dramatic shrug. "Well, Frau Goebbels, normally, I prefer to let my films speak for themselves, but with such august company, especially the Führer, how can I possibly refuse?"

I agreed with Fräulein Hatheyer, and since I was about to screen it, I had no interest in hearing it laid out before its time, but I had no vote.

"Well, all right then," she began, "I play a woman diagnosed with multiple sclerosis. My fictional husband and I decided—"

Suddenly, the Führer stood and quickly raised his arms, motioning down for all to remain seated. "I must undertake a short journey tomorrow and so have several important matters to take care of in advance. Therefore, I leave you in Dr. Goebbels's capable hands while I retire to my quarters. I've been assured that the film you're about to see will both entertain and inspire." With that, he hurried out, leaving his guests murmuring and staring at each other.

Goebbels collected himself sufficiently to request that Fräulein Hatheyer continue, seconded by Magda, who wondered aloud where multiple sclerosis would lead the heroine. The verbal disarray only ended when Fräulein Hatheyer resumed.

"As I was saying, when I'm diagnosed with multiple sclerosis, my husband and I decide that I should poison myself. This way, I die peacefully instead of living a life of pain and suffering. And so, he does for me. And since this isn't a ghost story, my 'compelling performance,' as my director and the Reichsminister call it, is over as well. The rest of the movie concerns a courtroom filled with doctors, lawyers, and judges, all debating if they should charge my husband with murder. They ultimately decide that euthanasia is entirely ethical. And that's it. Not exactly a romantic comedy."

"So it was for your own good," Morell piped in.

She stared at the ugly physician, some of his dinner caked along his upper lip. "You mean my death," she quipped, "or my absence from one-third of the movie?"

All chuckled, except Himmler, who never chuckled;

Bormann, who'd resumed his note-taking; Magda, who stared at her husband as if hoping that the actress would come down with the dreaded disease; and I, who, as I left to set up the film in the projector, marvelled at the coincidence of such a film following immediately on the heels of Klara's extermination. It was then that I knew escape was no longer possible, for resolution had made its way through the depths of my brain to the surface.

Günsche led the guests into the projection room and bade them sit while I finished spooling the film into the sprockets, clicking the latches shut, and adjusting the lens. Then I flipped the projector switch, and the black-on-white numbers flickered down to a solid image of the credits. Remembering Fräulein Hatheyer's synopsis, I strained to force down the bile without sound, leaving a raw throbbing in my throat, but sufficiently loud that I failed to hear Hess approach from behind me.

"Are you all right, Herr Linge?"

"I'm… uh… fine, uh, Herr Deputy. Is there a problem?"

"I sense no problem your pistol can't handle."

I glanced down to discover my hand gripping my service revolver aimed directly up at the screen.

"If you don't like the movie, Herr Linge," he quipped, "at least see it before shooting it."

I was aghast, more by Hess's rare display of wit than by what I'd done. I quickly replaced my revolver in its holster and snapped the fastener shut. When I turned to thank Hess, he was no longer beside me but in his plush theatre seat next to Keitel, gazing straight ahead at the screen. All the while, my face was on fire, my pulse, the rhythmic pounding of hammers in my ears, chest, and brain. Only the words of Tolstoy rose above the internal clamour:

It was that feeling on account of which a volunteer recruit drinks up his last kopeck, a man on a drunken binge smashes mirrors and windows without any apparent reason and knowing it will cost him his last penny; that feeling on account of which a man does… insane things, as if testing his personal power and strength, claiming the presence of a higher judgement over life, which stands outside human conventions.

When the film began, I was forced to exert a degree of control nothing short of heroic to not break down. So instead of watching, I studied the faces of the audience, most of which were rapt, save for Fräulein Hatheyer, who looked bored, and Magda, whose glacial mien couldn't entirely conceal a burning envy of the star and a resigned antipathy towards her lecherous husband. Despite my avoidance, all the while, the timing and subject matter of the film tormented me, and I couldn't rid myself of the uncharacteristically hubristic sensation that this entire event was for my benefit, not for the Führer's, and that somehow, fate (or something more intentional and sinister) wished to deliver another message to me.

Once the tail of the film flapped noisily to a halt, the applause subsided, and I switched on the lights, Günsche moved to the front.

"If I may speak for the Führer, we are most grateful to Dr. Goebbels once again," he announced, "for securing us the first viewing of—"

"Normally yes," the propaganda minister interjected, holding up a halting hand, "but the person responsible in this particular case is not I, but Reichsleiter Bormann. It's him you must thank."

❧

When I finally returned to my quarters and was removing my tunic, I felt the rustle of paper in my outer pocket. When I extracted and lifted it to read, the tinted notepaper and perfume were unmistakable:

> *Please don't grieve for me, my love, because I'm here for you, in your thoughts, for as long as you want me there. I can hear you now, perfectly, and so it's no longer necessary for us to face each other. I have one last request, dear one, and it's this: that you make what happened between us, even for so short a time, mean something—something beyond the two of us. Can I ask that of you? With all my love, forever, your Klara.*

Even through my tears, I could see that it was in her hand. When it was written and how it got to me was one more mystery that I knew would plague me until I solved it—somehow.

19 *January 1941*

AFTER THE EXCRUCIATING torment I experienced last night, I knew I had to quickly establish some semblance of closure with Schroeder and saw no pressing need to waste time with yet another mysteriously fruitless attempt to contact Brückner. So, after preparing the Führer, I went straight to her quarters.

"You took your sweet time, Herr Bereaved," she carped when she opened her door a crack and eyed me standing there.

To a vicious, warped crone like Schroeder, setting the proper tone was no simple matter. I had to seem caring but ruthlessly patriotic, an ingenuous-but-dedicated Nazi, selflessly serving a ruthless-but-benevolent Führer while his minions—those "fastidious men" and their savage underlings—worked his will: in other words, an idiot. Fortunately, years of perfecting my persona helped, but I was still apprehensive about my ability to maintain discipline and focus long enough to endure her vile presence. Since her response to me would determine my next course of action, I strained to be civil.

"My apologies, Fräulein Schroeder," I began, hands jammed into my pockets. "I didn't think—"

"You could begin every sentence with that phrase," she sniped. "For weeks, you've seen me with the Führer, you've seen me in the hallways, you've seen me in the lunchroom, and this is the first moment you can present your condolences?"

Take it, Heinz! "As I was about to say, I apologise if I seemed insensitive or uncaring, but when Günsche informed me of your reaction to the news, I naturally assumed you were deep in grief, and I had no idea how long that would continue. I hoped you'd let me know, that is, when you'd recovered sufficiently."

She stared at me for a moment with an expression just short of disgust, then her head performed a perfunctory nod, her version of acceptance. "You might as well come in," she conceded, opening her door a bit wider, but I still had to slip in sideways.

As with Morell, I'd never been in her quarters before, and if one could imagine a space as opposite in every way, this would be it. As astringent and devoid of human personality as Schroeder herself, the room stank of disinfectant and exuded all the warmth of the transparent plastic covering all the seating surfaces. She motioned me to the one unyielding armchair, and she took the very corner of her tiny, stiff sofa, choosing to pose at an uncomfortable angle, her knees jammed together. I waited for her to speak, all the while masochistically attempting to picture her bathroom and keep from laughing.

"It's just as well that you come now as any other time," she explained, "since I may never fully recover." Her obdurate expression had softened, and even the creases in her face seemed to become shallower. "It was a complete and terrible shock, like having a stroke. You can't know."

It was as if she'd completely dismissed my own relationship with Klara, as if it had never existed.

"But—" I tried again.

"There are no buts," she said. "Klara was my only living relative, a good and generous heart, and I was extremely fond of her, as you well know."

Now was the moment to test her authenticity.

"Of course I know," I countered as gently as possible. "In fact, I feel a great responsibility for what happened."

Her heavy-lidded eyes widened slightly. "You do?" she demanded. "That's nonsense."

"Well, my memory is not the greatest, but as I recall, you were adamant that she move into the Chancellery. I imagine you believed her to be safer here with you than on the outside with me. And when she balked at the idea, you tried to warn her, but she wouldn't, ah, hear of it, and I'm afraid I encouraged her to stay where she was, and even accompany me to Poland. You know the rest. Unless I'm mistaken, of course."

"You're not mistaken," she replied tersely, "but there is no cause to reproach yourself. For a long time, I had the sense that certain forces harbouring sinister motivations were closing in on her, and not even the Führer's protection would be sufficient, so I wanted to keep her as close, physically, as possible. But she was stubborn, as you say, and paid the price. If it hadn't been you, it would have been someone or something else. Or nothing. You shouldn't overestimate your importance."

A typical Schroeder compliment, her choice in decor was not accidental. And she didn't have to spell it out. Certain forces: Bormann. Sinister motivations: a warning to me.

"Are you saying that even the *Führer* could no longer protect her?" I asked with an expression of ostentatious incredulity.

She flattened and spread her lips in distaste. "You couldn't possibly have the sophistication of my insights, but you know the Führer almost as well as I do. In the laying on of hands, he is generosity itself, but when he believes that the removal of those same hands is called for, he dons surgical gloves and keeps his distance. You understand what I'm saying?"

I understood. Now it was my turn. "I'll take your word, as always, Fräulein Schroeder. Then," I pressed on, "despite your generosity, permit me to console you. From what you say, Klara was living on what I've heard called 'borrowed time.' That being the case, I believe what happened was for the ultimate good of the Reich. We knew that shielding her was a violation of one of the basic and sacred doctrines of the Führer and the Party—and we were, in a large way, accomplices in that violation. So, a cleansing was long overdue, don't you agree?" I could hardly get through the obscenity I spewed, but it had to be done.

When I looked squarely into her face, it was a different Schroeder: pale, exhausted, suddenly fragile and melancholic.

Her eyes welled up. "Console me, you say? An overdue cleansing, you say? The ultimate good of the Reich, you say? My Klara? Your Klara?" She forced herself up, and I followed. "I was right about you, Linge," she declared. "You're a doctrinaire and simplistic young fool, no different from any other of Himmler's vicious lockstep kindergarteners, merely balder. I loved Klara. A pity you didn't. Now, if you'll be good enough to leave." Her face returned to its granitic abandon.

I obeyed her with a secret sense of relief, for I believed her. And so, despite my own grief and her exacerbated hostility, I was comforted, knowing that the Führer, soon to have enough on his plate, would not be losing a valued secretary through a fatal "accident" I engineered. I couldn't save Klara, but in a manner of speaking, I saved Schroeder—and she'll never know how close she came.

20 *January 1941*

YESTERDAY, WHILE MUSSOLINI's train headed for the small railway station of Puch near Salzburg, I snatched the necessary time to think by feigning another migraine and passing my morning duties onto Schaub (who likened me to Wolf). Temporarily freed from the quotidian, I paced my tiny quarters, repeating to myself something that Brückner had told me years before: "First the what, then the how. If you don't know what to do, how to do it is illogical at best—not that it stops fools and fanatics, of course." For that moment, I had the urge to contact Brückner but immediately thought better of it, both logistically and strategically. From the Berghof, a telephone call to Paris by a valet was inadvisable, and in any event, he'd proven himself continually—and inexplicably—unavailable to my calls. However, I possessed enough Brückner in my brain to make an educated guess of his responses. I knew that he would counsel me to rethink all my experiences, from my first meeting with the Führer—if not even further back—all the way to the present. I also knew that he would have me reconsider Hedwig's warning and, perhaps, even stand it on its head.

And there was something far more significant, even revolutionary: the not-so-simple fact that I'd gained sufficient confidence to see the connexions among the data crowding my brain and, in doing so, detect the basic flaw in his aphorism: *Not "first the what," Brückner, my good friend and mentor, but the why! For without the why, the what and how are nothing more than purposeless exercises in meaningless motion.*

All right then, I told myself, *rethink all my experiences, whether real or imagined, and reconsider Hedwig's warning and, perhaps, even stand it on its head. Adding up to what?* I asked myself as I answered the knock at my door.

"Signore Linge."

Stunned into silence, I hesitated for a long, sweaty moment, my hands shaking, the distended blue veins on their backs throbbing visibly. I'd been caught completely by surprise and, instantly, regretted my display of puerile astonishment.

"Herr Mussolini will do," he said in passable Swiss-German. "You're probably remembering my feet more than the rest of me," he joked about our last encounter.

Disarmed, I managed to recover sufficiently to respond. "I… I remember all of you, Herr Mussolini," I said with some hesitation, despite his charm.

"Yes, I must say I'm difficult to miss." He simulated his jutted-lower-lipped expression, his head tilted up at a pugnacious angle. Then his face relaxed into a smile. "I hope I don't disturb. I may come in?"

"Of course," I said. "Please forgive the mess."

"You should see what my chambers would look like if I didn't have people to tidy up after me." The smile again, a little broader this time. "When I arrive, I expect to see you, too, but instead, I was obliged to deal with that—forgive me—moron, Schaub. But now, since I have you, I ask a favour."

I glanced down. "If Herr Mussolini will permit me to remove his boots, I—"

Laughter exploded from his mouth, and he clasped his hands before himself, bobbing them up and down. "Bravo, bravissimo!" he whooped. "I wish my own personal valet had your sense of humour—or any sense of humour. No, not for my feet this time. Something of less pain and more importance."

I hadn't enough information, but I did have the distinct sensation that this visit would prove fortuitous. "Of course I'll assist you in any way I can."

Mussolini nodded and punched my upper arm lightly with the side of his fist. "Good man," he said, his tone comradely. "You must know why I come here. In a few hours, I meet with your boss, so I would appreciate your advice."

"But—"

"It is without saying," he cut in, "the ritual, yes? It is not your place. But with my own experience, I know that valets, by their position, are made acquainted with the opinions of their employer that others are not permitted to know. Now, I'm soon to ask your employer for military assistance. Much is at stake for me and my country, and so I must know how best to approach him."

I stifled a smile. *He wants to use me, and I want to use him.* It occurred to me that in such a circumstance, Jung would smile. Now I had enough information but, as yet, no plan. I had to think quickly, for I might never get such an opportunity again. Since returning from Auschwitz, all my concentration had been at the service of giving meaning to Klara's death. *But what was that meaning? Bad luck to be born deaf? To be born deaf in the Third Reich? To be associated with me? A warning to me? Of what?* They euthanised Klara. That fact had become my sole focus. From it, all else proceeded. It motivated everything, justified everything, explained everything. But now, after meeting with Engel (whether the meeting was fact or fantasy) and putting all he'd told me into the context of my experiences, Klara devolved into merely one victim of a massive plague. And so there was nothing more to be said about Hedwig's warning. *But where does the Führer fit into this world he created?* Even after years of intimate proximity, I must confess to no greater insight into him than the average factory worker, common soldier, farmer, shopkeeper, or hausfrau who viewed him as the solitary, pure, magical, visionary genius who would make Germany a paradise at home and supreme in the world. I had no capability to fully comprehend the nature and breadth of his vision, and despite his placing unbridled trust in those who debased and debauched that vision, and then hiding his face from the consequences of that trust, I refused to assign evil to the vision, or to its holder. Be that as it may, somehow, I had to prevent the fastidious men who gave the orders from above and those less-fastidious men who happily did their bidding below from benefitting from that vision in any way. That was to say, I had to, somehow, thwart the perverted twisting of the Führer's vision—both physical and metaphysical. And as I see it, that demands the success of several specific objectives, the first, I decided instantly, involved the fortuitous request of the hapless posturer standing before me, so I had to play him to the bone.

I wished I had Brückner to guide me, or at least tell me that it was the very moment to become the principal actor in my own drama, to exercise volition in my dream. But he'd maintained a strict "radio silence," as Baur would say, unreachable to my calls and unresponsive to my messages.

"Of course I would be only too happy to oblige, Herr Mussolini," I said with a shrug, "but considering my untutored ignorance of the affairs of state, not to mention the humdrum nature of my duties and, of course, the Führer's natural reticence, I seldom receive confidences."

Mussolini crossed his arms, tilted his head back, and nodded with theatrical gravity as if on a reviewing balcony, his bulbous lower lip jutting out even more than usual. "I understand completely, Herr Linge. However," he pursued, "if—I only say if—in the course of those duties, in disregard of understanding, you had overheard and somehow recalled something to provide some clue to his attitude towards my request, or at least give me something to, ah, how is it you say, sweeten his decision?"

I swivelled my right eye heavenward in simulated thought, saying nothing, stretching the moment for all it was worth. My bowels churned with fright since this had to be astute and still be consistent with my image. "Well," I finally said, holding out my hands, palms turned upwards in humility, "I don't know, but... well... the only thing I can think of, maybe, is the Führer's anxiousness with Stalin."

Mussolini scrunched his face into an expression of puzzlement. "Stalin?"

"I could be wrong since I only hear random snatches of conversations while performing my duties and I forget most of them. He's never mentioned it to you?" I asked, eyes wide with simulated wonder.

"In passing, yes. He is certainly not such a great admirer of Stalin, or the Soviet Union for that matter, but never to where I would call it a—what did you say?—anxiousness. This is a word?"

"But Herr Mussolini," I replied, "with respect, you don't attend to him every day."

He nodded again. "Of course this is true. All right then, an anxiousness. But what is this anxiousness to involve?"

"From what the Führer says, Stalin is... how did he put it...?" I scratched my head. "I think, 'buying time,' or words like that. My memory, you know."

"Buying time, eh?" Mussolini mused under his breath. "And by this, he means?"

Prod to your heart's content, Duce. "Well," I continued,

spreading caution on my words like butter on bread as I shrugged, "I think he said this to Foreign Minister von Ribbentrop, though I could be mistaken, but he considers Stalin to be 'an Asiatic tyrant who trusts no one and so cannot himself be trusted.' Or something like that. I can't be sure." I tapped the side of my head as if to say, *You must allow for my limitations.*

"Please go on," Mussolini bade, ignoring my tap, now visibly excited. "I am finding this most interesting."

I'll give him more now that he's in too deep to notice that I'm giving him far more than I claimed to know. "The Führer stated on several occasions—in privacy, of course—that while we've been operating on a 'guns-and-butter economy,' I think he called it, 'Comrade Stalin's been operating only on guns. His people can starve,' I think I remember him saying, 'but they'll all have rifles they need to mask the pangs.' I'm not sure what he meant, but—"

"I believe I do," Mussolini interrupted, "but more will help."

"I'll of course do my best," I told him. "The Führer also said, I think, that 'Stalin may be burdened by the vastness of his domain and a prehistoric population, but those two realities can also become my burden,' or something like that." I was still afraid I'd said too much, too well, but the risk had to be run.

"And the consequence of this?"

I could discern by his face that the Duce seemed too absorbed by the tale to give any thought to the teller. "Well, the only thing is, to me, for what it's worth, that up to now, I believe his attitude to be—how to put it—in words, no, in theory only? But the last thing I remember him saying—and this is quite recent— is: 'Better a two-front war now than wait for a Soviet Europe.'" *Enough said,* I decided. "You seem troubled, Herr Mussolini."

"I will admit it, Herr Linge, to a problem. I still need to determine how what you are telling me can be of benefit when I meet with him."

I shrugged again. "I wish I could be of more assistance." I simulated another thoughtful pause. "I daresay that even from my limited faculties and menial position, it seems to me that if you were to… I don't know… support and encourage the Führer in his anxiousness, he might be more favourably disposed to your requests."

"Herr Linge, I am but a simple Italian. If you could be clearer?"

Could such a man be that dense? I took a deep, audible breath to demonstrate my struggle with ideas. "Well, Herr Mussolini, if you could indicate to the Führer that helping you would go a long way towards weakening Stalin and thwarting his ambitions… well, you know what I mean."

After a moment, Mussolini swung his chubby hands round and clapped loudly. "Again, to you I say bravo! In fact, *bravissimo!* What you suggest is pure genius. Even my feet are feeling better."

I smiled tentatively. "I'm glad to have been of assistance, even in this small way. I know that the Führer has only the highest regard for you." I was careful to omit the "despite everything."

Blaise Pascal wrote that "We are only falsehood, duplicity, contradiction; we both conceal and disguise ourselves from ourselves." Towards the end of my first year at the Chancellery, Brückner casually mentioned on one of our garden strolls that the Führer was the undisputed master of duplicity. When my persona asked him what duplicity was, he told me that it meant deceit, double-dealing, and cunning. He'd added that in the gifted hands of the Führer, duplicity was both an art and a craft: that art without craft would be bizarre or ineffectual and craft without art would be laughable or catastrophic. Brückner, being Brückner, went on to provide several amusing examples, both historical and hypo-thetical. At the time, it meant nothing tangible or useful, and so, as with all such things, I forced it back into the crowded recesses of my brain.

Without either art or craft, and on the lowest and most elemental level, even I'd employed duplicity to survive on the mean streets of Berlin. People like me used to call it "conning," not cunning. But as I considered the matter now with experience and hindsight informing observation, I was convinced that duplicity seemed to be a natural human action, not only for survival or even to assuage the vulnerable but to seek advantage, whether economic, social, political, military, even emotional. And our greatest achievement, it finally occurred to me, was that we were so easily able to fool ourselves. And in this also, I believed the Führer was the undisputed master.

◈

At the very least, my advice to "Herr Mussolini" did him no harm, since today, the Führer spoke for more than two hours in the presence of several military leaders about his decision to intervene in Greece. To my purpose, it was a stunning success.

As I straightened out his conference room, the Führer remarked to me from my usual place before the bookshelves, "You must see Morell again about those migraines, Linge," he counselled. "You missed a splendid meeting with the Duce. Wasted on that idiot Schaub. I tell you. For all the internal problems he faces, not to mention having to lead Italians in a war, he still has more military sense than all my generals combined. Unlike them, he understands that the true threat is from the east and urged me to end it before it ends us."

Shuddering with satisfaction over my coup, and as a loyal follower of tradition, I attempted to edge a word in, but as always, the Führer pressed on like an invading army, as I hoped he would.

"When I assured him that I'd been considering such a response for more than a year, he said that he considered it to be a masterstroke of strategy and that he'd be more than happy to accompany me in such an effort. Of course I was gracious, but I knew that such largesse would only come once I'd achieved total victory. I also shuddered to think of having the Italian army between us and the Soviet hordes, serving as anything more than cannon fodder."

"I'm sure the Duce appre—"

"I tell you, Linge, sometimes I'm ashamed of myself. You'd think that by now, I'd be numb to the timorous shudderings of the reactionary incompetents managing my military. But I still boil every time I attempt to explain the most elementary parts of my military strategy to their blank or hostile faces. One day, I tell you, one—"

This time, as the Führer spoke those words I'd heard repeatedly, year after year, I attempted to get a true and comprehensive fix on my position relative to him, like a sailor with a sextant. The results shocked and overwhelmed me, for what should have been a worshipper's blind disregard of the flaws in the *übermensch* I'd been serving was, instead, heartbreak and anguish over his emotional cowardice, crushing shame over my blinkered worship, intense grief over my vanished innocence, and mortal terror over the consequences of leaving his real-world affairs in the hands of Hedwig's "fastidious men."

It must be now, I decided, *come what may.* So as he spoke, I shook my head, then turned away from him, moved somnambulistically round his massive desk, sat down, lowered my head sideways onto my crossed arms, closed my eyes, waited a few moments, then began murmuring out of the corner of my mouth in as authentic a burble as I could manage and still remain articulate: "Within the year, comrades, make no mistake. That timid fool with his little moustache procrastinates at his peril. Once our troops invade, Germany will quickly become one enormous collective farm, and that shrieking nonentity will be in a gulag or dead."

I began another sentence but let it trail off into an inarticulate mumble, then silence. I could sense the Führer coming towards me, then felt his hands move my shoulders gently.

"Linge?"

I didn't respond. Too soon.

"*Linge.*" More strident.

Still too soon.

Then I heard him reach for his phone and lift the receiver, presumably to call Morell, something I didn't want.

"My… Führer," I groaned, lifting my head with effort. "I—"

"Who are you?" he asked.

"Don't you know, my Führer?" I asked him. "I'm Heinz Linge. Your valet. Shall I summon Dr. Morell?"

The Führer pursed his lips in genuine concern. "I'm quite all right, Linge. I was about to summon that very Morell—for you."

I raised my head. "I… don't understand."

The Führer smiled benevolently. "Look at yourself."

I made a point of studiously glancing round me, then shooting up to attention. "I… don't… know what to say, my Führer."

The Führer lifted his hands in a comforting gesture. "Relax, Linge" he soothed. "But I need to ask: Do you remember anything while you were seated at my desk?"

"My Führer," I replied, "I don't even remember sitting at your desk." I feigned a complex visage of embarrassment and alarm.

He didn't answer for a moment as he clearly struggled with

something. Then, he said, "You need to compose yourself. Take the rest of the day off. There's nothing that Günsche and Schaub can't handle."

"But do you still think Dr. Morell should—"

The Führer's face went rigid, and what little colour there was in it all but vanished. "No," he cut me off quickly—as I'd hoped. "No need to disturb Morell. You seem recovered sufficiently, so a little rest, I'm convinced, will be just the ticket." As I reached the door, however, the Führer added, "But make yourself available for quite late in the evening."

"Yes, my Führer," I answered with heightened satisfaction and anticipation, for I suspected that he required confirmation, and I assumed that he would waste no time in securing it. In the meantime, I had more to accomplish, and I didn't know how long I would have.

22 *January 1941*

I'D MADE MYSELF available until midnight, but no summons came. This morning, before I could proceed to the next phase of my foray into intrigue, I was obliged to stand by while Field Marshals Keitel and von Blomberg informed the Führer of the Italian defeat at Tobruk in North Africa at the hands of the British.[52]

"Would you care for details, my Führer?" Keitel ventured.

"Would that alter anything?" The Führer shrugged. "Can you, instead, tell me that the Italians actually routed the British and are, at this very moment, bombing London into submission?"

"I'm afraid not, my Führer," he replied to the Führer's snideness.

He smiled thinly. "Then what good are details?"

Given the Führer's traditional approach to bad news, I could only conclude that he had little if any concern about Italy or the British. I hoped it was due, at least in part, to my efforts at redirection, but I had no evidence yet to support any inference.

"However," the Führer added, "to plane out your furrowed brows, I've taken steps to redress the setback that so concerns you. I've appointed General Rommel to command my newly created *Deutsches Afrika Korps*. Of course, to placate the Duce,

---

[52] The British attack on the coastal fortress of Tobruk was finally launched on the twenty-first, and it fell the next day, yielding 30,000 Italian prisoners, 236 guns, and 87 tanks.

Rommel and his crack troops will be technically subordinate to the inept Italian commander-in-chief. Technically. But I've given Rommel strict orders to utilise all means at his disposal to… overcome these technical impediments. And you know how intrepid and cunning Rommel can be."

If they didn't know, I did.

"All right then," the Führer concluded, "are we now satisfied?"

Huzzahs, smiles, and salutes answered the Führer's question.

As they filed out, I found myself pitying the British, who would soon face a brilliant and prodigious steamroller. I also pitied myself, since I would need to redouble my efforts to get to the same place. I never needed Brückner's counsel more than I did now, but I was alone.

As if he'd somehow divined my anxiety, waiting at the Communications Centre was a coded, perfumed, pink-tinted message from "an especially ardent admirer, who is thinking of you" as she took a "thoughtful stroll in her garden." She hoped that "tonight, we can meet at the Cinema Capitol on Budapesterstrasse[53] to watch your favourite actress in her latest, aptly named film, *The Road to Freedom*, for the 2200 showing. And afterwards, who can say?" It was signed, "Hopefully, H." A ticket was enclosed with the note. I knew who'd sent it. Brückner had used "H" for Hannibal[54] before.

Since the Gestapo ran the centre, Brückner and I knew that no message to or from anyone at the Chancellery was secure—knowledge made immediate and obvious when the clerk winked as he handed me the "sealed" note. Why Brückner chose not to rely on my recently restored personal "mail slot" or some even more clandestine method troubled me, but at the time, I was too

---

[53] Located in the Charlottenburg district of West Berlin, this famous cinema was designed by architect Hans Poelzig in 1925 and opened with a screening of Charlie Chaplin's *The Gold Rush*. Seating was provided for 1,284 patrons: 737 in the orchestra, 32 in loge seats, 405 in the front balcony, and 110 in the rear balcony. The cinema also had a 50-piece orchestra and an organ.

[54] Hannibal, the Carthaginian military commander and tactician, is popularly credited as one of most talented commanders in history. He lost one of his eyes during the crossing of the Apennines.

elated to concern myself with logistics. Considering it now, as I write, he was the one who'd recommended hiding in plain sight.

I needed to concoct a plan for manipulating the Führer, a notorious night owl, into allowing me to make the 2200 show, but while contemplating, I received a mysterious, ungrammatically written summons from Günsche to meet with some unnamed party in a relatively small side room of the Führer's enormous reception gallery. I arrived to see a small, precise, baldish man with a small, beakish nose, protruding ears, and priggishly pursed lips—the face of an arrogant vulture. He was attired in an SS lieutenant colonel's uniform similar to mine, but unlike mine, his was bespoke. We saluted and shook hands, and I waited while he reached into his inside jacket pocket and lifted out a narrow blue box of Gauloise cigarettes, carefully selected one, screwed it into a yellowish-beige ivory holder, lit it ceremoniously with an exquisite gold lighter, and took a deep drag.

"Would you care for one?" he offered once he'd returned the box to his pocket.

"No, thank you," I said. "I don't smoke."

"Ah, like our Führer," he replied with a crooked smile and a short nod. "Admirable. Incidentally, I just came back from a visit to Auschwitz, and I have been asked to convey to you Commandant Höss's sincere regards. He hopes you had an adequate opportunity to appreciate that, under his creative and assiduous stewardship, his camp will soon become the microcosm of a new, pure Reich."

"One day there was more than sufficient," I replied with an icy stare. "Please convey that to him. Now, how can I help you, Herr Lieutenant Colonel?" It sounded like a sensible prompt, since I was still waiting for a name and a purpose.

He took another tip-glowing drag, this time letting the holder and its contents jut from the corner of his mouth,

Roosevelt-style. "Yes, of course, forgive me, Herr Linge. Nothing serious. Merely a social visit. We spoke on the telephone a few months ago. You may remember me. I'm Eichmann, General Heydrich's specialist on Jewish affairs."

I knew who he was. Aside from his visit to my quarters with Heydrich some years before, when the Führer had proposed his well-meaning-but-fanciful Madagascar Plan, he'd told me he'd sent it to a thoroughly disinterested Himmler as a courtesy. Himmler, in turn, had passed it all the way down to Eichmann, who, when victory over Britain had become a shattered dream, tossed the plan onto the RSHA's bureaucratic rubbish heap. He was also the first officer I'd asked for the whereabouts of Ziggy.

"You asked me about locating a friend of yours, as I recall. I trust you were successful?"

You filthy bastard! You fucking "recall"—and you know damn well about my success! "Yes, thank you for your interest. I did locate my friend. A most memorable reunion, all things considered."

"Yes, I believe I heard something. Well, I'm pleased to hear it." With a watchmaker's delicacy, he pinched out the stub of his cigarette, replaced it with a fresh one, and lit it. "Ah, you noticed my lighter," he said, quite gratuitously. "A gift from the Hebrew community, you might say. Solid gold, painstakingly fabricated from gold fillings from Jews who had no further need of them."

Calculated movements, casual sadism, no verbal contractions: one of Hedwig's "fastidious men." *But why is he here? What does he really want? Why me?*

"How can I be of service?" I asked the swine once more, hoping to get the ordeal over with and resume planning for this evening.

"Yes, of course. I can be quite the chatterbox at times." Another drag. "We heard that the Führer may have determined to attack the Soviet Union quite soon. Now, if these reports are accurate, an almost incalculable influx of Slavs and Jews will grace our camps. But these are only rumours. We need to know if they are, in fact, true. In this, you can be of enormous assistance with your… tangential relationship to the Führer."

First, Mussolini, now this filth. "Tan… what?"

"Yes, of course. Forgive me. I mean a relationship not connected to him politically, socially, or militarily."

"You mean a servant."

"Exactly. You are in an especially unique position to hear what the Führer really means and intends, where others have no such access and ability, you understand?"

I understood. "But I still don't understand. If what you want is a spy, why not someone far more… sophisticated, like my superior, Günsche, for instance? His job is to listen."

Eichmann forced a muffled chuckle round his cigarette holder. "Yes, Günsche. Ordinarily, an adjutant would make an ideal infor—ah, source, but you have been with the Führer far longer and so obviously acquired a degree of affinity and trust unavailable to someone so new and untested."

What Eichmann really meant was that Günsche was an idiot and hardly an intimate of the Führer. "But Herr Eichmann," I continued, "even if I were to change the attitudes and habits of a lifetime, not to mention venture beyond the capabilities of my memory and boundaries of my position, you must be aware that the Führer is notoriously secretive, and—"

"I know what you're thinking"—an attempt at placation—"you are concerned about violating your oath of personal loyalty, a quality to be prized and encouraged. But I can assure you that what I am asking is based upon an even higher loyalty, namely loyalty to the Führer's vision. For, with the proper information, the Reichsführer can adequately prepare the way and so make the Führer's prodigious task far simpler and infinitely more comprehensive. Do you see?"

I saw. This was nothing new in kind, my friend, only in degree. *How many of these needy nabobs had there been and, at the time, meant nothing to me?* But now, after Mussolini, my pulse was racing. Over the years, I'd been urged furtively by the loftiest dignitaries—whether financial, industrial, ecclesiastical, political, artistic, scientific, or military—to assess the Führer's mood before and after a critical meeting, and I would attempt to be as accurate and detailed as my persona, discretion, and the clever Führer would permit. But never, until now, had I ever been asked by anyone to spy and relate secret information. Short of another imaginary assassination entreaty from the imaginary Emerald, I wouldn't have believed that even Himmler would stoop to snoop on the Führer—and through me, of all people. But now, Eichmann ended even that paltry residue of innocence left in me.

"I understand, Herr Eichmann," I told him. "For the sake of the Führer's vision, I'll do my best, but I can't promise anything. If he chooses to remain closed unto himself until he's ready to announce his decision, I'll have nothing to convey to you."

Eichmann raised his hands in a conciliatory gesture. "We could not ask for more than that. And regardless, you will have earned the gratitude of the Reichsführer—and that is no small thing."

You and *the Reichsführer can go to hell, along with his gratitude!* "Then I hope for a most worthy outcome," I said.

Eichmann slid out his cigarette holder, removed the remnants of his cigarette, leaned over, dropped it daintily into the nearest ashtray, and returned the holder to his inside tunic pocket. A faint smile insinuated itself around the edges of his mouth.

"Yes, Herr Linge, 'most worthy,' and most appreciated." He held out a gloved hand. "To seal our bargain?"

I extended my own hand, sans glove. "Yes, Herr Eichmann," I promised, "a bargain then." *That will be the fucking day!* I thought as his perfectly tailored little figure receded down the hallway.

⁂

I was so shaken by Eichmann's extraordinary visit that, by the time I reached the Führer's antechamber, I still hadn't worked out how I could get leave to see Leander's film. I was about to enter when Günsche caught me.

"Did you meet with Eichmann?" he inquired with calculated blandness, a subtlety of which I thought the dolt utterly incapable.

"We met," I answered him with equal blandness.

"Anything you can tell me?"

"Nothing earth-shattering, Otto," I said. "Just a social call concerning an old friend I'd asked him about, and some small talk about nothing in particular."

Günsche shrugged. "What do you think of Eichmann? I've never met him, you know."

"Same here, except by phone," I lied. "Those RSHA boys keep to themselves."

"Kinda glad of that," he admitted.

"I hear you," I concurred. "How's the Führer?"

Günsche smiled his dopey smile. "Oh, great—now. Before, he was chewing out General von Rundstedt for, I think, being only lukewarm on the Russia thing. I didn't understand the general's point, and it was pretty hard to hear him over the Führer's screaming. But now he's in a great mood."

"Von Rundstedt?" I asked jokingly.

"No, Heinz," he responded with the testy tolerance of a moron trying to explain something to an even bigger moron. "The Führer."

"Ah, the Führer," I said. "And why this sudden change in weather?"

"Weather?"

"Sorry, I meant the Führer's mood."

"Well, now he's with Speer, and you know how that is. He'll probably be with him all afternoon and way into the evening, you can bet."

I experienced an internal shudder of delight at the news that only required official confirmation, and I was free.

I entered the study, the vast region strewn with enormous furled and unfurled white-on-blue architect's drafting paper lying ankle-deep on the carpet and scattered willy-nilly across the trestle-length table, just in time to hear the Führer declare:

"All right then, draw up a decree in my name ordering full-scale resumption of work on the Berlin buildings. You're quite right. Paris was beautiful. That I grant you. But Berlin must be made far more beautiful, as befits the new capital of Europe. You and I must design it so that Paris will be only a pale shadow. Then," he said, "there will be no reason for me to obliterate it."

I could see from the colour draining from his face that, despite his long association (and the brutal example of blitz-krieg-demolished Warsaw), the elegant and urbane architect was startled by the Führer's nonchalant and wanton willingness to raze a treasure of Western culture. I was far less troubled since my own long association taught me to take much of the extravagance of the Führer's assertions with a healthy measure of scepticism.

But in any event, I cared little about the matter, one way or the other, as I stood in a corner directly in the Führer's sight line, my brain occupied solely by the hope that the Führer would excuse me from my evening duties. With Arndt away[55] and Schaub in the hospital, without me, the Führer was fresh out of menials. After I stood like a stone sentinel for an hour, becoming desperate, Schroeder arrived with some papers requiring a signature, and I had an idea. Unnoticed by the architecturally absorbed Führer and a discreet Speer, she placed them on top of a growing stack on his desk. On her way out, she stole a glance at my calculated eye shift towards the door, and she wagged her index finger for me to follow, which I did, also unnoticed.

"What's wrong now, Linge?" she asked in the hallway with mock curtness, Schroeder's version of warmth.

I shrugged. "I didn't mean for you to see that."

She *tsk-tsk*-ed and shook her head. "When are you going to realise how transparent you are? All right, what's the big problem?"

"I have an important late-evening appointment, and I haven't been able to speak to the Führer about it."

She chuckled crookedly and rubbed her hands together, in the manner of a cartoon wicked witch, Schroeder's version of humour. "Is this your first day here?" she chided. "Get Arndt to stand in. You should know that when the Führer's sequestered with Speer, he's in another world, unaware and uncaring of all else round him. The Führer won't know the difference and so needn't give you permission."

"Unfortunately, Arndt's on leave. Anyone else you can suggest?"

"Linge," she said with no little consternation, "I provide advice, not staffing services." Schroeder's version of assistance.

---

[55] Wilhelm Arndt, born in 1913, was sent to the Dienerschule Pasing (servants' school) and eventually became one of Hitler's sub-valets.

I shrugged and scrunched my face in helpless perplexity as a last chance.

"All right," she finally said. "Get that huge oaf Günsche to do it?"

"To find a valet?" my persona asked.

"No, dumbhead," she said. "Get him to take your place. One night won't kill him, and the Führer's so involved with Speer that he'll accept whoever's in front of him."

Pour it on. "But, Fräulein Schroeder, Günsche outranks me, even though I outrank him. I can't ask him to take on valet duties as well as his own."

"A coward as well as no imagination," she sniped, fists jammed into her waist. "What the Devil did Klara see in you? All right, Herr Confidence, he doesn't outrank me. I'll ask him for you. Let him refuse me."

I smiled broadly. "I do see what Klara saw in *you*," I sniped back, well over her head.

"Now, go to your appointment," she commanded, then turned and walked away.

∾

At 2145, sans uniform, I slotted myself into the undulating crowd as they streamed into the theatre. I made my way up the majestic staircase to the rear balcony and took the seat that corresponded to the number on my ticket. As I sank into the plush seat, I suffered a momentary stab of sorrow and rage, as it occurred to me that, due to Klara's deafness, it had been ages since I'd watched a film while seated, rather than standing by the Führer's projector.

Within five minutes, all the seats were occupied, save for one on my immediate right by the aisle, presumably for the eye-patched Brückner to arrive inconspicuously and unobtrusively once the lights had been extinguished but before the movie began—a critical interlude of complete darkness.

It happened as expected. In the blackness, I could make out a vague shadow, hear the faint clunk and pfshhh of a cushioned seat being lowered and compressed, and then hear a whispered voice I knew so well.

"It's a good thing I chose the back row," he whispered, "or we'd be getting complaints from normal people who can't see over you." Brückner snorted approval of his little joke. "I missed you, my friend."

There was an awkwardness I'd never experienced with Brückner, even from the beginning of our association. I suspected he felt the same, and it was disquieting, like meeting a relative you never knew you had, with all its expectation, tension, awkwardness, caution, and suspense.

"I missed you too, Wilhelm," I whispered back, "though trying to contact you would give someone quite the opposite impression."

"Yes, I regret that, more than you could know, mainly because I couldn't tell you why I maintained my detachment."

"Couldn't? Can you tell me now?"

"Have you seen this film?" he asked, still a master of deflection.

Indulge him as always; he'll tell you in his own good time. "No, she's extremely popular with the public, but not so much with Goebbels, who still has a hearty dislike of social and political aloofness, especially if it's towards him and the Reich—in that order—and so, no special screening."

"She was also popular with you, as I recall."

"Was," I replied. "Like you, she suddenly dropped all communication with me, no warning, no explanation. I took the hint."

After a conspicuous pause, "I've seen the film," he informed me. "It's mediocre at best, but we should have mercy on those who don't know that yet. Let's go somewhere reasonably sequestered, that doesn't discourage frank talk, and do some catching up. What do you say?"

There was nothing to say.

❧

With its location, and no sign or lights outside, it would have been easy to miss. Huddled beneath the Anhalter Bahnhof railway terminus, well off the beaten track (no pun intended), the enormous iron door at the entrance suggested that if it were not a warehouse, then privacy was paramount, with secrecy not a distant follower. Three-and-a-half discrete knocks, followed by a pause and two more, and we were ushered into a cramped space with bare walls, a ceiling resting only inches above my head, and a floor of unevenly dried cement. The meagre light emanating from the low-wattage bulb within the geometric labyrinth of a Tiffany lamp was eye-squintingly dim, but I could still see that, aside from a barman, we appeared to be the only patrons. We took a rickety, slapped-together wooden table against the far wall, which Brückner angled so that both of us faced the door.

"Does this place have a name?" I asked.

"None that's spoken of. The Party had such places shut down as too unsavoury for the new, immaculate Germany. This one managed to survive, I imagine, because of the delightful fact that not all Germans are yet immaculate."

"How did you learn of it?"

"From Bella, who learned of it through her unnamed SS friend. She said it promised privacy, and I think you have to admit"—he waved his arm—"it delivered. Even our famous German efficiency must sometimes yield to humanity."

His wave seemed to signal the barman, who hurried over to us in character, a small, dark, stocky person of no particular account, a folded towel draped over his arm, and an eager expression. Perfect, even if counterfeit. "What can I get you gentlemen?"

Brückner looked at me.

"How about a drink in Bella's honour?" I suggested.

"Fitting. Go ahead."

I glanced up at the barman. "Two Zombies, please."

"Zombies," he repeated with a quizzical expression, as if suspecting I'd used a code word to which he wasn't privy.

"Right." I explained the formula.

He nodded dubiously and scurried away.

I turned back to Brückner and made the kind of face a dog makes when tasting something unexpectedly disgusting. "For his sake, I hope he doesn't try to sample it."

"We'll soon know," he quipped.

"Speaking of privacy," I asked, "what about the bartender?"

"I've been assured that he's a master of discretion. He'll leave once he's served us. I promised I'd lock up after him. Private enough?"

I didn't reply to a question I considered rhetorical, so I merely nodded.

We sat in silence for a few moments, and soon, our drinks arrived, and the server made ready to leave. We waited until the massive iron door thudded shut behind him.

"He didn't lock the door," I ventured. "What's to prevent—"

"Engel's adjutant is stationed right outside, freezing in the cold, I might say. And for good measure, there's another exit not so easily discovered. So a toast then." Brückner raised his glass.

"Yes," I said, raising mine, "but to what?"

After a moment, "I have it. How about a favourable change in the weather?"

I laughed to myself, recalling my ridiculous exchange with Günsche. I knew better than to assume Brückner meant anything even remotely meteorological, so I merely said, "Yes, to a favourable change in the weather." I clicked his glass, took a prudent sip, winced, and left the toast's meaning to eventual revelation. Sitting there, I sensed hesitation in both of us, which I attributed to distance and time, and their possible connection to Brückner's agenda. At least that was my case, for I'd taken a page from Hugo's *Les Misérables*:

Everyone has noticed the taste which cats have for pausing and lounging between the two leaves of a half-shut door. Who is there who has not said to a cat, "Do come in!" There are men who, when an incident stands half-open before them, have the same tendency to halt in indecision between two resolutions, at the risk of getting crushed through the abrupt closing of the adventure by fate. The over-prudent cats, as they are, and because they are cats, sometimes incur more danger than the audacious.

We were both being over-prudent. *But,* I wondered, *how long before audacity overtakes one of us, or both?*

Brückner drew a breath, smiled, paused for a long moment, then spoke very slowly, emphasising each word. "I must confess that I hesitated before contacting you."

"But why?" I asked, with an honest expression of incredulity.

"I was afraid that I'd caused you to feel betrayed and that you would hate me for it."

I was struggling with something and so didn't reply for a moment: *Why did he seek me out now, after being incomprehensibly incommunicado? What does he know? What does he want?* These were questions I would never have asked about Brückner before. But now...

"For a time," I said, "I had reservations about the nature

and degree of our friendship. But later, I became too involved in other betrayals, other hatreds, and other priorities."

He nodded sadly. "You've grown, Heinz."

"You should see Günsche," I quipped.

"I mean you've evolved."

"Yes," I said, "maybe it was an unexpected effect of your departure. No longer a reactive ape, I can now stand upright and sentient but, unfortunately, with a slight, lingering stoop." I regretted my lapse of persona, the double entendre, and the snideness of my words. But it was still Brückner, and regret was a useless emotion, so I dismissed it.

"Hardly noticeable, and useful when negotiating bunker doorways," Brückner replied, joining in my imagery with an admiring and conciliatory smile. "From orphan to urchin to petty criminal to bricklayer to valet to… what? A fascinating but incomplete trajectory."

I had no response to give, so I gave none. Like the Führer, he would get to the point in his own time, in his own way, but I suspected that it was situated somewhere within the word "incomplete." *But how much of my evolution, my "trajectory," could I allow him to know?* So many years, so many laughs, so many confidences should have meant something—everything! But here, now, with a matter about which I'd never have hesitated, a voice in my brain counselled caution. Tears began to gather in the corners of my eyes, and I wiped them away with my sleeve.

"We haven't much time," Brückner said with an edgy, unpleasant laugh, once letting loose a string of trivialities about his life in Paris, "so I'll get right to the point. There are those of us no longer with direct access who wonder what the Führer's playing at with this Soviet thing, and what you might know about it."

It was plain and to the point. *What did those who were wondering know or suspect—and why did they care?* The critical why. I took a long time to consider my response, then, "I had a visit from Heydrich's man, Eichmann," I told him, "who wanted to know the same thing."

"That prissy pencil pusher? I don't blame him. Himmler can taste the massive infusion of Slavs into his inferno. And he wanted you to—"

"Spy on the Führer and report. He was so anxious his cigarette could hardly stay in its holder."

Brückner grimaced, reached inside his jacket for his own cigarette holder, then appeared to decide against it. There was a pause, just enough for him to take a deep breath. "What do you think?"

I was tormented by my decision to dissemble, but Brückner's elusion and sudden emergence tormented me more. "Think? Think about what? An attack? Eichmann's request? Your people—whoever they are—who are wondering? Look, Wilhelm, I didn't suddenly wake up as an alert and astute political and military strategist. I'm still a fundamentally ignorant valet who stands mindlessly in corners or clears tables, floors, and toilet bowls while the Führer is conducting complex affairs of state." Then I laughed, instantly aware of the idiotic insincerity of my words in the presence of the one man who would know otherwise, and by his ironic expression, he did.

Brückner folded his hands as a theatrical manifestation of infinite patience and forbearance. "All right then, Herr Ignorant Valet," he quipped, "I'll enlighten you. Our sources tell us that the Führer's right on the cusp of deciding to attack the Soviet Union, an invasion to be launched quite soon. Am I right?"

"Eichmann certainly seems to think so," I answered to buy time.

"Eichmann's thoughts don't concern me," Brückner said with a slight frown. "Yours do."

I could stall him no longer and maintain any semblance of credibility. "The Führer appears determined," I said.

"He's had some encouragement, I think."

"Mussolini has been lobbying him."

He laughed. "That bombastic, strutting puff pastry? The Führer would give more attention to a dripping faucet. No, my friend, he's had some strategic prodding from someone for whom he must have the highest regard. Nothing short of that would persuade him to make such a momentous and catastrophic decision."

I didn't bother to affect any silly, infantile wide evenness. "Catastrophic? From what I've heard—from you, actually—it's just a matter of time before that paranoid maniac Stalin decides to attack us."

"Yes, my friend," he replied, "nothing short of catastrophic. And 'just a matter of time' is exactly what we don't have. We thought you might have an idea who that someone might be. Think about it, Heinz. Think about it hard. And quickly, for there's far more at stake than that person might imagine. And should you discover who that influential person is, please be good enough to ask him if he's ever heard of the Law of Unforeseen Consequences."

From that moment, I knew that this entire conversation was a charade, an absurd pretence, but I also knew that both of us were prisoners of that charade and had to play it out to its inevitable conclusion.

"So, what is this law?" I asked, though I'd read of it years before.

Brückner smiled in his faintly superior way, a characteristic that had amused me before but now rankled. I tried fighting it, but as I gazed at my old friend and mentor, I saw only a stranger.

"It's a phenomenon," he began, "in which any action has results that are not part of the actor's purpose. These consequences may or may not be foreseeable or even immediately observable. For my purposes, even though the intended consequences are successful, there are negative consequences that make the original problem far worse."

To underscore my assumed incomprehension, I moulded my face into an expression of artless bewilderment.

"Look, Heinz, I'll tell you a true story. I'm amazed Baur didn't beat me to it. When our movement was still in its infancy and populated with more crackpots than serious ideologues, one of these characters placed a crude-but-effective bomb on a government mail plane. After the bomb exploded in flight, destroying the aircraft and killing the pilot and co-pilot, the bomber was arrested for intentional murder, and his defence—and he clearly believed it—was that he merely intended to destroy the plane, not to kill anyone. A poor example perhaps, but you get the idea."

"So, am I to search for a crackpot?" I asked, partly in jest.

"Not this time." He chuckled dryly. "Oh, he may sound like one from time to time, but he definitely is not. That's the real tragedy. With all the best intentions, he may well cause the Führer to actually give the order to attack that savage, aboriginal colossus to the east, thus plunging us into a calamitous two-front war. And while this would be a boon for those simpletons who would, in their ignorance of the law I just described, welcome merely a change of regime, it would actually be at the cost of the obliteration of an entire generation of Germans in a military and political defeat from which she would never recover. An unqualified hellish disaster for the Reich. So, given what's at stake, this someone must be found quickly and persuaded at all costs to abandon his efforts."

Though we seemed to have resolved to communicate at oblique angles to each other, our words managed to intersect, and a cold sweat trickled down my neck as the implications folded their tendrils round my brain and began to squeeze. I imagined an extension of our conversation:

Me: But, Wilhelm, what if I can't find this someone—or if I do, he won't change his plans?

Wilhelm: Guess.

But my thoughts now weren't tranquil or linear enough to ask Brückner why those concerned parties with so much at stake wouldn't just eliminate that "someone" here and now and be done with it. I started to reply, but Brückner shot up his hand when there was a reverberating crash.

"We'd better check outside."

"How about using that second exit?" I offered.

"One was arranged as a signal to come out," he told me. "He probably considers it time to leave without undue fanfare."

When I swung open the massive door with a grunt, a fist of frigid air struck my face, and I almost stumbled over the corpse, whose identity in the moonlight I could only determine by the mangled badge of rank dangling from his shoulder boards. After both of us scanned the area in all directions and determined that we were surrounded only by emptiness, Brückner placed his hand on my arm.

"You're the young giant. You do the honours—but don't get any gore on your nice civilian suit."

I nodded, puffed some visible air from my nostrils, shrugged, bent down, grabbed the dead man's legs at the ankles, and dragged him inside while Brückner pushed the door shut and fastened the bolt.

Now in a lighted area and even from a slight distance, I could see that the corpse's face was almost devoid of skin. Without eyelids, the cloudy blue eyes stared sightlessly ahead, and the lipless mouth below the cavity where his nose had been hung open in the J-shape of a briar pipe. I could see—and smell—that at the point of death, his bowels had been released. Thick blood crept over the rim of the jagged slash across his abdomen, spilling out coils of glistening grey intestines. A messy end to this sentinel's mission. Having seen Adelsheimer and Ziggy, I believed I was inured to mutilation, but inside, I still recoiled at the sight—and the stench. I craved a deep breath but resisted, knowing what I would encounter if I did. My forehead, despite the chill, ran with sweat. The urge to urinate was almost overpowering, and I tensed my entire body, afraid that I would wet myself.

"General Engel's adjutant?" I asked, a gratuitous, tension-induced formality.

Brückner's mouth puckered in dismay. "Hard to tell for certain. But as an educated guess, I'd say it was. A battlefield right here at home," he remarked, seeing my face. "Between Auschwitz and Berlin, many of the delightful sights you missed in the last war you're getting in this one." The lightness of his words aside, his face was very composed, though I could detect a justifiable edge of concern in his voice. "Perhaps after this, you'll give some thought at least to what certain others consider at stake."

"If these 'certain others'—whoever they are—go to this extent, what kept them outside?"

"Excellent question, Heinz. I'm afraid I can only conjecture at this point, but I'd say it was to deliver a message, not unlike others you've received, only a bit more emphatic: for you to perform an action or to desist from performing an action. You'd need to be intact for either task. Or maybe they suspect..." He let whatever he was about to say trail off.

"In any case," he went on, "you need to get back to the Chancellery, and so tonight, I'll be the valet and sort this out." He nodded down to the former adjutant. "But first." He bared his nails and scratched my face with just enough force to sting and draw a little blood, ripped one of my lapels, and let it hang by a few threads, then reached into his inside jacket pocket and brought out a tiny ornate vial. He unscrewed the top, dabbed some pale-yellow liquid onto his palm, and patted me on my suit jacket and trousers, then screwed the lid back on. When he replaced the bottle, he took out a tiny tube of lipstick and applied the greasy redness to his lips. After, he asked me to bend down, which I did with a quizzical expression, then he leaned over and pressed his painted lips hard against my neck, managing to smear some lipstick on my shirt collar. I strained not to flinch.

"For cover and credibility," he explained, "to validate the perfumed note. Don't fiddle with yourself before you make certain that enough of the right people see you. Just don't tell them how you actually received it," he added drily. "Also, you needn't know what the film was about, since you obviously didn't see much," he added with a sneaky smile. "And consider this evening well, my friend," he said as we parted company.

I considered more than that as I made my frigid, dishevelled way back to the Chancellery. The great Nietzsche wrote: "I'm not upset that you lied to me, I'm upset that from now on, I can't believe you." Brückner's attitudes and recommendations over the past year, his recent dodging, his sudden emergence, and the terrible death of Engel's adjutant grievously tested all I felt I'd gotten to know about my old friend and mentor since joining the Führer's household. *Have I lost Brückner as well as Klara?*

AFTER AMPLY DISPLAYING my "amorous adventure" at several strategic and a few superfluous checkpoints (eliciting the desired coarse rejoinders), washing up, writing to you, and ruminating over the previous several hours, I was afforded little sleep before the Führerbuzzer yanked me into consciousness. Of all that had happened, I mused on Brückner's cryptic words as I dressed. *"Or maybe they suspect…"* troubled and perplexed me even more than Brückner's "request" or the mutilation-murder of Engel's adjutant. *They? Suspect what?* I harboured no doubts that Brückner and those "someones" knew it was me and what I was attempting to do, though the why probably eluded them, assuming they cared. But it was different with me, the why of it, and it troubled me then and still did, but I hadn't the wherewithal to pursue it today. My head was in such agony that I needed one of Morell's elixirs, so I groaned myself dressed and was making for the Führer's rooms, hoping the doctor was getting his patient ready to greet the day, when Baur and Kempka stopped me.

"Well, if it ain't Herr Jockstrap," Kempka called, and several heads turned to both the source and the object, then resumed their activities.

"The Führer," I sputtered, "I was buzzed—"

"I know what it's for," Baur interrupted, "so there's no rush."

"Speer's still there," Kempka said. "All fucking night. You may need to tend to him before dealing with the Führer. And by the look on your face, the Führer may have to tend to you. And poor Günsche. He's still there too. I figure you owe him a keg of his favourite lager."

"We're just glad to see that you finally got over Klara," Baur said.

"What are you talking about?"

"Come on, kiddo," Baur remarked with flattened lips. "It's all over the Chancellery."

"What's all over the—"

"Coy dog."

"One of Kitty's vicious vixens?" Kempka ventured.

"No, some stupid arranged date?"

"A date's only stupid if the female's *not* stupid," Baur declared. "I worry about you, Heinz. You always seem to need intelligence and sensitivity in a female. A disaster, my friend. By now, you should know that better than most."

"Believe me, Hans," I countered, "you can see that she was anything but smart and sensitive. By halfway through the evening, she was so sloppy drunk that when she finished with my face and my only good suit, she couldn't even find my belt. Then, when I tried to sober her up by taking her into the cold night air, she started shouting slurred insults at me in the street, so I had to flag down a taxi, throw her in, and race back to the Chancellery."

"My God, how the fuck did you find this creature?" Kempka asked.

"She was recommended by one of the Führer's temporary secretaries. I imagine she'll be gone when I visit to convey my appreciation."

"You should have the Gestapo convey it," Baur suggested.

"The less Gestapo, the better," I said. "It's enough to have gotten away in one piece."

"True," Kempka admitted, "who the fuck needs the damn Gestapo when we have Bormann?"

"Bormann's worse than the Gestapo," Baur added with a sneer. "At least the Gestapo sleeps from time to time."

"You should have seen the fuckin' Bear when he was told that Günsche would be taking your place last night," Kempka said. "He was chatting away with Kaltenbrunner,[56] when one of his unofficial snoops came up to him, whispered some shit in his ear, and left. Then Bormann said to Kaltenbrunner, 'You asked me what that pampered bastard is up to? I'll tell you, Ernst, just a feeling, but I say that nothing's what it seems with Linge. He plays the village idiot well and seems to fool everyone—including the Führer—but he doesn't fool me. I know he's up to something. But for the Führer's indulgence, I'd have the answers, you bet, and quick.' Then there was a pause. 'But maybe you can—' he started to say, but Kaltenbrunner cut him off, saying, 'Not a chance, Martin. As you said, the Führer has this thing for the fellow, and my boss won't interfere without absolute evidence of serious double-dealing.'"

"How do you know all this, Erich?" I watched him intently, severely distressed.

"From one of my own unofficial snoops," he said.

"Business as usual at HQ," Baur added. "Look, Heinz, promise that from now on, you'll come to me or Kempka here before accepting the dating recommendations of strangers."

Headache still pounding, I nodded a painful agreement, relieved that the subterfuge had achieved its desired result and

---

[56] One of Himmler's favourites, Ernst Kaltenbrunner was, like many of the regime's ideological fanatics, a committed anti-Semite. Under Kaltenbrunner's command, the persecution of Jews picked up pace. Kaltenbrunner stayed constantly informed of the status of concentration camp activities, receiving periodic reports at his office in the RSHA. He is reputed to have said, "Whenever I hear the word culture, I reach for my revolver."

more determined than ever to steer clear of Bormann and his clandestine army of snitches.

"All right then," Baur asserted, "when your 'war wounds' have healed, I think I may have the perfect female for you. I'll tell you all about her later, but now, you'd better relieve Günsche before he starts to shrink."

With Rommel poised to show the Allies what for (the Führer presumably arranging for a test of the "unconscious prescience" I demonstrated after Mussolini's visit), I had no time to lose in proceeding to my plan's next phase: raising someone truly loathsome over someone merely pitiful. I'd read that "the enemy of my enemy is my friend," an ancient proverb suggesting that two opposing parties can or should work together against a common enemy, and its efficacy had been historically proven. I needed Hess for one thing only, then once that was accomplished, I would release him to the wolves, or in this case, a bear.

I knew that Hess was haunted by his health to the point of hypochondria, consulting many doctors and other practitioners for a long list of illusory ailments involving his kidneys, colon, gallbladder, bowels, and heart. Since, as I'd hoped, the Führer had called his deputy and heir to Berlin from his home in Munich without warning or explanation, it wasn't terribly difficult to track him to Morell's unofficial surgery. With my history of authentic migraines, "member dysfunction," not to mention my fabricated episode in front of the Führer, it would be perfectly natural for me to be sitting anxiously in Morell's antechamber as the doctor escorted Hess out with a joke that only Morell seemed to find funny. In all my years at the Chancellery, I'd never seen Hess even smile, much less laugh, even at some witticism of the Führer's. And now was no exception.

"Anyway, I'm certain that will suit for now, Herr Deputy," Morell told Hess as he handed him a small blue box.

Hess merely nodded.

"And should—" Morell started to say, then stopped abruptly and turned from Hess when he spotted me shooting up from the couch and saluting. "I'll see you presently, Herr Linge. As soon as—"

"I didn't… know, please… forgive my intrusion," I stammered with as much awkward humility as I could realistically muster.

Two sets of pursed lips responded. "No intrusion, Herr Linge." Morell smiled. "This is, in a sense, my waiting room, yes, Herr Deputy Führer?"

"Indeed," Hess confirmed, with his usual absence of expression, his bony face shadowy with a beard and his dark eyes sunken into their sockets. Then he saluted, shook Morell's hand, peeled off his surgical gloves, handed them to the doctor, and made for the door.

"Now, Linge," Morell began, "what's the—"

"No, Herr Doctor," I corrected. "Actually, I've come to see the deputy Führer."

Hess halted at the door and turned. "You wanted to see me?" he asked, his translucent eyelids set at half-mast.

"Yes, Herr Deputy, I have a matter in which I require your advice, if you'll permit me."

Hess glanced quickly at Morell. "Thank you, Doctor," he said.

With that, Morell nodded, turned, and quickly disappeared back into his surgery.

Hess turned to fix his hypnotic gaze on me. "Is this from the Führer?"

"He doesn't know I'm here, Herr Deputy," I said. "I'm here for myself."

"Hmm," Hess murmured. "Most intriguing. Well then, can I buy you a cup of coffee?"

"I'd be grateful," I answered.

He had no idea how intriguing.

❧

We sat at a relatively small table in the Officers' Dining Room, Hess's back to the door, which I appreciated. I had no sense that his choice of position was anything but casual. Of all the most intimate members of the Führer's inner circle, Rudolf Hess was, without question, the most unassuming. Unlike the rest, Hess had not built a power base or developed a coterie of leeches or sycophants. It seemed to me (and to Brückner, who, even with his insights, never ceased claiming to be dumbfounded by Hess) that he appeared motivated solely by his loyalty to the Führer and a desire to be useful to him. He did not seek power or take advantage of his position like Goebbels and Himmler, accumulate personal prestige and wealth like Göring, or envelop the Führer like Bormann. And no less important—and no less dangerous, at least to my purpose—I knew that Hess was deeply concerned that the Führer's rabid antipathy towards Stalin might cause Germany to face a war on two fronts, an unqualified disaster, in his estimation.

Now Hess sat, hands folded, with a benign expression of infinite patience and forbearance on his face. "And now, Herr Linge, what can I do for you?"

I had to choose my words carefully and well: on the one hand, to show ignorance, and on the other, to ensure I made a point that would be understood and appreciated by someone steeped in the occult.

"This is difficult for me, Herr Deputy," I began. "I would not presume to… involve you in my feeble problem, were it not for your reputation as a man with vast sensitivity and knowledge of things not easily or necessarily explained by logic."

He looked at me in dubious silence for a moment, his eyes seeming to have receded even further into his skull. "Go on," was all he said, so I did.

"I don't mean dreams, Herr Deputy, though I can't rule that out, but it's more than…" I hesitated in order to measure any interest I might have generated. I saw none. "I thought that perhaps the Führer may have spoken to you of it."

"I've heard no 'it' yet, Herr Linge." He shrugged patiently and sat back, lacing his hands across his lap. "But of such matters in general, at one time he would have, but as you must be aware, considering your unique position, we speak very little of late—of anything. I say this to you in the strictest confidence, of course."

"Of course, Herr Deputy," I assured him, then leaned forward onto my elbows. "If I may continue. Mysterious to me, many times over the years I've been asked if I exercise any volition in my dreams, and each time I answered with all honesty that I didn't know. However, recently, I've had the feeling that I do. Not necessarily as myself," I added, "but as others, who speak through me. Like… like a…" I held back to allow Hess to fill in the blank for greater authenticity.

"Medium?" he asked impassively.

I widened my eyes in rapt recognition. "Yes! Herr Deputy!" I exclaimed. "I think that's what it's called: a medium. Like with spirits, you know." Then, for a few pregnant moments, I let all the possible implications of my words circulate in the air round him. When he remained phlegmatic, I went on to describe in murky yet intelligible terms what I'd experienced in the Führer's study on 20 January, emphasising my complete yet removed awareness of what I'd said as Stalin, but that I had no memory of having moved like a sleepwalker to the Führer's desk chair to say it.

It was the merest flick of Hess's left eyelid, but I could tell that I'd touched a nerve, which I pressed home by adding that a voice I couldn't place—attached to a faint image, like a ghost image—had said that the only way for Germany to survive was for the Führer to make peace with Great Britain. Somehow, I must have related this to the Führer because he told me to calm myself and not to worry; the Germans were fully prepared, in both body and spirit, to utterly crush their enemies from any direction, so peace with Great Britain was both unnecessary and utterly out of the question.

I watched carefully as Hess drank his thick black coffee. An odd look passed over his face, and I tensed.

"And you say the Führer heard all this?"

I hesitated for a second and glanced round, as though to make sure no one was about to enter, then turned back. "I think so, Herr Deputy, but not everything." *Draw it out. Make Hess work for it.*

"All right," he said, "if not everything, then what?"

"I… I hesitate to say it."

"Clearly," he replied with a slight wry turn at the corners of his mouth—nothing short of unbridled hilarity for Hess. "But it seems that not telling me would defeat the purpose of this meeting, yes?"

Despite the dispassion in his tone, I sensed a sudden urgency, so I blurted, "What I didn't tell the Führer was that the same voice told me that only you could broker such a peace and so save Germany from destruction, and that it had to be done in complete secrecy."

Hess gazed at me for a moment, then, in a tone of utmost

earnestness said, "Is that the sum and substance of what you wanted to tell me?"

"Yes, Herr Deputy, except for the fact that he'd spoken in English, and yet I understood it, even though I know no language but German."

"Have you had visions, visitations, and astral projections before?"

I knew what he was referring to, but he was not to know that. "As… as… I… don't…" I stammered dramatically and underscored my feigned ignorance with a helpless shrug.

Hess nodded indulgently. "You must know what visions and visitations are. Astral projection means a wilful out-of-body experience that assumes the existence of a consciousness called an 'astral body' that is separate from the physical body and capable of travelling outside it throughout the universe. Have you had any of these before?"

To demonstrate thought, I pursed my lips tightly. "So far as my poor memory will allow, Herr Deputy, I haven't." I said no more.

There ensued a long, painful silence, during which he sipped his coffee quietly and sullenly. It seemed to me that he expected me to say something, was waiting for something in particular, but I knew from years of experience that the best thing to do was remain absolutely silent and listen. I'd seen enough to know that.

"Can you tell me," he finally asked, "anything about the voice you couldn't place and the image, no matter how faint, that told you that it was I alone who had to negotiate a peace agreement between Germany and Great Britain?"

The question was unexpected, though perfectly logical, and I had to buy time to conjure up the magic words. I sipped my now-cold coffee in such a manner that it produced a welcome bout of expectoration that took a waiter's napkin and Hess's dry expression to finally conquer. All the while, I was thinking that compared to Hess, Himmler was a hysteric.

"I'll try, Herr Deputy. I could only make out what seemed to me a corpulent frame, an enormous head, and gleaming eyes. I could make out no distinct features. His voice was resonant but with a stammer and lisp. I remember that whenever he said the word 'Nazi,' it came out as a drawled 'Naahhzee,' you know, no 't.'" Brückner would have appreciated my purposely leaving out the signature cigar. "That's all, I'm afraid."

A look of near transfiguration spread over his face. "Another coffee, Herr Linge? Yours seems to be mostly on your uniform jacket."

"I... my apol—"

I started to stammer, but Hess cut me off.

"None called for." He gestured to the waiter for two more coffees, which arrived almost instantly.

"I will tell you," he began after a careful sip, "that I've known of these... call them... episodes of yours, for some time now. As have select others. So, I'm not surprised at hearing of this latest one—although quite divergent in kind and degree. How much do you know of the occult?"

"I know little of anything, Herr Deputy."

"The perfect valet," he informed me. "Then I'll try to make it understandable for a simple fellow like you. The untutored masses consider the occult to be connected to the supernatural, with magical beliefs and practices. To them, it's not especially different from religion, which relies totally on faith and so is totally passive. However, to the initiated, the occult is knowledge of the hidden, and once discovered, that knowledge provides a set of instruments, mechanisms, and procedures to change the world round them and methods to take an active role in bringing about that change. To put it bluntly, occultists don't sit back and hope for a miracle; they create the miracle they need."

I gazed at Hess hesitantly. I was curious to know what "instruments, mechanisms, and procedures" he referred to, but my purpose demanded discipline, and his expression unmistakably counselled silence. In any case, I knew of at least one, sitting directly across from him.

I thought he began to say something, but instead, he nodded slightly towards the door, and I saw a large group of middle-rank Wehrmacht officers enter boisterously.

"I must say this to you quickly," Hess whispered. "The Führer will not know of our conversation. It's good that you came to me with your tale, for even if others would have believed it, they would not know how to act on it. I do. You've told me enough, so let's leave that clamorous horde to their own devices and go on our way, yes?"

We consumed the rest of our coffee in one swallow, then, with casual furtiveness, left, my errand for the moment completed.

12 February 1941

THIS MORNING, I learned that Rommel had arrived in Tripoli with his mission to do his worst to the Allies in North Africa. I hoped that this was just a bare beginning. Even with the Führer's obsession with Russia reinforced and Hess primed, I realised that for my plan to succeed, it was vital that Germany gain more effortless victories as soon as possible to set up the Führer for a prolonged main event.

❧

Considering the precarious sensitivity of my operation and Bormann's obsession with my situation, I needed to attract as little attention to myself as possible, so I finally resolved to end my bereavement over Klara and join the world of savage virility expected of all able-bodied SS officers. Instead of lunch, I ordered transportation and headed over to Baur's domain at Tempelhof Airport[57] to take him up on his request and my promise.

---

[57] After the Nazis took power, they set about redesigning Berlin. Tempelhof Airport was designed to wow visitors to the new Third Reich capital of Germania. It represents the monumental thinking behind Nazi architecture and stands as a landmark in civil engineering. The enormous facility was built by the Nazis on the site of a much smaller pre-existing airport between 1936 and 1941. Intended to be a statement of Nazi Germany greatness as well as a stage for Hitler to address the masses, the airport was only ever 80 percent finished. Ironically, the Nazis never actually used Tempelhof as an airport. During the war, they used it as a factory for building combat aircraft and weapons, including several Ju 87 "Stuka" dive bombers, which were built in the hangars. All of this work was done by forced labour.

I was obliged to wait in Baur's "office" while he was out testing some new aeronautical contraption. His office wasn't really an office but an immense, lavishly appointed foyer. After forty-five minutes, Baur came breezing in with a toothy grin and a hearty salute.

"It just hit me, Heinz, that you've never visited. How do you like my humble workplace?"

"Don't tell the Führer, or he'll order the Wehrmacht to invade and annex it."

"Not to worry," he said with a twinkle as he threw himself down on a plush executive chair that would have been Göring's envy. Instead of a desk, there was an immense, rectangular Art Nouveau trolley with a staggering number and variety of alcoholic beverages virtually smothering the surface. An incongruous, ersatz wooden table also supported a telephone, a locked letterbox, and a device similar to my Führerbuzzer, only more elaborate.

"With the Führer, nothing's too good for his pilot," he kidded, waving to a plush armchair. "Here, take the co-pilot's seat."

I sat.

"Care for a drink?" He leaned over, spreading his hands magisterially over the trolley.

"No thanks," I said. "I need to be able to drive back. In the car, I'm the pilot."

He chuckled and poured himself a sizeable tumbler of French brandy, which he downed in one gulp. "So, what brings you all the way to Tempelhof?"

I forced a shy smile. "I… came to… take you up on your offer of—"

"Excellent!" he shouted and poured himself another shot.

"Forgive my bluntness, but I always say that when it comes to dating, it's more fun with the living."

I forced a laugh. "You have a point, Hans."

"All right then," he said with a decisive handclap. He reached into his tunic pocket and brought out a key, which he held up ostentatiously, then he unlocked the box, removed a colour photo, and handed it to me.

In *The Perfect Wagnerite*, his 1886 analysis of the *Ring* drama, the Irish writer George Bernard Shaw described Rhine maidens as "thoughtless, elemental, only half-real things, very much like modern young ladies." Contemporary critique aside, he might have been gazing at this photograph when he wrote it. As an amateur, I considered the photo to be several degrees short of a theatrical publicity still, but even so, I could tell that the girl was right out of Göring's *The Nine Commandments of the Workers' Struggle*, in which the corpulent hedonist succinctly summarised the future role of German women: "Take a pot, a dustpan, and a broom, and marry a man."[58] The only thing the photo didn't show was the pot, dustpan, and broom. A gigantic strawberry blonde, of course, and pigtailed, with perfect milk-white skin and peach-coloured cheeks. Robust and sturdy in her dairymaid costume, she was the consummate poster-girl for the BdM[59] or a Hollywood film.

---

[58] Göring was merely following the alliterative slogan of former Emperor William II of Germany: "*Kinder, Küche, Kirche*," meaning "children, kitchen, church."

[59] The BdM, or Bund Deutscher Mädel (Band of German Maidens), was the only legal female youth organisation in Hitler's Germany. In 1938, a voluntary organisation called "Faith and Beauty" (Glaube und Schönheit) was added for girls aged seventeen to twenty-one. It was intended to groom the former BdM members for marriage, domestic life, and future female-career goals.

An uneducated naïf fresh off a turnip farm and heading for a prenatal farm, she was exactly what Baur would recommend to someone he believed me to be. I knew I should seize the chance to hide behind his image of me and her infantile Nazi perfection, but—

"Perfect, eh? Like a poster? And a real Aryan, to boot. You can always trust your uncle Hans," he boasted and poured another brandy. "Just don't ask me how I got access." He smiled broadly. "As for brains, you needn't worry about her catching any spelling errors in your love notes. And," he added with a broad grin, "hardly less impor—what's the matter?"

I wanted to know what was behind his phrase "got access" and why. But that could wait, because in a strategic sense, she was just what I needed for my purpose—not an idiot, but nothing even close to being a curious, sophisticated challenge. And a genuine Nazi to boot—to the extent she could harbour an ideology. I should have leapt up, rushed over, and kissed Baur, but of course, I didn't. Instead, he saw my face, and his lips spread in mild annoyance.

"Well, Hans," I explained, "she's not exactly—"

"I know, I know, not your type. You're a real character, Heinz. Nothing wholesome and purebred for you. You know, when I was a kid, the family next door consisted of crazy dog lovers. Though they were royalists, they were idiotically democratic when it came to dogs. Nothing even remotely purebred for them. Having a mangy mongrel wasn't even enough. It also had to have been whacked by a tram and left shaking, moaning, and dragging its ass before it even got their attention."

I heard a distant loudspeaker call Baur's name, and I glanced at him.

"Pay it no mind. All this fucking foreign labour. They can't even wipe their behinds without asking me in what direction.

Now they'll need good old German ingenuity or else, eh? Anyways, Annagret—that's her name—she's just the ticket for you right now: somewhere between polished and primitive, bred for sex and service. Perfect for a valet, and I'll bet the Führer would even jump for joy to give the bride away at your wedding. At last report, she's still available. But I'll double-check to make sure. Whattayasay?" He reached for another brandy.

Flying with such a lush, I thought, *the Führer is in greater peril than walking alone on a Warsaw street.* Bred for sex and service. Somewhere between polished and primitive. Perfect for a valet. He already had me married, with the Führer as best man.

"Well, Herr Snooty?" he mocked benignly. "I know she's not a phantom, Jew, or deaf, but those aside, is she up to your strict standards?"

"She sounds ideal," I told him, suddenly formulating my own hazardous two-front social strategy. "When can I meet her?"

"You'll hear from me soon, I hope. Now, I gotta get back to those fucking idiots, or our planes will behave like panzers."

IMPORTANT THOUGH IT may have been as a symbol for Rommel himself to arrive in Tripoli, today was even more important, as the first units of his Afrika Korps arrived to provide the substance behind the symbol. Of course, the Berghof was aflame with elation, though it being the Berghof, the flame was set low.

We'd arrived the day before to provide a preparation period before the Führer, Göring, Von Rundstedt, and Von Ribbentrop were to meet with Yugoslav President Dragiša Cvetković and his minister Cincar-Marković—names only pronounceable with a mouthful of razor blades. Normally, the Führer would have merely arrived on the appointed day, initiated perfunctory salutations, issued obstreperous threats, and sent them on their way—with the Wehrmacht not far behind. But with what I hoped would be the imminent invasion of the Soviet Union, I suspected that the Führer desired even more imminent easy pickings with a minimum of military fuss and bother. This pleased his generals, who also suspected a Soviet invasion and dreaded being the hollow centre of a "lazy Susan" [60] of enemies.

The Führer had modified his earlier demands, making special concessions to Yugoslavia, of whom nothing "contrary to her military traditions and her national honour" would be asked. He did not demand troop passage, use of the railway, installation

---

[60] A lazy Susan is a turntable (rotating tray) placed on a table or countertop to aid in distributing food.

of military bases, or military collaboration, and additionally, he would guarantee Yugoslavia's national sovereignty and territorial integrity. Finally, he said, "This that I am proposing to you is not, in fact, the Tripartite Pact." However, and amazingly so, they managed to delay the negotiations by employing the absurd rationale that the decision lay with Prince Paul, the first regent.

Göring was aghast. Von Rundstedt was surprised. Ribbentrop was confused, but the Führer was entirely relaxed.

As for me, I wasn't aghast, surprised, or confused. For, while I timed his dressing this morning, he'd told me, "You know, Linge, I should probably remain in my nightclothes, for this entire affair is a ridiculous formality." When I dared to ask him why, his little moustache bobbed up and down in merriment. "Those stupid Slavs want little; we want everything. They have nowhere to go; we go where we please. So I dress up, and we play their little game."

All that was fine with me, so long as the Führer kept to his resolution to invade. I just wanted to get back to Berlin, where I was told a message from Baur waited for me. I wasn't certain that it concerned Annagret, but I was certain that if it did, I would be the last to know.

BACK IN BERLIN, and relieved this morning by Arnt, I fetched
my now well-examined note from Baur and received more than
a few winks from the Message Centre clerks. Since speaking with
him, I had learned that members of the BdM and FB, many of
whose homes were far away, lived in special dormitories in Berlin
and its suburbs, hardly the most alluring venue for a potentially
romantic encounter. So I laughed when, in Baur's note, he
arranged that "instead," Annagret and I meet at the only slightly
less peculiar "Wild West Bar" at Haus Vaterland.[61]

Peering through the louvres of the swinging doors, I was duly
impressed. Over the years, as the Führer's projectionist, I'd
shown enough cowboy films to appreciate the accuracy and care
with which the proprietors had fabricated a cinematic simulation of a saloon in an Old West town: walls festooned with
enormous covered-wagon wheels, Indian headdresses, oil paintings depicting a romanticised notion of the American frontier,

---

[61] Occupying almost the entire Potsdamer Platz, Haus Vaterland (Fatherland
House) was a food and entertainment centre in central Berlin. It was
preceded by Haus Potsdam, a multi-use building. From 1928 to 1943, it
was a large, famous establishment featuring the largest café in the world, a
major cinema, and numerous theme restaurants, promoted as a showcase of
all nations. During the Nazi years, the mix of restaurants was modified, and
the Jewish Kempinskis had to sell the building for a pittance to "Aryans" and
leave the country.

and other imagined Western-saloon paraphernalia, with waiters wearing ten-gallon hats, swaggering round the well-attended
room. A bandstand held musicians and a singer, all decked out
in glittery, dude-ranch opulence, as they performed American
popular cowboy songs in German while dancers pranced horsey
style about the stage, twirling their lassos in synchronisation
with the music.

I waited only a few moments, before all six feet of Annagret,
clad in the drab, shapeless, vaguely masculine FB uniform,
marched round the corner. Despite her garb and true to Baur's
photograph, the girl looked like an astonishingly flattering
woodcut from *Hansel and Gretel*. In turn, she must have recognised what Baur had described to her and halted before me as
if she'd been ordered to stand at attention on a parade ground.

I rushed to her and said, "At ease, comrade," meant only as
a calming joke, but apparently, she interpreted it as a command
and rushed her hands behind her back and spread her legs apart,
not the most subtle of actions in a pleasure-palace hallway.

"Annagret, please," I urged, "it's a date, not a military parade
inspection," and she loosened up like a puppet with its strings
suddenly slackened. Even the Führer would have been impressed
with such instantaneous compliance. "Let's go in, sit down, have
some refreshments, and get acquainted," I suggested.

She nodded shyly and obediently, and we made our way to
the nearest vacant table as far away from the band as possible.
Once seated, and with a few whisky-augmented sarsaparillas
behind us and another round ordered, she seemed to unwind
even more. She stopped calling me Herr Colonel, and we actually started to converse.

"Why are you staring at me?" I asked her lightly.

She shot an embarrassed hand to her mouth. "I'm so sorry. I

couldn't help noticing that you have lots more hair than General Baur said."

I smiled through a chuckle. "Well, it's not 'lots more,' but Baur would have people think that I'm Nosferatu's balder brother."

"Who?"

"Never mind. I'm just glad you're satisfied. You know, I wasn't much older than you when I started working at the Chancellery." I dared not evoke the Führer, lest she swoon, or worse, bolt up, heel-click, and give the Nazi salute.

"But such an unthinkable honour!" she exclaimed in wide-eyed awe. "To be at the very heart and soul of the Reich. And to physically service the Führer." All the colour suddenly drained from her face. She'd caught herself too late to prevent my once-repressible sense of humour from asserting itself.

"Fortunately, my duties don't extend quite that far," I told her, and she laughed, I was certain, with relief that I hadn't been offended. But to be sure, I said, "I know you meant serve," and she nodded vigorously. "But I can tell you, the Führer puts his pants on one leg at a time, the same as everyone else, the only dif-ference being that everyone else doesn't have me timing them."

She squinted at another of my futile attempts at humour, lifted her hands, and in one fluid motion, flung her long blond braids behind her broad, athletic shoulders. "I have so little to say…"

"Heinz, please," I appealed, "call me Heinz," and she smiled beguilingly. In the light provided by bulbs protruding down from suspended wagon wheels, she was quite lovely in an earthy sort of way, and out of uniform, she might actually be dazzling.

"I'm nothing… Heinz. I have barely a grade-school educa-tion and not much to show for that. I have three brothers: two in the Wehrmacht and one in the Hitler Youth. I'm a farm girl, so I worked on the farm. Now, I work on a different kind of farm, you might say. I, too, serve the Führer and the Reich—not like you, of course, but in my own small way. I know nothing of medicine, but I'd like to be a nurse. For the military, of course."

I could see the whisky working. She was talking more and more rapidly—and with less inhibition.

"With my three brothers gone, I was needed on the farm, so despite my application, I was not taken into the BdF. But I can't tell you how proud my parents were when I was finally accepted into the FB, and so here I am." She paused for breath and a sip of her third augmented sarsaparilla. I was still sipping my second. I decided not to ask her what had changed on the farm to allow her to leave.

The band began a Teutonic rendition of "Don't Fence Me In." I couldn't help but marvel at the lyrics:

> *Oh, give me land, lots of land under starry skies above,*
>
> *Don't fence me in.*
>
> *Let me ride through the wide open country that I love,*
>
> *Don't fence me in.*
>
> *Let me be by myself in the evenin' breeze,*
>
> *And listen to the murmur of the cottonwood trees,*
>
> *Send me off forever but I ask you please,*
>
> *Don't fence me in.*
>
> *Just turn me loose, let me straddle my old saddle*
>
> *Underneath the western skies.*
>
> *On my Cayuse, let me wander over yonder*
>
> *Till I see the mountains rise.*

I want to ride to the ridge where the west commences,

And gaze at the moon till I lose my senses…

Ironically, with its unbridled (no pun intended) worship of *lebensraum*, it was no less in tune with Nazism than the "Horst Wessel Lied."

"Would you believe that these lyrics are originally American and not German?" I asked Annagret.

"I'm sorry," she said. "I wasn't listening. I'm not very musical."

I repeated them verbatim, and her luminous blue eyes widened. "I'm truly impressed; you really know that song."

"It's one of my favourites," I lied. "What do you think?"

She gazed up at the ceiling then back. "I think maybe the cowboy would be lonely. I, myself, have no such need."

I nodded as if I agreed but said nothing, after which there ensued a long silence. It seemed to me that Annagret expected me to say something in particular, but I had no idea what.

"I heard that you were recently bereaving the loss of a loved one," she suddenly blurted. "I hope I am not being insensitive."

"No, Annagret, you're not being insensitive," I assured her, if only to generate more conversation. "I'll confess I had some bad moments for a while, but I'm as right as rain now."

She smiled benignly. "I'm glad. It's so difficult to keep the past from remaining in the present, sort of like an unwanted guest."

"Well said," I told her truthfully, impressed. "You're wise beyond your years."

She smiled. "That's what they tell me in my dormitory. They say I have an old soul."

We ordered another round as the band switched incongruously from twangy cowboy songs to boisterous Dixieland jazz, the result made even more ludicrous for being played in Western costumery.

"I've told you all about me," she said, "what little there is to tell. But you, I can't even imagine the things you've seen, the people you've met."

"Is that so important to you?"

"Sure it is," she blurted, wide-eyed. "I'm a daughter of the Fatherland. The kind of contact we get from the occasional radio broadcast, rally, and parade, you get every day from the Führer himself. If we're lucky, once in a blue moon, we're visited by some middle-level civil servant; but you meet the Führer's glorious inner circle every day. God in Heaven, who wouldn't be impressed?"

"Did you know that I once tended Mussolini's feet?"

That incongruity stopped her in her idolatrous tracks. "You're funny," she finally said.

I shrugged with false humility. "That may be true, but I'm being serious now. I can assure you that I did, and I can report that the Duce's feet are no different from anyone else's, despite what the Italian press claims. They don't walk on water."

The server snaked his way to our table with our drinks. In keeping with the new musical motif, our waiter had corked himself into blackface. "I'ze brung yo lyebayshunz," he singsonged in what I assumed was a German version of a theatrical rendition of American Negro patois, then left with a practiced shuffle.

"What was that?" she asked, eyelids lowered to half-mast.

"A crazy simulation of a people the Party would exterminate," I answered, with no attempt—or need, it seemed—to engage in my own simulation.

Her eyes narrowed again, and she started to say something but stopped herself, paused, then resumed. "Please, you may have my drink. All right?"

"Is something wrong?"

"I've had too much. I'm not much of a drinker. I should have informed you. Maybe I should have something to eat, or I'll be of no use to you later."

"Use to me?"

"See?" She raised her palms upward resignedly. "There I go. When I have too much to drink, I say things I shouldn't and don't do things I should."

What did Baur know? What had Baur told her? And why had she consented? "Would some coffee help?"

"Funny, they all ask that, but I tell them that all coffee does is make me a more frantic drunk. Not so good in a public place, wouldn't you agree?"

They all? Them? Hardly a farm-fresh Fräulein. "I would agree."

"Food helps," she repeated.

I nodded and called over the waiter. "Soup okay?" I asked her.

"Anything but alcohol. Best things are food and sweat."

I ordered her some soup.

Continuing its dazzling foray into incongruity, the still-cowboy-attired band began playing bucolic German polkas, while the cork-faced waiters continued their ludicrous Teutonic interpretation of Stepin Fetchit.[62]

The soup duly arrived, but before she could tear into it, a

---

[62] Slow-witted and lazy, Stepin Fetchit exploited whites audiences' sense of superiority and thereby became a very wealthy man. He portrayed "the laziest human being in the world," the quintessential "coon" stereotype: shuffling, mumbling, slacking, and dozing off whenever he could, with his heavy eyelids and loose lower lip forever dangling, and scratching his shaved head in befuddlement whenever a white actor upbraided or barked orders at him— as they did often—he was a living cartoon. Animated cartoons of his day often featured a thinly veiled Stepin Fetchit caricature that was hardly more exaggerated than his own shtick. He also spawned a legion of imitators.

voice behind me announced the arrival of Dr. Hugo Blaschke,[63] and I turned to see him go round me. As always, his face looked as if the features of the bottom half were jammed into whatever space remained after his prodigious forehead had been formed. His tiny nose (a nose I'd been obliged to look up more than once) was always corrugated in revulsion, as if he were constantly assailed by the foulest of odours, which, as a dentist, he probably was. Both Annagret and I stood, and we all exchanged salutes and introductions, after which, he sat down as if he'd been asked. Another Morell.

"Please don't let me interrupt your dinner," he offered, having done just that. Though we shared the same rank, Blaschke always treated me as a patient, never as an equal.

"Not at all," I prevaricated. "Can I order you something?" I desperately wanted him to leave, but propriety and discretion dictated a host-guest relationship.

"Yes, actually," he said, and I signalled for the waiter, who shuffled over.

"Whet cain ah'z gitchuzz?" he drawled with a Thuringian version of an Alabama accent.

"Well, my fine dark friend," Blaschke drawled back, "I'll have an Erdinger Weissbräu."

"Yowzzahmassa," he chirped brightly, like the good house slave he was playing, and pushed off.

"Now, if we could only get our new subjects to behave like

---

[63] Hugo Blaschke was born in Neustadt, West Prussia, and studied dentistry in Berlin and at the University of Pennsylvania. He trained as a dental surgeon in London and opened his own practice in late 1911. During World War I, he served as a military dentist before returning to private practice in Berlin. After treating Hermann Göring in 1930, he joined the Nazi Party on 1 February 1931 and the SS on 1 May 1935. In addition to treating Hitler, he also treated Eva Braun, Joseph Goebbels, Heinrich Himmler, and Heinz Linge.

that," he lamented, "but it takes generations to teach some types their place, does it not?"

I shrugged. "I leave such cultural matters to Heydrich and you, Herr Blaschke." The two dentists.

He laughed. "Always the comedian, eh, Linge? Even under the drill."

"That's when it's most needed," I answered drolly. I noticed that Annagret hadn't touched her soup but was studying it intently.

"For some reason, Linge, I never imagined you in this sort of place."

"Where did you imagine me?" I asked.

He smiled thinly and said nothing. Then his head turned, and with narrowed eyes, he slowly scanned Annagret from the top of the table to the top of her head, then Blaschke turned back to me. "I know I've seen her somewhere," he announced. "I knew it when we were first introduced, and my feeling is even stronger now."

As a servant, having been spoken of in the third person so often, I'd become inured to the slight, yet I took instant offence at her being treated the same way. "I'm just here to ride the range," I told him. "Why don't you ask her?"

Then he regarded me in a way I found, even now, difficult to attribute, then he said, "Not necessary, Linge, I'm sure. Perhaps I was mistaken. In any event, it's not that important."

At that moment, I knew he wasn't mistaken, and it was that important, but I chose not to pursue the matter.

Blaschke's drink came. He downed it quickly, made his apologies, and left, much to my surprise and, by the look in Annagret's eyes, much to her relief.

"Do you know him?" I asked.

"No."

"He seemed to know you. Sure you haven't met him? Even professionally?"

She smiled ambiguously. "Professionally? He said he was mistaken. Anyway, he'd never treat the likes of us in the FB. We have our own dentist, who I have to say, should be torturing Jews, not Germans."

I pursed my lips and ignored the Schroederism. "But why do you think he was so positive he recognised you at first?"

A slight twitch of her lips indicated to me a minor irritation. "I think you would have to ask him. I have no idea. But such things happen to me a lot. They tell me it's that I look like all those recruiting posters rolled into one. You'd be shocked how many think they know me personally because they've seen pictures of FB girls like me plastered all over Berlin and also in the newsreels and newspapers. I'm just a larger version."

I nodded. "Before we were interrupted, I was going to ask you about the FB since I know little or nothing about it—or the BdM, for that matter. At their age, I was the guest of various hallways, alleyways, and jails, and at your age, I was breathing brick dust." The chronology wasn't particularly accurate, but the situations were. "Now, I prepare baths, time dressing, clean privies, arrange bookshelves and desks, clear floors, stand at ease in corners during meetings like the three monkeys, sort mail, and run errands. The glamour never ceases."

She nodded with the knowing expression of a professor. "You see? Is that not the beauty of National Socialism? Yesterday, a jail cell, today, the Chancellery. Just like our Führer."

I laughed ironically. "'Just like our Führer.' It's *you* who is funny." But my brain wasn't laughing, for it realised that in a sense she couldn't possibly know or understand, but in a greater sense, she was right. In my relatively short time in the Chancellery, I'd undergone a quantum leap of sentience and a recognition of actual intellect. It was both exhilarating and frightening.

After a slight hesitation, she began spooning her soup, by then well cold, a condition which didn't appear to matter to her. What mattered to me was her tone changing instantly and drastically, from formal, shy conversation to clever, authoritative lecture, as if she'd been asked to recite from a text in a high school class. "But I understand… Herr… Heinz. It's unreasonable to expect someone in your position to know of commonplace things," she said, completely disregarding my attempt at humility, "so I will explain. The BdM is intended to groom racially sound females of the Reich for marriage, domestic life, and for a select few, more… how to say… specialised service. I myself am in such a category. Ideally, girls are to be married and have children once they are of age. So, as you would imagine, for the BdM, most days involve domestic training. But Saturdays involve strenuous outdoor exercise and physical training to promote good health, which will enable them to serve their people and their country. Evenings include worldview training, with instruction in history, geography, German culture, the inevitable destiny of the Aryan race, and the critical importance of self-sacrifice for the Reich."

Through all her internalised propaganda, I nodded dutifully and, I hoped, convincingly. "The Führer," I told her, "spoke highly and often of Youth Leader von Shirach, though I never had the opportunity to meet him."

Her eyes rounded with a disciple's awe. "The same for me. He had already joined the Wehrmacht and was succeeded by Deputy Reichsjugendführer Axmann. He hasn't visited but once. To be expected; it is wartime, after all."

"I noticed," I said jokingly, but her expression remained

fixed. "But what of the FB, your own group? I'd love to know more."

"Another soup then?"

"Bribery, eh?" I joked again, and this time, she winked.

"Just the beginning," she teased. "Food now, sweat later."

I ordered her another soup. Even in her dreary uniform, she exuded Valkyrian sex. And a sophistication she kept under strict guard. As did I.

16 February 1941

THERE WAS LITTLE activity of interest to me this morning, save for the Führer cautioning me to make myself available late in the evening. Why, he failed to mention, but his tone told me that only I would do, so there would be no substitution of personnel. However, on my way out, I happened to spot a scribbled entry in the Führer's calendar: "W." It was enough.

Do you exercise volition in your dreams?

I didn't know for certain what my necessary presence indicated, but I had an educated guess—and a hope.

❦

Entering the Führer's antechamber after his toilette, Günsche reminded me needlessly of my duty that evening.

"Any idea of what's going on?" I asked the giant, just for the sake of displaying an inclusive camaraderie I didn't possess to the slightest degree.

After a shrug and pursed lips, he said, "Beats me. Alls I know is that the boss wants you and wants all of us gone."

"Hmm, and how does the Reichsleiter feel about that?"

"When I told him, there was no change in expression, but I knew just from knowing him that he was fit to be tied."

When I told him. Brilliant! "That's tough." I shook my head slowly, my mouth downturned in pity. "I know how much he likes to be involved in things."

"Yeah, well, don't worry yourself about it, Heinz," he soothed. "You know Bormann; he'll find out everything, one way or another, right?"

Quite right, I laughed to myself. He would be fit to be tied, not loving it, if he only knew of my plans for him. "Quite right," I told Günsche. "He certainly has one way or another." With that, I excused myself and headed for the Communications Centre to retrieve the mail.

❧

"So?" Baur asked as he caught me lugging the enormous leather sack with the mail I was to share with Günsche. "You maybe have some news for your uncle Hans?" he joked seriously.

It was obvious what he wanted to know, but I was more concerned with how I would negotiate the evening's activities. I lowered the stuffed bag to the floor. Baur always meant well by me and so deserved a serious reply. But what to say was another matter.

"I met her at the Wild West Bar."

He tilted his head sideways and pressed his thin lips together in tolerant impatience. "That, I know, Heinz, since I arranged it. Tell me something I don't know, eh? Like, was she all I described? Were you captivated? Did you enjoy yourself? Did it lead to anything? Is it going to lead to anything?"

I fixed him with a deadpan gaze. "Yes."

"Okay, kid." Baur nodded. "You wanna be that way, just wait till I've got you alone in a plane with me."

I smiled. "Please, Hans, anything but that," I relented. "Only the Führer can withstand your piloting, so I'll confess. I meant yes to all your questions. But the most amazing thing about her was how she's able to be so transparent yet mysterious."

He nodded sagely. "Do I know you, or do I know you?"

Baur crowed, employing one of those ridiculous Kempkanesque repetitive-statement queries, like, "Is it true, or is it true?" Despite his rank and achievements, Baur was a prole, right through, but a fundamentally decent one, all told. *Am I right, or am I right?*

"She can be gorgeous or deformed," he continued, "brilliant or an idiot, tall or short, blonde or brunette, but she'd better be mysterious if she's to have a chance with you. Kempka—and most men, for that matter—will schtup anything with a pussy, but Heinz must have mystery."

"And I'm really grateful, believe me. With her looks and situation, she can be mysterious and still hide the mystery in plain sight." *Be careful, Heinz,* I warned. *Intellectual audacity is for Goebbels and Speer, not for Linge.*

"No offence taken, my son," Baur said. "I get it. A complex übermensch like the Führer must surround himself with relaxing simplicity, but a simple fellow like you, well, that's another story."

"Another story, yes," I assured him—but not one I would ever tell.

"But all told, you had a pleasant get-acquainted evening, yes?"

"No question about it," I told him with veracious ambiguity, "that is, until we were interrupted by Dr. Blaschke."

Baur shook his head. "The 'Tooth Fairy'?"

"Tooth Fairy?"

Baur fixed me with a gaze of incredulity. "My God, man, then you're the only one in the Chancellery who didn't know the worst kept secret in the Reich. What the fuck did that pervert want?"

"You tell me. He just came over, invited himself to sit down with us, ordered a beer, told me he recognised Annagret right in front of her, then retracted it and left."

Baur nodded in resignation. "He's an odd duck. Like Morell. Even the Jew, Bloch. All those medical types have a screw loose, I think."

"Even so," I pursued, "what possible connexion could he have with the likes of Annagret?"

"Ah, well." He smiled crookedly. "There's another mystery for you, then. You should be ecstatic."

Sitting alone during a lunch break at a partially obscured table in the officers' mess, I pondered, undisturbed, the coming evening with Weisthor and the Führer. Another precious opportunity—and it was being handed to me without the hazard of a conspicuous initiative on my part. And yet, it was precisely that which distressed me, for lurking beneath the moment was another kind of hazard that was potentially catastrophic: being the object rather than the subject. *Given that, how much could I plan, and how much would I be able to improvise as events developed?* "A goal without a plan is just a wish," Antoine de Saint-Exupéry wrote. *And yet, what was my goal in the absence of context? How can I plan without it? Can any further mulling be of benefit?*

Enough! I shouted silently. From the longest experience, I knew that any attempt to empty my brain was impossible, but concentration wasn't, so I forced myself to focus instead on Annagret, the mystery that Baur seemed to think I require. *And yet what was there to focus on? The subtle lapses in her ingenuousness? Blaschke's cryptic comments? Her consummate bedroom acrobatics? Masochistic fascination? Would Hess be there with the Führer and Weisthor and spoil everything?* Concentration impossible, I conceded. It was out of the question as well, and so I went to my quarters to wait for the Führerbuzzer to end all speculation.

❧

I entered the Führer's vast study to discover the ponderous velvet drapes drawn, everything in the room rendered as translucent shadows by a murky light emanating from no source I could detect. I eased the door shut, moved into a familiar narrow intersection between two long walls of bookshelves, and assumed an at ease position. Straining into the distance, I could barely make out a figure sitting at the Führer's desk, presumably the Führer, speaking to someone hidden from me by one of his two oblique-angled, high-back armchairs, presumably Weisthor. I say presumably because I could hear only the slightest of murmurs. Eventually, and with unnecessary stealth, I glanced down at the illuminated dial of my watch to learn that over forty-five minutes had passed. *Perhaps I wasn't needed after all,* I conjectured with a disturbing combination of dismay and relief.

I considered sneaking off, when I distinctly heard the Führer call, "Linge, join us, won't you?" Then the figure behind the desk rose and disappeared into the bedroom.

I didn't know how to join "us" since, with the Führer gone, there appeared to be only the figure in the armchair. I peered round the vast space to locate anyone else but could see no one. However, under the circumstances, I couldn't remain against the wall, so I moved to the adjoining armchair, slowly lowered myself into its plushness, and saw her.

❧

"Pity you can't see your face—it's quite a sight. I don't blame you for looking startled, but advance notice is a luxury in wartime, don't you agree?"

"The… the Führer—"

"He didn't wish us disturbed. Always the perfect gentleman."

"But I thought—"

"Oh, the 'W' on the Führer's calendar? 'W' was, I confess, a minor conceit, a lure, if you will. Would a 'K' have drawn out your curiosity? The general made the—not unreasonable—presumptive leap that you would prefer me to him." A beguiling smile followed.

"Another perfect gentleman?" I asked.

"Not always," she answered. "Would you like a brandy? My own private stock." She leaned down, removing a metal flask from her handbag. Unscrewing the cap, she poured some of the dense liquid into it and handed it to me.

The philosopher Karl von Möller wrote that "Everything is real, especially dreams." The only question—asked me several times since I joined the Führer's household—was whether I exercised any control in them. *Did I? Was sitting across from Katrin my psychological construct, according to Engel?* It now became the bullfighter's "moment of truth," a time when a person was truly tested. Perhaps the answer to that question would be provided here and now. I downed the drink in one gulp and handed the cap back. *In for a penny…*

From her raven-black hair to her amber eyes to her aristocratic cheekbones and nose, sensuous mouth, pale skin, and smooth, elegant neck, she was exactly as I remembered her: astonishingly enigmatic, mysterious, alluring, and unattainable. *But is she real?*

"You're staring at me as if I were an apparition," she asserted softly.

"I… was told you were," I answered haltingly. In case the brandy was more "exotic" than it seemed, I employed the extravagant care that a drunk takes to unmistakably demonstrate his sobriety. Unfortunately, at the moment, I didn't know whether I was drunk or sober.

Katrin nodded, her lips compressed into a snide smirk. "I see. You've been listening to the concocted fantasies of the traitor Brückner and his puppet, Engel." Then she raised a perfectly manicured hand in a placating gesture. "But please, let's not have any rancour, shall we?"

"It's been such a long time, Katrin." I forced myself into a more natural tone and cadence. "And not one word. What have you been up to?" It was far from an idle pleasantry.

The smile again, but this time, charm had replaced ritual. She reached over and placed her hand on my knee. "That's what I came here to ask you." It was also not an idle pleasantry. She drew her hand back gently, as the shadows began to envelop what scant light there was.

It had to be now!

"I'm afraid I'm as uninteresting as ever," I told her with a shrug. "The life of a valet, even a valet to the Führer, is not one of glamour and adventure." I paused to make a thoughtful face. "Except in my dreams, of course."

Adjusting to the shadowy dimness, I could detect a slight flicker in her eyes, and it told me that this was what she'd come to hear. Conscious or unconscious, I believed I had the opportunity to assume control. *But how much and for how long?*

"You may be many things, Heinz," she countered, as I'd hoped, "but never uninteresting. And as for your dreams? I couldn't begin to imagine."

No, Katrin, you couldn't. I smiled to myself. *Because I'm about to imagine them for you.* "No," I agreed, "not even you could imagine them. To be frank, even I can't imagine them. Sounds crazy, but true nonetheless. I don't know," I teased, "maybe I'm more interesting in my dreams because, well, because I'm not myself in them." My eyes strained to see any effect my words had on her, and it seemed as if her breathing had become deeper and more even, and a little blue vein at the hollow of her throat moved slightly. I had no way of interpreting this, short of an accompanying verbal response from her.

"Who are you, then?" she asked. Not much of a verbal response but enough.

I shrugged. "Many people. Just not me. Don't ask me how or why."

"I won't. Recently?"

"Is last night recent enough?"

"It'll do; anyone I know?" she asked with fabricated blitheness, her manicured eyebrows raised slightly.

"It was—" I began, then stopped abruptly and stared at her for a few moments, as if she were a total stranger. I shook my head ostentatiously, as if to clear it, then winced with frustration, as if unsuccessful. Then I rose and moved to the enormous world globe immediately adjacent to the Führer's long conference table and turned the switch on the base, causing the transparent globe to glow with a stunning display of differently coloured nations—like attached puzzle pieces covering a ball.

"Come," I commanded Katrin stentoriously in Russian-accented German, one of my arms pulled in slightly to make it shorter than the other. "*Gospozha*,"[64] I boomed, "come, and I show you future."

Care, notwithstanding, I feared that I might have become subsumed without control into my own design. Whether it was "augmented" brandy or an authentic hallucination, as I glanced round, I was suddenly no longer in the Führer's study but in a moderate-sized, vaguely shabby, narrow, rectangular, dark-wood-panelled office, a spare wooden desk on one end, facing

---

[64] Madame.

two long rows of ragged, wooden, high-back chairs with arms on the right row and none on the left. No table sat between the rows. A multitude of heroic portraits and photographs adorned the walls, but I couldn't make out their features. Only the globe remained of where I'd been standing only a moment before, and it was in the very centre of the room. But the most significant alteration of reality was my removal from the scene as participant and re-emergence as spectator, watching the action, observing me standing by the globe. I wondered if Katrin had noticed this, but her expression remained opaque, her body immobile.

She eased herself up and walked towards the globe with a quizzically apprehensive expression. "What is all this, Heinz?" Her eyelids pinched, as if staring at a face she seemed barely to recognise, then before I could answer, she shifted to no expression at all.

"In matter like this," my Soviet alter ego told her, "with such seriousness, strutting Nazi fool and menial lackey will defer to me, so you should listen with great care. Not repeat generosity, you understand."

"Yes," she answered, "I understand. Please continue."

"You maybe know of army ants?" I asked her.

She shook her head.

"Not matter," I told her. "I instruct you. During raids, fire ants attack prey in groups of more than hundred thousand. Sheer numbers, powerful jaws, creatures ravage and slaughter animals entirely larger than themselves. Not fanciful or incorrect—but instructive—that are called 'nature's Mongol hordes.'" I chuckled maliciously. "And what this has to do with you, eh?" I turned and rotated the globe to the enormous puzzle piece labelled the Soviet Union and jabbed at it. "Lesson in mathematics, yes? I give you two set of numbers: 170.6 million." Then I wheeled the globe west to the relatively tiny piece labelled Germany. "Seventy point seven million," I declared with a crooked smirk. "Army ants face rabbit. Simple truth for you: We lose half our population and still we devour you. You can afford to lose half of yours?" I coughed out a brutal laugh, hoping Katrin was suitably impressed.

Suddenly, a bone-chilling cold reached out savagely and firmly from the globe and a change in the globe's illumination sent strange and frightening shapes leaping out, then slipped back silently.

"You see, giving you taste of real world," I continued. "You conquer territories I permit you to conquer. You have pretty strutting army that wage successful war against helpless midgets, wasting time, all while giving me time. If in front of me, I would present ranting rabbit with Soviet medal."

I spun and spun the globe until it was a whirling, blurry kaleidoscope, then stopped it dead, back at the Soviet Union. "Why I am telling you is entirely simple, my bewitching comrade. Is that I am risking nothing, for little man you serve will do nothing. He is hysterical rabbit and soon be meal for my ants. Even should feeble screamer at long last, deciding to attack, is much too late with far too little. So have only one advice for you and rest of Germans: learn Russian."

As I watched, she studied me for a moment, then smiled a crooked smile. "So, are we truly lost… comrade?" Then she reached up, took hold of my shoulders hard, and moved me away from the globe. "Truly?" she repeated with urgent emphasis. "Forgive me for saying so, but if all were as lost for us as you say, you would not be here, even to gloat."

I stretched my lips into a broad, wily grin. "You are clever woman, but entirely wrong. Am here absolutely to gloat, since fool you serve too stubborn and gullible to appreciate and use what he possess."

"Gullible?" she asked, skipping stubborn, her eyes slightly widening. "What do you mean by gullible?"

"What I am meaning, is that rabbit has in hands, decisive weapon, but waits like arrogant fool for something that does not exist."

"Does not exist?"

"What I said. You need repeated?"

"And just what is this weapon?" she asked, her expression now ambiguous, half-defensive, half-indignant, yet a slight tremor in her voice diluted the usual haughty confidence.

I spread my lips disdainfully and shook my head slowly. "News to you? Jew toy, little top with the symbols—and the essential one who speaks the symbols and spins, yes? So long the rabbit has them and doing nothing, might as well be giving as present to your Magda Goebbels's swarm of Nazi brats."

"But the second—" she started to ask.

I cut her off with a hearty laugh, all the while hoping it was still me and that I wasn't hamming it up too much. "Rabbit swallows yarns from man with dead eyes and no smile. Second? Fool is slave to two-top old-grandma tale, so will delay and dither while I strike."

"What are you saying?" she asked, somewhat nastily, I thought, and so I replied in kind.

"Madame," I said, "no second one. *Nekorreky*—incorrect—information fed to rabbit who swallows entirely, which naturally, is good for me—and for ants. So I gloat."

Katrin's eyes narrowed again, just a little, then a relaxed, clever smile. "All well and good, comrade, but you made one mistake. Since with all your bluster, you haven't attacked, there's still a chance, yes?" she ventured.

This was a critical moment, and so I didn't answer. Instead,

I forced lines of concentration to slowly crease my face, a study in silent perplexity.

"I suggest… comrade…" she pursued snidely, "that there might still be a chance, despite the misunderstanding, despite the delay." Her tone was more strident, more authoritative, more arrogant, more Katrin.

"You're thinking so? If the case, incentive to tell you is what?" I sneered.

"If nothing else," Katrin replied, her eyes narrowed, her voice granite hard, "to further display your cleverness and supremacy, and incidentally, satisfy my curiosity. Since you claim it's too late anyway, you have nothing to lose by telling me what the… rabbit might have done to avoid the ants."

I kept my eyes hooded for effect since she was not to know or even guess that I'd orchestrated the entire scenario to provide the answer. And I'd given it to her and prayed that she would realise it. I was gambling on her mental sharpness, inventiveness, and keen intelligence, not to mention her very existence, despite Engel. And no less on her sense of reality. So all I said was, "You are smart woman, so be smart and…" I shifted my eyelids from hooded to fluttering, wobbled slightly, and sank to the floor in a synthetic swoon.

GÜNSCHE, GIFTED WITH the size and strength of an ape, if not the intelligence, managed by himself to haul my purposefully limp body to my quarters—a journey I quite enjoyed. Yet, once settled, and all the way into the earliest moments of the morning, my brain twisted and turned, questioning whether anything I'd experienced had actually occurred. Engel had told me that Katrin was a phantom, one side of an imagination warring with itself on the battlefield of my brain. *And yet what of last night?* She'd called Engel a puppet of Brückner and his tale of her unreality a traitorous concoction. *So, what was I to conclude?*

Alexandre Dumas wrote, "When you compare the sorrows of real life to the pleasures of the imaginary one, you will never want to live again, only to dream forever." *But,* I reflected morosely as I showered, *what would Dumas say if there were no differences to compare, or if there were differences, they couldn't be distinguished?* Standing there with the jets of icy water assaulting me, something emerged that I'd jammed into the most obscure crevice of my brain since I hadn't the wits to divine its devastating implication: that fantasy and reality might be, for me, interchangeable. Abraham Lincoln declared that "a house divided against itself cannot stand." *But did that morsel of wisdom apply to the human brain as well? Would I stay endlessly divided against myself?*

In the officers' mess a while back, I'd overheard someone complaining that after fourteen years of marriage, he didn't really know his wife, that she was a stranger. His companion asked how that could be, and the fellow replied, "Habit and deception, my friend. They eventually replace intimacy."

Then the other fellow remarked that such a condition seemed advantageous. "Since you're strangers," he opined, "you owe nothing to her, certainly not loyalty, so you can enjoy intimacy without consequence."

At the time, it meant nothing, but now such sentiments ate at me since any intimacy I'd had with Klara had led to the most horrendous consequences. I'd come a long way in perfecting artifice with almost a master diplomat's facile duplicity. *Who had I not deceived?* I asked myself and answered despairingly, *No one—including me.*

1 *March* 1941

THIS MORNING, I hurried past Günsche into the Führer's quarters without looking at him, a technique I'd perfected, both as a way to avoid idiotic prattle and to irritate Bormann.

I came in on a Ribbentrop rhapsody, wherein the sycophantically cloddish foreign minister was regaling the Führer with his "inspired" diplomatic manoeuvres in persuading Bulgaria to sign the Tripartite Pact[65] by promising Prime Minister Filov that after the fall of Greece, Bulgaria would obtain an Aegean coastline between the Struma and Maritsa rivers. Ribbentrop waxed on and on about how, due to his adroit diplomatic acumen, the Reich would also gain an additional coastline. I knew the Führer only agreed to such an arrangement because the Soviet Union had made overtures to the Bulgarians earlier, the hell with the coastline. *Could even the likes of a Ribbentrop be ignorant of this? Yes,* I answered myself. *Most definitely.*

Since coming to the Chancellery, I'd had ample opportunity to compare the relative merits of the Reich's top three foreign-service "vons": von Papen, von Neurath, and von Ribbentrop. I'd never embraced any class prejudices, since virtually everyone

---

[65] Soviet diplomat Arkady Sobolev encouraged the Bulgarian government to sign a mutual assistance pact, which had first been discussed in October 1939. He offered Soviet recognition of Bulgarian claims in Greece and Turkey. However, the Bulgarian government was disturbed by the subversive actions of the Bulgarian Communist Party in response to these talks, apparently carried out at Soviet urging.

in the Reich outranked me, but I was forced to confess that the first two possessed more intellect, sagacity, nobility, and spine in their big toes than the third possessed in his entire body. And yet, the Führer loathed and despised the superior Neurath and Papen while harbouring the brilliant-commoner's contempt for the mediocre Ribbentrop. It was also that the former never engaged in slobbering sycophancy with the Führer, an activity at which the latter excelled and, oddly, the Führer seemed to favour.

Not long after I entered the Führer's service, I asked Brückner why a visionary of such incomparable genius like the Führer was so disdainful of those who disagreed with him. He smiled abstrusely and told me that "to ask the question is to answer it," a typical Brückner response. When I pursued, he said that at moments of danger and opportunity, a genius such as the Führer had no time for debate when the future of his vision and mission was concerned. Since, at the time, my self-confidence and powers of analysis were so feeble, irresolute, and unformed, I assumed sense in anything I heard and experienced or attributed confusion to inferiority. My powers had grown exponentially since then, and with them, my attitude towards intolerance. And genius.

I imagined to amply demonstrate the utter inconsequence of Ribbentrop and the even greater inconsequence of Bulgaria, the Führer turned away from the foreign minister to ask me what I thought of the matter. I took my time. Aristotle wrote, "Wit is educated insolence." One of my many regrets (and a minor one, if I'm to retain any humility) is that when I was nobody, I could not afford wit, and now that I am somebody, I can afford it even less.

"It seems to me, my Führer," I finally said, forefinger to my lower lip and my right eye just lowered from the ceiling, "that any gain for the Reich that costs nothing, even a beach, can only be a good thing. But," I added in case he didn't notice, "I'm hardly qualified to give such a weighty opinion."

The Führer laughed and turned back to the furrow-browed, crimson-hued Ribbentrop (as if he'd been concerned that the likes of me would disagree with him). "Well," the Führer said, "it looks like you've a champion in Linge here." Then he rose, signalling dismissal, and Ribbentrop withdrew with dispatch, presumably to crow about his triumph to anyone who would listen without sniggering, at least to his face.

The Führer turned back to me, waved me to the front, and sat me down in the chair I'd occupied the night before, then took the chair that had held Katrin. "Well," the Führer said, "now that we've given that clown something to trumpet, to a far more important matter: how did last evening go?"

Something within told me that this could well become the template for further private interactions, and so I had to weigh my words with extreme care. "I don't understand, my Führer. Go? Go where?"

His little moustache ascended slightly. "I meant what happened after I left. Even I can't be everywhere."

But you could have been here *instead of somewhere else, so why did you leave?* I ached to ask. "Well, my Führer," I answered, then hesitated to again demonstrate my poor memory and awkwardness at personal revelations. "I'm afraid I don't remember much. I remember sitting down where I am now but being extremely fatigued and... I... think I waited a few moments alone, and when you didn't return, I left, and I must have gone straight to bed." I smiled wanly to underscore my tepid disappointment. "So, as much as I can recall, nothing exciting, I'm afraid, my Führer."

The Führer pursed his lips, then leaned forward, tapped

me on the knee, and drew his hand back. "Excitement is sorely overrated, Linge. As a youth, I had enough excitement for ten lifetimes. You know that during the last war, I was an infantryman in the First Company during the Ypres Massacre of the Innocents, where approximately forty thousand men—that's between a third and a half of nine newly enlisted infantry divisions—became casualties in twenty days. My own regiment entered the battle with thirty-six hundred men and, at its end, mustered 611. That was excitement!"

I knew every word he uttered and those to come, for over the years, I'd heard him go on interminably to associates and visitors of all sorts about his heroic wartime exploits. Never mere reminiscences, they were always a calculated prelude to a point he intended to make, so I listened with a manufactured expression of rapt attention and artificial awe.

"By December," he continued, "my own company of two hundred fifty was reduced to forty-two. After the battle, I was promoted from private to lance corporal and assigned as regimental message Runner, moving among the trenches and often under fire. Even *more* excitement! I won the Iron Cross First Class after an attack during which messengers like me were indispensable, and on a day in which my depleted regiment lost sixty, and two hundred and eleven were wounded. And if *that* wasn't enough excitement, on 15 October 1918, several comrades and I were temporarily blinded—I also lost my voice—due to a British mustard gas attack."

He threw up his arms in a theatrical gesture of frustration. "I could go on and on—from the war into the dark and dangerous years of struggle—but I'm sure you get the idea. My point, though long in coming, is that with such experiences, I learned to savour the rare moments when absolutely nothing was happening."

Even without his "point," I knew he would be relentless in his pursuit of confirmation of my exchange with Katrin. And he should be. Much was at stake for him. *But how, and when?*

"I can only agree, my Führer," I told him in truthful ambiguity. "Is there anything else you require?"

He smiled enigmatically, as if he were a cat and I'd suddenly become a mouse. "Well, let me see. I have my correct mail, thanks to you and not that immense idiot Günsche. Bormann is running around doing everything else, and I have no speeches to make or guests until after dinner, so I'd say that for me, with the assistance of Morell, it's one of those rare moments I spoke of."

Who should be first, the chicken or the egg? I wondered. *And does it matter which one I am?* "Then, if there's nothing further, my Führer, with your permission, I'll see to my other duties and return at dinnertime." I stood, saluted, turned, and began moving away, knowing that whoever acted first, I must not make it to the door without learning the Führer's agenda.

"So, you say the evening was completely uneventful?" he asked my back, and I turned round to see his face a placid mask of innocent inquiry. "After I left, that is," he added.

Our brains astonishingly in unison, I shivered internally with relief, anxiety, and anticipation as I returned to the Führer but remained standing.

"Completely, my Führer," I answered, "at least for me. As I said, after you left, I went to where you were sitting—I think. I don't know with whom you could have been speaking, since no one was in the other chair when I arrived. It was all very confusing. I waited a few minutes, then I left and went straight to my quarters and to bed. As I said, nothing exciting. That is," I paused pregnantly to convey self-conscious doubt, "unless you consider dreams."

He wagged his hand to have me sit back down, which I did.

"Dreams, eh?" the Führer asked. "What dreams?"

"Just one dream, I think, my Führer, maybe more. I don't always know."

"But an exciting one?" he asked so quietly that I had to strain to hear it.

"It was only a dream."

"Tell that to Pharaoh," he jibed.

A rather obscure Biblical reference for the Führer to throw at someone like me, I reflected, and not a little ambiguous, considering it was a dream that caused Joseph's callously envious brothers to sell him into slavery in Egypt in the first place. "Who?"

"Tell me about the dream, Linge. I'm not the Jew Bloch, but I do know a thing or two about dreams."

"It's not that clear, my Führer, and it was also confounding," I began with deliberate clumsiness to emphasise my ingenuous and inarticulate perplexity. "I say confounding because my dream involved… I don't know how to say… the time, I think, once I'd returned to my quarters. It was like when I was in your study, the same… but different, so different that even to this moment, I'm not certain which was which—or if either one was real. So my account must be, at its best, unreliable."

The Führer lapsed into a long silence, during which his fingers worked the edges of his tunic jacket. I'd hoped for that sort of gesture but harboured ambivalent feelings over his readiness to perform it, for I knew that I was suddenly dealing with a desperate man. It was both comforting and disquieting. This was the Führer, after all, *the Führer I was attempting to undermine*—for his own good, mind you—a man of historic brilliance and greatness, yet with one character flaw that I felt diminished, perhaps even negated, that very brilliance and greatness. *But who am I to make that outrageous assessment?* An unlettered menial not even thirty. So, as I stood there dissembling, I loathed myself for the seeming disproportionateness of it all. *And yet…*

"Not to worry, Linge," the Führer soothed. "Oftentimes, impressions are more accurate than transcripts."

And more useful, I added to myself. "Yes, my Führer," I conceded, "I'll try. It's like this. I think I was just nodding off when I heard a low hissing sound like a rush of air that seemed to be coming from the gap below my door, and—"

"Ah, the notorious replaced door," the Führer interjected, perhaps to calm me with more levity and also to demonstrate the degree of his personal involvement in "family" trivia. But that remark only distressed me more and further steeled my resolve because he didn't feel the same about concentration camps and euthanasia.

"That very door, my Führer," I confirmed to show I'd gotten it, then continued. "There was that hissing sound, and when I flicked on my lamp, you were standing at the foot of my cot. You were not in your pyjamas and robe or uniform but in stained and tattered prison stripes. Your moustache was gone, and your teeth were broken or missing entirely, but I could still recognise you. I was so dumbstruck, I couldn't move or speak. Your bloodshot eyes seemed to beg me for help, I think, but help with what, I couldn't figure out. Then, I was no longer in my cot but standing in my bathroom doorway, watching someone else in my cot."

"Intriguing," the Führer observed. "Who?"

"I… don't know."

"Well, try to describe him then," he prodded.

After a thoughtful hesitation, "A man. An enormous head and a thick chunk of black hair combed straight back on his head. But it was his moustache, like a walrus's, that was most memorable. The thick black hairs drooping over his mouth and extending downward at each corner. He was wearing a brown uniform with no signifying markings, but I could tell it was not German."

"You've never seen him before?"

"I… don't know," I said. "I think I may have seen him. In your study. When you weren't here. But I know it couldn't have been real, even if true."

"Go on."

"The man, he… began laughing, a gloating kind of laughing, you know, not a joking kind of laughing. At least, that's what it seemed to me."

"Gloating over what?" the Führer pushed gently.

"To the best I can recall—you know my memory—I think his words were that… 'As you can see, fox has no chance against bear, especially bear who's possessing audacity and fox who listens to fools and tarries.' I say 'think' because he spoke with a heavy accent I couldn't place, but it wasn't German. And I didn't know what he meant by fox, bear, and tarries."

"What do you think he meant?"

"That's what you asked him, whistling your words through your broken front teeth."

"What did he say?"

I shrugged. "That's the thing, my Führer," I explained. "I turned away for a moment, and when I looked back, the man was gone, and a woman was in the cot instead. The man had just vanished."

The Führer nodded. "In dreams, Bloch once told me, events cannot necessarily be anticipated or predicted, interpretations after the fact, maybe—you know how Jews talk. Did you know this woman?"

I would never identify Katrin to the Führer, who had to already know. "I… think I'd seen her before, but it could be just… just another part of my dream. An older one. It was all very mystifying and troubling."

"I have no doubt. Did the woman say anything?"

"I… can't be sure, my Führer, but I think she said that you—please forgive me—were a gullible fool, that you had the means to, as she put it, 'assume absolute power and change reality as we know it'—I know it sounds crazy—but that you hesitated like a… I think she said… 'frightened virgin'—again, please forgive me—instead of 'immediately and decisively using what you had to slowly strangle them into submission,'" I added, to put the next phase of my strategy in place.

I thought I glimpsed a brief smile at the imagery. "Forgiven, Linge," the Führer soothed. "She used the past tense?"

"I think so. No," I corrected, "I'm sure it was the past tense."

"Go on."

"Yes. She motioned me over from the doorway, and I sat down on the edge of the cot, my head in my hands. I looked up, my chest tightening."

"And what was it that I had? In your dream, that is?" the Führer nudged.

I stared for a few moments, deciding to stretch ever tighter the rubber band of the Führer's need to know, then I answered, hesitatingly, "The… 'toy,' whatever that is, and… me. You see, my Führer, how crazy dreams can be?"

He regarded me for a moment, then rose, quickly motioning me to remain seated, moved over to the immense window, tugged slightly on the thick cord, admitting a pale wash of late-morning February sunlight, and returned to his seat. As he looked me up and down, I did the same for him, only far more surreptitiously. He appeared flushed, and a little line of perspiration shone on his forehead, tracing the glistening black slash of his matted hair. His right hand trembled slightly. His face had also stiffened, a change which I attributed to him no longer assuming the role of benign facilitator but engrossed listener, taking it all in. For my part, I was considerably more at ease than I had expected to be. He nodded for me to continue.

A cold sweat trickled down my neck. *How could I do this without revealing the nature of my memory?* Certainly not while awake and lucid, and I dared not risk another "episode" so soon. In the throes of incipient panic, only one thing occurred to me—not a great deal less of a hazard, but it had to be risked.

"I… I can't remember," I told him with trembling hands, fluttering eyelids, and a nervous shrug to underscore my embarrassment and embryonic infirmity. "You know my memory is meagre and faulty at best. And right now, I'm not feeling too well. But it's only a stupid dream, my Führer, and I'm mortified for taking up your priceless time with, ah, such… such…" I let the rest trail off, praying the Führer would supply the remedy.

For a protracted moment, he said nothing, then he leaned over and pressed a blue button on his console. "No dream is stupid, Linge. By stupid, I assume you meant trivial. But not true. Sometimes, our dreams are more significant than our waking moments. A bit esoteric for you? Well, it doesn't matter. Morell will be here in a jiffy and quickly get you up and running."

Within minutes, a perfunctory tap sounded on the door, and the doctor entered with his little case, moved immediately to the Führer, and spread apart the top of his medical case the way I imagined a midwife dealt with her patients' legs.

"Not me, Morell," the Führer said, jutting his chin forward. "Linge here."

The frog turned to look down at me for the first time since he'd entered. "Ah, Linge," he said, then turned back. "What can I do for him, my Führer?" The doctor was sweating profusely, despite the moderate temperature in the room.

"He was right in the middle of telling me about a dream he had, then he began feeling indisposed and couldn't remember the rest. Not that the dream is important, you understand," he added, "but we don't want him unwell. So perform your magic. Like you do with me, eh?"

Morell wiped the back of his neck. "May we have less light, my Führer?"

"Linge?" the Führer called, and I rose quickly, hurried to the window, drew the drapes shut, and resumed my seat. The Führer tugged on the chain of his green-glass desk lamp, and instantly, a circle of shadow replaced detail round the tiny area where the Führer and I sat. The doctor smiled, then moved the soggy handkerchief from his neck to his face, but the smile vanished at once, as though he'd wiped it off along with the sweat.

"So, you need to finish your story, eh, Linge?" Morell asked. "Well, let's see what we can do." He lowered his huge head and peered into his bag, rummaging with his eyes. "I think I may have what the doctor ordered." He chuckled over his lame witticism, extracting a small bottle of tablets.

I dreaded the physical effects of whatever concoction he'd conjured up but feared, far more, any potential mental inability to control those effects and get my critical message across without putting my memory into the equation. I was right since I could see that the label on one of the vials bore the name Bayer and the product, "sodium thiopental," was a powerful anti-anxiety drug. Furthermore, from an officer stationed at RSHA Headquarters, I'd discovered that it was used as a "truth serum" when less medicinal methods failed to elicit the required information. I was fortunate that the medication was in tablet form so I could let it dissolve slowly in my mouth, thus gaining time to simulate the appropriate behaviours before the real ones kicked in. An injection would have finished me and my plan.

Morell de-capped the bottle, shook out a pill, and handed it to me, then poured some water into a glass and did the same. "I don't have the liquid with me," he told the Führer, "so it may take a while," then turning to me, "Okay, Linge, down the hatch, and before you can turn round, you'll be as good as new, eh?"

I followed his instructions, counted to ten, and began my performance with no time to lose. "What's going to happen, doctor?" I asked, trying not to show in my speech the tablet jammed between my gum and cheek.

"You should experience some drowsiness, slowed breathing, and a general sense of relaxation and well-being. Not a trouble in the world, nothing inhibiting you."

"Yes," I replied, "I can already—" I stopped myself and slumped farther into the warm plushness of the armchair.

The Führer fixed his gaze on Morell and shrugged.

"He'll be fine now, my Führer," the doctor said.

The Führer nodded. "Thank you, Morell. I can see that. I won't need you until morning."

After Morell left, the Führer turned to me. "You were telling me about the woman and the top."

"Yes, my Führer," I replied in as lucidly somnambulistic a tone as I could muster and, at the same time, simulated Katrin's cadence. "I was saying—no, she was saying—to you, 'With all your hysterical bluster, you lacked the will to assume ultimate power. Being intoxicated by grovelling acquiescence and ersatz expertise, you blindly trusted the assurances of dangerous inferiors my predecessor on the cot would have had exterminated as a matter of routine. So, while you dithered with your only toy, he attacked, and now, all that's left of your vaunted Reich is you,' she spat with a contemptuous chin-jutting nod, 'such as you are.' Then she vanished, and the thick-moustachioed man reappeared in her place, stared at you with an expression of intense condescension, called out, and some odd-uniformed men came in and removed you. He rose from the cot, motioned me back into it, smiled crookedly, and left. Then your buzzer must have awakened me. At least I hope so."

The Führer breathed out a laugh, but it was a laugh muted by a minimum of mirth. He looked shaken. He removed a handkerchief from his breast pocket and mopped his forehead; the handkerchief came away grey with perspiration. But then a look of near transfiguration spread over his face, and I knew that it made enough sense for him to accept it. And where there were holes in my narrative—and I sensed that if he gave it some critical thought, he would find many holes—the anticipation of the benefits to be gained was enough to plug the gaps. He was ready to believe. It suited him to believe. He needed to believe. I saw it plainly and knew that I'd timed it just right. What I'd said had decisively overridden how I'd said it. And now, as the actual effects of the drug began to envelop me, I could surrender to them with far more than that sense of well-being that Morell had mentioned. I'd made my point.

IT WAS WHEN I was hurrying to put on my uniform jacket that I glimpsed the small envelope edging out from the breast pocket. Long ago, I'd ceased concerning myself with the how of such things. At this point, it was only the what and the why. Since the early Führerbuzzer prevented me from inspecting the contents, I pushed the envelope down and raced out.

The summons turned out to come from a frantic Dr. Morell. In the empty antechamber, presumably having dismissed Günsche, two sentries, and Arnt by virtue of physician's privilege, he informed me, with ragged breath and glistening acne scars, that the Führer was in the throes of a "crisis of mysterious origin" and had demanded my ministrations more than his—a concession of no small consequence for an egomaniacally self-obsessed creature like Morell. He mentioned nothing about the previous evening.

From the beginning, I'd known that the Führer was in delicate health, both physically and emotionally. But it was more than that, I'd concluded, as my self-confidence advanced, and I became increasingly capable of generating information from data and, in so doing, expanding the prosaic boundaries of the rules that governed *üntermenschen*.

"Crisis?" I asked him, genuine crimps of concern appearing on my forehead. "What do you mean?"

He didn't answer for a moment, merely closing his eyes and tapping his foot arrhythmically on the linoleum. It was clear that he was struggling with something. Whatever it was—fear for his position, fear of something he didn't understand—his survival instinct ended up defeating his reticence.

"Yes, of course," he began, "despite your overall ignorance, especially of medical matters, I must confess that the Führer's condition baffles even me. This morning, his face was beet red. Perspiration poured from his forehead. His hands quaked. His jaw was set in apparent pain. Now, normally, one of my special injections would do the trick, but this time, the Führer wouldn't allow me near him, screaming that he needs to be lucid and to send for you—"

"And what—" I tried to ask the condescending bastard, but he was too immersed in his agitation to listen.

"And the Führer was of no assistance, Linge. When I attempted an examination, he screamed away my questions. And when he wasn't screaming, he was pacing round the room, bent way over, mumbling to himself. I'm at my wits' end."

Considering Morell's description of the Führer, I was increasingly anxious about the silence on the other side of the door. "What exactly was the Führer mumbling, if you could make it out?" I asked.

"It was insane." He shrugged. "Insane! He kept repeating over and over, 'Places to go and I'm not dressed, places to go and I'm not dressed, places to go and I'm not dressed,' and on and on, then screaming, '*Where is it? Where is it?*' and back to mumbling, 'Places to go and I'm not dressed.'" Then Morell leaned over, grabbed me by the elbow, and aimed me at the Führer's door. "You need to get in there, Linge; the silence is more alarming than the noise."

⌁

Given only what Morell told me, I had my intellect and the proximity of the previous night to make an assumptive leap that whatever the Führer was experiencing, it might have something to do with my "dream"—perhaps everything. Of course, I needed more information, but as it stood, nothing Morell had related was inconsistent with what I'd told the Führer last night, save for the kind and degree of the delayed reaction.

His bedchamber being vacant, I walked warily into the bathroom to find the Führer sitting fully clothed in a filled tub of water, his eyes fixed on the ceiling and his lips moving soundlessly. I quickly emptied the tub, removed the Führer, dried him thoroughly, replaced his sodden uniform with fresh pyjamas, carried his limp body to bed, and tucked him in.

I'd just turned to leave when I heard a frail voice behind me, "Find it, Linge. Except for you, it's all I have."

᪥

Did my artifice push the Führer too far? I asked myself as I moved with considerable effort towards my quarters. It was as if the air had become a viscous substance. Morell had seen the Führer often in the grip of physical and emotional calamity, and I'd had to summon the ugly quack more than once. I knew him to be delicate, even fragile in certain circumstances, such being the nature of a genius. But this was different, and moreover, I'd suddenly been obliged to discover two other weaknesses in the man I once believed to be thoroughly infallible: credulity and dependency.

Finally back in my room, I bolted my door, caught my breath, and read the long typed note I'd been too rushed to read:

My Dear Heinz, much time has passed since I had the pleasure of your visit, and I would be remiss if I failed to provide you with a progress report. The construction that you witnessed on your tour is proceeding with dazzling Teutonic speed and efficiency, but not nearly enough, it turns out. The Reichsführer SS just departed after a brief visit. Before leaving, he informed my husband that because nearby factories use prisoners for forced labour, he is concerned about the prisoner capacity of the camp. As a result, he ordered both the expansion of Auschwitz I camp facilities to hold thirty thousand prisoners and the building of a camp near Birkenau for an expected influx of a hundred thousand more. The Reichsführer also ordered that the camp supply ten thousand prisoners for forced labour to construct an I. G. Farben factory complex at Dwory, about a mile away.

It is clear, at least to me, that Himmler expects a massive influx of "Meyers," among others, and I scarcely imagine they will come from Greece. It is also clear again—at least to me— that from Himmler's words, the meeting was to be completely internal to the RSHA and that it will be kept from the Führer (that such a development could be so kept is something I would ask you to consider). But at the very least, I felt you should know.

Needless to say, but I say it: your visit was most opportune— and most necessary. Details aside, it is clear, even to an idiot, that the Reich is gearing up for some momentous—and horrific— initiatives, and I fear that this is only the barest of beginnings. I have been in contact with our mutual friends in Paris and New York, and they share my deepest fears for our country. As Tolstoy wrote, "What then must we do?" What, indeed?

With my best and hopeful wishes, H.

Having experienced the likes of Magda Goebbels, Emmy Göring, Margarete Himmler, and even Eva Braun, I couldn't help but be amazed at how a woman as intelligent, sensitive, and humanistic as Hedwig could tolerate a creature like Höss.

What then must we do?

As I incinerated the note and viewed the remains of Hedwig's warning swirling down the drain, I was now more resolute than ever in the rightness and necessity of my actions. Yet at the same time, I felt a chill in my gut, a sure sign that I was overlooking something. *But was the sign as sure as I thought? Was it, instead, something I was ignoring? Was I such a masochist that I would force myself to consider all the possible implications of Hedwig's letter?* Since I didn't wish to consider myself so afflicted, the answer that came to me was both simple and stubborn: *No! But then, was I any better than the Führer?*

THE FÜHRER APPEARED to have recovered sufficiently but not completely, and so helping him dress took longer than usual, and he appeared to be in no mood to be timed. Later, as I tidied the bathroom while the Führer was hunched over, rummaging absently through his mail, I forced my brain to ponder the real significance of what I'd gotten the Führer to accept, it seemed, so easily. *How,* I asked myself, *could a man so flawed be worshipped by so many?* For the masses, I answered with ease—they didn't see the flaws. *What of his deputies?* Again easily: their ambition overrode the flaws they saw, even when they couldn't actually take advantage of them. *His acolytes, then?* Not a consideration, since those nothings were far too grateful to interpret what they saw, much less care. *But what of me?* I'd personally seen all his flaws, every one, up close and continual, and yet, despite what I'd seen and experienced, I… I couldn't say the word, but I felt it for him nonetheless. Absent that word, I was obliged to use the term venerate—for most, an unquestioning dedication; for me, a disregarding and, perhaps worse, a manipulating devotion.

But what had I really accomplished with my manipulation? What was the real difference between one magic acorn[66] and two, when the entire occult business was preposterous (despite hedging

---

[66] In Germany, the oak tree is considered sacred, and the acorn—the fruit, the seed, and the origin of the oak—is considered a symbol of good luck and even as a source of magic in numerous ancient tales.

my bets by "eliminating" the second top)? However, as I considered the matter, even the preposterous had consequences, and in this case, potentially catastrophic ones for the success of my strategy. As I considered this conundrum, I concluded that I would do far better to destroy the idiotic talisman altogether and assume its place. I dropped the small metal lump into my breast pocket.

I moved from the bathroom, and by the time I'd come round to face him, he'd straightened and was staring at me with such an excruciating longing that my imagination evoked a scenario in which I extracted the top from my pocket and handed it to him.

Once the item was delivered, his hands would be trembling so badly that he would have to hold one with the other to keep them still. After a few moments, the trembling would subside, and he would gaze intently at the tiny metal object as a connoisseur would a priceless gem.

"I believe that the Führer, in his… preoccupations," I would inform him, "overlooked an obvious place for the top."

"It has been in your pocket?" he would remark, his voice a bit dubious but beginning to brighten.

"No, my Führer," I would reply, "it has been in *your* pocket, in the jacket you seldom wear."

A long, ambiguous silence would follow, and suddenly, his entire demeanour would change. He would leap up from his chair and begin his iconic triumphal dance, its most salient feature being the vigorous thigh slap—but not before tucking the toy into his current blouse pocket and fastening the button.

But that scenario remained with me. *Who knew what even one toy could unleash in the hands of true believers, magic or no magic?* Without both, the Führer would be obliged to settle for a state of affairs in which control resided in me—or nothing at all. But I still needed to convince him of that and, at the same time, prevent him from confiding that to Himmler, Weisthor, Rahn, Katrin, and anyone else whispering arcane nonsense into his desperate ear.

THE FÜHRER'S WAR on religion continued. Just this morning, as I stood in the great hall waiting for Kempka, I overheard two industrialists pitying a cleric who had just been refused an audience with the Führer. I would think that Catholics, from that cadaverous Pope on down, would be content to take anything they could get from a demonstrably hostile regime and not make a business, but on and on, heedlessly, the sermons, pamphlets, and sanctuaries persist—and then they resented something as insipid as ostracism. Since the Catholic clergy's primary motive force was nothing beyond the self-interest of retaining its holdings and protecting its narrow flock, I couldn't care less about that particular war, its supporters, its soldiers, or its casualties, save to the degree it kept Heydrich and his fiendish minions occupied with more than Jews, Slavs, and political dissidents.

I was far more concerned with three other wars: One, my war against the evil intentions of the Führer's disciples; two, the war in my brain over the Führer and his grand scheme; and not least, three, the war between my persona and my increasingly impatient intellect. Regarding war number three, for someone who grew up in squalor, viciousness, and chaos, what at first was a game, and later a way of life, had morphed into an insufferable necessity and burden. Over the years, my close association with Brückner had put a progressive strain on my discipline, and my hunger to escape the prison of perceived ingenuousness had only become exacerbated. More and more, the juvenile inanities, the guileless evasions, the moronic reactions, stuck in my throat. And yet, I was beset by the agonising irony that now, more than ever, I needed my persona intact and operative, for my first war had to take precedence, if it had even the remotest chance of succeeding.

☍

Since my "first war" strategy required a further series of simple, swift, and complete victories to reinforce, expedite, and fuel the Führer's vision, followed by a protracted, full-scale invasion of the Soviet Union, serendipity appeared to be tossing roses in my path. I saw what Goebbels had already accomplished with the ridiculous Yugoslavia campaign, which was rapidly approaching its foregone conclusion and was mightily encouraged.[67]

While Rommel stormed Tobruk, the entire Chancellery personnel not on duty had their ears figuratively affixed to their radio receivers, as if there could be any doubt concerning the outcome. At first, I was surprised at what could be interpreted as

---

[67] On 25 March 1941, Hitler, in support of Mussolini, "prevailed" upon the Regent, Prince Paul, to declare Yugoslavia a member of the Axis powers. However, this move was highly unpopular with the Serb-dominated officer corps of the military and segments of the public. On 27 March 1941, military officers—mainly Serbs—executed a coup d'état, forcing the regent to resign. King Peter II, though only seventeen, was declared of age. Upon hearing news of the coup, Hitler summoned his military advisers to Berlin on 27 March. That same day, he issued Führer Directive 25, which called Yugoslavia to be treated as a hostile state. Hitler took the coup as a personal insult and was so angered that he was determined, in his words, "to destroy Yugoslavia militarily and as a state" and to do so "with pitiless harshness" and "without waiting for possible declarations of loyalty of the new government." The invasion began on 6 April 1941, with an overwhelming air attack on Belgrade and facilities of the Royal Yugoslav Air Force by the Luftwaffe and attacks by German land forces from Southwestern Bulgaria. The invasion ended when an armistice was signed on 17 April 1941, after the unconditional surrender of the Yugoslav army, which came into effect at noon on 18 April.

a minor twinge of concern, but it turned out to be merely rapt fascination with the general and a Teutonic thirst for the grisly details of a fait accompli. I harboured no doubt that no matter how routine and inevitable the shocks, miseries, and defeats Rommel inflicted on the enemy, they would be instantly hyperbolised by the Reichsminister and his propaganda machine into Führer-inspired conquests of biblical proportions. Catholics really should take note of the Germans' true religion before engaging in further indiscretions.

On my way to the Communication Centre, I bumped into Baur. I hadn't spoken with him for some time, and since he seemed eager to converse, I allowed him to lead me to the jammed Officer's Lounge, where we grabbed two just-vacated high-back armchairs positioned at right angles to each other, like in the Führer's study.

"It's great to see you, Heinz, my lad," he bubbled once our coffees arrived. "I tell you, now that we're committed in North Africa, the Führer really has me on the go."

"Doing what?" I inquired. "The Führer hasn't left the Chancellery, except to go on a few of his mysterious night outings with Kempka and Günsche."

"Yeah, well, I thought I'd catch a break with the Führer being home for a while, but no such luck. He, uh, loaned me out, you might say, to Göring, who's supervising test pilots so he can stay at Karinhall with his food, his loot, his concubines, and his Emmy."

I wanted to say, "And in that order," but self-discipline prevailed. "Too bad," I remarked lamely instead. "You sure look like you could use a vacation."

He bared some crooked teeth. "That bad?" he joked. "But I gotta say, I'm more bored than anything else. Hell, those pilots know their stuff. They sure didn't need me—or the Reichsmarschall, for that matter."

"Well, anyway, I'm glad you're back, I—"

"About the only thing that broke up the boredom," he interrupted, "was that loony, Hess."

I didn't resent the interruption. "Hess?"

"Yeah, a real character. I was at this airfield just outside Vienna, observing some tests, when Stöhr, Messerschmitt's chief test pilot, called out to me. Over drinks that evening, he told me that Hess went directly to Messerschmitt himself to try out the new Me 210, the very latest two-engined plane, a really swift job that hadn't yet become operational."

"So?" I inquired lazily with a feeble shrug and barely pursed lip, desperate to disguise my excitement.

"So?" he exclaimed lightly. "You know as well as I do that the Führer hates Hess flying and had even forbidden him to fly without a full flight captain with him."

"Yeah, right, I totally forgot about that," I admitted, bumpkin that I was.

"Well anyway," he went on, "despite the prohibition, Hess went right to Messerschmitt himself—who also knew about the prohibition—and told him he was to engage in a special mission he couldn't talk about. So, what was old Messerschmitt to do about the Deputy Führer claiming to be on a special mission, eh? You guessed it, so he let him fly the 210. But that was a little problem, it seemed. A bigger one was that Hess had several changes made to the plane. Like he had the radar apparatus installed so he could use it without assistance, not to mention showing a keen interest in instrument and beam flying. See what I mean?"

"Hmm, as little as I know about aeroplanes, I guess that's odd, all right," I mumbled, my finger tapping my lower lip just to show enough vague interest to spur him on. I was becoming concerned that Hess was drawing too much attention to himself at just the wrong moment—wrong for me.

"Odd's not the word. But there's more—even odder. A few

weeks after that, I happened to meet Hess outside the Führer's private apartments, and he came straight up to me and declared bluntly, 'Baur,' he said, 'I want a map of the forbidden air zones.' I had—"

"Forbidden air zones?" I cut in. I had a pretty good idea what Hess was up to, but the unstable audacity of his approach could spoil everything.

"Yeah," Baur said, "showing those zones over which even German planes aren't allowed to fly, or only at certain definite heights. I had such a map, for my use, of course, but I believed I wasn't to share such a top-secret item with anyone else. But since Hess was so insistent, I told him I'd approach Milch,[68] which I did, and when I told him what Hess wanted, he seemed bewildered, but after a few minutes, he said, and I'm quoting now, 'Well, after all, he is the Deputy Führer, and I suppose there's such a thing as being overcautious. I'd better let him have it.' Do you fucking believe it, Heinz?"

I shrugged with dramatic perplexity. "Well, if the likes of Milch is satisfied, who am I to—"

Baur nodded with reluctance. "Same with me, but hell, can you imagine him taking the Führer's place if... I can't even say it."

I forced a laugh, easier for me now because I knew Hess had gotten unofficial but efficacious enablement and the Führer would be none the wiser. "To be frank, Hans," I replied, "I can't see anyone replacing the Führer, except maybe Günsche," I added for a good guffaw, though my thoughts held no humour. *Who indeed?*

---

[68] Field Marshal Erhard Milch was chief of the Luftwaffe, directly under Göring.

WHILE I RAN the Führer through his toilette, Goebbels bustled in with the news that Yugoslavia had just surrendered—another leisurely triumph—and yet the Führer was unusually muted.

"Hardly a surprise, Joseph." He moved to his desk, easing his backside into his chair with hemorrhoidal delicacy.

"No, my Führer," Goebbels said, "certainly no surprise, but," he countered gently, "with Rommel trouncing the British, and now with the surrender of Yugoslavia, when I'm finished trumpeting your achievements, the notion of an unstoppable Führer and invincible Reich will become terms of art spoken round the world."

Goebbels's eloquence always amazed me. No matter the situational hurdles, he always seemed to pull out just the right rhetoric as swiftly and accurately as the star of a Western movie pulled out his revolver. But the Führer was still unmoved.

"Thank you, Joseph," he said with a few head bobs to signal his appreciation. "Of that, I have no doubt. Please prepare a radio speech for me this afternoon. And now, I must finish dressing and see Morell so I'll be in fine form when I make the announcement." That was Führer-speak for one of the doctor's recondite injections.

With that, Goebbels—never one to misinterpret the Führer's intentions—told him the speech would be ready for review before noon, saluted, and left almost as hurriedly as he'd arrived.

When the Führer remained seated, I asked him if he was all

right, Morell being mentioned, his lack of enthusiasm, and all that. Pure ritual on my part, and so, essential.

"I wish I shared Goebbels's verve." He sighed. "I know I promised the Duce to save his hide and not least, his pride, but although we won handily, an outcome I never doubted for a moment, I think I've—what's the saying?—bitten off more than I can chew."

I thought I knew what the Führer was unhappy about, but I wanted him to say it. It never mattered to me before, but now it did, for it could muck up my strategy. I widened my eyes in ostentatious incredulity. "Yugoslavia, my Führer?" I exclaimed.

The Führer nodded indulgently. "I can't expect you to know something of which even my esteemed generals seem ignorant, but in truth, there *is* no Yugoslavia."

"Not any more, of course, my Führer," I told him, while knowing that was not what the Führer meant.

He smiled thinly. "Not at any time, Linge. That's my point. What's called Yugoslavia is just one more bastard child of the last war—and a dangerous one at that—an ill-fitting mosaic of hostile ethnic pieces forced together into something vaguely resembling a nation."

"But—" I started to reply, knowing the Führer would ignore it, as usual.

"Do you know what irony is, Linge?"

He'd asked me that question so many times, anyone else would have lost count. "I've seen the word in your books, but…" I let my ritual ignorance trail off into a shrug, and his head performed a metronome of disappointment.

"Linge, how many times have I told you that seeing isn't reading? I'll have to arrange for a tutor to help you make some meaning out of all those books I've been loaning you—and a bookcase, since your cot must be close to scraping the ceiling by now. In any event, the irony is that what wasn't a nation before, is one now—and precisely because we conquered it."

I needed to know the implications for me of what he was lamenting. "But why should that matter, my Führer?"

He chuckled grimly. "Because, my innocent friend, so-called Yugoslavia isn't France. Those primitive ethnic tribes will now unite, and soon, my troops will become bogged down in fierce resistance fighting. Mark my words, the Balkans could well become another front, and I ask you: How many fronts can I take before I run out of backs?"

Even as dark as it was, I marvelled at the Führer's humour over such a potentially catastrophic development (no less for me than for him). In point of fact, I hoped that the chaotic tapestry of "primitive ethnic tribes" the Führer referred to would keep the Wehrmacht busy and so delay the Führer's occult master plan, at least until Hess completed his "mission." But now, I saw that it might well fatally interfere with or even cancel it. I was reasonably certain that Brückner would have advised against basing any plan on the predictability of such a savage, volatile, and hate-filled hodgepodge of peoples.[69]

But there was little I could do now, save harbouring the consoling notion that the Führer would have come to the aid of Mussolini, regardless of anything I might have said or done. And so I could only stand by and hope that soon, the Duce would come to shoulder the insuperable burden, and there would only be the blessed delay I needed.

"My Führer," I ventured, expecting that he would, again,

---

[69] A list of Balkan clans includes Greeks, Albanians, Macedonians, Bulgarians, Romanians, Serbs, Montenegrins, and Bosnian Muslims. Other smaller groups of people found in the Balkans include the Vlachs and the Roma (Gypsies), neither of whom has a national state.

take the credit for something I hadn't yet mentioned. "I know I'm not learned in these matters, but since no other of your possessions seems to require such… how to say… care, might you—"

"Yes, Linge!" he interrupted with a shout and a hard slap on his desktop. "As usual, your insight belies your ignorance. Deploy only negligible occupying forces to my other conquered territories and leave Yugoslavia to Himmler and his SS, assisted by a token complement of regular troops until the Duce can step up, thus leaving the vast bulk of the Wehrmacht free to fulfil my grand design. Brilliant!"

"I thank you, my Führer," I said, "but it was your—"

"Linge, Linge," he interrupted again with a benign *tsk-tsk* expression spreading out his little moustache, "after all these years with me, you really must learn to accept compliments, especially ones deserved."

"I'll try, my Führer," I promised him, and he seemed satisfied. It was a pity that any satisfaction I might have taken from the Führer's praise was diluted by a humbling sense that I was still operating astronomically beyond my depth and range.

"I'm sorely disappointed in you, Heinz," Baur informed me at breakfast.

"About what—this time?" I joked with some unease.

"Annagret, you idiot. If you didn't like her or the two of you didn't get along, you should have told me, and I'd have found you someone better—not that it would have been a walk in the park, considering you."

"She was fine," I told him. "We got along great."

"One date in a stupid cowboy saloon? You didn't even take her home. Shit, you could have even had a high old time in the taxi, for God's sake. But you? You do nothing."

"Nothing, Hans?" I replied with no little exasperation. "You say nothing? I saw her only two days ago."

Baur shook his head wearily, as if he'd tried explaining the theory of relativity to a lemur. "Heinz, you may know everything about being a valet, but about women, you never taxied out of the crib. Look, my friend, I virtually touted you to her as not only a stallion but the real power behind the Führer— well, close anyway—and so it naturally got her excited. But even without that, all women want—*need*—is to feel desired, and you're, frankly, no help in that department."

"I thank you for the promotion, but what should I have done, Herr Don Juan?" I inquired.

"Done? *Done?*" he shouted, then glanced round at the eyes that were now fixed on our table and lowered the volume. "Shit, man," he almost choked. "Do I have to tutor a strapping young lad like you? Look, you're an eager and smitten fellow, right? You can't imagine not seeing her again, right? And so you arrange the second date at the end of the first—if not sooner, right? That's how it's done. It's for the female to play hard to get, not the male. So you need to do something quick, am I right, Anna?"

I looked up to see Anna Döhring looming over me.[70]

"The least you can do," she said with compressed lips. "And you'd better be damn quick too. From what even I hear, she's quite the catch—way up on the list of eligible Party females. Don't lose her to one of Himmler's uppity robots, eh?"

She moved round to stand beside Baur. *How long had she been standing there?* Not unlike a balloon receiving more air than it was made to contain, my brain felt stretched beyond its capacity with schemes, counter-schemes, implications, anticipations of foreseen consequences, and fears of unforeseen consequences— not the least of which was exposure. But I also realised that I needed to rid myself of Baur's and Kempka's ceaseless efforts to provide me with a sex life.

"Blaschke's been sniffing round her," Baur continued, "and despite his vulgar appearance and manner, and maybe even his preference, he's no small potatoes. Plus he's medical." It seemed the entire Reich knew of her desire to become a nurse.

"You're right," I conceded with a dramatic gesture of concession, "both of you. There's no time to lose. I'll do it now, straight away."

⋰

---

[70] Along with Constanze Manziarly, Anna Döhring worked as a cook at the Berghof from 1938 to 1945. According to her memoirs, on this date, she was at the Chancellery visiting her old boss, Martin Bormann.

"I so hoped you'd call," Annagret exuded after several minutes of me waiting for the FB bureaucracy to reluctantly unwrap. "I hope you don't think that's too eager of me. I had lots of doubts that you would, since you must have your pick, and who am I?"

I noticed that she'd begun using contractions—and seeking compliments.

"Not as much as you'd think," I assured her. "Hard to believe, I know, but few have mistaken me for anyone important. I certainly did want to see you again, though, and I do apologise for the delay."

I heard some light laughter. "I'm right off the farm, Heinz. Patience is bred into us. I would love to see you again, is what I'm trying to say—even though you're not important." More light laughter.

Her open, humorous attitude made my heart jump a beat. "Then it's settled," I said. "How about a movie?"

On her end, I heard a muffled, "Get the fuck away, I'll tell you later," then she was back. "A movie? Yes, that would be great. When?"

I needed to demonstrate quick action to all my well-meaning promoters.

"How about tonight?"

Another barely muffled, "Shut the fuck up, damn you!" and she returned. "I'm sorry to put you through this, Heinz, but since I met you, I'm quite the celebrity. I need to check, but I'm sure that tonight will be okay."

"Why the need?"

"Here, we have to requisition everything, even time, like it's toilet paper."

"I can clear it with your superior, if—"

"Not necessary, Heinz," she assured me, rather excitedly.

"Just the mention of your name and position will be fine. You're important enough to these types."

I laughed, more to calm her than anything. "That's more than I can say for the Chancellery personnel."

"I really love your modesty," she said. "What shall we see?"

"You choose," I told her, since the movie was merely a device to begin my campaign as Chancellery stud.

A slight pause. "Well, okay. I told you that I intend on becoming a nurse, yes? Well, one of the girls here saw *Ich klage an* and said it's a really great movie for someone like me. She refused to tell me anything more, so can we see that one?"

I felt as if a light bulb had exploded in my brain. An entire milieu swirled round me, with its sounds, smells, and movements, but I was numb to it. Instead, I was borne back to the horrible moment when Günsche told me about Klara. Sheer force of will wiped it away and enabled me to remain attentive and composed, even nonchalant. I forced a chuckle. "You know, I'm so accustomed to showing Goebbels's American films to the Führer and his guests that I never pay much attention to them or what they're about, so any real German movie's fine with me. Tonight then. Eight. But one favour, yes?"

"What?"

"No uniform."

"I'll do my best," she promised, though I wasn't terribly optimistic. "Eight, yes. I'll be waiting. Heil Hitler," she asserted with no little vigour and rang off.

⌖

On my way back from the Communications Centre, I ran into Anna Döhring again, who told me she was returning to the Berghof but, before she left, she hoped she and Baur hadn't been too heavy-handed, that they cared about me and it was all for my mental and social well-being. I needed their concern and their matchmaking, as Adelsheimer used to say, "like a hole in the head," but as I reflected, having an active social life helped make me seem more normal, that was to say, less conspicuous.

"No, not at all," I assured her. "I really appreciate your interest. I don't mean to be a hermit, but you all know how I am."

"Well, that's what we thought," she said solicitously. "So, did you call her?"

"I did, right after we spoke. We're going to a movie."

"Well, all right then, have fun tonight." She gave a sly wink. "Nice and dark. And afterwards… well, who can say, right? Just don't disappoint Baur," she added with a well-placed elbow, then nodded, heiled, and left.

⌘

Any thoughts I might have had about being inured to the movie were dispelled the moment it began. As Annagret and I sat in the packed theatre, my heart pounded and my stomach felt as though it were brimming with bile, working its way like a relentless snake into my throat. I was only able to tune out the horror in front of me by gaping peripherally and constantly at Annagret's rapturous attention to all the medical aspects of euthanasia, both displayed and implied. Afterwards, as we walked in the bone-cracking chill to my borrowed saloon, her enthusiasm was still so palpable and my dark curiosity so persistent that I acceded to the necessity of searching for a café that was still open at such a late hour.

The place I finally found was well off the beaten track, oppressively loud, dim, vaporous, and crowded, the stink of heavy tobacco, stale beer, and grease heavy in the air. Out of uniform, we were obliged to take whatever crappy table was available for nonentities despite Annagret's striking appearance (a statuesque, pigtailed, FB poster model in a milkmaid costume).

Once seated, a waiter in a shabby blue jacket came over. He was about forty but looked twenty years older. I ordered brandies for us, and he shuffled off, I imagined, praying that we were his final customers of the night. After the drinks arrived, I waited for Annagret to wind down by having her review the movie. I certainly didn't want that, but if I were to continue seeing her, I needed to gauge the boundaries of her enthusiasms and to demonstrate a visible interest in them. And no less important, I needed her to believe in my complete sincerity—all of this requiring extraordinary effort, forbearance, and discipline on my part.

"Will being out this late cause you any difficulty?" I asked her after our drinks arrived and she took a sound sip.

"Not if I can prove I was with you," she cracked. For a farm girl, she had a surprisingly sophisticated sense of humour—or an ingenuous one that made what she said sound deceptively similar.

I should know, so I needed to discover which. "Well then, getting us past all the sentries, bringing you right to your dormitory, and knocking on the door should do the trick."

"Oh, that and more." She winked. "Especially if your tie is crooked and your hair—oh, I'm sorry, I—"

"Not as much as I am," I told her, "but not to worry, it's not hereditary. But the tie will have to do, I'm afraid."

"And maybe a few shirt buttons?" she added.

With that, I concluded that her sophistication appeared real, as well as the intelligence behind it. "Consider it done," I assured her with a wary chuckle.

We ordered a second round, which she drained in one swallow.

I merely took a sip, since I needed to drive both the car and the conversation. "So," I began, "was the movie all you hoped for?"

She nodded her twin blond ponytails to and fro with considerable vigour. "Oh, it was really good. But for someone like me, who wants to become a nurse, it might have shown a lot more clinical stuff. You know, this might sound crazy, but the whole thing reminded me of when I was still living on the farm. My brother had this pet hen that was always sick. I don't know with what, but it could have been something hereditary. It looked awful, could hardly walk. You see, even then, I had this scientific sense of things. Anyway, we'd argue every night about it. I said it needed to be put down. She could breed and would create more chickens like her. Naturally, my brother said that he loved that hen and, even if her condition was hereditary, he would keep it away from any possible breeding situations. My folks, both good Party members, mind you, sided with me, but were too lily-livered to do their duty. Even then, I could see that doing the right thing would be met with resistance. Imagine, Heinz, if all this was over a stupid chicken, how could the Reich do what had to be done, right? And my God, you were there when the Führer himself recognised this necessity and ordered it put into practice! Didn't it give you a thrill?"

Her face had become damp and flushed. She'd been speaking a little too loudly, and a couple of leather coats at a table not far away stared.

I made a subtle calming motion to her with my hand. "So, how was the hen matter resolved?" I hoped we could soon change the subject.

A sly expression replaced her passionate openness. "Well okay," she said, "I went to our local political officer and told him the story. He agreed with me that my family meant well but that my parents lacked the necessary Teutonic will, and my brother, the sense of duty to rid the barnyard of a pestilence. He said that the Führer was engaged in a war to rid the Reich of those who would sap its strength, and could we do less? Then he thanked me for my patriotic diligence, and the next day, he sent someone to our farm and removed the chicken."

"Your brother must have been pretty upset."

"He spent a lot of time beating me—big guy—but my parents, who'd finally seen the light, stopped him from causing any permanent damage, as you can see. And eventually, he came round and now, as a sergeant in the Wehrmacht, is doing his duty and then some."

I noted that he'd not joined the SS. "Still a lot of trouble over poultry, wasn't it?" I tossed out. "Did you have any regrets?"

She shrugged and pursed her lips. She stared at me with a distant look in her eyes, then returned. "Poultry? Heinz, please be serious," she said, almost in jest. "Even then, I didn't see the thing as poultry. Would you? Would the Führer? It was so much bigger. But now that you mention it," she added, "I did have one regret: I wish I'd put down the hen myself."

At that, a feeling of black exhaustion crawled over me like the roaches I'd encountered when I had to sleep in doorways, alleys, and jail cells. For a horrible moment, I struggled with something nameless—at least to me. And yet, I finished my brandy with a sense of macabre triumph. She would have personally exterminated Klara as if Klara were that chicken, only with more patriotic verve. I hated her guts. *Thank you, Baur,* I thought. *She's perfect.*

IN 1937, THE American social philosopher Talcott Parsons wrote that desire and belief jointly cause action; that a desire plus a belief about the means of satisfying that desire are always behind an action. Of course, being a product of academia, this almost laughably elementary notion was smothered with a viscous coating of pedantic argot, but I eventually drilled through to the essence. To me, viewed from the vantage point of the Crusades, Thuggee murders, the Inquisition, witch hunts, Roman persecution of Christians, human sacrifices—and Nazism, Parsons's notion was both obvious (even to an idiot) and empirically incontestable. If they required even more evidence, they would only need to study the Führer's relentless obsession with the occult.

Therefore, it became unavoidably clear that my fantasy scenario must become tangible: at least one top *must* be in the Führer's possession, and that any attempt to substitute myself for both, no matter how subtle and adroit, would be disembowelled as heresy. Though the whole notion was utter hooey, he believed it to the bone nonetheless, and that was more than enough for action inimical to my plan. Then the question was only whether Weisthor and Himmler would—even begrudgingly—accept the Führer's claim that one would do. *Shall I choose today, the day before the Führer's birthday, to give him an early "present?"*

"Does the Führer still insist on not being timed this morning?" I asked.

When he didn't respond, listlessly rearranging the chaos on his desk into different patterns, I started for the bathroom to deal with that particular chaos. At the door, I turned to see the Führer take a small dark-blue bottle from a desk drawer, pour himself a shot glass full, down it, and sit for a moment with his head tilted back while the mysterious Morellian elixir did its work.

As I once more cleansed the urine-and-shit-soaked mess off the floor, the Führer shouted, "Linge!"

I raced out to answer his call. "Yes, my Führer?"

Again, silence. While waiting, I made a surreptitious appraisal of the man I served—and needed beyond desperation. Even at almost fifty-two and not at his best, he was still dazzling in a faintly dissipated way. I believed that it was precisely this faintly vulnerable quality, the stamp of frailty all too visible, that made him so appealing to certain men. They saw in that face on its way to ruin the proof that men no better looking than they could rise to power. And as for certain women, it went without saying. But all knew, deep down, no less than the Reich itself, that the Führer was uniquely splendid in spite of his apparent ordinariness—and so, irreplaceable.

"You've defeated so many enemies on the battlefield, my Führer. Please permit me to defeat the enemy on your desk," I offered.

The Führer blurted out a laugh and a fart, then pushed himself up. "Hilarious, Linge. What Rommel is doing to the British, you'll do here, eh? Well, Herr Field Marshal, I'll go and create a second front in my bathroom while your battle rages in here." Apparently bereft of more martialisms, the Führer turned, padded into his bathroom, and shut the door.

THE ENTIRE DAY, and well into the evening, was dedicated to the ineluctably clamorous and effusive celebration of the Führer's birthday, crammed with the traditional—and for a long time, numbingly ritualistic—celebrations, military parades, commemorations, and birthday gifts. For the population, a necessary jolt of joy; for the minions, another opportunity for calculated sycophancy, but for me, only stiff-upper-lip tedium to be endured and discarded once done. It would have been the same for the Führer, but all had been transformed after last night.

"I'm afraid you're no mystery, Linge," the Führer told me as I helped him undress. "I can see it in your face. You're as bored as I used to be. But I can tell you now that there's one conclusive consolation: this will be the very last time for such nonsense."

"What do you mean, my Führer?" My eyes widened slightly as I prayed it was what I'd put in place.

"Ah yes, you wouldn't know, would you?" he answered. "That the next year will be my first. A true birthday. I see that confounds you."

I shrugged. "I… must confess," I responded with infantile innocence, "but so long as *you* know."

He smiled faintly. "Well, now that I've convinced you, I must convince Himmler, a far less compliant audience."

"With your permission, may I ask why the Reichsführer?" I hazarded, knowing that the Führer wished to convince Himmler that, if found, one "top" would do the trick, against all the information the latter had accumulated and all the time, money, effort, and (mainly) reputation and influence he'd invested.

The Führer chuckled bleakly. "I shouldn't have to, should I? But he's an old, loyal comrade and an indispensable—and discreet—soldier in the war against the Reich's internal enemies."

I knew what the Führer meant by "discreet": *Don't tell me about it; just do it!*

"Convince him of what, my Führer?"

He glanced down his pyjama shirtfront. "The buttons seem askew," he said, then his eyes returned to me.

"Everything is in perfect order, my Führer," I assured him as I examined each one with my fingers. "I have no doubt that you can convince the Reichsführer. If I may say: When have you ever failed to do so?"

He nodded with a slight smirk. "Of course you're right, Linge," he declared. "On your way out, put him on my calendar for tomorrow, will you?"

MARCEL PROUST WROTE: "A book is the product of a different self from the one we manifest in our habits, in society, in our vices. If we mean to try to understand this self, it is only in our inmost depths, by endeavouring to reconstruct it there, that the quest can be achieved." It meant nothing when I first read it in the city library to escape the snow and the police. But as I awoke today, Proust's declaration occurred to me: *Yes, to Proust, a book—but what of a plan? In the chaos and vicissitudes of war, what are plans but immediate and continual adjustments, adaptations, improvisations—and no rational means by which to predict outcomes unless we imagine them and then live our imaginings?*

With no warning, the Führer had Baur fly Günsche, Dara, and me to the Berghof. As the Führer put it, "Perhaps a last time to bask innocently in the sun." It didn't take diplomas or divination to interpret his remark, for the Führer had ordered the Wehrmacht to begin massing troops near the Soviet border, even before the campaign in the Balkans had finished. By now, the Führer had secretly moved upwards of three million German troops and approximately six hundred ninety thousand Axis soldiers to the Soviet border regions. Moreover, he had Göring include numerous Luftwaffe aerial surveillance missions over Soviet territory. My plan was proceeding.

And to all this, Stalin appeared to be entirely nonchalant, if not oblivious, to a matter about which he should have been alarmed to the bone and prepared to the last detail. It certainly didn't correspond to my masquerade. *Had such a paranoid creature actually been beguiled by that meaningless pact?* Even I, who had planned, schemed, and helped to manoeuvre the key German "players" into position, was confounded by Soviet inertia. However, I have no complaint, despite my incredulity.

WE REMAIN AT the Berghof. Having to be ready and able to adjust my plans to constantly shifting circumstance, I'd learned not to look a gift horse in any orifice, not merely its mouth.

At 0930 this morning, as I was on my way to the Communication Centre, Hess's adjutant, Pintsch, and Bormann's brother, Albert, rushed to me in a state of extreme agitation. The fact of Pintsch, a small, dark, stocky person of no particular account short of his position, told me enough, and I forced myself into some semblance of composure, not looking at Albert at all. "What is it?"

"Please awaken the Führer at once," Albert said, virtually breathless. "Major Pintsch has a very important message from Deputy Führer Hess."

At once? I considered. Perhaps it was my extreme antipathy towards his older brother, but I invariably ignored the relative cultivation and intelligence of Albert and treated him like the pig Martin clearly was, though both outranked me. Also, I thought I knew what was coming and wished to milk the moment.

"I understand," I told them, "but the Führer stayed awake until very late and ordered me expressly not to awaken him before midday, so I'm afraid I'm unable to oblige you."

Pintsch went slack and kept shifting his weight from one foot to the other and waited for a long, sweaty moment. His hands shook a little, the distended blue veins on the back throbbing visibly. Albert merely stood there, eyes fixed on me, but otherwise expressionless.

"Well then," I said, to move the situation forward, "what is so important that it would require me to awaken the Führer?"

Ignoring Albert's stare, when Pintsch spoke again, his voice held a harsh, genuinely terrified edge. "Deputy Hess has left Germany in an aircraft."

I looked incredulously at the major. "Yes? So he's left in an aircraft. He's an experienced pilot. Forgive me, but I fail to see the emergency."

Now it was Albert's turn. "All right, Linge, here," he said, a distinct note of displeasure to his tone, as though he resented even the slightest impediment to his errand. He reached into his jacket pocket and took out a crumpled envelope, which he held out to me.

The back of the envelope was covered with scribbles, scratchings, and cross-outs. It was clearly from Hess. I took it.

"Open it and read for yourself," Albert uttered icily, "then tell us that the Führer shouldn't be disturbed."

I lifted the flap gingerly, extracted the letter, and glanced at the salutation. "This communication is to Deputy Hess's wife," I told them, "not the Führer."

"That's not important," Bormann countered, now a nasty resonance in his tone. "Kindly read it and you'll see." If there was a way to express violent patience, Bormann had mastered it.

"Yes, of course, Herr Bormann, Herr Major," I replied, now all eagerness and cooperation.

I'd already gotten the gist, but they weren't to know. The letter detailed Hess's intentions to open peace negotiations with the British. He planned to initially do so with the Duke of Hamilton at his home, Dungavel House, believing that the duke was willing to negotiate peace with Germany on terms that would be acceptable to the Führer. More important to me, Hess expressed that the idea had been inspired in him in what he called a "dream generated by supernatural forces." I folded the pages and handed them back to Bormann. "Do you really want to interrupt the Führer's direct-ordered slumber with the news that his Deputy Führer is insane?" Knowing Albert's brother as I did, I knew he wanted that exact thing as did I.

Before Albert could respond with a resounding yes, Pintsch said, "Look, it was my boss's final order to me, and I feel an obligation to carry it out. I have no illusions about the consequences for me, but I have to put loyalty above personal considerations. You of all people can appreciate that, can't you?"

Can I? It was a good and devastating question I was in no position or mood to answer honestly. All I knew was that I'd pulled the rubber band as tight as I dared without it breaking and slapping me in the face. I needed the Führer to read the message in a state of shock and agitation and these two desperate characters were handing me the opportunity on a polished silver tray.

"Of course, Herr Major," I told him, again, not looking at Albert. "No one reveres loyalty more than the Führer," I told him truthfully. "This will devastate him, you know." At least I hoped it would. "Wait here," I instructed them. "I'll deliver the news personally." I left them and went at once to the Führer's door and knocked.

After a few moments, he asked, "What is it, Linge?" His voice was loud and harsh, grating. I was immediately on guard. With a trembling voice, I reported that I had some news about the Deputy Führer from his adjutant and that he had a letter from Hess to deliver. Before I had the opportunity to shock him, he shocked me by appearing in the open doorway fully dressed and shaved, his face livid, and the veins on his neck inflated and throbbing.

"Bring him to me," he commanded.

"He's with Herr Bormann," I told him.

"Just Pintsch," he commanded, and I raced off and brought him back.

"Do you know the contents of the letter?" the Führer snarled through clenched teeth after reading it.

When Pintsch stammered his admission, the Führer had me fetch Lieutenant Colonel Högl[71] and had Pintsch placed immediately under arrest and taken away.

Once gone, the Führer motioned me into his bedchamber. "I know you're surprised to see me all gussied up," he remarked, as if it were just any ordinary morning, "but you were on one of your errands, Günsche was handy, and so I had him do the honours while I was on the telephone with Reichsleiter Bormann. God, for all his tireless efficiency, he's a coarse oaf. In any event, you know why I had Pintsch arrested?"

I shrugged. "I have no—"

"Then I'll tell you. Not because he knows what that lunatic Hess wrote, but for not informing me of Hess's elaborate preparations. My deputy!" he screamed, "Second in command of the entire Reich! He just decides to take a plane and fly off to England to make peace? And I'm left in the dark without warning or clue? I have to hear about it by telephone, and then this idiot Pintsch with his letter!"

Under the circumstances, I had no intention of telling him about my conversation with Baur. "This… is truly monstrous, my Führer," I declared with an ostentatious display of shocked umbrage.

____

[71] From April 1935, Peter Högl served as deputy to Johann Rattenhuber in the RSHD and was later appointed Chief of RSHD Department One, responsible for Hitler's personal protection on a day-to-day basis during the war.

"You haven't lost your flair for understatement," the Führer said. But suddenly, his features softened, and I even thought I saw the trace of a grin. "Calm yourself, Linge. I was merely testing my reaction on you before displaying it to the rest."

I just gazed at the Führer, once again in wonderment at how perfectly and brilliantly self-orchestrated and extemporaneous he was, a natural actor who needed no director or writer. But now it struck me that only he knew the real Führer—that was, if there really was one.

"To be frank," he continued, "I knew there was a screw loose with Hess, even as far back as Landsberg, and so this latest escapade holds little surprise for me. But since he was Deputy Führer, I certainly can't treat it as if I sent him, which I'm quite certain my enemies will claim. So, for the immediate present, we need the Furious Führer, eh?"

I just nodded vigorously, astonished to learn that the Führer had made someone he considered to have "a screw loose" Deputy Führer. My brain was in turmoil but lucid enough to still appreciate how well my own orchestration was proceeding.

He had me send for Goebbels, Martin Bormann, Himmler, von Ribbentrop, and Göring, who all arrived promptly, and all (save for Himmler) sporting their individual versions of astonishment and perplexity. I was dismissed to wait with the others in the Führer's antechamber. For obvious reasons, Luftwaffe Chief Göring was seen first and had to shoulder the initial brunt of the Führer's orchestrated rage.

After Göring waddled out in purple-faced humiliation, I sent Goebbels in, assuming a more strategic session—at least a quieter one. Von Ribbentrop's I knew would be just as quiet but hardly strategic, the Führer probably telling him to work with Goebbels on a multipurpose, face-saving cover story. With Himmler, I was certain the Führer would be ordering him to leave Hess to stew in his own futile madness, no reprisals necessary, and the Reichsführer would just have to swallow his bitter disappointment—and be grateful the Führer didn't blame him for the astonishing breach of security. All this contrivance was both boring and inconsequential to me since all I cared about was Bormann, my entire purpose in prepping Hess in the first place.

After the brother had left, but not before a withering glance in my direction and a snarling grin stretching his bulbous lips, I returned to the Führer, who informed me that Reichsleiter Bormann would replace Hess. "Certainly not as official Deputy Führer," he emphasised, "since the title left with Hess and will never return. And since the fellow never sleeps," he joked, "he can easily take on a few extra duties without even breaking a sweat."

And claim that he's the Führer's unofficial deputy, I wanted to add, but of course, I didn't. Success was enough.

BACK AT THE Chancellery, I encountered Baur and Kempka after lunch while on my way to the Secretarial Office with revised notes from the Führer. Happy for the break, I allowed Baur to coax me back into the mess for some coffee and conversation. I knew what it would be about but was interested in their view since I was confident they represented the mentality of those below. Also, considering Baur's position and our previous conversation, I wanted to know if I'd missed anything at the Berghof.

"See, Heinz," Baur crowed, imitating Kempka's whimsically redundant parlance, "did I tell you, or did I tell you?"

"About what?" I teased, as I knew he would expect.

"Right," Baur replied. "Even Kempka here knows." He nodded towards the chauffeur. "So you can imagine."

"Well," I said, "I was there when Pintsch and Bormann—Albert, that is—broke the news to the Führer, but nothing beyond that." A minor fib.

There was a pause, just enough for Baur to take a deep breath. "Well, from the beginning then. You know I was hoping for a few days' R & R and some family time, but at oh eight hundred on Sunday morning, the telephone rang, and I was told by Bormann—Martin, that is—that the Führer wanted to fly back to Berlin as soon as possible. I knew that he had intended to spend the weekend quietly at Obersalzberg, and I wondered what on earth was the matter. In any case, I got you all back to Berlin that morning, just as soon as I could, and by thirteen hundred hours, we were back in the Reich Chancellery for lunch. You went off to run some errands, and I went to the Smoking Room for some peace and quiet.

"From there, I noticed the Führer and Göring in the garden, talking pretty excitedly to each other, so I decided to go out and see if I could find out what was up. As I approached, I heard the Führer say, 'Come to think of it, Hermann, maybe something good can come of this fiasco. Perhaps they'll think I put him up to it and so consider me crazy too. At the very least, it will confound the British and keep them guessing, maybe even frighten them. Since your Luftwaffe can't seem to do the job, perhaps their reaction to my mental state can. What do you think, Baur?' Now, I ask you, Heinz, how does one respond to such a question?"

I reached down and pounded Baur on the shoulder a few times in a comradely fashion. "Look, Hans, I've been with the Führer long enough to know when he's leg-pulling, and I definitely think this was one of those times, don't you agree?" Even before this, I'd concluded from his own words that the Führer was less than serious about Hess's "mission" while, at the same time, desiring to keep his options open. For what if, just if, Hess succeeded and a battered Britain saw this as an opportunity to lessen its losses. Not a good outcome for me, certainly, but I could appreciate the Führer's position: one less front and little risk in eliminating it. And if Hess failed, the more likely outcome, no harm, no foul, as they said.

After regarding me for a moment, Baur nodded and smiled. "Yeah, sure, that's all it was. Anyway, you should see the Reichsleiter. He's not one for displays, but I could tell he was having a fucking orgasm over Hess's departure. Not really surprising, but there's something curious, though."

"Yes?"

"I heard him tell the Führer with no little malice, 'He must have gone mad. Flies to Britain, parachutes down, and hopes to meet friends with whom he can work out a political deal.'"

I shook my head, bewildered. "And what's curious about that?"

Baur lit a cigarette, took a few puffs, and stubbed it out. "Well, Heinz, I asked myself, just how did Bormann know that Hess had used a parachute?"

✦

Excitement wasn't confined to Baur. When I arrived at the Secretarial Offices to deliver the marked-up letter draft to Dara, Schroeder quickly hurried over to me, grasped my elbow with no little force, and tugged me into the hallway. Despite her obvious enthusiasm, her face was pale, exhausted. Her coarse features now seemed fragile and brittle. With her furtive whisper, it was impossible to tell whether the faint tremor in her voice was induced or genuine.

"You just missed Keitel," she told me. "The fat's really in the fire now."

"What fat, what fire? I think I missed more than Keitel, Frau Schroeder."

Her face lost some of its tautness. "Yes, Linge, my apologies," she sniped, a bit of the old Schroeder peeking through. "I forgot for a moment that you serve our Führer with your ears and eyes closed. You've heard nothing of Barbarossa?" Her smile was quick, nervous, almost fearful.

I hoped it was unnoticed by her, but my heart began sending mallets to my temples. Of course I had. As early as 5 December 1940, the Führer had received the final military plans for the hypothetical invasion of the Soviet Union, which the German high command had been working on since July 1940 under the codename "Operation Otto." The Führer, however, was dissatisfied with these plans and, on 18 December, issued Führer Directive 21, which called for a new battle plan, now codenamed "Operation Barbarossa." The operation was named after medieval Emperor Frederick Barbarossa of the Holy Roman Empire, a leader of the Third Crusade in the twelfth century. *But why does she care what I know? And no less important, why does she care, period?*

"No, Frau Schroeder," I told her. "What's the big deal?"

She looked up, her expression ambiguous—half-defensive, half-angry. "You can be quite exasperating, Linge. At times it seems to me that you're no more than a simple but efficient tool, like a screwdriver or a hammer. They also see and hear nothing. They're just used and put away until they're needed again. All right, you know nothing of Barbarossa, so I'll explain. Maybe at least your ears will work this time.

"I was called to take dictation while the Führer and Keitel[72] discussed 'The Barbarossa Decree,'[73] then gave it to me to type up the final draft for the Führer's signature, which I did, and he signed it without even reading it."

"Yes? So?" I shrugged with indifference. I was hardly surprised that the Führer had signed the thing unread. In actuality, I'd seen the document while tidying up after putting the Führer to bed and before placing it in his safe for the night. The decree was a major aspect of the preparation for what was now called "Operation Barbarossa," the all-out invasion of the Soviet

---

[72] Wilhelm Keitel, Chief of the Oberkommando der Wehrmacht (high command).

[73] Full title: "Decree on the Jurisdiction of Martial Law and on Special Measures of the Troops." On 27 July 1941, Keitel ordered that all copies of the decree should be destroyed but without affecting its validity.

Union. The document concerned German military conduct in relation to Soviet civilians and Soviet partisans. It instructed German troops to "defend themselves against every possible threat from the enemy civilian population without mercy." The decree also stipulated that all attacks "by enemy civilians against the Wehrmacht, its members, and retinue were to be repelled on the spot by the most extreme measures up to the destruction of the attacker." I'd remarked to myself at the time that Himmler himself couldn't have dreamed up a more satisfying protocol. It gave me some pause, but I mollified myself that anything short of a pitilessly long, brutal—but unsuccessful—attack on the Soviet Union would be an even greater disaster for the Reich and the Führer. The "toy" was another matter I would have to deal with separately.

"I would never presume to second-guess the Führer on any-thing," Schroeder said, "but don't you see what this means?"

I shrugged again, this time accompanying it with a facial suggestion of helplessness. "To me, it means that we're edging closer to an attack. By now, is this so surprising?"

She nodded slowly, exasperation and disappointment mixing in equal proportions in her voice. "That's the total-ity of your analysis? You know, Linge, there were times when I thought you were putting on an act, that you were trying to have people believe you were some genial simpleton without a serious thought in your head. But I must tell you that I now believe it's no act. You are surface, right through. No offence intended, of course."

"Of course," I replied with a "genial simpleton's" smile. "None taken. But I'd still like to know what you think the docu-ment means." The crone represented a type, and I needed to gauge its reaction.

She paused just long enough to take a deep breath and

spread her lips in disgust. "I don't see the point with the likes of you, but in memory of Klara, I'll indulge you. There is no way, no conceivable way, that the decree, even with the SS, not to mention the Wehrmacht, can ultimately prevent the Reich from... from inheriting hordes of miserable Slavs, not to mention the few clever Jews that manage to slip through. And you know what that means: racial pollution, mongrelisation, crime, a catastrophic drain on our precious resources, poisonous attempts at assimilation, resistance movements, and so on. It was bad enough with the Polacks, but now, incorporating the Slav capital of the world? Even Himmler could never keep up with it. I tell you, Linge, our inevitable victory will be our ruin."

I certainly hoped so. "Perhaps you should tell the Führer about your concerns," I advised, mostly in jest.

Schroeder rolled her hands into white-knuckled fists and jammed them into her waist. "Klara loved your sense of humour," she hissed through clenched teeth. "I don't." Then she pivoted round and stomped back to her office. Another constituency heard from.

13 May 1941

THE BIG NEWS of the morning was Kempka informing me that the Führer asked Bormann if he would like a uniform befitting his new position, but Bormann respectfully declined. I cared nothing about Bormann's attire, save that it indicated something about his attitude towards his "few extra duties," as the Führer put it.

"Did the Bear give a reason?" I asked.

"No idea, but it woulda been great if he'd said—which I'm sure he didn't—that a pig wearing lipstick's still a pig."

We both chuckled at that.

"No," I agreed, "a response like that would make him a whole lot wittier than he is, and also it might invite unwanted attention to his envy of Göring."

"Fuckin' true," Kempka admitted. "But like Göring, he is how he dresses, right?"

"To quote a famous philosopher," I kidded, "'When you're right, you're right.'"

"Fuck yourself, Heinz," Kempka kidded back, as I would have expected. "Shit!" he then added, "can you imagine if that fucking pig overheard us?"

"So what?" I soothed. "He can't drive, so your job's secure."

He nodded with some gravity. "You say that, Heinz, but that fucker would take lessons if he had to; just one more job. Him and the Führer, that's all he feels the Reich needs. Everyone else can drop dead—and would, it being up to him. To hell with him. Say, what's up with you and your giant dairymaid?"

I was caught completely off guard. "You shift subjects the way you shift gears," I told him. "She's fine, I think. I told you she wants to be a nurse, right?"

"Yeah. But with her farm background, you should tell her she should become a vet."

"Well, she… told me about her 'farm background,' but I think that now she wants to apply her skills to humans."

"She plays vet with you, though, eh?"

I considered our post-film conversation. "She does," I said, submitting to a brief lapse into irrepressibility. "But I have to keep reminding her I'm not a defective chicken."

He suddenly shivered like a naked man in the snow. "Say no more. Just so long as you're gettin' it, right?"

"Right," I replied with a simulated smirk.

≪

I heard the rustling before she came in. That's what taffeta was for, among other things. Then the breathing. As she entered, I could hear her breathing. Breathing was different in taffeta, especially when it served as a glossy veneer over an agonising lace-up corset. I sat back and closed my eyes. When I opened them, she stood there, staring down. She had glided into the bedroom with her sharp, narrow heels clicking rhythmically on the hardwood floor.

"Did you do what I told you?" she demanded needlessly. She knew I had, but she wanted the affirmation. She swung round to face me, her painted face hard, her blue eyes narrowed. "Show me what you bought today," she commanded, pushing some errant strands of hair from her eyes with an imperious flourish.

I wobbled to my feet, turned my back to her, and started to unbuckle my belt.

"No, no, not so fast," she barked. "Turn back. I want to see this."

I turned, my face flushed with shame, but I remained silent as I slowly undid the buttons of my skin-tight uniform trousers. As I peeled them down my muscular legs, I exposed a pair of small, tight pink panties. I stood, hands across my exposed crotch, staring defiantly at her. She gazed up and down for a theatrical minute, then rustled over to where I stood. The tightness of the panties contained my erection—but just barely.

"Very nice," she observed. "Small but tight—your panties, I mean." She ran her hand over my satin-clad tush and gave it a little pat. "These look much sexier than those stupid cotton jobs you usually wear, don't you agree?"

I nodded reluctantly.

"Yes," she affirmed, "very feminine." She ran a bright red, long-nailed finger round the tight waistband of the panties. "Now, if I remember correctly, I told you to buy the right kind of matching bra. Show me!" she commanded.

I glanced down at my own stiletto-shod feet. "I didn't get it," I admitted.

"Hmm," she snarled. "I'll deal with that." She drew in her breath. "Not to worry, dearie. I have something even more fitting for you. Now take your clothes off—everything except the panties."

I wiggled precariously as I pulled my uniform trousers over my patent leather pumps and onto the floor. Then I pulled my undershirt over my head and dropped it next to my trousers. All the while, she stood, hands judgementally on her hips, as I coated my body with the oil she handed me until I glistened, which was the way she liked it.

She moved to the armchair and brought out a bag. "Let's begin," she announced, and walked back to me, swinging a padded pink leather lace-up corset bra. She dangled it in front of me and said, "Turn round and lift those big, muscular arms."

When I did, she slipped it on and laced it as tightly as she could, fastening the catch just high enough that I couldn't reach it. "Now go and lie on the bed like a good little girl." She had gone again to her bag and retrieved four pairs of padded leather cuffs. "You know the routine."

I went to the bed and did a spread eagle while she fastened my wrists and ankles to the head- and footposts. By now, the tiny panties couldn't control my throbbing penis.

She then took a pair of rolled socks and tape from her bag, wadded them into my willing mouth, and affixed them there. "Now wait here." She laughed teasingly in my ear, went into the bathroom, and shut the door. After a good long time, she emerged carrying a straight razor glinting in the overhead light. She looked down at me, my taut muscles straining uselessly against the cuffs, my useless mouth emitting only muffled grunts. "Now the fun really begins," she murmured as she placed the blade at my throat, and then—

"I need to stop it here, Heinz. That okay with you?" Annagret asked, snapping the book shut and placing it on the bedside table. "My eyes are starting to hurt. All those damn science books I have to read all day. You're not disappointed?"

We'd met at a relatively squalid, seedy hotel off the beaten track. By now, my evenings with Annagret had settled into an exotic familiarity.

I sat up and swung my legs over the side of the bed. "Of course it's okay with me," I assured her, glad for the ordeal to be over. "I was fine just with the taffeta rustling." I was also drained, an unfamiliar lethargy having suddenly come over me.

"I thought my reading arouses you." Her lower lip pushed out into a pout.

"No, Annagret," I corrected. "Your reading arouses *you*. Remember, I'm the simple one. I just need you naked and willing."

For a seemingly artless farm girl, Annagret's lovemaking—especially her literary foreplay—was quite kinky, sadistic, frantic, and violent, yet in the act itself, tender and generous, with a dollop of irony thrown in. The first time, there had been an element of desperation in her, as though the act was done more out of hate than out of love or even pleasure. Now it was entirely different: She would remove her book from her bag, recite its obscene sado-masochistic tales (always with me as the powerless subject), and ultimately take me in a frenzy of bouncing, plunging, and scream-ing, time and time again, until she was entirely spent.

She smiled and pushed her loose blond hair back from her forehead. Her stare was ambiguous, but her mouth was relaxed. "Caught me," she teased, moving next to me. "I'll be better next time, I swear," she assured me while sliding her hand down the inside of my boxers. "And once I finish my nurse's training, we can play hospital, with me as the—"

"No," I interrupted, "let me guess: you as the doctor and me as the patient."

She giggled as her hand began its work.

THIS MORNING, THE Führer was altogether sprightly in accomplishing his toilette. He was already halfway done by the time I arrived, passing Goebbels, Keitel, Himmler, Göring, Canaris, Heydrich, and "Gestapo" Müller, all waiting in the antechamber and being tended to by a harried, sweating Günsche.

"Remarkable, remarkable," the Führer muttered to himself over and over, as though I weren't there, despite my standing directly in front of him with my stopwatch. When he had finished, he sent me to the door to bring in the seven officials, most of whom I knew.

Once all were seated before him, the Führer said with lightness, "All right, gentlemen, who's to be first?" Then, without waiting for a volunteer, he said, "Why not you, Canaris, since it was your information in the first place?" All eyes turned to the admiral, save for Himmler, who was occupied with his little notebook and pencil.

Canaris sat even straighter than his usual rodlike attitude. "Yes, my Führer," he began. "As I alluded to in my memo to you of the twenty-third, my source in the Kremlin reported that the Central Committee, War Section, met in Moscow to report, with disturbing accuracy, intelligence concerning an imminent attack by Germany. However, quite amazingly, Stalin utterly dismissed the report, claiming it was nothing more than disinformation from the British attempting to draw the Soviet Union into the war. And when the head of Soviet intelligence expressed a contrary opinion, Stalin had him arrested and shot."[74]

"My God!" Göring exclaimed. "Are you sure of *your* information?"

The elegant admiral turned his head slowly towards the corpulent martinet. "Even more accurate than your bombing missions over Britain, Herr Reichsmarschall," he answered, rather impetuously, I thought.

That seemed to shut down a narrow-lidded Göring for the moment.

"Any opinion, Joseph?" the Führer inquired of his minister of propaganda.

"Only extreme disappointment that I cannot use this information, my Führer. We certainly cannot disabuse Stalin of his delusions, can we?"

"And you, Keitel?" the Führer asked.

The OKW chief hesitated a few moments, then, "My Führer, you are aware that I have harboured—and expressed—serious reservations about attacking the Soviet Union. However, if what the admiral says is true, we have a truly decisive advantage over the Soviets that we must not squander."

"If what I say is true?" Canaris asked Keitel, his tone a study in dry ice. "Does the Herr Feldmarschall doubt my word?"

I'd observed that nearly all the field marshals and generals viewed Keitel with disdain for succumbing to the Führer's

---

[74] Though not every report proved reliable, Soviet intelligence reportedly named the exact, or almost exact, date of the invasion no fewer than forty-seven times in the ten days before "Operation Barbarossa" went into effect. The Soviets even recorded wiretaps of Germans discussing Hitler's plans, including one officer who declared, "They haven't even noticed that we are preparing for war," and another who said, "The Russians, of course, will be taken unaware."

influence and transforming himself from what they called an "honourable, solidly respectable general" into a sleazy yes-man with all the wrong instincts, whose only job was to allow the Führer to take control of the army. This was why I was surprised that such a compliant ass-licker could openly question the Führer's judgements regarding Barbarossa—something that momentous and in which I had more than a casual interest—and remain in command.[75] Keitel had even advised against invading France. If fools wished to consider the Führer and Stalin as equally paranoid and ruthless dictators, they needed only to sit in on this meeting.

"Of course not, Admiral," Keitel rejoined. "If the Führer is convinced, I couldn't be less so."

"Of course you couldn't," Göring muttered under his breath.

Based on the expressions round me, I believe I was the only one who heard him.

"And what of you, Heinrich?"

With excruciating precision, Himmler closed his notebook, put away his pencil, and looked up. "My Führer," he said, "I have no particular interest in debating the truth or accuracy of the admiral's report or Stalin's response." He paused—pregnantly, I thought—then, "But I am interested in"—he slowly lifted the notebook cover, flipped through a few pages, and glanced down—"the person who supplied the intelligence report with such… disturbing accuracy and how he obtained it. I imagine the admiral would be no less interested."

To be frank, at first blush I was astonished that the Führer hadn't already called his chief of Reich security onto the carpet for such an outrageous breach. But I should have realised that

------

[75] Even stranger, it was this same Keitel who authored the infamous Barbarossa Decree. See Linge's 12 May entry above.

the latter would be able to calmly and deftly shift any blame onto someone outside the inner circle.

All nodded vigorously and turned towards the Führer, who now eased himself back with his hands clasped behind his head.

"Gentlemen," the Führer began, "as you well know, I'm hardly a stranger to mixed blessings and two-edged swords, so I have some perspective on this latest… development. Heinrich, you, Heydrich, and Müller must make every effort to discover the traitorous swine, deal with him to the fullest extent of your ample resources, and take any and all steps, no matter how comprehensive or severe, and make certain there are no further occurrences. But my concern over security is more than compensated for by the wonderfully bizarre behaviour of Marshal Stalin. You must admit, Joseph, that for him to utterly dismiss the intelligence and shoot the lone dissenter could not have been richer fare had you and Canaris concocted it. Very soon, my friends—and mark my words—Stalin will be shaking his head amidst the rubble and ashes of what was once his crude, untapped domain—that is, before we cut it off," he added, running his forefinger across his throat to laughter and shouts of "Hear, hear!"

To me, the entire situation seemed queer. *Why would someone as reputedly paranoid as Stalin dismiss an attack by Germany out of hand, to the point of executing someone who dared to question that dismissal? But then, I considered, had I answered my own question?* I knew what Brückner would say.

❧

"And the world press says *I'm crazy!*" the Führer exclaimed after the others had left. "Aside from the treason, what if that Slavic dog had actually taken that report seriously?"

"Not possible, my Führer," I told him, no less rhetorically

than his question. "It occurs to me that you might have considered this just one more failed assassination attempt."

"An interesting analogy, Linge," the Führer remarked with an appreciative nod. "In your own simple way," he went on to my great delight, "you really mean luck."

"Yes, my Führer," I replied. "I was at a loss for the right word."

"I've always had luck, as you well know. But in this case," he said, "you're far too modest. Without the incalculable benefit of that dream of yours, who knows how the matter would have unfolded?"

Yes, my dream, for it was *my luck* that allowed the Führer to have his. I waited to explain this, but it was a test, and the results hadn't arrived until today. Yesterday, while the Führer and Morell were occupied in the bathroom, I was arranging the chaos on the Führer's desk and carpet for the day ahead and was fortunate to be the first to see Canaris's memo. A priceless opportunity had presented itself: I might be able to instantly establish what I hoped would become a working protocol with the Führer. Before he had a chance to read the memo, and just after Morell had left, I approached him in the bathroom doorway.

Whatever masterwork of pharmaceutical legerdemain Morell had conjured up this time for the Führer, I couldn't begin to guess, but the results were truly spectacular.

"Ah, Linge," he sang, an almost transfigured look on his face, "timing me today, you'll need a more precise stopwatch, I think. My clothes should fly onto me with no human assistance."

"I'm glad the Führer is feeling better," I replied. "I, too, am—"

"I'm ready for anything, Linge," he said, visibly excited, his angular face flushed with enthusiasm. "How is that Annagret of

yours I keep hearing about? The nurse, yes? You have something
to announce?"

"N… no, my Führer," I stammered, caught totally unawares.
"Nothing like that. I… I had an excellent dream this time, and I
wanted to tell you of it, that is, if you have the time."

The Führer clapped his hands and smiled. "The way I feel, I
could learn that I was Jewish, and I'd just pass over it—you get
it? Passover?"

"I… think so," I responded vaguely. *That fucking Morell*, I
mused, *a quack, to be sure, but a gifted quack, for all that.* "Well,
my Führer, in my dream, you were sitting at a dinner table in
a… what must have been… a bombed-out restaurant. Russian
lettering was scribbled on the two remaining shattered walls,
glowing embers of what were once tables and ceiling beams, dis-
membered bodies in foreign uniforms heaped and scattered all
round. A waitress brought over a tray with Stalin's head on it.
You informed her that you don't eat meat, but she could serve
it to your victorious troops. As she was about to remove it, the
head began to speak. It said that he had grossly underestimated
you, ignored all the warnings, and deserved to be devoured, and
that it was only right that you should be the one to eat it. 'No,'
you told him, 'I'll stick with vegetables. I have other plans for
your head. I believe I'll send it as a present to that fat stam-
merer in London, with a note telling him he's next, and that
both heads will be sent to that grinning cripple, Roosevelt, with
a note saying he needs to keep himself out of my business.' Then
I awoke."

I stood in stony silence for a time, and when no response
seemed forthcoming, I turned, went over to the enormous
window, and pulled the drapes aside to admit some apathetic
early-morning light. When I returned to the Führer, I saw
that the almost beatific expression on his face throughout my

recounting had not changed. I watched with growing concern. *Had Morell put the Führer into a drug-induced trance?* I thought to myself. But then he spoke.

"'I'll stick with vegetables?' Did I actually say that?"

"As far as I can recollect, my Führer. It was a dream, after all, and you know my memory."

"True, true." The Führer gave an appreciative chuckle, then moved to his desk and plopped down with spring-shattering abandon. "Thank you for sharing it with me. My own dreams, I'm sad to say, are seldom lucid, and when they are, they're of the past, while yours appear to be of the future—and a triumphant one at that. So dream on, Linge, dream on." Then he glanced down at his freshly arranged desktop. "And now I must see to my mail, eh?"

A friendly dismissal. I saluted and left, fairly confident that he would be able to properly read the memo I'd strategically placed as number three in the stack.

I WAS STARTLED awake by a firm rap at my door. I leaned over, switched on my lamp, and checked my watch to see that it was four-thirty in the morning. Not a little alarmed, I shouted that I would be right there, padded to the door in my pyjamas, and opened it. Heydrich stood before me, a tangible apparition, a sinister grin slitting his lips just enough to reveal a thin line of white. Normally, I would have been woozy with sleep, but the ominous context caused an ocean of adrenaline to surge through me, accelerating my heart rate and blood pressure, expanding the air passages of my lungs, enlarging the pupils in my eyes, redistributing blood to the muscles, and altering my body's metabolism so as to maximise blood glucose levels (primarily for the brain). I knew it was the brain I needed most.

"I hope I didn't disturb you." His SS policeman's idea of wry humour.

"Absolutely not, Herr General," I replied. "At this hour, I'm seldom busy."

The slit widened, accompanied by a touché nod that caused my persona no little unease. "Unfortunately," he replied, "we at the RSHA have no such luxury. May I come in?"

The adrenaline receded somewhat; I realised this had to be a social visit (of course, social by Heydrich's standards), for if it weren't, he wouldn't have come alone. It was only the hour that still disquieted me. "Of course, Herr General. Make yourself at home, such as it is," I offered, directing him to my only chair. "Please forgive the clutter."

"Policemen like clutter," Heydrich said, taking a seat. "Disorder suggests furtiveness."

"I hadn't thought of it that way."

"Doubtless. Your job is to create order out of chaos; mine is to discover the reason for the chaos and locate what the chaos is meant to obscure. It's really very simple."

"Simple for you, Herr General. But still, it's a pity you must come at such an ungodly hour."

"Well, not unlike you, we're slaves to our duties."

"But Herr General, I cannot imagine… you… with such power… would need—"

"Unfortunately, Linge, I'm afraid I must disabuse you of your innocence. With more power comes less freedom."

"I never realised that."

"Of course not," he replied with his customary superciliousness. "I wouldn't expect you to understand the subtle exigencies of command. But you can take my word for it or ask the Führer."

"Of course, Herr General," I assured him. My primary concern was when he would get to the point of his visit, not the "subtle exigencies of command," which he seemed intent on displaying at that very moment.

"I see you've made good use of those bookshelves I sent you," he remarked. "Soon, your collection of proscribed books will rival the Führer's."

"It's very possible, Herr General, since they are the Führer's. Now, all I need do is read them."

Heydrich chuckled in his usual malicious manner. "You might begin with *The Communist Manifesto*," he offered, aiming a languid forefinger at a particularly thick volume on a lower shelf. "Double your money there: a Jew *and* a Communist."

I nodded, agreed that it was a matter I would consider seriously, and otherwise remained silent, letting whatever passed for nature in him take its course.

He crossed one long, narrow, red-striped leg over the other with a balletic motion. "I imagine you're wondering why I'm here. Well, I'm here for a letter of reference for a young lady who has applied to train and ultimately join our exclusive nursing corps."

After six years at the Chancellery, serving the Führer, I believed that little could still stun me, but this did—and not merely because I knew this couldn't be the main or even the real reason for his visit.

"I… know of such a person," I told him, "but I hardly imagined she'd apply directly to—"

"Me?" He chuckled again. "Yes, hardly. But since she appears to have a… connection with you, and your name was mentioned in her application, it naturally ended up on my desk. Are you able to vouch for her? As a potential nurse, that is."

I smiled in such a way as to avoid acknowledging that I understood the implication. "I can say unequivocally, Herr General"—considering her chicken story—"that Annagret has all the makings of an ideal nurse for the SS and will be a credit to its sacred mission." I planned to say a bit more, short of rhapsodising, but hesitated and stared for a moment at the Reich's chief policeman.

His face, oddly enough, struck me at that moment as not at all evil, and this made me all the warier. I knew such faces well (his especially), and it was a terrible danger to take them as they appeared.

"That's good news," he said, "since, from what I hear, we're going to need as many such creatures as we can get. That primitive Slavic horde can't possibly win, but like the mindless brutes they are, they'll put up one hell of a fight. In any event, I should permit you a few more moments of sleep before the Führer summons."

"Thank you, Herr General," I said, waiting without breath for his real purpose in coming. "I appreciate—"

"Would you like to hear something quite amusing?" he interrupted, as I knew he would. At least he didn't wait to get to the door.

"Amusing, Herr General?"

"Well, we think so at the RSHA, but you know how relative humour is and how we are. Be that as it may, there's a rumour circulating that you might have been the source of the information that ended up in Stalin's hands. I thought you'd appreciate it."

The adrenaline returned with tidal-wave ferocity, and I fought to contain it. "Yes, amusing," I replied hesitantly, "and I am appreciative. You know, Herr General, I never thought, when I entered the Führer's service as a menial six years ago, that I'd ever achieve the prominence that would warrant a general of the SS relating an amusing anecdote to me in my quarters at oh-four-thirty in the morning." And if the general would care to tell me the origins of this rumour, I so wanted to ask him, but I waited to see how many prongs his pitchfork contained.

Heydrich barely stifled a hammy yawn with the heel of his hand, his usual way of displaying elegant aloofness, not unlike the faux fop Tyrone Power displayed in *The Mark of Zorro*, a film I showed the Führer at the Chancellery last year to *real* yawns.

"And how does such a thing begin?" he asked. "Who can tell?" Heydrich answered himself, clearly lying through his gleaming slit of teeth. "Probably from someone close to the subject of the rumour, I've discovered in my experience. I merely thought you would be entertained by the fancifulness of it."

"And so I am," I replied as nonchalantly as I could. "Thank you."

"I'm gratified," he said with a self-deprecating smil. "And now I must be off." He uncrossed his legs and rose, saluted, and left.

I just sat on the edge of my cot, numb—both mentally and physically—and waited for the Führerbuzzer.

I DIDN'T KNOW, or for that matter, care, what might be occupying the Führer's mind as I assisted him with his toilette, for I was
immersed in divining the reason, meaning, and implications of
Heydrich's extraordinary visit. Arthur Conan Doyle wrote: "My
mind rebels at stagnation. Give me problems, give me work, give
me the most abstruse cryptogram, or the most intricate analysis, and I am in my own proper atmosphere." *Good for him,* I
brooded, *but I'm not Doyle: I possess neither his brain nor his need.*

But as always with me, there's the *and yet…*

*What could be Heydrich's purpose in pulling the "rumour" out
of a deranged nowhere, and no less perplexing, who originated it
and why, and how should I react to it? Should I discuss it with
someone and, in doing so, bring to consciousness something no one,
even in his wildest imaginings, would ever consider? Or should I
keep it to myself and, by containing it, draw suspicion among those
who might gain by promulgating it?* As with Jung, "It seemed to
me I was living in an insane asylum of my own making." All I
knew at the moment was that I would keep the matter from the
Führer until I had a reason not to. *But without Brückner, do I
have anyone in whom I could safely confide?* Desperate, I sought
out Kempka and Baur in the officers' mess, told them my tale,
and spun the roulette wheel.

"See, Heinz," Kempka said, "is that creature something, or
is she something?"

"She's definitely something," I replied with no vocal inflection, not knowing what the fool meant.

"Shit," Baur piggybacked, "to be brazen enough to send an application that would make a smooth landing on Heydrich's desk and prompt him to visit you. Man, I'd never do that in a million years. A real prize, just like I said. Don't do anything stupid to lose her, eh?"

"That's what you got from my story?" I asked, amazed that the rest of it seemed not to matter—or even register—with these obsessed matchmakers. "*It was at oh-four-thirty in the morning. It was Heydrich. The rumour!*" I stressed in an intense whisper.

"Well… yeah, okay, but then it might have been just another one of those screwy dreams of yours," Kempka ventured.

I held back for a moment, not entirely certain of my timing—or my footing. "It was no dream," I assured them. "So, what the hell do you make of it? The rumour part, that is."

I was faced with two sets of pursed lips and helpless shrugs.

"Hell if I know," Baur said. "The Gestapo's idea of a joke?"

"It's their speed," I told them, "but it's not Heydrich's. His humour carries pliers."

"Right," Baur agreed. "Definitely not Heydrich's. So, then was it his idea, or was he acting for—"

"Himmler?" Kempka blurted, followed by the turning of a few heads.

"Discretion, Erich," Baur advised.

"Fuck, sorry," Kempka murmured through gritted teeth. "But hey, if not Heydrich, it could only be his boss. Am I right?"

As the chauffeur spoke, I noticed something seemed to be wrong with Baur. His head was cocked back at an odd angle; his eyes appeared to be focused on the ceiling, searching for something.

"You all right, Hans?" I asked him, and he returned, his eyelids narrowed.

"Look, Heinz," he said, "maybe we're going about this back-asswards."

"Yes?"

"Instead of worrying about Heydrich right now, the end of the trail, eh, you should think about the beginning of it. Like who you know who'd want to brand you as a traitor."

"Yeah, like an enemy," Kempka explained.

"Exactly," Baur confirmed.

I barely heard him. I was trying hard to remain calm and finding it very difficult. *Who indeed? If I did as the rumour suggested, what would be my motive? Why would I, of all people, do such a crazy, traitorous thing? More to the point, who would believe it of me in the first place? The Führer? Never. And who else mattered? Moreover, even if I discovered the bastard's identity, what then?* The whole notion was so absurd, it hardly merited pursuit. But of course, the inevitable: *and yet…*

"Is it paranoia for the wolf to complain that the sheep are out to get him?" I joked, while I thought about what Baur had suggested. "And anyway, how can a valet have enemies?" I asked, with some slight disingenuousness.

Baur laughed. "First you're a wolf, then you're a sheep. Mainly, you're muddled, my son. Am I right, Kempka? You should know. Look, Heinz, you've been with the Führer long enough to know that to him, you're not just a valet. Hell, even I know that, so I'm confident that everyone else knows. That being a given, you only need to ask one question: Who would benefit with you gone? Simple, eh?"

"Yeah, simple," Kempka echoed. "It worked for me, you bet."

"That's it?" I asked them. "What if I take what you say and discover who the piece of shit is?"

Baur shrugged. "Ah, well, of course that depends on who it is. You're an SS man. Now think: What would an SS man do? I'll tell you: if he's below you, eliminate him; if he's above you, kiss his ass and get someone else to eliminate him; if he's beside you, become his best friend, watch, and wait—then eliminate him. Also simple. Am I right, Kempka?"

"When you're right, you're right," the chauffeur answered. "And who should know better than you and me, Heinz, eh?"

I was forced to admit the truth of what they were telling me. And not only the truth, but the prospect of success as well. I nodded with calculated reluctance for effect. "Okay," I told them. "I get it. But what about the rumour itself? What do I do about that?"

Kempka was the first out of the corner, swinging. "I'd fuckin' deny it and challenge anyone who said otherwise to meet me someplace quiet and without our uniforms on."

"Sounds like you want a good brawl more than anything else, my friend," Baur kidded. "Remember, you're not in a 1925 Munich alleyway. I'm sure that our brawny Heinz here could acquit himself just fine there, but let's adjust to the present day, eh?" Then he turned his head towards me and fixed me with a Heydrich-like glare.

"Did you do it?"

"What?"

"Did you leak the information?"

I just stared back, mute and incredulous.

Then he stretched his flabby, fishlike lips into a broad grin. "Just pulling your leg, Heinz. You think the Führer believes you did it?"

"Absolutely not," I assured him of the idea's complete absurdity. "Never."

"Right. That's all that matters. The rest is a game, so play it. You ever hear of hiding in plain sight?"

I smiled to myself. "What's that?"

"If you're obvious, no one will see anything because you're so obvious."

Both Kempka and I shook our heads.

"It's not so complicated. I did it after the last war and look at me now. I constantly tested planes we weren't supposed to have right under the enemy's nose, and they didn't even notice me because I was so fucking brazen about it. They couldn't believe their eyes, so they didn't. Get it?"

Of course I got it, though I had my doubts about Kempka. "All right," I said, "I get it, though it doesn't make much sense. But what does that have to do with the rumour?"

Baur shook his head slowly. "*Ach!* How the Führer can tolerate your feeble-mindedness is a bigger mystery to me than who leaked the information. Look, if I were you, I'd milk the fucking rumour for all it was worth, and more. I mean, if and when it comes up, not only would I claim ownership of the deed, I'd crow it to anyone within earshot. The more you admit something outrageous but possible, and even brag about it, the less anyone will believe it. You'll get ribbed, but you won't get caught. Both the rumour and the perp will dribble away. Get it now?"

I'd gotten what I'd come for. It was late. We were almost alone in the enormous room, and I hadn't even gone to retrieve the mail. I gave Baur and Kempka my heartfelt thanks and reminded them of my duties. It was when I got up to leave that Baur reached up and banged me lightly on the arm.

"Hey, kiddo," he said, "before you go flying under their

noses and suspicion of you becomes a joke, you might still want to identify the comedian, eh?"

Kempka snapped out a laugh. "Man, is that the truth," he declared. "The asshole might try that shit again."

In their own inimitable styles, they were both right.

ON MY WAY to prepare the Führer, I slowed down to assess the value of seeking out Baur and Kempka, my own Rosencrantz and Guildenstern.[76]

"Who would benefit with me gone? Simple, eh?" Baur had tossed off. Simple for simpletons—or for those who know nothing of my singular life. *On the other hand, would Brückner have provided anything better?* But I got no further in my mulling because I ran into King Kong with epaulettes, my alias for Günsche, who informed me, half-jokingly, that my leisurely pace had forced him and Arnt to perform the rituals of the toilette but that the Führer still had duties for me to perform and I needed to get a move on. I could more than live with their mindless griping.

Standing in a corner after removing a snowfield of balled-up foolscap from the floor, I waited for instructions while the Führer and Field Marshal Keitel listened to Count Ciano, the Duce's son-in-law, explain the Gondar debacle.[77]

---

[76] Characters in William Shakespeare's tragedy *Hamlet*, Rosencrantz and Guildenstern are childhood friends of Hamlet. They are summoned by King Claudius to distract the prince from his apparent madness and, if possible, to ascertain the cause of it. They often stumble upon deep philosophical truths through their nonsensical ramblings.

[77] The Allies captured Gondar in Ethiopia, thus completing the elimination of the Italian Empire in East Africa.

Though the faces of the Führer and Keitel remained blank throughout the telling, I sensed in the former's gaze an aura of intense disenchantment, for I knew that, unbeknownst to the hapless Italian, the Führer was privy to an unfortunate remark Mussolini had made prior to Ciano's leaving for Berlin: "I've had my fill of Hitler," he'd said. "These conferences called by the ringing of a bell are not to my liking; the bell is rung when people call their servants. And besides, what kind of conferences are these? For five hours, I am forced to listen to a monologue, which is quite fruitless and boring. You go."

"Is that all you have to tell us?" the Führer asked Ciano once he'd completed his sorry tale, a faint smile informing his lips, as if he knew more but had no intention of disclosing it.

A grim smile answered him. "I am sorry," Ciano said, a downcast expression seeming to round out his normally angular features. "I can, of course, provide you details. For example, there were Italian casualties of four thousand killed and eighty-four hundred sick and wounded, that sort of thing, but I imagine you are already aware of these numbers."

"We are only too aware," Keitel said.

"Yes." Ciano looked so much older than when I had last seen him. "So, what more need be said besides—"

The Führer cut him off with a broad, conciliatory gesture and a look that counselled caution and diplomacy. "A pity, yes," he said, "but we'll take it from here. Please tell your father-in-law that I understand fully and that no further burdens need concern him."

I was sure that the count understood the Führer's reference to "father-in-law," instead of Duce, and that further joint adventures were out of the question. Mutual admiration had passed into diplomatic cordiality. A sadness hovered over the room like a shroud, and I was awash with relief when Ciano left with Keitel.

The Führer oomphed up from his desk, moved to the armchair before the fire, eased himself down into it, and extended his legs. "That was a grim episode, wasn't it, Linge?"

"I assume so, my Führer, though I only heard small portions of what you said and nothing of the count."

"No need to hear more." His pale-blue eyes made a furtive movement. A faint tremor ran along his cheeks. "I'm afraid my charm has worn thin with the Duce. But you know, despite that, and against all logic and experience, I admired the fellow, all the while knowing his failings as a leader and the Italians as warriors. I allowed him his delusions of reigning over another Rome, but the Rome he harkened back to had a different government and different enemies. I'm a rank sentimentalist, I'm afraid, despite what the world chooses to call me. Mark my words, Linge, if I'm not careful, it will be my undoing."

THE DAY'S COMPARATIVELY quotidian events were overshadowed by Annagret's exhilaration when I telephoned to confirm our date for the evening. When we began our association, I agreed that we would meet at a different hotel each time, and at her request, the sleazier and more remote, the better, for the insulated child in her longed to experience the aphrodisiac of furtiveness. Having lived most of my life with the hide-in-plain-sight concealment of my persona as a constant companion, I found the arrangement inconvenient at best—and fodder for more jokes from Baur's "comedian" at worst.

She'd asked me to bring a bottle of champagne to celebrate her "amazing good fortune," which I did, and she greeted me at the door wearing only a Cheshire cat grin and holding up a corkscrew.

"I hope that's not for me, since you don't use one for champagne," I joked with no little unease, as the stories she'd been reading aloud to me for her sexual arousal had possessed a distinctly sadomasochistic quality.

Still smiling but without a word, she pulled me into the small, shabby bathroom, tossed the corkscrew into the rust-stained bathtub, took the bottle from me, and with practised surgical precision and carnal slowness, removed the foil and discarded it. She loosened the wire cage, flipped down the small wire key, and pressed up against the neck of the bottle at the bottom of the wire cage that enclosed the cork. Turning the key to loosen the cage, she removed and discarded it, then draped a tattered towel over the bottle, leaving only the cork exposed. Inserting the corkscrew, she angled the bottle away from us at forty-five degrees and twisted the bottom until there was a soft pop of the cork leaving the bottle—nothing like the explosive, foamy waterfall effect displayed in so many films. She extracted two champagne glasses from her oversized handbag, which hung over the shower nozzle, poured only about an inch of liquid into each glass at first, waited a few seconds for the bubbles to subside, then continued filling to just below the rim and handed me a glass. *From the farm to the FBN?* Despite the tantalising anomaly, I didn't dare ask her where she'd gained her expertise—and choreography.

"From what you told me when I called, we have something to toast, yes?"

She eyed me up and down with silent, seductive suspicion, as if to ask why I was still dressed.

"Ah, I get it." I put my glass down on the end table, removed my uniform and underthings, tossing them aside with a striptease artist's theatricality, and retrieved my glass. "Now, what is this amazing good fortune we're drinking to?" I asked her.

"I just heard from General Heydrich's office. I've been accepted into the elite SS nursing programme and begin my training at a top psychiatric hospital under the direction of Commissioner Dr. Brandt himself.[78] You must have done one terrific sales job for me. You see, you're no ordinary valet. I'm so happy and so grateful to you."

The sight of a grateful, naked Valkyrie was far more erotic than her stories of a pigtailed dominatrix with restraints,

------

[78] Dr. Karl Brandt was not only one of Hitler's long-time personal physicians but also Reich commissioner for Health and Sanitation.

corkscrews, and razor blades. "I'm pleased for you. I just told the truth. When do you begin your training?"

"'With immediate effect,' the letter said, so I'm leaving tomorrow. I can't wait to get out of those sterile barracks."

How does one characterise relief and disappointment, something pleasant but tinged with sadness, a mixture of pain and pleasure, a movie with a bittersweet ending? I needed her, but now... Ambivalent was the only term I could come up with. "A toast then." I raised my glass. "To the next Florence Nightingale."

She stared at me with an expression that told me she had no idea who that was, so I risked an explanation.

"In 1853, the Crimean War broke out," I began. "The British Empire was at war with the Russian Empire for control of the Ottoman Empire. By 1854, no fewer than eighteen thousand soldiers had been admitted to military hospitals. Nightingale received a letter from the secretary of war, asking her to organise a corps of nurses to tend to the sick and fallen soldiers in the Crimea. She quickly assembled a team of thirty-four nurses and sailed with them to the Crimea just a few days later.

"The hospital sat on top of a large cesspool, which contaminated the water and the hospital building itself. Patients lay in their own shit on stretchers strewn throughout the hallways. Rodents and bugs scurried past them. More soldiers were dying from infectious diseases like typhoid and cholera than from injuries sustained in battle.

"Nightingale quickly set to work. She procured hundreds of scrub brushes and asked the least infirm patients to scrub the inside of the hospital from floor to ceiling. She herself spent every waking minute caring for the soldiers. In the evenings, she moved through the dark hallways carrying a lamp while making her rounds, ministering to patient after patient. Her work reduced the hospital's death rate by two-thirds.

"Nightingale became a figure of worldwide public admiration. Poems, songs, and plays were written and dedicated in the heroine's honour. Young women aspired to be like her. And you could be the next one—even better." I took a deep breath. "Impressed?"

She stared at me for a moment, squint-eyed, as if I'd been speaking in tongues, then she smiled. "With you, more than with Nightingale. But don't you find this whole thing titillating? I mean, the two of us standing here naked, holding champagne glasses while you give me a history lesson on nursing? Almost as good as my stories, don't you agree?"

"I never thought of it that way," I confessed. "The lecture part, that is."

"Oh yes," she said. "It was amazing. While you were telling the story, I pictured myself assisting in a euthanasia procedure, a hysterectomy, or an amputation, and almost experienced an orgasm. And speaking of orgasms…"

At that moment, I needed to race from the room but held on, lest she report me to Heydrich, so we drank up, clinched, and struggled with awkward abandon to the shabby bed.

THIS MORNING, GOEBBELS announced the invasion of the Soviet Union to the waking nation in a radio broadcast, with the Führer's words I'd heard him dictate in shifts to Dara and Schroeder in his study the night before. "At this moment," Goebbels declared, "a march is taking place that, for its extent, compares with the greatest the world has ever seen. I have decided today to place the fate and future of the Reich and our people in the hands of our soldiers. May God aid us, especially in this fight!"

I was certain that invoking God was Goebbels's idea: belt and suspenders. A Morell-augmented Führer had dictated until 0500, after which the speech was copied for the press in the adjutant's room, and I'd brought the pages from the Führer every fifteen minutes.

At 1000 hours, the Führer, dressed in his military-grey uniform (for what he told me was "grand theatre befitting the occasion"), drove to a session of the Reichstag and delivered a rousing speech to ear-splitting applause and shouts.

Later that morning, the Führer declared to his inner circle, "Mark my words, gentlemen, before three months have passed, we shall witness a total collapse of Russia, the like of which history has never seen." Then the Führer addressed the German people via the radio, presenting himself as a man of peace, who reluctantly had to attack the Soviet Union as a crucial part of a "European crusade against Bolshevism."

Many, it seemed to me, considered the attack on the Soviet

Union to be just one more prologue to a swift and dazzling German epilogue, only writ larger. For even more, steeped in relentless Party propaganda from the mid-1920s onward, fear and hatred of Bolshevism, Stalin, and the Soviets were so palpable, they were like a living thing, a virus permeating all the Reich, all the way down into the marrow of each German's bones. For them, the attack was both natural and inevitable. However, at bottom, these attitudes were not true of the Führer and me, but for different reasons, and with different objectives—both, I hoped, unbeknownst to each other. I was particularly perplexed by the Führer's three-month timetable.

Now that the invasion had come—the actual reality of it—I sensed a critical point of inflection that drove me to my "commode of contemplation," a *nom de guerre* for my toilet, where I attempted to sort out my extreme unease. The eminent nineteenth-century psychologist Manfred Weber wrote that "Trusting in your instincts is the supreme act of self-regard." But that was the Führer, not me. *Then what was it with me?*

Despite being a mute sentinel in the Führer's quarters and elsewhere, and despite my encounters with Brückner, Katrin, Emerald, Bella, Engel, and Hedwig, when it came to political and military matters, I'd never even had first thoughts, much less second ones. But after Klara, and as I listened this morning to the fruits of decisions I'd helped make and actions I had helped to be taken, I was having actual second thoughts—that my decisions and actions were based not on advice from those considerably wiser, more learned, humanistic, and accomplished than I, but instead on a severe gut reaction to a personal tragedy. A tragedy that had worked its way back through all that I'd heard, seen, and experienced over the years (perhaps even from a horrific childhood and a wretched adolescence) and then forward into that part of my bowels that now harboured a bitter rage.

Under such circumstances, did I merit such self-trust? Was I equipped to accept the consequences of that trust? Compounding my insecurity was the fact that in all this machination, I'd confided in no one, sought no one's counsel, and so received no guidance or advice. This gnawed on my conscience like a starving dog with a meatless bone. I'd been so absorbed in my masochistic ruminations that I failed to hear the Führerbuzzer and only came to when I was jolted by the insistent banging on my door. When I opened it, Kong was positioned at parade rest and peering down at me with a peevish squint.

"Goddammit, Heinz!" he declared through clenched teeth, a bad sign in the normally gentle giant. "We've been tearing the fucking place apart looking for you. The Führer wants to go immediately to his Eastern HQ, and in your absence, the Reichsleiter had Arnt, Schaub, Kempka, all the other adjutants, and even the secretaries hopping, and where the hell were you?"

"On the pot, Otto," I explained, "tending to a diarrhoea worthy of the day's events. Can't you smell it? Just excitement, probably. I'll apologise to the Führer personally when I see him, and please convey my apologies to the Reichsleiter for having put you all to such inconvenience."

That rapid-fire display of slobbering grovel seemed to mollify the oaf. "Well… okay… sure, Heinz," he said, as if caught stark naked in the great hall. "No big deal. Anyways, we're all ready to go, so get a move on, eh?"

"Consider it done," I assured him, and late that afternoon, the Führer and his entire entourage (this time even including Göring) left from Bahnhof Stettin for Rastenburg.

23 *June 1941*

WE ARRIVED AT Wolfsschanze in the frigid evening.[79] Anyone who doubted that the Führer had had Russia on his mind for a long time need only have seen the complex and had it explained to them by Speer (who explained it to me as we all advanced through two heavily fortified security zones to the Führerbunker).

"About two thousand people live and work here," he said, "or will, at least, quite soon. Mostly men, of course, but also several women, you know, the secretaries, cooks, food tasters, Fräulein Braun from time to time"—a wry smile accompanied this news—"and so on. The installations, while secret, are served by a nearby airfield and railway lines. As you can see, the buildings within the complex are camouflaged with bushes, grass, and artificial trees on the flat roofs. Netting is also erected between buildings and the surrounding forest so that the installation looks like unbroken, dense woodland from the air. You're impressed?"

---

[79] Wolfsschanze, or Wolf's Lair, was Adolf Hitler's first Eastern Front military headquarters. The complex, which became one of several Führer Headquarters in various parts of Eastern Europe, was built expressly for the initial invasion of the Soviet Union. This top-secret, high-security site was located in the Masurian woods, about eight kilometres east of the small East Prussian town of Rastenburg (now in Poland). Three security zones surrounded the central complex, where Hitler's bunker was located, and the site was guarded by personnel from the SS Reichssicherheitsdienst and the Wehrmacht's armoured Führerbegleitbrigade.

"Very much," I told him in truth. "Had you anything to do with the design?"

He smiled. "Linge, please. Does this hideous concrete concoction look like one of my designs?"

All I cared about was where Hoffmann's studio was and how to gain access. "I know nothing of architecture, Herr Speer," I answered, also in truth, but more in diplomacy.

"Clearly," he said, keeping the smile and nodding sideways towards Dr. Todt,[80] then moved off to accompany him. It was when I looked back that I caught sight of Weisthor, whom I'd not seen on the train, walking with another man I'd never seen before.

---

[80] Fritz Todt (4 September 1891–8 February 1942) was a German construction engineer and senior Nazi official who rose from "Inspector General for German Roadways," where he directed the construction of the German Autobahnen, to Reich minister for Armaments and Ammunition, where he directed the entire wartime military economy. At the beginning of World War II, he initiated what Hitler named Organisation Todt, a military engineering company that supplied industry with forced labour and administered all construction of concentration camps during the late phase of the Third Reich. He died in a mysterious aeroplane crash in 1942.

MY MORNING ROUTINE with the Führer was punctuated by intermittent reports from Keitel and Jodl on the progress of Barbarossa—all spectacular. According to them, the initial momentum of our ground and air attack had completely destroyed the Soviet organisational command and control within the first few hours, paralysing every level of command, from the infantry platoon to the Soviet high command in Moscow. This news was greeted by the Führer with an air of supreme nonchalance to them, and a subtle wink at me, as if he felt I had understood the real meaning. I had. It was, as many had predicted, swift and dazzling, but for me, it was far too swift. I needed time for others to respond.

The Führer underscored his attitude of didn't-I-tell-you insouciance by leaving his briefers and taking a walk alone with Blondi. I confess that I had no great liking for dogs, never having had one as a child (or anything else, for that matter), and as an adolescent, encountering them only as particularly vicious rivals for food. Even the Führer was no natural dog lover. Blondi behaved badly at first, but the Führer was determined to bend her to his will, and of course being a man of unparalleled intuition and judgement, he knew just the way—he treated her as he treated the Reich: by being the only one to feed her, he made himself Blondi's master.

When he returned, he went directly to his narrow War

Room, with its enormous oblong table, strewn with military maps, dispatches, and coloured pencils.

Surrounded by field marshals and top generals—including von Brauchitsch, the Supreme Commander of the German Army—Admiral Canaris informed the Führer that Moscow not only failed to grasp the magnitude of the catastrophe confronting the Soviet forces in the border areas, but Stalin's first reaction was also disbelief. "It appears as if—"

"As if Stalin has an immunity from facts, eh, gentlemen?" the Führer interrupted, prompting a raucous round of guffaws. "Continue, Admiral."

"At approximately zero seven sixteen," Canaris resumed, with meticulously equivocal attention to detail, "Stalin issued NKO Directive Number Two, which announced the invasion to the Soviet Armed Forces and called on them to attack Axis forces wherever they had violated the borders and launch air strikes into the border regions of German territory."

More laughter followed, even without the Führer's incentive.

"And at around zero nine fifteen," Canaris continued, "Stalin issued NKO Directive Number Three, calling for a general counteroffensive on the entire front, quote, 'without any regard for borders,' unquote, that we presume he hoped would sweep us from Soviet territory. Stalin's order," Canaris concluded with a shrug of incredulity, "is not based on a realistic appraisal of the military situation at hand, but commanders passed it along for justifiable fear of retribution if they failed to obey."

At this, Göring chimed in. "You know, my Führer, all this brings to mind the old joke of '39: Did you hear about the Polack criminal who turned himself in for the reward? I tell you, gentlemen, I believe that Stalin would even order an attack on himself to have the taste of victory." More laughter.

"Well, then, Hermann," the Führer said, "let us hope you're more accurate about Stalin than you were about Churchill."

The laughter stopped dead in its tracks. I couldn't imagine a painter capable of reproducing the red that suddenly appropriated Göring's fleshy face.

Then the Führer smiled. "A joke, Hermann," he declared, "just a joke." He glanced round the table. "I can joke, too, eh?"

This prompted more laughter, though more hesitant and tentative, but the redness did ebb from Göring's face.

3 July 1941

THIS MORNING, I helped dress the Führer while Canaris and Goebbels (not the chummiest of colleagues) briefed him on Stalin's latest broadcast in which he called on his people to pursue a scorched-earth policy and conduct guerrilla warfare against us.

"Shall I inform the others, my Führer?" the intelligence chief asked.

"What do you think, Joseph?" the Führer asked while I clocked his tie-tying.

"To be frank, my Führer, I think Stalin's full of shit," the propaganda minister answered. "The blustering fool has his own version of me—no match, of course—and I think he was advised to play on our fear of losing precious Russian resources."

"Do you agree with Joseph's… colourful assessment?"

"When it comes to leaders being full of shit, I defer to the expertise of the propaganda minister," Canaris mocked with no little recklessness.

"Thank you, Admiral Canaris, for the compliment," Goebbels said coldly, as though marking the name down for some future unpleasantness. I wondered if the Führer caught the breadth of Goebbels's reference.

"My pleasure, Minister," Canaris replied. "However, I'm not convinced that we have a fear of famine for Stalin to play on."

The Führer turned to Goebbels and shrugged. "I appreciate your concern, Joseph, but in this, I must agree with Canaris. Stalin reflexively reverts to scorched earth whenever he feels

threatened. It's his own fear, not ours, at play here. I tell you—
and I'll tell my military leaders tomorrow after my meeting
tonight—that we'll scorch Stalin's earth before he can even get
to it. Just enough scorching, mind you, to preserve those very
resources and hordes of Slav scum to work them for us. Now, is
that all?" the Führer asked by way of dismissal.

They had nothing but each other, so they saluted and left.

"You can put away the stopwatch, Linge," he told me.
"Those two fussbudgets threw me off my game. I tell you, Linge,
after the meeting tonight, even my most rabid critics will be
struck dumb. No need to tend me after dinner," he added. "I'll
see you in the morning, and we'll have another go with that
stopwatch, eh?"

I'd grown so accustomed to this sort of below-the-throne
sparring and sniping, before a Führer-directed facilitation, that
I'd paid scant attention. But now, I wished I had listened. *No
need to tend him until morning? What meeting tonight?*

"Oh yes," he said as I prepared to leave, "and you, Günsche,
Junge, Arnt, and the rest, will coordinate with Bormann tomorrow as well. I need all my focus, and this place won't run itself."

He must have seen something in my face that I couldn't
conceal, because he quickly added, "Albert Bormann, Linge, not
Martin. So perk up."[81]

Even though the Führer didn't require my services, I required his,
so after the Führer finished dinner and retired to his quarters, I
stationed myself at a furtive distance and waited. At 0130 hours,
I observed two unaccompanied men enter without knocking. It

---

[81] General Albert Bormann, Martin's brother, was chief of Main Office I,
Personal Affairs of the Führer.

was Weisthor and the man I'd seen with him on that first day and not since. With the predictable onset of another migraine, I barely made it back to my quarters.

4 *July 1941*

A TERRIBLE MORNING after a migraine night (no sleep, but wel-
come-yet-fitful unconsciousness). Shapes, sizes, and distances
had returned to normal, but the monstrous headache remained.
Fortunately, the Führerbuzzer didn't interfere with my recuperation. Still and all, I wondered who was substituting for me, and
more importantly, why.

By lunchtime, I'd recovered sufficiently to greet the hermetically cloistered world of Wolfsschanze, and specifically,
the conference with Albert Bormann and selected staff in the
officers' mess. I needed to know the nature and content of the
Führer's previous night's meeting, but that would have to wait.

We followed the Bear's brother through the massive wooden
double doors into the vast space, an elongated, white-painted
room set quite deep in the ground. The ceiling lights were bare
and harsh, protected by little wire baskets, and the room itself was
deserted and calm, like an enormous hospital corridor at night
but far chillier, since Todt had yet to install efficient heating. The
walls and doors were soundproof, so the only disturbance was
the harsh pounding through the high-placed windows of march-
ing soldiers, regular and methodical, on the concrete outside.
Since all the others had remained in their greatcoats, I felt no
awkwardness in my own.

Round the overlong trestle table sat Günsche; Junge, my assistant (back from extended duties elsewhere); Arnt; Schaub[82]; Baur; and Kempka, with Bormann positioned at the head. I'd been late, a mortal sin in the Führer's household, the Führer having always condemned it as fit only for decadent aristocrats, mindless Slavs, crafty Jews, and the French. However, Albert was brimming with bonhomie, and the rest took their cue from him, so I was merely given a perfunctory wave to the only vacant spot on the bench.

"Now that we're all here," Bormann began, "let's get this meeting over with and move to where it's warmer, yes?"

No one said a word, but the expressions of gratitude, including mine, were unmistakable.

"All right, gentlemen," Bormann continued, "the Führer has made it quite clear to me that Wolfsschanze is not intended for an overnight stay, like a hotel. He will be here as long as it takes to personally conduct the Eastern War. What that means is the Chancellery moves with the Führer, and here we are. So things must run as if we were back in Berlin, and of course, it will, since I think no one wishes to explain to the Führer why it won't."

Light laughter followed.

"So then, gentlemen, the duties you performed at the Chancellery must still be performed, and with even greater efficiency since much more is at stake here in the East. Everyone understand?"

All nodded their confirmation.

"No questions? You all must be colder than I thought,"

---

[82] An "Old Fighter" with Hitler, Julius Schaub became Hitler's chief adjutant in October 1940. Among his duties was giving day-to-day operational orders to Hitler's personal protection chief, Johann Rattenhuber of the Reich Security Service, and ride herd on Hitler's other adjutants, such as Otto Günsche.

Bormann joked. More laughter, though somewhat heavier. "Okay then, if there are no questions, the meeting is adjourned." As we all got up, Bormann said, "Oh, Linge, would you be so good as to remain for a moment?"

I felt like hell from the remnants of the migraine and knew I looked worse, but I had no choice. I sat back down and watched the rest leave, imagining (though I couldn't see) their expressions of pity for me.

Bormann moved over and sat next to me. Later, when I thought back on it, I was reasonably certain I'd heard a barely audible exhalation, not quite a sigh, but almost. Albert was much different from his older brother. He was tall, cultivated, and eschewed internal power politics, believing he was serving the greater good and, to my knowledge, never using his position for personal gain.

Bormann nodded. "I kept you back to alert you to a potential problem so it can be nipped in the bud, so to speak. Are you all right? You look like shit, if I may say so."

Could I have stopped him? "Perhaps I'm coming down with something, Herr General, but I'll be fine."

"You should see Morell about that. We don't want the Führer becoming indisposed at this critical point, do we?"

"You're quite right. I'll see Morell as soon as we finish."

"Good man. Now, what do you know of the Barbarossa Decree?"

I shook my head, accompanied by a shooting pain behind my eyes. "Nothing, Herr General," which was the truth. Barbarossa itself, yes, since I was involved, but I knew of no decree, which was troublesome. Drops of perspiration began to roll down my armpits and back despite the chill, and I waited for Bormann to continue.

"I can see from your face that you didn't know," Bormann

said, his lower lip pursed in concern. "That's good—surprising, but good. However, now you need to. It's a top-secret directive that my brother believes might be, ah, misconstrued to the detriment of the Führer if its details were to be revealed. You must—"

"But, Herr General," I interrupted, "since I can't tell what I don't know, wouldn't it be better not to tell me?"

"Call me Albert, please. I'm sure you didn't 'Herr General' with Brückner all the time. So informality between us, yes?"

What could I say? My head was splitting, and I was freezing. "If you say so… Albert," I mumbled. "It seems strange."

"I'm hoping it will become less so," he replied with a beguiling smile. "Perhaps you may even come to see me as a friend. In any event, theoretically, what you say is true, but as a practical matter, you may find out about the decree from… shall we say, inappropriate sources? And I'd rather you hear it from an appropriate one."

"Do the others know?" I asked, referring to my table companions.

"The ones at the meeting? One way or another," he replied. "But you need to know differently, and I'll tell you why. Now that the Chancellery has been transferred here for the indefinite future, the Führer will have several visitors, as he had in Berlin, both from the Reich and elsewhere, who may wish to know about some decree they've merely heard about. It's unlikely that they will come into contact with the others, but you know how much your advice means to those who wish to influence the Führer by learning of his moods, thoughts, plans, and so forth. There's another reason," he added, "but that's for another time." Then he proceeded to explain the contents to me.[83]

---

[83] The Barbarossa Decree was laid out by Hitler during a high-level meeting with military officials—including Himmler and Göring—on 30 March 1941.

Whether it was the residue of the migraine or what I was hearing—or both—I almost collapsed, and Bormann had to lean over and prop me back up.

"You see, Heinz?" he said. "You must have Morell look at you."

I could only stammer, "I… will… uh, straight away."

"But now, if you're feeling up to it, what do you think of the decree?"

What did I think of it? The most horrible answer to a prayer I could imagine! A blitzkrieg would be terrible enough, but if I managed to manipulate the Führer into a protracted invasion? Suddenly,

---

During the meeting, Hitler declared that the war against Soviet Russia would be a war of extermination, in which both the political and intellectual elites of Russia would be eradicated to secure a long-lasting German victory. Hitler underlined that executions would not be a matter for military courts but for the organised action of the military. Then he left, placing Himmler in charge of the briefing. The order, composed by Himmler and to be implemented by Heydrich and his top generals in the field, specified that "partisans are to be ruthlessly eliminated in battle or during attempts to escape," and all attacks by civilians against Wehrmacht soldiers were to be "suppressed by the army on the spot by using extreme measures, till [the] annihilation of the attackers; every officer in the German occupation in the East of the future will be entitled to perform execution(s) without trial, without any formalities, on any person suspected of having a hostile attitude towards the Germans," (the same policy applied to prisoners of war). The decree characterised "Judeo-Bolshevism" as the most deadly enemy of the German nation, declaring: "It is against this destructive ideology and its adherents, that Germany is waging total war." The decree went on to demand "ruthless and vigorous measures against Bolshevik inciters, guerrillas, saboteurs, Jews, and the complete elimination of all active and passive resistance. The war against Russia is an important chapter in the German nation's struggle for existence. It is the old battle of the Germanic against the Slavic people, of the defence of European culture against Muscovite-Asiatic inundation, and of the repulse of Jewish Bolshevism. The objective of this battle must be the demolition of present-day Russia and must therefore be conducted with unprecedented severity. Every military action must be guided in planning and execution by an iron resolve to exterminate the enemy remorselessly and totally. In particular, no adherents of the contemporary Russian Bolshevik system are to be spared."

the terrible conflict within my objective struck me, as if I'd fallen and smashed my brain against the sharp corner of a cabinet.

The philosopher Manfred Schiessl wrote that "Even the most human of motives can lead to extreme inhumanity." *Albert wanted an immediate opinion. And where would my opinion travel, after relating it to my new "friend"?*

"What do I think?" I asked him, wide-eyed. "I'm a valet… Albert, not a soldier. Valets run baths, assist in dressing, sort the mail, clean up messes. They don't make battlefield policy. Please, may we speak outside where it has to be warmer?"

"I appreciate that you and Brückner like the great outdoors, but this will take only a moment more."

What did Bormann know about us and how—and why did it matter to him? I had no intention of asking him but hoped he would reveal it, somehow.

He gazed at me hesitantly, his face blank, expressionless. "You probably know that my brother despises you. In fact, but for the Führer's extraordinary regard, you would simply disappear, a mystery no one would bother to solve. You should also know that he and I are not always in agreement."

"About me?"

"About many things."

"All right," I said. "But I don't understand why—"

He nodded with some solemnity. "You wish to know why I'm being so forthright with you. I'll be even more forthright. It's true that my brother told me to speak to you about this, but what if I were to tell you that my decision was based on my relationship with someone else, someone you know well, even an intimate?"

"I'd say he or she has placed me way out of my depth. I have no idea what this is about. I seem to be important only to the Reichsleiter, and that just because of my apparent importance to the Führer. Regardless, I'm still simply a twenty-eight-year-old valet, an uneducated menial. Please don't let my rank or SS insignias fool you."

Bormann removed his cap and patted down his thinning blond hair. His eyes seemed to shine, his breath pluming out before him. He paused, then nodded again, as if he'd been considering alternatives and had finally decided. "He told me you'd react that way, and I can appreciate your prudence. I would do no less in your situation."

My situation? What situation? He was as abstruse as—

"Brückner told me a great deal about you before leaving Paris to go on active duty in North Africa."

He'd answered my unasked questions but left me with even more, not the least of which was why he had brought up Brückner three times already.

"At his age and with one eye?" I joked, to help relieve some of my anxiety. "Are we at that point in the war?"

"He hopes so," Bormann replied with an enigmatic smile. "He told me you would appreciate his decision and that you would consider me a friend."

How was I to respond to something that provocative and hazardous? Especially when presented by Martin Bormann's brother, no less. Style and reputation aside, I had no reason to believe that one Bormann was more benign than another, just because one had a better bedside manner, especially when there were things—critical things—I could divulge now, about which even Brückner didn't know. It might be different had my old friend and mentor contacted me and vouched for Bormann, but in any event, my physical and mental condition were not up to dealing with any of this at the time. I needed to play for time on a promising note.

"Yes… Albert, I must get used to that," I said. "If Brückner considers you a friend, well, that's another matter."

"By the way, Hans Junge has been released from Göring's gilded cage and is back with us, so you'll have a real partner instead of that scurrying lump Arnt. Junge's a good man. You should get to know the fellow."

"I'll make every effort," I assured him. "Now, Albert, you've told me all this about the decree and why I needed a special briefing. Then what is it you wish me to say about it if I'm asked?"

"Nothing, Heinz. Exactly nothing. You never heard of it. You're just a young, simple valet, an uneducated menial. Now, let's go outside and warm up, shall we?"

SINCE MORELL'S MINISTRATIONS freed me for a time from being on immediate call, I strolled over to the compound's abbreviated motor pool to see what Kempka was up to. The tiny "autocrat," as I was fond of calling him behind his back, was ensconced in his office, tilted back in his executive chair, unbooted feet propped up on his desk, gazing with lustful languor at a well-thumbed copy of *Aryans' Forbidden Desire,* an open-secret, pornographic periodical. His eyelids were set at half-mast.

"You seem bored, Erich." I closed the door to shut out the noise.

Kempka moved his chair forward to a more vertical position, shut the magazine, and tossed it aside. "Bored ain't the word, my friend. Fucking numb'd be more like it."

"Not enough action?"

"Not enough for me. Not here, anyways. Eastern Front my arse. The only action I get to see is from the driver's seat, and believe you me, a saloon ain't a panzer. And since the Führer don't travel much here, well, just keeping stored cars from losing air in their tyres ain't much of a job. It's different with Baur and you. Baur at least gets to take his chances with the RAF once in a while, and with you, the Führer's needs are the Führer's needs. A different story when we're in Berlin, eh?"

"In Berlin? For you, maybe, but for me, it's business as usual. As you said—as only you can—'the Führer's needs are the Führer's needs,' and so it goes."

He appeared to think about this for a moment, then turned his head, placed one index finger on his left nostril, pressed in, and blew out some yellowish-brown snot from the other nostril. I'd gotten so used to Kempka's vulgar, locker-room rituals that I just waited for it to end, meaning the evacuation of his other nostril.

"Rallies, parades, mucky-muck transport, principal-garage command," he went on, now that his practice was complete. "Shit, nothin' beats Chancellery duty. Even you manage to break outta routine." He paused for a moment, then, "Hey, remember that night when you came with me to deliver the Führer to that apartment building?"

Of course I did, but my persona must prevail, so I shook my head in puzzlement. "Apartment building? What apartment building? When was this?"

"Come on, son, even you can remember the night we delivered the Führer to that apartment building."

"Repetition doesn't jog memory, Erich, but more information might."

"Fuck!" he shouted in exasperation. "Okay, right, you know, when there was that shot? You asked me about it? Now do you remember?"

"Not with any accuracy," I lied. "I mean, that was a long time ago. Best as I can recall, the shot seemed to come from the building where we deposited the Führer, but I wasn't sure, so I asked you about it, and you told me in so many words that it was none of my business. Am I right?"

He shrugged. "True. When you're right, you're right."

I didn't know about him, but while I had been content then, through ingenuousness and inexperience, now I wanted to know more. "That was the excitement you were talking about?" I teased. "Maybe excitement for you, but not much from where

I was sitting. What the hell was that evening all about anyway? What was the shot about? Was the Führer ever in danger? Were we? Maybe you'll tell me now what you wouldn't then, eh?"

His eyes narrowed just a little. Then a relaxed smile spread over his face. "No harm in that, I guess, since you must hear shit all the time round the Führer that would clamp even my sphincter."

Good old colourful Kempka.

"There was lotsa nights like that, no mistake," he began. "Same thing as when you came along. Like then, the Führer wasn't the only one going into the building. A few minutes after we got there, behind us was Himmler and some others I didn't know. They wasn't in uniform, but they sure looked like big-wigs. In fact, one sorta looked like that chap who came here on that first day with that whatsisname? Some Jew name, Weis-something-or-other. Oh yeah, there was always one female, a different one each time, not bad dishes, at least from a rear-view mirror. No chance to add 'em to my book though. Hey, speaking of my book—"

Enough with the book, you uniformed pimp! "Any more shooting?" I interrupted.

"Yeah, every time, one shot, always around forty-five minutes into it."

Into what? Shots, Himmler, Weisthor, and his mysterious associate. Now intrigued became ensnared—I had to know since I thought I was privy to everything (and letting relevance sort itself out later, if at all), but obviously, I wasn't even close.

"How often were these… affairs?"

He *tsk-tsk*-ed me with his index fingers. "Ah, gotcha by the short hairs now, eh? You're more bored than you let on. Well, every two weeks they were, regular as clockwork."

"Anything else?"

He squinted at me hard, as though by so doing, he could force out more information than he had. "Nah," he admitted, "nothing more. After an hour, he came out, got in the car, and no words between us. I'd take him back to the Chancellery. No expression on his face the whole time, neither."

"You said 'they *were*.' Sounds like those trips stopped."

"Yeah, well, suddenly, no more outings like that, no reason given—and you think I'd ask? Ol' Frau Kempka didn't raise no dummy, you know."

"Do I know, or do I know?"

Then there was another squinting glance. "But hey, how is it you don't know alls I been telling you? Shit, you're with the Führer morning, noon, and night. You wake him up and tuck him in, and the Führer never told you what went on?"

"Nope," I told him with easy-but-disturbed honesty. "Not a word. Or maybe he did, and I just forgot."

"Most likely the second one," he kidded and threw his magazine at me, which I caught and tossed back.

"Well, even without those outings, as you said, you can't beat the Chancellery for motoring excitement."

He smiled at that, and his little piggy eyes shone. "Shit yes! I sure hope this part of the war ends real quick, so we can get back to it—or at least put me in a panzer."

THERE WAS CONSIDERABLE effort for me, Junge, Günsche, and particularly Morell, to prepare the Führer for his meeting to "discuss" the Reich's occupation policy with, I assumed, special emphasis on Russia. I imagined this was the sort of thing Albert had cautioned me about knowing and discussing, but as of today, no one, high or low, had approached me, save for Albert.

I knew what the Führer would say because, for three days, I stood by, watching him dictate to Schroeder and Dara. As always with the Führer's pronouncements, they were bountiful on generalities but sparse on specifics, what Brückner had characterised as "so long as they get what you mean, you can't be held accountable for what you didn't say." As usual, Brückner was spot on.

The conference began at 1500 hours and, including a break for coffee, lasted until about 2000 hours. The Conference Centre, a narrow rectangle, not unlike the mess but shorter—and warmer (the Führer had ensured Todt heated the place properly)—easily accommodated the six of them and me, standing in the corner closest to the Führer. Even though Himmler was joined by his ever-present notepad and pencil, Bormann was to be the official taker of the minutes, something he did regularly during dinners in the Chancellery. I noted that Martin's brother was absent, whatever that signified, if anything.

"By way of introduction, gentlemen," the Führer began, "I wish first of all to make some basic statements. It was essential that we should not proclaim our true and comprehensive aims in

Eastern Europe before the whole world; also, this was not necessary, but the chief thing was that we ourselves should know what we wanted. In no case should our way be made more difficult by unnecessary declarations.

"If required, therefore, we shall then continue to emphasise that we were forced to occupy, administer, and secure a certain area, that it is in the best interest of the inhabitants that we provide order, food, traffic, and so forth, hence our measures. It should not be recognisable that thereby, a final settlement is being initiated. Nevertheless, we will take all necessary measures—no matter how ruthless and brutal—and we will take them without hesitation or mercy. Am I clear on this point?"

Nods all round, with an especially vigorous jowl-swinging one from Göring. Himmler merely jotted down something in his little notebook.

"But," he continued, "on the other hand, we have no wish to make any people into enemies prematurely and unnecessarily. Therefore, we shall act as though we wanted to exercise a mandate only. It must be clear to us, however, that we shall never withdraw from these areas, so I assume that is clear as well.

"All right then, in principle, we now have to face the task of cutting up the giant cake according to our needs: to first, dominate it; second, administer to it; and third, exploit it. Thanks to our unlikeliest ally, Stalin, the Russians have been given an order for partisan warfare behind our front. This has a great advantage for us: it enables us to exterminate everyone who opposes us, by any and all means necessary. I'm confident that Göring and Himmler will not shirk from the task. And where they go, my generals and their troops will be sure to follow."

Finally, he'd made a reference to the decree, which was met with faces blank with obvious prior knowledge.

"Now," the Führer declared, "to codify my comments into

some basic principles for immediate and continual execution: One, never again must it be possible to create a military power west of the Urals, even if we have to wage war for a hundred years in order to attain this goal. All my successors must know that security for the Reich exists only if no foreign military forces exist west of the Urals; it is Germany, and Germany alone, who undertakes the protection of this area against all possible dangers. Our iron principle must be and must remain;

"Two, we must never permit anyone but Germans to carry arms. This is especially important; even when it seems easier at first to enlist the armed support of foreign, subjugated nations, it is wrong to do so. This will prove, someday, to be absolutely and unavoidably to our disadvantage. So only the Germans may carry arms, not the Slav, nor the Czech, nor the Cossack, nor the Ukrainian!

"Three, we must create a Garden of Eden in the newly won Eastern territories; they are vitally important to us. Compared with them, colonies play only icing on an already-rich pastry. But however we act, we shall always proceed in the role of protectors of the law and of the population. Göring and Himmler will ensure this in their own unique fashion, and it will be accomplished in complete accordance with my wishes.

"Four, we must give some thought to Finland and counter the natural tendency to annex it since they are ably assisting us in our subjugation of the Soviets. The area around Leningrad is wanted by the Finns, and as a present, I will have Leningrad razed to the ground to hand it over to them, properly wrapped."

Titters. I waited for the Führer's usual *coup de grâce*, and it came.

"Of course," he said, "all that I've just told you is to be considered by all—and I mean all—as top secret, to be shared with no one not personally authorised by me. And," he concluded, "be mindful that should my parallel strategy, to which you've not been privy, succeed"—stealing a quick glance in my direction, then back to the nonplussed group—"all that I've announced today will be utterly moot. Comments, gentlemen?"

The assembled performed the time-tested theatrical gesture of glancing at one another, as if looking to see if someone, anyone, possessed the answer to a particularly complex and burdensome question, then turned back to the Führer with a unanimous "nope" written on their pursed lips. That was, except for Rosenberg, who felt obliged to introduce a topic ignored by both the declaration and today's pronouncements.

"But, my Führer," he asked, "what of the Jews?"

"What Jews?" the Führer asked and adjourned the meeting.

Though I worked hard not to show it, I was becoming more and more perplexed and troubled. Since Weisthor's arrival, I hadn't been called upon even once to visit with the Führer after dinner, save for a few minutes before putting him to bed. I still didn't know who Weisthor's companion was, nor had I even seen him since the day of arrival. As I had no intention of asking who he was, where he could be, or the nature of his connexion to the Führer, he continued to occupy a large and troubled portion of my consciousness, so I had to find a way to somehow insert myself into the mysterious equation.

The Führer was in an especially ebullient frame of mind this morning, racing through his toilette at peak efficiency, even without Morell's increasing pharmaceutical encouragement. I assumed it was due to the report by Canaris of Churchill's response to Stalin's desperate request. According to the admiral, Churchill wrote back to Stalin, explaining that opening a new front was out of the question. "You must remember," Churchill said, "that we have been fighting alone for more than a year, and that, though our resources are growing and will grow fast from now on, we are under the utmost strain, both at home and in the Middle East, by land and air." I was desolate but knew I needed to demonstrate hysterical enthusiasm if required.

"What did I tell those limp noodles in my military?" the Führer asked while I put away the stopwatch and began arranging his chaotic desk. "Since '33, I've given them nothing but success after success, and still they doubt me. Now Stalin's alone, crying in the wilderness of my making, but I tell you, Linge, when I announce that fat, stammering, British oaf's response, those arrogant knobs will still counsel caution, mark my words. Well, unfortunately for them, I decided on immediate annihilation, not for petty spite against those 'military geniuses' I'm saddled with, mind you, but through instruction I've received from a far more knowledgeable and reliable source."

A vague, expectant look shone in his eyes, a signal that he awaited some sort of response.

I maintained an outer calm, but my insides churned. *Far more knowledgeable and reliable source?* A miserable and terrifying dawn began to break in my brain.

"The Führer continues to have a sixth sense," I remarked, straining to hold in abeyance any quavering, "concerning the value and source of his inspirations, well beyond my powers of understanding."

He emitted a resigned sigh. "True, Linge. True. Ironically, like our friend Stalin, I, too, am alone, but unlike Stalin, I'm alone in my superiority, not in my inadequacies. There will be immediate annihilation of that Slavic sewer, not an incremental devastation. The Russians are nothing. We have only to kick in the door, and the whole rotten structure will come crashing down. I have a far bigger fish to fry."

Immediate annihilation! Was there nothing I could do? I can't think. All I can do is photograph this awful day.

WE HAD JUST received reports that the Luftwaffe bombed Moscow for the first time, but I took no comfort after hearing the Führer's alarmingly discordant decision. He'd been told by people he needed to believe that blitzkrieg was not merely a successful strategy but a particularly Hitlerian phenomenon, not unlike the emperor Nero being advised that burning Rome as entertainment was something only a god like he could conceive of and implement.

Not for me, I vowed. Yes, the Reich must survive, but not as a vast, evil runaway locomotive powered by hatred, greed, and madness. And the Führer must also survive, but not as the supreme engineer who, eyes always averted, runs the train off the rails, killing all on board and those the careening behemoth rams into.

It was what Klara would want.

So, my friend, aside from the "mystery" of the Führer's sudden need for speed, this situation is potentially disastrous for me and, more importantly, for Germany. Lightning war would be a calamity beyond measure. I know I'm harping, but I can't help myself. Instead, there must be an incremental advance, yet so relentless and barbaric in its ferocity that the Allies, no matter how unprepared and skittish, will be compelled to intervene, and the Führer will be surrounded quickly and thoroughly— with a minimum of military and civilian casualties on all sides. *But how to snatch back the reins before it's too late?* My only causal link to this catastrophic development was Weisthor and, I presume, his influential companion. However, any attempt at access might prove more hazardous than the results could justify. My position and persona were my only protection, and to risk either would be to position myself before the cannon's ready mouth.

It was on my "commode of contemplation" that it came to me.

THE CRITICAL SCENARIO had to be performed quickly, without distractions, and natural within the context I created. As for distractions, I primed Günsche by telling him that, by the Führer's express command, for the next hour there must be no visitors or other interruptions of any kind. When the giant inquired why he was not told this personally and directly, I suggested that he complain later to the Führer, which ended the matter. As for context…

"That one?" the Führer asked me, once he'd secured his tie in record time and saw the tan jacket draped carefully over my arm like a headwaiter's towel.

"Yes, my Führer," I told him.

"I didn't mention which jacket. With that one, I have to change every—"

"I'm sorry, my Führer, a mistake. But I could have sworn you told me… but if you'd prefer—"

He held up his hands in a conciliatory gesture. "Not to worry, Linge. I haven't worn that one for some time, and it's good to thwart people's expectations every once in a while, eh? So let's redo the whole business."

I thought back to my hypothetical scenario of 3 March and so was considerably more at ease than I expected to be. I laid the prepared jacket with exquisite care on the arm of a chair, then helped the Führer redress to coordinate with the jacket. Nothing must happen before or after its time. I lifted the jacket gingerly and began to move towards the Führer, then halted in mid-stride.

"What is it?" he asked, raising his arms above his head to receive the sleeves.

I lowered my eyelids and pursed my lips. "My Führer, I believe I felt something in one of the pockets." I looked down at it, my chest tightening with apprehension as I took back the blazer.

The Führer nodded sideways. "Perhaps it's money. Before, I didn't have it; now, I don't need it. You may keep what you find."

I made a show of feeling round the garment until I got to the inside breast pocket, felt the tiny angular piece of metal, and, with uncertain hands, shook the garment with vigour.

"Be careful, Linge. It's to be worn, not worn out."

I held back for a moment, still not entirely certain of my timing. "Sorry, my Führer." I paused meaningfully and gave it one last jolt, and the top fell to the floor.

The two of us stood there, staring down at the little piece of metal for a long time without saying anything. I stole a glance at the Führer with growing concern. An odd look passed over a face as white as candle wax, jaw slack, and his eyes glazed over. I watched carefully for any sign... *of what?* I had no idea. Then his eyes rolled up, showing only the whites, and I grabbed him before he could hit the floor.

With utmost gentleness, I carried the Führer to his bed and laid him out as a mortician would a corpse: feet together, arms bent, and hands folded over his chest—one of his hands I'd balled into a fist to grip the top I'd placed there. I went quickly to the chamber door, opened it a crack, and informed Günsche that the Führer still wished to have no disturbances of any kind, emphasising the word "any," and woe betide the transgressor. I shut the door before he could react, returned to the bedroom, took the straight-back chair by his side, and waited until I could hear some murmurs, then a feeble, "Linge?"

I shot up and bent over him. "You look much better, my Führer," I said. "I was quite terrified. I was just about to call—"

He brought his fist up to his face and unfurled his fingers with maddening slowness, the action of a desperate sceptic. "No!" he shouted, then shifted to a whisper. "No Morell."

"But, my Führer," I ministered with no little theatricality, "you passed out, and when I placed you in your bed, you began to say—"

"Say? Say what?"

"I… can't remember everything, my Führer. Between my panic at your condition and my poor memory, I—"

"Whatever you can tell me, Linge, tell me."

I chose my words very carefully now, testing, watching the Führer's expression. "You were saying that you'd… obtained—I think that was the word you used—the, ah… 'key to infinite power,' at least that's what I think you said, 'obtained it at last.' And while you held it, you said you heard a voice telling you to 'prolong the agony. Don't let that… Slav shit off the hook; let them starve, bleed, burn, and flail, while I alone hold the rod. They'… the voice said, 'must endure prolonged, untold misery,' for the 'scum Stalin and his prehistoric, ragtag Slav army do not deserve the mercy of a blitzkrieg,' or something like that. It's all so crazy. I must have had another episode. There can be no other explanation."

The Führer was silent for a moment; then he said, "Yes, there can be, Linge." He held up the top.

This was the moment. I could feel the sweat starting to trickle down from my receded hairline and across my forehead. My hands had suddenly grown cold, and I could hardly breathe. "The voice you heard, my Führer, did you recognise it?"

Here he paused meaningfully and turned his head towards me, his face flushed with confirmation. "Yes, Linge," he said. "I most certainly did, no mistake. It was yours."

§

Goethe wrote, "It seems to never occur to fools that merit and good fortune are closely united." Goethe was right, and I was no fool.

WHEN THE NEWS arrived about Moscow, the Führer ordered an immediate visit to the headquarters of Army Group North concerning Leningrad, the Soviet Union's second largest city. Field Marshal von Leeb's army had been tasked with destroying Soviet forces in the Baltic States, then driving on to Leningrad and eradicating it.[84]

As I helped the Führer dress, considering this situation to be the first major field test of my new strategy, I waited with a pounding headache and sweaty palms for his next move. By the time I'd finished timing him, I knew that my audacity, not the top, had worked its magic, for the Führer now reversed himself and ordered von Leeb to stop some sixty miles south of the city and not to take it. To this, von Leeb demurred strongly, but to no avail.

"You're so far out to sea, von Leeb," the Führer declared. "You should ask for a transfer to the navy. Food," the Führer said. "Food. I shouldn't need to instruct you on such an elementary matter. If we take the city, which we could do in our sleep, they eat our food. If we lay siege to the city, instead, they eat each other."

------

[84] Militarily, Leningrad was prized because it lay across the path of the Germans' advance into the north of Russia. Hitler ordered von Leeb to take and destroy the city "immediately." Six weeks later, von Leeb's army had completely encircled the city and was poised to destroy it.

This grotesquely brilliant strategy failed to mollify the field marshal, who argued that a delay would prove disastrous to the momentum already generated, but all this did was anger the Führer, and it catapulted us onto the Führerwagen for a not-so-friendly visit to Army Group North.

The Führer's problems with von Leeb were his own at this point. My only concern, as I sat alone in the dining car, was the rumour of my treachery, the identity of that mysterious companion of Weisthor and his role, and the consequences for me of the Führer's hundred-eighty-degree turnabout, in sudden and total disregard of their influence. *But who would know and also be safe for me to probe?* Those two questions absorbed so much of my concentration that I didn't notice Junge sit down across from me.

"One hell of a situation!" Junge declared by way of a greeting, shaking me back to my surroundings.

"Hello, Hans," I greeted. "What's wrong?"

His smile was quick, easy, too easy. "I shouldn't complain."

"But you are complaining, so at least tell me what's the problem."

He shrugged, as if I'd forced him to tell me, and for the sake of fellowship and diversion, I allowed the shrug to succeed.

"If you force me," he said, "when I was transferred out of Göring's household, I hoped it would be to the front lines. Instead, I'm just shining a smaller pair of boots."

"As I recall, you never were a soldier," I reminded him. "From bodyguard to valet, same as me. Not much of a military trajectory. Anyway, you should count your blessings. Only paper and rumours fly round here, not bullets and artillery shells."

Junge stared back at me as I regarded him. His hair was

SS blond, his face was narrow and oval, his forehead high, lips full, nose thin and upturned, as if attempting to avoid a noxious odour. "I suppose you're right." He sighed. "God knows I have no real training. I'd probably be the first in my unit to be killed."

He wasn't a lout like Günsche, but no great intellect either. I smiled at him with indulgence. "In such matters, my friend, it's my own civilian opinion that where you are in that particular queue is unimportant."

His smile shifted from uneasy to anxious, and his voice plummeted. "I think, better a discussion for another time and place, yes?"

"Sure," I said. "Any time and place you say. Assuming anything more need be said."

He took a mouthful of his meat and chewed in silent thought.

"By the way, Hans," I said, "notice any people round the Führer you don't recognise?"

Junge seemed shaken. "Shit, Heinz, I've been away so long that aside from you and the Führer's illustrious long-time companions, everyone's strange to me." His lips compressed. "Why do you ask?"

"I don't know," I said. "Since we've been stationed here, I've seen a few people with apparently direct access to the Führer that I can't account for. I don't feel right asking him. Just curious, nothing earth-shattering. If you think of it."

"Hmm," he murmured, lips pursed and right eye aimed skyward. "Sure, I'll be alert. Anyways, what are we supposed to—you know, that is," he interrupted himself with a decisive tap on the table, "if you don't count some types I've seen schmoozing every now and then, always came with Himmler when he visited Göring and are here now. But what they did there, I have no idea. Whenever they were with him, I was dismissed for the night. Less work for me, right?"

"Yes?" I nudged, careful that my tone remained casual. "And who might they be?"

"Shit, you must have seen them. Only at night, mind you, but they're in and out of the Führer's rooms. Don't even knock. They must have lotsa juice, I can tell you that. Know what I mean?"

"I do. Any names to go along with them?"

"Well." He scratched his head. "I forget the old guy's name, but I overheard Himmler introduce the younger one to Göring as Herr… uh, Kracht, Graff, something like that."

The name hit me like a fist. Not Kracht, not Graff, but Krafft. Karl Ernst Krafft, to be exact, Hess and Himmler's astrologer. Originally a member of a group persecuted by the Party, this particular occultist was propelled into the exception column in November 1939, when he made a remarkable prediction: that the Führer's life would be in danger between 7 and 10 November. On 2 November, he'd written to a friend named Fesel, who worked for Himmler, warning him of the attempt on the Führer's life, but the friend filed the letter away, unwilling to become enmeshed in something dangerous. However, on 8 November, when the bomb exploded at the Munich beer hall, the target was unscathed because he'd been "advised" to leave the hall a few minutes before the explosion. When newspapers reported the near catastrophe, Fesel dispatched a telegram to Hess, drawing attention to Krafft's prediction, and Hess showed the telegram to Himmler and to Weisthor. Hess had related the story to me, so I made a mental note to thank Albert for his advice about befriending Junge. Good man or bad man, at the very least, he was a useful man. I'd defeated—at least for the time being—a dangerous rival for the Führer's attentions.

"Name means nothing to me," I told him. "Probably some ultrahigh-level chap that even we aren't permitted to know of."

He chuckled. "Shit, I thought valets are supposed to know everything."

"Well, Hans, I imagine that here at Führer Headquarters, you'll just have to get used to *almost* everything."

❧

At von Leeb's headquarters, Junge and I stood by while the Führer, bug-eyed and screaming, dressed down the field marshal for his unimaginative and incompetent military judgement. His staff, huddled in the adjoining room, couldn't avoid vicarious participation in the verbal bombardment.

"But, my Führer," von Leeb protested again with self-assured slowness, "is it possible that you fail to recall demanding a 'lightning bolt of ordnance to instantly and utterly raze the city to smouldering ash'?"

This show of elegant defiance only made the already-irate Führer hysterical.

"You see?" he shrieked and slammed his foot down on the plank floor like a Japanese sumo wrestler. "What I say seems to go in one ear and out the same! It's you and your obdurate, incestuous kind that will be the ruin of the Reich! A complete failure of imagination! A complete failure of flexibility! A complete failure, generally!"

Junge and I were too transfixed by the Führer's tirade to even risk a glance at each other. I'd experienced many such scenes before, but they were so long ago, and pre-Morell, that I assumed some alteration in the Führer's personality, if not his attitude.

With Führer-like suddenness, he turned and began "iceskating" round the room, finally stopping in close to the field marshal, who'd remained at rigid attention all the while.

"All right," the Führer said, his tone down several decibels, his face closer to its normal neon pallor. "Of course Leningrad must be erased from the face of the earth, but now hear me and make no mistake, by starvation, not a full-scale assault. We are fighting Slavs, not soldiers, so I have no interest in saving the lives of its civilian population. Since you seem incapable of providing detail to simple commands, I will supply it. The city will be hermetically sealed. Any and all requests for surrender resulting from the situation of the city will be rejected, as the problem of housing and feeding the starving and defeated population cannot and should not be solved by us. Moreover, Herr Field Marshal, my strategy will be employed for as long as it takes to succeed, and succeed it will, and to hell with your sacred momentum. You understand me?"

"I understand fully, my Führer," von Leeb said, his tone flat but definitive. "Is there anything else?"

The Führer answered by turning abruptly and striding out, followed by Junge and me, and returning with our military escort to the Führerwagen for the trip back to Berlin, Krafft be damned.

WHILE DRESSING, I felt a familiar ungainly stiffness in the inside pocket of my tunic. Since there was no time to deal with it, I left it where it was and hurried to the Führer's quarters, where he was sitting at his desk in his bathrobe, listening to Goebbels recite from Bishop von Galen's third sermon, concerning euthanasia.

Stationed at the door, I didn't at first notice Himmler in the other high-backed armchair, but when I looked more closely, there he was, accompanied as always by his vacant expression and trusty notepad. My throat constricted, but I made sure nothing registered on my face.

"That cassocked fool actually called it murder?"

"I'm afraid so, my Führer." Goebbels continued reading from his sheet of paper. "'Unlawful by divine and German law, a rejection of the laws of God.' Galen also claimed that 'productivity is not a justification for killing,' blah, blah, blah. Galen then remarked that a regime that can do away with the fifth commandment can destroy the other commandments as well. He went on to raise the question of whether permanently injured German soldiers would fall under the programme. He also cited several specific instances of euthanasia procedures, carefully choosing the most grisly ones, I might add. For instance, there was—"

"And what do you see as the impact of this claptrap, Joseph?" the Führer interrupted, as I knew he would.

"In the most Catholic areas, especially in the south," he said, "there will be protests, but not against the Party per se, against our cleansing policy. And if the protests should expand in location and substance, well, I defer to Heinrich."

With that, Himmler closed his notebook with exaggerated slowness and faced the Führer. "The resources under my command are fully prepared to deal with any and all disturbances. I know it, and they know it. And if they need reminding, we can accommodate them."

"Short of that," ventured the propaganda minister, "I would counsel restraint. In time of war, we need the support and morale of all our citizens, no matter how misguided."

"Be that as it may," added Himmler, "I see no reason to halt or even mitigate our T4 programme. I would only—and I'm sure Joseph can appreciate this—make its implementation more... unobtrusive."

The Führer's lips formed that thin smile reserved for lesser beings who stated the obvious. "So, all well in hand," he said. "Good. I have far too many military vons to handle without being beset by a fucking holy von. But mark my words, gentlemen, the fact that I remain silent in public over such affronts should not in the least be misunderstood by the sly foxes of the Catholic Church. I'm quite sure that a man like Bishop von Galen knows full well that, after the war, I shall extract retribution to the last pfennig."

⌁

"Dreadful, Linge," the Führer groused once Goebbels and Himmler had left. "As if I'm going to turn the Reich topsy-turvy over some arrogant asshole who fancies he speaks for God. You heard. Von Leeb is no different. All those fucking toffs who believe they know more than I do merely because they were born. I've had to fight such entrenched aristo idiocy all my life, and it seems I must continue to fight it until the critical moment. But I have no intention of working up a lather over it now. When we've done our work, you and I, and war is needless once and for all, I'll give them all the meaning and attention they deserve."

Of that, I had no doubt. *But what was the meaning behind the emphasis on "we"?*

"Would you like to dress now, my Führer?"

"Yes," he said. "It looks like, from now on, you and Morell will be waking up earlier and earlier. Like me. By the way, I have a treat for you."

I shook my head. "A treat for me? What is it?"

"A surprise. While I hate getting surprises, not counting Blondi, of course, I do like giving them—ask our enemies. I especially like giving them to members of my family. After dinner, you'll receive it, so don't nag me in the meantime."

I never understood the desire to tell someone about a surprise and then not tell what it is, rather than just springing it on them and letting that speak for itself. "I'm most grateful, my Führer," I told him.

He shrugged. "Well, let's hope you're still grateful afterwards," he joked. "Now, let's put me together, eh?"

∽

It wasn't money, but whatever that envelope contained was burning a hole in my pocket, as the saying went. So, I paused my scheduled journey to the Communications Centre, proceeded to the nearest WC, chose a central stall, locked myself in, and read the contents: *My Dear Heinz, it's only right that you receive a progress report so long after your visit to Auschwitz, so I attached a memo from Göring to Heydrich. Peruse it in all secrecy, and please consider its implications.*

Official Transcript:
The Reichsmarschall of the Greater Berlin, 31 July 1941
German Reich
Plenipotentiary for the Four-Year Plan
Chairman
of the Ministerial Council for the
Defence of the Reich
To
the Chief of the Security Police
and the SD
SS Gruppenführer HEYDRICH

BERLIN

Supplement to the task which was entrusted to you in the decree dated 24 January 1939, and based upon the Führer's wishes, namely to solve the Jewish Question by emigration and evacuation in a way which is the most favourable in connection with the conditions prevailing at the time. Due to the logistical and racial impracticality of the aforementioned task, I herewith commission you to carry out all preparations with regard to organisation, the material side and financial viewpoints for a final solution of the Jewish Question in the territories in Europe which are under German influence.

If the competency of other central organisations is touched in this connexion, those organisations are to participate.

I, furthermore, commission you to submit to me as soon as possible a draft showing the administrative material and financial measures already taken for the execution of the intended final solution of the Jewish Question.

The Führer is aware and supportive of my efforts in principle and wishes not to become encumbered by details.
(signed) Göring

If you remain opposed to the only thing that will guarantee no more loss of life and the creation of a Reich governed by moral principles, then at least, before conceding the failure of your efforts, look to your successes, Herr Dreamer—and keep dreaming. With great affection, E.

I reread Göring's memorandum, not doubting for a moment its authenticity or that the Führer had no knowledge of its specific contents. I also harboured no doubts that Heydrich himself had initiated this commission with his boss's blessing. From Brückner, I already knew that Heydrich had some experience in organising such a plan, having reintroduced, in 1939, the cruel, medieval concept of the ghetto in Warsaw after our occupation of Poland. In such hellholes, Jews were jammed into tiny walled areas and held as prisoners, their property confiscated and given to either local Germans or non-Jewish Polish peasants. Between Himmler's obsession and resources and the Führer's hyperbolic generalities and averted eyes, their eventual condition was a foregone conclusion.

For a time, I just sat on the pot, staring at the document and note without blinking until the letters turned into black birds in a white sky. I felt as if the cells of my brain were colliding, rendering me incapable of rational thought, and yet, thoughts I had in unfortunate abundance. Since General Engel was erroneous at best about Katrin—or deceitful at worst—this communication indicated that Emerald, too, was far more than merely the other side of my addled brain. *But did any of this, including my manipulation of the Führer into a new protraction strategy, alter anything for me? What were the implications for the people of Leningrad and other Soviet cities, the ghetto Jews, the "Meyers" in Auschwitz (and a vast influx yet to come), and so on?* To all this, no less than the Führer, I averted my eyes. I tore the note into tiny pieces, flushed them, and resumed the trek to retrieve my half of the Führer's mail.

❧

Dinner was more elaborate than usual, attended not only by a few of the usual inner circle regulars, but by all of them, including Göring, Himmler, "Scarface" Kaltenbrunner, von Ribbentrop, Keitel, Speer, and someone I'd seen once, years before, but not again until this evening: Director Hermann Schmitz, CEO of I. G. Farben.[85]

Save for my brain and later my camera, neither Bormann (Martin) nor Himmler appeared to be taking notes this time. After a spate of innocuous banter, the Führer shifted seamlessly to the war.

"Personally," he began, "I think we're doing the Russians an enormous service. By instinct, the Russian does not incline towards a higher form of society. Over centuries of inbreeding, the Russian has come to comprise two entities: mindless, decadent autocracy above, and mindless, coarse subservience below,

---

[85] Interessen-Gemeinschaft Farbenindustrie AG (Dye Industry Syndicate, Inc.), commonly known as I. G. Farben, was a German chemical and pharmaceutical conglomerate formed in 1925 through the merger of six chemical companies. In its heyday, I. G. Farben was the largest company in Europe and the largest chemical and pharmaceutical company in the world.

with nothing in between. The autocrats have no function, so they will be eliminated, once and for all, not a remnant to remain of these hereditary leeches. As for those hordes below, we will gain an endless supply of slave labour, freeing up Germans to perform the higher tasks required of any great civilisation, and the drudges won't know the difference."

"Perfectly put, my Führer," simpered von Ribbentrop, lackey extraordinaire, "and I might add that the sow Churchill, no friend of communism, will bless you for taking Russia out of the picture without him firing a shot."

"And that," the Führer added to Göring, "also takes *you* off the hook, eh, Hermann? You aim at Stalin and hit Churchill, a manoeuvre your Luftwaffe could profit from, since you can't seem to get to him directly."

The Reichsmarschall executed a jowl-swinging guffaw but made no verbal reply, the bespangled pretender to elegance being nothing if not discreet. I still marvelled at the way the Führer treated Göring, whose demonstrated military incompetence would have got anyone else sacked—and worse. I assumed that their history, and Göring's more easily accomplished role (along with Himmler and his RSHA) as Überpoliceman of all areas external to the Reich, more than compensated. Writing memos was far easier than bombing a resolute nation into submission.

"Even with my new strategy," the Führer continued, "it should all be over by December, right, Keitel?"

A potential disaster, even with the "even," and I could do nothing!

Keitel's eyes widened slightly. "I… foresee no impediment, my Führer," the field marshal hedged with what I thought to be the merest hint of a smile. "It would appear—"

"It should be possible," the Führer cut in, "for us to control this conquered region to the east with two hundred fifty thousand men plus a cadre of competent administrators. I've instructed Heinrich here to draw up a list of candidates, using Heydrich as a model, who will govern a subhuman population in full accordance with my wishes."

The mere mention of "Heydrich as a model" was enough to give me an internal headshake and eternal gratitude that I wasn't a Slav.

"Whoever he is, I wish him luck," von Ribbentrop said. "Millions of Slavs. My God, what a task."

"Luck is irrelevant, Ribbentrop," the Führer countered. "Let's learn from the English, who, with two hundred and fifty thousand men in all, including fifty thousand soldiers, govern four hundred million Indians."

"You are correct, as always, my Führer," Himmler said, his face a mask of blandness, save for the light glinting off his round spectacles, making them look like silver coins on his eyes. "As with a chicken, once the head is cut off and the neck wears a tight leash, there is precious little uncertainty in the barnyard."

All laughed at that analogy, especially Göring, who anointed it with, "That's a good one, Heinrich. Soon we'll control the biggest barnyard in the world."

"And nothing would be a worse mistake on our part than to seek to educate the prehistoric masses there," Kaltenbrunner added. "It's in our interest that they should know just enough to recognise the signs on the roads. The women, not even that. At present, none can read, and they ought to stay that way."

"My Führer," a cultivated voice interjected, "just one thing, if I may: Are you certain that finishing this Russian business before Christmas is compatible with your new siege strategy?"

All heads swivelled to Speer, then to the Führer, in dead silence. I needed to pay particular attention to this, since Speer occupied a special position in the Führer's inner circle. *Would he help or hurt?*

The Führer smiled benignly, his right hand patting the air in front of him in a soothing gesture. "Ah, Speer." The Führer sighed. "You know, I once heard of a film actor who considered himself so gifted a thespian that he believed he could direct his own picture. It was a complete disaster, of course, and he returned to acting with a renewed sense of purpose. I hope my anecdote isn't lost on such a brilliant architect like yourself."

For a moment, more dead silence, then, "I believe I'll stick to buildings," Speer answered by way of apology and escape.

I considered the Führer's response and asked myself whether I should stick to valeting. And again, I averted my eyes.

"Have you anything to add, Herr Schmitz?" the Führer asked.

The tiny chemical magnate in his bespoke suit looked like a prosperous gnome, like someone's well-heeled grandfather about to tell a tale. He glanced round the table and shrugged his padded shoulders. "This is all very interesting and even more promising, my Führer. But," he added, "I think that my part in this is somewhat premature. As the Reichsführer and Herr Speer are well aware, we're still experimenting with the means of—"

"Gentlemen," the Führer interrupted, "I've had a long day, as my valets and adjutants can attest. I'll leave you now, but please, continue your discussion. Junge, you stay here and see to them. Don't bother to get up," he told the rest. Then he rose, crooked his index finger, and wagged it at me to follow him.

Escorted by his personal guards, the Führer guided me into the hallway, then called a halt. "Like that December remark? Made Keitel's day, I'll wager."

"I… but—"

"I know what you want to say. But don't berate yourself.

The field marshal just has a bit more savoir faire, the ossified idiot."

The Führer's sport. My entire body shivered internally with relief. "So you didn't mean December, my Führer?"

"Oh I meant it, all right, but it meant nothing. It might be December—or later, depending on the stubbornness of the Slavs, not on my strategy. On that score, the later, the better. Let them suffer before annihilation. But it did shut Keitel and his fellow cadavers up for a while. The most I can hope for with a command structure and commanders from the nineteenth century."

"You had Herr Speer fooled too, my Führer."

A look of undisguised amusement lit the Führer's eyes, but it was a look of disdain. Cold, cynical, and knowing. "That was the *coup de grâce* to Keitel's belief that I'd changed my tune, and he didn't even know it. I worked with Speer for an hour this morning to get it just right, even to the dressing-down. In this case, *I* was the architect, and Speer the structure. Ah, Linge, sometimes I even surprise myself."

That, I could never imagine.

The Führer shrugged, his lips pursed. "Anyway, I didn't bring you out here to listen to me gloat. I have a surprise for you. Turn and look."

I did, and that was when I saw Annagret, her majestic torso stuffed into her drab nun-like nurse's uniform. No more braids, her strawberry-blond hair was now rolled and pressed tightly into a bun, held precariously in place by a tiny nurse's cap.

"You're sufficiently surprised?" the Führer asked me, even after witnessing the pallor of shock on my face.

"I... I'm..."

"You're sufficiently surprised," the Führer concluded for me, "so make the most of it."

"But won't you be needing me later?"

"No. I wouldn't want to spoil a party I arranged, now would I? Go and enjoy, relax. Günsche can fill in, since I have other duties for Junge." Then he turned, motioned to his massive escort of guards, and they all journeyed back the other way towards his quarters.

∾

"My God!" she gasped when I approached. "Can you believe it? I was brought here by the Führer himself!"

"He's gone now," I informed her with a grin to calm her. "You can relax, unless you prefer standing at attention."

She paused, as if she were thinking about it, then assumed a normal (for her) civilian posture. "Heinz, you should have seen the other girls' faces when I got the Führer's personal summons."

"I'm sure they were impressed."

"Impressed? *Impressed?* You know, I wasn't a particular favourite of theirs from the beginning. Those jealous cyphers don't even have the skills to be patients, much less nurses. Envy, Heinz, the pure envy of inferiors. It was a lot different when I showed it to the doctors and administrators. They thought I was special before, but now, I'm a *wunderkind*, a true prodigy."

"But it was only an invitation to the Chance—"

"Yes, to see you. I get that now. But it didn't say that, and so it could have meant anything, you see? And signed by the Führer himself? What do you think they thought?"

"That you were taking Hess's place as deputy?"

She made a mock frown. "Now you're being silly."

"Sorry. I get it," I assured her, and I did. "You're a celebrity."

"Even more, Heinz," she said, "and without signed invitations too. I've been given the honour of leapfrogging the others to personally train at Hadamar,[86] under T4 Director Dr. Karl Brandt, Chief Administrator Klein, and SS Sturmbannführer Dr. Karl Gebhardt, Medical Superintendent. And I owe it all to you. Do you have any idea what this means? What I'll be able to accomplish for the Reich? For the Führer?" Her sapphire-blue eyes glistened with pride and zeal.

I had more than an idea of what it meant: she'd graduated from chickens to Klaras. My stomach heaved, my face reddened, and I felt a slight wobbly dizziness.

"You, too, are excited by my news," she observed. "See? I told you: Heinz Linge is anything but a mere valet. You should listen to me."

Her message returned my composure. "I agree with you and will listen, I promise. Though, unlike your situation, Principal Valet is as high as my position goes. But of course, I can't complain." I expected the ambiguity would escape her, and by her expression, it did. "Well," I went on, "now that you're here and the Führer was generous enough to make that possible, shall we go somewhere and celebrate your success? But not to the clinic," I added with ironic jocularity.

She laughed. "Hardly the clinic. It seems that the Führer not only arranged for me but also for a hotel room at the same hotel

---

[86] The Hadamar Euthanasia Centre was a psychiatric hospital located in the German town of Hadamar, near Limburg in Hesse. Beginning in 1939, the Nazis used this site as one of six for the T4 Euthanasia Programme, which carried out mass sterilisations and the mass murder of "undesirable" members of German society, specifically those with physical and mental disabilities. In total, an estimated 200,000 people were killed at these facilities, including thousands of children. The programme lasted until Germany's surrender in 1945. Nearly 15,000 German citizens were transported to the Hadamar hospital and killed there, most in a gas chamber. Additionally, hundreds of forced labourers from Poland and other Nazi-occupied countries were also killed at the site.

where we used to meet. Not the same room, of course, but the same hotel. Can you believe it?"

I could believe it.

To this moment, I still couldn't be certain that it had happened and, more important, whether I could be an objective, coherent, and accurate chronicler. If I appeared nonchalant, it was probably the final wearing off of whatever Morell had given me—if he had. Even now, I strained to accommodate a linear narrative.

After a quotidian morning, I'd been told by Albert to remain in my quarters until the Führerbuzzer summoned me, then to proceed straight to the main garage without speaking to anyone on the way. This might appear unusual, to say the least, but with the Führer, the unusual was normality itself. So, I did as I was told—but not without a wariness borne of native perspicacity and harsh experience.

"What's up, Erich?" I asked Kempka as I eased into the saloon's plushness and clicked the door shut. "All very mysterious."

"No idea." His shoulders lifted, and his lips pursed. "The boss wanted you delivered, and I'm just the delivery boy. Maybe a surprise birthday party."

"It's not my birthday."

He nodded indulgently. "Yeah, well, you get what I mean, eh? I don't fucking know. You'll know when we get there, I figure. As usual, I just sit on my ass and wait." He nudged the accelerator, and the car lunged up the ramp and onto the animated Wilhelmstrasse.

The constant migration of country dwellers into the city at the end of the nineteenth century had converted Wedding into a "blue-collar"—as the Americans called their common labourers—district. These urban peasants lived in cramped tenement blocks, many in the Wilhelmine Ring. After World War I, the district became known as "Red Wedding," renowned for its militant, largely Communist constituency and, by the late 1920s, the scene of violent clashes between Communist and Nazi sympathisers. The Communists lost, but the area was not to experience renovation under the new regime. Perhaps it was a form of punishment.

We arrived at a wretched apartment building on a seedy residential street bereft of light and life, its lowly inhabitants long tucked in bed to prepare for a pre-dawn rising. The only sound came from the always-jarring *E-ah! E-ah!* hiccup of a distant police car siren.

"Okay, my friend," Kempka said with a friendly punch on the shoulder, "this is it. Not exactly the Adlon, eh? Top floor, number three-oh-three. No need to knock. On your way now."

"Sure you don't know anything about this?"

"I drive the Führer; I don't ask questions. That's why I still drive the Führer."

⊸ß

I heard no signs of life, save my own, as I clumped up the three dim floors on the rickety, piss-stained stairs. No one was stationed outside 303, so I went straight in and was forced to squint through light provided by a single candle. Even in the shadowy darkness, I could see that it was one vast, open space that must have taken up the entire third floor, the other outside doors and numbers being mere stage setting. Scant furniture decorated the space: an ornate liquor trolley and a tight circle of high-backed, plush armchairs adjacent to a massive, interior-lit world globe (now dark), not unlike the one in the Führer's study. Any windows must have been covered, end to end, with heavy cloth or boarded up.

"Come, Linge, take some refreshment and sit with us. No ceremony." I knew that voice and the words well; they were the Führer's.

I'd been through enough similar scenarios at the Chancellery to trust nothing of what I saw and heard, but I made for the trolley, knowing better than to drink, for, at best, I needed my wits intact, and at worst… Morell. But as I didn't consider declining to be an option, I was faced with one shot glass and two "identical" bottles of aptly named Jägermeister,[87] not unlike the two doors in "The Lady, or the Tiger."[88]

In the story, the reader never discovered what lay behind the door he chose, but I had no such luxury, so I eeny-meeny-miny-moed, chose, poured a fifth, and moved to the circle. As I came closer, I could see the Führer and Weisthor, and when I took the only empty chair, I saw Himmler (sans his notebook and pencil) and Krafft. Now, the furtiveness began to make some sense—and my brain filled with effervescent ice water.

---

[87] Jägermeister (meaning "master hunter") is a *Kräutorlikör*—an herbal liquor—composed of fifty-six different ingredients. While the entire recipe is a closely kept secret, the company has acknowledged using a few specific ingredients in the recipe, which has remained unchanged since its creation in 1934.

[88] A semi-barbaric king arrests his daughter's lover for daring to love someone above his station. The lover is forced into an arena, where he must open one of two doors. Behind one door is a tiger; behind the other door is a lady whom he must marry.

Becoming more accustomed to the murk and utilising the time it took me to sit, I surreptitiously studied the only man I hadn't already encountered. Around forty, I guessed, and skinny, he was wrapped in an ill-fitting double-breasted suit with the jacket still buttoned, creating a pointed-hat-shaped gap at the chest. His face was long, dark, and solemn, with a small, slightly open mouth and sunken steely-blue eyes that made me instantly uncomfortable. His skin had the colour of old newspapers, faintly yellowish, and his teeth were none too good. If Goebbels and Hess could have copulated and one of them given birth, Krafft would be their son.

All held shot glasses in varying stages of completion, but I hesitated, letting the first move be theirs.

"A toast." The Führer raised his glass, paused, then nodded towards Weisthor. "You make it."

"Of course, my Führer."

Himmler and Krafft then raised theirs. *So, what was I to do? Say to hell with Leningrad, pour my drink on the rug, and stomp out? In Kempka's parlance, "Frau Linge didn't raise no dummy. Am I right, or am I right?"*

"To the eradication of time," Weisthor proposed.

"A most fitting toast," the Führer declared, "since time is the ultimate enemy."

I had no choice but to raise my hand as well—a hand that seemed to have separated from my arm—and swallow, all the while praying for control.

After several moments, the Führer reached into the breast pocket of his tunic and pulled out the top I'd given him. He handed it to Weisthor, who leaned over and passed it to me. Since my now-inflated eight-fingered hand hadn't returned to me and was numb in the bargain, I dropped it, to no one's reaction.

"What is that in your hand?" Weisthor asked me.

So it hadn't dropped. Control was slipping away on an unknowable timetable. Since they couldn't have anticipated which "door" I would choose, they must have placed a "tiger" behind both. The only questions for me now were how sharp its teeth were, how hungry it was, and whether, somehow, by force of what will remained to me, I could transform the tiger into Androcles's lion. Just then, something vile assaulted my nostrils.

"Do you smell something, Herr Weisthor?" I asked. "Something foul, like decaying fish or a decomposing body?"

Weisthor smiled. "No, Linge, no smell. Do you smell anything, Karl?"

"No, nothing," Krafft answered. "Herr Himmler?"

No smile. "Nothing," he said. "What of you, my Führer?"

The Führer turned his head towards me. "I don't smell anything, Linge, foul or otherwise. It's your imagination."

"The… Führer's top!" I blurted. By then, there were two of me, and one had floated to the top of the globe. The other me sat on the Arctic Circle, but it was quite warm.

"Now, please give it back," he said, and I obliged. Then Krafft reached into a pouch he held and drew out another top that looked identical to the one I'd given back and the one I'd secreted away. *Was there a third?* He handed it over to where I sat, seeming not to notice the other me on the globe. I leaned over, took the top, screamed, and dropped it.

"What's wrong, Linge?" the Führer asked in his most solicitous tone. "Are you all right?"

Now, from my perch atop the globe, I watched the seated me answer. "It was like sticking my fingers into boiling sugar, my Führer."

"You should pick it up again," said Krafft. "I think you'll find it a pleasant experience."

As the seated me looked down at the floor, I could see that I was naked but untroubled by it, as if nakedness were my natural state. I reached down and retrieved the top, which, as Krafft predicted, was quite cool and comforting to the touch. Then, with my other hand, I peeled back a chunk of flesh on my forearm, took the "new" top, inserted it, and pressed down the flap. "You were right, Herr… Herr—"

"Krafft," he answered, and I knew I'd retained some degree of command.

Only how much, for how long, and were they aware of it?

"What are you doing, Linge?" Weisthor asked.

It seemed that I'd leaned down again, picked up the pair of pliers lying beside me on the floor, and began extracting my front teeth. "Extracting my front teeth, Herr Weisthor," I answered with somnambulistic nonchalance.

Krafft reached over and gently removed the pliers from my hands. I couldn't have cared less, since I was now absorbed by the top that had been under the flap but was now in the palm of my hand.

"You see the… implement before you, yes?" Krafft asked.

I looked up. "Yes, Herr Krafft." My mouth had separated from my face, floating free, and possessed all its teeth. "I see it."

"Now," he said, "if you would be good enough to decipher and recite for us the symbols engraved on its sides." Krafft's face, illuminated only by the meagre light that emanated from the candle, was neon white, with eyes sunk so deep into his head he looked like a skull, but his voice was so soothing, it was like falling into an endless sea of meringue.

I had to resist, but my brain seemed to be missing, and when I looked up at the globe, my doppelgänger had it in his hands, fondling it like a tiny, depilated animal.

"We're all comrades here, Linge," Weisthor said, "and with

only one mission: to ensure that the Führer realises his vision and fulfils his destiny, wouldn't you agree?"

Focus! Control! Use what tools you've been given! I held up the top to my face and squinted in deep concentration. "I'm afraid I cannot decipher the symbols, Herr Weisthor. Perhaps if I possessed my brain, but the fellow sitting on the globe has it. If you could retrieve it for me."

The Führer, holding the other top—the one I'd given him—was totally impassive, but the others leaned forward, face to face, conferring in whispers, as if it were a huddle in football. Then they leaned back, and Weisthor turned to me.

"You realise that the implement you hold," he said, ignoring the problem of my missing brain, "is identical to the one you gave the Führer. You do realise that, don't you?"

Now, I couldn't move, immobile from head to toe, like a costumed mannequin. *Was my brain immobile as well?*

Weisthor leaned back, fixing his pale eyes on me. "The truth, Linge, eh?" he said, his tone somewhere between snideness and mockery. "You have no power over the implement, do you? It's merely a toy, yes? And it means no more to you than an encyclopaedia to a snail."

A deep silence followed Weisthor's self-serving accusation. Even though my body was inert, it seemed my brain was not. I was certain now that this candlelit exercise was a test—no, a *contest*—between Weisthor and me, with the Führer as referee.

Focus! "But it isn't," I said. "It isn't, you see, and that's why I can't decipher it and recite. That's why the symbols mean nothing to me." *Fuck you, Weisthor, with your snail together!*

Another huddle, and even in that stingy light, I could see Weisthor's face grow dark. When he spoke again, it was in a low, barely controlled voice.

"All right, Linge, we understand. We understand and

appreciate your predicament. But you see, a brain is not necessary, only will."

I glanced up just in time to see my doppelgänger toss my brain back to me, leap off the globe, scamper to the Führer's liquor trolley, and disappear into one of the bottles. I was still in the tiger's mouth.

Weisthor reached over and took the top from my hand. "You deny this implement's authenticity. All well and good. But I trust you can decipher and recite the symbols on the Führer's own object."

It had to be now! Strength! Will! Guile! "Yes, I can, but I… I cannot decipher and recite with everyone here. It must be for the Führer's ears and his alone."

Staring intently, letting his displeasure gather visibly in the seams of his face, Weisthor nodded to Krafft, who took up the baton as if they were partners in a relay race.

"And you know this how, Linge?" Krafft inquired.

I hesitated for a long, sweaty moment. My hand had returned to my arm, but both were shaking, the distended blue veins on the backs throbbing, though I couldn't move—just one more oddity I ignored. What concentration I still had needed to be focused, for historic decisions were riding on the next few minutes.

"I… uh… in much the same way… the Führer understands—as only he can." Toss the ball with calculated clumsiness and see where it lands.

Weisthor, Krafft, and even the impassive Himmler, turned their heads to the Führer. After an interminable pause, "Linge's quite correct," he said. "As should be expected, only I can understand this. But we're getting nowhere, so we must now proceed to the next phase. Karl?" His tone held a distinct edge of nascent displeasure.

"As you wish, my Führer," Weisthor acceded, though I thought I could detect some hesitation I couldn't interpret.

"No gun this time?" the Führer asked with no little jocularity.

"No gun, my Führer," Weisthor said with no jocularity at all. "Linge's finally here."

"Ah yes." Then the Führer stood, motioning for us to remain seated. "To realise my vision, absent of distractions," he announced, "I must maintain my detachment even from this. I'll return when it's done." With that, he turned and exited alone through a side door I hadn't noticed.

Weisthor turned to Krafft. "Have her brought in while I prepare."

Krafft rose and moved to the front door, eased it open, and muttered some words I couldn't make out. Moments later, as I squinted in the sparse light, he was joined by Annagret in full SS nurse's uniform and an equally statuesque, naked female I couldn't quite make out. Meanwhile, Weisthor had us stand while he spread the chairs into a wider circle, then he went over and cleared the trolley, placed a large wicker basket on top, and wheeled it into the centre, removed the basket and put it on the floor beside it. Then he beckoned Annagret to deliver the female, and when they got closer, I could see that it was Emerald, unmistakably so. Still immobilised, I was also transfixed, no less by the situation than by her splendour.

Weisthor whispered something in Emerald's ear, and she eased herself up onto the trolley, taking up most of its surface. Then he nodded to Krafft and sat down. At no time did she look at me.

Krafft turned from us and gazed down at the naked Emerald. "Is there anything you wish to say?"

Without moving, she said, "Not to all, just to one."

"And who might that be?"

"He knows—and without words," she added.

"And what would you say to him without words?"

"He knows."

"Is that all?"

"It's everything."

After some fluttery blinking, Krafft went over to me. "Linge, the implement, if you please." He took it from my hand, brought it over to Annagret, who lowered it to Emerald's open mouth and inserted it between her upper and lower teeth. Then Annagret reached into her pocket and drew out a pair of pruning shears, and as I watched, immobilised, she began amputating all of Emerald's fingers and toes, dropping each item into the basket as she went. Emerald was silent all the while, gazing blankly at the ceiling, her face bearing no more expression than Himmler's. Since I couldn't move, my face must have displayed shock as I gaped in disbelief.

Finished, Annagret laid the shears on the floor and turned to Krafft, who removed a serrated flint knife from his other pocket and handed it to Annagret, who began sawing off Emerald's limbs and dropping them into the basket as well. In all this atrocity, there was no blood. My brain screamed for me to intervene and tear Krafft and Annagret to pieces, but I was held fast, compelled to witness the ghastly spectacle. When she'd finished, all that was left of Emerald was a torso, an elongated chunk of her former perfect self. Annagret took the knife and made an incision down the centre of her chest from just below the Adam's apple to just above the navel. She cut the breastbone in half, called for Krafft to come and separate the two halves, and spread them apart, while Annagret cut her heart free and removed it (as well as the implement from her teeth), and proffered them to Weisthor, who accepted them and told Annagret to remove the trolley and its "passenger," which she did and left without even a glance at me.

"Since the Führer is a vegetarian," Weisthor said, "the pleasure of eating it, Linge, falls to you." His tone was so insouciant that he might as well have been speaking about a perfectly prepared leg of lamb.

My hands trembled so badly that I had to hold one with the other to keep them still. "I… I can't—"

"Why, of course you can," Weisthor said, I knew, facetiously, carefully modulating his voice and speaking very slowly, as if he actually intended something benign. "It was prepared with you in mind. Perhaps after a few nibbles, you'll feel more like providing the Führer—and us—the information he must have."

At that moment, incapable of motion and beset by a stunned and rattled brain, I didn't know what I could do, but I had to do something. Of that, I was as certain as I'd ever been. But could I do what was necessary? Not a question, I concluded: I had to do it! With whatever control I had left. And it had to be then!

"Herr Weisthor, please give me the Führer's top," a voice said suddenly, "and call for the Führer."

Weisthor emitted an edgy, unpleasant laugh. "And the reason is?" he asked with no little insolence.

"Just do as I say."

The authority in the voice must have been both unmistakable and impressive, for Weisthor pursed his lips, rose, went to the side door, and knocked. A moment later, the Führer emerged and moved to his seat, followed by a clearly disturbed Weisthor. As they sat, the candle, now almost a nub, erupted with a blaze of light and a loud, breathy "*Whuh!*" startling all, save Himmler and me, then returned to its flickering ebb. It was then that I realised it had been my voice.

With Emerald's heart in one hand, I began fingering the top

with the other. "Herr Weisthor," I began, "the Führer is not yet ready for his sacred destiny to be realised. Far more is required than the paltry performance of ritual on the female. All of you, now gaze at the globe."

All heads swung to see the translucent orb now glowing from within and casting no external light. I pointed the implement at it, and a viscous red substance began oozing down from the Arctic in rivulets to engulf the entire Soviet Union and moved no further.

"There you see the blood of the woman," I said, "the blood you didn't see on the trolley or floor. Your sacrifice of the woman was both feeble and futile, Herr Weisthor. You, and especially Herr Krafft, should know that there must be a vastly more cataclysmic offering before the implement and I gain the power to guide the Führer to the final stage. And as a path to that glorious end, there must be mass sacrifice in the form of starvation unto death, starvation on a biblical scale. It must be in Leningrad. And it must take as long as need be. The Führer knows this to be true, and that is all that matters, gentlemen, is it not?" Then, with newfound mobility, I took some hearty bites of the heart and tossed the rest to Weisthor, who fumbled and dropped it, leaving it on the floor.

I waited, watching the others, waiting for a change of expression. Several silent minutes passed. It was Weisthor who blinked first. The colour drained from his face. He wiped his forehead and turned to the others as though he could not really believe what he'd heard, but no response came from Krafft or Himmler.

Finally, the Führer spoke. "I've heard enough," he declared, turning to Himmler. "Linge speaks for me. Heinrich, things will proceed as I've directed." He glanced at me. "Linge, can you stand?"

I didn't know. "I'll try, my Führer." I raised myself up with woozy awkwardness.

"The top?"

I glanced down at my hand as if I'd just discovered I had one, then reached over to the Führer and handed him the top.

"You've had a busy evening," the Führer said. "I'll have Arnt tend me in the morning. Lunch will be soon enough."

"Thank you, my Führer," I told him and turned to leave without looking at the others.

"Linge." It was the Führer again.

I turned back.

"You might do well to put on some clothes before you hit the street."

❧

"You're a real lady-killer, Heinz. That I gotta tell yuh." Kempka's head was a metronome of disappointment.

I'd found myself in the back seat of Kempka's moving saloon in full uniform but had no idea how I'd got there.

"What?"

"Whudduyuh mean, what? Here the Führer wanted to surprise you with that nurse of yours, and before I can even get you out of the car, you have one of your fucking spells and conk out."

"You mean I didn't go in?"

"Go in? *Go in?* You was sprawled out in the back seat for three fucking hours while I diddled. At one point, you came to and tore off your uniform, like you was sleepwalking, but I shook you real good, dressed you, and that was that. Still out cold, though, but at least you wasn't naked."

"So, it was all a nightmare?" I said this more to myself but loud enough for Kempka to shake his head over.

"I don't know what the fuck 'it' is, but your nightmare sure had to be more exciting than me staring out the fucking window."

"Can we go a little faster?"

"Why?"

"I need to get to a toilet. My stomach's killing me."

He shook his head. "Probably something you ate."

THIS AFTERNOON, JUNGE and I sorted out the vast chaos of unfurled military maps of Eastern Europe scattered all over the floor, desk, and tabletops, while the Führer "debated" strategy with Generals von Bock, Guderian, and Hoch concerning an attack on Moscow. It was a short meeting—the Führer saw to that.

"But, my Führer," protested Guderian with no little vigour, "my panzers are only two hundred twenty miles from Moscow, their troops are utterly unprepared, they are cut off from supplies, Stalin has no remedy to offer his troops, and the blow to Russian morale will be incalculable."

The other two generals *hmmed* and nodded in agreement.

"You yourself—"

I knew what Guderian wanted to say. At a military planning meeting just before we attacked Russia, the Führer had told the assembled generals, including the three standing before him now, that: "British strategy is founded on hesitancy and fear. If the fools had but gone on once they had been cleared out of Greece, they could have marched straight on to Tripoli and taken the place. Instead, they chose that very moment to call a halt without the slightest reason. It is a classic example of a lack of imagination and orderly thinking. And why this desperate desire to take Salonika? Was it because they were less anxious to bomb us and wanted instead to attack some Italian town each night? For us, things are much simpler," he instructed them. "In most cases, we have no choice. In the East, if I don't attack, the Russians will gain the initiative."

But that was the "old Führer," I considered, the "pre-top Führer." So, I also knew that Guderian was in for a classic Führer reversal and, with it, a strategic thrashing.

The Führer splayed his hands so firmly on his desktop that the skin became a blotch of red and white, his face a rictus of barely controlled fury. "Again, this ex-corporal must instruct generals," he said, his voice a time-tested study in slow, guttural tension. "British strategy," he told them, word-for-word from his previous pronouncement, "is founded on hesitancy and fear," but now it contained a crucial alteration—"and I'm not too hidebound to say that it *works!* Of course we have the means to quickly annihilate the Russians, but at a needless cost that I refuse to countenance. You ask why? Because my strategy, unlike yours, is not confined to the battlefield. That is to say, we also have the means to exterminate them from within, through siege, starvation, and subversion: I call them the 'Three Ss' of my inspired master strategy. At this moment, a meaningless city is of far less importance than the resource-rich Ukraine. Along those same lines, priority must be given to the conquest of the Crimea and the Donets Basin. Gentlemen, the matter is beyond debate." The Führer's way of saying that permitted no debate.

After receiving that lesson in how to use the same facts to arrive at a completely opposite conclusion, the generals could only stare at each other again in perplexed awe before being dismissed.

❧

Sitting across from Junge and Albert in the crowded, raucous officers' mess, I strained to concentrate on what they were saying, but I was far too elated from the Führer's military rebuke to do more than hear random snatches and attempt to appear engrossed. Jean-Paul Sartre wrote: "It would be much better if I could only stop thinking. Thoughts are the dullest things. Duller than flesh. They stretch out, and there's no end to them, and they leave a funny taste in the mouth." He must have been referring to his own thoughts, for mine were anything but dull. But I was forced to admit that, like his, they did leave a "funny taste," that was to say, dreadful: the Führer's Three Ss, implemented.

A blow on my arm roused me from my ruminations.

"Heinz," Junge said, "you look so far away, I was expecting a postcard."

Now slightly self-conscious, I performed a stagy headshake. "Sorry, very little sleep last night, you know how it is."

They winked at each other and chuckled. "Well, Heinz," Junge said, "yes, we know… up to a point, but not how it is with a Valkyrie in nurse's training. You'll need to help us out on that, eh?"

I had to shut my eyes for a second to process "Valkyrie." I suspected they were using the term to signify a woman whose physical dimensions rendered her sexually formidable. But I knew what the term actually meant, and my definition was far more accurate and dark: one of a host of female figures who chose those who may die in battle and those who may live. It seemed that even in Norse mythology, there was a selection process, T4 being only the most recent and most abominable, but I had no intention of burdening them with irony. In fact, had I described our last "real" rendezvous (not counting her operation on Emerald), they would have been disappointed, since she had spent most of the night regaling me with grisly anecdotes of her medical prowess, accolades from her superiors, and expectations of the patriotic services she'd soon be performing for the "racial betterment of the Reich." She'd spoken of euthanasia with the exhilaration other women reserved for orgasms and childbirth, and it was all I could do to remain in the room without dealing with her the way she'd wanted to do with that chicken.

"She's very inventive" was all I said, leaving the erotic implications to their particular fancy.

"I'll bet," Junge said. "I'm amazed you even had the strength to show up today. You know, Albert," he remarked, shifting subjects and recipient with uncommon lubricity, "that Kaltenbrunner's a real piece of work. After you and the Führer left, he was discussing the Führer's new starvation strategy for Leningrad with your brother. He actually said, and I quote, 'the Führer is brilliant, as always. Before long, those fucking animals will be eating each other until there's only one left, and the one who'll be left will end up eating himself.' You know, like the man in the cartoon who jumps into a hole and pulls the hole in after him."

Unworthy of a laugh, we all proffered a thin smile.

"I'll tell you something," Albert said, "that scar on Kaltenbrunner goes a lot deeper than his cheek."

"How did the others react to all that?" I asked.

They glanced at each other, pursed their lips, then went back to me. "As you'd expect," Junge answered, "no surprises. Göring continued stuffing down his food. Keitel and von Ribbentrop left the moment they wouldn't be noticed, and Himmler, as usual, sat like a blank, staring straight ahead as Kaltenbrunner babbled on to the Reichsleiter about the fun he and his men would have once they entered what remained of Leningrad. That's it, meeting adjourned."

"What about Speer and Schmitz?" I inquired, wondering if they were excluded from the narrative by design or by accident.

"Oh yeah, those two," Junge said. "Right you are. They were the farthest away from my station, so I could only hear stray bits and pieces. It was only when they were leaving and stopped at the door for a few moments that I heard Speer tell Schmitz it would be a substantial problem but solvable because it was a matter of logistics and so subject not to human laws but to scientific laws. Schmitz then replied that he agreed but added that it was also subject to economic laws, and Speer laughed and said—and I think this is accurate—'Good engineering, my dear Schmitz, is always good business.' That's all. Boring as hell. Be happy you were in that hotel room with Annagret."

"Just out of curiosity, Hans," I said, "just what was the problem they were talking about?"

Junge lifted his shoulders. "No idea; I think it was some hypothetical project they were tossing about."

12 August 1941

AFTER COMPLETING MY morning duties, I was leaving the Führer's quarters in Sperkries[89] when I spotted Field Marshal von Bock sitting in the antechamber, ramrod-straight and ignoring Günsche and Keitel (who sat directly across him) with stoic abandon. Over the years, I'd become fairly adept at reading faces, if only to alert the Führer, but I was always stopped dead in my tracks by the military "vons," who seemed—not unlike Himmler—to make deadpan an art form. They entered the conference room as I reached the door, and by the time I shut it behind me, I could already hear the Führer shrieking obscenities, nothing worth reporting.

Given all the attention my strategy required, I needed a diversion more than ever, and it was good to have the comic team of Kempka and Baur to provide it. This afternoon, I was sitting

---

[89] Sperkries 1 (Security Zone 1) was located at the heart of the Wolf's Lair, ringed by steel fencing and guarded by the Reichssicherheitsdienst. It contained the Führer Bunker and ten other camouflaged bunkers built with two-metre-thick (6 ft 7 in) steel-reinforced concrete. These shelters protected members of Hitler's inner circle, including Martin Bormann, Hermann Göring, Wilhelm Keitel, and Alfred Jodl. Hitler's accommodation was positioned on the northern side to avoid direct sunlight. Both Hitler's and Keitel's bunkers featured additional rooms for holding military conferences.

facing Frau Becker[90] in the officers' mess when they arrived. Becker was no Christiane, Annagret, or Klara, but she made the other tasters, secretaries, and housekeepers look like barnyard animals by comparison. She was also, unlike the other tasters, secretaries, and housekeepers, an intelligent, decent human being with a sense of humour as a bonus. She was also married.

"Hey, Becker," Baur said as he and Kempka took seats on either side of her, facing me. "Somebody make you an officer?"

She shrugged. "Heinz spotted me coming from the tasters' room and invited me over. He called it a battlefield commission."

"If you weren't married," Kempka said, "I'd call it something else."

"I'm sure you would," I told the boor. "Now, unless you intend to arrest her for impersonating an officer, is it okay if she joins us?"

Laughs from Kempka and Baur.

"She can be my co-pilot anytime, officer or not," Baur declared, "husband or no husband."

"Think Karl would mind?" I asked her with no great risk. From what she'd told me before, her husband was at war, and having heard nothing from him in two years, she had long since assumed he was dead—and had told me so.

---

[90] Johanna Becker was a German secretary among fifteen young women selected to taste Hitler's food at the Wolf's Lair in East Prussia for two-and-a-half years to ensure it was safe to eat. She and the other tasters were brought to a barracks where cooks prepared the food for the entire Wolf's Lair. Each morning at 0800, Becker would be rousted from bed by SS guards shouting, "Johanna, get up!" from beneath her window. She was picked up by bus daily from her mother-in-law's residence and was only needed if Hitler was present at the Wolf's Lair, though she never actually saw him in person. The food tasting took place daily from 1100 to 1200 hours. After the women confirmed that the food was safe, members of the SS transported it in crates to the main headquarters, where Hitler's primary cook, Constanze Manziarly, prepared his meals.

"My fear of heights would override any approval of Karl's. I don't even like standing on a chair."

"Then in bed, you like being on bottom, eh?" Kempka's customary venture into vulgarity.

"Be nice, Otto," Baur advised. "Have some regard for Becker's and Linge's sensitivity."

Becker's expression seemed fixed at zero. She probably knew that Baur didn't mean a word of it, only intending it as a way to prod me into responding.

"Have pity, my friends," I told them. "She has to eat that baby food first."

"True," Kempka said, "every bite could be your last. What keeps you going?"

"Well, I'll tell you." She pursed her lips, and for a moment, her features softened. "There's a hidden benefit: if I encounter something unpleasant, I won't have to do it anymore."

Baur laughed. Kempka looked confused, and I smiled with admiration at her wit. Her face told me that she'd expected those very responses, and a chill of satisfaction—and something else—coursed through me.

"You must be quite a patriot," Baur said. "I don't think the Führer appreciates your sacrifice. Like having an insurance policy; something you don't think about, and if you do, you hope you never need to use it."

She shrugged, no doubt having heard this many times. "I don't imagine the Führer knows me, but the SS do, and that's enough appreciation for a lifetime, no offence meant. I have to go now and make sure the baby can eat his dinner without it eating him, so if you'll excuse me, gentlemen." As she left us standing, she gave perfunctory glances at Baur and Kempka, but her eyes lingered a fraction longer on me, I thought (*or did I hope?*).

"Quite a dish," Baur remarked.

"Someone ought to taste her," Kempka added, or it wouldn't be Kempka.

"She's very nice," I said, hesitant to go further.

"'Very nice?'" Baur remarked. "Is that all you can say? From the way she was looking at you, my friend, you might as well have been an item on her food table."

"A possibly poisonous vegetable?" I kidded, hoping he was right.

"Heinz, Heinz," he chided with a swivel of his head. "When will you realise that National Socialism liberated men as well as the Fatherland? Under the Führer, we're as much in demand to females as nations are to him."

"And we're SS to boot," Kempka chimed in. "Shit, we're any woman's wet dream."

Kempka, a woman's wet dream? That particular image didn't recommend German females to me, Annagret excepted. "I know, fellas. Himmler, the Reich's premier sex symbol, would be ashamed of me."

"Look, Heinz," Baur said, "the hell with Becker. I can secure a pass, fly Annagret here, and you can have a kinda conjugal visit."

"Conjugal visit? She's a long way from being my wife," I said.

"I said 'kinda.' You know I have lots of those. Kempka here has even more. He's the King of Kindas, you might say. And in the field during wartime, 'kinda' is plenty good enough. Especially considering the talent employed here, no offence to Becker."

"When we signed on to serve the Führer," the chauffeur added, "we... I don't know, joined a fucking monastery. We do all our shit in a world of men, no less than the troops. And a world of men ain't gonna do the job, that is, unless you're in fucking prison and have no choice 'cause, in prison, everyone's a homo, get me?"

I got him. I'd been in enough jails to affirm his alluring insight. I only escaped being a brownie[91] to an arse bandit[92] by being larger and tougher than my prospective suitors.

"So how about it?" Baur asked me again, eyebrows lifted. "I can get her here and back without breaking a sweat, and the only proof she was here will be in your sheets."

It would be nice, I thought. But something aside from interrupting her euthanasia training and enduring her sexual kinkiness held me back, and I was troubled by not knowing what it was. "I appreciate it, Hans, but I don't want to get her in trouble with her bosses at the hospital. She said they keep a close watch on their students, especially their star pupil. No, I'll just—"

"Well, then what about that luscious Johanna?" Baur asked. "I bet she's superb in the sack."

"She's married," I told him, in vain, I imagined.

Both laughed with vigour.

"You gotta be kiddin' me, Heinz," Kempka said. "Two fuckin' years and no word? She thinks he's dead, and he probably is, and who the fuck cares if he isn't?"

"Erich has a point," Baur seconded. "If she doesn't care, why should you? But I'd get on it right away. Her job's like bomb disposal. You know, the next one could be the one."

By then, I was sick of the subject. "Yes, fellas, you're both right. I'll get on—"

Baur's hand jerked up, almost the Führer's right-angle salute.

---

[91] A person penetrated in anal sex.

[92] A gay male who has anal sex, especially with a boy as the passive partner.

"No-no-no." He grinned. "I can't leave such a delicate job to someone who hesitates because the female wears a wedding ring. I'll do the grunt work. Anyway, I outrank you, so it'll be more impressive, not to mention persuasive."

I shrugged with weary resignation, secretly relieved that the matter was being taken out of my hands to be performed by another.

Like the Führer.

20 *August 1941*

THIS MORNING, I was awakened by one of the sentries who had been assigned "Führerbuzzer" duty until all the facility's electronics could be made at least more predictable, if not more efficient. After getting dressed, the Führer began his day by taking a walk alone with Blondi, then returned to glance at the mail that Günsche and I had sorted and delivered. After he dismissed us, we made for the officers' mess to join Albert, Junge, and Pfizer[93] for a late breakfast.

[Unreadable]…

He took another mouthful and chewed thoughtfully, his round eyes narrowing until he looked like a near-sighted raccoon.

"Too complicated for this poor clerk," Junge said, making a rare, honest concession to inferiority.

"I gotta go." Turning to Albert, Pfizer lamented, "Your brother has another errand for me. Since oh-four-thirty this morning, that's four so far, and it's not even afternoon."

Albert smiled. "There are no mornings and afternoons for my brother. No evenings or nights, for that matter. He's always run on a numberless clock and expects everyone to do the same, unfortunately."

"Yeah, well…" Pfizer started to say, then clammed up, rose, saluted, and left.

----

[93] SS Captain Erich Pfizer was one of Martin Bormann's army of loyal menials.

"He's a snitch," Albert said. "Good he left before things got serious."

An Übersnitch, I thought. I wouldn't even yawn in his presence, for the certainty that he would run to the Reichsleiter with the news that I was a slacker.

"Now that he's gone, what's so serious?" I asked.

"Nothing really, I was just flexing my wit. But if you need something, how about the Führer's ongoing military tennis match with himself?"

Günsche shook his head. "Tennis match? What tennis match? I don't get it."

"Of course you don't," Albert quipped. "All right, here: originally, the Führer was fighting with his generals to defend his blitzkrieg strategy, and now that he's been successful, he's fighting those same generals to defend his new siege strategy."

This was serious, and I listened with both ears.

"With all due respect, I was never thankful to not be a general until now," said Herr Clumsy Lout, as I'd named him.

"Not to worry, Otto," Albert answered. "I'm confident you're giving me all the respect that's due. But to relieve your mind, you need never worry about being a general. Feel better?"

Though I sat Himmler-like, I was laughing my guts out at Bormann's elegant squelch. His brother he wasn't by a quantum leap.

"I'm most grateful, Herr—"

"Now that we're being informal and disregarding rank for the present," Albert finished for him, "is what I said serious enough for you?"

"Uh, plenty serious, but I don't see where it matters, so long as we win. The Führer knows what he's doing, so the generals should go along with him, right? Whichever way he sees fit."

"Well, I'd—" Albert started to say, when Junge cut him off.

"I agree with Otto; the Führer's a genius, so who are we—or even the generals—to question such a man's judgement?"

"I see what you mean," Albert said, tongue embedded in cheek. "Command is complicated, no question about that."

I'd never tell them, but I always thought of the Führer the way Schopenhauer did: "Talent hits a target no one else can hit; genius hits a target no one else can see." But I wondered if Günsche and Junge ever considered Aristotle's comment that "there is no great genius without some touch of madness." I doubted it, but I was beginning to think that Albert had, and that to him, it mattered.

∾

"They have all the loyalty of dogs but without the intelligence."

A chill shot through me. It was like listening to Brückner, as if he and not Martin Bormann's brother were sitting here after those two oafs had trundled off and he'd had me stay behind for the real discussion. But it wasn't Brückner, I had to keep telling myself.

The clatter and chatter that accompanied our lunch had ebbed, and now that we were among the few remaining customers, Albert's voice dropped several decibels.

"I couldn't help noticing that you said nothing all through lunch. Are you feeling all right?" Albert's hands were folded in front of him, an expression of patience and forbearance on his face, the critical question hanging in the air without having been spoken.

He wasn't keeping me here out of concern about my lack of volubility or vigour, of that I was certain. The issue for me was an ancient and beguilingly simple one—and possibly devastatingly complex for all that: *What can I allow myself to reveal?* I'd read that gold miners in America in the last century were so fearful of thieves, they actually ate their gold to provide the safest hiding place, expecting to expel it in the natural manner later. Instead, they repeatedly vomited, suffered sharp abdominal pain, severe bleeding, rupture of the intestine, and septicaemia, all leading to a miserable death. I imagined the lesson was that even with the best of reasons, one can be too careful. *Should I eat* my *"gold" as well?*

"I feel fine, considering," I told him, hoping for Albert to fill in any blanks.

"What do you think about the Führer's radical shift of strategy?"

The veins at my temples bulged and throbbed, and I was afraid that Albert could see it. I shrugged. "Why do you think I have any opinion and, if I did, that my opinion would be different from his?"

He smiled his benign smile. "I don't know, one way or the other. That's why I'm asking."

Trust no one! "I've been with the Führer a long time, not near as long as his inner circle of course, but plenty long enough to know my limitations—in memory, knowledge, and curiosity—and my place."

Albert chuckled with seeming good nature. "Heinz, my friend, this isn't an interrogation. I'm merely asking for an opinion from one man to another. Nothing sinister, I assure you."

"But you know me," I probed. "Who and what I am, and what I do. How could my opinion on anything matter to someone like you?"

He smiled in a faintly superior way. "To be frank, I don't know you at all. Many seem to believe they know you, but I'm quite certain that they don't know anything of value. Personally, I think you may know even more than you think you know and certainly far more than those two lummoxes who just left."

It *was* an interrogation, I concluded, perhaps just one degree short of a classic Heydrich. *But do the degree—and the person—make a difference? Or am I attempting to put together the pieces of what may not be any kind of puzzle at all?* I needed to know since, in the relatively cramped quarters of Wolfsschanze, we would be thrown together often.

So I turned up the palms of my hands. "Well, if after all I've said, you still feel that I have something to say, for what it's worth, I'll accommodate you. I've heard that superior men tend to appear unpredictable to ordinary men. And so, while I was surprised by the Führer's change of strategy, to the extent I understood it, I accepted it as just another example of the behaviour of someone with exceptional intellectual and creative power. Is that what you were looking for?"

His lips compressed and spread in disappointment. "I would be, if you were a village clergyman or an ignorant peasant, both of whom employ 'God's will' to answer any difficult question. Granted, it's convenient, comprehensive, and above all, safe— but hardly useful as a tool for analysis and discussion."

"But I am an ignorant peasant, Albert," I told him, hoping for a concession and retreat. "I'm afraid your expectations are far too grand for me." I forced a smile.

Lines of concentration slowly creased his sleek features. I could sense that he was considering where to go next, if anywhere.

Then his face smoothed again. "What if I were to tell you that there are those who believe the Führer is basing his strategies entirely on conflicting advice he's receiving from malevolent and exotic sources? What if I were to tell you that?"

Shit! I narrowed my eyes just a little, followed by a relaxed smile. "Well, Albert, I'd say that they are the priests and peasants you mocked. We all have beliefs, but unlike us, the Führer has insight. I would say that there is his inspiration and not some… what did you call them? 'Sinister and exotic sources.'"

Why was he asking me that question and not my tablemates? What did he know, or at least suspect, and how did he know it? And even more important, on what side of the answer would he fall? I dared not continue my response to such a loaded question. Instead, I swallowed the last of my coffee with as much nonchalance as I could gather and shrugged. "So, you think that what I just told you is half-baked."

Albert nodded with no little gravity and finished his coffee. "Not in the least half-baked," he said, "partially baked, perhaps." Then he laughed. "Heinz, don't fret; I'm only playing with you." He rose and bade me remain seated.

He turned to leave when I asked him, "Before you go, Albert, I'm curious. If Junge and Günsche are dogs, what animal am I to you?"

He turned to gaze at me for a pregnant moment. "A fox." He smiled, turned back, and went on his way.

A fox, he called me. My sleep was ruined with it. *Who was this obscure brother of that vicious and ubiquitous, subhuman electric blanket who would seek to envelop the Führer and make him his own? Was he an ally, an enemy, an amused observer? Or, like Brückner, a would-be deus ex machina?* I gazed for a time at my image in my bathroom mirror, marvelling at the evolution of my sentience and active intellect and, at the same time, despairing over the pace and the nature of what I'd become from it. I leaned forward, kissed myself on the reflected mouth, then sat down to tell this to you.

THE FÜHRER'S LEGENDARY volubility seldom interfered with our morning routine, but this morning, he was so loquacious, my stopwatch was rendered useless. I placed the responsibility right at Morell's door since that medical warthog, standing in the corner, had been continually experimenting on him with every manner of potions. Given this, the last thing he needed at the moment was the presence of Goebbels and Himmler, his "natural" stimulants. Once I finished arranging his bathroom in such a condition that none of his army of housekeepers could seem to manage, I entered his study with only perfunctory attentiveness.

"…request a meeting with me here," the Führer was saying, his voice elevated in outrage, "and written as a demand! The cheek of the bastards! In wartime! As if I would interrupt my destiny for one second to palaver with them. I tell you, what could be more fanatical, more exclusive, and more intolerant than Catholicism, a pernicious cult which bases everything on the love of the one and only God whom only it reveals? They're no better than the Jews, I tell you, and in brains and stealth, far inferior. Even you admit this, Heinrich. Personally, I would prefer Jews to Papists if I were forced into the choice and had the freedom."

Himmler remained silent.

"As for Leningrad, who asked about it?" He glanced at Goebbels and Himmler, both of whom shook their heads in the negative. "Never mind. Soon, they'll be eating each other, and only stripped bones will greet our troops as they enter in triumph. Of course, they'll have to bring in their own food." He chuckled at that.

This was nothing I hadn't heard before, sometimes in the same words, sometimes in different words. But regardless of the familiar jabber, I forced myself to listen for any meaningful nuance or sudden shift in subject.

Then, without skipping a beat, the Führer's face reddened, and his right hand began to tremble. "The fools don't understand!" he shrieked. "Or worse, they do and are attempting to undermine my vision! To my face, they lie and tell me that they alone know what's good for me and the Reich. THEY are the true criminals. THEY are the diseased remnant of treasonous scum and must be eradicated before their contagion can spread!"

His face had taken on a purplish cast. He stamped his feet, and both his hands shook and judo-chopped the air beside him. The words tumbled out in a torrent so precipitous that he became almost incomprehensible.

"They hate me. They've always hated me, the limited, useless filth! And they'll be taken care of, you hear me? You can BELIEVE they'll be taken care of! Soon, very soon, they, this war, nations, and all of YOU will be moot, since all will vanish as if they never existed, and I will be transformed, the hand in an empty sleeve, mark my words. My new strategy is nothing, a trifle. When I put what has just come to me into play, something that—"

He never finished, for Morell moved with remarkable speed from his corner to the Führer, took him firmly by the shoulders, and held him fast. Goebbels rose, but Morell removed one hand from the Führer's shoulder and motioned the propaganda minister down, then returned his hand, which held a syringe, and pumped it into a vein on the Führer's wrist.

"My Führer," he whispered, "you told me to warn you when you were becoming overwrought. You must be at your best for this evening's—"

Morell's words—or, more likely, the injection—must have held magical powers, for in a fraction of an instant, the Führer was his old self again, no colour, no shaking, no screaming. He glanced round at the distressed Goebbels and the placid Himmler, then back to the concerned Morell.

"Right," the Führer said, "no time for idle chatter." He looked back at Goebbels. "I've ordered Army Group North to form an impenetrable ring of steel round Leningrad, dealing a sustained crushing blow to those miserable Slavs and, incidentally, providing Heinrich here an opportunity to have his way with the few survivors," to which Himmler, with studied languor, lifted and lowered his eyelids behind his round, rimless glasses, like a poisonous snake. "All right, Joseph, apply your usual sopping veneer of exigency and morality to my speech for the Reichstag tomorrow justifying my actions. A final draft to me by early tomorrow should give you sufficient time, eh?"

"More than sufficient, my Führer," Goebbels said.

Once Goebbels and Himmler left and the Führer retired to his bedroom, Morell held up his hand in a halting gesture as I attempted to follow.

"The Führer," said the doctor, "has expressly required that you attend him this evening—in full-dress uniform. The scheduled dinner and informal outing are cancelled. Tell Günsche to inform the intended guests of that and be here at ten hundred hours sharp. Can you remember all that?"

"I'll write it all down as soon as I enter the antechamber," I assured him.

I left, sporting an internal smile, but soon, the thrill of

personal triumph was tempered by my curiosity over what the Führer had planned for the evening that required his best.

⁕

I spent most of…

[The rest of this entry was corrupted.]

IT WAS OUR last day at the Chancellery before we travelled to Wolfsschanze, where the Führer would meet once again with Mussolini. This morning, I stopped off at the Communications Centre to find a letter from Annagret along with the Führer's mail:

> *Hadamar Euthanasia Centre*
>
> *22 August 1941*
>
> *My dearest Heinz:*
>
> *I write with awkwardness, for my early years on the farm betray me. I miss you terribly. I console myself that I am so occupied with assisting with the Führer's sacred work that I know you would be proud of me. The doctors are so pleased with my progress that they have chosen to ignore procedure and promote me to a full nurse's position with rank. My dream is a reality at last.*
>
> *All are despondent here, for we have received the news that our vital programme will be shut down soon because of stupid and disloyal protests.*[94]

---

[94] Despite precautions taken to cover up the T4 programme, the local population was fully aware of the events at the Hadamar hospital. The people murdered in the hospital were brought in by train and bus, only to seemingly vanish behind its high fencing. As the crematorium ovens often incinerated

However, I must overcome my disappointment and make the most of what the future brings. I have been reassigned and given the high honour of assisting the brilliant and renowned Dr. Josef Mengele in the Ukraine, who works at the SS Race and Settlement Main Office, where he is tasked with evaluating candidates for what is called Germanisation.[95]

How this can be done medically is something I am eager to learn.

I am, of course, hoping that I will soon have the further good fortune to earn some leave and see you. I do not expect you to remain celibate in my absence, but if you choose to satisfy yourself with the stories I read to you, I would, of course, be pleased.

Sent with love, gratitude, and admiration,

Heil Hitler!

Your Annagret

---

two corpses at a time, the process was less than perfect, resulting in a thick, acrid smog that hung over the town. According to a letter sent by Bishop Hilfrich of Limburg to the Reich Justice Minister in 1941, local children taunted one another with the words, "You're not very clever; you will go to Hadamar and into the oven."

[95] The Nazis considered land to the east—Poland, Ukraine, Belarus, and Russia—to be *Lebensraum* (living space) and sought to populate it with Germans. During the Nazi period, the policy of Germanisation carried an explicitly ethno-racial, rather than purely nationalist, meaning. Its aim was the spread of a "biologically superior" Aryan race rather than the expansion of the German nation. Hitler, speaking with generals immediately prior to his chancellorship, declared that people could not be Germanised—only the soil could. Later, Himmler declared that Slavs were fit only for unskilled labour under the harshest and most primitive conditions. "Those unable to work," he proclaimed, "must be exterminated in accordance with the Führer's wishes."

I'd heard of the closing days ago. In fact, I'd heard of it even as far as the hallway since Himmler had to break the news to the Führer. I'm certain the Reichsführer didn't want to but was concerned that the Führer would hear of the complaints by other means; that is to say, means lacking his ameliorative filter. Though I wasn't present, Himmler must have been quite persuasive, for when I entered the Führer's chambers, he was in his pyjamas, dictating to Schroeder the order suspending the T4 programme. In the room with him sat Himmler (scribbling in his little notepad), Goebbels (watching him scribble), Von Ribbentrop (staring at the Führer), and Dr. Karl Brandt, administrator of the programme (staring at the floor). I went about my business tidying up and sorting until he'd finished his dictation and sent Schroeder on her way, then moved to the bathroom, where I could listen in while rearranging the Führer's toiletries.

"Well, gentlemen," the Führer began, "that's that, I'm sad to say. I know you're all disappointed, but it had to be done."

I needed to know why. So did Brandt, it seemed.

"My Führer, I completely understand and appreciate your point, but may I still suggest at this late date that you reconsider? Our cleansing programme has worked miracles. This is undeniable. But exterminating useless eaters and the handicapped is merely a means to a glorious end, namely the public health of the Reich, and in this regard, there is so much more to be done."

I could sense, even without being in the room, the tension caused when the oblivious Brandt said "the handicapped," since Goebbels had a deformed right foot that turned inwards, thicker and shorter than his left foot, all due to a congenital condition. According to Chancellery lore, he'd undergone a failed operation to correct it just prior to starting grammar school and was rejected for military service in World War I due to the deformity.

What wasn't lore was that he wore a metal brace and special shoe because of his shortened leg and walked with a limp.

"I entirely agree with the Führer," said von Ribbentrop, who by now was universally regarded as arrogant, vain, stupid, snobbish, and servile—the perfect upper-level lackey.

"Of course you do," Goebbels said, then, to place some salve on the sting, added, "and rightly so. Considering the information leakage, unfortunate negative publicity, and ignorant outrage surrounding T4, something had to be done."

All I could see in my brain was the pulsating dimple on Brandt's chin, a depression so deep that it seemed formed by a bullet.

"There's an additional reality." Himmler removed his round, rimless glasses and scoured them with a handkerchief. "That I hadn't considered at first blush. As usual, the Führer saw beyond the immediate and convenient. With the start we've made, the Reich can be cleansed at leisure, but now that we've invaded the Soviet Union, many T4 personnel will be required to begin the even more vital work on the Jewish—"

"Since the programme's death has been established," the Führer interrupted, "I see no need to be present at the postmortem."

With that, he rose and moved to the bathroom, where I was quickly engrossed in scrubbing some errant grout when he entered.

"Ah, Linge." He sighed. "Will I never escape the sycophants and second-guessers?"

I wanted to say, *Only when you dismiss them from your service, my Führer,* but instead, I said nothing—the safest, and expected, course—and struggled to call a cease-fire to the war within my brain over the indefinite suspension of T4. You ask why I shouldn't be jubilant over this development, and under other circumstances, I would be. But my strategy tossed a wild card onto the table, and it tormented me with its propulsive and unassailable logic. To put it bluntly, I needed horror.

Mussolini must have taken my advice with an advocate's zeal, for the Führer now received him with excessive pomp and circumstance. The Duce, long a favourite of the Führer's beyond circumstance and reason, was now the beneficiary of the latter's enthusiasm—stemming, I knew, from his desire to demonstrate that the former's moral support had been amply justified. And in return, Mussolini congratulated him with no less exuberance. To make that support tangible—now that the heavy lifting had been performed by our soldiers—he'd recently sent some Italian troops to the Eastern Front, much to the whispered titters of our generals, who felt that they now had the additional burden of protecting those troops from the battle-hardened, desperate Soviets.

While I took some pleasure from Mussolini's subtle wink at me while being greeted so effusively by the Führer, I took even more pleasure from the chaotic delays that would inevitably be caused by the late infusion of Italian troops. But I knew better than to wink back.

﹅

A boring lunch with Günsche and Junge was interrupted by Johanna Becker's startling news that one of the Führer's food tasters had died after sampling some bread pudding with cherries.

I thought of Mussolini first, then amended it after realising that no one would miss him, save for the Führer and the Duce's nepotistic relatives. My next thought was for the Führer, so we shot up and raced to his quarters, where we found him, Mussolini, and permanent interpreter Dollmann standing serenely with Baur, bent over some aircraft-engineering blueprints.

"To what do we owe the honour of your intrusion?" the Führer asked, levity tempering his tone for his guests, I imagined.

Günsche was the first to speak. "My Führer, we... we heard about the attempt on—"

Baur's laughter rang out.

"Have you ever read Mark Twain?" the Führer asked the giant.

"Who?" he answered, squint-eyed.

"The American humourist, yes?" Junge ventured.

"The very one," the Führer said. "He told mourners that 'rumours of my death have been greatly exaggerated.'"

I'd seen that remark underlined in one of the Führer's books, so I was not surprised by the quote, but I was struck by the optimistic wit it took to relate it to such a dolt.

"Yes, my Führer?" Günsche's bewildered expression confirmed my accuracy.

"I meant to say that I'm not dead, Günsche. The Gestapo have already caught the culprit, interrogated her, and discovered that the intended victim was not me or even the Duce but Morell, of all people. They imagine that whoever put her up to it didn't realise that Morell eats what I eat and so gets the same attention. Pity she expired before providing a motive."

The motive must have been their thirty-third question—she just ran out of teeth. Ironically, Morell could have gotten it out of her with one injection.

28 August 1941

THIS MORNING THE Führer, Mussolini, the elusive Engel,[96] Dollmann, Griess (Hoffmann's photo reporter), Schmundt (another of the Führer's army of adjutants), Kempka, Günsche, Junge, and I boarded a Focke-Wulf 200 and were flown by Baur to Uman[97] to inspect the Italian Blackshirt[98] troops, who were on the march near there. A long table had been set up for the Führer and Mussolini in the open air. In a hangar nearby, the position of the armies was explained to them.

The Führer grasped the promising situation right away, and when he smiled and turned to explain the explanation to Mussolini, the latter replied, "There is no need, Führer. Originally, I was a journalist, not a soldier, and so I, of course, defer to you. If you are pleased, how can I be otherwise?" How much the Duce had grown since our clandestine conversation in January.

After the briefing, they wished to see the Italian Blackshirts,

---

[96] Gerhard Engel was one of Hitler's adjutants. See Volume Two for his mysterious interaction with Linge.

[97] Uman is a city located in Cherkasy Oblast (province) in central Ukraine, to the east of Vinnytsia. In 1941, the Battle of Uman took place in the vicinity of the town, where the German Army encircled Soviet positions. Uman was occupied by German forces from August 1941 to March 1944.

[98] An all-volunteer militia of the Kingdom of Italy under Fascist rule, similar to the SS in Nazi Germany. After 1923, they were integrated into the army as an elite unit.

and so we set off in three Krupp all-purpose vehicles (the one that held the Führer and Mussolini was helmed by Kempka). On the way, the Führer had us all stop while he presented his "new possessions."

"Look, Duce." He swept his arm in a wide arc over the vast fields of black soil. "Here is the most fertile soil on earth. Your poor Italians must toil endlessly to work their parched and stony dirt. Here, however, are huge regions with this kind of rich earth. Through the success of our troops and the labour of those miserable Slavs, grateful to even be alive, what you see is going to be the breadbasket of the new Europe."

Miserable Slavs, indeed, I thought. Mussolini—and even, I was sure, the Führer—didn't know the half of it. I'd heard from Günsche that Himmler had plans for the Russians that, as the latter put it, "will make what we did to the Poles seem like summer camp—and that's not even counting the pestilential Jews." Günsche had some trouble with "pestilential," expending three bumbling attempts before even coming close, but I got the message. I abhorred what was to come but hoped it would be thorough, and its thoroughness widely publicised—such was the Gordian dilemma of my strategy.

Moving on, our cavalcade reached a point where two wide roads crossed. The Italian division was supposed to march past the Führer and Mussolini here, and when, as is common with the Italians, it was late, the Führer made the decision to drive towards it, and soon we could make out the forward units of the Blackshirts. The Italian commander must have assumed that Mussolini would be at the appointed place and so drove past us without even a glance. However, we were finally recognised, and the commander, visibly shaken, sprang from his vehicle and ran over to the Führer and Mussolini, holding onto his steel helmet as it bounced up and down on his head. A comical sight if there ever was one.

He was completely out of breath when he finally stood to attention before the Führer's vehicle. It was clear that he was too flustered to know to whom he should report—the Führer or Mussolini. The Führer gestured towards Mussolini, and that was that. The Führer had a slight smile on his face as the commander stammered his report, and on the return trip, as I learned, Mussolini assured the Führer that he would send more Italian divisions to the Front and, naturally, only the best ones. I thought that bit of middling comedy ended the matter, but as I learned over coffee from Dollmann, it was far from over. According to him, instead of the Duce's usual great good humour, he was infuriated over the incident. Then Dollmann related his memory of Mussolini's dialogue with his adjutant once the Führer was out of earshot:

"That stammering clown dares to humiliate me in front of Hitler?" Mussolini shouted. "We have enough reputation to contend with. Make the arrangements, Luca."

"But, Duce, it—"

"But? *BUT?*" he screamed. "You dare? Do you see Hitler's minions braying, 'But, Führer, but, Führer'? That is why we are a joke to the Germans. You know what to do. DO IT!"

"So what happened?" I asked Dollmann.

"The commander was summarily taken out and shot."

Normally, I would have shrugged and mentally moved on, but now, such things took on an importance out of all proportion, so I was gratified by Mussolini's ruthless rage. He was becoming a fitting ally of mine, no less than of the Führer.

THIS IS TURNING out to be the longest visit Mussolini has ever made to Germany, one that Kempka guessed stemmed from the fact that his troops were, as he put it, "so fucking successful, you wouldn't imagine they was Italians." I believed him.

Aside from the rewards of his latter-day conversion to cruelty, Mussolini is still the source of endless amusement, sometimes dangerously so. The Führer invited the Duce to fly with him to the war zone in his Fw 200 Condor, the *Immelmann III*.

Before take-off, Baur told me that the Führer was eager to savour his triumphs in the East and to view the conquered Ukraine, where his Army Group South had destroyed twenty enemy divisions and taken over two hundred thousand prisoners, and he wished to impress Mussolini with this.

"God knows why," Baur concluded with a bewildered headshake.

During the flight from Uman to Lvov that carried the Führer; Mussolini; Anfuso, his ambassador to Germany; Himmler; Ribbentrop; a "nameless" representative from I. G. Farben; Günsche; and me, Mussolini asked to pilot the aircraft himself. Baur said nothing, but I could see from the deep furrows on his face that he was concerned for the Führer, who was speechless with surprise, managing only an awkward smile and a gesture of surrender with his hands. I knew that Mussolini had earned his pilot's licence years before and fancied himself a talented aviator, but I also knew Baur too well to doubt even for a moment whether he would remain nailed to the co-pilot's seat as insurance.

During the flight, the passengers, including me, sat with knuckles white with tension, and I overheard the strained whispers.

Herr Nameless: "I can't believe the Führer permitted that Italian circus clown to put himself as well as all of us at risk."

Von Ribbentrop: "I wouldn't fret, Mein Herr. At the first sign of trouble, the behemoth Günsche there would remove Mussolini by force if necessary, and Baur would continue as if nothing had occurred. What do you think, Heinrich?"

Himmler: "As chief of Reich security, I worry every time the Führer enters an aeroplane, even with Baur piloting. Göring has fallen catastrophically short of making the skies safe, and the planes themselves are none too sturdy for my liking. But on the other side, Baur is still in reserve, the Soviet Air Force has been nearly destroyed, so it poses no real threat, and even if it did, as you can see out the windows, the Luftwaffe have deployed an escort of Messerschmitt Bf 109 fighters to ensure the Führer's safety. I'd say the risk is there but minimal."

Knowing Himmler's mania for understated accuracy, all breathed a tentative sigh of relief.

Of course, nobody asked me, but if they had, I would have wanted to tell them that a nice comprehensive plane crash would have made Emerald more than delighted.

30 *August 1941*

Mussolini was finally gone, and the investigation continued into the attack on Morell. *Was it an assassination or accidental murder?* The untimely demise of the perpetrator made the answer elusive at best, so the Gestapo were focusing on her associates and associations, but it remained a mystery. As for the intended victim, what began as hysterical blubbering quickly turned into a matter for humour. As he told the Führer this morning while I watched him administer his daily volley of injections:

"I love this one, my Führer," he said. "It's about Churchill, where a woman says to him, 'If you were my husband, I'd poison your coffee,' and he replies, 'If you were my wife, I'd drink it.' Hilarious, eh? I told it to my Hannelore, and she said, 'I sympathise with the woman.'"

The Führer sniffed. "With Churchill, I'd feel the same way. But seriously, ruling out your wife for the moment, we must get to the bottom of this. Clearly, there are those who would try to get at me by depriving me of your services."

Frederick the Great again, I thought with amusement. To get my mind off the subject, I busied myself with the immediately insoluble task of trying to discover the purpose of a representative of Farben on the flight. Another mystery. But after learning from Albert at breakfast that Himmler recently experimented with Farben's Zyklon-B on selected prisoners in Auschwitz, things became much clearer—and more promising for the success of my strategy.

To satisfy Kempka and Baur and, I will confess, to satisfy my own needs as well, I used lunchtime to get to know Johanna Becker better, by way of asking her for an opinion about Morell. I began by telling her what the Führer said about deprivation, and she pushed some lank pale-blond strands from her forehead that had escaped her professional bun and laughed.

"That's a good one," she said. "Though it's possible, I suppose. But I'll tell you, from what I've heard, what's really necessary is having someone between Morell and the Führer to check out first what he's being administered. Don't you agree?"

I wondered how many on her level and below knew this, but I laughed just the same. "To be frank, Johanna, I don't think even the SS would volunteer, and if they did, how many of them would make it to the next day?"

An earnest look, and she leaned slightly forward. "Well, to be serious, if the Führer is right, the entire inner circle's at risk, including you, so there's no time to lose."

"In getting protection?"

"No, Heinz, in getting me into bed."

THIS MORNING, OUR dressing ritual was disrupted by Goebbels, who travelled all the way from Berlin to regale the Führer with news that the famous Swedish American aviator Charles Lindbergh had made a speech on behalf of the isolationist America First Committee in Des Moines, Iowa. Quoting from a sheet he held, Goebbels said, "'The—ah—three most important groups who have been pressing this country towards war are the British, the Jewish, and the Roosevelt administration.'" He went on to mention that Lindbergh said he admired the British and Jewish races but claimed that, "'The Jews' greatest danger to this country lies in their large ownership and influence in our motion pictures, our press, our radio, and our government.' There's more to the steak, my Führer, but that's the sirloin."

The Führer's eyes narrowed. The impression of gentle indulgence vanished from his features, and his face took on a hard, uncompromising look. I couldn't tell whether the bitter frost in his tone was artifice or genuine. I could see nothing negative in it for the Führer. In fact, it illustrated the extent and influence of isolationism in America that could only further inhibit Roosevelt from coming to Britain's direct assistance. But there followed a long, pained silence. I wanted to leave, but unable to do so with delicacy, I merely shifted round to a position directly behind the Führer, still holding up his tie. I knew that it was classic Führer to demonstrate constant shifts of mood to keep even his closest associates perpetually off balance, but I wondered if this was one of those moments.

"Are you a complete idiot, Goebbels?" the Führer screamed. "With Leningrad and Moscow on my plate and with generals fighting me at every turn, you couldn't telephone me, or at least wait for me to get dressed, to give me this critical news?"

Even with his long association with the Führer, Goebbels was visibly shaken, his pitted face bleached white, his hands tremulous. The Reichsminister appeared to be calculating his next move as if his life hung in the balance. But after a few deep, shuddering breaths, he straightened his tiny, distorted frame to his full five and a half feet.

"For a moment," he said, his orator's voice returning in fine form, "I thought I was speaking to my Führer, the greatest political and military figure in history, and not a mediocre, mercurial maniac like Stalin. Was I, perhaps, mistaken?" It was one of the very rare times since I came to the Chancellery that Goebbels stood up to the Führer—and with alliteration to boot.

The Führer shook his head as if he were clearing it, turned away from me, moved to his desk, and fell into his seat with a creaking crash, staring vacantly at his empty desktop and leaving me standing like a moron with my arms raised, holding his tie. Goebbels, with a bewildered expression, turned to me, and I could only shrug. But it was then that it struck me. Goebbels could have added one more "m" to his alliteration: Morell.

"Herr Reichsminister," I said, "the Führer is clearly indisposed. May I suggest that we leave him for the present? I will summon Dr. Morell, and I'm sure that he'll be as good as new in no time."

He stared at me for a long moment, trying to compose himself. The difficulty showed. Then, "I daresay," he said with a sneer. "Only that can explain it. Yes, fetch the arrogant quack.

Tell the Führer that I'll return in a few hours to witness the outcome of his magic." With that, he turned and limped out.

I called for Morell, and while I waited, I considered
Goebbels's news. A small part of me was pleased that Roosevelt,
never a man to defy public opinion, might need to keep dangling substantial aid to Britain in front of the porker Churchill,
as if it were bait kept just out of reach. But the rest of me—the
lion's share, so to speak—hoped that the American president
would either succumb to Churchill's charms or react to the horrors already perpetrated by Himmler and the Wehrmacht (with
far greater horrors to come). Or both.

I OMITTED TO mention that the lummox Günsche, in the throes of a latter-day paroxysm of Slavophobia, had begged the Führer to be transferred to the SS for active military duty in Russia, to which the latter agreed, joking to me later, "I just hope he isn't captured inside Leningrad; those Slav scum will have food for a year." Long time a "bridesmaid," Schaub was now elevated to chief adjutant, a position once held by Brückner. Despite the rank of general and being no stranger to hubris before (Schaub considered himself, as he put it, an "amazingly important, significant person"), I found him to be a distrustful and mediocre fellow for all that, but not entirely stupid.

Today, Günsche stopped off here on his way to SS Officer School in Bavaria to visit with friends. I hadn't included myself in such company, but Günsche seemed to, for he sought out me and Schaub first.

"This is some place," Günsche said, eyes wide to underscore his wonder.

"But fitting for the Führer, wouldn't you say?" Schaub asked.

A tiny row of sweat dots sprouted along Günsche's hairline. "Oh, that and more," he answered.

"How have you been?" I asked to shift the tone from insinuation to reunion, but not before making a mental note to trust Schaub no further than I could toss the bunker.

A smile dried the sweat. "Oh, just great, Heinz. Nothing like battle to keep things clear…"

I knew what he meant, and a part of me envied him.

"The Führer's enemies are everywhere, Günsche," Schaub remarked, "not just on the battlefield. We—"

"Put it this way, Otto," I cut in, "you protect the Führer from his enemies, and we protect him from his friends."

"Heinz, I gotta tell you that you're as looney as ever. I miss that a lot," he told me after a crushing embrace. "But hey, guys, do you think the Führer plans to spend the winter here?"

Schaub laughed. "My dear Otto," he said, with no little pomposity, "spend the winter? What are you thinking of? We are fighting a blitzkrieg against Russia. At Christmas, we will certainly be celebrating on the Obersalzberg, as usual."

I certainly hoped not. *And where did Schaub's "blitzkrieg" come from, after the Führer's continual siege-strategy pronouncements and conduct?*

"So, how's the Führer?" Günsche asked me.

"Why don't you ask him yourself?" I suggested. "Right, General?"

Schaub's mouth formed a crooked smile. "Of course, Linge. I imagine the Führer would be delighted to see Günsche here."

We accompanied Günsche to the conference room, where the Führer, in a Morell-enhanced mood, walked straight up to him with elongated strides, greeted him, then raised his arm for an effusive handshake.

"So, Günsche, how are you? What are Sepp[99] and my Leibstandarte[100] up to?"

"Success after success, my Führer," he said with no little passion. "Morale is excellent; they enjoy making war in Russia."

The Führer nodded. "I would expect no less. They—"

"The only thing, my Führer," the clod interrupted (it seemed he'd been away too long), "they only bridle at the pace. The Russians are resisting all the way and—"

My heart dropped, and my stomach felt as though it was filled with broken glass.

As I expected, the Führer's fatherly expression round the mouth became a rictus of barely contained fury. "And this is the shared opinion?" he asked, teeth clenched.

Even this dolt had some sensibility. "N-n-o, no, my Führer," he stammered, "only a very few stupid malcontents, and we dealt with them as you would." An anxious laugh followed.

---

[99] Josef "Sepp" Dietrich was a German politician and SS commander during the Nazi era. Prior to 1929, Dietrich served as Adolf Hitler's chauffeur and bodyguard. He received rapid promotions within the SS after his participation in the extrajudicial executions of political opponents during the 1934 purge known as the Night of the Long Knives. Despite having no formal staff officer training, Dietrich became the highest-ranking officer in the Waffen-SS, the paramilitary branch of the SS, attaining the rank of Oberst-Gruppenführer (Colonel-General).

[100] The "Leibstandarte SS Adolf Hitler" (LSSAH) began as Adolf Hitler's personal bodyguard, responsible for guarding the Führer's person, offices, and residences. Initially the size of a regiment, the LSSAH eventually grew into an elite division-sized unit during World War II under the command of Sepp Dietrich. The LSSAH was involved in the Battle of Uman and the subsequent capture of Kiev. According to a post-war report by Waffen-SS journalist Erich Kern, the division murdered four thousand Soviet prisoners on 18 August, after finding the mutilated bodies of six of its members who had been executed at Nowo Danzig, north of Kherson. Members of the LSSAH were later responsible for numerous atrocities and war crimes, including the Malmedy Massacre. They killed an estimated five thousand prisoners of war in the period 1940 to 1945, mostly on the Eastern Front.

After what seemed a millennium, Schaub broke the silence. "My Führer," he began, "it's clear that—"

But the Führer cut him off. "Good, Günsche, these traitors must be exterminated in the harshest possible way to serve as an example for the rest. What you did to those traitors, I wish I could do to my generals who question my strategy at every turn. All must realise that I shall break the Russians utterly, and time is less importance than method. Leningrad, Moscow, they will be crushed, and we will have won the war, in preparation for my new order." His face turned bright red, and his voice rose. "You go back, you go back, and let all know that as the reformer of Europe, I shall make sure that my new order is imposed on this land and according to my laws. You go back and tell them that!" he shouted. Then, as if nothing had happened, the Führer made a fist and gave Günsche a friendly pound on the arm. "Glad you stopped by," he said by way of dismissal, and we left.

Once out in the corridor, Günsche almost collapsed. "Shit, guys, I thought for a moment there that I would be arrested and executed on the spot."

"Aw, Otto," Schaub mollified, "you know the Führer. He gets agitated, and it goes away as fast as it comes. He's always had a high regard for you, and nothing's changed. He's just frustrated at those stupid generals who fail to appreciate his genius, right, Heinz?"

I hadn't been listening until I heard my name, since they were both useless founts of insignificant gossip—like Kempka and Baur, but at least the latter team were entertaining.

"What was that, General?"

Schaub cocked his head. "Please, spare me the 'general' stuff. I'm Julius, and you're Heinz," then he added, as I knew he would, "just so you know who's who, eh?"

"Never to be forgotten… Julius," I answered. "Now, what were you asking me?"

"I was about to tell jumbo here"—he thumbed at Günsche—"that it's good he didn't elaborate what he just told us now to the Führer about the zeal of the Leibstandarte, considering his mood."

"What elaboration? Günsche? What elaboration?"

"You need to listen more, Heinz," Schaub chided, "and not be off in your head someplace, where you usually go when anyone of consequence talks. Günsche was telling us that a Leibstandarte division executed four thousand Soviet prisoners in reprisal on 18 August, after finding the mutilated bodies of six dead divisional members who had been murdered at Nowo Danzig, north of Kherson. And I was telling him that I didn't think that the Reichsführer wanted anyone to divulge the details to anyone, especially the Führer."

"Or the Reichsminister?" I suggested.

"Especially the Reichsminister," Schaub said. "My God, if the world press were to get ahold of such potentially inflammatory material, well, I needn't tell you."

No, you needn't, I almost said but kept silent on that point, mainly because it just struck me that I needed such news to appear in the world press, but I also needed a conduit. I pursed my lips and nodded in tacit agreement.

"When do you leave?" Schaub asked Günsche.

"Just as soon as I see some friends in the Führer's bodyguard."

"Then, perhaps you should see them," Schaub suggested with a less-than-subtle nudge in his voice.

⤐

After Günsche left, a sweating Schaub drew out a handkerchief and mopped his forehead. "With Günsche's mouth disconnected from his brain," Schaub sighed, "the Führer was well rid of that giant circus clown."

"You do him an injustice, Julius," I corrected in a jocular tone. "His brain and mouth *are* connected. That's the trouble."

Schaub laughed and replaced his handkerchief. "I see why the Führer keeps you around," he said. "Humour has its place but," he added, "within limits, you understand."

"Fully," I answered, having just come up with the name of my conduit.

❦

At last, I had the opportunity to speak with Morell without the Führer present. I was in the main garage, waiting for Kempka to return from one of his daily "dressing down" sessions with a hapless underling, when the doctor came in to pick up a saloon the Führer had secured for him.

"Ah, Linge, you're travelling somewhere?" Morell asked, his usual ugly, repulsive self.

"Not to my knowledge," I joked. "Just waiting for Kempka. I should ask you that question."

He shrugged. "A drive, Linge, just a drive. Cooped up here day after day can be burdensome. At least the Führer gets to go off campus, so to speak. And so do all you little minions who follow him. I just wait, like the homeliest girl at a dance."

I wanted to tell him that he must be in some demand by women, even if only by poisoners. "Have you fully recovered from your near miss?"

He pursed his violet bladder lips. "To be frank, I still can't imagine the fool was after me. I satisfy all my patients—or kill them," he kidded. "Either way, I'm safe. Seriously, Linge, I'd have liked to have questioned her myself, my way. I'd have gotten to the bottom of it, you bet. The Gestapo still think it's 1934. And speaking of the Gestapo, I think one of those fellows is looking for you."

❧

Oscar Wilde wrote: "Some cause happiness wherever they go; others whenever they go." He must have been thinking of Heydrich, the "fellow" Morell said was looking for me. He was waiting for me in the empty Old Tea House (empty by his order, I assumed). We saluted and sat.

"I just came to say farewell to the Führer," he said. "But I'd be remiss if I didn't say it to you as well."

"Farewell, Herr General?"

"I'm afraid so, Linge," he said, head cocked, his slash of a mouth ever so slightly downturned. "As of today, I'm *Reichsprotektor* of Bohemia and Moravia. It would seem that the Reichsführer needs a firm hand in Czechoslovakia, and who has a firmer hand, I ask you?"

I didn't need to be asked, realising that there wouldn't be a tooth left in Prague when he got finished. *But a cultivated monster like Heydrich, a master administrator,*[101] *a provincial governor?* The whole notion was absurd. Himmler could have sent bureaucratic thugs like Gestapo Müller or Herr Reach-for-His-Revolver Kaltenbrunner for such a numbingly nothing assignment. Then an internal alarm sounded in my brain. Something was up, and I hadn't a clue to what it was, but this was what I did know: it wasn't just Czechoslovakia.

---

[101] For example, in early 1941, Heydrich was given responsibility for carrying out the Nacht und Nebel (Night and Fog) Decree. According to the decree, "persons endangering German security" were to be arrested in a maximally discreet way—"under the cover of night and fog." People disappeared without a trace, with none told of their whereabouts or fate.

"No one, Herr General," I told him. "I'm just surprised that the Reichsführer could spare you."

The slash widened to permit a laugh. "Well, my friend, I appreciate the sentiment, but only the Führer is indispensable. I will miss our stimulating chats, so I won't depart until I've given you an update on matters we've spoken of."

"Yes?"

"Yes. Like the case of the alleyway murder. Sounds like the title of a cheap pulp fiction, doesn't it?"

"Yes, Herr General."

"Anything but cheap and hardly fiction, though. In fact, we've spent a great deal of money and time in the attempt to solve it."

They had nothing better to do? Who the hell was *the SOB I killed?*

"And?"

The slash spread into a full Heydrich smile. "And nothing. We kept hitting dead ends until I concluded it wasn't for us to discover… or at least acknowledge."

The pause said it all. "I don't under—"

"—stand?" he cut in. "Of course you don't. The only important thing is that the matter is closed… at least for now."

The pause said it all. "Javert never rests."

"Ah, I see you do occasionally dip your brain into that massive informal library of yours. No, Linge, Javert never rests. And the culprit should never think that he'll be saved by this Javert committing suicide."

I didn't ask whom he thought was Jean Valjean.

Change the subject! "You must be eager to begin your new assignment."

"Eager isn't the word," he said with typical calculated

ambiguity. "Well, I should be going. A few more goodbyes, and I'm off."

He turned, and I waited for the other shoe.

He turned back. "Oh yes, this Morell business."

The other shoe.

"I thought it was solved," I ventured into the dark. "The woman—"

"The woman? Yes. But until we have a motive—beyond aesthetics, that is—we have no way of gauging the nature and extent of the threat."

"Yes," I said with a shrug, "I can see where—"

"By nature and extent," he interrupted, "I mean who could be next and why?"

"I understand."

"I'm sure you do. Would you mind some parting advice?"

Not really. "I would welcome it."

For a moment, an absolute, deathly silence settled over the room while he pulled his spent cigarette from its holder and dropped it into an ashtray.

"You need to realise," he began, "that National Socialism is not a philosophy. It's not even a programme. For the greedy, it's a means. For the faithful, it's a reason, and for the barbaric, it's an excuse. But for all, at bottom, it's a man. If you wish to survive what is to come, you must focus on the man and him alone. The innocent indifference you display with such adroitness must be real and not merely a clever artifice that a few of your kind have perfected. I hope, for your sake, it's the former. But as I said, just some parting advice."

Advice? "... and not merely a clever artifice"? He "hopes"? Since when does the fiend care about my "sake"? Be that as it may, I told myself with no little unease, *whatever he thinks he knows or suspects, he can't act upon it, or he would have done so.* I was far more concerned about "what is to come." I had a damn good idea what he meant, and I also knew that it must be trumpeted to the world to end it, once and for all. *But how?*

2 October 1941

Employing the Führer's (and, I may say, my) strategy of incrementalism, envelopment, and erosion, the war in the East had brought success after success, but I continued to fret about the Führer. Never one to maintain a mood, his role as supreme military commander, with Morell as his medicinal "morale officer," had played havoc even with that, and serving him had become an unceasingly rotated kaleidoscope of action and reaction.

Today, the Führer ordered a full-scale progressive attack on Moscow, an action he "predicted" (meaning, in Führer-speak, ordered) would be accomplished within four months. To me, this was satisfactory, though eight would be better.

After our dressing routine, I busied myself while listening to a one-sided version of the Führer discussing on the telephone with Goebbels:

"I must never be photographed from the back. I've given the word."

"No, I have no neck from the back, and I look as if I'm slouching, drooping forward."

"Don't fuss, Joseph. Morell is working on ways to provide me with more hours in the day."

[Pause.]

"Yes. Yes. For my troops as well. My new strategy takes time, and commanders must provide it, no less than weaponry."

[Pause.]

"I understand, Joseph. Must I hold a course in military tac—"

[Pause.]

"Yes, I've always maintained that Moscow is secondary, but—"

[Pause.]

"Yes, economically, naturally. But for that, we need—"

[Temperature rising.] "I'm fully aware that the fool Halder—"[102]

"And I'll tell you what I told him: You see Leningrad? Now see Moscow."

[Short pause.]

[Ice.] "And if I may, I overruled those idiots in favour of pocketing the Soviet forces around Kiev in the south, followed by the seizure of Ukraine. The hell with Moscow then, and I was right. I would remind one who shouldn't need reminding that the move was successful, and by the end of September, it resulted in the loss of nearly a million Red Army personnel killed, captured, or wounded, combined with further advances by our forces."

[Pause.]

[Hot fists clenched, knuckles white.] "I'm surrounded by timorous fools with no vision or imagination to counter their lack of skill and knowledge. Halder is merely the tip of an iceberg of incompetence!"

[Lava flow.] "I want more than surrender! I want such a complete extermination. There will be only memory left, and that memory will be planted in the very marrow of not just the few Russians left alive to do my bidding but also anyone in the

---

[102] Fritz Halder was head of the Army General Staff.

ossified high command who dares to question my decisions or outright traitors who would attempt to thwart my will and prevent the fulfilment of my destiny!"

[Pause.]

[Instantly calm.] "You must come—and bring your family. There's nothing as bracing as a battlefield. Junge told me a joke yesterday: This angry Russian sergeant says to a lazy private, 'I ought to drag you out into the open field, shove you face-first against a wall, and shoot you between the eyes with a shotgun so you'll remember it for the rest of your life!' Get it? *This* is the enemy! And do get busy with my radio address, will you?"

[Slams the receiver down.]

This was what I meant. Craziness. Every day now, from minute to minute, all these instant volatile shifts and reversals. All I could do was wait for my turn at bat.

IT SEEMS THAT even Stalin faces reality sometimes, for today, he proclaimed a state of siege in Moscow. The Führer erupted into hysterical laughter over this, but I knew that victory by siege would not be without cost. I overheard two colonels in the mess lament that, though up to two million German troops were committed to the operation, along with 1,000 to 2,470 tanks and assault guns and 14,000 guns, German aerial strength had been severely reduced over the summer's campaign. The Luftwaffe had 1,603 aircraft destroyed and 1,028 damaged. *Luftflotte Zwei* (Air Fleet Two) had only 549 serviceable machines, including 158 medium and dive bombers and 172 fighters.

When their conversational tone descended to furtive, I could still make out that Halder was criticising the Führer's "underestimation of the Russian army's numbers." That he, among other high-ranking military figures, wanted to "make straight for Moscow," but the Führer insisted that they meet up with Field Marshal von Leeb's army group, which was making its way towards Leningrad. "Another one of the Führer's fucking side trips," they called it.

Nothing was shocking to me in all this, for many of the Führer's top generals, not merely Halder, believed that the time-consuming combination of siege and side trips only assisted two of Russia's most formidable military strategists: General Winter and General Mud.[103] Once again, ambivalence enveloped and gnawed at my conscience. *How much destruction and devastation was I prepared to counsel in the name of moral restoration?*

❦

Ambivalence aside, I made a tentative decision to approach General Engel at the first opportunity to seek his advice on ways to get the story of Himmler's atrocities and crimes out to the world, the only way I could see to spur the creation of a vigorous second front to end the horror once and for all.

---

[103] Generals Winter and Mud refer to the brutally harsh winter climate of Russia as a contributing factor to the military failures of several previous invasions of Russia.

TODAY, STALIN MADE a radio address broadcast worldwide declaring that "Hitler's crazy plan" to draw Britain and the United States into a coalition to destroy the Soviet Union had failed. Stalin said that a coalition of the United States, Britain, and the USSR was "now a reality" and expressed his hopes that a "second front" would be established "in the near future." I was certain that no one hoped for this more than I did, but I feared that it would take far more than Russian distress to accomplish this. I still felt that Himmler was the key, not Stalin, and he must be exposed.

Baur roped me into a lunch date with Johanna at the officers' mess. "Roped" was, perhaps, too harsh a word. I harboured no reservations about seeing her—quite the contrary. But I could have lived without my "matchmaker" tagging along. When we arrived, she was already seated and speaking with the officer across from her, Lieutenant Colonel Georg Betz, the Führer's co-pilot and desultory substitute for Baur. I sat down directly across from Johanna (by needless guidance), and Baur planted himself next to Betz.

"Ah, Betz," Baur said, "no feats of aeronautical derring-do for the Führer scheduled for today?"

"Sitting here is dangerous enough, wouldn't you say?" Betz

ventured. He was tall and lean and far from unsightly, a man the featureless Baur could hate with little effort.

"I predict turbulence ahead," Baur said. "I suggest you bail before it hits." He nodded sidewise towards the door. "As the pilot, I must stay with the ship, burdens of command and all that."

I could see that Johanna was enjoying herself, though she couldn't have known their years of nasty rivalry.

Betz's mouth wrinkled in dismay, and he wiped angrily at the back of his neck, I thought, weighing indignity against retaliation. Then his face went slack. "If you'll excuse me," he said to Johanna, got up, and walked out without looking back.

She turned to Baur. "I hope you don't do this in a plane," she kidded.

He shrugged. "I wish I could," he told her, and she smiled.

"Okay," Baur said to Johanna, "now that the clown's gone, what's the good word?"

"I'm still here," she said. "In my job, that's no small thing."

I marvelled at her sense of humour as well as its quality. But it was a sensation stained with sadness, for it reminded me so much of Klara.

"Are you all right?" she asked me.

Her question startled me, though it made sense once she asked. I sniffed and wiped at the corners of my eyes. "I'm fine. Just fighting off a cold, I think. Temperatures vary from room to room in this place."

"Like in a plane," Baur chimed in. "They never get it right."

Whatever that meant, I was grateful for the diversion. "You were saying?" I asked her.

"I was just saying that since the Morell mishap, they hired more tasters, and Manziarly's even more ill-tempered than her usual harridan self."

"Mishap?" Baur hooted. "That's a good one. He's getting a taste of his own medicine for once, you might say."

We both laughed at that one.

"Well, children," Baur announced, "it's been nice, but I've gotta be off to brief the Führer on some new aircraft design. I tell you, in another life, the Führer would have been no mean aeronautical engineer." He rose, saluted comically, and departed.

"Your friends think you're simple." She quickly raised her hand in a conciliatory manner, then lowered it. "I don't mean simpleminded, just uncomplicated. They're wrong, of course, but I would never dare tell them that. Also, you like wit in a woman," she went on. "I can tell. Most men don't. They think that wit implies intelligence, and men don't go for intelligent women."

I smiled. "It does, and I do."

She smiled, too, but said nothing, another sign of intelligence.

"I'm sorry that Morell spoiled your workplace," I followed up. "If it's any comfort to you, he's done the same to mine."

Her sharp, penetrating, wily eyes fixed themselves on me, and she pursed her lips. "Well, if it's any comfort to *you*, if the Führer can stand the food we're forced to taste, he can stand even Morell, not to mention *real* poison." Any hint that her observation might be construed as cold and cynical was rebutted by the look of undisguised amusement that lit her eyes. "May I ask who she was?"

I shook my head. "I... I don't—"

She shrugged. "I embarrassed you. I didn't mean to. I was merely asking about the last witty woman of intelligence who'd captured you."

At that moment, I was overcome, and a migraine began peeking round the corner of my brain. *How she knew wasn't difficult to figure out, but should I acknowledge it, and if so, how much?*

"What did they tell you?" I asked her.

"I *did* embarrass you. I'm sorry. I only—"

"You didn't embarrass me," I told her gently. "You can't be friends with Baur and Kempka and embarrass easily. They're decent chaps who mean well, and they were probably just trying to get you interested, but—"

"They succeeded," she cut me off with a broad smile, "but did they get *you* interested?"

With an eyebrow-lifting glance of theatrical lasciviousness as my answer, I forced a grin through the ache of the migraine and told her that, of course, I was interested, and because of that, she shouldn't follow up on her hapless co-worker's mission, and she laughed.

"Not a chance, Heinz," she assured me. Then she cupped her hand round her mouth to simulate a confidence. "Frankly, I think any self-respecting poison would run at the sight of him. Shall we order? It's such a luxury to be eating my own food."

After arranging a more informal date, I left the mess with a chaos of conflicting emotions trailing me. I decided to try locating Engel, when I encountered Albert, who suggested a hefty stroll round the inner perimeter, which we began in silence. All I could think about was why the sudden desire for a stroll, especially one so out of earshot.

"I noticed you earlier in the mess," he finally said as we passed the RSD Command Post, "but you seemed so immersed in conversation with that delightful-looking food taster, I didn't dare disturb you."

"It was nothing earth-shattering. I was just admiring her bravery, dedication, and—"

"Ah," he teased, "you were conducting a performance review. I should have realised. In any event, now that we're getting some air, I heard that you used to do this sort of chatty amble often with Gen—ah—Colonel Brückner, well, a general then."

"Yes, Albert," I replied. "Many times. He was very generous in allowing me to indulge my photographic hobby while he stood by."

"That's Brückner, all right. Generous to a fault. You know, given the number of times, you must have quite a sizeable collection of photographs. Have you shown them to the Führer?"

I forced a laugh, hoping it sounded sincere. "Sizeable, yes, artistic, another matter. With the Führer's access to Hoffmann, I would hardly wish to embarrass myself and waste the Führer's time with my amateurish snapshots."

"No," he said. "I imagine not."

What the hell was all this prosaic blather really about?

"I say, do you get many letters?" he asked me with what I thought to be studied casualness, as we reached the relatively isolated Firefighting Pond, and he stopped.

Finally a clue? "Not really." I shook my head nonchalantly. "I have no family, and all my friends and associates are at the Chancellery or here."

"Well, you've received one. In a way." He smiled benignly, as was his custom.

"May I ask who it's from?"

He smiled. "It's whom, Heinz. Justifiable cynicism on your part aside, I didn't look at it—though it came to me for you."

In a fraction of an instant, ice-cold seltzer water replaced my blood, and I fought to keep my hands from shaking. "To you?"

"Yes, odd as it may seem—and is—it's true, nonetheless. Still, I didn't consider it proper to peek."

He intended to show it to me, that I knew, but types like Albert seemed to require preliminaries, so I indulged him. "Then, why not just place it in my mail slot?"

"Out of my hands into the malign void? Then, I'm afraid your cynicism would be justified."

Did he really believe that I would understand his grandiloquence? "All right, Albert, but why you?"

"Perhaps because then it wouldn't end up in your mail slot. But you should read it. Now. Perhaps there's a clue." He reached two fingers into his inside jacket pocket, pulled out a small blue envelope, and handed it to me.

"Now? Here, in front of you?" Sirens went off in my aching brain.

"Come come, it wouldn't have been sent to me if there was any danger to either of us by its contents. Go ahead."

I tore open the envelope, but not before observing that the stamp had been removed, and I held the typed contents to my face, slightly out of Albert's view:

> *My dear H., my friend who is always a source of protection, comfort, and guidance has informed me that you have an unquenchable need and has urged me to tell you that the fulfilment of that need is nearer than you ever imagined, and therefore, he would urge you to wait before proceeding further. Please consider this my own urging as well. With my fondest regards and highest of hopes, B.*

I didn't understand the totality of Bella's cryptic meaning, but certain words gave me a sudden frisson, any manifestation of which I had to hide. Even if he had already read it, the adroit Albert would ask me what the note said, but I had no safe response at hand. Whatever answer I gave would doubtless be bumbling—*but could I make it convincing?*

"I imagine," I said, to get ahead of the obvious, "you'd like to know what it said."

He smiled again, that beguiling, Brückneresque smile. "After all, technically, it *was* addressed to me, but only if it won't compromise you."

Now I smiled. He had read it. I was certain. "It won't compromise me, I can assure you, but it will embarrass me."

"Ah, a lady?"

"No," I corrected, "worse." *Draw him in and leave him flat.* "Far worse."

He pursed his lips so tightly he looked like a drawing of a *Placidochromis phenochilus Mdoka* I'd once seen in the library.[104] "Ah, now I am intrigued," he said. "What if I promise not to cause you any embarrassment?"

Show shy reluctance! I cocked my head in slow deliberation.

"The word of a gentleman," he coaxed, his eyes incandescent with anticipation of my answer, if not of the information. I handed him the note and waited. He glanced at it twice and handed it back.

"It means nothing to me," he said. "If it's a code, you should send the writer to Canaris for immediate employment, or to Himmler for immediate interrogation."

I simulated an awkward chuckle. "It's far from a code, Albert," I told him.

----

[104] A remarkable fish with large, pouty lips resembling those of a human female, its distinctive lips are primarily used for fighting and for picking up objects in the ocean.

"Then what?"

I performed a foot shuffle, reminiscent of the sophisticated American actor Jimmy Stewart's put-on, aw-shucks drawl. "All right, but you must promise not to tell anyone, especially the Führer."

"A gentleman's agreement."

"All right. You know that I've been sorely lacking in formal education, a condition pointed out by many and, unfortunately, not inaccurate. I read books the Führer loans me but understand little. I'm told things but understand even less. I try to express myself, but I'm too inarticulate to even provide understanding, much less respect. This is especially true with females. So, when I was in Paris with the Führer, I happened to meet this Wehrmacht officer who told me he had a brother, a teacher named Bernhard, and he agreed to provide me with a correspondence course. That's it."

"And the note?"

"It seems this Bernhard has a flair for the furtive. He doesn't wish anyone to know he's helping me. I don't know why, and he's only saying that he's not ready and for me to be patient. I waited this long, so I can live with it." I liked that explanation, lame as it was. *But what of the stamp?*

He moved his index finger to his lower lip. "I always wondered why you never went back to school."

"Opportunity, I guess. And my jobs never called for any special knowledge I couldn't get while working—even this." *Albert removed the stamp! I know it!* But not knowing the purpose nagged at me.

"I think the Führer would be happy to get you a tutor, the best there is."

"But—"

He placed his hand on my shoulder. "Consider for a

moment, Heinz, why this… Bernhard would send a message to you through me, no matter how innocuous."

I did consider it for a moment. The pause, and stress, ended the nagging for me. I was now certain he knew who sent it, and from where. I was reminded of a prohibited Kafka novel, in which he described a character as "a man of extravagant intelligence, urbane, of consummate ability, the proper sympathies and cautions. And completely untrustworthy. An opportunist of the worst sort. But necessary." Regardless, I still needed to know more.

"Innocunus?" I queried, still in character.

"Innocu*ous*, my friend—that is to say, innocent," he said, eyes fixed on mine, "like you. But you do need a tutor." He grinned. "No question about that."

In the Führer's study, tidying up while he again castigated Halder in the conference room for vehemently pushing for a blitzkrieg assault on Moscow, I happened upon some wadded-up dispatches on the floor from that very Halder. They insisted that although much had been accomplished and Army Group Centre still possessed considerable nominal strength, its fighting capabilities had been thoroughly diminished because of wear, fatigue, and mud, and since there was no more strength, a withdrawal might be necessary. Had Halder asked me, I could have told him that both alternatives were abominations to the Führer and could only result in a hysterical dressing-down. What I *wouldn't* have told him was that a blitzkrieg was the last thing I wanted. I swear I could actually hear the commotion, despite the substantial distance, the thickness of the walls, and the constant growl of dogs and military vehicles.

Eventually, it subsided into silence, and after a few tense minutes, the Führer, red-faced and shaking, burst into his study accompanied by Schaub and commanded me to send for Morell, which I'd already had the foresight to do, and who waited in the bathroom with all the exotic elixirs at his command.

IN THE COMMUNICATIONS Centre, I finally received a typed letter from Annagret:

My Dear Heinz,

You cannot know how much I have missed you. I have such news!!! It has truly been an inspiration, and I am so fortunate to have the honour of assisting Dr. Mengele in the Ukraine. The man is not only a superb physician, but he is also a gifted scientist who goes far beyond the mere treatment of patients and into the causes of their conditions. His qualities have not gone unnoticed by the Reichsführer, who has entrusted him with the sacred task of protecting and treating our troops through exhaustive experimentation on captured Slav prisoners. I cannot discuss any of this in detail because it is considered to be a secret. But I can tell you that it is most gratifying for a true daughter of the Reich to make the Slavs suffer for the greater good of the superior race. Dr. Mengele regards me with high esteem and so has trained me in all the medical arts of which he feels me capable. He also has me assist him with all his experiments. I cannot be happier, except when we are together "reading" my stories. I must go now, but I will try to come and see you before the year ends.

Heil Hitler!

Your Annagret

Amazing creature. I wished she'd provided more detail about those experiments so I could relate them to Bella for general distribution. Perhaps I would discover more if she could visit. She'd found her true calling, that was clear.

Heydrich, Weisthor, Krafft, Bella, Albert… Johanna. I continued to be oppressed by possible connectivities, but at the moment, I had no time to agonise or investigate.

This morning, I dusted at a distance while the Führer was on the telephone, screaming at Guderian, the general commanding the panzer army before Moscow. "You gutless fogey!" he bellowed into the receiver. "You maintain your position at ANY PRICE, do you hear me? Stop your quaking. I'll mobilise everything I have. Just stick it out, damn you—just stick it out!" He slammed down the receiver, took some quavering breaths, and lowered his head into his open palms.

Even before there was time for him to recover, he received a report that Guderian was retreating. He just lifted his head and shook it in slow, slack resignation.

"That fucking Jew-cripple Rosenfeldt can be Rosenfeldt, and the voters lick his behind, and that fat, cigar-chomping nonentity in Britain can slur and stutter his way into oblivion and the people still slobber all over him. But your Führer? Until the transformation, he has to be all things to all people—constantly. And if that weren't enough, he's afflicted with an obsolete general's staff with their minds still mired in 1917. I tell you, Linge, sometimes, the burden is insuperable."

I nodded with appropriate gravity. "Who but the Führer could bear such a burden?" I asked. It was only partially rhetorical.

After several moments of gazing off into the middle distance, the Führer nodded. "You're right, Linge," he admitted. "As always."

The Führer convened a noon situation briefing in Keitel's and Jodl's long, low-ceilinged bunker. Also present were Goebbels, Halder, Field Marshal Wilhelm Ritter von Leeb, Schaub, and Albert. I was there too, more than happy to be the ignored stick of black and silver furniture in the corner with Keitel's adjutant, Gabriel.

The meeting hadn't even formally begun, when the Führer started screaming, thumping his fists on the table, and accusing the generals of being dull-witted fossils and regimented fools and cowards incapable of fighting. I could tell that the august military men seethed inside, despite their granitic exteriors, and I wondered how long they could—or would—endure the Führer's hysterical broadsides. In fact, things got so heated that Gabriel and I took the opportunity to steal into the corridor for some rest and relaxation before returning to the "battlefield."

We hadn't been there for more than five minutes before von Leeb burst through the door and began striding back and forth in a visible state of agitation, finally coming up to Gabriel and saying, "What am I supposed to do? How can we fight a war when we are not believed and when our assessments and opinions are called shit?"

Since he hadn't addressed me (or even looked at me), I had the occasion to consider his questions privately. Had he asked me, I would have wanted to counsel tactical caution and strategic audacity. By that, I meant I would have advised him to go along with the Führer in word but follow his informed instincts in deed. I admit to you that there was no little self-interest in my undelivered advice, for it was to my advantage that the Führer's siege strategy continue and that he and his military leaders would be at such loggerheads that there would be chaos of command—a simulated third front, if you will—and an even quicker end to hostilities—and to Himmler.

5 *December 1941*

Today, the Führer reversed himself and agreed to temporarily abandon the Moscow offensive and approved Army Group Centre's retreat to safer defensive positions. *Why?* Even he had to take one "general" seriously: General Winter.

One, I won't burden you with numbers, but this season in Europe, and especially in the East, was the coldest ever recorded.

Two, our troops were freezing with no winter clothing, using equipment that was not designed for such low temperatures. More than 130,000 cases of frostbite were reported among our soldiers. Frozen grease had to be removed from every loaded shell, and vehicles had to be heated for hours before use. Of course, the same weather hit the Soviet troops, but they were better prepared.

Three, a massive Soviet counteroffensive for, as Stalin called it, "removing the immediate threat to Moscow from the Nazi scourge" started on the Kalinin Front.

Guderian, the prime beneficiary of the decision, related his elation to the Führer, laying it on thick when he oozed, "The brilliance and flexibility you've demonstrated today, my Führer, will be an inspiration to your troops and the Reich and will become a major chapter in military history."

The Führer, for his part, was less sanguine, telling the general, "Don't pack your bags yet, Guderian. When I said temporarily, I *meant* temporarily," and "At the first hint of thaw, we will resume in full. And don't you think, for a single moment, that I will let up on Leningrad. Moscow is only Moscow."

Did this development advance my strategy? Not necessarily, for I learned that day that, as Kempka would say, there are delays, and there are delays. This was underscored when I was leaving the Führer's office and noticed that, on his calendar for that night, was pencilled in the letter "W."

AFTER COMPLETING HIS morning toilette, the Führer hadn't told me to wait around, so I took the opportunity to arrive on time for my luncheon date with Johanna—but not before notifying Schaub of my plan and receiving his reluctant blessing.

❧

She'd taken the trouble to change out of her drab taster's garb (replete with a long rubber apron to protect her and anyone nearby from potentially toxic vomit, drool, and blood should she encounter some less-than-desirable cuisine), applied some makeshift makeup, and looked encouragingly comely.

"How was your morning?" she asked, seeing my serious face. "As you can tell since I'm here, mine wasn't too bad."

I laughed. She was as funny as ever, and her subject was not surprising in a job that would elbow considerable gallows into anyone's humour.

"The Führer's unhappy with his generals again," I told her with considerable understatement. "At first, General Halder said we'd won. Then he said we'd lost. Now he says we're not great, so we need a blitzkrieg. Needless to say, the Führer was ready to fire you all and take his chances with the food. I joke, of course."

Her smile was quick and earnest. "As I've often said—usually to myself—if the Führer can survive Morell's nostrums, he can withstand any intentional poisoner."

I laughed again but this time with less ease. "I hope more than usually. That's dangerous talk."

"Dangerous, smangerous," she mocked. "The only one I worry about," she said with a surprising and, it seemed to me, deceptive calm, "is that shrew Manziarly, and she's too busy trying to concoct something different for the Führer while using the same swill. I wish her luck—among other things."

"I admire your pluck is all I can say."

She spread her newly lacquered lips in mock disappointment. "Is that all? And here I removed my rubber apron just for you."

I wanted to eat her up and take my chances. "No, it's far from all, but I'm not the most articulate fellow."

"Well, if you use words like articulate, you'll do." She moved some errant strands of hair over her ears like the handles of eyeglasses. "Now, who is this Annagret I keep hearing about?"

I shook my head. "'Keep hearing about?' Who's doing all the talking?"

"You know, your chums, Mutt and Jeff."[105]

I smiled at the easy—and accurate—reference. "Oh, them. We go back a long way in matchmaking history. They're just trying to make you jealous and me more exciting."

"Hair isn't everything," she said. "You were going to tell me about Annagret."

I wasn't.

"Just more Mutt and Jeff matchmaking." I was going to say cupids, but the image of Baur and Kempka as winged, naked

---

[105] Originally, Mutt was a tall, dim-witted racetrack character—a fanatical horse race gambler motivated by greed. Jeff was an inmate of an insane asylum who shared Mutt's passion for horse racing. Over the years, popular culture made them into any dopey pair of individuals of differing sizes.

infant boys with bows and arrows stopped me dead in my tracks. "Annagret was a simple country girl who longed to be a nurse," I told her with somewhat sanitised candour, omitting her sexual and political eccentricities, among other things. "I saw her a few times in Berlin, but she had nursing on the brain. All she could think about—and all she talked about—was how she could best serve the sick and wounded of the Reich. All the time we were together, I had the impression that I was merely affable filler between the farm and the hospital. At last report, she's on the front lines as some SS doctor's personal assistant. That's it."

"Maybe she'll meet my husband," she said, almost to herself. "She can have him," she added a bit louder. "Did they ever figure out why someone targeted Dr. Morell?"

Since so many people I knew were masters of the non sequitur, I was far from disconcerted. "No. It seems the lady in question ran out of teeth and nails before the Gestapo ran out of questions. The rest are just bad jokes about Morell. Did you know her?"

She shrugged. "We all work side by side, but we don't know each other, short of naughty nicknames and grim humour. Easier that way, as you can imagine. I'll tell you something I've kept to myself all this time. That evening, the one where... well, she'd asked me in the morning if I would take her place that afternoon so she could go on a date, and I said all right. But then I, too, was asked out and had to retract. Imagine if I hadn't."

"I'm sure she asked others," I ventured, hoping to mask my sudden anxiety.

"So far as I know, she only asked me. Is something wrong, Heinz?"

"Not a thing," I answered. "I'm relieved, is all."

After studying me for a moment, she smiled. "How well do you know Herr Bormann?"

Another non sequitur, or was it an extension of the previous one? I could feel trickles of perspiration begin to descend. "Which one?"

"The one here. The one I've seen you with."

"Ah, Albert, the brother. I don't know him at all. In truth, I don't know anyone, not really."

"But surely the Führer—"

"Him, least of all. To be frank, Johanna, I'm not sure he's even knowable. But I would like to know *you* better." I said it and noticed her stare—a vague, distant look in her eyes.

"There's nothing to know."

I knew she would say that. To someone like me, there's no better way of unconsciously signalling one's mysteriousness than by claiming transparency.

"In that case, I want to know as much nothing as I can. For instance, why did you want to know about Albert?"

Her stare remained but was far less vague and distant. "He's the one who asked me out."

End of Volume Two